STORMBITE

BOOK ONE OF THE STORM SERIES

T. HEARTS

Stormbite was first published in 2018.

Text copyright © T Hearts, 2018

Cover Illustration and Header illustrations by T Hearts.

Edited by T Hearts

Twitter: @StormbiteBook

Wikia: https://stormbite.fandom.com/wiki/Stormbite_Wiki

ISBN 9781718052789

ISBN 9781-7180-5278-9

Typeset in 10 pt. Garamond.

Cover font typeset in Libby

Stormbite

For Joelle

No matter how horrible things can be and how far away you are, always remember that I am here for you, and I will continue to do my best, correct mistakes and keep on creating things that will make you smile, cry, and laugh.

STORMBITE UNIVERSE BOOKS

The Storm Series

Stormbite

Silverbird

Skybourne

The Compass Projects Series

Sirocco

Gregale

Libeccio

Mistral

Far Horizons

Broken Arrow

Ten of Feathers

Glasswing

CHAPTERS

0

"…Alive…"

"Storm! Breathe!"

A scream filled the air around her with a piercing echoing note. Her own scream. She gasped as the adrenalin hit her system. Heart pounding in her ears and hungrily gulping in lungfuls of sour air. Everything felt cold and sharp against her skin, a sickly metallic taste lingered in her mouth, as oxygen was forced into her through the mask that was pressed to her face. Head throbbing with every heartbeat, the world before her swam before her, blurry in distorted colours of grey and white shapes, until the blue uniform of a nurse came into view as she lolled her head.

Where was she? What was happening?

A shone a light in her eyes, the shock of the brightness making her flinch.

"Patch Professor Mira in immediately. Tell her we have a problem and can't scan her. The claustrophobia makes her panic, and we can't administer any more sedatives because it'll put her at risk of respiratory failure."

Their voices were distorted, barely audible against the noisy throbbing of blood in her ears but growing clearer. Senses returning, the bright white room, and clinical stink of hospital disinfectant was an assault on her, sharp and burning. She squirmed and struggled, pain shooting across her back, held down by a crushing weight on her chest making it hard to breathe.

In panic, she screamed; a piercing raptorial noise that drove the doctor and nurse away from her, clutching their ears at the sound.

"Doctor Sang! Help!"

"Oh Jesus Christ- How much adrenaline did you give her?"

"I didn't! The sedatives just wore off!"

"What do we do?" Another nurse shouted staring as the girl began thrashing wildly. Her left arm came free from the cuff, giving her the means to tear at the remaining restraints, still shrieking.

"Loosen the straps! She'll break her bones!"

"What about us?"

"Just do it!" The doctor rushed forward, hands scrambling to loosen the restraints on her. She slashed at the doctor with sharp talon-like nails that sliced cleanly through the blue plastic gloves and cut into the skin. The nurse fared no better as the girl caught him across the face, leaving four deep slashes through his cheek, forcing him back.

"Storm! Storm please! It's just an MRI scan, we're not–" The doctor tried to assure her, releasing the straps across her chest, but her assurances fell on terror-deafened ears.

She struggled to take the girl's arms as the last restraints were freed. A jolt of electricity shocked her, forcing the doctor to reel back with a shout and release the girl.

Rolling forward onto the balls of her feet and perching up upon the rolling bed, for a split second she caught her reflection in the one-way mirror.

She saw herself, distantly familiar in her state of confusion. A lean little girl face sharply featured, pale eyed and body oddly proportioned with her deep chest, her long limbs and even longer wings.

Slate-grey feathers, banded with dark midnight blue and edged in silver, the same colour that ran in a gradient across her shoulders and up her neck to face, all the way down her back to an ankle length fan of a tail. Rolling her shoulders, the wings moved with her arms, their actions subconscious and refined.

They flexed softly, reaching to the ceiling where the meter-long primaries had to bend as they ran out of room. Every feather on the ventral side a stark white with narrow bands of charcoal grey, sliding softly and smoothly over each other with a gentle rustle. Her tailfeathers fanned out wide, patterned with the same dark bands as the upper side of her wings, tense in aggression and fear.

All as much a part of her as her heart in her chest.

Seeing the awe in the eyes of the doctor's reflection as she moved them, and noting their empty wingless backs, she was struck with an awareness that they were not the same species as her.

There was movement behind the mirror, the ghosts of figures running to the door on its right. A pale membrane flicked across her eye in an alien blink, though she could still see through it. She bared her mouthful of sharp cat-like teeth at the figures on the other side with an angry hiss, drawing her wings back, she crouched on the edge of the table, tensing as the door swung open. As it did, she launched herself across the room, drawing her legs up and catching the guard in the face with her heel, knocking him down to the floor.

They were so slow to move and before they could even react, she had bounced from his body and off the wall behind him, out the door and charging blindly down the hall, barrelling through several porters, and knocking them over.

"Stop where you are!" A second guard shouted, firing at her. It missed, the projectile clattering and ricocheting off the floor tiles as she raced towards the doors. Wings straining to beat in the confined corridor, the porters and guards were hot on her heels.

They fired again and this time the dart sank into the back of her leg, stinging like a wasp and throwing her off her sprint. Falling flat on her face at the sudden paralytic shock of the dart, the porters quickly pounced upon her, wrestling her strong arms and flailing wings into restraints with considerable difficulty.

She snapped her fangs down onto a nearby hand. Tasting their blood in her mouth, she spat it back out into the face of another trying to hold onto her wings. Their shouts were a cacophony of incoherent sounds that she cut through with another piercing scream, then with a sharp heavy blow to the back of her head, she fell still and back into unconsciousness.

Black.

Quiet.

Calm.

Then an agonising jolt of electricity shot through her, lighting up the world and bursting through the blackness.

"Wake up!"

A familiar voice and another shock with a high-pitched siren of tinnitus. The shock made her aware of her physical body, each nerve ending on fire as the shock leaped across each synapse and startled her back into consciousness.

"Please wake up! Don't be dead! PLEASE!"

'I'm not dead, don't worry…' she thought loudly, wondering how long she had been lifeless for.

With a third shock and the sound of the real world began to breaking through the haze. Blurry at first, the sounds distant as though she were underwater, then it all snapped into focus. The alarm was blaring in the distance, an oscillating drone doing nothing to cover the screams.

"We can't leave her!"

"I'll carry her out, just get the doors!"

Gunshots, screams, shouts, the sound of shattering glass and explosions. The metallic smell of blood and burning plastic overpowering the cleanly disinfectant stench.

"Wake up!"

Her eyes snapped open with the world back in focus, her limbs numb from the dart still, the floor moving below her as she was carried away. Flames flickered up from one passing hallway, followed by piercing screams from other children.

Terror set in at the bombardment of her senses, overpowering the paralysis of the dart. The feeling in her limbs returning rapidly, she flailed, kicking and lashing out at her captor, beating her wings against his head in panic. She clawed his neck and shoulder, ripping at his shirt and skin with her sharp talons slicing into him. The doctor swore at her as he dropped her from his bleeding shoulder, cursing and calling after her as she scrambled to her feet and began to sprint down the hallway.

"Storm! Storm no! Come with us!" The familiar voice.

Stopping dead in her tracks, she spun around to face the doctor and a girl.

It was like looking into the mirror again. At the other end of the hall stood a small and feathered girl with long limbs and even longer wings, grey-blue like her hair and the same sharp pale green-blue eyes. Behind her were more winged children, just like her and just as terrified.

"This way!" Her sister shrieked ushering her towards herself, the other children and the doctor, "Come with us! It's not safe that way!"

Tentatively, fearfully, she took several steps towards them, but a blast of fire erupted from the hallway she had run past startled her. With a scream she bolted away from the group.

Fight or Flight; no time for thinking it through.

Flight was always her answer.

"Storm!" Her sister shrieked as she was lifted off her feet by the doctor and dragged off down the hall to escape the blaze. Hands reaching out towards her, she thrashed in his arms.

"Don't leave me! STORM!"

Run.

Run.

Fly.

Too frightened to remember the layout of the building her only goal was to get up and away. She broke out into the stairwell, fire above and below and screaming all around. She didn't want to run the entire way up through the many basement levels and so launching herself out into the square space she beat her wings hard, struggling to gain any height in the stairwells, which were now acting as chimneys to the rising smoke. The heat and smothering smoke made it hard to go more than four levels, forcing her to land before she reached the top.

Rumbling explosions echoed from down the hallways, bursts of flames gutting the building quickly. The dense smoke was making it impossible to breathe and stinging her eyes. Fire licked at her tailfeathers and scorched her arms as she darted past a blazing doorway, turning the edges black and curling them up, she'd never realised how quickly feathers burnt and how awful the smell was.

Coughing, she stumbled out of the basement levels onto the ground floor of the stairwell, following after a crowd of fleeing people, shoving the door open and falling to her knees.

A hand grabbed her by the scruff of her neck, pinching at her hair and the feathers of her nape, hauling her to her feet. Unable to breathe at the smoke and fumes, she struggled to fight back against him.

"Is this one of *those* ones that Rex wanted?" A mask man asked, dragging her towards two other men dressed from head to toe in black, both in fire masks and armed with guns. One crouched and took her by her chin, twisting her head until the membrane blinked across to wipe away the tears. She snapped her sharp little teeth at him, hissing like an animal but the man didn't flinch.

"That's one of them," He growled, "but one's enough, now let's go."

She snarled at them, trying to slash and kick her way free, but she was lifted and tossed over their shoulder as they broke into a sprint away from a bomb that they had planted.

The people in black charged for the exit, breaking out onto the balcony above what once was the reception area. The glass doorways that once were the entrance were shattered by armoured vans that had been run through it into the foyer. More armed masked men patrolled the foyer, wingless, faceless beings that were carrying children and dragging adults into the back of vans.

"Charges are set! We've got two minutes people! If you're not out by then you're barbeque!" The leader shouted into a radio, kicking the body of a huge abomination of a dog that had been gunned down. "Get the kids in the van and go!"

"There's still Synths and men in here Rex!" A voice crackled in response, but the leader didn't seem to care.

"Collateral damage."

"They'll die Rex!"

"They'll produce more Synths in time, just take whatever is closest and leave the rest. The less they have, the better for the world!"

Fury pierced through her fear, snapping the world into logical focus of what was happening. Armed and dangerous, he didn't care there were people there who had done nothing wrong, he was just going to burn everything to the ground no matter who was there.

"Rex! I got your bird!" Her captor shouted, holding her up by her arm. Their leader with his red hair glowing in the light of the fires, looked up to them. Even beneath the mask that covered half of his face, she could see the glee in his eyes.

"That's the one! Give that one to me."

They lifted her over the balcony and dropped her into his arms. There wasn't much she could do, but she couldn't get away. He hooked his arms round her chest and began hauling her kicking and screaming towards the vans.

Out.

Out!

Need to get out!!!

His nails bit into her skin, inflaming the burns she had received from her escape. The pain gave her a nudge of realisation.

His fingers were exposed.

All that armour and he'd left his fingers exposed.

Yanking his hand up, she bit down hard. Her sharp little teeth piercing his skin and crunching though the bone, she shook her head like a dog with a toy. The man shrieked, tightening his hold on her. The more he tightened the harder she bit until she felt a crunch in her jaw and the man dropped her, holding his hand in agony.

Her head snapped round, taking in her surroundings in a single glance, processing all the possible escape routes and letting the world seem to fall into slow motion again.

Fire flickered all around, glinting off broken glass and blackening once white walls. Between the armoured van and the ground, a gap too small for a grown man in Kevlar to get through, but small enough for a tiny ten-year-old girl.

Spitting out the finger she had bitten off, she slammed her wings back against her captor, winding him and throwing herself forward. She could move faster than them, she knew she could. Her slate-grey wings flared out and beating hard as she ran for speed. The other men were slow to turn and follow her as she dove beneath the van. Wings drawing in tight, she slid beneath it out into the open darkness, the stones tearing at her stomach and knees.

There were more armoured vans outside, some already driving away, whilst a few lingering men who were waiting, were startled by her eruption from beneath the van. The fire cast a dull orange light on the landscape, a blazing beacon in the night, glittering off the lake the facility stood by and the patches of January snow. She bolted as the men turned to stare at her. They couldn't chase her across water. Icy frost stung at her burnt feet as she raced towards the dark lake at a full sprint and beating her singed wings down.

With a leap, she had lift off, rising into the air and sailing over the loch. Several of primaries were missing and damaged, and her tailfeathers were still smouldering with the fire, but she had enough power in her near fifteen feet of wings for her to get skyborne, driving herself up with all her might.

Chest burning with the effort, she arced round in the sky, circling back over the estate, trying to locate one of the other exits where her sister may have escaped from. So much of it was on fire, the people pouring from it like ants, silhouetted black against the flames. The large buildings were engulphed, with the sign that read *ARCDA: The Arcadia Corporation*, which hung above the entrance crashing to the ground as the mercenaries threw grenades at it. Even the homes on the hill were burning with the wooden playpark reduced to scorched embers.

The north end of the facility exploded into a ball of fire, illuminating the valley and catching the light on the whites of her wings. The shock of heat seared her and she was knocked back. Catching herself before she could drop too far, she looped and righted herself into a hover to see a second explosion in the western end closest to the mountains and village.

They were razing it to the ground. Everything.

The lights on the vans began to glow, the attackers evacuating themselves from the devastation. She looked down, trying to pick out any semi-familiar faces of doctors or even her sister, but she shouldn't have lingered. Scanning the people escaping she made direct eye contact with the leader of the attackers through the sights of a gun.

The bullet cracked through the air, tearing through her chest before she even registered what he'd done. Pain ripped through her, a white-hot agony that blinded her and stopped her wings from beating.

And then she fell. Blackness and cold enveloping her.

No!

No.

Too cold.

She blinked in the light, awakening for a third time.

Her head throbbed rapidly in time with her pulse at the brightness and the sudden cold, her chest aching in exhaustion and pain. Ice clung to her hair and feathers, the cold gnawing at her bones, leaving her senseless and exhausted. Half in the water of the lake, with all her might she dragged herself out, soaking winged and soaking haired, onto the frozen land.

Looking around she tried to remember where she was. The grey clouds and snow-covered ridges of a featureless mountainous land were reflected perfectly in the flat teal-grey waters of the loch. It was familiar, but…her memory of why it did so was so faint that when she tried to grasp at it, the thought dissipated into smoke.

The cold frosty grass beneath her feet made her toes feel sore, as though she had been walking over burning coals. She put her hands to her face to feel her cheeks. They stung the moment she touched them. The pain was very real, and too intense for it to be a dream. The more she thought about it the more she became aware that she was hurt all over and began to sob, dropping to her knees in pain. Her face, her feet, her arms, and her wings and tail too with the awful keratin smell of burnt feathers that had melted right to the skin. But her chest-

She felt her chest where a gaping hole was, just below her deep Y-shaped clavicle and above her lungs and heart. An inch either way and she'd have been dead. The icy water had helped in a way, making it too cold for her to bleed out with the gaping bullet wound, though she could barely remember how it had happened or how she had survived it.

Explosions and fire, glimpses of bright orange flames.

The images dissipated into smoke as the pain worsened as tears rolled down her cheeks and stung at the scorched skin. Had she lived there? Visited there? She didn't know, it was just… She was missing something…no…everything…. It just all faded away like a dream.

Whatever had happened it didn't matter; she just wanted the pain to stop.

"Are you alright?" A voice asked from behind her, soft and filled with concern.

Head heavy and mind lethargic, slowly she looked over her shoulder at the speaker. A woman was knelt next to her. Wingless but not like the doctors. She had a strange face. Yellow eyes and white canines bright against her dark olive skin that shimmered with sparse ashy white fur. It was hard to focus, but she was certain the woman had a twitching tail of an animal.

"What's your name?" The woman asked softly, holding her rough clawed hands out for her to hold. Things moved behind her, drawing in closer, people probably, but it was so hard to focus.

Turning fully, she staggered forwards and fell into the arms of the woman, exhaustion overcoming her.

"Hey now, it's alright, you're safe." She cooed, gently brushing the little girl's hair from her face, "Are you hurt? Can you tell me your name?"

"Storm…my name is Storm."

STORMBITE

BOOK I

1

London at three in the morning was one of the quietest hours possible for the metropolis. It was humid, the earlier rain evaporating and carrying with it the earthy fresh scent of petrichor and mint throughout the city, drawing out the insects and night-time wildlife with it. Southbank was almost deserted, leaving the luminescent artworks and glowing fireflies unadmired in the semi-darkness.

Almost, save for the five individuals stalking down the embankment path alongside the Thames, past the gently bobbing cruisers and barges with their golden solar sails moored close to the stony banks. Amidst the wind turbines, and dozens of towering new skyscrapers draped with plant-life that transformed the city into a vertical forest, the iconic London skyline remained relatively unchanged across the decades. The Houses of Parliament and the London eye behind them were all illuminated by a warm gold light, although the men didn't seem too interested in admiring the scenery. They were too busy hunting.

Coming to a stop, they scented the air for their target.

Canids. One ARCDA's many synthetic creations. Two Coyotes, a Dog, a Wolf, and a Fox. Hardly a uniformed and united pack, but they didn't need to be a pack to work. ARCDA had assigned them with the task of recapturing a rogue Synth, and a job was a job; it didn't matter who they worked with.

Although Canids were based upon canines, they didn't look particularly dog-like, yet they also didn't look human. It was subtle enough for the most part that the humans could easily ignore and walk past them in the street like any other stranger. However, if they were to stand just a few feet away and take a good look then the more inhuman and almost Anubis-headed the elder Canids appeared.

Their jaws protruded from their faces an inch more than would be normal on humans as they were full of pointed canine teeth, only visible if they grinned or snarled. Their nostrils split along the sides separating them from the rest of the face allowing them to twitch. Fur covered their faces, arms, and large mobile triangular ears, a trait that continued down their thick muscular necks and along their spines to their tails. They had hidden their tails down one leg of their pants and occasionally they would twitch involuntarily, which for anyone stood behind them would have been the one thing that would have drawn attention. They even had whiskers, which were hidden amongst the sparse fur across their faces and could easily have been mistaken for being part of their beards.

Strange and inhuman, but all part of their design as Canid Synths.

"Your nose had better be right, runt!" The leader, a Wolf based Canid, snarled to the youngest of the five, the Dog. "I don't want to have run all the way down from Camden for nothing!"

He scratched at his neck where the collar of the shirt was beginning to rub against his still damp fur, clearly irritated at the long journey; they would have taken the underground, but as always with London, the trains were delayed.

"Maybe he's lying." Jabbed the Fox. The Wolf growled at the idea.

"If this *is* a fucking goose chase, I'll use your tail as a feather duster." He sneered, making the young Dog flinch.

The three others chuckled at their leader's remark and grinned at the runt, their amber eyes flashing with eyeshine as they caught the low light cast upon them.

The young Dog-Canid's green eyes were wide with panic, and too young to have grown a fully furred beard, his whiskers tremored along his jaw. It was his fault they were out so late in the first place and he didn't want to be punished for any mistakes. The conventional methods of tracking their target through technology had failed and so he had been dragged from the wilderness of the Ardèche to work temporarily as a Scent-Hound. He detested it. This wasn't what he had trained for at all; he had wanted to be part of the Crisis Aid unit where he could help people, not part of the Hunting unit.

But a job was a job, and he couldn't get further from what he was accustomed to, as London was a complete contrast to the mountains and gorges with its incessant noise and crowds. Dodging cars and road works, hopping on the backs of the solar-powered trams, running through the backstreets trying to avoid the police who seemed to be everywhere. He wasn't used to any of it and the current task had resulted in spending two days running around one of the world's largest cities, testing his abilities to the absolute maximum.

And the smells; trying to distinguish a single scent out of a million more overpowering ones was far more difficult than any test set up by Core – ARCDA's military faction.

A combination of metal, dust, human, foods of every origin, pigeon, rotting rubbish in bins, seaweed from the river, car fumes, deodorant on humans, dogs, cats. With a population of ten million humans who never stopped moving, and transport all around the city, it was a perfect place to hide. He just wanted to explore every inch of it, as he hadn't spent much time out in the real world and half the things which he saw he had no name for.

"I-it's always right. I wouldn't lie." He protested, English coloured by his French accent.

"Hah!" The Wolf scoffed, scratching his head with a black clawed hand, "The number of times I've heard kids like you say that. They always lie and end up in trouble, not always with the bosses though."

"Like that one Pard tied up in the park and stripped naked!" One of the Coyotes laughed, nudging the Fox, in the side with his elbow. "Didn't he get transferred after he got back?"

"I think he got sold to Atlas, or maybe even Delta." The Fox responded with a twitch of one of his huge ears. They both cackled at the misfortune of the cat-based Synth. The young Dog however didn't find the idea of being sold to Atlas or Delta and *recycled* a very appealing one.

His nose twitched as they drew closer to the target, focusing upon the distinctive perfume of magnolia and sweet lemon on top of unnatural fur and feather, a sweet contrast to the salty clay scent of the river that grew stronger with every step.

The tide was out, revealing the stony banks of the Thames along the edges of the river wall and the bases of Waterloo Bridge. Shielding his eyes from the glare of the streetlights, he could see a figure standing in the shadows of the bridge, able to see far greater detail in the darkness than humans could ever achieve.

"Over there, *monsieur!*" He said pointing, though not very confidently, as something did not seem quite right, "She's under the… *waterloo bridge.*"

A new word he had recently learned in English and wasn't too sure if he had pronounced it right. Even so, they didn't seem to misunderstand his pronunciation and accent. The Wolf grinned wryly, somewhat relieved that they had found her after two days of searching and being led on a wild goose chase. The other four sniffed the air peering into the darkness under the bridge, leaning over the wall for a better view. Even in the low light they could see long honey-brown hair trailing out of the hood of her coat, and what they presumed to be the tips of her wings and tail pointing out from the bottom. It was easy to see her now, catching her breath against the wall of the riverbank and using the stench of the river to try and hide.

"Well done runt, you've saved your tail." He chuckled and loosened his tie and the buttons on his shirt.

The second Coyote's grin widened as he finally caught the scent, salivating with excitement.

"Is that it? It smells strange."

"She's a Tribrid. Hasekura made from the information I was given, worth at least eighteen million…" The Dog hesitated slightly now that he had gotten a better look at the target. Although he could see no one else beneath the bridge or near it, he felt as though there was something wrong.

"Well let's go say hello to the *little lost kitten.*" The Leader growled, clawing open his shirt. From his pocket he withdrew several small patches and pressed them against his chest. The effects of the Nitro, Boosters, and EPI+ patches hit his system immediately, and he shuddered and gagged at the sudden spike in blood pressure and the intense sensory overload as all sounds and scents became acutely clear, followed by the high of the chemicals that would help him to heal in case of a fight. The drug patches had a terrible effect on the older Canids, making their fur grow rapidly and bringing on a half-feral state but that didn't stop them from enjoying the high it brought with it.

The Wolf shook his Anubis-head with a deep and throaty growl, itching and clawing at his skin watching as the scratches healed into thick patches of grey fur. Clawing at the tight clothing, he begun to rip it and free the itching coarse fur spreading across the rest of his body and scratching at his dog tag engraved onto its thin metal band around his bicep, its spiked undersides embedded deep into his skin. It hurt like hell, but he couldn't take it off.

The other three Canids applied their patches shortly after, taking their lead from the senior and biting into their own arms or smacking each other in the face with a laugh to check the drugs were working.

"Now this is more like it." The Wolf growled, voice strangled and deepened a few octaves by the rush of drugs. The green-eyed Dog flinched, uncomfortable with them being so visible in the middle of a big city.

"*Monsieur!* Sir! Should you really be doing that?" He babbled, quickly shooting a glance around, "I-I mean, what if we are seen?"

"Who cares," The Fox hissed, flexing his clawed hand so that all the joints cracked, "It's not like there's anyone around right now."

"But we shouldn't-"

"What are you gonna do about it? Howl for your Alpha, little puppy?"

The Wolf swiped at the Fox, ripping out a chunk of skin and making the Canid bark with shock.

"Shut up and do your damn job!" He snapped, and with a shake of his shaggy head he lunged forward snarling, sprinting on all fours towards the Tribrid Synth with the other three Canids following close behind, lumbering awkwardly on two legs.

"Wait! We really shouldn't be..." The Dog yelled after them, trailing off as he realised that they would never listen to reason.

He started running after them, doing his best to keep up with their lolloping pace. However, as he drew closer a new scent caught his attention.

Honey. Why could he smell honey? He focused harder on the sub-notes of the scents, metal, feather keratin, chamomile detergent, adrenalin, coming from two...*no...three* different sources including the Tribrid. Ears straining, he slowed so he could focus. Then, over the background rumble of the city, he heard it.

Wingbeats.

In that moment he realised why the chase and location seemed odd. No one would stay in one spot and allow their pursuers to get this close, they'd even hear them coming through the din of the city, unless–

There's more than one Synth!'

"Wait! *C'est un piège!*" He shouted, but they had already vaulted over the wall that ran along the river edge and were rushing at full sprint to meet the Tribrid.

"*Merde!* Why do these idiots never listen and just charge in–" He complained to himself as he too vaulted over the wall after them.

The four Canids charged up to the girl, slipping in the mud but cornering her with snarling and snapping jaws before she could make a run for it.

"Hello kitty." Chuckled the Wolf, snapping at her and making her jump back so she was pressed against the wall. The other three surrounded her, one on either side and two in front.

The Dog landed on the pebbled bank but refused to go any closer. His nose twitched as he tried to pick up on the scents of any more nearby before he got too close, but the salty stench of seaweed, rust, and clay overpowered him.

Her wings were tucked under her coat, with the longer feathers sticking out from the bottom reaching her knees and tufted lion-like tail twitching in agitation. It would be difficult for her to take off and fly with the coat around her wings, although if she tried, she would be caught and her head ripped off before she could even take her coat off.

"It's not safe for a little kitten to be out on her own especially at night," The Fox mocked, "There are plenty of big bad men who might eat you."

"Don't come any closer! I'm warning you!" She panted, sounding exhausted but turning and tensing to spring away from them at any second. She wasn't a Pard, but they didn't doubt that like them, she could still leap over them if she wanted to, although the slippery mud would have made it difficult.

"Why not? Are you scared of me?" He mockingly swiped at her face. "Are you scared kitten?"

She ducked as he sliced his thick claws at her, this time not so teasingly. Her hood fell back, revealing a pair of rounded, furred ears that were flattened back against her hair. It gave them a better look at what she was; not quite an Avio, but not a Pard either. She was something entirely different and not at all designed by ARCDA. They growled and stared in surprise and awe at the girl, not having expected Hasekura, a rival bioengineering company, renowned for its terrible bootleg Synths, to have produced such a beauty.

And she was *beautiful.*

Narrow, monolidded, hazel eyes dark against the unblemished olive skin and mane of silky golden-brown hair gave her a sweet and innocence appearance, even with the rounded ears and tiny blue feathers that were visible along the sides of her neck and scattered throughout the fur of her tail.

"Don't touch me." She warned again with a subtle growl in her voice, trying to shrink as a Coyote raised a paw to grab at her. Reactively, the Tribrid blocked and snapped the Coyote's fingers back with a meaty crunch and burst out into a melodic peal of laughter as they reeled back at the Coyote's pained yelping.

"I said, *don't touch me.*" Her round ears flicked forward with excitement, and she smiled with a wry fanged grin. "How stupid are you mutts? One cute girl and you forget how to be hunters?"

The Wolf frowned as much as his fur allowed him to, about to snarl at her when the Lioness chuckled. Her stance changed from meek to predacious within a blink an eye, as though there had been a jump in a video and they had missed a scene, leaving the Canids with a burning sensation tingling in the back of their skulls.

"S-Sir!" The Fox stammered. The Wolf snapped his head round to look at his comrade, only to watch as the Fox staggered, clutching at the deep bloody gouges across his throat and collapse lifelessly to the floor. The remaining Canids leapt away from the bleeding corpse and the bloody handed Lioness with panicked barks.

"What the fuck?" The Coyotes yelped wildly, huddling close together and backing away from the Lioness. "*What the actual fuck!*"

A mocking whistle from behind them revealed a second person, lurking in the shadows of the underside of the bridge. Snapping their heads round at the sound, a flash of red eyeshine caught their attention in the dark.

With a thrumming blur of iridescent blue-green feathers, he launched himself out of the shadows onto the bank and threateningly flared his narrow wings out.

An Avio.

With a wingspan of at least sixteen feet, they made the already tall young man appear much larger. The two long, glossy, peacock-like tailfeathers that held two huge, feathered disks flicked and caught the light behind him. With opalescent blue eyes that contrasted against the rich amber skin and glossy brown hair, he was equally as handsome as the Tribrid was beautiful, but he held himself with a manner that alerted them they were dealing with a well-trained Elite and not a delicate Risio product.

The Canids moved closer together, knowing that if separated they were an easier target against an Elite.

"Are they really letting unranked Quartzes like you out into the wild?" The Hummingbird snorted, brandished a hunting knife with an elegant flourish. "At least you dogs make good practice."

The Wolf's fur bristled, spinning and dropping into a lunge towards the Hummingbird with a roar of, *"You fucking-!"* only to be cut off as from their right swooping in on silver wings with tremendous speed was a third Synth.

Wings pulled in close to avoid scraping them on the wall as well as to gain speed, she struck them feet first at full momentum, knocking the closest Canid into the remaining two, taking them off their feet and throwing them across the riverbank.

Her momentum carried her forward, gliding speedily over the fallen bodies as she banked back towards the river, smacking the Dog in the face with a single wing hard enough to knock him backwards. He yelped in pain as he fell, cracked his head against the stony riverbank and was knocked unconscious.

Downed by the strike and the shock the Wolf lay under the body of the remaining two, snarling angrily as he tried to regain his senses and breathe.

With the Canids down, the Lioness launched her attack, swiftly pulling a pair of knives that were hidden on thigh belts beneath her coat and stabbed the closest Coyote viciously and repeatedly in the jugular whilst he lay stunned on the floor.

"Is it fun to hurt girls now?" She snarled as she stabbed furiously. "Is it? *Is it?*"

He gurgled out a cry for help, blood spluttering from his jaws with the booster patches unable to heal him quick enough, clawing at his wounded throat until he too lay dead.

The Wolf however was not so easily kept down.

Shoving the unconscious body of the remaining Coyote off him and sitting up he swiped a clawed hand at the Lioness's face. She reeled back in time, falling back against the wall.

The Wolf roared, rolling onto his haunches and fixing his sights on the Lioness. He drew his arm back to try to swipe her again, but within a blink, she had moved five feet away from the spot she was in, holding the bloodied knives up and prepared to pounce and attack. The Wolf however, was left with the burning sensation again and agony in his arm as it struck the seaweed covered wall. A muser. They had a muser with them.

He howled in pain and snapped his head round to where the Lioness now stood and made a lunge to attack again, only to be struck by the Hummingbird who rushed forward and stabbed him in the back, missing his target of the spinal cord, as the Wolf twisted into the attack. The drugs and bulked muscles gave him more resistance to the attacks than the slighter Fox and Coyotes, but it didn't stop him from feeling the pain.

Swinging his arms around to swipe and snapping his head round, the Wolf gnashed his long teeth at the Hummingbird behind him. He caught the young man's chest with his claws, managing only to graze him as he reeled backwards. Knife still in his back, the Wolf lunged at the Hummingbird, jaws open wide to bite down on the young man's throat, but his attack was cut short.

The silver-winged assailant struck him with another aerial attack, kicking him sideways in mid-leap. She held onto the Wolf and skidded with him as he splashed into the river.

She snarled down at him with a raptorial screech, sabred cat-like fangs bared at him and talons ripping into his throat. Her wings flared out either side as she balanced, she drove her the talon on her thumb into his eye, piercing it and gouging it out. Howling and thrashing, the Wolf managed to catch hold of her hair, dragging the girl's face closer to his jaws.

She resisted and dug her talons in deeper. There was a sudden cracking sound, and with a spasm the Wolf kicked violently as he was electrocuted and gave out a last dying strangled scream before his head lolled to one side, dead in the water.

Slamming the Wolf away with a smile and arms still buzzing with a tingle of electricity, she shocked the dog tag that the Wolf wore, ripping it from his arm.

Spinning on her heels, she headed back to the others and neatly folded her wings away, doing her best to keep the tips off the muddy ground.

"Done and done," She chirped playfully, tossing the metal band into the air and catching it, pleased with the results of their trap.

"Storm, what the *fuck* were you doing?" The Hummingbird yelled at her angrily, stepping in to stop her from going any further. Storm rolled her eyes at him, already prepared for his criticisms. "Can you not keep to a plan at all? I was going to deal with him, you were meant to just stun them and catch any that ran!"

"Does it really matter, Wilny? They're dead, aren't they?" She shrugged her shoulders, rousing her feathers up and shaking her wings out before resettling them. Wilny's frown didn't change and his two long tailfeathers whipped about behind him in agitation as he continued with his criticism.

"What if there had been more of them? Using Kat as bait was risky enough. She would have been completely outnumbered there if you didn't take your time getting down from the sky. I had to give away my position and stall because you were taking so long and came in at the wrong angle!"

"I'm sorry that I delayed you by two seconds, *sweetheart*, but I had to change my angle of attack." Storm snarled, brushing past the bigger man, intentionally bumping him with a wing. "I was *trying* to keep to the plan, like you keep bitching at me to do."

"And what if they had guns too? No chance, she'd be ripped apart!"

"Kat's a big girl, she could take them."

"I seriously doubt that."

"I'm right here you know!" Kat snapped as she wiped her knives clean, tail twitching angrily. Kat beckoned Storm to her side, leaning down so that she could wipe the blood from Storm's face.

"I'm hardly a damsel in distress, Wilny." She continued. "I could have dealt with them, even without any knives on me. Canids are slow."

"I'm sure you could have done it on your own Kat," said Wilny sourly "it's just I was concerned about...*her*." He nodded towards Storm who smirked.

"Concerned that I might have fucked up and hurt Kat too?" Though she said it in amusement, there was an edge to her words. Wings flicking in and out in a sharp twitch, Wilny stood upright and glowered down at her, blue eyes narrowed.

"Of course. Idiots are always dangerous, especially out of control ones." He said with cold sharpness. "The overkill was completely unnecessary; you both could have killed it far more efficiently and cleanly than you did."

"Whatever you say, now stand down and lighten up." Storm said with a smirk and playful slap across his buttocks, walking over to the body of the Dog who lay face up on the stony bank with a darkening bruise across his face. She glanced over her shoulder at him, her eyes glittering mischievously.

"And despite what you love to believe, *Wilma*," She chirped, "I'm always under control. It's why I let the puppy live. The overkill was because they deserved it after what they did to that girl."

With her light Scottish accent, and sweet sunny tone of voice she made the sentence seem far more disturbing than she intended, it might have unnerved Wilny if he was not currently mad with her.

Frowning, he just shook his head and retrieved the metal tag from around the Fox's arm. One of the Coyotes which Storm had attacked, stirred. She hadn't killed it. It looked up at Wilny with a bleary orange eye. Before it could make a sound, he put his hands round its jaw and the back of its head and snapped its neck, quickly and quietly so as not to alert the girls and to finish the job. As he did so, Wilny realised what she said. His feathers roused angrily and tailfeathers thrashed about behind him.

"Wait. You mean you didn't kill that dog either?"

"It's for interrogation purposes, not just kindness."

"*Kindness?* Are you completely insane? This was elimination not interrogation!" Wilny snapped flourishing the knives in his hands about in anger. "Are you completely incapable of thinking of the consequences of your actions you ignorant-"

"Oh, calm your arse-feathers *Winnie*. I've got this."

He stopped and stared at her. He was used to the retorts but was shocked that she had come up with one so weak.

"*Arse-feathers? Winnie?* Really? That's the best you've got?" He cocked a scar-split brow at her in bewilderment.

"I'm tired." Shrugging, Storm looked over at Kat who was equally unimpressed with her decision but was keeping quiet about it. Unlike Wilny who had only dealt with Storm's behaviour for a few months, Kat had had well over a year to become accustomed to her behaviour and found that it was always best to keep quiet and wait until she'd finished before criticizing.

Sighing, Storm gave a little gesture to the Lioness to join her.

"Kat, can you be my wing-woman to shut him up please?"

"Storm. Are you sure this is a good idea? We don't even know if this is worth it or not." The Lioness asked. Her ears and tail tipped with black both twitched in agitation as she eyed the unconscious Dog.

"I'm sure. There's nothing to worry about." Storm assured her, crouching down next to the body, placing her hand upon his neck and giving him a small shock of electricity.

The jolt woke the Dog with a yelp of shock, clutching at his chest and coughing.

"*C'est des conneries.*" He swore, rubbing his face as he felt the throb from the bruise and bringing tears to his eyes. Both his face and the back of his head ached from where he had been hit.

Then someone near him laughed and he caught the metallic scent of blood.

"Aww he's so adorable, look at him the little Puppy. Hey Kat. What do you think he's based on?"

"Probably a husky or a spaniel since he's a Scent-hound."

The Dog flinched and almost scrambled backwards into the river as Storm crouched in front of him smiling, wings tensely arched in preparation to launch at him. She hopped forward, barefooted with only four long toes on each foot but with every one of them ending in a long sickle shaped talon.

'*Avio!*' the word was like an alarm in his mind at seeing the wings.

A Synthetic species he had never encountered in person, having only seen them within diagrams during training and as a skeletal taxidermy, but up close they were far more terrifying than he had anticipated.

"Don't move and you won't be hurt, little Pup." Storm said sweetly, but only sounding menacing. Her fanged smile and piercing eyes only made it more frightening to the inexperienced young Canid.

"I just want some information from you. It'll be better if you'd just cooperate with us. Understand, Puppy?"

He glanced behind her to see the Lioness and Hummingbird watching him. There was a tickle across the back of his head as their muser – the Hummingbird – tested his state of mind. Three against one, he wouldn't stand a chance against them all together.

'Run! Run!' his mind screamed. He had seen how quickly they had killed the Fox, and although he could not see the bodies of the others because of Storm's banded wings shielding him from the sight, he could smell the blood.

'She killed them, and she'll kill you too!'

He started to shake.

'I don't want to die!'

Adrenalin kicked in out of fear, triggering the fight-or-flight response. He lunged forward at her, aiming to scratch her face with a well-aimed swipe with his thick claws.

He may have been fast, but her reactions were faster. By the split second he had bought his shoulder back to power the swipe, she had seen what he was going to do as much as Kat and Wilny had. Both had flared their wings out to power themselves forward into a lunge to defend her, but Storm reacted fast enough on her own. She blocked the swipe with one arm, and with the other snapped her fist forward and flicked him on the nose, giving him a small shock in doing so.

"Bad puppy," She said, calm smile never faltering and pushing the Dog back as he rubbed his nose.

He gawped in bewilderment, leaning back on his hands, staring as he tried to think of what to do next. Wilny was watching him warily, unsure if the Storm had control of the situation or not. Knife in hand he wasn't about to let his guard down for a single second. If he thought the Dog might try and attack again, he would strike.

Kat also stepped up behind Storm to be closer in case the Dog tried to attack again, but upon getting a closer look, she started to laugh as she saw how young he was.

"He really is a puppy." She chuckled quietly to Storm, "He hasn't grown into his paws yet."

She gestured to the lumbering sun bronzed arms, covered in sparse cream and grey fur the same colour as his hair. The Dog's jaw hung open slightly as it failed to contain the oversized sharp teeth, and his fern-green eyes wide with fear.

Cocking her head to one side like a bird, Storm spoke softly to him. "When you've finished behaving like a Feral, we can have a quick and civilized chat; I might even let you go afterward, if you cooperate."

"W-why did you kill them?" He whimpered, retreating away from her further, "Why did you do this? This trap?"

Storm held up her hands trying to explain the situation as best she could.

"It's nothing personal Puppy. None of this is because of you, we only intended to kill that big Wolf."

"But why?"

"We did it to help people who were hurt and save people who they could hurt in the future. Our technician found several..." She paused, and her expression darkened as she thought about it, "*graphic* recordings of these bastards assaulting and abusing people in the Core. They seriously hurt one girl in particular who was meant to be a field nurse they were working with."

"Killing her would have been kinder than what they did." Kat bristled protectively beside her with an enraged growl that he felt in his bones. "They deserved this."

The Dog's shoulders slumped slightly as he felt a pang of pity for this girl he had never met. He didn't doubt for a second that the Lioness was right, knowing how they were from having worked with them. In fact, he felt glad that the Wolf was dead.

"Did you save her?" He asked, speaking before he realised what he was saying, already picturing his commanding officer scolding him for showing the slightest amount of care and compassion.

"We did, but they were still on the loose and hurting others. Then they got transferred to the Hunter Unit and who knows what kind of damage they would have done to humans and Synths alike." She twitched her wings slightly and straightened up. "So, Beth, our technician, organised for them to come out here so we could punish them."

"You mean *kill* them."

"Either, *either*. They deserved everything they got. I would rip his heart out and eat it had I the chance." She said with jokingly but with such sweetness that his blood ran cold.

The Dog swallowed nervously as the translucent lid of the nictitating membrane, blinked across her eye, reminding him that they were incredibly different species.

"Now," She shrugged her shoulders, making her wings shrug too, "can you tell me which bunker you're from Pup? And what kind of Puppy you are. Malamute? Akita?"

"A-Ardèche. France. An err...Core Bunker. I am an Elkhound base, not an Akita." He felt that had to be honest with her. He was scared she might shock him again or worse if she found out he was lying. Storm nodded sagely.

"A French Hound then. That explains the accent. Are you hunting anyone else or was it just the trap that Beth laid down with Kat?"

"I-it was just the trap...they brought me in because their last Scent-Hound and medic went missing."

A smirk shared between the girls told him that they most likely had something to do with it.

"Do you have a name then? A callsign?" Storm asked, head tilting to one side again in curiosity.

"No callsign. My ID is *V-Vingt-deux*- sorry, I meant Hound V-twenty-two-twenty-four," He said slowly for them in English, rolling up the sleeve of his shirt and showing her his dog tag which, like the Wolf, was on the metal band around his bicep. Storm gently took his arm and examined the tags for a moment. There was a sharp shock across his upper arm and the clasp for the band sprung open, allowing Storm to remove it carefully so as not to slice through any blood vessels with the sharp spikes.

Satisfied, she placed it into the pocket of a bag she wore on her thigh and stood, placing her hands on her hips and grinning down at him while he inspected his arm.

"Well, I'm going to give you a proper name then." She chirped gleefully. He looked surprised, as did Kat and Wilny.

"What? Why?" He frowned, warily.

"Because you're not a bad person, and you deserve to have a chance to do something good." She shrugged, then clapping her hands together as she thought of a name for him, "I'm going to call you...*Raoul*."

"Raoul?" Kat questioned, "Why?"

"Because he when he fell in the water he didn't bark or howl properly, it came out as a little puppy *Raoouuu*." She laughed and rubbed *Raoul's* head making him blush a shade darker. Her rolling R's and extended Oo's mimicked the pathetic baby howl he had made earlier.

"*Raoul.*" She said again, rolling the R so it sounded like a puppy growl and giggling. She held her hand out and helped Raoul to his feet, leading him out of the river and back onto the embankment. "I'm sure we can get you some dry clothes back at the house."

"Storm. *No.*" Wilny cut in, stepping up to her, and pulling her back by her shoulder, "We're not taking him back, he'll betray us! Cut his head off and let the Rioteers clean it up with the rest of the bodies."

Storm rolled her eyes at him, brushed his hand from her shoulder and reached up to poke the tiny beauty mark on the right-hand corner of his chin, remaining unintimidated by him.

"You're not in charge here, *sweetheart.* This is my decision."

"Beth won't agree to this."

"Beth knows any mistakes I make are mine to deal with. We are *not* killing him."

"We can't trust him."

Glaring at her, he flourished his knife in Raoul's direction, gripping the blade tightly. Now he was closer, Raoul could see that almost every inch of exposed skin across Wilny's arms were covered in battle scars in groups of parallel lines that indicated claw marks. His stomach knotted. The Hummingbird knew how to deal with Canids and survive.

"Just kill him now! He's not like us, he's an animal! He'll rip your wings off the moment you turn your back!"

"*You* are hardly behaving *civilised* yourself, Wilny." Slate-grey feathers bristling, she stared him down. His iridescent wings thrummed as he beat them in fury, large disked tailfeathers rattling.

Storm stood on tiptoes, as Wilny stood a whole foot taller than her, and flared her sleek wings out either side of her, shielding Raoul from him.

"If you want to start ordering me about, how about you try being less of a twat first."

Kat clapped her hands together, growing tired of their bickering.

"That's enough you two." She snapped, "Wilny, back off or she'll deck you,", but Wilny ignored her. He tensed up, gripping the knife tighter, about to make a lunge for Raoul, but Storm reacted fast.

"I said *no!*" She snarled, springing into a wing-powered kick to the torso that brought him to his knees, coughing and swearing.

Storm tucked her wings back, calming down quickly. Wilny glowered up at her, silently admitting defeat as he rubbed his chest, trying to calm his fluttering heart and feeling for any broken ribs. It wasn't as hard as her usual kicks, but it still would leave a bruise.

Smiling victoriously, she turned to Raoul.

"You can come home with us Raoul. You'll probably like it more out here than being ARCDA's mutt."

He forced a smile out, unsure if he would be safe if he had to go to the same house where Wilny would be, Storm defending him or not.

"Storm, I know your intentions are good, but you do realise Beth will kill you for this. She doesn't like it when you don't follow her plan. And Rex will hate it even more." Kat groaned in both exhaustion and aggravation, rubbing the bridge of her nose.

"Firstly, you're mistaken in assuming that I give a fuck what Rex thinks," Storm grinned cheerfully, heading back up to the ladder of the riverbank wall, Raoul and Wilny following close behind, "and secondly, Beth loves me, she'd never kill me, only lightly stab me. It'll be fine, trust me."

2

Cherry Tree House, Battersea Park, London.

"YOU ABSOLUTE ARSE-BUCKET! WHAT THE FUCK DID YOU DO!"

"Beth, I am so sorry. I really am, honest!"

"*Bullshit!* You do this every time! I give you a simple plan – *A SIMPLE PLAN* - AND YOU COMPLETELY BALLS IT UP FROM TIP-TO-TAIL!"

As the group's second in command and technician, Beth was beyond angry with Storm, holding up a kitchen knife threateningly and making no effort at all to hide the murderous tone in her voice.

Not the usual greeting they were used to, but it was to be expected.

"Why the hell did you bring a Wolf back without consulting me first?" Beth snarled at Storm, her harsh Kentish dialect a contrast to Storm's sweet lightly Scottish one. "You could have told me if you'd checked in you featherbrained tit!"

"Firstly, he's a *Hound* not a Wolf, secondly I can explain." Storm smiled sweetly down at her, trying to sound apologetic as possible. She wasn't scared of Beth. In fact, she found Beth brandishing a knife somewhat amusing, but it did not mean that she wouldn't put it past her that Beth might use it.

"You better had!"

"Will sugar appease you for the moment, while I explain what my intentions were? It's a very good reason," She said taking out a pack of blueberry muffins she had insisted on buying as they made their way home.

Beth narrowed her eyes, contemplating if she should take them or not before accepting with a huff and putting the knife on the coffee table next to her sofa.

Whilst Raoul remained tensed at the situation, the others relaxed, removing their coats and unbuttoned their jackets so that they were freeing up the wings they had kept hidden on their walk across London.

With Avios being so rare to come across and having never seen one up close before in person, he couldn't help but to stare at them all, observing the differences between them all as well as himself.

As Avios, the bases of their designs mimicked different birds with their shapes and colours, but it wasn't a perfect representation. They weren't designed to be birds, or humans or even anything in between. They were designed to be Avios.

Each set of wings held a different shape, texture and colouration, all individual to their owner. Glossy scalloped peacock blue-green, sleek slate-grey edged with silver iridescence, ragged and badly maintained soft mottled tawny brown, brilliant azure to black gradient highlighted by pale turquoise and marked with faint stripes.

There was no sudden contrast between skin and feathers, but a gradual gradient of small plumes that ran through their hairlines and contoured their bodies from the neck, across the shoulders and upper arms, to the entirety of their backs although he did not know if this extended to their chests also.

He noted how much muscle there was to their shoulders and chests, more than he had anticipated, even on Storm. Even their backs were muscular with a smooth curve into the wing from where just below the shoulder– as he remembered from his classes in anatomy– there was a secondary socket within the modified scapulae, altered collar bone and a deep keel that protruded from their sternums to support their wings.

It wasn't as if the wings had been stitched on to a human body like what occasionally happened with transhuman Avios; they were limbs not accessories, their entire anatomy had been meticulously designed and altered far beyond the designs of any mammalian based Synthetic creation. Even the very material composition of their bones and muscles was different.

Getting herself comfortable once more, Beth shrugged her shoulders so that her short, tattered wings laid themselves across the top of the sofa to prevent any further damage to the flight feathers.

Beth was far smaller than the other two girls were by at least half a foot. Her chest lacked the pronounced muscles that were built up from flying when he compared her to Storm, and despite being an Avio, a Synth-type renowned for their superb eyesight, she wore thick glasses with a tiny crystal optics screen. But then, Raoul knew that she wasn't an Avio from birth. With no feathered ear tufts, facial feathering, or tail feathers, he knew that she was a Transhuman Avio. Now these he *had* come across before.

As Raoul looked down to her hands, he saw that her left arm from the shoulder down was a red and black bionic, as were her legs from the thigh down and designed in such a way that the feet resembled those of a bird, which he assumed provided her with more balance. For all intents and purposes, she was what Core would call a horribly faulty product, yet her disabilities did not make her any weaker or less intimidating. He wondered if it was part of the process of becoming Transhuman that caused her to lose her limbs, although he dare not voice these questions in case she got offended and stabbed him then and there.

"Oh, for fuck…" Beth muttered quietly to herself as a short clip displayed itself in the crystal square on her lens. She snapped her head round and glowered at Storm once again. "Storm! Did you fly down Brixton high-street this morning?"

Storm grimaced for a moment, noting the tone of Beth's voice and how much trouble she was in already, dropping her gaze to the banded feathers on her inner wing as a rueful smile spread across her face.

"No…*maybe*…yes…"

"For fucks sake Storm! What if Rex finds out?"

"Relax. It was clear and quiet this morning and nobody saw! I need to fly at least once a day; you should know that by now."

"It doesn't matter, we agreed upon no flying in streets during the daytime, during lockdown week! Only take off from parks and covered areas. Rex is already on my arse about what you've been doing, how many times do I have to remind you-"

"It's fine, I blacked out the area first. I know what I'm doing, don't worry. It won't get back to Rex."

Beth was far from impressed with this excuse for flying in the streets, but there was nothing she could do about it now. She turned her glare from Storm onto Raoul. Large rust-brown eyes peered over the red-rimmed glasses with an intensity that made him feel incredibly uncomfortable.

She may have been small with soft owl-like wings – the right one noticeably smaller than the left– but she was ferociously intimidating.

"So, tell me," She said sharply to Storm who was busy preening her wings and pretending to ignore her, "Why did you bring a dog home without taking him to the headquarters first for a check-up? It's not because you wanted a puppy is it?"

"How did you know?"

"*Storm!*"

"I'm joking." She laughed, hopping up into a crouch on the back of the sofa and using her wings to balance. "I gave him the once over, he's an honest kid. Hunter Unit scent-hound, as you know. I'm pretty sure he managed catch Wilny's scent from the sky before they fell into our trap. Also, he's French so can probably update you on some of the other bunkers and translate things for when Grace forgets what language to write in."

"You're making assumptions again, Storm. What makes you think he's going to tell us anything?"

"I'm sure I can get something out of him if he refuses," muttered Wilny darkly. Storm rolled her eyes and reached up to mess his brown hair up, revealing an iridescent blue sheen to every strand in much the same way as his wings.

"Down boy. No violence in my house."

He frowned at her, batting her lightly round the head with one of his tailfeathers with a mumble about honey.

"Look, Beth. Just trust me on this." She jumped off the sofa and dangled Raoul's dog tag in front of her, so she could see the identification code on it. "Be kind to him and I'm sure he'll tell you whatever you need to know. You stuck with me when I brought Wilny home so stick with me on this."

Beth stared unblinkingly at her for several moments, then with a deep sigh she took the tags, turned back to her laptop and began muttering to herself as she began typing away. Beaming, Storm patted Raoul on the shoulder reassuringly.

"It's all good Raoul. Beth is just naturally the angriest person in the world. All you have to do is be honest with her and she'll not stab you. Now if anyone needs me, I'm making tea and some midnight snacks." She made a move to leave, then paused and lent into whisper to Raoul.

"But just to warn you, she does like to talk a *lot*, so just nod and look interested even if you don't understand her."

With a ruffle of his shaggy grey-brown hair, she left the room, heading to the back through an archway to what Raoul assumed would be the kitchen, leaving him in the room with the others.

Raoul gulped nervously, remaining in the centre of the room, glancing around at the furnishings and size of it, looking for an escape more than anything but being astounded by his surroundings.

Having seen the occasional film or television programs that were sometimes shown to them to keep them entertained as young Synths, it wasn't as if it was all entirely alien to Raoul, but it was still rather odd; especially when he remembered that these four Synths were *living* here.

It was a huge room with a tall ceiling with an eclectic mismatch of furniture and house plants. A wooden bookcase stood against the stairs leading up to the next floor, overflowing with books of nearly every variety and a fireplace with an actual log fire, decorated with plenty of photos and mementos. In the centre of the living room were two sofas with a glass coffee table between them, angled towards a large TV that sat against one wall with various wires and accompanying screens hooked up to it.

It may have been messy, jackets and bags strewn over the backs of chairs, books lying about in piles by the sofa doubling as tables for their phones and laptops, the strong smell of coffee and honey, and the odd bright blue or green feather floating about on the floor, but it was welcoming.

Beth paused from her typing and held out her hand, but not looking away from the screen.

"Where are the tags for the others? I need to change their status on the database and call Owen to make sure he cleaned the bodies up you left behind."

"Here." Wilny handed over the dog tags he had collected from the bodies, and leant over the back of the sofa, trying to see what Beth was doing. Smirking, she began typing away silently, ignoring Wilny.

Standing awkwardly in the middle of the room, Raoul felt a little isolated as he waited for Beth to start asking questions. His damp clothes were starting to itch, and it was now becoming uncomfortable to have his tail hidden down his trouser leg.

Nearly all mammal-based Synths had tails with different lengths, textures, and patterns between species and even between batches. Because Canid Synths were so numerous and often identical within their batches, they often used tail traits as a method of differentiation. He'd once asked why they had been made that way, since Preternaturals bore no such morphological traits with their very human appearance, but never had received an answer.

"*You*," Beth snapped sharply at Raoul, and pointing to the second sofa, "Sit."

Obeying her orders, he sat down, not leaning back against the cushions on the thought that she would appreciate having her sofa smell of wet dog. His arm hurt from where Storm had shocked him, his face however was feeling better and the bruise had gone from purple to yellow very quickly, thanks to his rapid healing.

"Katana, go take a shower, feel free to stand down for the night. Wilny can deal with any problems."

"Got it."

He forgot the Lioness was there she was so quiet. She stretched her azure wings out and headed up the stairs, Raoul finding himself glancing at her bare legs and elegant tufted tail smattered with tiny blue feathers, as she left the room.

He caught himself when he realised what he was doing and stared at the floor in embarrassment, half expecting Wilny to leap across the room and batter him across the head for looking, but he didn't seem to have noticed. Despite having encountered very few girls in his life he still knew enough from the female doctors to know not to stare.

"Now," Beth looked up at him over the top of her glasses, brushing her auburn hair from her face, "Since Storm decided to let you live you better prove yourself to be both trustworthy and useful. I've disabled your tracking chip. I assume Storm dealt with it herself, but I am taking no chances. ARCDA will not be able to find you and will assume you dead. The moment you decide to backstab us, reach out and contact them or run, you will be torn limb from limb by both Wilny and Katana, then electrocuted by Storm, who will be *very* angry at your lack of gratefulness towards her. Do I make myself clear?"

Her sharp and clearly murderous tone made the fur on the nape of his neck stand on end. He swallowed, for a moment forgetting to speak English.

"*Oui, Madame.*"

"Good. You can start by giving me the location of the Bunker you're from and which faction it works under."

Raoul paused before he spoke. He did not want to make a mistake and have this aggressive little Owl lacerate his throat with the knife that was still on the table in front of them.

"Ardèche Gorge. The *Haut Baravon* Bunker near *Saint-Remèze*, it was Core, but it's part of the Delta faction now." He said, making a little sour face as he thought about ARCDA's technologically focused faction, Delta.

Wilny frowned at him. "He speaks very good English for a French Dog." He muttered to Beth, bitterly.

"All Synths from mainland Europe are taught to speak three languages fluently, usually just French, English and German– Any other ones you've been to and their faction?" She asked briskly, cutting through her own sentence and getting back on subject, still typing away.

Raoul shifted about on the sofa, growing increasingly uncomfortable, the more he was watched. It felt as though he were talking to a doctor for a transfer interview.

"Schwarzwald in Germany and more recently Arkhangelsk in Russia, they're both Core factions. I also speak some Spanish, Italian and Russian, but my standard Arabic is not very good. I've also received medical training and other transferable skills as part of my original batch purpose."

"You must be very intelligent then to be so multi-lingual, most people can't even fluently speak one language let alone seven, especially for your age."

"*V.31.12:CanisFamil;NorskElghund-22-24…*such a long ID. Wait. You're part of V-gen?" Wilny blinked, looking between the screen and Hound mouth agape. "But that would make you just *seven*."

"Yes? Is that wrong?"

"No just…Wow you're younger than you look. I thought you were about fifteen." He shook his head and let his wings extend with sharp little flicks, "You're a really smart kid then."

The compliments caught him off guard and he felt his face flush red.

"Your handler's callsign?" Beth asked, glasses slipping down her nose as she peered over them.

"Montfort."

"And your original purpose was intended towards being part of the Crisis Response and Aid Unit? You went through Quartz and first year Emerald Elite training correct?"

"*Oui*- yes, until the commander at Arkhangelsk changed us over to the Hunter Unit."

A small smirk played across her lips as she stopped typing and read what was on her screen. "And how well that transition went." She sighed sardonically, making the fur down Raoul's nape prickle.

"Two years ago, you were put into the testing rings against CY-NX prototypes in a team building exercise with your team, but you refused to fight. Tell me, what your exact reason was for refusing an order?"

He blinked in horror, palling immediately as the memories of what happened flashed up into the forefront of his mind. He paused, so tense he felt sick and trying to put the words into English without sounding like a coward or allowing emotion to overcome him, acutely aware of both Avios' focus on him, although Wilny's expression read more as one of empathy.

"Answer me."

"I refused because …I didn't want to fight little girls, but– I thought it was unfair, but-"

"But they wiped out the rest of your batch because they listened to the orders and attacked. Only you were spared by them, is that correct?"

-The howls of agony as their EMI weapons exploded in their hands, yellow eyes glittering with glee, telkens slicing through bone, the area around them being set alight, the putrid smell of burning fur and boiling blood- No! No-

He forced the memory back and clenched his jaw, focusing upon one of Beth's mottled feathers to bring himself back into the present.

"I should- should have…H-how do you know all of that?" He gulped, voice wavering, clutching his side where a blistered scar covered his skin. He didn't want to remember, didn't want to think about it or let her indulge in his terror.

Beth shrugged and carried on typing. Wilny looked between Beth and Raoul, then peered over her shoulder to look at the laptop screen. Beth had Raoul's profile up with the event recorded onto his page.

The Arcadia Corporation– ARCDA– had profiles for all the Synths they made, listing from everything from their birthdate and base, to the genes that made their eye colour and if they had any talents or family in ARCDA. They were only accessible through their custom-made laptops and the faction doctors accounts inside of the facilities, and then there was Beth.

Raoul did not need to tell her anything because she had it all right in front of her; she was merely testing him to see how truthful and reactive he was, even if it was a little cruel to be poking at such a bad memory. Wilny scowled at the back of Beth's head disapprovingly.

"Good boy. No lies at all so far." She trilled and looked up, "You can relax, Storm was right you're a good kid."

"S-so you *can* see if I'm lying?" Raoul swallowed. "I was not sure if it was true or not that Avios could do that."

"We do process visual information fast enough to detect lies or tells– well, Storm can since she's got the eyes for it – Never play poker with her, she'll always win– You don't need to worry, we're not going to hurt you…" She paused and looked cautiously at him as she was unsure if he had a name or not, or if she had missed it earlier.

"Raoul." He responded with a tentative smile. His new name sounded strange and rather like a puppyish growl in his mouth, but it was better than a set of letters and numbers.

"We're not going to hurt you Raoul. As long as you don't attack or betray us."

"R-right."

"Do you have any questions?"

"Yes…um. What is this place?" Raoul asked, gesturing to the house.

"Cherry Tree House. Our personal base. Set up by the Rioteers about twelve years ago now. Storm's been here the longest and was part of the first Rogues when they were all still here, so she's the first in command due to experience rather than…*maturity*." She set the laptop on the table, stretching her arms and wings out, the soft feathers not making a sound.

A sudden knot of terror formed in Raoul's gut at the mention of the Rioteers. He'd heard about the Rioteers- almost everyone in ARCDA had. Nearly every story about them was of the horrible things they did such as kidnapping children and doctors, destroying medical supplies that could help thousands of people, and bombing buildings with doctors and Synths still inside. They were terrorists.

"The Rioteers...that is the renegade group, yes?" He posed it as a question, trying to keep his tone level. As much as he wanted to tell them this is how ARCDA saw them, he feared doing such would give them a reason to attack him.

"That's right."

"You are Rioteers?" He asked cautiously.

Beth laughed aloud.

"The Rogues *aren't* Rioteers, no. We work with them, but we're not '*with*' with them, if you get what I mean."

"I uh...I think my English is not...Could you repeat that please?"

"The Rogues is *us*." She gestured to herself, Wilny, and Storm in the kitchen. "The Rioteers are *them*. We help *them*, *rescue* people, then give those people safety and they go on to help other people by putting their knowledge, talents and skills to use, so they become *Us*. Tit-for-tat, vivé la libera et freedom, and all that Rioteer propaganda."

Raoul stared at her, trying to process what she was saying. There was something in the word *rescue* that sounded like a lie or sarcasm, though he couldn't tell what it meant.

"But *us*- we do other things, from simple tip-offs and break outs, to international heists. It's all about justice." She explained arrogantly, wafting her bionic arm about.

"Like, I can get into ARCDA's system and give the Rioteers information on which Synths are loose or are in a position where they can easily be rescued and change the statuses on the freed ones to say that they're dead or missing in action. Or even hack into the accounts of dodgy businessmen and expose them for their crimes, find trafficking routes, and all the secrets people don't want you to find out. You know, easy simple things which no one else seems to be capable of."

"You do this for justice?"

"Eh, occasionally for shits and giggles if I'm honest, but if it helps people then it helps. You can't do good by just being good."

Raoul shook his head in shock, undoubtedly certain that Beth was the most dangerous one there after all.

"So, they give you a house to yourselves?" He asked, drawing them back on track, "They don't watch you or order you to go places? You don't have to report in like the Elites?"

"No. We're completely free to do as we wish in the house so long as we keep it clean and don't attract too much attention. We do what we like and do our best to help other people."

"We do *sometimes* behave like Elites." Wilny pointed out. "Though that's mostly on the missions Beth finds and gives us."

"It'd be all too easy to just give up, stop doing anything and overindulge in freedom, but maniac Synths like these need regime and goals to complete." She nodded her head to Wilny who shrugged in agreement.

"Most of our work is Search and Rescue. Occasionally we attack them and anyone who has hurt one of our own. Like tonight for instance, the plan was to avenge a girl who they had hurt so that they never do it to another person again. We help others learn to be people and not just numbers or soldiers or studies or products. We get a chance to *live* and *help*. We are not *products* or *profit*. We are our own people out here. Helping is what we do, and we will do whatever we can to help."

Storm was correct about how much Beth liked to talk, but he could hear the tone of pride in her voice as she spoke. She was proud of the Rogues, the way they lived and what they did.

"That sounds…nice…really nice actually." Raoul stared wide-eyed at her, leaning forward with interest at what she as saying, despite not understanding half the words she said. Even though he did not trust the Rioteers, was intrigued that they would work with the Rioteers and were allowed such privileged freedoms. The only people he had known to have such freedom and power were the doctors and Diamond ranked Elites.

"It is, but hard to come to terms with." Said Wilny flexing his shoulders and stretching out an iridescent wing. "I've been here for about eight months, and I'm still not entirely used to it."

The feathers were neatly scalloped and glossy along the tops, shimmering from pavonated blue and brassy golden-green, to dark indigo-violet primaries tipped with ice white, colours that were echoed in tiny feathers scattered through his wavy brown hair. For such a rugged warrior-esque man his wings seemed almost too pretty for him, and the lack of ear tufts had Raoul wondering if he was a very old Risio design or not.

"It's unusual not having to follow orders, eat at certain times, or train every day. And having so much privacy and freedom is wild."

"Privacy?"

Wilny nodded. "You get a shower all to yourself and you can spend as long as you want in it…with hot water and nice smelling gel which gets blood off much easier than just water. The honey scented one is the best." He smirked to himself, his long-disked tailfeathers swishing about behind him. His comment made Beth laugh and roll her eyes at him.

"You have a very strange obsession with the shower, Wilny. And honey."

"You never had the same treatment as I did, Beth. When you've been forcibly hosed down with ice cold water in a line with thirty other people, then you appreciate it as luxury."

She rolled her eyes, as she had heard this anecdote at least fifty times before.

"You're as bad as the Daggers."

"Daggers?" Raoul questioned, shifting slightly on the sofa as he made room for his tail, taking it out from his trouser leg and brushing the fur back into place.

"One of the main groups who have territory here in the UK." Beth answered, noting the tightly curled tail with a wry smile. "The Daggers are more into sabotaging ARCDA and affiliates, so they can be taken out more efficiently."

"There's not just you people out here?"

"Fuck no. There are at least seven other major groups in west Europe. There's–"

"–The Rogues, which is us." Storm cut in before Beth could answer, carrying in a tray of tea, biscuits, and honey and setting it down on the small coffee table for them all.

"The Daggers, Sienna, Avarken, Matagot, and then Fen and Asena pack. Asena is like the alpha group and are constantly traveling the world to manage other groups in other continents. But there's also smaller groups like Xana, Sea-mist, and Aurelia."

She offered Raoul some tea, and he politely took it, warming his hands on the cup. He sniffed it first to make sure it wasn't toxic. When he looked to Wilny to see if it was drinkable, he found the Hummingbird downing the entire bottle of honey in one go.

"Pack?" He asked looking away from Wilny, who was now shaking the bottle vigorously to coax more honey out. "There are Canids out here too?"

"Yes, tonnes. Asena pack is a purely Canid group, with fifteen members including their boss." Storm said with a smile, brushing her blue-grey hair, the same shade as the backs of her wings, from her feathered face. "Asena Canis. She's the alpha boss. *The Empress*."

"Fifteen is nothing compared to Taurus, one of the North American groups. They have twenty-one members." Beth smirked, sipping her tea.

Raoul choked on his tea and spat it out in shock. "Twenty-one?"

"They're by far the biggest of the forty-nine main US groups. France has seven, Canada eleven, Germany four and I think Russia has nine, but New Zealand has only one." She smirked at him over her glasses. "I'm in contact with just about every known group, but there's still a lot of people out there. It's important for us all to keep in contact with one another just in case one of us needs any help or not but it's hard, especially when you get lone Avios flitting around the place."

"We all help each other." Storm nodded.

Raoul breathed out slowly as he took a moment to process it all.

"I...never realised there were so many..."

"Yeah, and it sounds like there's a lot of us out here, but really there's not many at all." Storm shrugged, giving her wings a little shake, "Barely sixty-thousand of us known Synths, when there's still a few hundred-thousand locked away. And who even knows how many Ferals there are out here, but we do our best to help those we can."

"Risio who usually have buyers in the cities and mansions in countryside. They're the easiest and top of the list for getting rid of. Delta, Core, and Atlas bunkers that get rebuilt pretty much as soon as we clear them out." Beth interjected, irked that Storm stole her thunder. "Aura Bunkers we rarely touch, because we can't fucking find them anywhere. Then there's Hasekura, those bootlegging motherfuckers, the various human gangs and traffickers who get in the way or do damage...we're very busy people."

Raoul sat staring ahead as the information slowly sunk in. It was a lot to get his head around, and he was certain that he was still a little in shock from the earlier events of the night.

"But...how do you survive out here? Do humans not notice? I mean...your face." He gestured to the tiny white and slate-grey feathers that contoured her cheekbones and shoulders.

Wilny burst into laughter.

"Is that a serious question?" He snickered, turning to Storm with a flailing gesture for her to explain. And smiling she did so, letting the feathers across her face rise and flatten.

"Humans in London are too busy focused on their own lives to pay attention to one more stranger passing by. It's not always the case, but a long coat, not letting them look at you for more than ten seconds and going out when its darker usually helps to avoid attention. And if they do notice, they rarely stop and ask."

"Though you have stopped and taken pictures with tourists before now." Beth pointed out. Storm giggled and flicked her hair over her feathered shoulder.

"Well, I couldn't exactly say no when they were so amazed."

Raoul stared into his tea thoughtfully as he came to terms with the fact that at any point, he had been outside he could have made a run for it and been free years ago.

"You help people." He mumbled to himself, mulling everything over. ARCDA wasn't bad, but it wasn't good either. They had made him and educated him yes, but they were also the reason that his team was dead. His side ached at the thought of it.

"I...if I had known..."

"You weren't to know, Puppy." Storm said softly, sitting on the sofa beside him. Her wing brushed against his back, taking him by surprise at how warm and heavy it felt. His cheeks flushed.

"I'll tell you anything you want to know," He said snapping his head back up to face them all.

Beth raised an eyebrow at him.

"There's nothing else I need." She patted her laptop. "The only thing I do need is information on any if Delta has opened any new Bunkers."

"I...don't know that information I'm sorry...but I'll help in any way I can."

"What?"

"I was made and trained to help people who were hurt and in bad situations before I was transferred," Said Raoul with a determined look, "you're helping people and so that's what I'm going to do to, if you'd let me stay."

Beth blinked at him over her glasses, then stared at Storm who was smiling warmly at him, proud at his enthusiasm and willingness to help despite having just been dragged into an unfamiliar world.

"How is it that you found a pure cinnamon roll for a Puppy?"

Aquamarine-green eyes glittering, Storm laughed and downed the rest of her tea.

"It's not that hard to tell if someone is a good person or not Beth, you don't always need a computer to find that out. You've just got to trust them."

"*Urgh!* Please go back to swearing and being violent, the bleeding-heart sweetness is killing me." Wilny groaned, pulling his wings over his head with a dramatic sweep. Rolling her eyes, Storm flicked a biscuit at him.

"Hey. I'm pretty good at judging characters, why do you think I didn't kill *you* even though you can be such a twat at times?"

"But you *did* kill me."

"Only *temporarily*. I did also give you CPR and resuscitated you. I could have left you dead at Gibraltar if I wanted to. You *did* shoot me, remember."

"But you didn't leave me because you think I'm a- what was it? *'Damn fine piece of man-flesh who's good with his guns'* wasn't it?"

Storm tilted her head to one side, recalling if she really did say those words. With an approving smirk she nodded and looked Wilny up and down, admiring his physique.

"That's true, though I like Kat more because I can't resist a beautiful woman, but your pretty boy looks and toughness do make up for your general fuckmongery."

"Ah, she doth swear once again! Balance is restored to the world." He clutched his hand dramatically to his heart and smirked down at her, batting her in the face with one long tailfeather. "Such poor manners you have for a lady."

"I'm as much a lady as you are." She scoffed, trying not to smile at his insult, throwing a small yellow bottle at him, which he caught and looked at. Upon seeing that it was another bottle of honey rather than marmite, he happily began to drink it from the bottle making Beth and Storm laugh.

Raoul started to laugh a little too, seeing how relaxed they all were. They may have been killers, but it was something they could turn off and let go of.

Beth's laptop made a chime and all three turned their heads.

"Storm. Message from Grace."

Storm leaped from the sofa Raoul was sat on, landing on the arm of the chair next to Beth and eagerly peered at the screen.

"What is it?" Kat asked, drying her hair as she entered the living room with a towel around her, not seeming to mind too much that it was the only thing that she was wearing. Raoul did his best to avert his eyes and instead focused on her wing, and now that he had the time to admire them, he was amazed by how vibrant they were.

Velvety feathers of brightest azure to black with the shape of a kingfisher's wing, with tiger striped patterning along the marginal coverts with a pristine streak of turquoise down the vanes of every feather and edged in black along the primaries. The undersides contrasted the bright blue with a flaming red along the secondaries that turned to purest midnight blue with a lone white band along the tips of the primaries. They were stunning.

"One of the African groups which were migrating this way disappeared after they crossed the channel. Senegalese and calling themselves Ciel. The Rioteers in the Calais outpost saw them and checked them in five days ago. They should have made it here by now, but they haven't and there's been no word of them."

"Are there any *suspicious* reports?" Her round ears flicked back as she emphasised the word suspicious, meaning any non-Rioteer or ARCDA reports on the matter.

"Kent police got a report about people lurking in an orchard outside Canterbury covered in blood, and the only thing that I can see that connects is that the RSPB got a call that a giant eagle or buzzard or something crashed landed in the same orchard."

"So, they were attacked or something? Maybe they got hurt and took cover."

"Maybe…I don't think it's ARCDA however, I'd have picked it up." Beth patted the top of her laptop with pride. "I think we just need to go find them and make sure they're alright. It's just a simple search and rescue mission. We'll test run the pup and see if we can use him on heists later."

Storm grinned and hopped back onto her feet.

"Well Raoul, this is your chance to prove yourself and see if you can still remember your Crisis Response training."

"I can help?" He looked up at her hopefully. He wanted to prove himself almost immediately, especially to Kat and Wilny who both seemed to be keeping a close eye on him.

"Actually, this is the perfect opportunity for you to show us what you can do Raoul. First to track them down, and secondly to talk to them and translate. They come from one of the bunkers in Senegal where they speak French mainly. And if there's any injuries then I'm sure you can assist."

"I can help with that." He smiled, feeling strangely valuable.

"Fantastic! Wilny, let him borrow some of your clothes and show him where the shower is please."

"Why me?"

"Because Kat will take forever to dress him." She said, looking across to Kat who pouted a little at the missed opportunity.

"But I can make him look half decent!"

"Kat. We don't have time for an entire modelling session with the new Puppy."

"Fine. I'll dress him." Wilny sighed loudly, gesturing quickly for the Hound to follow him up the stairs before Kat set her sights on him.

"Don't take too long, we'll be heading for the train station in about two hours," Beth smiled "You're not going to waste time with this. It'll be no trouble at all."

"We, Beth. I heard you say *We*."

The smile vanished from Beth's face as she snapped her head round to glare at Storm.

"No." The Owl snapped, "You are not bringing me with you, and that's final."

3

Two hours later, they were on the first train out of London Victoria towards Canterbury, greeting the early sunrise and passing through sleeping towns.

Dressed in long light coats to hide their wings, it gave them all a bulky hunchback appearance with their slouching postures. They would have looked an odd sight for anyone who cared to glance at them for longer than a second, but as Storm had said, no one paid them any notice. Even if they did look then they might have thought twice about seeing wingtips pointing out from the bottom of their coats, but at five in the morning, no one they passed was in any mood to take an interest at all in other strangers. Even the station staff didn't care to look at them for more than a second in their exhausted jaded way before ushering them on through the barrier.

The quiet train also gave them some cover as very few people made the early journey, and their tickets had already been checked leaving them all alone in the carriage with no one to bother them.

Beth took a table to herself and her laptop, whilst adjacent to her sat Raoul and Kat, both of whom were staring out the window. Storm and Wilny were sat behind them, next to each other with Storm asleep on Wilny's shoulder whilst he stared out the window in a daze. They were all sat rather awkwardly, leaning slightly to one side because of their wings or tails, which were hard to accommodate on trains designed for humans.

Tail wagging in excitement as he watched his first sunrise of freedom, Raoul was the most awake of them all. Knelt on the chair, with hands on the window ledge staring out, he looked like an excited puppy about to go on a walk, eyes flicking back and forth, as they followed passing trees or tried to read the signs of the stations they passed.

"*C'est incroyable.*" He breathed as pale pinks and turquoises backlit an array of wind turbines that were slowly turning across the estuary, the still waters reflecting the image perfectly. To humans it would have been such a mundane thing to see, but for Raoul it was amazing. Even though he had been outside may times before, most of the time it was in secluded areas of wilderness for training purposes, and television never did reality justice.

"It's not Kagoshima, but it's still good. A few more people than there should be that want to start knife fights for no reason, but still good." Kat chuckled to herself at the memory, the sound almost like a purr, and adjusted the woven wide-brimmed sun hat that was helping to hide her ears.

Raoul blinked in surprise at her, not sure, if she was talking to him or not, one of his own ears twitching slightly in response. They may not have been as mobile as Kat's, but he along with all other canids, still had muscles to move them accordingly.

"It may look pretty out there, but it doesn't mean that it's completely safe." She hitched up the short blue dress she was wearing to show the Hound a small knife hidden on a thigh belt underneath. "Never can be too careful."

He glanced at the knife for a second and then averted his eyes, so as not to stare at her legs.

"I didn't think you were armed." He mumbled, suddenly feeling nervous about sitting next to the Tribrid who had murdered other Canids in front of him only hours before hand.

She shrugged and brushed the dress back down over her legs. "Only Storm and you aren't armed. Knives are far easier to hide than guns."

"You are from Core then?" He asked cautiously, "I thought you were from Risio because you are...are...what is the word?"

"A Tribrid?"

"*Joli.* Pretty."

"Pretty? Yeah I guess I am. *Pretty and pretty fucking badass.*" She shrugged. "Looks aren't everything, Puppy. Before this, I was in training as a bodyguard and hitman in Japan for an investor of *Hasekura.* They're the ones who made me rather than ARCDA."

The information shocked him, and he looked her up and down once again, slack jawed and confused.

"Hasekura? *Pas question*. Really, I thought that was a lie for the trap you set. That does not seem- but they make such terrible *faux* products! Risio produces sturdier stock than Hasekura and they're useless decorative- ah!" He stopped before he could go any further, looking sheepish as she stared dryly at him. "*Désolé*. I didn't mean to offend you."

"None taken. Hasekura isn't great at anything other than genetic modifications, but they did try with me and my siblings, although that was only because a *lot* of money was put into our commission."

"You were commissioned? That explains the uhm…combination." He grimaced and tried to show that he meant no offence by the fact that she was a very strange Tribrid. ARCDA, despite its proficiency and speciality in creating Synths, rarely made such designs. Even Risio, the faction of ARCDA dedicated to aesthetically designed Synths and other work, didn't intentionally create Tribrids.

"It's a strange look, I know. If you want someone to act as a stealth killer, then why give them big butterfly wings?" Kat rolled her eyes and laughed, taking off her hat, shaking out her honey-brown hair, and brushing the fur of her ears back into place. "*Panacea regina*…I'm still not sure why he wanted to have me made this way, but he did. He was pretty eccentric though."

"*Eccentric*? What is that word?"

"Strange, odd. His office was covered with real butterflies pinned to the walls. Sometimes he'd point to a pretty blue one and say to me, '*this one is you if you misbehave*' then throw a knife at its wings." She shuddered at the memory, her wings tensing at her back.

"Why would he have a knife in his office?"

"To make a statement. He collected a lot of historical weapons, mainly swords and knives and often gave me them to use whenever he had business partners who needed ending. I got my name, Katana, from his favourite kind of sword," She said with a wistful smile. "It used to be Akemi, but Kat suits me more, even if it's one of the third most-common names for Pards."

It was a sudden bit of honesty from her, and it surprised him. Having just been given a real name of his own he could see that her name meant a lot to her and had meaning behind it. However, he could see what she was trying to do by telling him about herself. She was trying to make him feel more at ease with them and help him place some trust in them so that he didn't feel as though he was still under interrogation.

"How long have you been …*free*? If you don't mind if I ask?"

"I've been *free* since I was seventeen, but I've been with the Rogues for a little over a year and a half now, and I'm nothing like what I was when I first arrived. I would never have tolerated any of the humans in the Rioteers."

"And you are…*twenty*?" He was cautious to guess her age as some Synths could look thirty, but be only ten, and others the total opposite.

"I'm nineteen, nearly twenty actually." She sat up, arching her back in discomfort at the seats. "For the few months I wasn't with the Rogues, I was a Feral living in the forest with my brother and sister. It wasn't great but I did what I had to, to keep them safe."

"Feral?"

"Wild, not completely civilised or able to communicate in a civilised manner like we are doing now." Kat explained, "Ferals are Synths who switch to animalistic behaviour when they get out of ARCDA. Like forgetting how to speak, or hunting small animals, attacking and killing humans, or running on all fours."

He knew what she meant. Feral behaviour was not tolerated in Core. However, Raoul found it hard to imagine this pretty lion-Tribrid running on all fours. Some Canids had a need to run on all fours as it was far faster and less cumbersome than running on two legs, despite the limb proportion being out of balance in comparison to an actual canine. Nevertheless, he could quite easily see himself forgetting how to speak if he were left all alone in the wild with nothing, but his instincts to rely on. The thought of being lost in the forest was tempting.

He shook his head, trying to get back to the original point of the conversation. "Are you saying that you killed humans?"

Kat dropped her gaze to her lap and her ears flattened back in shame.

"It's very easy to fall into a Feral state and forget everything you are taught not to do." Her voice soft with remorse. "It wasn't even out of revenge or hatred of humans, it was just…necessity. Anyone who seemed to be a threat, I'd kill. My only priorities were Tanto and Tachi. I probably wouldn't be here if I wasn't thinking of them and their safety."

She made circles on the table with her nails, scratching into the surface, but she didn't raise her eyes to look at him.

"I murdered the man owned us because he hurt them. Just the once. He hit Tachi. I can't remember why, but he ordered me to punish her by cutting her feathers from her wings. I just…saw red and attacked… we escaped through the windows. I did everything I could after that to make sure that they were safe since I was eldest and was the only capable one."

"What happened to them?"

"We got separated during an ambush. I was followed back to our camp by a team of Elites hired by Risio who had been casing us for months, because as Tribrids we were all valuable."

Her lowered tone made him nervous. "Were they…Canids?" He asked, concerned is the event had marred her view of his species and if the honesty and civility she was showing him was a façade.

"No, they were Reptiles and Preternaturals. That's the human looking ones. I'm not sure what you'd call them in French." She explained, nose wrinkling in disgust as she recalled the foul sent of the reptilian-based Synths, their scaled skin and for the more dangerous ones, venom.

"The serpent Synths scare me." Raoul shuddered.

"You're not alone there, Puppy- uh, *Raoul*. I much prefer to fight Canids, much slower and less dangerous too… no offence."

"*Il n'y a pas de quoi,*" He shrugged and smiled, pleased that she considered Canids better than Reptiles. "So, what did you do? Did you kill them?"

"I tried to, but they were armed Sapphire ranked Elites and were all wearing ExoArmour. It wasn't exactly a fair fight." She laughed dryly. "So, I tried to hold them off long enough to give Tanto and Tachi a chance to escape. They broke my knives, broke my arm, my wing, my collarbone, they even broke my tail in five places."

"That's horrible!" Raoul reeled back in horror, feeling empathy pain in the base of his own tail. As fast as they could heal, they could not regrow an entire limb. Kat nodded sadly, holding her tail and stroking the tufted brush idly, continuing with her story though her voice became strained as she started to upset herself.

"Tanto and Tachi got away I think, but…"

"But?"

"I never saw what happened to them. I only got away because Storm caught up with them just as they were about to enter the Risio bunker after *literally* dragging me back by my hair." Her pupils became pinpricks within her hazel eyes, and her entire body tensed. Breathing strained, Raoul could see a flash of anger and pain cross her face.

"I promised I would protect them, and I don't even know if they're alive or not. Even Beth can't find anything on them."

"I'm…" He hesitated, unsure of what to say. Her bottom lip trembled, and she slammed her fists down loudly onto the little table. The sudden slam made Beth flinch and look up. Coolly, she blinked slowly at Kat who was glowering murderously at her.

"You *promised* me you'd find them." She snarled, shaking with rage. "You promised me!"

"They'll turn up Kat. Just be patient," Beth said softly, trying to reason with the Lioness.

A deep growl resounded loudly in her throat and came through in her words. "It's been a *year* though! You can find obscure humans in remote parts of Russia and know what their internet activity is, but you can't find two Synths!"

"Only if I knew they had a computer or contacted the Rioteers, I could know where they were."

"But you—"

"—*Katana*, you're getting stressed. Stop talking about it already and get back in control, before you break something. I don't need you going all berserker on me." Beth shrugged and carried on playing with her laptop. "Keep it together."

Kat swore under her breath and clawed at the table, leaving marks in the plastic. Raoul remained silent for a moment, observing her behaviour. He had never had to deal with women in his life, as almost all Canids were male, but he could see that he should be nothing, but gentle and kind to Kat, unless he wanted to test just how good she was with a knife.

"I'm…sorry." Raoul apologised placing a warm hand on top of hers to show sympathy, "I shouldn't have asked."

She froze for a moment, neither flinching nor attacking him in response.

"It's alright… I'm sorry if I scared you." She sighed, taking several deep breaths to recover before smiling and trying to laugh it off. The sunlight caught on her honey-brown hair, casting a golden glow about her, making the smile warmer and appear as though nothing had happened to distress her at all.

"S-so…" Raoul gulped and glanced back at Storm and Wilny, hoping to change the subject so that he didn't upset Kat further.

"What is their story?"

"Whose? Wilny or Storm's?"

"Both. And Beth."

"Well, there's not much to say about Beth because she won't tell me and as far as I know, has always been like that."

Beth gave her bionic feet a drum on the floor and without looking away from the screen, threw them both a momentary pair of finger guns and a click of her tongue before going back to scrolling through her computer, clearly wanting to say nothing more on the topic.

"And she would be the better one to ask than me about what the deal is with Storm and Wilny, but she's always going to be cryptic when it comes to histories. I did try to ask them myself, but they didn't tell me much."

She gave a little defeated shrug and looked to Beth to see if she was willing to explain any further only to have her roll her shoulders and muttered something about confidential information. Raoul chuckled a little at her nonchalance. From what he had seen of Beth, she knew a whole lot more than she was willing to tell people and he would not put it past her to know him better than he knew himself.

He smiled sweetly at Kat, trying to remain on her good side.

"What about the short version of what you know?"

"Short version; they're both a little complicated. Wilny was the leader of a team of Elites, so if he seems like he's got a gun up his ass, it's because he probably has. Ruby ranked apparently and trained as both a sniper and a melee attacker."

Raoul's fur prickled in a sudden jolt of terror at the mention of the rank and the connotations of it. A Ruby ranked Elite was a dangerous special operative soldier, equal to Sapphires and outranked only by the Diamonds. As if he wasn't intimidating enough.

Raoul didn't know why they used gemstones as ranking names, though from what he had heard it was due to the director of ARCDA and Core wanting to differentiate them from the human military.

"And Storm…" Kat continued before biting her lip and thinking hard, "Storm I don't really know much about other than that she's been free for the last eleven years, has a killer kick, and was some kind of prototype Avio from what Beth has let slip. Don't expect her to tell you anything, she's very much a '*live in the moment*' kind of girl, so if you want any funny stories about her, I'd talk to Crow."

Raoul's jaw dropped.

Eleven years outside of ARCDA.

She had been out of ARCDA longer than he had been alive, making her anywhere between fifteen and twenty. Meeting a Synth so old was rare, as the majority of the Synth population– excluding the variable ages of Transhumans– were all under the age of eighteen.

"So long…but she's an Avio prototype?" He glanced back at Storm in confusion. She was curled up into a ball against Wilny's shoulder with one wing pulled slightly around her like a blanket, peacefully sleeping. "Is that why she can do that…*thing*?"

"The electric shocks? I think so. How about it, Beth?"

Beth cast the pair an exhausted look as Kat gestured for her to elaborate and explain.

"I don't know what the full details of the project she came from," Beth shrugged, Raoul sensing immediately that she was lying, "but the electroplaques were apparently a rare side effect to the genotype they were trying to produce that you usually find in strong musers. So instead of being electro-sensitive, she's simply bioelectric. Standard Type-4 Avios sometimes have this mutation too, but it's rare."

"Her name suits the talent." Chuckled Kat, relaxing now that the conversation had turned away from her own issues.

"Also," Raoul continued, still looking at the pair behind him, "What is their relationship? Wilny and Storm I mean, because earlier they were fighting and insulting each other, but now they are...being close. I don't understand. Is this normal for Avios?"

A sly grin spread across Kat's face.

"It's complicated. When we first rescued Wilny, Storm got his heart beating again and revived him after kicking his ass, so I guess he thinks he owes her. Even if he does think she's *dangerous* and *immature*." She gestured for Raoul to lean in so she could whisper to him, which he did so. Her hazel eyes glittered mischievously as she whispered, "And I think when they insult each other they're actually flirting with each other in a way, though it's hard to tell with Storm because she *always* sounds like she's flirting. But he does give her these puppy eyes whenever she gets irritated with him or calls him other names-"

"-I *can* hear you Kat." Wilny growled from behind them making both Raoul and Kat jump.

"Shit! I thought you were asleep!"

"No, your snarling and gossiping woke me up. And don't you even dare start to tell him about your *head-canons*! I heard where it was going. Just because two people argue does not mean there's some sort of erotic tension between them!" He glowered at them both, blue eyes sharp and dangerous beneath his glossy hair.

"Ugh! You're always ruining my fun."

He focused his glare on Raoul most of all, voice low and cold. "Don't ever ask about me again, *Dog*. The girls may trust you, but I don't."

"Wilny stop being a fuckwit to the kids and *carefully* wake Storm up." Beth ordered, cutting in with as much diplomacy as she could manage, "We're nearly at the orchard where the reports came from."

Straightening up in his seat, he left Raoul alone and turned his attention to Storm as ordered. Raoul breathed a sigh of relief and sunk down in his chair.

"Wake up." Wilny said softly, shaking the girl's shoulder, "Storm...wake up now...we're nearly there."

"I don't want to..." She grumbled, pulling her wings and the coat that covered them up over her head. She hadn't slept in nearly forty-two hours and was catching up on as much sleep as she could manage.

Irritated at her lack of cooperation, Wilny pinched the feathers on her cheeks.

"Wake up already!"

Without warning, she gave him a shock, making him yelp and leap in his seat.

"Dickhead!" Storm snarled, now awake, eyes blazing angrily. She dug her talons into his bicep hard enough to leave a mark, but not so deep that she drew blood. He grabbed her wrists and pulled her arm up, then proceeding to catch her other wrist and hold it back as she went to hit him.

"Bitch! What was that for?"

"Why'd you pinch me, you *arse-feathered bell end*!"

"Because you wouldn't- Ow!" He flinched as she shocked him again and then proceeded to knee him in the side as she brought her legs up to kick him.

"Beth! Make her stop!"

"I did warn you to be careful."

"I was- *OW*!"

-x-

Once they had ceased fighting, the train had come to a stop at Selling station, a tiny village outside Canterbury, surrounded by the rolling hills and woodland of the countryside. For miles around there were only orchards and fields of hops and wheat, which broke up the woodland areas, with a soft warm breeze rustling the grasses and leaves. The sun had risen, and the day was starting to become warm, bright azure skies overhead with very few clouds drifting across the sky.

The Rogues stretched joyously. The clean air relaxing and refreshing after their uncomfortable journey.

The village was almost silent, save for birds chirping in the hedgerows. The few residents were either not awake or had already set off to wherever they needed to go for that morning, meaning the Rogues could walk freely without being given odd looks by the more attentive people who lived there.

Tasting the sweet early summer scent reminded Raoul of France and training outside in the sun, one of the better moments of his time in ARCDA. As there were very few people around it was safe for them to give themselves a little freedom. The girls removed their coats, shaking out their feathers and splaying the primaries wide under the sun. Kat removed her hat immediately as they entered the first orchard, her ears beginning to twitch and flicker, listening to all the little sounds made by the wildlife. Wilny uncoiled the two-meter long tailfeathers he had wrapped around his waist and set them free, Raoul following his lead with his own tail.

"Okay so the report was made by a farmer who owns an orchard about a mile from the station on the other side of Oversland." Beth stated as they headed down the narrow road towards the gated entrance to the orchards, being wary of oncoming cars as she navigated them with her phone. "He says that it was a very large bird, or something like a buzzard that fell out the sky."

"But if it was bird-like, aka an Avio, wouldn't they have just flown off somewhere? There's plenty of woodland round here to hunker down in, and the trees are large enough to support one of us in the branches." Storm pointed out.

"Maybe, but that's where Raoul comes in." Beth nodded towards the Hound. "You can probably sniff around to see if they've left or not or have been in that area. The air here is clear enough that you won't make much of a mistake or get too confused by other scents."

Raoul nodded in agreement. Too many scents were troublesome, especially.

"There's a few crows flying about here Storm," Kat said ears turning in the direction of the trees, which were chattering every now and then breaking the silence of the countryside. "Do you want me to ask if they've seen anything?"

Storm nodded, tying her blue-grey hair back into a ponytail and deliberately whipping Wilny in the face with it, still annoyed from the rude awakening. With her hair pulled back Raoul saw that her ears were covered by small white feathers with hints of grey and soft down, nothing like his own and Kat's ears or even the other two Avios who had somewhat human looking ones. It was just one of the varying phenotype expressions for their species, just like some Canids he knew had a permanent covering of fur, or dark paw pads and claws on their hands and feet like he had.

"Go for it," She smiled, brushing the hair off the ear-feathers, "They should be politer than the London crows, but probably warier so don't be irritated if they fly off."

"Got it." And with that, Kat skipped off down the hill towards the black birds, short dress snagging on the thistles and fool's parsley and butterfly-blue wings held tight at her back. Raoul stared after, not too sure of what the girls were talking about or if he had heard correctly and trying to keep himself from looking at her legs again.

"Um…she can understand animals?"

"Not really?" Storm explained with a little smile uncertainty, giving the Owl beside her a nudge in the side. "Uh…Beth, clarify please."

Rolling her shoulders, a small smug smirk tugged on the corners of Beth's lips as she cleared her throat.

"Decades ago, when ARCDA was still focused on genetic modifications, they modified crows to be hyper intelligent, enough so that they could talk and comprehend human language. These birds were smart enough that they escaped into the wild and now part of the corvid population are able to talk and think on a higher level than wild crows."

"They can talk?" Raoul stared down the hill as Kat flicked her wings in and out, the crows gathering closer and closer to her. Storm grinned.

"Yes. My brother, Crow, raises some of their chicks from time to time. He has seven right now."

"Yeah," grumbled Wilny, "and Blackheath is the worst of them."

"You only say that because you don't like that it can talk."

"It's. *Creepy.*"

Tilting his head to one side, Raoul listened. They were talking, in croaky inhuman voices. It was odd to hear.

Then in a mad flurry, the birds took to the sky and scattered as a sparrowhawk rushed them from the bushes. Unable to call the crows down, Kat came skipping back, swearing at the thistles prickling her legs. Summer dresses and sandals were not suitable for skipping through meadow fields full of prickly plants, but she had insisted on wearing them.

"The crows say that they saw '*an odd small wing girl*' in the orchard behind this one." She relayed, rubbing her legs and checking for any cuts or scratches. Both Storm and Beth looked surprised at her whilst the boys frowned in confusion.

"An odd small wing girl? Then that's definitely a young Avio."

"I couldn't get any more details out of them than that. I'm sorry." Her ears flattened back, annoyed that she couldn't find anything else out to help them.

Storm smiled.

"Don't apologise. You did great." She chirped warmly with a little wink, causing Kat to blush profusely and the fur and feathers along her tail to fluff up. "Any little detail is helpful. Now let's go!" And with that, she led the group onwards up the hill and through the first orchard.

Being late-spring-early-summer, all the trees were bearing semi-ripe apples and pears of varying varieties. The branches creaked in the breeze, heavy under the weight of fruit. Occasionally, there would be sparrows and rabbits darting out of their path as they walked through the trees, and Raoul had to control himself so as not to lunge after them.

"These orchards are...*huge*. They are like the vineyards in France and Germany." Raoul reminisced, looking around with a smile. "It smells better here too. I like this more than London, *je me plais ici*."

"Got a scent yet, Dog?" Grumbled Wilny from behind him, idly rubbing the scar that sliced his left brow in two.

Flinching, Raoul's tail went between his legs and he stepped a little closer to Beth and Kat for protection. He was certain that if Wilny got the chance, he would kill him. The scars on his arms and face told Raoul that this man was very familiar with fighting clawed Synths, a skinny boy like himself would be crushed in seconds if it came down to a fight.

Rolling her eyes at his bad attitude, Storm hooked Wilny's ankle with her foot, making him trip and flail, nearly ripping his wings through the coat he was still wearing as they tried to flare out to balance him. Aggravated, Wilny opened his mouth to swear at her, but she stopped him by putting her hand over his mouth and smiled sweetly.

"He has a name, *Vanessa*. I suggest you use it properly unless you'd rather be ordered to remain silent." She chirped. Silently, Wilny stared at her as she bared her fangs in a warning smile. Looking away in defeat and huffing, Storm knew Wilny was not going to say another word against the Hound, so removed her hand and kept walking. He sighed to himself and started to catch up.

When they reached the edge of the next orchard, Raoul stopped and scented the air.

"I have found something."

"Is it the girl?" Storm asked patiently.

He curtly nodded. "Permission to examine the area?" He tentatively asked, unsure of how to proceed in the situation. Smiling softly, she gave a wordless sweeping gesture towards the orchard, allowing him to carry on with what he needed to do.

Cautiously he stepped away from the Avios and crouched so that he was closer to the ground and able to find the scents with more clarity, inhaling deeply.

The main scent was of the apples, wood, pollen and grass. Warm, heady and sweet, but this didn't disguise the other scents there; fox, rabbit, hedgehog, at least four different kinds of native bird and one scent neither native nor natural. He focused in on this one and dropped to the ground and began padding on all fours through the grass between the trees until he found a tiny rust-orange feather. He lifted it to his nose and sniffed, locking the scent into his mind and comparing it to his memory of other birds and Avios behind him. Continuing on all fours, Raoul followed a trail through the trees for a short distance before doubling back and checking again to be sure he was on the right one. He found several more feathers near by the trail, the grass there were flattened patches from where they had been buffeted down by wings dragging or flapping too close to the ground. It was very recent and was enough to see that they were in the right spot.

"She's definitely around here." He said, heading back to them, examining the feathers he had found. Handing Storm the feather, she gently brushed her fingertips over it, then holding it to the sky to examine it in the sunlight, letting the wind blowing up the hill tussle the soft down about wildly.

"It looks like it's a baby feather. Not even the first real quills." She muttered to herself, then her whole posture changed, and she stood up straight and looked serious.

"If she's really little then she might just be a fledgling and unable to fly for long," She said with a commanding tone, rolling her shoulders as her wings began to ache, pocketing the orange feathers. "We should spread out. That way we can cover the area faster."

The corner of Wilny's lips twitched upwards into a small smile.

"For once a reasonable idea, I'm impressed."

Storm stood on her tiptoes, even though they were at the top of the hill, she still wasn't tall enough to see to the very end of the orchard. "Wilny and Kat take the far end, Raoul and Beth can you take this end."

"And you'll take the middle then? Good strategy, but-"

"-Nope." She grinned slyly. He blinked slowly at her.

"What...?"

Wilny didn't pick it up right away, but Beth, who had known her longest saw what was coming and scowled at the Rogue leader as she took two steps back to give herself room, tensing up her shoulders.

"Storm. *No.*" The Owl chided coldly, "You are not flying out here! You'll get seen and I'll have to deal with it! As usual!"

Shrugging with a playful smile, Storm ignored her, roused her feathers with a little shake and tightened the long purple sash around her waist.

With a sound like the billowing of a sail in the wind, Storm flared her wings out above her head. In the sunlight, Raoul could see them to their full extent, eighteen and a half feet of sleek slate-grey scythes that reached from shoulder to knee in breadth, with a short feather covered tail ruined by deep scars, jutting from just below the sash. Each and every feather of the upper wing was edged in iridescent silver, whilst the undersides were stark white and marked with fine charcoal grey barring. They weren't as dazzling in colour as Kat or Wilny's wings, but they were extraordinarily elegant and built for speed.

She beat them down once with a testing stroke, splaying the feathers out to their correct positions and stirring up small tornadoes of dust. Before Beth could have a chance to scold her, she kicked off powerfully from the ground into a leap. As soon as her feet had left the ground, she had powered her wings down, lifting her higher, using the wind to her advantage. With a surge of air, dust was billowed into the eyes of the other Rogues and by the time they had rubbed it away, Storm was high above them.

"For fucks sake! Storm!" Hollered Beth angrily, still rubbing the dust from her eyes, "Get back here right now!"

But the rush of wind and the distance made it almost impossible for her to be heard by Storm.

Up, up, up she went into the sky, powerful down strokes sending her higher and catching the wind until she was high enough that from the ground she looked like any other bird in the sky. With a trilling a sigh of happiness, she found a thermal rising from the valleys and began circling the orchards from a thousand feet above, the sun warming her back and the wind caressing her feathers.

Beth glowered up, shielding her eyes from the glare of the sun.

"That idiot. She's such a pain in my arse." She grumbled.

"She has a point though. She can keep an eye out from above in case the little girl moves or tries to fly away." Kat smiled, her own wings starting to ache as she watched Storm flying up above them. She wanted to join her up in the sky, but knew they had to rescue the girl before she could relax and take off into the blue expanse. She looked across to Raoul who was staring open mouthed at the sky. She could see his awe on his face, along with the slightest glimmers of envy as Storm defied gravity.

Beth huffed angrily to herself. "I suppose...*urgh*. Let's split up then..."

4

Oversland Orchards, Selling, Kent.

It was hard to describe the feeling of flying to someone who had never done it for themselves. The only way she could think to describe it as would be that it was what true power and freedom felt like.

The strain on her back as she beat her wings against the summer wind, and the ache in her chest when she held them steady to soar. How the wind rushed over her wings sending little tremors down every single feather, allowing her to detect the tiniest change in the air currents so that she could adjust the position of a single flight feather to change the angle of attack. The drowning sound of the air buffeting across her feather tufted ears in a roar, cracking her sash like a bullwhip behind her in the stead of her missing tailfeathers. Her blood rushing hotly through her veins and heart pounding a hard drummers-tattoo against her ribcage. Words just weren't enough to describe it.

And when looking down at the hilly green patchwork of orchards and woodland broken by small villages and roads where humans were trapped by a mundane life of work and school, she truly did feel powerful and free. The very awareness that she was hundreds of metres above the ground and not falling towards it, filled her with euphoria that lit every nerve with a golden glow; victorious over pull of gravity.

Even after years of being skyborne, she never grew tired of the feeling, and every Avio she taught to fly soon came to feel the same way, no matter how horrible they were at it.

Flying could be easily learnt by Avios who had never even seen the sky before, once they had built up enough muscle to maintain powered flight that is, but flying *well* took practice and understanding of how the world affected you. The wind and weather were the two factors which had the most affect, but also clothing and where exactly you were flying could change how easy it was.

Despite having a short feather covered tail, she was missing her lengthy tailfeathers that would usually help her balance, and so she had to twist her body and use her legs to counteract the lift of the wind to allow her to turn. But she had years of practice under her belt and found little tricks which helped her, such as using a long sash around her waist, much like the tail of a kite, could help as well as to tuck her wings in and roll to change direction sharply.

Caught up in her delight at being able to fly in the sunshine, she loop-de-looped and corkscrewed through the sky, skirting the edges of a low cloud, almost forgetting what she was meant to be doing and almost failing to notice a kestrel gliding past her.

The bird circled around her with a cry of surprised trilling pips, its tiny, speckled orange and brown wings were dwarfed by a single banded flight feather of her own wing. Storm stopped messing around and smiled at it as she levelled out her flight, gliding lazily upon the breeze. It hovered close to her, head perfectly still as it examined what this strange not-bird was doing in his area.

Most birds would never get closer than a few meters to her when flying, but corvids and birds of prey would, just to see what she was out of curiosity as well as to defend their hunting grounds.

The kestrel remained hovering for a moment, its dark eye still focused on her before it reeled back in the air and twisted its body into a dive, flying out of her way and looking for a new spot to hunt in.

She watched its flight, angling its wings in and twisting to make a sharp turn before catching a fresh gust of wind and soaring away. Eleven years and she still was learning, and the best to learn from were from those who had evolved to fly. Half drawing her wings in and twisting her body, she mimicked it, practicing the move over and over, using the wind and thermals differently each time to find what had the best effects, as she set her mind back to the task at hand.

-x-

"I don't think we should leave that dog on his own with Beth, who knows what he might do." Wilny complained as he and Kat patrolled the far end of the orchard.

"Do you have to do this now?" Kat rolled her eyes at him, "Can't you hold it for your therapy sessions with Jenna? Just so you know the whole brooding angst thing does *nothing* for me."

Ex-Elites were the worst. He was never normally so vocal about his complaints, preferring to mutter quietly under his breath or roll his eyes about Storm's decisions, but having a Canid– who's unit they had killed several hours earlier– help them had truly riled him up.

"I'm *worried*. And you should be too! He could be a pathological liar!"

"And there you go again. Back into *Work Mode*. God K-pop, you're such an asshole like this." Kat sighed, ears flicking back and forth as she tried to pick up the sounds of movement through the rustle of leaves and Wilny's whining.

"Trying to be the heroic knight and defending the damsels in distress from the tiny little Puppy."

"I am not! Why are you Pards so cantankerous?"

"Ugh! Can you go back to regular Wilny, please? Brooding isn't sexy. I want my K-pop to come out to play."

"I'm just saying that Canids are-"

"-Oh my god! Just stop already. You don't know anything about him." She snarled, marching off ahead. Her temper was already stirred by Raoul's questioning about what happened before she met the Rogues, and Wilny's whining was only infuriating her more.

He jogged a few steps to keep up with her, "Neither do you or Storm. You don't know if he's got history or how loyal he is to ARCDA."

"We've all got history, Wilny! He's just a kid." She stopped and turned to face him; ears flattened back against her hair. "You saw how he reacted to what we told him, what we did to those other Canids. He was terrified. The only harm he could do would be to himself and Beth really isn't as weak as you think she is, trust me! That robot-arm packs a punch."

"But–"

"–*But nothing*! If Storm says we can trust him, we can trust him. If she asks Beth and Raoul to search together then that's her call not yours. She's the boss and Beth agreed to it." With a flick of her tail, she marched onwards, scouring the area to find more feathers.

"Why do we even take orders from her? She is no leader. Beth's the one with the plans." Wilny growled.

Seeing that he was going to go off on another rant, Kat sighed, humouring him one last time and beginning to flex her fingers, letting her claws curl across her palm.

"Because she's experienced."

"So?" His lip curled up into a sneer. "She's dangerous, undisciplined, selfish, and completely oblivious to everything and their consequences. Improvisation only gets people killed quicker."

"She knows when she fucks up and sticks to her guns on her choices. And for all your training I bet you never had to improvise at all in Core. It's so clinical and predictable in there, I bet you memorized all the routes in the labyrinth."

"I'm the commander of an Elite team! Ruby ranked, almost a Diamond!" He snarled, letting his anger get the better of him and stepping up towards her, pulling his coat off and letting his bristling feathers flare out and beat.

"She's just a-"

"*Were.*" She cut in. The gold flecks within her hazel eyes turning them to a golden tiger's eye gleam, sharp as the blade she carried. Far too fierce to fear, and far too feisty to resist a fight with him. Wilny paused, staring down at her.

"What?"

"You *were* the commander of a team back in Core, but you're not anymore. *Bluebird.*" She stepped up to him and held her ground as he loomed over her.

"Don't call me that-"

"-And murdering your own team doesn't make you a very good leader now does it. Is that why you hate him? Because he reminds you of your Wolf friend?" She teased coldly, baring her fangs in a smile.

"You feral fucking *bitch.*" He moved quickly, grabbing her by the front of her dress and pulling her towards him. "Did Beth tell you that?"

She retaliated by grabbing his wrist, letting her claws sink sharply into his skin and drawing blood.

"Do you really want to fight me Wilny?" She snarled, "You dare even make a mark and Storm will hand your balls to you on a silver platter, if I don't cut them off first that is."

Her knife was pressed against his groin, its tip pricking him right above his femoral artery. They both knew that if she cut that, he would bleed to death far quicker than if she simply stabbed him in the chest.

They glowered unblinkingly at each other, waiting for the other one to back down first. After a long and hostile pause and swallowing their pride, they released each other at the same time and took three steps back so they were out of each other's space. Kat put the blade back away and adjusted her dress, watching Wilny carefully out the corner of her eye. Neither was afraid of the other or disliked the other enough to truly attempt to kill each other, but their pride and training made them volatile when anything to do with their past mistakes were brought up.

"I still think she's a poor decision maker." He huffed and straightened up his jacket before marching off ahead. Sighing, she decided not to argue with him anymore about it before there really was bloodshed over the whole situation again.

She flicked her hair out over her shoulders and put it up into a ponytail, trying to find something more amusing to discuss.

"The way you keep going on about her and ranting at her, anyone would think you had a little crush on her." Kat smirked at him, wanting to see how he would react. He gave her exactly the expression she wanted to see, horror mixed with bewilderment and fear, long tailfeathers whipping about behind him. He really did not know how to react to the new line of conversation since not even thirty seconds prior they had literally been at each other's throats.

"We've covered this. I have *zero* feelings for her, unlike *you*."

"Of course, you don't, K-Pop." She purred mischievously, flouncing past him with a playful tap across his buttocks that made his wings flick out in surprise. "But fear is a very powerful aphrodisiac, and you are *very* scared of her."

He gritted his teeth and glared at her, iridescent feathers rousing.

"Kat, I swear if you're thinking about Storm and I-"

"I'm not, I'm just pointing out how much you talk about her when she's not in earshot."

"I don't."

"You do, more than you think." Smiling she strode off, leaving him standing there with an angry frown.

"You brought her up!"

"No, I didn't, you did."

"Didn't."

"Did."

"Kat, I swear to fuck–"

-x-

"Bloody hell, I can hear them from here." Beth grumbled rubbing her eyes, "You can't leave him alone with anyone or he'll just start an argument for the sake of it."

Raoul sighed. "He's not going to trust me, is he?"

"He will do. He's just a bit of a tit sometimes. At least he's not as bad as he was."

"Those scars on his arms…" He asked tentatively, not finishing his sentence, as he did not know how to ask Beth about it without sounding nosy. He wanted to know how he had come to gain so many and if the story behind them had anything to do with the way he was.

"He has them all over." She responded with a shrug. "Even has a few on his wings, but they're not as easy to see since the feathers grew back."

"Really?" It didn't really answer his question. If anything, it only made him all the more curious. If he was a Ruby Elite, what rank was he? Where did he train? Who was his team?

"It's private information, not to be disc-"

"-Beth." He grabbed her arm, stopping her from walking. Beth pulled her bionic back into a fist about to hit him for touching her but saw that he was focused on something up ahead. Nose twitching, Raoul smelt the little girl close by. He could smell her blood and tears.

There was a rustling sound from the apple trees and grass, which could have just been the wind, but with their acute hearing there was no mistaking it.

Wingbeats. Small ones.

"I heard that." Beth whispered, focusing on the spot where the noise came from. A small patch of rusty orange smuggled within a leafy apple tree caught her attention and she squinted, certain that they were feathers and nodded towards it. Raoul let go of her arm and slowly took a step forward.

Without warning, an apple crate came flying at them from over the treetops.

"*Merde!*" Raoul shrieked, raising his fists and smashing through the box. The box splintered on impact, the fragments and splinters puncturing his skin and drawing blood. With a growl he held his arms close, pulling out a thick splinter that had pieced his shoulder.

"*Allez-vous en!*" Shouted a small voice, and a little girl dressed in a tattered yellow dress, darted out of the tree she was hiding in and ran for cover, her cinnamon-coloured wings flapping weakly behind her, with one limply dragging across the ground. It looked as though at least one of her wings was broken and the other was missing several darker brown flight feathers.

"*Vous devez calmer!*" Raoul yelled, although with the shock of being attacked, it came out as a snarl.

The girl looked back at him, golden eyes bright against her dark skin.

"*Loup!*" She cried, stumbling as she ran through the trees as fast as she could until she tripped and fell face first onto the ground. Raoul chased after her, Beth close behind.

"*C'est okay, je ne vais pas te faire de mal. Je ne suis pas un loup.*" He said softly as he could manage in his strangled growl, holding his hands up to appear less threatening, but with claws for nails, it didn't work.

"Raoul put your hands down! You're scaring her you idiot!" Beth yelled as the girl crawled backwards up against a tree. Beth stepped forward, wings flaring slightly in the hope that she would not attack her since she was an Avio too.

There was a loud snapping sound as one of the branches off the trees was severed and hoisted into the air by an invisible force. Raoul leapt in front of Beth to defend her as it was hurled at them, but the branch struck them both, knocking Beth off her feet and winded Raoul as he was struck in the gut.

The little girl began sobbing loudly, curling up and pulling her wings around her in a protective cocoon.

"Je ne veux pas mourir!" She wailed, as more branches were severed from their trunks and hurled at them.

Beth retreated behind a tree, whilst Raoul was beat to the ground by the branches, forcing him to curl up and pull his arms over his head to defend himself from the attack.

A rush of feathers flew over Raoul's head. There was a sudden shriek and suddenly the branches dropped to the ground around them.

Cautiously Raoul peeked out from under his arms to see what had caused her to stop, only to see Storm crouched down with her wings spread out either side of her. Rising to her feet, she turned to face Beth and Raoul with the little girl unconscious in her arms, carefully tucking her wings back up against her small body so that they didn't drag and damage the feathers.

Kat and Wilny came sprinting through the trees, Kat with her blade drawn and Wilny holding a thick branch as a weapon. Both were ready to fight whatever they came across.

"What's going on?" Kat asked breathlessly. "Were you attacked?"

"Yes…" Beth squeaked hoarsely, crawling out from under the tree holding onto the laptop bag for dear life. "The kid has telkens!"

Kat looked at the damage done to the area then at the little girl in Storms' arms and burst into a peal of laughter.

"It's not funny!" Beth continued to squeak, pulling splinters and leaves from her hair. "She could have taken our heads off!"

Catching a glimpse of her bionic arm and noticing a crack running up the plastic casing around it, Beth swore furiously under her breath. Flexing the fingers on it, they responded with little effort and indicated no damage to the wiring much to her relief, but she was still angry at the crack. Bionics were not easy to replace, unless you were part of Delta.

Raoul sat back on his haunches, rubbing his sparsely fur covered arms and trying to catch his breath, too exhausted to ask what Beth meant by *Telkens*. His arms were bleeding and some of the splinters had caught his face, but there was no serious damage.

Regaining her composure, Beth stood, brushed herself off and went over to Raoul, holding her hand out.

"Thank you, Raoul." She said softly. Raoul looked surprised at first but took her hand and allowed her to help him up. She awkwardly ruffled her auburn waves up, trying to find a compliment in her somewhere to give to him, only able to manage mumbling a simple '*You did good*' for him. The compliment made him feel oddly proud of himself, that he had done something worthy of appraisal.

Wilny stared at the little girl in Storm's arms, and then around them at the damage she had done. The broken branches which looked to have been ripped from the trees and crates splintered to pieces. He was rather impressed by the amount of devastation caused for such a small person.

"She looks like a toddler..." He noted, and then began to frown and look around again. "Where's the rest of her group?"

"Not sure, I didn't see any signs of any other Avios or anyone else." Storm said adjusting the girl in her arms and gently rocking her from side to side, holding her as carefully as a butterfly.

Her dark hair was matted with dirt and leaves, her umber skin was marred by dust and scratches from running through the trees. Rows of tiny grey spikes lined her cheekbones, as blood feathers were beginning to emerge and grow, and brushing back the mats of hair saw that her ears were also starting to form little feathers around a small ear hole. She had so little chest muscle that the sharp keel of her sternum could be seen protruding through the torn dress, and from beneath the dress jutted out a knee length set of dull grey-brown tailfeathers.

"She was dragging her wings when we chased after her, Storm." Beth said, unpacking her laptop and settling down on the floor with it to work out who the girl was. "I think one might be broken, but I'm not sure."

Nodding, Storm checked her wing for any breaks in them, carefully extending them out one at a time. Opened out, they were approximately five foot each – longer than she was tall - cinnamon orange mottled with grey baby down, with sharp little pin feathers pointing through. Some of the flight feathers were still sheathed in hard grey casings with the tips of the plumes just starting to be exposed, but those that were, were a rich dark brown.

She gently felt along the thin bones from the tip to the bony process on the shoulder blades which, like all Avio scapulae, stuck out of her upper back forming a large muscular hunch. Although Storm couldn't find any damage to the bone, she carefully checked the thin propatagium membrane that stretched between the shoulder and the wing-wrist in case the skin and ligaments had torn too. The girl tensed and scrunched her face up whenever she got near the biceps of her wings.

A small smile twinged at Storm's lips. This was no Risio product, someone had tried to make her flight worthy.

"Just some strain. No breaks. She's just getting some muscle built up for flying properly and overstretched herself there. See her wings," she stroked the few dark fully formed flight feathers, which contrasted the rusty orange of the coverts, "those primaries are fresh. She can't have been flying on her own yet. Kat, can you check behind her ear and neck for an ID for Beth? I'm betting she's in Z or AA years. She looks like a baby."

Nodding, Kat stepped up to them, and brushed back the little girls' matted hair from her ears and neck to check. There was a white tattoo in miniscule clean print, beneath a long barcode that was only just visible under a layer of hair and soft downy feathers.

"X.02.08: Neo+:FalcoBiarm-ZenaiGrays-2-10."

"That is a hell of a long ID code." Wilny noted, hand absently pressing to the back of his own neck where his code was tattooed.

"Neo-plus huh. I've never heard of that prefix before...*Zenaida graysoni* and *Falco biarmicus* morphology bases," Beth muttered to herself, as she opened the laptop and scanned the screen and summarised the girl up from what she saw before her.

"Socorro Dove and Lanner Falcon morphology bases; damn, she is going to be a power flyer when she gets going. From Linguère, Senegal. Atlas owned bunker– that explains the Telkens then. In the *X* year, so four years old, five soon. In August actually. She's a slow grower this one."

"Interesting."

"No. What's interesting is that the project she's classed under is a confidential one called *Libeccio,* and I can't access the folder."

"*What.*" The Rogues all shuffled closer with intrigue. If Beth couldn't access something, then it was usually important or dangerous.

Wilny's face scrunched up at the name.

"*Libeccio?* Isn't that a dance?"

"That's called flamenco, Wilny." Beth sighed.

"No, pretty sure a flamenco is a big pink bird."

"That's a flamingo."

"Then why is she a falcon-dove if the project is named for flamingos?"

"What are Telkens?" Raoul asked, trying to switch the conversation as Beth began to glare furiously at the smirking Hummingbird.

"Telekinetics. We call 'em Telkens for short." Answered Storm, sitting on the grass and continuing to check the girl over, gently brushing her fingers through her hair to untangle it and preen the encased feathers.

"They're like a mind-controlled force particle or something weird like that, that can be used as an invisible murder knife or sledgehammer. I'm actually not sure what it is or how in the flying fuck it works since my area of expertise is aerodynamics."

Again, some of the words were lost on Raoul and made him feel dizzy and uneducated, despite what he had learnt from the science lessons in Core. He understood the part that telkens could lift and move things without touching them, and that Atlas were responsible for their production. Everything else however, was lost in translation, and so he proceeded to nod and pretend to understand yet again.

"All the actual info is patent protected, but that's as much as we know on it." Beth rolled her wings, a glint of excitement in her eye. "But as far as Atlas goes, she's super new compared to the VE-RA Preternaturals they use for telkens. Home-grown at that– she's not a Transhuman, look at the ears. Feathers. A tail also. And she's only got four toes. This is not a Standard Type-4 Avio."

Raoul looked down to Storm's bare feet to compare. Both had four long scaled toes that ended in sharp talons. Wilny had his feet hidden in a pair of mismatched coloured sneakers, and Beth of course had bionics, making comparison between them all hard. At least with the ears and tailfeathers, it made it more obvious as to if an Avio was transhuman or not.

The Rogues crowded in, each with contemplative scowls talking in low voices between themselves.

"Though it's odd that Atlas would make an Avio with telkens." Wilny pointed out. "They stopped all grown telkens experiments completely in most bunkers thanks to all the aneurisms."

"Preternatural origin bases have them still. The ORION, LYRA, and VE-RA Preternaturals mostly."

"Even then there aren't many because of all the brain damage that it causes…no one needs a super strong Synth with psychosis or who's prone to seizures."

"Maybe they're re-trialling it? Trying to use different brain structures and mixed morphologies to counter the issues?"

"But then they would use faulty Risio products and mess with them to do that because it'd be cheaper and faster. Growing an Avio from scratch is super-costly and time consuming, even for Atlas."

"True, but if it's a project then they would be more dedicated to figuring it out. This Libeccio project might be what it's about."

"I'll see what I can dig up." Said Beth. "We've been so focused on Core and Risio recently that I forgot to keep tabs on Atlas- She's registered in the group named Ciel, their leader is Rust." She cut through her own sentence frowning in confusion. Eyes flicking across the screen, Beth's face began to pale.

"They were recorded onto the database just a week after they were freed. There should be five others, three Avios and two Chiros. There should be another little girl. Another Avio like her."

"They have another little girl with them? Why would they just leave her on her own and not leave them both together?" Questioned Raoul, sniffing the air. Other than the little girl in front of them, he could not scent any others. "If that was Atlas bunker, then they all must be talented enough that they wouldn't just disappear. Right?"

Storm's brow furrowed, and she rose to her feet, the girl still in her arms.

"I don't like this. This is no recapture from ARCDA, or we'd have known, and I doubt she was just abandoned."

The little girl stirred in her arms with a low groan. The Rogues held their breath and remained completely still as bleary eyed she looked around at them all, still not fully awake to understand what was happening.

"Où… suis-je?" She murmured in confusion, asking where she was, a pale membrane flicking slowly across her eye. She looked up at Storm and frowned a little, raising a tiny hand to tug on Storm's blue-grey hair. Her eyes were a rich honey colour, bright and warm. Storm smiled and raised her wings up, extending them before her so that the little girl could see what she was, and that they were alike. Seeing Storm's wings immediately calmed her, and she spoke again in dazed quiet tones.

"Vous n'êtes pas Miel. Où sont-ils? Où suis-je?"

"I'm sorry sweetie, my French isn't very good." The Rogue chuckled softly, brushing back the girl's hair from her face. "Raoul, can you help translate please?"

Raoul took a step back before he spoke to her, not wanting to scare her too much. The little girl had ripped the branches from the trees with no effort, she could quite quickly rip his head from his shoulders if she felt scared enough.

"Ne vous inquiétez pas, nous n'allons pas vous faire de mal." He said softly. The little girl flinched and stared at him in terror. She clung to Storm, pulling her wings up to shield herself from him.

"Loup!" She squeaked, burying her face into Storm's shirt and pulling her wings over her head.

"Stop that, you're scaring her!" Wilny snapped from behind Raoul, hitting him round the back of the head making him flinch. In response to it, Storm thwacked Wilny hard in the chest with her wing. It was a strong enough hit to send him stumbling backwards.

"Stop being a dick." She snarled at him, as he regained his balance. "He's trying to help us out here."

Wincing at what was sure to become a bruise, Wilny pouted. "Why are you so violent?"

"I thought you preferred me this way to being a bleeding-heart, or has it grown on you?" She purred. He smirked slightly at the reply, and with that, she stuck her tongue out at him and turned to Raoul. "Can you ask her what happened? Ask where her family has gone?"

Storm set the girl on her feet– revealing her legs to be also covered with scales– and allowing the girl to hide under her wing whilst Raoul talked to her. The little girl watched the Hound warily as he cleared his throat and knelt to her level, speaking softly in French.

"Um…where is your family?" He asked her calmly. *"You can tell me; these other Avio don't speak French."*

The little girl bit her lip, unsure if she could trust him. She glanced up at Storm for support. The elder Avio smiled and stroked her head in reassurance, nodding to encourage her to speak.

"I don't know…Miel told me to hide here until they came back." She said in a tiny nervous voice, her dialect one that was very unfamiliar to him. She frowned at him, amber eyes narrowing at him in suspicion. They were stunningly bright against her dark skin.

"Why? You're not with the doctors, are you?"

"No, no, we're good people. Miss Storm is a good person and we just want to help."

"The girl…she said she would help us too."

"Girl?"

She nodded and tugged on her matted brown hair. *"Orange hair. She said she'd help us if we joined her. She said we would be safe."*

"Orange hair? Ginger? Was she working for the Arcadia Corporation? The big place where you came from."

"I'm not sure, I don't know those words…she was an Avio, but not a real one like us. She had other people with her. This many." She shuddered slightly, holding up seven fingers. *"We flew over the big white cliffs by the sea with big ships and a big castle, and they found us. They seemed nice, gave us sweets."*

"But she attacked you?"

"Yes…no…the boy did." She hugged Storm's leg tightly, little voice wavering as she spoke.

"She said she wanted to go home, then the boy got angry and I don't know why, but he told us to go with him and Rust and Miel said no to them and they chased us through the air. We split up and Miel flew me here and told me to wait, but she hasn't come back yet."

Tears welled up in her eyes and trembled. A whine caught in Raoul's throat as he saw her distress. She was so small, and far too young to be left alone, but shaking his head, he composed himself.

"We can help you find them."

"Are you sure?"

"If we can find you in a whole country, then we can find them. And we'll stop these bad people. I promise you that." He smiled reassuringly, tail wagging behind him. *"Do you have a name?"*

She fluffed her rusty orange feathers up and rubbed her eyes dry on the corner of her filthy, ragged dress.

"Malana." She said quietly. *"Miel named me Malana."*

Smiling, Raoul straightened up and began translating for the others. "Her name is Malana and she says that her group was attacked by a group of eight, including a red haired Avio…I think."

Storm cocked her head to one side.

"Odd," She muttered, "there are no other groups in Kent. It is part of our territory, so we'd know who's living here. And it's not ARCDA because Beth would know about it."

"Strays from Europe then?" Suggested Kat with a twitch of her tail.

Beth's frown intensified to the point her glasses slipped down her nose, as she put her laptop away into its case again.

"Probably. The Rioteers took out five Bunkers in the last month and plenty of Rubies and Sapphires escaped which didn't want to go with them." She pushed her glasses back up her nose and considered the likelihood of it.

The Rioteers had been very busy, systematically making their way through the Core bunkers in west Europe; Norway, Denmark, Germany, the Netherlands, Belgium. Bunkers that were owned by Core, usually trained the higher ranked Ruby and Sapphire Elites – ARCDA's own personal military - which would account for why they might have been on the attack, but also explain why they were in the UK. Between Dover and France, it was little more than an hour's flight across water.

"Don't worry sweetie, we'll find your family for you." Storm reassured Malana, picking her up and curling her wings around them both. With a disapproving tut, Wilny rolled his eyes and folded his arms across his chest.

"Storm we don't even know if they're alive or not. Don't get her hopes up…if she can even understand you that is."

"We don't know, but we can still try."

"And then what? When we inevitably don't find them?"

"Well in the *inevitableness* of that happening, she can join us," She smiled impishly at him, and put Malana in his arms, much to both Malana and Wilny's surprise. "And until we find out what has happened *you* can look after her."

Wilny stared at her in horror, frozen to the spot, going pale as he realised he was holding a tiny child.

"W-why me? I don't know how to deal with children." He choked, setting Malana down onto her feet, worried that he might accidentally hurt or drop her. Storm grinned, fluffing her feathers up in amusement at his expression.

"Well, you like looking after damsels in distress. Plus, you'll only moan that I'm dangerous or a bad influence and you don't trust me or Raoul with children, or Kat's shouldn't play with knives around her." She mused counting off the list of possible complaints that he could come up with if anyone else were left in charge.

"But Kat had a sister, she could-"

"No. Knives and toddlers *do not* mix." Kat glowered at him, cutting him off before he even had a chance to finish. "Storm asked you, to do this, not me."

Still pale faced he looked round at the only other person left in the group.

"Beth?"

"I don't like small people" Said the shortest of the Rogues, cradling her laptop to her chest, before Wilny could attempt to place the girl in her arms.

"But-"

"*Wilny Mira.*" Storm's cut in sharply with a flick of feathers to get his attention. Wings spread wide, she cornered him, aquamarine-green eyes narrowed and fixed unblinkingly on his him as she calmly asserted her authority over him.

"I'm now *ordering* you to look after and protect that little girl, not because I want to piss you off, but because I think you are best for this role to protect her and I trust you to do it."

Wilny blinked at her. He was always surprised when she ordered him to do something, but even more surprised when she gave a valid and legitimate reason for it.

She straightened up and crossed her arms. "Do you understand me?" She asked coolly.

Head cocked to one side; he considered her logic. Although it was a little arrogant of him to assume so, the way he saw it, as an Elite he was possibly the only one amongst them truly able to protect this little girl given both his talents and training. And yes, he didn't trust Raoul to take care of her – although remembering that the canid was only seven, it made him a child too. He stared at her, impressed with her reasoning.

"I understand." He nodded, tone softening, and with a coy smirk began to chuckle. "I'll protect her, although I thought you'd want to do it since it takes a child to know a child."

"Dickhead." She stuck her tongue out at him again and then flicking her wings neatly back she turned to lead them all back down the orchard. With everyone behind her, she smiled to herself, happy and amused by Wilny's shift in attitude.

Malana and Wilny stared at each other for a moment whilst the rest walked on ahead of them. Golden eyes watching him he realised one thing that Storm had forgotten.

"Um. Storm. I can't speak French."

5

White Cliff Walk, East Dover, Kent

Wilny was hyper vigilant during the train ride to Dover now that there were more people traveling. Raoul and Malana became increasingly nervous of the humans around them, and so he kept them close by to ensure that they were safe. Kat had given Malana her coat so that her wings could be hidden, whilst she flew overhead. They received more odd looks than when in London, and even had one overly interested child loudly and incessantly ask their mother as to why Storm had *freckle feathers*. Upon leaving the train station, Storm passed the child one of her feathers with a wink of the pale nictitating membrane, leaving them gawping in amazement.

After a short stop for food, they slowly trekked over the cliff above the port and past Dover Castle, to which Storm gleefully began telling them about the history of the castle as they walked along the cliff tops, of the secret tunnels beneath it, its wartime uses and the various weapons inside. An hour of walking later, and they had reached an old Victorian lighthouse where they all took a rest in the sun. Beth sent a text to Kat of their location, to which Kat responded by sending a picture of the lighthouse they were by through the branches of some trees with the caption *'let's play hide and seek'* in response.

"I blame you for this." Beth grumbled to Storm who looked at the picture and chuckled.

"I'm a bad influence, I know."

"We're busy! We don't have time for pissing around! Be serious!"

"Beth, children pick up on when adults are tense or worried." She straightened up and gave Beth a smile. For an instant, the smile became forced and her eyes narrowed, but with a blink, it became natural once again. Subtle as the change was, Beth caught it;

she doubted that the rest of Malana's group were alive, but she didn't want to let the others know her doubts. She wanted them to have some hope.

Beth threw her head back and groaned towards the sky. "Fine!" She snapped, "You're the boss, just be prepared for me to mutiny if you carry on pissing around!"

Smirking at her threat, Storm placed a hand on Raoul's shoulder.

"Kat wants to test your nose. She's asked you to try and find her." She said softly.

The Hound looked slightly dazed but nodded and stepped away to try to pick up any scents he could. With a little pacing, he picked it up quickly. Two days of chasing her had left the magnolia perfume etched into his mind and so lead the Rogues on their way along a dirt track.

They came to a small, wooded area at the edge of the cliff, closed off by a fence and a sign that read *'private property, keep out'* and very cautiously slunk through the trees, careful so as not to draw attention to themselves. Heading to the largest tree that sat far too close to the edge of the cliff, Raoul paused and looked around for Kat.

"You're late." Kat's disembodied voice chirped, followed by an amused chuckle from above. Raoul looked up and jumped back just as Kat leaped out of the tree, landing gracefully in front of him with her azure wings flared out, revealing their velvet-and-fire undersides.

Grinning, Storm strode over to her, holding a paper bag in one hand. "Sorry Kat, we stopped for some food. The girl looked hungry and Wilny complained."

"Nothing new there."

Wilny rolled his eyes at her. He had put Malana down and was holding her hand, allowing her to walk next to him since he deemed it safe enough with no humans around. The cliffs were not a very crowded place; in fact, the only people to be seen were either a hundred meters below them on the beach. Only the seagulls soaring across the waves, the kestrels hovering over the fields, and the constant buzz and chirp of crickets gave them any indication that there was life there at all.

"This had better be cod." Kat said excitedly pulling at the bag, which Storm then handed over to her to get to its contents. Almost purring with happiness as she gave it a sniff, Kat began tearing into it, unbothered by it being cold. Flying took up a lot of energy and that morning they had not had the chance to eat a proper breakfast so a large portion of fish and chips each sufficed, along with some fruit and water to wash it down with.

"So, did you see anything unusual from up there?" Storm asked leaning against the tree as Kat continued to eat.

"Nothing yet." She responded, shaking her head and licking the grease from her fingers. "Though we might be in the wrong area."

"Hm." Storm tilted her head to one side, considering what they should do then turned to Raoul. "Raoul ask Malana if anything has been familiar so far."

Nodding Raoul crouched down to Malana's level and asked her Storm's question softly in French. The little girl looked around for a moment, at the sea and the cliffs falling away before them then nodded, pointing towards to another lighthouse peering through the trees, holding tightly onto Wilny's scar covered arm.

Kat sighed with relief. A little flick of her ears as she surveyed the area, she scowled a little. It was a very hilly landscape, split between fields of growing crops and towns nestled away between the hills.

"I might need an extra pair of eyes to help me," said Kat, "there's too much ground to cover on my own."

"Done!" Storm beamed, rousing her feathers to shake the dust from them. She never missed an opportunity to fly, especially on such a sunny day. Beth however, grumbled in irritation as she realised there was no way that she was going to talk Storm out of it.

"You two had better be careful, there aren't any clouds for cover."

"Then we'll just have to stay out of visible range. We'll text if we see anything." She grinned stepping towards the edge of the cliff before stopping and looking over her shoulder.

"Raoul."

"*Oui?* I mean…yes?"

"Stay on the alert for any non-human scents, and please try and teach Wilny some French so he can communicate with Lana."

Raoul nodded in assurance. With a wink, Storm spread her arms out and let herself fall from the edge of the cliff, vanishing for several moments before rocketing back up into the sky with Kat following after. The two girls soared up into the blue, leaving behind the others in the woodland edge. Beth sighed bitterly, and with a sharp tug on the strap of her laptop bag, she led them onwards, carrying on down the chalk path.

After a few minutes of walking in awkward silence between them all, Beth coughed and pointed across the vast expanse of water to their right. Raoul blinked and looked to where she was pointing, a thin strip green against the blue sky and sea on the horizon.

"Over there is France, Raoul." Beth explained.

He smiled to himself. "I didn't think we were that close…"

"It's pretty quick and easy to just hop on one of the ferries or on the Eurotunnel and head over there."

"Do you…get many assignments that take you there?"

"Not that many anymore. Sienna and Matagot usually deal with the ones in France. They're like us, except Parisian and have more Preters and Pards than us or the Daggers do. Which reminds me, Matagot owe me three favours now."

"Favours?"

Wilny sighed to himself as Beth and Raoul began to talk. Beth's need to be seen as being intelligent and all knowing, was often frustrating. However, he was getting used to it.

Running a hand through his hair, plucking out one of the shiny indigo feathers that grew through it, he glanced down at Malana walking beside him.

Her amber eyes fixed on the sea, the hem of Kat's coat dragging on the ground as she walked. She wasn't comfortable, and with the strain on her wings and the heat of the sun it wouldn't have improved anything He could relate how uncomfortable she felt, as he regularly had to hide his tailfeathers by carefully wrapping them around his waist and keeping them under his shirt.

He gently squeezing her hand, getting her attention. The little girl gazed up at him questioningly. Storm had cleaned her face up with the napkins they had gotten with their food, now revealing almost iridescently gold freckles that had been hidden beneath the dirt.

"So Mal," Wilny said nervously, scrunching his face up as he tried to remember the vague sounds of basic French, "Uh...keys apple Mal…uh…Jammy apples."

"No, no don't call her that." Raoul cut in, falling back and began walking next to Wilny. Beth had stopped talking and was now on her phone texting someone, furiously swearing under her breath.

"What?" Wilny frowned in irritation. "What did I say?"

Now that they were standing so close Raoul could see the flaws of Wilny's face. His right eye held a section of stained red within the blue of his iris, his nose had several breaks within it, and the scar which split through his eyebrow and ran up into his hairline as a set of parallel marks that appeared to have come from Canid or Pard claws.

Nervously Raoul swallowed, holding up his hands in defence, remembering that this young man was no pretty Risio product but a Ruby ranked Elite.

"*Mal* means bad or evil. She speaks French differently to me so it's probably not a good idea to call her that."

The Hummingbird narrowed his eyes at him, then looked back down at Malana's perplexed face.

"Lana it is then." He sighed softly, ruffling her matted brown hair. "Commey vous apple...err...fromage?"

Malana stared at him in confusion. With a quiet voice, she looked to Raoul and asked him why Wilny was talking about cheese. Raoul snorted with laughter.

"What? What did I ask?" Questioned Wilny.

"It's *Commet vous appelez-vous,* if you really want to ask for her name."

"Oh. Right. Uhh...how do I ask if she's okay?"

"*Comment allez-vous,* say that. It means '*how are you*' and if she says '*Je suis bien*', it means she is fine and if she says *mal,* she is not. Simple." He shrugged, then quickly looked to Malana to explain what he was saying to Wilny. The little girl made a small '*Ooh*' noise and nodded quickly, patting Wilny's arm to try to get him to talk.

"R-right." Wilny hesitated and looked down at Malana. "Uh...Commen ally voos?"

Both the Hound and little Dove winced at his terrible pronunciation mixed with his cocktail accent, but both managed to force a reassuring smile, glad that he was at least trying.

"*Bien, je suis bien.*" Malana nodded shyly, speaking slowly so Wilny could try to understand what she was saying. With a half-panicked smile, Wilny looked back at Raoul, trying to remember what he said.

"Uhh…she said she was alright, right?"

Raoul smiled and nodded, opening his mouth to tell him that he needed to pronounce the words a little better, when a pungent and revolting scent, drifted past him. A sickening stench of burnt flesh and hair hit him and made his stomach churn. At first, the smell was just passing wisps of a scent on the breeze, then they stepped into the full gust, downwind of the source.

The sharp metallic sent of blood, keratin and flesh mixed with the earthy smell of damp hay and dust, with a familiar odious scent beneath it that made him recoil as it set off alarm bells in his head.

Raoul choked as he caught the scent and covered his nose quickly, but it didn't stop him from feeling nauseous and falling onto his hands and knees to retch.

Beth blinked at him, taking her eyes off her phone, as Raoul recoiled and began coughing. Wilny instantly picked Malana up into his arms and held her close to protect her.

"What is it?" Asked Wilny cautiously, head to one side and eyes glancing about the coastline. He was prepared to rip his hot heavy coat off and fly off with Malana if the Hound so much displayed a fang to them.

"What do you smell?"

"Flames and Serpents." Raoul spat, pulling a sour face. He pulled the shirt Wilny had let him borrow over his nose to try and stop the scent, not that it helped.

The Hummingbird frowned. "Serpent? Oh, snakes."

"Not just that…there's blood too, and feathers, and burning…I think it's…" Raoul shuddered, unable to finish the sentence as he began to pant for breath as his chest tightened in anxiety. His hands trembled and eyes glazed over, Wilny immediately recognised what was happening as Raoul stumbled and fell to his knees. A PTSD attack.

"Kid. Kid look at me. You're safe with us." Wilny said in a low voice, setting Malana down and pulling the Hound to his feet. He shook Raoul by his shoulders gently and made him look him dead in the eye. "Keep it together kid. We can't have you scaring Lana. Focus."

Raoul shook his head and apologised, swallowing down the acid in his throat. Watchfully and patiently, Wilny made sure that Raoul had levelled his breathing out and was steady enough to stand before he let him go. Beth quickly sent a text to Storm to inform them of what to look for.

Gliding on a thermal, a few thousand above, Storm and Kat had been circling above, scouring the ground for anything that might be of interest as well as just enjoying the airtime. Storm's phone vibrated in her pocket as she received Beth's message. Steadying herself in the thermal with a few sharp flaps, she took her phone out and read the text.

'Look for any signs of a fire. Raoul said he burning and snakes. Might be them.'

Her heart dropped and putting her phone away with a disappointed sigh she angled her wings and caught the wind to rise. Kat followed suit, having to flap several times before she could get the same height.

"What did Beth say?" Kat asked, gliding alongside Storm.

"Look for anything burning." She said softly, looking down at the patchwork of field, towns and countryside. "It needs to be large enough to contain bodies."

Kat looked horrified by the latter part of the sentence. She nodded furiously, shook off her shock and focused her sights on the ground below.

They soared over a small village nestled between the hills, which had little plumes of smoke drifting out the gardens where people were barbequing, not what they were looking for. If it were burning bodies, they were looking for then it would have attracted attention if it were in a town, as even humans would be able to smell it. Flying on, they drifted back over the fields, broken by narrow country roads and patches of woodland.

"Could that be it?" Kat asked pointing down to a cross section of fields where a small plume of smoke drifting across in the breeze. Storm looked across at where she was pointing to, where on the edge of a field there were haystacks being burnt. Storm and Kat circled the blackened bales from above. It lined up with the direction that Raoul and the others were in. This knowledge added with what of what Beth had told them it was a simple deduction.

Just to be sure, Storm swooped down and circled the burning haystack, examining it without landing when she too was hit by the revolting stench and she shot back up to Kat's side, retching as she went.

"That's it." She confirmed as Kat banked out the way, rising higher on the thermal. Kat looked across to the Rogue leader, unnerved by the coldness in her voice. Her face was impassive but Kat knew that beneath this mask was a murderous rage.

Taking out her phone, she sent a message to Beth to confirm to her that Raoul was right.

'We found Ciel.'

'Where?'

Several aerial photos soon followed, to help Beth navigate their way to the scene. It wasn't far, not even a mile away when Beth compared to the map on her phone.

"Storm's found them." Beth said to them, adjusting the strap on her laptop bag. "I think we'll have to look after Malana from now on."

Wilny frowned as he processed Beth's cryptic message and picked Malana up, holding her close.

"Are we sure they're...y'know." He asked. Beth could only sigh, offering them no answer as she led them off. Silently they walked round the edge of the town that Storm had told them to go through; passing several humans on the way who all gave them odd looks but said nothing.

As they drew closer to the location, they noticed the smell more and more. Raoul was becoming even more perturbed by it and anxiously clawing at his arm. Wilny allowed him to walk beside him so that he would feel safer, but also so that if Raoul did go into another panic attack then he could easily get hold of him.

After about fifteen minutes of silent walking, they drew closer to the burning hay bales, getting off the road and walking along the tractor paths that broke up the fields. They spotted Kat standing several meters back from the bales.

Though no longer on fire, the blackened bales were still smoking profusely, a damp rotting stench of damp hay which became mixed with the sickly metallic smell of barbequed flesh and keratin as they got closer. The thought that there may have been people in the burnt mass made both Beth and Raoul feel sick, and the thought of that inside it was a little girl's family made Wilny shiver in rage, iridescent feathers rousing into an angry display.

Malana looked up at Wilny's angry expression, bright amber eyes confused by the behaviour of the older ones. She clung onto his neck, frightened by it all; She did not like the smell either and their silence was alarming her.

Kat made no greeting to them when they reached her, her eyes were fixed on the bales perfectly still with the exception of her tail twitching with anger. She didn't want to investigate and glanced at the others, hoping that one of them would be brave enough to check for bodies.

With a lamenting sigh, Wilny made the decision for them.

"Beth, Kat, keep Malana here." Wilny said in a low voice, putting Malana down and shrugging off his jacket to free his wings. Malana instantly grabbed onto Wilny's arm again, refusing to let him get any closer or leave her alone. Kat and Raoul pulled Malana away from the smoking pile, trying to get her attention so she wouldn't see whatever came out of it whilst Wilny investigated.

Though she was not fully aware of the situation, Malana understood it had to do with her family and when she looked down at the ground as she was being led away, she saw distinct feathers caught within the grass. The small feathers lay scattered about the grass. Cinnamon orange, deep brown, and shining burnished gold feathers, far too bright to belong to any native bird but they were familiar to her. She dropped to the ground, gathering them up into her arms.

"Rust, Miel, Leilani…" She muttered, looking down at the feathers. A second look at them and she could see that they were covered in dried blood at the quill tips where they had been ripped from the skin, and all over the ground there were dark patches of blood splashes. Then she understood.

She would never see her family alive ever again.

With great gasping sobs, she began to cry heart wrenchingly, the only sound to break the uneasy silence.

Finding a stick, Wilny cautiously poked through the black ashes, which disintegrated away under the gentle pressure until it hit something hard. Leaning in over, he blew on the ashes creating a small black cloud of smoke, and when it cleared revealed part of a fire charred face.

He recoiled in horror, back pedalling with his wings away from the ashes. The blackened skin had cracked from the flames, the red muscles exposed under the broken skin, their mouth was open as though it were screaming, eye sockets empty and steaming, all hair, clothing and feathers a melted mass. Swallowing his disgust, he silently brushed more ash away from the body, unearthing it further and finding the burnt figure of another person laying beneath.

Both figures were lain out on their fronts, simply piled one on top of the other, their backs horribly burnt and mutilated; the blackened broken bones that would have once been the long radius of a bat-like Chiro's wing, shattered with flesh still clinging to it, the spindly elongated fingers still attached at the wrist. It looked as though someone or something had broken their wings and ripped them from their back.

Raoul watched Wilny as he investigated the ashes. The strong scent and the sight of the burnt corpses overwhelmed his senses, flashing back to dark and unwanted memories of his brothers, he felt sick to his stomach. Looking down to where Malana was curled up on the ground sobbing with Kat and Beth knelt beside her and attempting to comfort her, Raoul's heart ached. Loss was familiar to him, and it hurt.

He wanted to help her.

He *needed* to help.

Swallowing his disgust, he crouched down on to all fours and took a deep breath, trying to focus on the scents of anything, but the corpses.

It was difficult to block out the sickening stench, but he persisted, padding around on his hands and feet trying to find the culprits and distinguish them from the Rogue's scents.

Seven individuals; At least three unfamiliar Avios, two Reptile Synths – the serpents he had smelt before – a Chiro, and the bizarre scent of a Preternatural.

"There were Reptiles here, Avios too," He said as Wilny returned to Malana. Nodding silently, Wilny lifted her up into his arms and carried her away from the burning bales, not wanting her to see the bodies. She flung her arms around his neck, wailing louder as she buried her face into the feathers on his shoulder.

Wilny ground his teeth, tail feathers rattling behind him in disgusted fury. Elites didn't kill unless they were ordered to. The Rogues and other Synth groups didn't kill unless they had no other choice. This was different.

Malana was a little girl – if they had caught her, they would have done the same thing to her? The thought chilled him.

"Comment allez-vous?" He asked Malana quietly, using the phrase Raoul had taught him, glancing to the Hound to make sure that he was saying it right. She shook her head.

"Mal…" She sobbed. He sat down with her in the field, gently rubbing her back and shoulders to try to comfort her.

"I've called Owen…Storm wanted to be alone…" Kat softly murmured to Beth; eyes still fixed on the ashes. "He'll be here soon to…clean it up…" Her voice trailed off into a wavering whisper.

Beth nodded, patting Kat's shoulder and motioning for her to go sit down before she collapsed or threw up. Casting a glance to the sky, she saw Storm still circling up above. There would be no reaching her when she was angry, and Beth knew well enough to not ask her if she was okay.

"Was anything else here? Storm needs to know so she can decide what our next action is." Beth asked Raoul, phone out and ready to let the Rogue know what was happening on the ground.

Between tremoring breaths, explained what he had found whilst Beth immediately texted Storm, looking up to the sky where she circled as a silhouette above. The message was received and Storm shot higher, vanishing into the blue in anger.

With a sigh Beth patted Raoul's shoulder in reassurance. "You've done well, Raoul. You can stand down now."

The Hound nodded and quickly made his way over to the others, leaving Beth alone. With a little stretch of his wing, Wilny brushed his feathers against Raoul's back and nodded for him to sit close with them. Sighing loudly, she sent a short text to Storm to keep watch above and sat down, waiting for Owen and the Rioteers to arrive.

-x-

Owen arrived in a marked police car followed by two vans full of officers and forensic team. All were Rioteers or at least had some affiliation with them and could be trusted to keep their activities secret.

When Owen stepped out of the car in full uniform, and made a beeline directly for Beth, who was sat alone on the edge of the field staring up at the sky with her laptop open. The others were sitting together in the field, only visible from the tops of their heads, and avoiding all sight of the ashes.

"Twice in under twelve hours you've called me out, I need to sleep you know, Beth. I'd much rather sleep than deal with all this bullshit." Owen grumbled bitterly, running a hand over his cropped greying hair.

"People have died, show a little respect, Owen." Beth scowled at him over the tops of her glasses, snapping her laptop shut and returning it to its bag.

"People die every day, and I'm far too old and tired to care." He grumbled with a shrug and helped her to her feet. He jerked his head to the ashes and signalled for the other men getting out of the vans in forensic gear to get to work setting up the tents.

"So, five bodies all under there then?"

"All Avios and Chiros, and probably all with their wings ripped off. I haven't got their full ID's through from Grace yet."

"Urgh, *ripped*? Then burnt?"

"And apparently, from what our newest Rogue said, there were three Avios, two Reptiles and a Chiro and a Preternatural which did it, but I can't find any record of a group like that."

"Your *newest* Rogue?" He gave her a quizzical look, then cast a glance over at Raoul sitting in the field. He whistled for his partner, who was still sat in the car, listening to the police radio.

"Anthony are you getting out or what?" Owen called.

Anthony, the second officer, stepped out the car, put on a pair of shades and made his way over to the Rogues sitting in the field.

Raoul lifted his head up, looked at the police officer, and sniffed. Right away, he knew this person wasn't human and with a frown and tapped Wilny's shoulder lightly.

"There's a Canid here." He muttered to Wilny. Looking round, Wilny spotted Anthony and nodded.

"That's Anthony. Second in command to the Asena pack so make sure you behave yourself."

Wilny stood and motioned for Raoul to stand also, both being quiet and calm so as not to wake the little girl curled up in Wilny's arms. It had taken a lot to get her to calm down and sleep, Wilny didn't want to have to stress her any further.

"New boy?" Anthony asked in a gentle voice, watching Raoul cautiously beneath his shades, the pointed ears twitching subtly. Raoul stood to attention and nodded, not about to forget his manners when talking to an older and superior officer.

"*Oui, Monsieur.*"

"Anthony Scarlett." The Canid extended his hand to Raoul to shake it. Now he was closer Raoul could see sharp canines flashing as he spoke, thick black whiskers hiding amongst his furred beard, and like Raoul's own hands, he had rough pads to protect the skin beneath. He looked rather human, more so than the Wolf did, even with the hairy arms, which was until he removed his shades to reveal large yellow eyes.

"No need to call me sir, Anthony will do...umm...have they given you a name yet?"

"Uhh...Raoul..."

"You've been helping the Rogues?"

"*Oui mons-* I mean...yes Anthony, sir."

He gave the boy a small smile of confidence. "Good." He said. "These birds need a lad like you to help them really. I am going to need a full report of what happened." Giving them a nod to follow he led them over to Owen.

A shriek and a gust of dust drew everyone's attention as Storm had bolted from the sky and landed next to the tents, startling several of the forensic team and officers who had been too busy with their work to notice her circling above. Tucking her wings back, she skipped over to Owen and Beth, ignoring the ashes that she had disturbed with the downdraft of her wings, and the irritated men whose white suits were now greyed with ash.

"I've found a farm three miles from here which looks like it's been raided." Storm reported to them. "It's off the main roads and surrounded by fields, perfect for camping out in if you're a group of psychopathic Strays."

Beth noted the smile and level tone to her voice but knew this was just a mask. There was an electrical charge around Storm, she could feel it as every nerve in her body screamed for her to run from Storm as fast as she could, because at some point soon she was going to lash out and bite. It was almost like the effect musers had when they let people know how they were feeling, but much more deadly. Musers couldn't stop your heart from beating.

"I've alerted the force so if we need help, they'll give it. We'll deal with that in a while after we've cleaned up this mess," Owen said, stretching out his arms behind his back and taking a subtle step away from Storm, sensing the threat too.

"I can handle it Owen. We can get there and be done with it in ten minutes."

"Don't get cocky missy," Owen sneered, "you may be able to stop a man's heart dead with a shock, but you're not invulnerable."

Storm grinned at him with her mouthful of serrated teeth. "Aww, you're just worrying that *Wolfie* will rip your head off if I go back injured."

"I wouldn't put it past her. Asena doesn't like any of you kids getting hurt." He shuddered at the thought of Asena's angry snarl.

Anthony stepped up to Storm's side with the other Rogues, acknowledging her as the leader with a small salute.

"Evidence?" He asked, in his low soft voice, whiskers twitching.

"What looks like several dead animals, upturned cars and blood in this farmyard. No humans about or any other signs of life." Whipping out her phone she showed him the photos she had taken from above, both close and far. "If whoever was barbaric enough to do this to the Ciel group, then they're definitely up for something like this."

"Are you sure? The owners might be away and they're taking advantage of it."

She rolled her head to one side and gave him a snide smirk.

"I am very well versed in the logic and behaviours of the impulsive. If they're up for murder once, then they're up for it again."

"Want me to head over there in the car with you Storm?" Anthony questioned after a brief pause to contemplate what she said.

Storm thought about what she wanted to do about the farm and how to make it work so that Malana was safe. Wilny was still cradling the little girl in his arms, though his eyes were fixed on Storm as he waited to see what her plan was. She knew he was ready to cut in and deconstruct it if he did not like it or did not think it was safe, now more so than ever.

"Take Raoul, Wilny, and Malana in the car," she said carefully, "that way if you need to you can drive them all back if it turns out to be nothing, and Malana can stay in the car if we do need a hand. Flying there it should only take us all of five minutes, so Kat, Beth, and I will investigate."

"Nice idea, but I don't want to." Beth stated, clinging onto her laptop bag and staring unblinkingly at Storm. Storm shrugged, her wings also shifting and extending a little as she moved her shoulders, feathers rousing with anger.

"Tough shit. You're coming with Kat and me."

"I make plans, I hack into things; I do not do dirty work!" She snapped, gripping onto the strap tighter. "And I do not *fly*."

"I repeat: *Tough shit*." Storm said sternly with a growl in her voice, exerting her leadership over Beth. "You're coming with us. Unless you want to stay here with the dead and help with the forensic crew, I'm sure they can find a few skulls for you to identify and put a name to."

"*Urgh*. Alright. Anthony I'm putting my laptop in your car." Beth grumbled as she considered the alternate option, then span on her heels and marched towards the car to put her beloved laptop away.

"Storm." Wilny said sharply.

Storm looked over at him, eyebrow raised in question as to what he wanted to say.

"Don't do anything reckless okay?"

"Like I'd do that!" She laughed, then with a powerful kick and a stroke of her wings, she shot skywards.

6

Poison Wood, East Langdon, Dover, Kent.

"This is a bad idea, Storm." Grumbled Beth bitterly. She held her hands above her eyes to shield them from the sun as well as to keep her glasses in place. "Just us three taking on several killers without assistance from Anthony or the Rioteers or even the police? *Seriously*? What use will I be if it comes to a fight? You know I can't fight for shit."

Storm rolled her eyes at Beth's complaining.

"It's not like we haven't done something like this before."

"I know, but we had six other people and the Rioteers behind us with *that*. And even with all that support, we still lost Koi and Lilly."

"You don't need to remind me. If you're so scared you can always throw something at them while me and Kat handle it." She stated, brushing the hair from her face. "And the lads will be here in a few minutes anyway, so we won't be totally alone."

Beth huffed and began pulling at the collar of her shirt as she started to sweat. Red faced and sweating, her chest and lungs were screaming with pain from the use of her near atrophied wing muscles and the exertions of flight.

She hated flying. Soft-feathered wings trapped heat very well, but unfortunately made her far too hot for comfort and even the wind from flying couldn't keep her cool. It didn't help that her right wing was slightly smaller than her left and that it threw her balance off, so much so that she had to work hard to swing her arms and keep twisting to stop herself from spiralling through the sky.

"How can you even be sure this is where they are?"

"If I'm wrong then I'm wrong." Storm shrugged, sharply angling her wings and banking in a tight arc, looking down at the farm.

From their aerial view, they could see what looked like several upturned vans, the glitter of smashed glass, dark stains pooling under the bodies farm animals. Even if it wasn't due to the Synths they were looking for, there was no doubt that something bad had happened down on this farm.

Storm shot the Owl a scornful look and then sweeping her wings back, she arrowed out of the sky, aiming for the strip of woodland behind the barns with Kat quickly following behind.

Gritting her teeth and wishing she were back at the house in her comfy chair with a pot of tea and some cake, Beth tucked her soft wings back with an agitated sigh and swooped down after them.

What took them several minutes to climb to the right altitude where they were not clearly visible to human eyes, took only seconds for them to get back down again. The rush of diving was exhilarating, but for Beth there was always the terror and anxiety that she might fall or hit the ground too fast when landing and shatter her bionics or even break her bones. She hated flying, but she hated landing even more.

Splaying her wings wide, Beth tried to use them to parachute to the ground after half-crashing into the trees on her descent, coming to a stumbling landing that threw her onto her hands and knees. Cursing, she dusted herself down and checked her arms and legs for any further cracks or dents, praying that they'd one day heist a Delta bunker to provide her with new and updated limbs. Satisfied that she had suffered no damaged, she jogged over to where Storm and Kat were waiting for her in the shade of the woodland, wings tucked back and standing still. The only sign of movement was their hair which caught and tussled in the breeze and the alert twitching of Kat's ears. She was listening for any signs of life, holding a blade in each hand, prepared for an ambush or sudden surprise of any kind. Storm remained as equally still so as not to distract her.

"House." Kat muttered, glancing towards Storm. "Definitely a group of Synths in there."

Rolling her shoulders, Storm thought carefully about what their next step was. It was hardly a safe move to attack the house straight away. What if there were humans inside being held hostage? Unlikely as it was, but there was always a possibility of things not being quite what they'd expect them to be.

"How many?"

"Four…maybe…I can smell the blood too."

The feathers along Storm's spine rose in agitation and she hopped easily over the high barbed wire fence into the woodland strip, Kat swiftly following after. Huffing in annoyance at the two women's graceful athleticism, Beth followed them after taking a small running start and a good leap to make sure she cleared the fence.

Used to having scratches and stings on her legs, Kat easily ignored the undergrowth and pressed forward, focused on the task at hand, whilst Storm and Beth kept their wingtips raised up, so the feathers wouldn't be damaged by the sharp thorns or caught in long arches of the bramble fronds.

'I wish I'd stayed at home' Beth thought indignantly as she picked her way carefully through the brambles and nettles that covered the woodland, grateful she couldn't feel the stings on her bionics. She really hated having to run, jump, and or fly; that was Storm's area of expertise whilst hers was sitting down and keeping everyone safe from behind a computer screen.

When they escaped the rough undergrowth, they came out behind two large containers and vans were parked at their end closest to the woodland, giving them cover from the sights of the house. Wood, crates, and farming debris was piled up against a barn off to one side of the yard. The sharp metallic sent of blood caught their attention and they all dropped into a crouch, pressing up against the container until Kat could assess the situation and make sure they weren't about to be ambushed.

Beth hissed in anxiety, her feathers rousing across her wings as she grew increasingly tense.

"I don't like this. I want to leave."

"Not now Beth." Storm breathed as they crept carefully onto the property, remaining out of sight of the house.

As they peaked through openings between the containers, they could see that the bodies two dogs and a few sheep, caught against the side of an upturned van. It looked as though they had been thrown and must have been there for a day or two in the baking sun, as they were beginning to smell and attract the flies.

Kat's ears twitched, picking up sounds of laughter from the direction of the house that she could now see from their hiding spot. Other than the laughter, there was also quite an audible buzzing sound of possibly thousands of flies. The Lioness' ears flattened back as, they crept round towards the barn, from which the sound of the flies resounded loudest.

"Storm," Kat swallowed, as she began to smell fresher blood the closer they got to the barn. "I think there's something dead in there. It might just be more livestock, but...I'm not sure."

Storm peeked out from the container to check if there was anyone on guard, but the area was deserted.

The entrance to the barn was no more than three meters from where they were crouched, its big doors shut, even so, this did not seem to stop the flies from finding their way in through the gaps and cracks to get inside.

Beth covered her ears, the drone of the flies starting to both irritate and unnerve her further.

"You're not going to go in there, are you?" She hissed at Storm, watching her stand and cautiously step out from their cover. "You don't know what's in there!"

Storm didn't answer, only rolled her shoulders and extended out her wings, preparing them to be ready to backpedal right away.

"It's only dead things." She muttered, as she put her hand to the door. Now she was close she could smell the blood and hear the low buzz of flies, her stomach turned to a hollow pit in disgust and alarm.

Taking a breath, she pulled the door back, sliding it open in a swift movement. The droning buzz intensified for a moment then rushed towards her in one giant mass.

She yelped loudly as a swarm of gigantic flies scattered from the barn in a mass of black and flew into her face. Throwing her arms up to her face to protect herself from swallowing any of the flies, she beat her wings as hard as she could, driving the flies away. When the buzzing had dimmed to just a few individuals rather than a swarm she slowly lowered her arms to look and then with a horrified gasp, she snapped her wings shut and stood motionless.

Before her, suspended from the rafters and hanging by their feet as though they were pigs in an abattoir, were three humans. Two adults and a teenage boy. They were lifeless, their eyes glazed over and arms limply hanging down with blood dripping from their fingertips.

Kat and Beth appeared at the barn doorway behind her, half-curious half terrified as to what she was seeing. Horror overwhelmed them at the sight. Suppressing down the urge to vomit, they took a moment to calm themselves before they stepped inside the barn, keeping their wings high off the ground.

"This is disgusting." Beth grimaced, stepping around the bloody pool on the floor. "Now I'm definitely not going to sleep for a month."

"Why would they-" Kat swallowed, forcing down the nausea. Her feathers and fur bristled. "Why would they kill humans and Synths?"

Storm shook her head and rolled her shoulders in agitation, pupils little more than pinpricks within her piercing eyes. She took a few deep breaths and tried to calm her fury by pacing back and forth across the barn floor with low snarling growls, but only winding herself up into a knot of anger.

"Whoever has done this *really* needs to die." Storm stated coldly, the mantle feathers rising in anger and stepping towards the bodies to examine them. Snapped necks and bite wounds. Synth teeth were different to human teeth, not only in how many they had but what they could do. From what she could see they looked like Reptile bite marks, but there was other indication of other damages. Broken arms. Talon cut skin. No hint of a scrappy fight, but instead deliberate injuries.

"They're not Feral. They know what they're doing." Her feathers rattled with tempestuous rage, her entire body shaking as she restrained herself from lashing out at something. "They know *exactly* what they're doing, and I know *exactly* what I'm going to do to them."

"They're quite high up…" Beth frowned at the bodies. Crossing her arms across her chest, she shivered at the sight and at the coldly logistical thoughts that sprung to mind. "Did they use a ladder to get them up there or are they just really strong?"

"Does it matter?" Storm snapped, baring a flash of white fangs at her. "Just call Owen, tell him more bodies are here and then we'll get these murderers and *kill them*."

"As justified as your murderous intent is, Storm, is it necessary?"

"They've killed at least eight people, three of them kids! For humans this counts as a massacre, I consider it *very necessary!*"

"But we could–"

"Beth." Wings flared, and sharp teeth bared, she stepped up before Beth who shrank back from her wrath. An electrical muser-like energy surrounded Storm and every nerve in Beth's body screamed for her to run away.

"They're serial killers. We can't just lock them up like humans do. Where's the justice in that? This has to be done for the safety of everyone."

Kat made a little gasp for breath as the smell of blood and the sight of the bodies became too much for her to handle. It wasn't the sight of the dead that bothered her – she had killed humans before, but that had always been quick and clean, these people however had ever so clearly suffered before they had died.

She had to turn away from the sight whilst the other women argued, and as she did, she was caught by surprise that they were not alone.

"*Fucking hell!*" She shrieked, leaping back several feet with her blades raised to strike. Storm threw her fists up and leapt in front of Beth so that if any fighting were to ensue, the least prepared Rogue would have a chance to drop back and find a weapon to arm herself with.

Sat along the wall of the barn behind the door were three partially dressed men staring straight ahead, not seeming to hear or notice the noise that the Rogues had made.

The three Rogues held their ground, tense and ready to spring into action, but the men barely batted an eyelid. It was almost as if they were dolls; they were so unnaturally still.

Cautiously Kat adjusted her grip on her blades and quietly padded over to them. She stepped into the view of the first man, a huge titan of an Avio with vast broad wings that were spread limply either side of him. Each was at least ten feet long, with brown with white bands, but with no tailfeathers or feathered ear tufts it meant that the man was a Transhuman.

His deeply bronze skin and dark mane of hair was splattered with dry blood, covered in old scars and fresh cuts, and from the size of his bare chest and breadth of his shoulders he looked to have the strength to rip their wings from their backs. However, even this giant didn't move or blink when the blade came into his line of sight. He just stared ahead; deep brown eyes fixed unseeingly on the other side of the barn.

"Katana, keep your knife on them." Beth said coldly, watching the three motionless men.

She side stepped around Storm and slowly made her way over, crouching down in front of the giant Avio first and cautiously checking his pulse and eyes before moving onto the human looking darkhaired man in the middle – the Preternatural, although she couldn't tell what Origin his base was. Slow pulses, no reaction to touch or sound, they were sleeping with their eyes open.

Even the third Synth didn't even flinch. A Chiro with large rabbit-like ears that would usually be hypersensitive and twitching constantly at even the slightest noise. His silky, leathery, bat-like wings that flowed down his back to a flexible tail, were hooked around him in a sleeping posture. She checked further up their arms for any signs of the little square patches that ARCDA used for their drug administration and found the shimmery holographic patch for Hax.

Furrowing her brow, her glasses slipped down her nose as she looked to Storm uneasily.

"They've been drugged, or they're being controlled by a muser. Or both. Probably both."

"Are you sure?"

Beth pulled off one of the patches of Hax from the Chiro and held it up.

"Hax. Not only that, but their pupils are also fully dilated. They've a slowed pulse and breathing rate, and they're not reacting to anything. Look," She pinched what little skin she could on the muscular Avio. He didn't even twitch. "They're basically unconscious. Although, most musers couldn't do this unless they were hopped-up on Nitro. And if we've got Hax, then we've probably got a whole bunch of other drugs going on."

Beth stuck her tongue out in disgust. Hax was usually recreational, a relaxant that made people happy and calm, slowing their reactions. Many Synths took it; however, it was addictive, but it was nowhere near as dangerous as Nitro.

Storm glanced at the men then back at the bloody bodies hanging from the metal beams.

"So, these three are *not* to blame for the deaths? If they have no control over their actions, it's not their fault?" She questioned, not content with Beth's deduction though it was enough to still her anger.

Beth had to think, recalling what she could about the effects of muser control.

It was one of the more common talents or abilities that Atlas faction had developed. Many Synths had this ability, even Wilny had it, as it was highly useful for Core's Elites to spy and communicate with in their teams. Whilst Wilny was himself a muser, able to augment people's perceptions he was unable to control anyone directly, and with past experiences, had no intention of learning to either. Others could however, although they had to be within range of a person to do so and could leave people unconscious until mentally nudged into being awake again.

"My best guess is that they possibly won't remember it, or they would have been in control of their actions. So, no, they aren't really the ones to blame." Beth frowned for a moment. "It would be manslaughter more than murder."

Thoughtfully, Storm rolled her shoulders a little, shaking off the disgust and beginning to recalculate a plan. The muser in control would be the priority, along with whoever had been involved in the murders.

"Are you both alright?" She asked looking at the other girls' pale faces.

"It's disgusting," Kat muttered, swallowing a little and trying to focus on something else other than the smell of blood and the hanging bodies of what was once a family.

Storm roused her feathers, pacing back and forth once again beneath the suspended bodies. "If we can stop whichever one of the remaining five is doing this then we can probably get these three guys to fight on our side if we need to."

"Do we need to?" Kat asked, rubbing the goosebumps on her arms. "What if they just attack us and think we're with ARCDA?"

"Then we'll crack their skulls if we have t-"

"*Shit!*" Beth shrieked as all three men suddenly turned their heads in unison to face the girls. The Rogues span round, wings, flared, fist clenched, teeth bared, and knives raised ready to fight.

She leaped up and back to Storms' side, feathers ruffled up in shock and glasses askew. Storm flared her wings out and shielded Beth from the men, lip curling into a snarl. The men rose but made no further movements towards them.

"What the hell is this?" Asked a voice.

They found themselves confronted by an Avio girl, no older than sixteen, watching them from the doorway of the barn. The girl observed them with a wary glare, bloodshot yellow eyes boring into them and her tangled ginger hair flowing over her shoulders.

Stepping forward, Storm swept her wings out and held her ground much to Beth's surprise. Storm assessed the girl with a critical eye. No tailfeathers, no feathered ear tufts, she was another Transhuman Avio, but that was not the thing that held her attention.

The girl was *heavily pregnant.*

Alarm bells rang in the Rogues' heads, with Beth immediately trying to think of a solution as she whispered a horrified *'oh no'* to Storm. This complicated things.

Straightening up and resettling her feathers with a thin-lipped calm smile, Storm extended her wings out in a silent but warning greeting. Warily the girl stretched one wing out, to reciprocate the greeting. The long wide wing, with its shaggy grey feathers streaked with cream and splayed primaries, Storm presumed that she was a vulture based Avio from the shape – a common base used by Core.

"What are you doing here?" The girl asked cautiously, eyeing Kat's knives and the shape of Storm's wings, frowning down at the four toes on Storm's bare feet with a slightly disgusted frown. Kat could see clearly in the girl's tensed pose that she was looking for the familiar uniforms and mannerisms of Core Elites, watching to see what they might use as their weapons and how they might fight.

"I thought Vultures only scavenged." Storm said snidely, rolling the R of the word and suppressing a growl that would have naturally arisen from it. "You seem to have gone predatory and territorial. Is this a side effect of the transgenics or was this your human home and I'm missing out context on an old abusive family here?"

"It's that obvious that I'm transhuman?" The girl reeled back warily, hands going to her chest where the forcibly grown keel grew from her sternum. Storm snorted, giving her wings a sharp little beat, watching as the girl flinched away from them.

"Yes. Though I'm still trying to figure out if you're feral or not."

With a moment of thoughtful comprehension, the girl sneered. Standing straight and brushing the dust from her loose dress, her large wings shifted slightly as she moved away from the doorframe, revealing a blond-haired teenage boy who was stood behind her. He was not much taller or older than the girl himself, and with a stretch of his buff-coloured wings in greeting, it was apparent that he too was Transhuman- another Vulture-based Synth, just like the girl.

Beth gave Storm a gentle tap on her wing, whispering a second '*oh no*' as she realised the ever-increasing complexity and complications of the situation.

Transhuman Avios were uncommon and were often over worked in genetic design to reform a human body into an Avio one. It created a lot of psychological damage in the subjects and instability, and now they had three of them on their hands.

Behind the boy, two lanky men lingered in the sun.

Their scaled grey skin marked by dusty brown diamond patterns and elongated bodies that characterised them as snake-based Reptiles; Toxicoferis Reptiles, most likely.

Storm counted. Three Avios, two Snakes, one Preternatural and one Chiro, just as Raoul had said.

"You're very far from home." The teenage boy said, his accent not one the Rogues could fully place, whilst the girl had a clearly East-London accent.

"We're from just up the road in London." Storm snorted. "You're the one who's come far."

The young man brushed his scraggily blond hair from his face, revealing the left side to be marred by old horrific burn marks that had scabbed over in dark scaly brown blotches. Many patches covered his arms, and Beth gave her third '*oh no*' as she spotted the patches of Nitro, Parax, and EPI+ covering every available bit of skin.

Another alarm bell rang out in the Rogues' heads at the sight of Nitro. It was a drug that Avios were not allowed to take without boosters and EPI+ as even though it could boost abilities and talents, it was lethal in their Synth species, as well as causing insanity and psychosis.

Beth stepped a little closer to Storm and Kat, noticing out the corner of her eye movement from the three men, as they made their way behind the Rogues.

"Uh....*Sekhmet*?" Beth murmured to Kat and made a slight gesture with her tawny wings. Kat spun on her heel; blades raised up in defence but Storm didn't take her eyes off the girl.

The two Vultures muttered something between each other, the male eyeing the girls in glee, much to the disgust of Storm. She could feel him trying to muse, a tingling sensation that ran across her skin but was rebuffed by her own bioelectric field. She tried not to smirk as he looked bewildered, knowing that he couldn't do anything to affect her. Brow knotting in annoyance, he softly crooned something into the girl's ear, and kissing her neck, he gently pushed her towards the Rogues. The girl stepped forward towards Storm, hand outstretched with a surreptitious look of excitement behind her smile.

"Kathy."

"Storm…" Was the Rogue's cautious reply, refusing to shake her hand.

Behind her she could feel Beth grip her feathers in anger at using her own name rather than a callsign, but it was too late to change it.

"You're Scottish. Aren't *you* rather far from home?" She echoed what the boy said, drawing her hand back and looking Storm over, seemingly having changed her mind about being frightened and suspicious to now being impressed by her.

"What's your reason as to why you're trespassing on our patch?"

"Your patch?" Storm smirked, trying to play it calm though it was impossible for her to keep the rage from her eyes. "Were these people trespassing on *your* patch too."

"Yes. Now what are you doing here?"

Storm snorted. Keeping her wings wide but folding her arms across her chest she strode forward, intimidating the girl into stepping back. She needed space to give Kat and Beth a chance to escape the barn. They couldn't perform vertical take-offs like she could and if it came down to a fight, she needed them to be able to get airborne.

"We found several dead Synths. Avios and Chiros." She told them, watching the reaction on their faces. Their smiles couldn't hide shadows of alarm in their eyes. "ARCDA doesn't dispose of bodies like, that so naturally we had to investigate, and it led us to here to you kids."

The boy chuckled and stepped forward, wrapping his arms around Kathy and resting his head on her shoulder. Though it seemed affectionate, the way he gripped Kathy's arm seemed more possessive than tender.

"Investigate?" The boy said, nuzzling the neck of Kathy lovingly and making her giggle. He watched them all lasciviously, teal-grey eyes flicking between them to size them up.

"Are you a detective Miss Storm? Are we to be arrested for defending our property?"

"This isn't your property, *boy*, it was theirs." Storm's pale eyes narrowed at him, regarding him with disgust as he tried to use his muser abilities on her in an attempt to persuade her.

'*That's not going to work with me boy, give it up now.*' She sent to him loudly, letting her fury colour the thoughts.

His head snapped up and puffing his chest out, he opened his mouth to snarl something at her, but she cut him off with a feral hiss and flash of fangs before he could even start.

"So, you kill Synths and humans alike? Why?" She pressed head cocked at an angle. They were panicking, glancing at one another with increasing uneasiness. The boy stepped before Kathy, blonde hair swept back, and face scrunched up into a sneer.

"What are you? A handler?" Teal snorted mockingly, infuriating Storm further. For all his pomp and brazenness, as well as his bordering upon lecherous gaze, the boy couldn't hide from Storm his terror as she bared her sharp little fangs at him and flicked the translucent membrane across her eye.

"Or maybe you're a Diamond."

"I'm not an Elite."

"Then we don't have to answer to you."

"No, but you will do." A growl caught in her throat.

Behind the two teenagers, the Reptiles began shifting from foot to foot anxiously. They still wore the grey and yellow accented uniforms of Topaz Elites, a rank much lower than the Ruby Elite that Wilny was. They sensed the electricity and how hard the boy was trying to muse and tiptoed forward to try and persuade the two transhumans to back off. The boy refused and hit out at the Reptiles with a shaggy wing.

"Why did you kill them?" Storm demanded. "Kathy, your answer?"

Kathy looked startled at being asked a question directly.

"I didn't like the way them birds thought that they'd be safe if they ran into the arms of them humans. Whatever they're called. Idiots, I don't care." She gave a little shrug, flicking her waves of red hair over her shoulder with a hand, adorned with a sparkling ring, which Storm presumed belonged to the human woman hanging behind her.

"So, you killed them because they wanted to go to the Rioteers?"

"Well, *I* didn't kill 'em. Teal and the boys did."

"Why didn't you just let them go? They had kids with them."

Kathy opened her mouth to answer, but no words came out. Her face scrunched up as she tried to find a reason until the boy, who Storm assumed was Teal.

"Because we hate humans, don't we Kathy."

"*Boy*, you shut your mouth until I ask you a direct question." Storm snapped at him, fangs bared and head cocking sharply with a feral intensity. The nictitating membrane flicked across her eye in an alien blink and Teal backed away quickly, half cowering behind Kathy's shaggy wings.

"Kathy. Answer."

"We *hate* humans." Kathy continued darkly, echoing Teal again, her feathers rattling as she shook, "Disgusting creatures. Vermin, the lot of 'em. They're as bad as those doctors are. They try to make you one of 'em. They try to control you. *We aren't them*, we aint *humans*. Anyone who wants to be should just die."

"You *were* human."

"I'm not anymore!" She shrieked and threw her hands over her ears, "We hate humans! We hate 'em! We just want somewhere safe to live! *I just want my baby to be alright!*"

"There's that *we* again. Are you saying that because he thinks it or because you want to?"

"You're scaring her." Teal pulled Kathy back, and protectively wrapped his arms around her as best he could with the large bulge of her stomach between them. "I'm not making her think anything that she doesn't want to! She's my mate. She loves me, and I love her!"

Kathy's face lit up at his words and she threw her arms around his neck and kissed his cheek with a squeal of delight. The display that Teal put on didn't fool Storm, who mockingly retched at them both.

"But of course, you do. Young love at its finest right here. Pretty sure I've seen how this story ends for dumb kids like you."

"*Thunderbird!*" Beth hissed, gripping Storm's sash as she felt the buzz of electricity buzz across Storm's skin. "Stop pissing off the crazy people! Now is not the time to psychoanalyse their relationship!"

"Why not? I think he's manipulative, and you're an idiot to even do or believe a word of what he says." Storm stepped forward, feathers bristling. "If you want to live safely and quietly, *murdering* people is the *opposite* of what you need to be doing."

"As to the alternative of letting *vermin* like them take care of us like pets?"

"You'll need help if you want your kid to survive. You have no idea what you're doing." She nodded to Kathy's bulging stomach. "And if ARCDA hears about that, then they'll hunt you to the ends of the earth and tear you apart to figure out how it was even possible to have kids."

"Oh, and you'll help, right. You know exactly what you're doing right? Or will your human *masters* just take them and sell them?"

"This isn't my first rodeo and they aren't our fucking masters you idiot, who even uses words like that?"

"They're terrorists! They blew up the bunker we came from!"

Storm's jaw clenched in anger. She would be having a serious debate with Asena and the Rioteers when she returned to their headquarters if what Kathy said was true. Asena had been doing her best to make sure that the Rioteers weren't using explosives or anything dangerous to Synths in their attacks but getting the Rioteers to listen was difficult.

"The Rioteers aren't perfect," she said carefully, hating that she was having to paint them in a good light, "but they could have helped you if you had just thought for one *fucking* second."

"You're just one of 'em! Of course, you'd say that!" Her wings flared out, a semi-subconscious attempt to look intimidating. Teal grabbed her arms to try and hold her back, but she shook him off sharply. "You'll lock us up you will! Then sell us back to Core!"

Storm stepped up to the challenge, beating her own wings with a sharp crack feathers, bearing the white and tightly grey-banded undersides at them. She lost her calmness, allowing the feathers to rattle and letting a sharp raptorial '*scree*' to escape.

The sharp sound made the Vultures shriek and rush back into the sun with the two Reptiles.

"You have one chance." Storm warned. "Stand down now and we can help, if not then I'm afraid we're going to have to kill you."

"Then kill us then!" Kathy snapped, beating her wings hard as she threw her arms wide in threat. "Fight me! We're not going anywhere with you!"

Without so much as a blink, Storm obliged the invitation.

She surged forward with a sharp beat of her scythe-like wings, with Kat and Beth at her back following her lead, rushing at the two Vultures, the male reacting faster than Kathy as he pulled her back quickly and beat his long wings to propel them away from Storm.

As soon as she was out in the open, Storm kicked off the dusty ground and with a single powerful downward stroke of silver-grey was airborne and vaulting over their heads, landing in front of them to block their escape.

"Catch them!" Teal shrieked at the three Synths under his control, half dragging Kathy across the ground as he dodged out the way of a hard kick from Storm. "Bring them down!"

The three men, who had not so much as blinked began to move, dropping into a fighting stance and running at the girls, chasing after them as they ran.

"Beth, hide!" Kat yelled to the Owl, giving her a small shove with her wing to make her run faster. Beth obliged without complaint, veering sharply left towards the upturned vans as the men flew out of the barn.

Kat span on her heels, ducking down as the Preternatural lunged at her. She dodged his grasp, slashing his throat on her way up and felling him with a kick to the back of his knee.

She expected him to suddenly drop immediately and bleed out on the ground, but instead the Preternatural only fell to one knee. He turned to face her, the wound quickly healed, the sliced arteries and veins stitching back together and the skin rapidly flushing across the pink gash as he pressed two Booster rapid healing patches and an EPI+ Patch to his arm. She swore under her breath, tensing up and bringing her wings up to try and take off. In the air, she would have the advantage of height and gravity against him.

The two Reptiles sprung at her, each grabbing a wing and jerking them apart so that she couldn't take to the sky, almost dislocating them. Kat screech with shock and pain as she was dragged along the dusty ground, her sandals catching rocks and her heels being grazed until she pulled her wings in sharply, tugging the Reptiles along with them. Wielding her knives in an X across her body, she sliced one across the eye and other slashing open his scaled blister covered cheek. They both screamed in anguish, releasing her. Adrenalin flooded her veins. She spun quickly, her dress flaring out around her. Swiping the blades again she caught them both on their faces and guts with a dual sweep, kicking their knees out from under them before sprinting through them to avoid the Preternatural behind her.

As Kat fought Beth lunged for junk and debris between the containers to look for a weapon, followed by the pale-winged Chiro who had decided to focus his attention upon her. He wasn't as heavily built as the Eagle Avio although was possibly just as strong, but the bright sunlight, the black uniform and the mask all slowed him down as he began to get hotter and struggled to see through the mask.

Finding a metal bar amongst the debris, she picked it up and held it up as a weapon. The Chiro lunged at her and swinging the bar as hard as she could succeeded in whacking him across the face.

Shaking off the initial pain, the Chiro started to laugh with hoarse rasping breaths, cut off by Beth striking him again with angry curses. Grabbing the bar and yanked her forward. Avio reactions were fast, almost instantaneous, however, her bionic arm didn't respond as fast and she was pulled forward, colliding heads with him. The Chiro grabbed hold of her neck, hoisting her of her feet and began to crush her throat.

Beth struggled as black spots appeared before her eyes and the blood pounded in her head. Grabbing hold of his arm for support, and flailing her soft wings about, she drew her legs up to her chest and with as much force as she could manage, aimed for his knees and groin. Her feet connected with the target areas and the Chiro toppled, releasing Beth. She hit the ground hard, landing on her left arm, shattering the plastic casing of the bionic.

Taking no time to assess the damage she scrambled to her feet as the Chiro began to recover and taking a few powerful steps she launched herself into the air with frantic flaps of her wings. She hadn't the strength of Storm for a vertical take-off and only just managed to land herself on top of the containers out of reach of the Chiro for the moment.

The Eagle Avio meanwhile had taken a running start after Storm as she bounded into the sky, along with the male Vulture. The pair of them beating their large wings as hard as they could in an attempt to scramble into the air. Their heavier weight and their transhuman differences made getting airborne difficult. Their broad wings and splayed primaries were meant for soaring, not fast take offs or agile manoeuvres.

The nimble Rogue darted past them, barely centimetres above their heads and forcing them to stumble in their take-off, the advantage of speed and experience on her side. Racing across the yard, she struck one of the Reptiles fighting Kat in the head with a powerful kick sending it rolling several meters away. Pivoting on a wing tip with the iridescent edges to her feathers flashing silver under the sun, she turned back to face them. Swooping down on the Vulture with lightning speed, she clipped one of his wings with her foot and sending him cartwheeling into the ground before shooting skywards again.

"Kill them!" Teal screamed in agony as his nose broke and blood poured down his face. "Kill them all!"

7

Poison Wood Farm, East Langdon, Dover, Kent.

The Eagle succeeded in getting airborne and was now rushing up to meet her. With every down stroke, the large dark brown feathers on the tops of his wings lifted and Storm could feel the powerful gusts created by them. Each wing was easily ten feet across and so broad that the lowest edge of his secondaries reached his ankle. Storm grinned wildly, the pale membrane flicking across her eye to protect it from the dust and wind as she watched him fly. He couldn't react as fast as Storm whilst he was being controlled; he could barely turn without dropping several feet and with no tailfeathers he had no additional lift or way to manoeuvre effectively. Noting the advantage, she had, she darted past, clipping him in the face with her foot and watched as he dropped and fell upon the roof of the barn.

Teal tried again to attempt lift off, and once again Storm stooped upon him. She kicked him hard on his right wing and the bones shattered with a meaty crack. The wing flailed and flopped; the buff feathers torn from the skin by the force of Storm's kick. Teal howled in agony, cursing as he rolled about on the ground, clutching a hand to his injured wing and as he did, the Eagle, Chiro and Preternatural all faltered for a moment in their assaults on the girls. They paused swaying slightly with bewildered looks on their faces until Teal recovered, to which they then returned to their attacks.

"Storm! Stop pissing around!" Beth yelled up to the Rogue as the Chiro used his wings to climb up onto the container she had escaped to.

"Get Vulture McFuckboy!"

"Give me a minute!" Storm shouted back, throwing a flourishing gesture towards the Eagle.

Leaping from the barn, the Eagle flew at her, pulling in his wings and stretching out his arms to grab her. In an agile move, Storm tucked her wings in sharply and dropped out of his way before flourishing her wings out before she could drop too far, arcing up into the air behind him.

Out the corner of her eye, Storm spotted the police car turning into the long drive to the house as she soared upwards. Glancing back at the Eagle who was banking in a tight arc to attack her again, she took a breath and then pumping her wings hard, dove towards them. The Eagle copied her as best he could. Angling his wings back to dive, his weight only increased his acceleration downwards, catching up with her.

Keeping close to the ground she missed the windscreen by inches and twisted to glide alongside them as the car drove down the road. The window was down, and Anthony stared at her with a startled look on his face. The Eagle overshot them as Storm dipped down and out of his way, forcing him to carry on soaring, heading upwards rather than banking and following Storm.

"We need backup! Nitro-boosted Avio muser!" Storm yelled into the window and powered over the roof, taking the short cut across the fields back to the yard. Slamming his foot down, Anthony sped up, racing the car up the drive to join them.

"What are you doing?" Kathy snapped at Teal, rushing to his side as he scrabbled and stumbled to his feet, his burned face contorted with rage "Just muse and control her mind or something!"

"You don't think I didn't try, Kathy? It's not working! Now get out the way!" Digging into his pockets, he pulled out another patch of Nitro, slapping it to his arm with a follow up of EPI+ and a Booster to keep it from killing him.

"Then try harder!" Kathy snarled angrily back at him. "She'll kill you! She'll kill me!"

He snapped his head round to face her, the Nitro flaring as it sent a rush of feral adrenalin through him.

"Get out the way or I'll kill you."

Kathy reeled back at the comment, about to question what he was implying when he recanted his words with a smile and a gentle hand on her shoulder.

"Get out of here, I don't want them hurting you. Fly somewhere safe and I'll come find you. I love you, remember that."

Kathy beamed at him, immediately forgetting his threat as he kissed her and spun to defend her. She began to run, shaggy wings splayed out and flapping slowly as she tried to get airborne and as she did so Storm spotted Kathy climbing into the air and dove at her, the Eagle on her tail. As much as she didn't want to harm the girl or her unborn baby, she didn't want Kathy to get away.

She slowed her descent, recalculating the strength of her attack to bring Kathy down when Teal charged into her path and leapt up, catching her leg. He dragged Storm down, and her momentum meant that the two tumbled and rolled over each other across the dusty stony ground.

Winded, Storm shocked the Vulture's arms, freeing herself and staggering to her feet. She hadn't crash landed since she was a child and it infuriated her. Flicking her wings out, she shook the dust off and resettled the ruffled feathers, watching to see Teal's next move and acutely aware of how many drugs he had taken.

Teal staggered to his feet, swaying a little from taking the full force of the crash, but he was focused solely upon Storm. Spitting a mouthful of blood onto the dust, he lunged at her with a roar to which she obligingly leapt forward and returned the favour of crashing with a high kick to his nose, snapping his head back and raking her talons across his throat and chest.

The police car streaked up the driveway, dust clouds billowing out behind. It skidded to a halt, the doors flew open and out leaped Anthony prepared to fight.

"Wilny, make sure the girl stays in the car!" Anthony ordered, charging forward. He lunged towards the Reptiles attacking Kat, snatching at the nearest one with his thick claws. Yanking the Snake Synth's arms backwards and kicking him forward in the spine, the Snake shrieked in agony as his arms were dislocated and was sharply thrown to one side, left to lay in the dirt.

The second Snake opened its jaws wide, far wider than any human could manage, revealing a pair of long curved fangs and bit into Kat's right wing, making her shriek loudly. She sliced her knives through the air trying to stab him without severing her own wing, at the same time as fend off the Preternatural who was now within choking distance of her.

Snarling, Anthony grabbed the second Snake's waist in his clawed hands and with a swift movement bit down into the back of its neck. With a sharp jerk, he snapped the Snake's spine.

Beth was doing her best, swiping and occasionally hitting the Chiro whenever he managed to get close, but her attacks only made him laugh. She danced with him around the containers, occasionally jumping up on top and off them, gliding a short distance away only to have him follow and shadow her every movements. Tripping her with his tail as she darted past him, he managed to catch her by her wrist and spin her round, slamming her into the container with a bang.

Black spots appeared before her eyes as her head struck metal. Her bionic arm dented upon the impact, the fingers twitching wildly as the connections inside the plastic casing were damaged. She swiped wildly at him again with her damaged hand but he caught the wrist of the bionic, pulling her arm high above her head with a sharp yank. Beth snarled at him, trying her best to kick him as the bionic was detached from its socket, the sensitive nerves the impulse receptors were connected to, firing off and stimulating an illusion of pain. Tossing the bionic to one side, he grabbed Beth by her auburn hair and slammed her back against the container hard enough to stun her.

He spread open his enormous wings, the sun shining through the ghostly translucent membrane and brought them forward against the container, the thumbs scraping against the metal loudly, trapping and surrounding Beth in a leathery barrier.

"Raoul!" Wilny snarled at the Hound, scrambling out of the car to join in the fray as he spotted Beth struggling to fend the Chiro off. "Stay here with Malana and protect her!"

"But I can-"

"Do it!" He ordered, then the iridescent wings unfurled, and he took off like a bullet in a blur towards Beth and the Chiro.

The flash of shimmering feathers caught Beth's attention, and in that instant, she let her legs collapse under her. She dropped down just as Wilny's foot connected with the back of the Chiro's head, slamming him into the container with a resounding clang.

Wilny grabbed the Chiro from behind and tore him away from Beth, pulling his shoulders back and crushing the fragile pale wings between them both. Time seemed to slow down right before them, and a disorientating feeling overwhelmed Beth as Wilny began to muse to gain control over the Chiro's reactions.

The Chiro's face contorted into a snarl, his long rat-like tail that the wing-membranes connected to, flicking about like a whip. The two wrestled before Beth, though it seemed to take forever with everything drawn out in detail. Wilny struggled to augment the Chiro's perception, rebuffed by Teal's control which sent painful jolts across the nerves down his spine to his fingertips. Two musers trying to affect the same person never fared well and so he withdrew his mental field, resorting to the old-fashioned way of attack: brute force.

Swinging him round, he tried to force the Chiro to the ground. The Chiro may not have had the power in his wings to knock Wilny away, but he had claws which scratched across his face and a tail that could grip and tangle up in Wilny's legs. With his sharp teeth, he bit into Wilny's arms and thrashed wildly about trying to tear out chunks of flesh as the two wrestled.

The Snake-Synth thrown by Anthony struggled up on to his feet hissing angrily and spotted Wilny wrestling the Chiro. Wilny's back was left exposed and with his arms around the Chiro, he couldn't do anything to fend off an attack from behind.

With Anthony preoccupied with the rapidly healing Preternatural, the Snake darted towards Wilny, tackling and staggering them. Wrapping his arms around Wilny's neck he began choking the Avio hanging onto the Chiro, who was biting hard into the arm closest to his sharp fangs. Beth was of very little help, lying on the floor holding her stub of an arm, but she tried her best to keep on kicking into the brawl.

Wilny hissed with fury as he felt sharp teeth of the Chiro digging deeper into his arm, and the Snake with his hands around his neck. Using his wings, he tried to hit out at the Snake to throw him off, but to no avail. The three struggled as they tried to kill each other, however, had Wilny had the opportunity to take a second to see the three Core trained Synths ungracefully, and unsuccessfully brawling in a conga line, he would have laughed himself into a stitch.

A loud snarl resounded from behind Wilny as he struggled, and all three Synths were jerked back, falling like dominoes as they hung onto each other. The Snake swore angrily for a moment then there was a sickening fleshy ripping sound and the arms around Wilny's neck were ripped away.

Beth looked in horror as she watched the Snake's windpipe be crushed as Raoul bit down upon it, then with a sickening and fleshy crack of bone as he snapped the spine. The Snake screeched hoarsely with agony as he died, legs twitching wildly even after his head lolled to one side.

Keeping his choke hold on the Chiro, Wilny glanced back at the Hound, after seeing the expression on Beth's face. The Chiro stopped wriggling in his arms as he lost consciousness from the lack of oxygen.

"Good Puppy..." Wilny muttered, horrified when he saw Raoul's mouth dripping with blood and the realisation that the *Puppy* was even capable of ripping a person's head off. Raoul nodded once and coughed, trying to spit out the blood in his mouth.

Grinning, Wilny shoved the Chiro off him and rose to his feet, clutching at his bloody arm. He raised a boot to stomp down upon the unconscious Synth's head, but was knocked sideways by Beth, who had gotten up and shouldered him.

"Don't kill him." She snapped. Wilny gawked at her in bewilderment.

"But he tried to kill us!"

"He's being controlled."

"Like fuck he is!" He snarled, kicking the Chiro over, rolling him onto his back. Beth shoved him again and turned back to the Chiro to make sure that didn't get up and attack once more.

"Go for him! The Scarface over there is the one controlling them! Help Storm!"

Wilny snapped his head round to where Teal and Storm were fighting, Storm kicking the Vulture back and shocking each time with a well-aimed punch to the face and chest, every time he got close. His broken wing was dragging along the ground and he kept tripping over it as he was being pushed back.

She was a strong fighter, but not a disciplined one. Fast and nimble, and with years of practicing vertical take-offs she had incredibly powerful legs, which when used to kick with could break bones if she was in the mood to do so, but she clearly didn't have the energy. Flying, fighting, and using her bioelectric talents took a lot of energy, as did the lack of sleep, and even though she was winning it didn't make her the victor especially against a Nitro-boosted muser.

Teal managed to land a punch to Storm's face, stunning her temporarily and causing her nose to bleed a little, when out of the sky swooped the giant Eagle, kicking the much smaller Avio in the chest. She skidded along the dirt ground with a grunt, wings dragging beneath her and tearing at her feathers. The Eagle stood on her chest with his broad wings stretched out either side like giant sails of white to brown. She struggled to shove him away but he was far too heavy for her to push off, even if she wasn't already exhausted from fighting.

Raoul shot past Wilny, charging at the Eagle on all fours, tail bristling and the fur on the back of his neck raised. Snarling viciously, he leaped at the Eagle attempting to tackle the Avio to the ground. He knocked the Eagle off Storm and staggering him Raoul snapped his jaws at the Avio, clawing at his face and arms and trying to force him away from Storm, who began to army-crawl a few feet away, gasping for her breath back as she did. The Avio threw his arms up to hold the Canid back at arm's length to avoid the long teeth, but Raoul lacked the muscles and weight of an older and better trained Canid like Anthony to wrestle him. The Eagle punched the Raoul hard in the stomach, then lifting him off the floor by his throat and hurled him towards the police car. Raoul slammed into the windshield of the car with a yelp, shattering the glass and knocking the boy unconscious.

"Feather!" Wilny hollered, voice constricted with fear, as Raoul rolled limply off the bonnet of the car and remained motionless. Malana watched wide eyed from the front seat. Grabbing Beth's laptop, she fearfully retreated into the back to hide from the violence in the footwell, out of sight from everyone outside.

Snarling, Wilny flew at the Eagle-Avio, wings thrumming loudly. He brought his legs up and kicked the Eagle hard in the chest, staggering him. Twisting his body and flipping himself round in the air, Wilny landed into a crouch, then tucking his wings back, sprinted at the Eagle. As he closed in, he leapt, striking the Eagle in the face with his right fist and as his face turned with the force of the hit, struck again with his left, aiming to concuss the man. It was like punching a wall; the man was solid muscle and didn't even seem to notice. Switching tactics and saving his aching fists, he kicked hard into his chest and gut, and then flicked his wings forward, powering himself back several feet again as the Eagle swiped at him, staggering backwards.

It was a quick attack and it seemed to have an effect, so he tried it again.

However, this time the Eagle was prepared. He tensed with his wings flared, and as Wilny landed the kick on his chest he grabbed the Hummingbird by his ankles so that when he pushed off, he could not get away. Wilny fell, head hitting the dirt and making black spots appear before his eyes with the force. Still holding onto his ankles, the Eagle spun round with him, throwing off all of Wilny's sense of balance and then released, sending him bouncing across the dirt with a series of angry curses until he rolled to a stop.

Teal laughed raspily as he got his breath back and straightened up. His face was bruised, and nose was bleeding, his wing limp and its feathers tattered from being dragged and trodden on.

"Amell." Teal snarled. "Throw her over here."

The Eagle snapped to attention, stepping forward to Storm, who was trying to scramble to her feet. Obediently he grabbed Storm by her ankle, yanking her upside down into the air and tossed her over to his Teal as though she weighed nothing.

Storm swore as she skidded along on her face, grazing her chin. About to push herself up off the ground, shaking with exhaustion, Teal took a swinging kick at her, knocking her sideways. Smiling through his bloodied face, he stomped down hard on her forearm several times with a foul crack of bone. Storm stared in horror for a moment as the pain started to seep through her fading adrenalin and she suppressed a screech of pain, as he did so several times more before attempting to kick her in the head. She evaded having her skull fractured with a quick dodge and smacked him hard with her wings. She shocked him, but flooded by adrenalin, it had little effect and so grabbing him as hard as she could, Storm brought Teal down onto the ground before engaging in a furious scrap of talons and teeth, lacerating him into a bloodied mess as he landed punches upon her, both fighting as fast as feral cats.

Shaking the dust off Wilny charged, leaping into the air with a thrum of wing beats, aiming to get in close enough to immobilise Teal. But he underestimated the reflexes of the Eagle.

Grabbing Wilny by his leg as he flew past, Amell threw him into the police car next to Raoul. His back slammed against the bonnet with a hard crack, Wilny certain that he had broken his spine in several places as he slid off and thumped to the floor. Immediately he flexed his fingers and kicked out both his legs to be sure of any spinal damage and much to his relief they moved. With a leap and a beat of wings, the Eagle landed behind the car, but there was no chance for Wilny to breathe a sigh of relief as the car moved. Amell lifted it up onto its front bumper, showing an incredible amount of strength as Wilny stared, then grabbing the unconscious Canid lying next to him by the leg and using his aching wings, Wilny dragged them both out the way as fast as he could manage. The car slammed roof down onto where they would have been, crumpling the vehicle and shattering all the glass.

Wilny froze, gut hollowing in a wave of dread and horror as he stared at the smashed car.

"No...No! *Lana!*" Shrieked Wilny. Leaving Raoul to the side, he scrambled to try and reach the car, only to be picked up and thrown again by Amell.

Teal didn't so much as blink when the car hit the dirt, instead he turned his attention back to Storm, knelt on the dirt clutching her arm, and kicked her down to the ground, pinning her there with a boot between her wings. She swore angrily at him, out of energy and charge to shock him and her right arm throbbing with pain and unable to move her fingers.

"You idiot." He smirked, pulling Storm's head back by her hair so that she'd face him. "Do you think you're better than me? Is this the best you've got?"

He snapped his head in Wilny's direction and gave a sharp nod. Amell turned and grabbed the Wilny before he could scramble towards the crushed car, lifting the man up off the ground by his head. Wilny snapped back into reality and began to twist and thrash, holding onto the giant man's arms so that his neck would not break. Then he began to squeeze. Thumbs pressing increasingly harder and harder against his temples. Wilny squirmed and kicked viciously at the Eagle as he felt his skull being crushed like a grape.

"Stop! I have to help her!" He shouted; his head felt like it was about to explode at any second. "STOP!"

There was a sudden sharp sound of metal being struck or torn, followed by a creaking noise. Amell, or it may have been Teal distracted by the rending and loosing focus, stopped suddenly and dropped Wilny to the ground, staring at the upturned police car, the source of the sound.

The car rocked a little then split cleanly into two halves, and out from her hiding place tumbled and uncurled Malana holding Beth's laptop close to her chest, looking a little pleased with herself.

"Thank fuck." Storm laughed with relief as she saw Malana stumble to her feet and shake her wings out. "Telkens!"

Glancing round Malana spotted Wilny and Raoul lying on the floor, with Wilny staring in disbelief at her. She ran to him, swatting the Eagle out the way with her telkens as if he were a ragdoll, and threw herself into Wilny's arms. She hid her face against his chest, talking too fast for him to understand and smiling happily through tears. Wilny hugged the little girl, brushed her hair from her face and checked her over for any more injuries before giving her a smile.

"Well done..." Wilny breathed with relief and pride, holding her close and ignoring the pain across his back and pounding head, "Well done Lana. *Merci*! *Bien*!"

"Ah, there's the other little girl." Teal smirked through a bubble of blood at his mouth and quickly purpling bruises, half impressed that she had survived.

Wilny glowered at him, swearing under his breath and bringing his wings up around the little girl protectively. Malana saw his anger and looked at the man who had murdered her family.

She wasn't afraid, she was furious.

With a little snarl and flash of tiny fangs from Malana, the Vulture's left wing was suddenly sheered from his body, as though an invisible guillotine had been dropped on him. Teal screamed. Blood pulsed from the clean slice and the rest of his wing lay on the floor, the buff feathers darkening as they became soaked with blood.

Lana smiled. He had made the Eagle rip the wings off her family, doing the same to him was an appropriate revenge. Wilny laughed, trying to disguise his shock and fear, and hugged the little girl.

"Bien!" He praised. "I think."

"You little bitch!" Teal snarled, Teal snarled, retreating away from Malana and Wilny, holding his stub of a wing as blood pulsated from it. "Amell!"

Amell stumbled to his feet, took several steps forward and before he could advance anymore, Malana used her telkens to slash him across the face. It was too far away to take his head off, but close enough to leave a deep gash. He ignored the blood now pouring from the slice across his face from chin to forehead and kept on advancing towards them. Malana focused and wrapped the Telken around his ankle, hoisting him up into the air with a squawk of surprise. The Eagle's huge wings flapped about gracelessly with awkward flutters, feathers flying everywhere as he struggled to right himself.

With Teal distracted by the display of an Eagle being taken down by a little girl and nursing his injured wing, Storm seized her chance. She rose to her feet and with her undamaged left hand she grabbed the Vulture by the hair, kicking him full force in the spine.

With a crack of bone, she broke his back.

Teal shrieked as he fell face first onto the floor, releasing his muser control on the men. They all instantly went limp, the Preternatural that Kat and Anthony were struggling to fight dropped face first onto the bloody floor, allowing them both to pin him to the down, with Malana dropping the limp Amell to the ground.

Teal twitched upon the floor, eyes wide with panic and gasping for air.

"No…NO!" He screamed, unable to feel his arms or legs. Storm staggered backwards nursing her broken arm and allowing Wilny to march forward.

Wilny grabbed the Vulture by the hair, kneeling beside him, he punched the scar-faced Vulture repeatedly, as hard as he could manage, bloodying his knuckles and Teal's face further. One hand went to his throat and began choking the life out of him as Teal screamed for mercy.

"Mercy? *Mercy?*" He snarled menacingly, throttling Teal as hard as he could before slamming his head into the ground several times, "*Shits like you don't deserve the breath to beg for mercy.*"

A small hand tapped his shoulder, and he stopped his assault, turning to look at Malana. She looked down expressionless at Teal.

"*Au revoir.*" She said curtly and without so much as a blink sliced her telkens through his neck, letting his body flop to the ground and leaving his head still gripped by Wilny, hang in the air. Wilny stared in horror at the head in his hand, his vision tunnelling before finally letting it drop to the ground. Shocked by Malana's sudden display of vengeance filled murder, he didn't even notice her throw her arms around him and hug him tight.

"Good…good girl…" He complimented her weakly, rubbing her back. They had rescued a truly lethal weapon. "But please don't ever do that again. *Ever.*"

She looked up at him with wide golden eyes, clearly having no clue as to what he had said, but smiled at him regardless, and wiped the speckles of blood from his face.

"Holy shit." Beth breathed, dragging herself to her feet as she stared horrified at the decapitation. "Was she even trying when she attacked me and Raoul?"

"Raoul!" Wilny remembered, leaving the body and running with Malana back to where the Hound was left on the ground. Both crouched beside him, checking along his spine and skull for any fractures and carefully trying to rouse him. He was breathing slowly, unconscious with several bruises blossoming across his face, but with no signs of any larger damage.

"Well, the girl's flown off." Beth grumbled, walking across to Storm and looking out behind them to the sky. The Chiro still lay unconscious with the blood now drying on his face, and the flies soon returned to crawl across the bodies. Storm looked between the body and the sky with a sigh.

"Is there much point in going after her?" She asked aloud. "I doubt Rex would let her live, even if she didn't kill herself fighting us after what we've done to her boy."

"I thought you were going to kill her."

"I don't think I could now." Her expression turned to a pained grimace, "I got qualms about hurting kids and I don't want to deal with that level of guilt."

"Well *qualms* aside, it's your call if you want to chase after her with your arm like that." She nudged Storm and flourished her stub with a small laugh. "I'd lend you an arm, but uhh…"

With a small chuckle Storm gently nudged Beth back in return, then stood still to allow her to take her sash and turn it into a makeshift sling for Storms broken limb.

The calm soon became interrupted by the angry yelling of the Preternatural. He squirmed beneath Anthony who was sat on him, demanding in a thick German accent to be read his rights upon seeing Anthony's police uniform. Across the ground Amell groaned from his crumpled heap on the, wings flexing awkwardly as he began to regain consciousness. Knives raised, Kat crept towards him, fighting off the nausea caused by the venom.

"Uh…hello?" She said gently, ears flattened back and a slight prod at his side with her foot, wary of how the Eagle might react now that he had been released from Teals control.

He ran his hands across his face, feeling at the blood from where he had been slashed by Malana's telkens, before looking up at Kat.

"*Kia ora.*" He replied eventually with a slightly dazed smile.

"He aha?"

Rising to his feet with a wobble, both Storm and Beth approached with caution and flaring her wings out Storm ushered for Kat to stay close by.

"Christ, I got decked hard there." Amell chuckled, hissing with pain and inspecting his injuries, voice deep and mellow. Now that he was standing next to Kat, they could all see how tall he really was, since Kat herself was five-ten, but she only came up to his shoulder putting him at least six-seven. Coupled with broad shoulders and a very muscular physique, he cut an imposing figure.

"Are you okay? Do you know where you are, Amell?" Storm asked, examining him closely to be certain that he was as confused as he looked.

"Yeaahnooooo...no. No." He shook his head slowly and started to pace as he looked around the area and at the sky, running his fingers through his tangle of long hair.

"This isn't...Where am I and how do you know my name?"

"Do you really not remember what happened?" Beth asked, attempting to fold her arms and forgetting the lack of bionic to do so. "Do you even know what month it is? Where you think you are?"

"It's February, right? And I should be in Denmark or somewhere like that since the air there was cold as dicks...but...this isn't there is it?" His accent was vague, but it sounded as though he was from New Zealand from his inflection.

Storm shared a little pitying grimace with Kat and Beth. Extended muser control or severe mental assault could cause severe memory loss. ARCDA often used it as a '*hard reset*' when they had very troubled Synths, and the effects of it were highly psychologically damaging.

"It's nearly the end of May, and you're in England." She corrected him softly.

He paced around quickly, muttering to himself as he did. The dark brown feathers rousing in agitation as he tried to think. His head hurt, his body ached, and he felt starved. He stopped by the body of Teal and stared down at it silently. The burnt face and light hair, he remembered it.

"Him... That girl..." His head snapped to the sky in the direction Kathy had flown and he staggered backwards. "I r-remember...oh god..."

His face paled and he clasped a hand to his mouth in realisation, falling back onto the ground, shaking as the faded memories of what happened returned.

"Take deep breaths, okay?" Storm told him softly, crouching beside him but keeping her wings flared. Wilny rose to his feet, watching Amell with suspicion, hands balled into fists and getting ready to attack, but Malana held onto him, keeping him from going forward.

"Tell us what happened."

"They made me kill those kids…the little girl and- Spice. Oh my god I killed her- I-I-I just- He just- *Oh my god.*" He dry heaved. "None of it was me, this was all her, that bitch."

"She wanted you to kill them? Not this douche-canoe?"

"Whatever she wanted; he gave her." He clutched at his head. "She wanted a dress, he made someone get it for her. She wanted a house, he made them give it to her. She wanted them to stop screaming, so he made me…"

"I'm so sorry Amell…" Storm reached forward to comfort him, but Beth grabbed her wing and held her back. The aftereffects of Teal's musing was going to bring about a wild ride of emotions in Amell. They all knew it; they just didn't know in what way it would come out.

Amell rose to his feet and flicked out his wings, beating them several times and sending the dust swirling in billows.

"I'm gonna kill her." He snarled darkly. His expression was murderous, and his fists clenched. "I'm going to rip her heart from her chest and shove it up her ass!" He shouted up to the sky, then kicked Teal's corpse hard enough to send it flying like a ragdoll several meters away.

"You're injured though." Storm pointed out calmly, head tilted to one shoulder, letting Kat and Beth stand behind her.

"I'll heal."

"Do you really want to go after her?"

Amell paused, contemplating himself before turning to look down at her with a nod of determination.

"I want- I need to stop her."

"Fair enough. Go on after her then, she went that way."

"What? *Storm!*" Wilny squawked in disbelief. "He's on the cusp of having a psychotic breakdown if you haven't noticed! Is that *really* a good idea?"

"He's a fully grown adult Wilny, he can handle himself and someone needs to catch her." She shrugged nonchalantly and gave a gesture to her arm in its makeshift sling. "I'd rather he burns off that fury chasing her, than lash out at people at headquarters. You know. *Like you did.*"

"He tried to kill me, tried to kill Malana and Raoul!"

"I did?" Amell blinked sadly at the Hummingbird, looking him up and down with genuine remorse.

"You tossed me about everywhere like a damn doll!" Wilny yelled. "You nearly crushed my skull! My brain matter could have been all over your hands."

"I'm sorry bro, it wasn't my personal intention to do that, but at least you're alive right?"

"That doesn't change what you tried to do."

"I could have been made to do a lot worse."

"I could have died!"

"But you didn't. Maybe you could think of that as more of a love bite than a grievous wound, okay handsome?"

"*You-*"

"Haven't we all tried to kill each other at one point or another, Wilny?" Storm cut in. Wilny's face reddened as Amell gave him a nervous wink. "And didn't you feel better after we let you kill that doctor? If he goes after Kathy, he's at least being productive in stopping a maniac."

Wilny snapped his mouth shut.

He couldn't argue with it. There was something visceral and essential about vengeance that he couldn't really deny Amell from seeking it. Instead of proceeding to argue with Storm on his thoughts of how it was a terrible idea, and would all be her fault, he rolled his eyes and went back to trying to wake Raoul up with Malana. Storm ignored him.

"But if you can't, you can find us in London. A big guy like you is sure to get noticed and get a call sent to us." She smiled warmly to Amell, Kat nodding in agreement.

"Thank you, um- sorry, I don't remember your name."

"Storm. My name is Storm."

"Well, thank you Storm." With a grateful dip of his head to the girls, Amell smiled sadly. "I'm sorry that we didn't meet under better circumstances."

"Next time. It'll be better next time we meet."

"I hope so."

Rolling his broad shoulders, Amell opened his wings out in preparation for flight. And with a nod and a wink at Wilny, he took a running start across the bloodied yard, beating his gigantic wingspan and took off into the sky after Kathy.

A rumbling came from the long driveway as a parade of police cars, vans, and an ambulance began streaking up towards them. The Rioteers had finally arrived.

Their speed alarmed Malana, and in an attempt to protect Wilny and Raoul, she slashed the tires with her telkens as the other police car drew up making it drop and skid to a noisy stop. Owen got out from the damaged car, took one look at it then at the bloody farm with the Rogues standing by several bodies of Synths and animals and with a deep sigh, swore at the sky.

8

Rioteer Headquarters, Camden, London.

The Rioteers' headquarters was quite a difficult place to find. For a start it was underground, hidden deep beneath London's surface, below the streets and railway tracks and the hustle and bustle of human life. Built in the nineteenth century the warrens of tunnels and catacombs stretched deep underground, reaching under Regent's Park nearby and linking up to several old warehouses or canal exits. With several years' worth of secret building work, the Rioteers had converted the great chamber into a structurally sound main hall from which they led their operations. Occasionally the rumble of the trains could be heard in the distance, but other than that, the headquarters was secluded from the outside world. Over the space of a decade, it had grown and expanded with new tunnels and chambers being made so that they had a medical ward, bedrooms, kitchens and a dining area, as well as offices and a newly made quarantine zone for any Synths that may be unsafe or infected with one of the ARCDA's modified viruses.

It was a hive of activity, as busy as the market aboveground, Synths and humans working together to try to cope with their freedom from the Arcadia Corporation – ARCDA – and their rivalling company, Hasekura.

The Rioteers were accustomed to treating people brought in by the ambulances, many of its members being former ARCDA or Hasekura doctors and nurses, so the Rogues were treated quickly for their injuries, their breaks x-rayed, bites treated, and bruises given ice.

Beth had gotten away lightly with her injuries. The only major damage she had suffered was breaking her bionic arm. In between her complaints about her arm, she had also spent a while explaining to the Rioteers the whole story with the Canids and Kathy, to update them and inform them of what had happened and who had died.

Kat lay sleeping on her bed, her wings had been treated from the Reptile bites, but it would be a few days before the bites would heal. For Storm and Raoul, however, who had received the worst injuries of them all it could take up to a week or more before they would be fully recovered.

Raoul was still stunned. He couldn't recall how he ended up in the headquarters, waking up to the confusing scene of being underground and in a hospital bed with a very large bruise to the side of his face and several cracked ribs.

"Raoul you can relax." Wilny breathed softly, noticing how tense the Hound was. The ECG beeped away in time with his heartbeat, the nurse at his side keeping a watchful eye on the regularity of the beats, aware of the heart condition that Wilny suffered with and which would occasionally trouble him. A side effect of being severely electrocuted by Storm.

"I cannot...I don't know... please tell me what to do..." Raoul muttered nervously, his foot bouncing erratically, and curled tail bristled. His eyes were transfixed on the other Canids and Preternaturals walking around freely, none of them in a uniform to distinguish who they were or who was the most senior ranking among them all.

Storm fidgeted in her bed, tapping the cast on her arm in boredom and flexing one wing out at a time, carefully realigning her feathers, after having to sit awkwardly on them for two hours in the back of the police van to reach the headquarters.

"Focus on something else. Why not ask questions?" She sighed, pulling the wing down so she could pluck a loose banded feather from underneath.

"Questions?"

"That calmed you down at the house and when we were out. Ask something to distract yourself."

The Hound swallowed nervously as he picked up what sounded like a scream across the other side of the headquarters. All the noise and unfamiliarity unnerved him. He did have many questions though.

How did this place get built? How were there so many people down here working for the Rioteers? Was that a Hasekuran style Canid over there? Who bought them here? His mind filled with questions, but he had one that confused him most of all.

"Wilny..." Raoul said quietly, reaching across the gap between their beds and pawing the exhausted Avios' arm. Wilny gave a tired sigh and rolled his head to one side to face Raoul properly.

"Hm?"

"Before, when we were fighting, I heard you yell um...Feather? What did you mean by that?"

Wilny tensed suddenly. The iridescent blue feathers on his shoulders rose, in what Raoul assumed must have been fear.

"D-did I say that?" He swallowed, speaking in a low tone, his blue eyes fixed on Raoul. "N-no. You heard wrong. I di-didn't-"

Wilny's breathing became ragged and his hands clenched into fists, his knuckles white, whilst the ECG began to show a quickening of his pulse. The nurse came over, asking if he was okay but Wilny couldn't answer as he had put his fist to his mouth to stop himself from speaking.

"*Will.*" Storm said sharply, with a commanding tone, catching his attention. He glanced past Raoul to Storm, shaking his head with some meaning that Raoul didn't understand, his blue eyes still wide and bloodshot with torment.

Wordlessly, Storm gave Wilny a stern look and flourishing her hand she made a small and silent gesture. The small gesture conveyed an entire dialogue, which the Hound didn't understand.

Composing himself, Wilny's voice cracked a little as he tried to give Raoul a little explanation.

"*Featherhead.* He...he was a friend of mine. A Canid." Wilny said softly, his bottom lip trembling slightly. Folding his arms and drawing them tight to his chest, Raoul noticed that he was tracing the scars that covered his arms with his thumb. "I...lost him."

"I am sorry." Raoul murmured apologetically, dipping his head and dropping his gaze. "I didn't mean to hurt you with this."

"You didn't hurt me I- I'm just- I'll tell you about him some time..." Wilny shifted in his bed in an attempt to relax again and not jostle Malana too much, who was curled up beside him, "Just not now. I'm not ready to talk about them right now."

"I understand."

"Thank you, Raoul."

Both sighed deeply and remained silent as they contemplated their memories and scars. Watching them both, Storm smiled softly as she noted Wilny's acceptance of Raoul by the simple way of using his name.

"How…how is Lana?" Asked Raoul looking across at the figure of the little girl sleeping by Wilny's side.

"Exhausted." Responded Wilny, sighing with relief as he turned his attention to the real world.

He looked down at Malana with her wings splayed over the edge of the bed and tangled dark locks covering her face. Smiling he brushed her hair gently from her eyes. The little girl grumbled and snuggled closer, comforted by Wilny's presence. The noise of the medical ward didn't seem to bother her at all.

"She's had food." Storm said as she managed to prop herself up against the metal headboard of the creaking bed. She stretched her wings out either side of her, spreading them to their entire extent and nearly knocking over the IV set up for Kat beside her.

"We'll really need to get her some new clothes, she can't wear rags. And give her a bath."

"Raoul too." Contested Wilny with a frown. "Don't forget about him."

"But I have clothes."

"They don't fit you."

"They don't?" Raoul blinked and looked down at the oversized sweater he was now wearing, given to him by the Rioteers after they took the shirt he had been previously wearing so they could fix his ribs.

"That's mostly because you have no chest muscle. You need to work out a little more; you're so skinny for a Canid."

"Need to work out…?" The phrasing was unfamiliar to him, so he presumed it was another way of saying he needed to exercise. Wilny nodded, beginning to propose a workout routine to build up his strength whilst Raoul smiled blankly at him. There were a few more words and phrases that he had heard that were unfamiliar to him, and halfway through Wilny's plan he decided that he would have to write them down later to translate it better.

"Storm," Beth sighed as she trotted over to her bedside with her laptop clutched to her chest, "Rex is here to speak to you."

Storm's wings snapped back to her sides and she winced.

"Aaah. Lovely…just what I wanted. I can't wait." She said snidely, running her fingers through her blue-grey hair.

"Don't piss him off, okay?"

"Why ever would I do that?"

"Just…try *not* to be yourself for a while, okay?" Beth suggested sternly, opening up the laptop and setting it up as the doors to the ward swung open.

The leader of the Rioteers strode over to them, followed by armed guards and a girl no older than Malana at his heels. Upon seeing Storm and the other Rogues, the girl let out an excited cry and charged ahead.

"Hey, Imogen." Storm smiled as the little girl ran up to greet her.

Giggling the little girl reached up and struggled to bring herself onto the bed to sit next to Storm. Even with one arm broken, it wasn't difficult for Storm to lift the girl up onto the bed with just one hand.

"Did you bring sweets?" The girl asked, grey eyes wide with wonder as she reached out to stroke at Storm's soft feathers.

"Not today Imogen, but maybe next time, so long as you share with all the other kids. Okay?" She laughed softly, ruffling her mess of ginger hair.

"Though I guess it depends what Rex has to say about it. He might think I'll poison you."

"You won't do that!"

"Of course I wouldn't, but your daddy is a very silly man."

The Rioteer leader gave a loud sigh as he made it over to the beds where the Rogues lay, gesturing for the armed men in tow to fall back several paces behind him.

In his mid-fifties, the Rioteer leader Rex Brisbane was a tall and fairly muscular man for his age, with short combed back hair, once red and now streaked grey with age. His expression was one of pure exhaustion and disappointment with the world; time and life had worn away the honesty behind his smile.

"How are you all? Wilny, Beth." He greeted them coolly, nodding to the two Rogues he named before stopping in front of Storm and staring her down.

"Ah, Emperor Palpatine, how nice of you to join us down here, I thought the Sith didn't do hospital visits." Storm smirked at him, clear eyes glittering with sly rebellion. Beth slapped her wings over her head with a muffled scream.

Wordlessly, Rex sharply whacked Storm's injured arm with the back of his hand. Storm gave an angry yelp, pulling her wings up around her like a feathery shield, the little girl at her side hugging her and looking furious with Rex. Raoul flinched and stood, prepared to start thinking of excuses for his existence, to try to lessen any blame on Storm, but Wilny gently tapped his arm and gestured for him to sit back down on the bed.

"Fucking ow!" Storm seethed, ignoring the fact that there were children present. "That fucking hurts, Rex!"

"Well, it's your own fault." Rex snapped with a sharp Irish brogue, ignoring her pain. "What the hell were you thinking! They murdered a whole family, not to mention the little girl's group, Ciel, and you let two of them *escape*?"

"The boy, Teal, was the one we needed to stop and Amell is already going after Kathy so that'll be sorted by him when he catches her."

"Oh, so we know them on a first name basis, do we? If you had time to learn their names, then you had time to kill them."

"She was both *pregnant*, and a *child*." Storm snarled, baring her sharp fangs at him. "Teal was the priority there, not Kathy. You weren't there so it wasn't your call."

"Stop making excuses! You had a job and you should have done it. You've put your whole group at risk with your pissing around, girl! *Twice!*" He accusingly jabbed his fingers at her, Raoul noticing that he was missing his right index finger.

"Don't even get me started on the Canid you brought back without permission."

"I don't need *your* permission to allow new people into *my* group, Rex."

"Bloody Feral. Do you ever learn?" Rex snorted. "Are you incapable of thinking about the consequences of your actions? Do you not see the damage you've done by letting two of them loose? Who knows what they'll do now or where they'll end up?"

Storm sat up abruptly, drawing her legs up and rocking forward so that she was crouched upon the bed gargoyleish, the movement so sudden that the little girl beside her flinched, as did the two Rioteers who had followed Rex. Rex however, puffed his chest out and held his ground.

"I'm so *sorry* that I had only four hours sleep out of fifty-three, and that I've issues about *killing pregnant women and-or children,* but it was my call and I chose to let them go!" Her voice rose to a roaring crescendo that drew the attention of the entire room, letting her wings flare out behind her and brush against the curve of the vaulted ceiling. Rex stared her down.

"A murderer is a monster, regardless of age and circumstance. You should have put them down."

Within the beat of a pause, she had bolted up onto her feet. Standing on the end of her bed, with her wounds raw and wings arched before her, she glowered down upon him with the fury and image of a long-lost goddess of retribution.

"Alright, how about we start with *you* first then, you hypocritical piece of shit." She snarled at him, enunciating each and every word so that everyone could hear.

The Rioteer leader stood up straight, bristling with rage, but said nothing. He knew the game. They'd fought this battle between each other many times before, each time with more and more risk of war.

Seeing the growing tension, Imogen scrambled off the bed and tugged at her father's arm sharply, catching his attention. Rex blinked and looked round questioningly at her as she buried her face into his side with a whine. He knew he would risk upsetting his daughter and losing face in front of the other Rioteers who were watching behind him. They already questioned how well suited he was to lead, as for half the year he spent time in America to deal with the Rioteers out there, leaving no one to govern the London headquarters; with the exception of Asena of course, who all the Synths listened to regardless of their opinions on her.

The doors at the end of the medical ward opened, and instantly every non-human head turned to look. Rex with a quick glance to see who had entered, stepped back away from Storm, giving her space and clearing his throat loudly as he recomposed himself. Even the guards who were at Rex's back lowered the grip on their weapons and retreated, trying to keep out of the way as a tall muscular woman strode across the floor with a few members of her pack of Canids in tow, Anthony among them.

Raoul stared in awe. He had never seen a female Canid before, let alone one so old and battle-scarred. Long silver-blonde hair flaring out behind her as she walked, graceful and dignified as a queen, but the ragged scars across her golden-brown skin that was covered by sparse fur, made her the warrioress she truly was.

The Alpha-boss, Storm had called her.

The Empress.

"What have you done now, Storm?" She chuckled in a husky voice as she stopped at the end of Storm's bed and leaned on it grinning, long canines flashing in the light. Sparse ashy fur and thick whiskers looked silver on her cheeks and arms. Like the Wolf that had been in Raoul's Hunter Unit, she too was almost Anubis-Headed with her split nostrils, long nose and jaw, and large triangular ears, however she appeared to be a far older version of Canid, more so than any he had met before.

"I got into a fight with a muser-possessed eagle, Wolfie." Storm smirked with an awkward laugh and patted her broken arm gently. She had sat back down, letting her wings drape either side of the bed.

The Empress laughed, and lightly hit Storm across the foot, meaning her no harm unlike Rex.

"You idiot. Eleven years teaching you how *not* to get hurt and yet you *always* come back with some form of injury. If you're not careful, you'll lose a wing next time you silly arse. Or more likely that arm. How many times have you broken it now? Seven?"

"*Eight* times actually. I promise I'll be a more careful."

"Good." A grin spread across her face, showing off her canines. "Now would you like to tell me how your two little missions went, or should I ask the Puppy over here."

She turned her gaze on Raoul, looking him dead in the eyes. Pale yellow irises striated with brown and very strangely shaped as there was no visible whites to her eyes. It was a little unnerving to Raoul as he had never met a female Canid before and didn't know the etiquette for the situation, so he kept his eyes down and kept his posture submissive so as not to have seemed a threat.

"He's from France, Asena." Anthony said softly with a small bow. "A substitute Hunter unit tracker."

As he did, Raoul realised that there was a small Canid-cub on Anthony's back, holding onto him like a koala. Auburn hair, tan skin and bright amber eyes, he could see a striking resemblance to Anthony in the boy's features.

Asena's ears twitched with far more movement than Raoul had expected. Scrunching up her face as she stepped away from Storm's bed to examine Raoul closer, Raoul felt the fur across his spine rise in uncontrolled fear.

"He's fine Asena." Wilny babbled, sitting up quickly in bed, his movement causing Malana to stir from her sleep. "He wanted to help, and he's proved himself to be a good kid. Crisis Aid trained."

A blonde ear twitched as Wilny babbled, listening to what he was saying, as she wordlessly looked Raoul up and down. A calming tingle ran across the back of Raoul's head and down his spine.

"Interesting." She remarked after several moments followed by a small chuckle. "There's certainly no need to give him any puppy classes."

Confused by what she meant Raoul turned to Beth with a questioning look, to which her response was a smile followed by her tapping her head.

She was a muser too. It was unusual. Canids were rarely ever Musers unless Atlas had bought them to experiment upon, or they were Diamond Elites who had been given the opportunity for upgrades.

He knew what musers were like and knew what Asena had seen from both Wilny and himself.

The bloody murder of the hunters - the walk to Cherry Tree House - the train ride – the scent of the orchard still in his mind - the taste of the fish and chips still on his tongue– the attack on Kathy's group –

Rex rolled his eyes at the woman, clearing his throat as a prompt for them to carry on assessing Raoul. With an indignant snort, Asena looked over her shoulder at him, but said nothing. She rarely needed to speak to express her opinion.

"Asena Canis. I rule Asena pack and govern all groups both in and out of Europe, though I'm sure the Rogues would have told you that." She gave a small head tilt towards Raoul as she officially introduced herself. "Have you got a name yet?"

She already knew the answer, but she wanted to hear him speak.

Raoul swallowed nervously looking to Storm and Wilny, as he was unsure if he was allowed to talk to her without permission. Back in ARCDA he would have only been allowed to speak to the highest authority if given permission by his handler.

Storm smiled, gesturing for him to answer with her free hand.

"Raoul." He said quietly, taking a great interest in his feet.

"Well Raoul, you're welcome to stay with the Rogues. They may be troublesome little birdbrains, but they seem to like you."

"He's a good kid." Wilny declared proudly, "I'm going to take care of both him and Lana."

They all turned to stare at the Hummingbird with the little girl at his side. The look of determination on his face showed clearly that he would fight anyone who disagreed. Raoul was the most surprised of them all by how quickly his opinion had changed of him. Storm chuckled a little, seeing Wilny puff his chest out.

'I only asked him to take care of Malana whilst we were out. He's only just decided that he's going to take responsibility of them both.' Storm mused loudly, directing the words towards Asena so she could hear.

An ear twitched as she caught Storm's thoughts, making her smile.

'He's making progress. Good.'

She rolled her shoulders back and smiled down approvingly at Wilny, her tail swishing.

"Then both of these kids are your responsibility. It'll be tough to teach them, but I'm certain-"

"Boss!" A black-haired Canid yelled, cutting through Asena's words as he burst into the medical ward, shirt stained red with blood. Alerted by the sight of blood Anthony tensed and ran to his side.

"What's wrong, Blake?" Anthony asked hurriedly, placing an arm around the smaller Canid and bringing him over. The boy on his back whined and scrambled up further onto his father's shoulder, trying to hold on tight as the big Canid moved about.

"One of the other Synths they brought back attacked one of the medics and me!" The Canid coughed and wheezed, holding his chest as he spoke.

"Which one?" Asena inquired. She remained calm, not even batting an eyelash at the blood.

"The Chiro. He's terrifying! I walked into accompany the lady and it...it..."

Putting a hand onto his shoulder Asena gently led him towards a bed so he could lie down. Rex gave the Wolf Empress a concerned look and hugged his daughter close to his chest. This was her call she heard Rex think, and if she thought that the Chiro was too dangerous to be rehabilitated or calmed or hurt anyone else then they might have to kill him.

"I can handle it, Blake. You just rest. Try to get your breath back." She said softly, gently rubbing the injured Canid's shoulder.

"Do you need a hand, mum?" Storm asked, swinging her legs out of bed to get up. The Empress held her hand up and gestured for Storm to sit down.

"I can handle it Storm. Stay here. You too Rex. Anthony, keep Caesar away from the blood please." She ordered, giving the same instruction to her entourage before striding off down the ward alone. She caught the slight whisp of a criticism from Rex's mind as she left but brushed it off. Some things were better dealt with alone and without the involvement of the Rioteers.

Quickly winding her way through the warren of the catacombs, Asena rounded the corner of the corridor and saw a small group of people gathered by the door of the quarantine rooms.

"Stand back." Asena ordered the small crowd, voice resonating with a growl. The people looked up and parted to allow her through to the medic who was sat on the floor shaking like a leaf. She was gaunt with shock, leaning against a food trolley with several people were standing by her to make sure she was all right, as well as guarding the door to the room. The quarantine rooms were secure, so if the Chiro was still inside then he would have no chance at escaping.

Taking a quick examination of the scene, Asena crouched down before the medic, head tilted to one side and keeping her tone soft.

"What happened?"

"H-he just-I was so scared- he bit me! He's a feral!" She babbled away, holding her bleeding hand to her chest, staining her white shirt.

"Calm down." Asena cooed softly, helping her stand. "From the beginning. What did you do that made him bite you?"

"He w-woke up a-and asked for f-food s-so..." She gulped and quickly shook her head. She was still far too scared to answer properly so Asena swiftly moved on with her investigation, turning her attention to the room and opening the heavy steel door.

As she opened the door, she instantly smelt blood, but it was not human or Synth blood but instead beef. A quick glance to the food trolley. There were different plates of food, one of which had a rare-cooked steak.

"It's alright, just calm down and take slow deep breaths, alright. Someone will take you to go get your hand looked at. I'll deal with this." She picked up a slab of steak from the food trolley. The medic nodded quickly and scurried off down the hallway back to the medical ward followed by several members of the crowd.

"You two." Asena said, pointing to two of the Synths in the crowd. "Stand by the door and make sure none of the Rioteers come with guns. They tend to overreact like that for these situations."

The Wolf Empress smiled, then proceeded to head inside the darkened quarantine room and shut the door behind her. She lingered at the door for a moment, ears twitching and listening to any sounds of rustling or even to pick out a heartbeat of the room's occupant.

The tall hospital bed and the ECG, which usually stood next to it, had been knocked onto its side with the electrodes tangled as though they had been ripped off. There was a metallic smell of blood, a mixture of human, Canid and several other older layers beneath that. Though it was not cold in the room, there was a lingering feeling of dread hanging in the air that made her shudder slightly and the distinctive tingle across the back of her head of muser abilities being used.

She heard a rustle from under the bed. Shaking off the dread, she crouched down, balancing on the balls of her feet with her tail aiding her and looked underneath.

Large pale leathery wings were tucked up and wrapped around his crouched figure, pale faced smeared with blood. With his huge oddly shaped rabbit-like ears solid black eyes staring out at her, he looked alien.

He remained perfectly still, although his large sensitive ears didn't as they flicked back and forth and twitched.

Asena held out the meat, projecting calming thoughts forward against him as she used her own muser abilities upon him.

"Hungry?" She asked, ear twitching as she watched the Chiro's expressions for any signs of hostility. "It's beef."

He frowned at her, then with a fluid movement drew his wings back from around him, tucking them back with a flick of his narrow and almost rat-like tail. Although as a Chiro, he mimicked the features of a bat, Asena knew that he was more closely related to Avios like Wilny and Storm. Designed to have six limbs and hiding a keel to his chest like the Avios, the only difference between them was that the featherless membrane of the wing connected down along the sides of the long tail.

The Chiro reached out his hand to take the meat from her but stopped before he took it. Although the entirety of his eye was black, even what should have been the whites of his eye, she could just about read his expression as being suspicious.

'*Poisoned?*' He thought quietly. The thought was charged with a strong sentiment of suspicion and caution. Sharp pains of confusion and

With a small smile, Asena bit off a large chunk of the steak to prove to him that it was safe, and then offered it out, the juices from the semi-raw meat dribbling down out the corners of her mouth.

"It's safe. It's beef."

She pushed against his mind, altering his suspicion to be calm. With a moment of deliberation, cautiously he took the meat from her hands and began scoffing it hungrily.

"Any more?" He asked in a low voice, grinning a little and showing off a mouth full of sharply pointed teeth. "Maybe something grilled?"

"Not at the moment."

"I suppose you wish to interrogate me then." The Chiro snickered, rocking back on his haunches and looking her up and down, unaware that his mood had been altered by her. "Did they send you in to rip my head off for biting that woman? Or maybe it was for attacking that dog? I disavow any knowledge of any assault, if that is the case, and I demand a full inquiry with a lawyer."

It caught Asena off guard to hear him speak with such a strong Australian accent, but with the articulation of a Synth who was ever so clearly Risio raised. Synths from other continents weren't uncommon, but it was still unusual to have one come in who was living *feral*.

"Not completely incorrect about the head ripping part," She chuckled wiping her mouth on the back of her arm. "Although they sent me in because I'm in charge."

"Oh?" He seemed surprised and he cocked an eyebrow, the only true indication of his expression. "I should call you Ser then. So, do you wish to interrogate me or not? *Ser?*"

Asena stood up and folded her arms across her chest. "Not right now, I would just like you to not bite people who are trying to help."

The Chiro sighed dramatically, ignoring her demand.

"So where on earth am I?" He asked sitting back on the hospital bed, head tilted to one side. "If I am on earth that is. You never know with ARCDA and all their plans for space colonies." Looking her up and down, she could hear the sentiments of his thoughts questioning where her handler uniform was or if she was a commander. He was thinking that he was in ARCDA, looking and listening to find anything familiar.

"Where were you last?"

"Oh…" He waved his hand about nonchalantly, leaning back on his arms, the image of an Atlas beta-tester bunker springing to mind. "Somewhere north heading even more north, because why not."

Asena's ears flattened back a little and she tried to keep her exasperation to herself. "Cryptic. You're in London."

"London? Really?" His posture changed, and he suddenly became alert and aware. He glanced past her towards the one-way mirror behind her on the wall. Frowning with suspicion he spoke in a low voice.

"And these humans are…not doctors?"

"No. These are the Rioteers."

"Aaah, I am behind enemy lines."

"Is there going to be a problem with that?"

"That entirely depends on what they want."

"What they want is for you not to bite people who are trying to help."

"That seems a reasonable enough request." He chuckled to himself then swiftly stood up and began stretching out his leathery wings, limited in range by the smallness of the room.

"I wish to shower and to eat a proper meal." He announced, folding his arms across his chest. "And I wish the opportunity to explore and a room to myself. I won't tolerate a shared room."

"I'd like a name first before I accept any demands. If you have one at least." She responded sharply, putting her hands to her hips indignantly. He was definitely from Risio. The Synths from Risio always held the same entitled attitude as this Chiro did, and it was often used as justification for their behaviour.

"As would I from you *Ser.*" He leant in, grinning. She was not sure if he was intending to be irritating or was usually like this, but either way it annoyed her. Risio Synths often did.

"Asena Canis."

"Hm." Black eyes blinked slowly as he contemplated his response for several moments before speaking. "I am Freeborn." Was his final response with a smirk and a bow. "Or if you prefer, *K.07.30:MacroGigas-6-6.* Or if you prefer the short version, *Ghost Bat-K-6-6.*"

Asena wanted to say something about the name, to ask if he thought of it right on the spot or had been given it before but remained silent. Synths were not really the most imaginative people with their names, but it was the only possession they had, and it was an offence to mock it.

"Well then, *Free,* welcome to the world." She sighed, knocking on the door for the Synths outside to open it. "Try not to kill anyone."

9

Beaufort Bunker, Haute-Savoie, French-Italian Border

Kathy awoke to blinding white lights and a painful throbbing in her lower abdomen as she slowly came around from the anaesthetic. Everything felt heavy and distant. With the waves of sedative still in effect, she struggled to recall what had happened.

"Professor Mira, *elle est éveillée*." A male voice, coming from her left.

She tried to roll her head to the side to see who it was, but with the bright operating theatre lights shining directly into her eyes, all she saw was a solid white blur. She felt exhausted, with pins and needles all over her body. Not even her wings would respond; she couldn't even tell what position they were in.

"*Tres bien*," A female voice from somewhere on the other side of the room, echoing slightly. "*Emmène la dans sa chambre s'il te plait*."

'*I must have still been on the French side of the Alps.*' Kathy thought sluggishly, the little French she had learnt in school surfacing and vanishing like a bubble.

The light switched off and black spots appeared before her eyes. The doors to the operating theatre opened with a soft hiss. Out the corner of her eye she could just about make out the blurry dark figures of several people, possibly porters.

"Take her to room three." The woman's voice again, speaking English this time and directing the orders to the porters. "It'll be a while until the sedatives fully wear off. That should give her time to recover. Make sure you give her the necessary boosters."

Wordlessly the porters obeyed, gently lifting Kathy off the operating table and onto a padded gurney before wheeling her out of the theatre. The overhead lights flashing slowly across her vision as she passed beneath, staring helplessly up at them. They eventually came to another room, which from what she could hear had two sets of doors.

The more alert and anxiety filled part of her brain awoke, telling her that it was probably a high security cell they were putting her into, maybe a quarantine cell, where they would strap her down to the bed to stop her trying to escape and observe her. Fortunately, the grogginess was far stronger than the anxiety and all internal thoughts of the worst happening were ignored as the porters gently lifted her off the gurney and placed her on a low bed.

They didn't linger for long, abandoning her to the room. She stared at the white ceiling, her thoughts beginning to become clearer and regain her senses, rebuilding the events leading up to the last moments she could remember.

She had always prided herself on her memory, it had always been good and becoming an Avio had only improved it. It was the only thing she could rely on.

She focused upon recalling her last memories before waking up, was of being almost doubled over in pain and flying low over mountains and forests as she tried to cross the border from France into Italy. Her wings were designed for long distance flights with minimal effort, but it was hunger and the sharp kicks of her baby that made it hard.

She had crossed over a beautiful bright blue lake that was penned in between several mountains by a huge dam. If she had not been exhausted and alone, she would have enjoyed the flight over the lake, maybe even flown through one of the waterfalls. And then the dark clouds, the biting cold and stormy weather. Amell catching up to her as she struggled to fly through the rain. Then sharp things that caught her wings and tangled them up– the feeling of falling– a damp leafy scent as she crashed through branches and leaves–the dark figures and beaming lights.

'*I'm in ARCDA again*' were her bitter thoughts as she put it all together. They must have found her, or she must have at least run across their radar. As ARCDA was so spread out, there was no way to know where the more minor bunkers were hidden or the size of the area they monitored. She only hoped that they had killed Amell.

'*If we had gone somewhere else...if we had done something different...if, if if...*' Jaw clenched she held back tears as best she could. Teal had in her mind been her soulmate, the one true thing in her life. They would have had a family, a home of their own, but the moment she knew that Amell was chasing her, she knew that Teal was dead.

'It's not your fault, it's not. It's all their fault. Them. It's all Storm's fault.' She snarled inwardly, picturing the Avio before her. *'This would never have happened if she hadn't 've barged in where she wasn't wanted! All her fault!'*

She wanted to scream and shout, punch a wall, slam her fist against something, anything, just to move and release the horrific pain in her chest, but the drugs were still in control and so she was forced to lay there, wings bound against her back only able to blink and cry; sick with fear and disgust, broken and exhausted.

After what felt like hours of plotting revenge and retaliation on the Rogues, thinking of the various ways she could make them pay, she found that she could move freely again without the effects of the drugs making her feel lethargic and heavy.

She was surprised that they had not strapped her down to the bed to stop her moving about, but she guessed because of her condition that they did not want to do that just in case they harmed her baby.

Glancing to her left, Kathy saw the far side of the cell had a large observation mirror which took up about three-quarters of the wall, in front of which was a white beanbag that she stared at in confusion. To the wall on right of the mirror there was a terrarium built into the wall behind a glass, mimicking a window into the outside world and giving the pure white room some green. The whole cell was very calming and tranquil; it was more like a minimalistic hotel room than a quarantine cell.

'I must be in Risio,' she thought loudly to herself as she stared at tiny, bejewelled insects flitting from flower to flower inside the tank. That seemed to be the only logical answer for the cell and the treatment. The aesthetic seemed to fit.

The feeling in her fingers and toes returned to her, along with the pain of the bruises across her body. Her wings throbbed in agony, having been strapped to her back to stop them opening and from having been laid upon for several hours. She curled her fingers and toes to make sure that she had full control back, before raising her arm above her and examining her arm for any cuts or scarring. It was all clear. The boosters had helped accelerate the healing process, and now she was feeling hungry.

She rolled onto her side and swinging her legs off the bed, she sat up. Pain seared across her lower abdomen as though it were on fire. Her hand went to her bump and felt…nothing.

Kathy looked down at her stomach in horror as her baby bump had gone. She felt her stomach beneath the white hospital pyjamas, hoping that it was just a delusion caused by the drugs she had been given. However, the sharp pain across her lower abdomen and what felt like stitches assured her that it was real.

Her baby was gone.

A sob caught in her throat and tears streamed down her cheeks, and holding her head in her hands, she cried.

They had taken away *everything* from her.

'It's their fault,' cold vitriolic anger hissed through her pain, *'those birds, Storm and the little girl. It could have been just fine if they hadn't have looked or Teal had killed the last girl, but no they had to ruin everything!'*

Slamming a fist down onto the bed and taking several deep breaths, she tried to calm herself down enough so that she could think straight, but the rage still bubbled underneath.

The door to the cell slid open with a soft hiss. Kathy's head snapped up and she leapt to her feet, ready to attack only to have the blood rush from her head and her tender scars screaming with agony at the sudden movement, forcing her to her knees.

The world still a dizzy black as she tried to regain focus, a person stepped through the door, alone. She could barely make out who they were.

"Touch me and I'll rip your eyes out!" She yelled slurring, her wings straining against the bonds when she tried to spread them out to seem more threatening.

"Calm down there!" The man said in surprise, throwing his hands up.

"Who are you? Tell me!" Her voice was sharp and strained with rage.

The young man lowered his hands and smiled, opening a pair of brassy-green and indigo-purple wings enough for her to understand that he was not a doctor, but an Avio.

He was well made, Risio-made Kathy presumed from his handsome looks. Rather than the usual uniform worn by the products of ARCDA, he looked as though he had just stepped off the set of a fashion shoot with his dark narrow eyes, warm olive skin, and dressed in a neat set of clothes that looked as though they had been tailor made to fit around his narrow, clipped wings. He flicked back tailing wisps of long black hair behind his ears, most of which was tied back in a high ponytail and shimmered an iridescent purple under the lights as he tilted his head. He was handsome, but it felt like a betrayal of her mate to admit it.

"Sit down, it's alright. I'm not going to hurt you." He said softly.

Kathy swallowed, uncertain if she should trust him or not, but with a glance behind the Avio before her, she understood that behind the large mirror there were probably doctors watching her. As easy as it could have been to attack him, she knew it was a bad idea.

With a defeated sigh, she sat down on the edge of the bed, one hand still clutching her abdomen, with the other brushing the long flight feathers back so they would not be bent if she sat on them.

"What do you want?" She asked warily, but still boiling with rage. Any indication of a threat and she would launch herself at him to take him out. He smiled warmly at her, brushing his glossy hair out his eyes.

"I don't want anything other than to make sure you're feeling better."

"Well I aint better." She snapped. "Where's my baby?"

"Calm down, they're-"

"Don't tell me to calm down!" She gripped the edge of the bed so hard her knuckles went white. "Where are they? Have they killed them? Tell me!"

"If you'd let me finish." His voice became ice cold, so suddenly and sharply from the sunny greeting that Kathy flinched. "They're safe and being cared for right now."

"C-cared for?" She faltered, heart beginning to race faster as the information sunk in. Her baby– babies rather–were alive and being cared for.

"You were given an emergency caesarean section because of the state we found you in was putting them at risk. We saw you flying over Roseland, so we sent Fell and Sabre out to get you." He explained, straightening up proudly.

"Your babies are in the nursery right now."

"Nursery?"

"Mum made sure she got them an incubator."

The words didn't seem to compute with her image of ARCDA. Was his mother a nurse here? Why would they have a nursery? What faction even was this bunker. She had so many questions, and her mind was reeling with mental whiplash.

"You're at Aura." He answered her thoughts, though she felt no familiar tingle of muser abilities being used.

Kathy gasped softly. Aura was a research faction like Atlas that focused upon creating and understanding Synths, not militant like Core who trained them. She didn't know much about Aura – few people did – however she was relieved, that it was a place without malice or foul intent for the children. But as her hope grew, her suspicions rose as well as to why and what they wanted with them.

"Can I…see 'em?" She asked cautiously, "Please?"

The young man looked down at her, folding his arms across his chest as he considered it. Behind him, two long tailfeathers twitched. They were nearly a meter and a half long and ended with a glossy plum coloured disk, much as if they were two large peacock feathers, but lacking the array of colours.

With a jovial shrug and a nod, he agreed to the request.

"Have you got a name?"

"Kathy Grey."

"Hello Kathy, my name is Wilheim Mira." He held his hand out to her, offering it forward for her to take.

She did not particularly want to be helped up, but she did not want to offend him when he might lead her to her babies, so with a sigh and quiet thanks she took his hand and got to her feet.

"Just stay with me, alright Kathy?" Wilheim smiled cheerfully putting a hand on a black square next to the door and smiling as it slid open with a soft hiss.

As she stepped out of the cell and began following Wilheim down the long hallway, and immediately she found herself flanked on both sides by two Avios, who seemed to appear out of nowhere.

"Shit!" She shrieked, backing away and into Wilheim in panic, her muscles flaring up with pain as she twinged the stitches. "Who the fuck are they?"

Neither man said a word as they regarded her with dark brown eyes, their unblinking stare made her scalp prickle. They were identical, more so than any batch created Synth she had come across before, even Preternaturals.

They were as intimidating as Storm had been, with very much the same commanding animalistic presence. Although they were smaller than Wilheim, they clearly had a wingspan that would dwarf them all, with long forked tailfeathers that were folded up behind them. Sleek black feathers with bold pristine white undersides which were so large that they were consciously poising their wings so that they were raised off of the floor to avoid damaging the tips.

"Them?" Wilheim asked looking over his shoulder at the twins. "This is Sabre and Fell. Don't mind them; they're just here to make sure you didn't kill me since you're a little crazy."

Kathy frowned at Wilheim.

"Crazy?"

"Well, you were flying through a rainstorm, up a mountain with another Avio on your toes. Logic clearly isn't on your side." He shrugged, his clipped wings rolling with his shoulders. "Clearly you're not the sanest of thinkers."

"He didn't mean to offend you." Spoke up the twin who stood on the right before Kathy could yell at him. "We presumed that your emotional state might make you rather...*volatile*."

"So, you'd 've leapt in if I attacked Heim there? Would you've killed me?"

The one who spoke cocked his head to one side sharply with a smile like a shark. "Yes. We'd have killed you on the spot. No negotiations."

The lack of emotion in his response made her shiver. There was no doubt about it that he was telling the truth, though she would admit that the thought of attacking them in a feral manner and taking them down with her had already crossed her mind.

She would have aimed for their throat and eyes, knowing there was no point in trying to punch or kick an Avio like this. Those were the two soft spots that were on Avios, not that she felt she would have been fast enough to strike at them in the first place.

"They're good guard geese. And friends. Watch out for Sabre though, he bites." Wilheim chimed, gesturing for her to keep on following. The twin who spoke grinned again and gnashed teeth mockingly at her. White fangs like the teeth of a lynx and an imposing set of wings that filled the hallway made her wish that she wore something a little more defensible than the white pyjamas she had been given, or at least for her wings to be free.

'You are quite bloodthirsty aren't you Kathy. Our eyes and throats first? Would you have used your teeth?'

They were speaking to her – musing to her. Sabre, she assumed. Kathy rolled her shoulders in agitation and glanced back at him walking to her right, uncomfortable with him being inside her head. Teal had used his muser abilities near enough all the time with her, but she didn't feel comfortable with it coming from a stranger.

'Don't panic, I'm not going to do anything bad. I agree with you actually,' he smirked, head tilting to one side, the scruffy locks of dark brown hair falling across his face. Tiny white feathers covered his cheekbones and ear tufts, stark against his brown skin. Kathy frowned at him, confused by the lack of tingling buzz that usually occurred with musers when they *spoke.*

'What?'

'Any person who wants to be human is definitely the crazy one, not us. We've got the better deal.'

A small reluctant smile twinged at her lips.

Fell – the other Avio, gave a small snort as he picked up on the musing and with a little nudge of his wing said to Sabre very simply, "Stop."

They past large open areas where doctors discussed reports and porters led Synths across to their cells or to the test rooms. Like the cell she was in, it had the same minimalistic softness to it, white bearing more resemblance to a hotel or a spa with its wall terrariums, open spaces, and air of calmness. There were even planters with fully-grown silver leafed trees and ferns growing in the larger open areas beneath arching glass domes that let in the sunlight, with the balconies and walkways of the upper levels coursing between them. It was nothing like Core.

"Are they twins?" She muttered, still watching the two Avios following them as Wilheim led her down the clean teal and white hallway. She looked them up and down and the more she stared the more unnerved she felt. They had only four toes, covered in fine scales, and their long tail feathers flicked and twitched to balance them as they walked, yet there was something else that didn't seem quite right with them that she couldn't put her finger on.

"Yes." The one on the left, Fell, said softly.

This twin was very calm and reserved, a contrast to his brother who was practically skipping alongside him with his feathers rustling noisily. He walked with his head held high and shoulders back, which made him seem regal and quietly confident.

"I didn't think they could make twins."

"Years ago, they did make twins and triplets in the place of batches, but that was under exceptional circumstances, either by commission or due to project needs." He had such a beautiful voice, calm, with a softness that made her chest hurt. She wanted him to talk more.

"So, you're old versions of Avios then?" They certainly looked older than her, and from what she knew Avios aged only marginally faster than humans meaning that they could have been at least twenty.

"Ours were prototypes. A model that never made it to the shelves."

"Why not?"

"Because we are some of the most dangerous creatures that they have ever made." He said quietly.

There was no malice to it, but the words sliced fear across her chest as she knew that he was not joking. Sabre she could easily see him laughing as he dropped people from great heights but Fell had the air of someone who would mourn the loss of a sparrow yet could also slit a man's throat without hesitation.

Heim led them through another corridor at the very end of which had a double door which needed to be opened with a handprint. Grinning, Heim tapped the screen and pressed his hand to the black panel, showing off the authority he had.

It opened with a soft hiss and inside the large room were seven doctors scurrying about, monitoring several pedestals with incubators on top of them. Seven was not very many at all in comparison to some of the bunkers of Risio and Atlas who had a minimum of twelve doctors on a ward at a time plus the nursing team and STEM interns who would work alongside them. Like the rest of the facility she had seen, it was open plan, bright and filled with plants that gave the room a fresh earthy scent and calming atmosphere.

A few small children scurried about the room being chased by a rather exhausted nurse who could not keep up with their pace, and in one corner of the room were some soft chairs where a few girls were sitting with their own children. Slack jawed,

Kathy gawped at the sight. Continuing on through and down a ramp to a lower section, Wilheim led them past more incubators into a darkened night room. Kathy stared in curiosity at the mixtures of strange eggs, kelpy seaweed-like pods in water tanks, and even sleeping piles of Synth-cubs curled up and nestled together as they slept.

'*So this is a nursery.*' Kathy mused loudly. A strange feeling of agreement, a sentiment not her own, brushed across her mind as she felt one of the twins return the musing with their own feelings. It was strange, dissonant almost as she realised that these two musers were on a completely different level to Teal.

"Here they are." Wilheim announced flourishing his arms and striding over to where Kathy's babies were, ignoring the clamour of kids above evading their bath-time.

Kathy followed Heim over to where a technician worked by one of the incubators, though she was bumped into by a small toddler who had run down the slope after them. The little girl looked up at her with narrow black eyes beneath waves of coppery hair, then without a word hugged her leg, then carried on running off as the nurse tried to grab her to give her a bath, a short cat-like tail flicking out behind her with every other step. It made Kathy laugh a little seeing how carefree the toddler was despite being in a laboratory surrounded by doctors.

"Kelly! We're here to see the newest arrivals!" Wilheim sang loudly to the doctor monitoring Kathy's babies. She looked over the top of her tablet at him in a very disapproving glower and clicked her leopard print heels.

"You're not supposed to be here." The doctor sneered at him, passing her tablet to a nurse who looked at the notes upon them and scurried off to input the data into the system.

Heim shrugged, giving the older woman a charming smile.

"Special permission from mum. You don't want me to have to get her now do you?"

The threat was given in a very charming light-hearted tone. The doctor backed down and backed away from the incubator as Kathy stepped up to it.

Inside lay two tiny babies, pink and new and almost too small to be real. They looked blind as baby birds with their eyes shut and dark behind their eyelids. Rows of raised goosebumps that held the beginnings of feathers lined the fresh red skin, and along the ridge of their wings were small finger like claws.

Wilheim watched her expressions carefully as she moved closer, pressing her face against the incubator. She reached in and placed her hands on their backs feeling their little hearts beating through her fingertips. Their little wings floppily extended and beat against the soft towels that surrounded them.

"Are…their wings meant to be like that?" She asked, letting a little wing claw hook around her finger and grasp with the same reflex as the baby's hand.

"Not sure, but since you're a transhuman they're likely to be different to a real Avio."

"What are they missing that doesn't make them real Avios?" She sneered.

"There's different organs, brain structures, and tails for a start."

"Are you saying I'm made wrong?"

"Kathy, you've just had three kids. For them to exist whoever made you must have done something outrageously wrong."

"He means that all Transhumans are thought to be sterile." Fell calmly corrected. "Under regular circumstances they wouldn't have been possible."

Scowling, she avoided looking at the other Avios and reached into the incubator again. She stroked a finger along the curve of her baby's backs, before checking the temperature on the incubator's panel.

Her memory flashed to lessons at school. It was only at thirty-three degrees Celsius, which even for a human, was below their body temperature.

"They're too cold. They're gonna freeze!" She panicked, turning to the doctor, Kelly, Wilheim had spoken to. "Turn the heat on these things up!"

The doctor opened her mouth to argue, but before words even had a chance to form in her mouth, another woman cut across her.

"Do as the mother says."

Everyone leapt to attention and turned to the direction from which the voice came. The twins stood up straight as though awaiting a military inspection whilst Wilheim smiled widely, not changing his posture in the slightest.

Before them stood a petite Korean woman in a white lab coat, her arms folded across her chest and watching them coolly. Although she was small, she had a very commanding presence about her. Her bistre eyes seemed almost black as they flicked from face to face, whilst a wry smile played at her scarlet lips. She pushed her glasses back up her nose and tucked a strand of wispy black hair back behind her ear, advancing towards them with sharp clicks of her heels.

"Professor Mira!" Doctor Kelly announced, turning pale and tensing.

The Professor gave her a charming smile and stepped forward towards Kelly, and said with the sweetest of voices, "Turn it up as she says, or I will fire you and I will send your body to Delta where they will have more use for you than I will."

Kelly dropped her gaze and went over to the panel of the incubator with some reluctance. Doctor Kelly complied, turning the incubator temperature up then hastily scurrying off to the far side of the lab so she was out of her superior's range.

"Professor Evelyn Mira." Smiled the woman sweetly, shaking Kathy's hand politely. "I am the Executive of the European side of the Arcadia Corporation, and head of Aura faction. I assume my son Wilheim introduced himself, yes?"

"Y-yes." Kathy stared at her in wide-eyed shock. "You're...you're the boss of Aura?"

"Of course, and you're very lucky that you ended up here and not with those Core faction barbarians." She gave a disapproving snort. "Imbeciles. They have no idea how to behave."

Feigning a smile, Kathy swallowed down the knot of fear, thanking her luck that of all the people that she flew across it was the head of Aura, though she was still aware of the danger she was in if she didn't behave.

"Thank you." said Kathy softly, tucking her hair behind her ear and straightening out her hospital gown.

The Professor laughed lightly and put the fans for the incubator on. She turned to the twins who, dismissing them with a silent wave of her hand. Nodding the twins bowed curtly to her and gracefully made their exit, holding their long forked tailfeathers high off the ground.

With a sweeping gesture, she indicated for Kathy to follow her across the room to the seats that surrounded one of the many planters in the room. The other girls saw her coming and politely stood to make room. Sitting she gestured for the other girls to sit and continue with what they were doing as the same small girl who had run into Kathy earlier toddled over. She reached her tiny hands up, wanting to be held. Eve chuckled and picked her up, sitting the little girl on her lap and playing with her hair.

"Norah, you haven't had your bath," She laughed softly, making the toddler screw her face up in disapproval. "My granddaughter, Norah." Eve said, indicating to the little girl.

"*Noa.*" The little girl mewed, pouting at the woman.

"Noa then. A little second generation herself– like your children– and too smart for her own good."

"She's your *granddaughter?*" Kathy questioned, looking to the Hummingbird Heim and back to the girl. The slightly feline Pard ears and tail, flecked with feathers, suggested that it wasn't by natural means. Heim's lips pursed, and he gave his mother a cold look, which Eve ignored with a light and musical laugh.

"Well after one of my sons decided that he'd rather build robots and bionics for the rest of his life than have children, and the other insists his bees are all the children he needs, I had to do something. I helped build the original Synth genomes, making her was a weekend job. Now, *your* babies." Eve said softly, patting the cushions beside her, gesturing for Kathy to sit.

"You...you're not taking them away from me?" Kathy swallowed, carefully sitting down next to Eve, sat sideways so that she was not damaging her feathers. Eve put the toddler down, letting her run off again, and gave Kathy a charming smile.

"Of course not! They will remain here, but don't worry your babies will be very well looked after," said the Professor, "and you'll be given the right treatment to get you back into shape, so you can mother them properly. You have to understand that we're very excited to be having you and your children here. It's the first time we've had any transhuman-Avio pregnancies which we've been able to record, but we'll try to be as gentle as possible to not do them any damage."

She nodded slightly to the other girls sitting on the chairs opposite and the lone nurse running around after the children whilst the six other doctors scurried between incubators and the computer systems trying to record data.

"I do want to ask some questions though about how you got into that...state." Eve said softly, trying to be delicate and polite.

"State?"

"Pregnant, injured and still able to fly. How long did it take? What happened? Where did you fly from?"

Kathy blinked at her, a little nervous about answering. She glanced towards Wilheim. He was avoiding eye-contact with his mother but gave Kathy a reassuring nod and a smile to prompt her to speak.

"England...I was from there before I ran away and ended up getting taken into Core." Kathy said quietly, swallowing slightly and trying to calm her nerves. Eve looked surprised.

"You remember being human?"

"Yes."

"Fascinating. How old were you?"

"Thirteen. It's a little blurry between that and when I first woke up like this. But I escaped with Teal, my mate, a few months ago when those people attacked the bunker."

"People?"

"The Rioteers. It was horrible, and we got away as fast as we could. We were just roaming with a few others like us and we ran into several others."

"*Oh?*" the doctor's curiosity rose, and she leaned forward in her chair.

"We killed most of them."

"*Oh.*" Her tone dropped in shock that she had put it so bluntly. "Why?"

Kathy's brow furrowed, and she glowered at the floor as memories of arguments with the various people bubbled up in her mind along with the rage she had felt.

"I didn't agree with what they thought. Stupid creatures. They thought that we," She gestured to herself and the other Synth girls, "could *be human.* That we could be *safe* with the Rioteers. They wanted us to join those people, right after we saw them kill our friends. Yeah, Core sucked, but they weren't the ones who hurt us. Why would I want any part of that?"

Eve looked shocked that rather than sticking together with whoever they came across, that they would kill the weak and take the strong.

"So, you hate humans a lot then." The doctor said calmly, unafraid of the girl.

Kathy made a little *tch* sound and rubbed the back of her neck where she knew there was a small barcode tattoo with her ID underneath that had forcibly been marked there.

"Understatement…" She muttered, rolling her shoulders and wishing that the doctor would take the bonds around her wings off already, so she could stretch them. Eve tapped her foot thoughtfully, twisting a strand of black hair around her finger. She was patient and calm, not at all what Kathy had expected and so with a sigh, she continued.

"The seven of us had just got rid this group from Africa who had a few Avios and Chiros who wanted to join the Rioteers, and then looked for somewhere to sleep for the night. So, we stayed in a farm."

"In a barn?"

"In the house. We killed off the family there of course."

"Why would you do that?"

"Well, the man pointed a knife at us when we trespassed, we retaliated."

"Did he stab you?" Eve asked.

Kathy gave a short sharp laugh, rubbing the stitches on her abdomen.

"He didn't have a chance to move. We slept in the house and decided to stay there for a week or two because of me and the babies, but a day or two after that we caught three girls, Avios, in the barn looking at the bodies."

"More Avios?" The doctor's expression seemed exasperated, growing angry though it was not directed at Kathy. Wilheim gave a furious eyeroll too, muttering under his breath to his mother about how bad Core and Atlas' management was.

They did have the advantage over other experiments in that they could fly which made them notoriously difficult to track and capture. She nodded in agreement to Wilheim's criticisms, whispering that would have to have words with the other factions about their security, especially for the factions who liked to give their Avios' flying room and caution them for allowing them to escape.

Kathy frowned a little, continuing to tell her story.

"Yeah, more of them. Except these didn't look like they had just escaped like the other African birds did. They were different."

"How so?"

"Well, they were clean weren't they, and had nice clothes, but they said they were from London, so I guess that figures. But none of them were the same." She thought hard about the girls, anger rising.

"Could you describe them?"

"One was Transhuman like me but missing her arms and legs. Had bionics instead. Another was this pretty Tribrid-girl, super strange looking, but their boss was this silver-bird. Some sort of falcon-based Avio because she was all sharp and dangerous looking."

"What did you say?" Eve sat up straight and lost her charming smile, expression becoming an impervious mask as she fixed her black eyes upon Kathy.

"What did she look like? The silver-bird. Describe her to me." Eve demanded.

"U-uh, nothing special or pretty really, just dangerous and like a feral."

"What did she look like?"

"Grey hair and wings, silvery feathers, green eyes, um…no tail feathers and only four toes." Her voice tremored. "Teal got angry because he couldn't muse on her, but I thought that was because she was just feral."

Both Wilheim and Eve went still and stared at her in silence. Heim looked across to his mother after a few seconds, his dark eyes wide and he opened his mouth to speak, but she raised her hand to silence him and gestured for him to leave. Without argument, he quick marched out of the nursery to find the two other Avios, long tailfeathers floating behind him.

"Continue…" Eve said softly, though there was not the same charm there had been in her voice before. Though it was one word it made the feathers between her wings rise in fear.

"There wasn't much after that. There was a big fight, a police car started to come close and Teal told me to fly so I did and…" She faltered a little, "And they killed him."

Pain flushed across her chest and she looked across to her babies in their incubator for a moment until she could speak again with tears welling up in her eyes.

"I just wanted a home and a family." She choked. "None of this. It's all her fault! It's all Storm's fault! We would have been fine she hadn't-"

"Storm?" Eve cut through, grabbing her hand sharply. "Did you say her name was Storm?"

"Storm, yeah. That's what she called herself."

Eve's face went a shade paler and her lips pursed. Releasing Kathy's hand, her shock grew slowly into a frown. The Professor remained still for a long time, contemplating, thinking. There was little emotion betrayed, but Kathy knew that she was angry.

"Do…do you know her?"

She snapped back to attention and gave Kathy a forced pitying smile.

"Not for a long time. She's a very dangerous creature. You're lucky to have escaped her. She killed your mate, I'm sure she would have done the same to you."

"Not if I kill her first." Breathed the Vulture. She clenched her fists as the bloodlust rose and she imagined herself ripping the feathers from their backs.

Eve noted her bloodthirsty smile, and held her hand out to the young mother, the warmth returning to her voice.

"I think I have an idea which can help us both Kathy, but first I need you to tell me again, everything that happened."

10

Cherry Tree House, Battersea Park, London.

Nearly three weeks had gone by since they had been inducted into the Rogues, Raoul and Malana were starting to find comfort and solace in their new life. The strange complexity of how things operated was still a little overwhelming to them at first; the lack of rules for bath and bedtimes, the television and music, freedom of having a choice in what they ate and what they wore.

They quickly learnt about the different boltholes around the many parks and stations of London and how to act in public, which was harder than Raoul had anticipated. Many things of which he thought he knew as fact about humans and city life turned out to be false. It was all a learning experience, but he caught on quick.

The Rogues' main priority however, had been on Malana.

Having lost her family and been dropped into a completely new world with very little understanding of the language, she had adapted surprisingly fast. They were wary as to how she would behave, and so far, she had been remarkably calm and stable but it only worried Wilny and Storm more as to what she could have been hiding from them. For the moment however, their focus was on gaining her trust and confidence before they began bringing up what had happened with her.

The most difficult part which both of the newest members of the Rogues had found was the language barriers. Having grown up with mainly military and scientific terminologies, their vocabularies lacked all the many metaphorical idioms, descriptive words and colloquial names for things, as well as the context of what these abstract phrases meant which was missing from both their French and English vocabularies.

"What is...*fluummozzed?*" Raoul asked cautiously as he scrolled through his new laptop, reading over the latest news. He sat outside at the garden table, basking in the late afternoon sun before it dipped below the row of terraces behind them, whilst Storm and Wilny cooked together inside.

Storm was usually the one who cooked, but since her arm had been broken Wilny and Kat had to help her, since Beth had a permanent ban from the kitchen. Raoul hadn't learnt why she was banned but could only imagine what she'd done to earn it.

Wilny looked up through the exterior French doors in confusion.

"Fluummozzed?"

"It's in this report. '*Portuguese health officials have been left fluummozzed as the town of Évora, which was recently placed under quarantine for an outbreak of an as yet unidentified virus, have found the residents to have been cured overnight'*. Is fluummozzed bad? Am I saying this correctly?"

"Do you mean *flummoxed*?" Storm cut in, poking Wilny's shoulder and gesturing to put the salad into a dish.

"I do not know the word or the French for it." Muttered Raoul in annoyance copying and pasting the word into google. Fluent as he was in English, the fact that he did not know words in his native tongue irritated him and made him feel as though he had the vocabulary of a child.

"It means confused, y'know, *discombobulated*." Storm answered for him with an amused smile, knowing he wouldn't know what it meant.

"Discomb…what?" He blinked slowly at her, half certain that she was just making the word up to tease him.

"Discombobulated. It also means confused."

He blinked slowly at her for several more moments, still not fully confident of what she had just said before responding.

"I am *that* word."

Both Wilny and Storm laughed, then seeing the distress on Raoul's face, Wilny lightly whacked Storm's broken arm with a wooden spoon, hitting the cast with a dull tap.

"Don't be mean. He's still learning." He chuckled, stirring a pot full of tagliatelle that was beginning to boil. Storm smiled apologetically and leant out of the doors to ruffle the Hound's hair with her good hand.

Raoul gave her a forgiving chuckle and tugged on her feathers in turn. He was getting used to her rebellious playfulness and he never took her teasing as an insult. The Rouges all teased and tormented each other a lot, but it was no different to how when he was young and used to play fight with his brothers. It actually felt comforting to be tormented as it felt like he was part of their family.

His curled tail wagging slightly, he continued to browse through the news stories, skimming over the words he didn't understand to finish the articles.

"These news reports are very strange." He said, thinking aloud. "I do not know many of these countries or any of these people. Who is the prime minister or president of Wessex and Yorkshire?"

Abandoning his post and striding out into the garden, Wilny looked over Raoul's shoulder to see what he was reading, squinting slightly as he tried to focus on the words before putting on his glasses.

"Those are counties, Raoul. Like little factions within a country." Winy shrugged, trying to explain it simply. "And most of these people are celebrities, you don't need to know about them at all."

Whilst Wilny struggled to read or focus upon anything too close to his face, Beth could barely see three feet in front of her without her vision blurring. When Raoul had asked why neither he or Beth got corrective surgery in ARCDA for their eyesight, both had groaned and hissed at the suggestion, stating that their eyes were too different for regular opticians to deal with and would much rather stick to the old-fashioned glasses to correct their vision.

"Wilny! The tagliatelle is gonna stick to the pan, you arse!" Storm complained.

"Oops!"

They both blinked and Wilny teleported back into the kitchen, using his muser abilities to distort their perceptions of time to appear to have gotten there quicker. Unamused by his use of his talent Storm gave a sharp tug on his long tailfeathers, making him yelp and nearly fling the spoon at her.

"What goes in next with this?" Wilny asked as he rubbed the base of his tail.

"You're going to need to fry the fennel seeds and onions first, you can leave it to stand for now and drain it later when all the vegetables are done."

"Humans give the strangest names to things. Tagliatelle. Fennel." He muttered to himself as he turned from the bubbling pot of pasta to the fridge, pulling the door open.

"I can't see any fennel things in here, Storm."

"I'll get them if you can just deal with this please."

Raoul watched the pair dance around each other in the small kitchen space, leaning over each other and gently sidestepping so that they could reach the things they were after. Even though their wings seemed to crowd the kitchen, not once did they bump into each other, at most only occasionally brushing against one another's feathers. He was amazed by how sensitive their wings were that they could use them to be aware of one another's presence. Even with Wilny's long tailfeathers out and occasionally twitching and flicking about, they seemed to have no problem with clashing.

"So, these people, the Daggers? Yes? They are coming to eat dinner with us?" Raoul asked noting down the word Fennel into his little notebook under the *F* section and searching for the French translation through the internet. The definition down, he packed his laptop away and returned to the kitchen to help them set up.

"Yes. The whole lot of them." Wilny muttered with a frown of concentration as he the drained pasta into the wok, being as careful and steady as he could so he didn't drop any on the hob or floor.

"In about ten minutes, so we're rushing a bit. They'd just be getting back from a sabotage mission in Portugal. They really want to meet you, Puppy." Storm grinned at him over her shoulder.

Having heard the Daggers mentioned once or twice he understood that they were a group much like the Rogues, but they specialised in breaking into ARCDA Bunkers, and occasionally banks or offices of politicians, and sabotaging the place. From what Raoul understood, the Daggers were *very* good at it.

"Are they all like you?"

"Avios? No. There's only one Avio in the Daggers and that's my brother Crow. The others are mammalian-based Synths, with the exception of Bubbles." Storm explained, standing on tiptoes to reach the pot of fennel seeds from the spice cupboard. With a bit of a jump she managed to grab the pot, then began sprinkling it into wok with the onions and peppers giving the kitchen an aromatic anise scent.

Raoul turned to the back of his book where he had noted down the different groups he had heard about, the names of their members and what they were, had been sectioned out beneath each one. So far, he understood that there were seven major groups who all commanded a different part of Europe, but there were several more subgroups within these territories.

"I didn't know you had a batch-brother."

"Well, it's more adoptive than from the same batch. Crow came from the same Bunker as me." She continued as she directed Wilny to mix the pasta with the onions and crème fraiche. "Or so he says, and will have a thousand stories to tell you if Bubbles will let him."

"That's his second in command who's...well you'll see." Wilny chuckled, nibbling upon the aromatic pasta.

"Bubbles? I don't know that word...or is it another human name for people like Beth?"

Giving each other strained looks, the two silently questioned each other how to explain what bubbles were to the Hound. They often forgot that mundane words like *bubbles, spatula, dishwasher* and *banana* were not often used by doctors in front of their wards for them to understand without visual context.

"Bubbles are uh..." Storm looked about the kitchen trying to find something to explain them, when she realised the most obvious way to do so.

Stepping away from the cooking, she plunged her free hand into the sink full of water meant for the washing up, splashing it around for a moment till the foam appeared, and coming up with a hand full of dishwater bubbles.

"These." She proclaimed holding her hand out before him, proud of her ingenuity. Raoul blinked slowly at the popping white mass in her hand, still confused by the name.

"She is named after the sink clouds?"

Storm tried not to laugh as she shook the bubbles off her hand and rinsed it off under the tap.

"No, Crow named her after she dyed her hair bubblegum pink."

"Bubblegum...pink?" The confusion on his face grew into distress again as he tried to pull together a mental image of pink sink clouds on a girl's head, all popping and disappearing. Wilny stifled a laugh and smiled at the Hound. He could see a little of himself in Raoul's confusion as several months prior he was just as confused by names.

"I'll buy you some and show you later Raoul." Wilny sighed with a smile.

Loud shouting, laughter and a loud thud came from above them, and all three looked up at the ceiling. Following the movement of the sound, they watched Beth as charged down the stairs, span herself round the banister and skidded across the wooden floor.

"God I'm good!" She laughed with a flourishing spin, pushing her glasses back into place. Storm frowned sceptically at Owl.

"What did you do?"

"I've may have just found a juicy bit of information which will pay well... in the right hands." Beth purred wiggling her hands and letting the scrappy skeletal metal fingers of the replacement arm she had been working on curl and uncurl.

"And I thought you didn't do blackmail anymore."

"That was my new year's resolution. You should know how hard it is to keep them, since you broke yours in the first week."

"Fair enough." Storm shrugged and turned back to the cooking. "Just don't spend the money on more screens okay."

"I'll save up to buy a motorbike with it then. Also, the girls are home." She smirked, picking up the sound of Kat and Malana from the street, and waltzed off towards the door, reaching it just in time to hear the bell ring. Upon opening the door, she was almost bowled over as Malana raced past her.

"Wilny!" She squealed excitedly, "Wilny! *Regarde!*"

Wilny's face lit up and he immediately dropped the spoon he was using and rushed to the kitchen archway.

"Lana!" He yelled back, dropping to one knee and throwing his arms open wide. The little girl beamed as she ran to him, throwing herself into the hug and wrapping her arms around his neck. Looking over to Kat, Storm gave the Lioness a knowing smile, proud at the quick connection the ex-Elite and the little girl had made.

Lana let go and pushed him back, so she could show him her new clothes and newly cut hair. What had once been a tangled and matted mess was now tied into bunches of bronze curls, smattered with small orange feathers growing from her scalp in the same manner as with both Wilny's and Storm's hair.

Wilny beamed at her, gesturing for her to spin to show him her new dress that they had picked up from one of the few tailors who was able to design and make clothes to fit Avio wings. "You look so pretty! *Jolie?* Jolie is pretty, right Raoul?"

He caught Raoul's pleased nod out the corner of his eye. He was picking up on his French, although it was still fairly amateurish.

"I got err…six er *drezzes et nous avons mangé tarte-aux-fraise…*they…*ils étaient trop sucrés pour moi…*" Malana said, scrunching her face up as she tried to remember the English. She turned to Raoul.

"*Drez? Comment dis-tu robe et fraise en anglais, Raoul?*"

"*Dress* and *strawberry* tarts." Raoul translated with a smile, glad that the little girl was no longer afraid of him.

"Six dresses? Wow. Kat spoilt you." Wilny cooed, picking Malana up and carrying her into the living room.

Putting the laptop away, something tingled across the back of Raoul's head and irritated whiskers in a peculiar way. His nose twitched as he caught a strange unfamiliar scent. It was an Avio scent, but not belonging to any of the Rogues. He turned to face the direction from where it was originating. For a moment he swore there was someone stood there, and as he tried to focus the scent disappeared.

"I couldn't have her dressed in rags now could I?" Kat laughed and dropped the bags of shopping down by the stairs, removing her hat and jacket to free her wings, tail, and ears.

Storm frowned at Kat, looking her up and down as she twirled in her new clothes. "You bought nine sets of clothes last week, how could you possibly need another dress?"

"Because I got blood on three of them, lost two, Wilny stole four of them-"

"*Borrowed!*" Protested Wilny.

"And ripped two of them! But also, because one can never have enough clothes." She purred with a grin and a small butterfly-like flutter of her wings and a twirl. "Oh, and Storm-" She began, but Storm stopped her with a gentle gesture of her hand.

"I know."

And with that she lashed her fist out towards the wall. Her knuckles made contact with something– or rather someone– invisible, making them squawk with both pain and surprise as they fell to the floor, revealing themselves to all. Raoul gawped, both vindicated that he knew there had been someone there and he was still shocked with himself that he had managed to slip past him undetected.

"Nice try Crow. She got you again. I make that eight-three to her." Wilny cackled, looking down at the man now rolling about on the floor who was swirling into focus.

"Sweet fuckery Storm! You didn't have to hit me *and* electrocute me! I could have broken a wing!" Complained Crow, rising to his feet.

"You've only yourself to blame." Storm flicked her hair over her shoulder with a smirk, then ducking as a huge black wing swept out to hit her.

As her brother straightened up and composed himself, Raoul's jaw dropped in bewilderment.

Crow was unlike any of the other Avios. Glossy black feathers covered nearly the entirety of his body, only leaving his forearms bare from what Raoul could see. His tail was longer, body oddly shaped, with his bare feet exposing four long bird-like toes on each foot, whilst two long fingers stretched out from his wings, ending in hooked talons. He had never seen an Avio of this variation before. Were there sub-species? He would ask later.

"What the...your head- hair I mean. *It's feathers!*" Raoul babbled. Crow turned to look at him. His huge eyes were such a deep shade of brown he could hardly distinguish them from his pupils.

"Oh? *Oh my,* I never noticed that before!" Crow chuckled, dark eyes glittering mischievously. He winked wryly, and the feathers roused emotively. The sight of them moving and reacting like the feathers on a bird, made Raoul continue to gawp.

"Crow." Storm said sternly. '*Stop showing off*'.

"Sorry, sorry." He laughed, removing the gloves he wore and extending a hand towards Raoul for him to shake. "You must be the new puppy then. Raoul, right?"

Raoul looked down at his four fingered hand, gawping still as he saw scales along it, much like what Storm and Malana had on their legs. He was so bizarre to look at and it made Raoul think of the Anubis-headed Canids.

"Crow Corvus. Leader of the Daggers, professional pain-in-the-arse, and former Rogue." Crow informed him with a smirk, carefully stretching out black wings which held two thin finger like digits along the wrist.

Behind him he heard a tiny whisper from Malana to Wilny, "*Pourquoi est son nom de famille* Corvus *et non* Strawberry-Swann. *Je pensais qu'il était le frère de Storm?*" To which Wilny tried his best to explain that Storm's surname was Fraser and not *fraise.*

Still dumbfounded by Crow's appearance, Raoul slowly shook his hand.

"You have the same voice as Storm."

"Yeah, we've the same accent, though I think yours is better."

"I…thank you?"

Grinning, Crow turned away from Raoul and with a roll of his black wings, strode over to Wilny and Malana. Malana, startled by Crow's appearance dug her nails into Wilny's arm as Crow approached, recoiling and drawing her wings up defensively.

"And this must be Malana." Crow chuckled, smiling at the little girl. She hid her face, pulling her rust-orange wings up about her head to shield herself. Her reaction made the boys laugh and Wilny lightly kicked Crow.

"Your face is scaring her, old man."

"I'm sorry," He chuckled, stepping back to give them space, "I should be used to kids being terrified of me-"

"Crow you bastard! You could have waited for us!" Howled a small girl who had stormed in through the door, interrupting Crow.

"Saffron! What have I said!" Crow snapped, head full of feathers rising and falling quickly, as he scowled at the little Monkey-Synth. "No swearing!"

"But you *always* get to swear!"

"I'm an adult! I'm allowed!"

"*But it's not fair!*" The little girl groaned dramatically, pouting and letting her long prehensile tail curl up across and around her chest. Shortly after, she followed by two boys and a young woman, who tossed down their rucksacks and bags against a wall and stretched in relief at being in a safe environment. All five Daggers had arrived.

Raoul remained where he stood, staring at them when he caught the eye of the group's Pard, who winked at him and grinned slyly. A jaguar or leopard based Pard, Raoul denoted from the spotted long tail and the markings that extended into his hair. Beside him stood a Canid with a short and silky white tipped tail and the largest ears he had ever seen and angry black eyes. A Fox-Canid of some variety. They both didn't quite look or smell right as Raoul's nose twitched. There was something human about them both.

With a gentle shove from Kat, Raoul was directed over to both boys to introduce himself and instead ended up standing awkwardly as the two circled him and commented to each other.

"A curly tail?" Said the Jaguar. "Is he a show dog?"

"He's a hunting dog," Replied the Fox. "Curly tailed dogs are hunting dogs."

"What about pugs?"

"Well, he's clearly not a pug is he."

"I'm based on an elkhound," Raoul said tentatively, taking hold of his tail in defence. "A spitz breed."

A sharp clap caught their attention, and the boys silenced immediately and turned their heads to look at their second in command, Bubbles.

Her skin was finely scaled, a pale beige with a mottling of darker browns and a streak of black and red that ran from her large round eyes. Though they were a bright cornflower blue, they held a very reptilian slitted pupil that sliced through the length of blue with dark veins that looked to flow into it. With the ridged eyebrows, flat nose and thick grey tail curled around one leg she would have looked somewhat disturbing if it wasn't for the waves bright pink hair which offset the reptilian appearance.

"Since you boys aren't doing anything helpful, you can set the table. You know where everything is." She smiled at them with a mouth full of tiny teeth giving her a piranha grin, folding her arms across her chest. "Go down to the basement and get some spare chairs."

Without a word of protest, they left Raoul alone and went through to the kitchen to the door that led to the basement.

"Bubblegum pink." Raoul noted the colour of her hair to himself, recalling the earlier discussion, though her hair didn't look like the sink clouds he had imagined her to have. Bubbles tilted her head at him, staring flatly.

"Pardon?"

"Err! Bubbles, *oui*? I am- I'm glad to meet you."

"Yes." She assessed Raoul unblinkingly, holding out her hand to shake. Rows of padded scales lined her palm and fingers, he expected her hand to be rough when he shook, but much to his amazement, it was surprisingly soft.

"Don't mind them. Jett is the Jaguar and Prince is the Dhole. They're harmless." She said softly, smiling her piranha smile. "So are we what you expected?"

"No. You aren't what I expected at all, you don't look-" He threw his hands up in a sudden panic as the stared at him- "not that I say that in a mean way, I didn't imagine any of you to be what you are. I didn't even know they made female Reptiles, I thought you would have been a bird or- or cat!"

"So, you thought I would have been something...*cute*?" Her eyes betrayed even less emotion than the Avios raptorial stare.

Raoul smiled awkwardly, trying to save himself before he caused offence. "You are...unique. And the first gecko-lady I have met."

"So, Bubbles! How was Portugal?" Beth cut through saving Raoul anymore embarrassment, linking arms with the Gecko and leading her to the kitchen.

"Hot." The girl laughed, thick tail slapping the ground with a sudden twitch.

"I really wanted to turn the van around and head to the sea."

"You just wanted to go to the beach? But I thought you loved sabotage."

"A beach is far better than an underground bunker full of half-made Cybers."

"Urgh. *Delta*." Beth grimaced. Having come from Delta herself she knew what it was like. "Okay, you're right, a beach would have been better."

The boys brought more chairs up to the long table that sat outside in the garden, since it was the only place large enough to host them all, whilst Crow, Wilny, and Kat brought across the food and plates. Fairy lights and citronella lanterns hung from the trees and fences, illuminating the long narrow stretch of grass in the dying evening light.

It had been such short notice that they hadn't even set the table or cleaned up the living room, not that the Daggers minded at all. They only cared that they were in the company of friends.

The two groups gathered and began arranging themselves about the table. With eleven of them there it was a tight squeeze, especially for the six who had wings and needed the room.

Raoul had been slightly concerned that the neighbours would look out of their window and see them, but no one else brought the matter to attention. None of them cared if they were noticed or not.

Storm smirked at Crow as he pulled her chair out for her.

"So, it was hell then?"

"We managed to save about thirty living people from being used as target practice." He responded softly, pushing her chair in.

"*We* are responsible for that." The little golden Monkey, Saffron, piped up, pushing Crow out the way and sitting down at the table next to Lana. "All you boys did was knock out porters and run around the building with hammers and water guns, shooting them at the electrics. Bubbles and I rescued the people."

"We helped though! And we didn't use water guns thank you very much!" Retorted Jett, his round ears flicking backwards.

"You nearly locked us in the building."

"We could have gotten out easily. Bubbles just needed to turn the generators on again and disable the systems."

The little Monkey stuck her tongue out at the Jaguar, only making him laugh loudly and throw a spoon at her.

As they began to pile their plates with food, the vegetarians, Wilny, Lana, and Saffron getting first pick, they began to break off into small discussions of their own. Kat and Raoul who were sat next to Jett and Prince began to have a discussion on various sporting events coming up and joking about how skinny Raoul was, with Saffron and Malana piping up every now and then with a childish need to be included, whilst Beth chatted to Bubbles about the mission and the technology of Delta.

"How long are you staying in London for?" Storm asked, letting Crow get the gammon for her.

"A week. Need to check in with the headquarters and see mum." Meaning Asena who had raised him as much as she had raised Storm.

Storm grimaced. "Ah, you'll probably hear a lot of bitching from Rex about me."

"I already have."

"*Yay.*"

"What did you expect? You didn't kill the Vulture girl, or bring her in. You knew she was a killer, yet you let her go."

Storm groaned loudly and pulled her wings up to shield herself.

"I know I know. Rex has been over this already and how I've put people at risk for not *'dealing'* with her because everything I do is a thousand times worse than what he does." She frowned at him from beneath the shadows of her feathers. "I didn't feel good about hurting a pregnant teenager, so I didn't."

She prepared for an in-depth lecture on how she could have been far more badly hurt or killed, but instead Crow gently draped a wing across her back and patted her broken arm.

"His face must have been a picture when you told him to get fucked." He smirked at her, dark eyes glittering. "I'm proud of you for putting him in his place. Heaven knows he needs it."

A small and pleased smile spread across Storm's face.

He hated Rex almost as much as she did.

"But it really was a stupid idea to let that Eagle go after her." He scoffed, making her face drop back into a frown once more. "What were you thinking?"

"That's what I said." Wilny chuckled. Storm bumped Crow into Wilny with her wing and gave them a reprimanding fang filled snarl.

"Can you both just *not.*"

"Well, it was a stupid decision."

"I don't want to talk about it anymore."

They both made a mocking *'Oooh'* sound, and Crow began to teasingly poke her side to annoy her further until she plucked a feather from his head.

"Oh, will you boys just go back to sweet talking each other with your talents and let me eat in peace."

"Fine then, we will. Miss Mardy-arse." Crow smirked, fluffing his feathered head up and turning his back to her to talk to Wilny. She rolled her eyes and let her wings stretch out behind her.

"You're expanding your talent well." He purred softly, to the Hummingbird sat next to him. "You should be able to move on to new skills soon. I'm proud of you."

Wilny's tailfeathers flicked about in pride, catching the light with a shimmer.

"Thank you! I saw you coming this time."

"I saw you had your eye on me when I entered."

"Well you're too large to slip into anywhere unnoticed."

A loud spluttering cough from Kat on the other side of the table interrupted everyone's conversation, and she began laughing hysterically to herself.

"Katana. Behave." Scolded Beth disapprovingly.

Kat however, didn't stop laughing and soon got Jett, Prince and even Storm going as she tried to explain herself between gasps of ragged breath.

Crow grinned slyly for a moment and glanced at Wilny. After a few seconds, he himself began to cough as he got a snippet of images from Crow on the innuendos.

"Stop with the mind reading stuff!" Kat hissed at him between gasps for breath, "Let them use their imaginations!"

Raoul looked back and forth in confusion, when a prickle across his scalp and suddenly a stream of knowledge began to fill his mind as Crow began to project thoughts to him. In a blink, he found himself staring at his own gawping face from the point of view of Kat, the feeling of irritation at Crow in his mind as the vestiges of an image in her mind's eye dispersed into a strange haze that left Raoul with a strange feeling in his gut. Then quickly altering the viewpoint to where Crow was sat. A peculiar sensation came over him as he felt his back muscles twist and flex, fingers and hands seemingly in the wrong place as his wings flexed, yet he felt himself holding the fork that Crow had in his hand and tasting the gammon as he ate it.

The sudden flood of thoughts left Raoul's head reeling with an uncomfortable disassociation. They weren't his thoughts; they weren't his feelings. He knew he didn't feel annoyed or gleefully mischievous at that time, and it was disconcerting to find himself looking at his body through Crow and Kat's eyes simultaneously.

"Kat!" Wilny rasped, trying to get his breath back from nearly choking. "No more *friend-fictions* at the dinner table! You're going to give me a heart attack!"

"Stop ruining my fun!"

Raoul frowned and looked over at Kat as the thoughts vanished from his mind as quickly as it had begun.

"What is friend-fiction?"

"Well-" She began, but she was stopped by Wilny throwing a lump of gammon at her face in order to silence her. Kat froze then swiftly picked up her knife and threw it at Wilny who managed to dodge at the last second.

"It's so nice to see the older ones getting along isn't it?" Saffron sighed to Malana who was staring in confusion at the scene, which had begun to escalate to an over-the-table knife fight as Kat picked up Bubbles' knife and began to fight with him. It caused a giggle amongst the others, but they carried on eating regardless of the mini sword fight that was happening in front of their eyes.

When they had finished fighting and eating dinner, they all went to the living room to play some games as they waited for their stomachs to settle before they had dessert. Humans would have found the after-dinner game strangely old fashioned, but the Daggers loved it as it usually reduced them to tears of laughter or brought out the competitive sides of the quietest ones, such as Malana and Bubbles who on the last round of charades had begun to have an arm wrestle to declare a winner.

They were broken up by the arrival of dessert, which calmed them all down to tell anecdotes of how the Daggers all met, and how Raoul and Malana joined the Rogues.

Raoul was surprised by the Daggers since all save for Crow, had been out for only two years and they had all rescued each other in some way, with most of them having come from Atlas.

Jett and Prince were both once humans who had been caught by Core after they slept in a youth hostel in Cambodia during their gap year backpacking holiday and had been made transhuman – which explained to Raoul how they didn't seem quite right.

Saffron was a standard quickly produced Monkey Synth from Atlas, made for whenever ARCDA needed to trial run new drugs and diseases, and didn't want to test it upon the much more valuable Preternaturals. Bubbles and Crow, as they had explained it, were two of the first non-mammalian-based Synths to have been produced, Bubbles having come from America and Crow from Scotland. Whereas Crow had been out of ARCDA for as long as Storm had, Bubbles had remained in Atlas for nearly all her life.

Even though they all had stories of hell in ARCDA they all were bright and cheerful people with plans and hopes for the future. Although, when it came to sharing stories, Crow avoided all topic of what bunker he and Storm had originated from and instead skipped to all the fun stories about how the two had been as teenagers, most of which had involved a lot of fighting, alcohol, nudity, and bets that escalated out of control.

They spoke for hours, all gathered up together in the small living room either squashed on the sofas or sat on the floor, until it became so late that the first rays of early summer sunlight began to tinge the sky green. The two youngest had fallen asleep and they others were all beginning to yawn. Wilny had to take Malana upstairs to her room and with that, the Daggers began to move.

"We should get going." Crow yawned helping the boys to their feet. "A short stop at headquarters and we're off to Wales once again."

"Back to the mountains once more." Storm smiled at her brother, getting the door for them and watching the boys stagger out and down to their motorhome.

"We'll see ya' again soon."

"Drag the boys over to me sometime and I'll introduce them to a few sports, maybe even make them do some decathlon training." He laughed quietly, gently pushing the languid Bubbles out the door ahead of him, before gently hugging his sister. "See ya later, Silverbird."

"Later, Crowbar." She smiled and shut the door behind him. Turning back to the living room she sighed at the peace. The house felt very empty and silent with almost everyone having gone to bed, but she was glad to have had the Daggers over.

Smiling, she took herself to the garden and began to tidy away the table until Wilny came downstairs to help her wash up.

"I've put Malana to bed, Raoul is asleep on the sofa and Kat is probably in her room writing." Wilny gave a little dramatic shudder at Kat's hobbies.

"And Beth doesn't sleep." Storm noted, looking to the kitchen ceiling with a smirk at Beth's room above them. A small thud made Beth's approval known as she heard Storm. Between them both they cleaned the dishes and moved the chairs back inside with a quiet efficiency, doing their best not to wake those who slept.

"You're going to have to sign me up for a mission with Crow." Wilny beamed at her as he scrubbed the plates, long tailfeathers swishing about behind him. "He said he might be heading out to Italy next time with what new information he received."

"You just want to hang out with your *Bro*." Storm chuckled quietly, looking over her shoulder at him as she put the dried plates away. The dinner with Crow having brought out her accent again, and she rolled her R's into an unintended growl.

"Try not to fall in love with him, he's already spoken for."

"I know my boundaries, and besides he's cool and he's teaching me how to expand my talents. What? Why are you giggling like that?"

"*Expand your talents.*"

"Oh sweet- You are so immature sometimes."

She bumped him with her wing playfully.

"*Aaah,*" she said, "but you wouldn't want me any other way, now would you?"

"The day you don't giggle at someone saying, '*There's a storm coming*' is the day I know they've replaced you with a clone." He smirked down at her, bumping her back. Storm turned away from him and began brewing a tea, which she then offered to Wilny.

"What's this?" He sniffed and recoiled away from it. "Urgh. Valerian and lavender. Again?"

"It'll help you sleep."

"I don't have a problem sleeping, give it to Beth." He brought up a glossy indigo wing to separate himself from the strange smelling tea.

Storm folded her arms and scowled at him. "Well, have you at least taken your beta-blockers for today?"

"My heart is fine Storm." He said with a little pat to his chest, before adding with a little smirk. "So long as you don't put six-hundred volts into it again at who knows how many amps."

"Hey now, you shot me. It was completely deserved."

"You killed me Storm. I was deaded."

"I resuscitated you too; why do you always leave that bit out! You owe me your undead-life you dick." She hooted, giving him a little shove. "Don't you forget who it was who gave you CPR and dragged your dead ass through Core to find a defibrillator!"

"Or who punched me full in the face when I came to."

"I panicked."

They laughed. It was the only way they could deal with their first encounter with one another when Wilny was still an Elite in Core. Dramatic and eventful as it had been, they had soon found that the combination of stress caused to Wilny along with the electroshock caused by Storm had damaged the cells of his heart, causing it to beat irregularly from there on after.

After a long argument over his wellbeing, he had agreed to take medication to help his heart, and while they had offered him medication for his PTSD, he refused to take them, instead opting for herbalist remedies such as lavender, chamomile, and valerian. They had no access to the medicine or care that Atlas could provide to fix it properly, and so they made do.

"Go on then, Wilny, drink up."

"I don't want this."

"Wilny."

"You don't need to keep giving me things to-"

"I know, I know. You don't want me to help you, but please just drink it before you go to bed." She kept her voice soft and gentle.

"I'm not a child! I can take care of myself Storm."

"No, but how are you meant to take care of Malana and Raoul if you can't focus? You're an arse when you're sleep deprived and if anything happens I know you'd never forgive yourself."

The two stared silently at each other, holding each other's gaze until Wilny submitted and looked down.

"Alright. For the kids." He sighed, drying his hands and taking the tea from her. With a sour face, he took one sip, then taking one of his many bottles of honey squeezed as much as he could into the mug to sweeten it.

"Oh! And don't forget," Storm stated with a smile as he began to drink, "tomorrow you have your counselling session with Jenna first thing."

Wide-eyed, Wilny paused and swallowed down the mouthful, staring straight ahead in realisation.

"*Shit.*"

11

"How are you doing out here Wilny? Have you been sleeping well?"

"Fine. Perfectly fine."

"You don't need to lie here. Remember Wilny, this is a safe space where you can speak freely."

"I am aware."

"You're tense. Are you uncomfortable?"

"*You* make me uncomfortable."

He *really* did not like the counselling sessions with Jenna Hart, the Rioteers' resident psychologist and made no attempt to hide that fact. Something always felt '*off*' about her in such a way that despite the fact that she spoke with a very hushed and calmed tone of voice. He didn't trust it. Part of him suspected that despite being wheelchair bound, that the psychologist might have been a Preternatural of some Origin or another, but it was hard to tell.

'*Maybe she's secretly an Ursa,*' he mused to himself, thinking back to the bear-based Synths he had encountered before. She certainly had the demeanour of a grizzly bear.

"Have you been having any more nightmares?" She asked softly, watching and noting down his behaviour into the tablet.

He was very tense and was making it painfully clear that he wanted to leave, despite only having just arrived. He impatiently drummed his fingers on the arm of the chair, eyes fixed on the bricks behind her head, foot bouncing erratically and shimmering wings that were tautly arced either side of him vibrating with anxiety.

"*No.*"

"I'm only asking you because you look tired."

"I've been going to bed late. We had the Daggers over yesterday and I didn't go to bed until four."

"And how did you feel about that?"

"Fine. I like the Daggers."

"Wilny…" She sighed, growing tired of the circular conversations they always ended up having whenever they were scheduled to meet. "We want you to get better, we can't help you if you don't tell us what it is that's troubling you-"

"-I'm *fine.*"

She gave him a hard look from beneath her eyebrows. Of all of the patients she had to take care of, Wilny was proving to be the orneriest of them all.

"Tell me about the last week. What has troubled or annoyed you recently?"

"Not much. I was pissed off when we ran out of honey and when I was told that I wasn't allowed to use the shooting range, *again*. Seriously, it's been months now since I fired a gun, when am I being put back in commission?"

"You know you're not allowed a firearms weapon until you are deemed fit to carry one without putting people at risk."

"And yet you let me have access to knives. Sound logic right there. Outstanding."

"You're getting on my tits with that tone of yours mister." She retorted sharply as she typed down her evaluation. The sharp reply caught him off-guard as usually Jenna had endless amounts of patience with Synths, however today she didn't appear to be in the mood for his attitude. The painted nails rapped on the screen of the tablet with small clicks as she continued to type.

Wilny shifted again in his chair, leaning forward to seem interested. He forced his wings to be still, aware that he was testing her patience.

"Jenna," He said softly, attempting a persuasive approach. He smiled at the psychologist, sat up straight with his hands folded on his lap. "I know you're trying to help me, but even Storm thinks I'm fine and she is my leader. She wouldn't let me take care of Malana and Raoul if she didn't think that I couldn't handle it. I'm sure that she'll tell you about it."

Jenna didn't fall for the smile; she knew better. As the Rioteers residential behavioural psychologist for both humans and Synths, there wasn't much that could escape her.

"She has." Jenna responded coyly, mimicking his charming tone. "She told me that since they both arrived your nightmares have been pretty much nightly. She said that after the second week you started having them and you woke the house up screaming, and any time she offers help, you insist you don't need it."

Wilny's smile dropped. It was true that he had been having a lot of nightmares recently, but he didn't think that they were connected to Raoul and Lana's arrival, or that Storm would tell anyone about it. He didn't remember screaming, but he did remember Storm pinning him to the floor and then held him and comforted him as he cried uncontrollably, before making him some honeyed tea and sitting with him until he fell asleep again. As much as he didn't want it, Storm had been the biggest help through his nightmares, and he had yet to thank her for it.

"You've not taken any lavender and valerian for the anxiety, have you?"

"I...drank some last night, so now we don't have any left," He grumbled, scratching his neck in discomfort as she began to stare judgementally at him again, "It smells like feet and makes honey taste weird."

"It helps you sleep. If not, I'll prescribe amitriptyline or-"

"*I'm! Fine!*" He snarled at her, leaping to his feet and flaring his wings out either side of him. "I don't need any drugs! Or any of this bullshit! I am not *sick*!"

The woman didn't recoil or flinch, she just watched him, waiting to see his next move. Seeing that his outburst had been uncalled for, when she was only trying to help him, Wilny apologised and sat down again.

Jenna shook her head and quickly typed another line of evaluation into the tablet with rapid little clicks. After a long and awkward silence, she sighed heavily and rubbed the bridge of her nose.

"It's been several months now, and you're still not going to try and come to terms with what happened?" She asked. "You're not even going to begin to speak about it even though you know and understand that it will help you?

Silence.

Dropping his gaze to the floor, Wilny remained still. He had only mentioned Featherhead to Raoul, but he still hadn't told him the full story. The girls clearly knew what had happened and so he had never spoken about it with them, and there was no way he would be able to explain himself to Malana. His nightmares were his alone to endure.

"I've had enough for today." He said sharply, getting to his feet again. "I'm sorry for wasting your time."

"Very well. I'll schedule another appointment for two weeks' time, for your five minutes as usual."

Wilny sneered to himself and grabbed the handle to open the door and leave, but as he did, Jenna spoke again.

"Wilny."

Trying to remain composed, he looked over his shoulder at her, trying to keep the irritation from his expression. Jenna's glare and grizzly bear demeanour overshadowed his forced composure.

"I know you don't trust me, but I hope you trust your team enough to confide your troubles in them."

"I…" He hesitated, before steadying himself. "I trust them."

"Can you send in Raoul and Malana please? I would like to see how they're both coping here."

With a sigh, he opened the door. Sat on the two chairs outside were Malana and Raoul, who stopped mid-conversation as soon as he stepped out.

"In you go. Jenna wants to see how you're both doing." Wilny smiled to them both, gesturing for them to head inside. Raoul looked surprised and slowly rose, helping Malana off the chair and taking her hand.

"Alone?"

"She's not scary, Puppy, well…not all the time she isn't, all she wants to do is talk to see how you are both doing and ask a few questions. You'll have to translate for Lana."

"Why aren't you coming with us?"

"I…need time to myself."

The concern on Raoul's face made him feel a little better, knowing that he was worried about him.

"It's nothing serious, I just don't like these sessions," He reassured him lightly patting his shoulder, "You're tough enough to handle it on your own."

"Thank you."

"I'll be by the rings. Meet me there when you're finished."

Raoul nodded and gently tugged Lana's hand to lead her into the small office. She resisted slightly, looking up at him with sad golden eyes seeing that Wilny wasn't going to join them. Wilny immediately dropped to a knee to give the little girl a reassuring hug.

"Trust Raoul." He said softly to her with a smile, brushing a loose coil of hair back behind her feathered ear tufts. She pouted a little, and though her English was limited she understood what he meant and nodded.

"That's my girl. We'll get ice cream afterwards. I promise."

The thought of ice-cream made her smile and hugging him tightly around his neck before she followed Raoul inside the room. Smiling wistfully, Wilny sighed.

He did not regret his decision to take care of the two newest and youngest Rogues, even if their presence did stir up nightmares and terror of failure. They needed him and he needed to take care of them, that was what was most important.

Straightening up, he pushed the clawing nightmares out of his head, turned on his heel and headed off to the sparring rings for some Recovery.

The Rioteer headquarters was a very elaborate warren of tunnels and chambers, which if you didn't know your way around could lead you into a circle around the same area over and over again. A few months ago, Wilny would have gotten himself lost after exiting the small psychologist office. Now however he could navigate his way through the redbrick tunnels with ease. He could now even find some of the emergency boltholes that were hidden at random intervals around the headquarters that would have been overlooked by any new or uninformed individuals. Not even many of the Rioteers knew where these exits were, and it was only thanks to Kat that Wilny even knew.

The sparring rings, however, were part of one of the three largest chambers, where people could go and practice self-defence or if they felt like fighting, could take it out on each other in a safe space. It may have seemed odd to have an area of their sanctuary dedicated to fighting, but since they were in a situation where they could be attacked by ARCDA or Hasekura at any time, they needed to be able to defend themselves so that they would not be so easily taken away or killed. Most of them enjoyed the sparring, and it had even become a form of recovery therapy for some individuals. All fights were to be refereed and were not allowed to leave the boundaries of the ropes.

As Wilny entered the chamber a pair of bright blue wings immediately caught his eye amidst the small gathering of Preternaturals and Canids who were sparring in one of the four dedicated areas.

He greeted Kat, joining her on the bench to watch the fight going on in front of them.

"Hey J-Pop."

"Hey K-Pop. You bailed on your session already?" She asked offhandedly, not taking her eyes off the fight.

One of Asena's pack members was fighting the darkhaired Preternatural they had rescued, and from the jeering he was hearing, he had managed to piss off more than a few people, who were all gathered around the ring edge. People cheered on a black Wolf-Canid in the ring. The flagging Preter slammed a fist into the Canid's jaw only to have the Wolf bite the Preter on the arm with a sickeningly loud crunch and toss him out the ring into the wall of the chamber. The crowd cheered and applauded, Kat and Wilny included, then when the Preter failed to lift himself off the floor, they sent forward two people to drag him to the medical ward.

"Yes. I told her I was coming here for some *Recovery* with Roux." He answered, finally taking his eyes from the fight to look at her. He stopped clapping and frowned at her hand, which she was cradling to her chest. "What happened to you?"

"Oh, this?" She showed him her purpling knuckles with impish smile.

Kat rarely got bruised in the Rings, she barely so much as smudged her eyeliner in a fight, and so it must have meant she had given someone a feral punch. Chuckling slightly, he gave a small nod for her to explain.

"So, we had a batch of new ZHANG-origin Preters come in from North America this morning. Turns out this entire batch have never seen a girl before in real life, let alone a Tribrid, and have only learnt from their TV screenings and occasional bit of *literature* how to behave around them."

"*Oh shit.*" He said softly. The ZHANG Preternaturals were just one of seventeen types of Preternaturals, and from his experience they were not made very well.

"How many did you kill?"

"None this time, although one is in a critical condition after trying to slap my ass and call me a pretty kitty and a *geisha*." She explained, knotting a wave of hair around her finger, and pulling it so it bounced. "I may have fractured his skull and several ribs in the process of bruising my hand."

"And the rest of the batch?"

"Oh, they quickly fell into line after four dozen broken fingers and a sliced-up face each. Their diamond skin was so fragile I didn't even bother with a knife; I just used my claws. I swear all the current versions of the Preters are made to be fuckboys, but I guess that's what you get for growing them quick and not spending enough time on teaching them manners."

Wilny smirked and shook his head, entertained by the way Kat spoke about fighting in the same tone she used as when she talked about buying a new set of clothes. There was little she adored more than a good fight, a new dress, a sharp knife, and a pretty girl. All four things combined was a cocktail guaranteed to make her week.

She laughed at him suddenly. "You're making that face again."

"Which one."

"The stunned one." She tilted her head and smiled sweetly at him, fluttering here eyelashes in mock flirtation, "Did you forget that I used to break men's fingers and *shinai* for fun?"

"Come on J-Pop, you make *everyone* forget that, not just me."

"*Aaah.*" She mused with a grin, stretching her butterfly-blue wings out behind her and arching her back until it clicked, "I love being a honey trap. It's so satisfying to me to not be what they expected when they end up getting their ass kicked."

"*Niña!* Shoulders back and cut that shit out!"

They both glanced down the room to the furthest ring. A glimpse of black hair and people beginning to quickly scurry away from the ring signalled that Roux Cuélebre, was present and pissed off.

"Though I guess her method of *be-outright-absolutely-terrifying* works too." Kats ears flicked back at the sound of the shouts. Wilny trembled at the sound of Roux's voice.

A rare and remarkable creation, she was one of the original Preternaturals and what the first two origins – DRACO and VIRGO – were based upon. However, as stunningly beautiful as she was, Roux was also a self-proclaimed, one hundred percent, cold-hearted undiluted bitch who struck fear into the hearts of men. She was not someone to mess with.

"You should probably go over-"

"-Where's Storm and Beth? Still in a meeting with Rex, Crow and Asena?" Wilny cut Kat off before she could finish her sentence. "Maybe I should go look for them."

Rolling her eyes, Kat stood up, roughly dragged Wilny to his feet and began to shove him across the room in the direction of the furthest ring. Wilny tried to dig his heels in, but with a pair of clawed hands pushing against the sensitive spot between his wings there was no way to fightback.

"Oh no you don't. You're not going to delay the inevitable that easily."

"Kat, why!"

"Because if you don't, she will *literally* incinerate you."

Reaching the ring, they found that the Preternatural already busy with another girl, an Avio, who seemed to be cowering in fear and crying.

"Maybe I should come back later–"

"No."

"But Kat!" He whispered, opalescent-blue eyes wide in terror. "She might *actually* kill me! It's Tuesday! Everyone knows she's more likely to kill on Tuesdays! Statistics are no joke!"

"Are you really that scared of her? And here I thought that you thought that Storm was the most dangerous thing out here."

"Storm, Asena, Roux, you, the traffic most days. You're all dangerous, but she's just a monster! The woman has diamond skin and is a certified psychopathic *arsonist*! I'm sure she's a dragon Synth or something, and you know; *Fire!*"

"Just because you're afraid of fire-"

"With good reason!"

Kat shook her head and shouldered him closer into the Dragon's view.

"You're still going to have to see her."

Despite his exaggerations, there was some truth behind her dragon-like descriptions as Roux Cuélebre was renowned for her fiery talents and rage.

The way she had been created resulted in her skin being near impermeable from sharp objects, the structure of her skin more resembling the fine microscopic scales of a shark which had been modified additionally to produce a crystalline casing on top, and so giving her the so called '*Diamond Skin*'. It couldn't be cut, couldn't be pierced and couldn't be burnt without considerable effort or force. Many other Preternaturals also had this trait because of her, but not to the same degree.

However, if having diamond skin wasn't enough, whoever had created her had sought to give her an additional talent of being able to ignite her skin on *fire*. This was done through releasing a gas through her pores that could be ignited by a single spark, usually created from the friction of rubbing her crystallised skin together. Roux called this dangerous and unstable ability, *Pyrros*.

"Keep your hands up, Comet! Away from your face!" Roux barked down at the girl, who kept shaking and hugging her heavily scarred arms tight to her body. The girl whimpered a pitiful apology, trying to compose herself and put her hand up in a defensive position.

Her long narrow wings fluttered behind her, a rich gradient of sea green to midnight purple with wingtips that looked as though they had been gently brushed with molten gold that turned back to white. As she fanned them and caught the light, each and every feather shimmered, mirroring the gold tipped primaries as the colour lined the filaments, giving her wings a gleaming warmth with every movement.

"Isn't that...the girl that Avarken rescued?" Wilny asked, frowning a little as he began to recognise her from her metallic wings. "We took the Canids out who abused her when we found Raoul, didn't we?"

"Comet? Yeah." Kat nodded, glancing at Wilny with a cocky smile. "It turns out that she's a Hummingbird-base just like you. Though I think a little prettier."

"How rude!" Wilny gave a dramatic gasp of feigned offence. "I'm just as pretty as she is-"

"Wilny Mira! *¡Ven aquí ahora, Azulejo!*" Roux barked at him, making him flinch. "Get over here now!"

"Yes ma'am!" He stood to attention with a salute, and then proceeded to march into the ring before he realised what he was doing.

She stared him down as he climbed into the ring, dressed in practical black gym clothes rather than her usual leather jacket.

"I'm over running slightly, but you can help out here." She spoke very quickly with a thick Spanish accent, which only emphasised her tone of irritation.

Comet's eyes went wide as she saw Wilny step up to Roux's side and stepped into a competitive stance. She retreated in fear, pulling her metallic wings up to shield herself, but she watched him with an expression of recognition and confusion.

"W-why-"

"You can't keep fighting me. Wilny here is a trained soldier and knows what you're going through, so he can find fault with your stance and technique, and I can kill two birds with one stone so to speak."

"B-but Roux I can't fight him! He's-"

"A man, yes yes, there are many of them about unfortunately. Face your fears Comet and stop whining." She pulled the cowering girl over by her arm, ignoring her fearfulness.

"Roux, are you sure that you should be-" He was cut off as the woman glowered at him. There was just something about her behaviour, which unnerved even a hardened soldier such as himself. It was near on feral, but Preternaturals couldn't turn Feral…as far as he knew.

Roux huffed angrily and pushed Comet forward, forcing her hands up into a defensive poise and then circled them both, checking Comet's stance from various angles.

"This is for her benefit not yours. Stand there, look pretty so she can practice."

Obeying the order with a sigh Wilny adjusted his stance so that Comet could attack.

"I…I can't Roux." She stuttered, not moving an inch closer to him than she needed to, "Not against him, I don't want to do it."

She had tensed up so much that her wings were visibly vibrating, casting a gold aura around them. Her dark amethyst-coloured eyes were filled with tears. each and every single pearly olive-grey feather that covered her face and shoulders, were raised in fear.

"Fine then. Watch his techniques and see if you can copy them." Roux snapped, whipping out a serrated hunting knife from a sheath on her thigh and thrusting it hilt first into Wilny's hand. Wilny adjusted his grip on it, knowing what was about to happen.

He focused, musing and causing time to appear to fall into slow motion between them as Roux's fist drew back and her stance shifted. Fast as his reactions were, with his perception altered and sped up every movement felt heavy and dragging as he drew his wings forward into a rapid series of beats and sprung backwards, but it allowed him to plan and premeditate a strike. However, it also meant that Roux too could plan an attack during this hyper altered time.

Time snapped into motion again as he stopped musing, and Roux swiped at thin air before spinning on her heel and sinking into a low foot sweep that caught him off guard. Wilny cursed internally.

Roux changed her fighting style regularly, always keeping people from understanding her tells and twitches, though today she was clearly fighting in Baguazhang style with the sweeping circling movements. Angling the knife, he parried a strike from her with a sound of metal on sandpaper as the blade skimmed off her skin without so much as leaving a mark.

The two circled, striking and blocking each other's attacks until Wilny foolishly made a lunge towards her that over stepped. She dodged and caught his wing as he passed, gripping it tightly and throwing him off balance with a kick to his knee. Before he muse once more, she had disarmed and had him pinned down to the floor with a foot pressed between his wings.

"Yield! I yield! *Cojeme!*" He groaned loudly, feeling a sharp stabbing pain down his spine.

"There," Roux said with an approving smile, releasing him and turning back to the girl, "now it's your turn, Comet."

Comet backed away from them both and then slumped to her knees hugging herself. Roux groaned in irritation.

"Comet, get up off the floor, you're acting like a baby."

Wilny felt a little sorry for the girl for the treatment she was receiving from Roux. He couldn't ask her to be gentler as Roux didn't do gentle, and she definitely didn't do empathy. She was a dragon right to her core; made of rage, cloaked in fire and diamonds, built to fight and burn the world to ash.

"I don't want to." Comet sobbed from the floor, pulling her exquisite wings around her to cocoon herself from the outside world. "I'm not like you! Let me go back to my room, I'm tired and I want to sleep."

Roux let out a snarl of frustration. Giving up wasn't an option that Roux would allow.

As much as he felt sorry for her, even Wilny was starting to feel a little irritable with the girl's attitude and unwillingness to defend herself. It made him question how she had even managed to survive this long.

"*Joder*, don't you dare try and make an excuse to me." She snarled, grabbing the girl by her arm and pulling her roughly to her feet. "You're using your experiences as a shield to hide behind. You may have had shit happen to you, but so has everyone, both in here and out there in the real world. If you keep running and hiding because you got a few scars well I got bad news for you *niña*, you can't hide forever."

"I'm not-!"

"There you go again!" She sneered, getting up into the Avios' face, dark eyes blazing with fury. "Acting like a little *pet* who runs for cover and cries her eyes out. I've seen Risio boys who are less whiny than you, *niña*."

"Stop-"

"-No. You've had it easy here for too long *Pet!* The humans may be sympathetic with your cry-baby attitude, but you're not fooling me. If you're going to keep acting like this then you might as well crawl back to the hole you were saved from you ungrateful immutable *pinche coña!*"

Comet gasped, clearly having understood the insult, and advanced towards the Preternatural with her wings and fan of short tailfeathers flared out behind her.

"Don't ever call me that you…you *bitch!*"

There was a sudden ripple in the world around them. Black wisps whipped through both Wilny and Roux's visions and pain burned across their minds with a siren blare. Wilny wanted to throw up as the ground shifted beneath his feet, but the sensation was familiar to him and in an instant, he realised that Comet had muser abilities like himself. It wasn't an uncommon talent, however the intensity of this was on a very different level to any muser he had experienced before.

"Bravo. You're finally showing your true colours." Roux chuckled, shaking off the black wisps from her mind and the punch that Comet had managed to land on her jaw. "So, you're not really scared at all. You're just angry."

The girl rubbed her eyes furiously in an attempt to not cry, red faced from the stress of being made upset.

"I'm no-"

"*Cállate*. Yes, you are. All broken people are quietly angry but cry because that's all they know how to do unless shown otherwise." She jerked her head at Wilny. "You're just as emotionally repressed as he is. You both need to bring up your regrets and rages and kick the shit out of them to clear your heads."

"I'm not emotionally repressed." Wilny said defensively.

"Yes, you are. You're hanging onto regrets and it is holding you down. You could both do with punching something. It's not good to hold onto anger. Do that and you'll turn into me." Roux sighed, brushing her mess of black hair from her face.

"Fists up! Wings out! Get skyborne since you're both birds." Stepping back and leaning against the elasticated barriers of the ring edge, arms folded across her chest.

Sighing with relief at the opportunity to not be training against Roux, Wilny snapped his wings out and took off, hovering five feet above the ring floor with a helicopter like thrum of wing beats. Being a hummingbird-based Avio, his wings beat fast, allowing him to hover very precisely and move about in pretty much any direction, but it exhausted him very quickly and caused a strain on his already damaged heart.

Comet looked to Wilny for reassurance from the ground whilst he hovered in the air, holding onto her hair with white knuckled fear. With a little silent gesture, he ushered for her to join him.

After a few small and very jerky wing beats, she managed to get into the air, into a very unstable hover in a blur of gold. Despite her being several inches shorter, her wings appeared to be far longer than his putting them at roughly seventeen feet to his sixteen, although she didn't seem to be a very good flier. Wilny lowered their height so that if she did fall, she wouldn't hit the ground too heavily.

"It's alright Comet." He said softly to reassure her. "You can hit me."

"A-are you sure?"

"Yes. Just don't hit me in the throat."

She took a deep breath and calmed herself before she struck out at him. With a very weak lunge, she flew forward, one arm outstretched to hit him and the other brought tightly to her chest.

Wilny avoided it easily.

"Don't punch with your wrist bent like that, you'll hurt yourself." He informed her. "And don't tuck your arms in it makes it harder to remain stable in the air."

"Go on *niña*, just let out that anger." Roux called to her, watching how Comet fared now that she was flying. She too seemed concerned about how poor her flying skills were. "Say out loud the words in your head if it helps just stop hitting like a baby."

Comet frowned and to correct her flight pattern, watching how Wilny used his body to move about the air and change the direction of his flight. Her short fan of tailfeathers twitched and tilted as she tried to emulate his movements. Their wings thrummed loudly as they darted quickly about their ring. Even with Wilny's long tailfeathers and their disk like ends which caused drag, he was still the faster and more agile of the two.

"Stupid…stupid…Stupid!" She began to mutter as she lunged and struck at him again, getting faster and more precise with each strike. Wilny watched the girl's expression. There was something about her face which reminded Wilny of Storm. Determined, focused, eyes sharp and teeth sharper, although even though she was chasing him around the ring, there was nothing feral about it. He slowed down a little to allow her the chance to actually hit him and when she did, her plum-coloured eyes lit up with a sense of achievement.

He knew that most the Rioteers didn't seen why Roux promoted them to release their anger and aggression by fighting when they were meant to be rehabilitating them, but he could justify it as a form of therapy to help people like Comet regain their confidence.

"Stupid…*bastards*!" She swore, now trying out an attack with a kick to Wilny's rapidly beating wings, which he managed to avoid easily.

Roux burst out laughing below. "Bastards, now that's something I've not heard you say before. *Gilipollas* is what you should yell!"

Comet ignored her and continued her attack, occasionally managing to hit Wilny. "Stupid wolfy bastards! I hope they die!"

Wilny shot upwards over her head as she lunged at him. She was beginning to slow down with her corrections and started to go red faced from the exertion.

"Okay Comet. That's enough for today." Roux signalled, clapping her hands as she saw Comet beginning to tire. "You did well. Wilny come down too."

Wilny landed quickly, taking several deep breaths after the small exercise. His heart rate was up, but it wasn't too dangerous that he'd need some time in the medical room, a few minutes to cool down would set it right. Comet however didn't come straight down. She lingered, hovering above them in the air.

"Comet?" Wilny called up.

Comet out a sob and stopped beating her wings suddenly, plummeting like a stone out of the air. She landed heavily, staggering and falling to her knees.

"I hate them, I hope they die!" She was shaking and beginning to cry again.

He watched her wings arch and tense, her tail feathers flicked sharply. She was nervous and mistrustful, anxious. Wilny stepped over to her, concerned that she might use her muser talent by accident. Musers could do a lot of damage if they weren't kept under control, often causing insanity or trauma for victims of unexpected mental attacks.

"Hey now, it's alright." He assured her, using the same gentle tone as he did for Malana when she had a nightmare or was upset. The same as what Storm did for him.

"Comet, look at me. It's alright." Wilny said softly, kneeling so he was at the same level as she was. "We took care of them. They're all dead. You're safe."

Comet looked up at him, unnatural purple eyes wide in disbelief, tears still rolling down her cheeks.

Up close and with her now still, Wilny's gut twisted in horror and pity as he saw deep slices from claws and punctures from Canid teeth which covered her arms.

They still looked very raw. The damage was deep but there were also the older twisted scars of burns. Wilny shuddered. Burn scars were hard to heal.

"You...you killed them?" She asked cautiously, narrowing her eyes at him. She didn't believe him. He could feel her beginning to muse, although there was no give-away sensation of a buzzing across the back of his skull, but instead the ghostly scent of fur, burning plastic, and keratin. Musers could affect all of the senses, as well as emotions and memories.

Thinking for a moment of how to help, Wilny mused, pushing forward his mental field to Comet so that she could feel his sentiments. Rarely did he muse this way, as he only allowed Crow to touch upon how he was feeling and what he was thinking, but with this Avio so distraught and anxious, he needed her to trust him.

"They're all gone now. You're safe."

"Are you sure?"

"I'm sure. They're not coming back."

Pausing in thought, Comet's face softened and in a moment of exhaustion, she slumped forward. Her metallic wings draped across the floor. The visual disturbances receded and Wilny breathed a relief.

Standing, Wilny offered out his hand to her.

"Come on, let's take you to the canteen and get you a nectarine and mango smoothie. I'm sure you'll love it, if you haven't tried it."

Bleary eyed and dazed, Comet cautiously took his hand and allowed him to help her to her feet. The moment she was standing, she brushed his hand away and hugged herself.

"I...I've not tried that before..." She said shyly, pulling her metallic wings around her shoulders. She was still mistrustful, but she was looking at him searchingly as if analysing him for ill intent. Wilny smiled, musing again so that she could see the truth in him and let her know that he just wanted to help.

"Also, honey! I'm sure that you'll like that!"

Roux cleared her throat next to him, casting a sudden spike of fear into Wilny's heart.

"You still have to do an hour here."

"I'll just take Comet to the canteen and then I'll be right back."

"If you don't return within ten minutes, I'm dragging you back by your tailfeathers." She promised, narrowing her dark eyes at him.

Comet gave a little bleat of laughter, feeling Wilny's genuine terror, before clearing her throat. Retreating, and so gently tugging Comet's hand he led her out of the rings before the Dragon could spit fire at him.

Kat watched them leave and smirked to herself, having been observing the scene from the bench. She quite enjoyed watching Wilny show Comet how to fight and fly.

As they left, she observed Comet flinch a little when they neared the Canids, stepping to the other side of Wilny so that she was further away from them, and how Wilny suddenly put his wing out behind her to shield her from the stares of the others.

"How come he never spars with me?" A despondent voice asked from behind Kat.

"Storm!" Kat flinched, nearly falling off the bench. "Don't sneak up on people like that!" She hadn't even heard Storm arrive.

"I've been here a while. You were just too distracted by those two up there to notice." Storm smirked, rubbing Kat's ears gently. Kat began to blush and the fur and feathers of her tail rousing in a fluster.

Storm didn't notice as she chuckled at the disappearing shimmery tailfeathers of their hummingbird-Avio.

"I see Wilny is getting out of his sparring with Roux by charming Comet there."

"Was that a note of envy I heard there, Storm?" Kat smirked, round ears twitching she smoothed her feathers down.

"Or are you feeling lonely and just want to dance with someone."

"Are you offering?"

"You know I'd dance with you any day."

"Ah yes! Come dance with me my beloved *Sekhmet!*" Storm laughed dramatically, vaulting over the bench, taking Kat by her hand and kneeling before her. "Come dance a *pas de deux* with me so that we might rule a queendom together with the thighs of goddesses and good hair to match! May the blessings of Artemis be upon us!"

The Lioness drew an azure wing up to her face to hide her scarlet cheeks and muffle her unladylike snorting laughter as Storm kissed the back of her hand with a playful grin.

"An...*interesting* image, *Thunderbird*, but how did the meeting for getting that queendom go?"

"Just as you'd expect." Storm released her hand and sat down beside her on the bench.

"Rex got loud and angry, Crow threatened violence, but then Beth and Bubbles saved Crow's skin by coming up with something *interesting*." She smirked and handed Kat a folder. "They gathered some intrigue on Risio buyers, imports and exports and an upcoming Gala."

Kats eyes lit up with glee. "Tell me more, *Thunderbird*."

"They found the place holding the gala as well as uncovering info on three minor MP's and five senior managers of a transnational company, all who have funded Risio or bought children from them." Her grin widened, and the mischief glittered in her eyes., "Feel like doing a little gossiping to the media, Kat? I'm sure you'd be able to keep the money they give you for it."

"What kind of gossip?"

"Well, we have many, many, flavours on offer. We've got human trafficking of asylum seekers, fraud, embezzlement, a few different investors for Risio in here taking money from people they shouldn't, and even one or two who are guilty of nepotism on Hasekura's behalf who may be pushing drugs that are not safe for human use out to people."

"Terrifying. I love it." Kat's grin grew, her long canines showing and her blue feathers fluffed up in excitement. She loved a mission which allowed her to play with news hungry journalists.

"Two questions though. Will I get to dress up, and will I get to go to a fancy restaurant? I really want to go to Soho or Chelsea."

"If you want. I'll make Beth pay for the coffees and cakes, or the steaks and bourbon sauce if the journalist we find doesn't pay for you."

The Lioness shot to her feet and took the file from Storm's hands. Flicking through the files she purred with excitement, tail flicking from side to side.

"So," Storm grinned, watching Kat pace in glee. "What do you think?"

"This is going to be so much fun!"

12

It took a less than a week for Beth to set her plan up, and have it agreed to by Rex, as well as find a journalist willing to talk to one of them in public. Many were wary to take the bait, but they eventually hooked a reporter.

"Are we ready Asena?" Beth asked as she and Storm strode into one of the headquarters' offices.

Although they had done this enough that they didn't need to be supervised– as Beth was always very thorough with her plans– Rex had insisted that a Rioteer or Asena was to watch them, due to his increasing paranoia on how the Rogues conducted themselves.

The Empress didn't take her eyes off the screens in front of her, white-blonde ears flattened back against her head in anger whilst the little Canid-Cub, Caesar, played with her tail, seemingly unaware of the mood of the room.

"Just give me two minutes; I need to sort out this territory dispute between my children- *No.*" She snarled, at the screen. "I am not giving you any more than you need. You can barely manage what you already have, and Silver has already warned you already about trying to take charge of eastern European grounds when she's already set people up there."

"But mum-" complained the Canid on the right-hand screen, whilst a Pard on the left rolled her eyes- "she's got way more territory than I have and a much smaller pack!"

Asena clapped her hands to cut him off from speaking. He silenced immediately.

"When you're done behaving like a toddler, Marlowe. She has just as much land as you do, and does twice as much work, now if you aren't going to settle this diplomatically I will half both of your territories and fly out two new groups to take the land you're fighting over!"

"That's not fair!" The Canid whined, "It's no fun here after clearing out all the Atlas bunkers!"

"This is not about you Marlowe!" Her volume increased, and a reverberating growl could be heard beneath her words as she scolded him, fur bristling across her arms and shoulders.

"It's *not* about how much fun you're having! It's about keeping people alive and helping them! If you have yet to understand that, then I'm taking the entirety of North Italy and the Alps off you until you get your shit together! Do you understand me?"

Marlowe dropped his head in submission.

"Yes mam…I understand."

Asena snarled, "Good. Dismissed."

The screen went black as he logged off. She turned to the second screen. "You too Inks. I have things to do."

"Merci."

"Oh, and Inks; please don't wind him up anymore. I don't want him going stray on us. It's bad enough as it is already with Rex, I don't want to tell him that one of ours has gone off the radar. He's already wanting you all to wear electronic tags to track you with."

The Pard grinned, a slice of white against her black skin. "Alright, I'll try and not invade Sicily anytime soon." And with a small wave logged off too.

Sighing deeply Asena slumped down into her chair, letting the cub climb up onto her lap to be cuddled.

"Are Marley and Inks at it again?" Storm laughed, sitting up on the table next to her and swinging her legs, she stretched her wings and arms out behind her. Her arm was finally out of the cast and was now only wrapped in a wrist support, soon to be fully healed.

"Cats and Dogs, what do you expect." Asena sighed, cradling the cub to her chest. A bright smile spread across his face and the tiny auburn ears either side his head twitched as Asena rubbed behind them. "To think that they used to adore each other as kids."

"What happened?" A new voice made Beth shriek as she felt the breath down the back of her neck, and the tingle of muser abilities being used. She spun round and swung her fist into the face of the speaker, only to have her arm caught and for a wide grin of ragged teeth to be inches away from her face.

"Sweet fuckery- Where did you come from?" She bellowed, kicking the Chiro in the groin and crippling him to the floor. Groaning and curling his wings about him, he tried to laugh off the pain of taking a metal foot to his balls.

"Well, it all started way back when with some doctors who went; '*you know, humans are a bit shit really, let's make something better*' and so synthetically created a brand spanking new creature based on some bats, and-" He started with tears in his eyes.

Beth raised her foot again letting the three talon like digits splay and flex before bringing it down close to the leathery membrane of his wing.

"I mean what are you doing here?"

"They wouldn't let me go outside to church."

Beth cocked an eyebrow sceptically. "You're religious?"

"No, I just wanted to see how they'd react to me."

"Kinda like this I guess," She snapped and kicked him again, bringing him to his knees as she caught him in the crotch.

"Jeez." He groaned in pain. "For a disabled bird, you're pretty vicious."

"I'll disable your fucking breathing!"

"Kids, not now." Asena cut in before Beth tried to lacerate him again. "Can you please leave us Freeborn, the Rogues have stuff to do."

The Chiro tilted his head, blinking his black eyes slowly at Asena. Few people refused Asena's requests.

"Well, what happened between those two? I'm curious." Freeborn purred leaning on the table, his huge ears twitched a little as he picked up sounds from outside the office. He gave Beth a sly wink to which with a disgusted noise, she snapped her laptop open and proceeded to ignore him as much as possible.

"He couldn't stand to see her leading her own group and got jealous that she wasn't his second in command, so they argued, and she stabbed him in a fist fight." Asena explained nonchalantly with a shrug, directing him to a chair. "If you're determined to stay then sit down and keep quiet, we're busy."

With an enthusiastic grin, the Chiro sat down and wrapped his leathery wings around him in a blanket.

"I'll be silent as the grave, *Princess.*"

Snorting with disapproval at the name, she flicked her hair off her shoulder and set the toddler on the table beside the Chiro.

"If he speaks, bite him Cesare." She commanded the cub. The boy nodded and grinned at Freeborn, showing off his sharp little teeth. Freeborn recoiled away from the toddler as he wobbled to his feet and growled at him.

"And who is this?"

"Caesar. My son."

"*Wow.* How old is he? His teeth are bloody sharp."

"Only three."

"Years?"

"*Months.*" Asena chuckled. "They grow fast."

Mouth agape in shock, Freeborn laughed a little and petted the boy's head flinching every now and then as his tiny jaws were snapped at his fingers.

"Are you all prepped and ready to go girls?" Asena asked, turning away from Freeborn to watch the two Rogues set up.

"As always mum." Storm smiled, letting the Wolf run her fingers down the arch of her wing to her shoulder and straighten up several stray feathers. "It's just a small job so Wilny took the kids out to the park to get ice cream and go to the zoo. I know this is targeting Risio, but there's no need to drag them all in just to watch Kat talk."

"*Risio!*" Freeborn gasped excitedly teasing the little cub with his long tail and letting him chase and try to catch it. "You're hitting up my old home?"

Asena ignored him.

"Has Kat got the hearing clip on?"

"Mum, *really?* We've done this how many times?"

"I'm just making sure, so I can tell Rex honestly."

"*Yes*, I've got it in and I can hear you too if you're wondering." Kat's voice purred through the speakers with the chiming clink of ice in a glass. "Are you sure that he won't be able to hear your voices from it?"

"We test ran it with some Preters, if they can't hear it then a human can't either."

"So, where is she?" Asena asked, tail swishing every now and then. Freeborn watched them silently from across the room, curious as to what they were doing since it involved his old faction, Risio, with Caesar chewing on his tail.

"I'm in *The Old Star*." Kat answered, the tone of amusement clear in her voice, "Personally I'd have gone to *The Feathers* just for the irony."

"A pub? Really?" Asena seemed surprised by the choice of location, checking on Beth's where she had a map of the area up. It was right in the heart of everything, parliament, Buckingham palace, the treasury, various offices, ministries and departments, even the Thames and the London eye were not even two hundred meters away.

"The guy chose it, not me. I'd have gone for *the Star Tavern* since its way more criminally appropriate." Apologised Beth.

Kat's soft sigh could be heard through the speaker, along with the faint click of a door opening and closing from where she was sat. The microphone she had was incredibly sensitive, just what they needed if they were to be able to listen into the conversation, no larger than a bead that she was wearing upon a bracelet around her wrist. Far less obvious than the larger headsets they usually would choose to wear. All she had to remember to do was not to jangle it about too much or play with it since it would create screeching feedback for those on the other end.

"I'm still mad that you made me miss breakfast." She grumbled and shifted in her seat. Glancing around her, she made sure to check that there were no humans around before she took her hat off to rub her ears.

It was troublesome having to wear hats all the time in public and finding one which suited her sense of style, but she was glad that the woven broad summer-hat matched her dress.

With the loose coral pink and blue bohemian dress, she wore with its loose flowing skirts and black and white patterns, her wings she could easily pass off as being part of the dress. To be sure that it didn't draw too much attention she wore a pashmina across her shoulders to disguise the little feathers on her shoulders and down her back where the wings grew.

"You can eat whilst you discuss things with him." Beth's voice hissed in over the ear clip. Adjusting the volume one last time, she put her hat back on and brushed out her waves of hair to hide the lack of human ears before picking up the menu once again.

The pub was reasonably nice and very quiet for the mid-morning as the lunchtime diners hadn't arrived yet and the journalist, she was meeting had reserved the upstairs vaulted function room with its leather sofas and pillows. She had chosen to sit at the far end by the pillar, allowing her to lean slightly so as not to sit on her feathers or damage them too much.

The pub door opened below. A few mumbling voices and the sound of footsteps told Kat that the man she was here to see had arrived. Quickly brushing hair again to cover the fur, she returned the hat to her head and adjusted her position on the sofa so as not to appear too oddly poised. She did her best to appear as nonchalant as possible, forcing her excited quivering wings to remain tightly folded against her back.

"Showtime." She muttered softly into the microphone, a grin spreading across her face as the journalist entered the room.

"So sorry I'm late, traffic and all that. He apologised as he straightened his clothes up whilst crossing the room. "You must be…" He trailed off and transfixed he remained frozen to the spot for a moment, an awe filled smile slowly spreading across his face as he stared at Kat. Hastily tidying himself up, Kat tried not to scrunch her nose up at the smell of heavily applied deodorant, he appeared eager to both meet her and to get his break in journalism.

"Cho Sekhmet." She smiled sweetly and held her hand out to shake.

"Darryl Graves, the *Observer*, we spoke on the phone," He blurted out, shaking Kat's hand and slowly sitting down, eyes still fixed on her though they had dropped from her eyes to the rest of her body for longer than she appreciated. He cleared his throat, switching from the excited babble to a smooth suave tone. "*Kon'nichiwa*. Can I just say how stunning you look?"

Hiding her cringing disgust, she heard a little giggle from her ear clip from Storm.

"Don't kill him yet, Kat." Storm warned, amused. With a flick of her eyes to the corner of the room, she spotted a glowing red dot from upon the security camera, that Beth had already accessed their CCTV to watch.

"Thank you." Kat purred sweetly.

"You haven't been here too long have you, Miss Sekhmet? Can I order you anything? A drink perhaps? Wine? Salad?" He babbled as he straightened out his jacket and tie, placing the tablet he was using to take notes on to one side of the table and lunging for the menu.

"How about some *real food*. Like gammon and chips, or steak and bourbon. It's rude to presume things about ladies."

'*Such as presuming they don't notice you staring at their breasts*', she almost added, but continued to smile politely, and leant forward to flutter her lashes at him.

"Oh…" He stared in bewilderment at her.

"What?"

"Oh nothing, I'm just used to interviewing clients who are always on diets." He tried to smile and recover himself. "It's nice to meet a woman who knows how to eat properly."

"I am pretty hungry," She leant forward a little with a small pout on her lips to try to appear meek and gentle, "If you'd be so kind as to run downstairs and tell them the order now. I know you have deadlines to meet." She purred softly, her voice silvery and sweet.

The journalist swallowed and nodded furiously.

"I-I'll go ask right now." He babbled and leapt to his feet, bumping into the table with a clatter, knocking the salt and pepper pots to the floor. Swearing under his breath, he quickly slammed the pots back on the table and rushed downstairs as fast as he could manage without wanting to seem too eager.

"Well, he seems like your average idiot." Kat mused into the microphone, giving her wings a little flex.

"Stop fluttering your lashes at the guy. He'll keep getting the wrong idea and you'll just want to hurt him." Beth sighed. "You know how simple the common-or-garden man is."

"He thinks I don't notice where he's looking."

"Don't get mad. Just smile sweetly while picturing yourself giving him a kick to his balls until we're done."

Kat smiled to herself, trying not to laugh as she took the tiny device Beth called her *Trojan Horse*, from the pocket of her bag and slotted it carefully into the tablet, being careful as to not move it or to leave fingerprints on the screen.

It would take less than two seconds for it to connect Beth's laptop to the tablet, and the moment it was done Beth would have access to all his files, contacts, passwords and any other notes and records he stored on his phone. Even though they were giving him information, Beth liked to have a little blackmail material on the side as well as to keep an eye on what he was doing with that information.

Her ears flicked beneath her hat as she listened for the sound of footsteps and voices. She could hear Graves snapping at someone, she assumed a waitress or kitchen staff, followed by angry stomping. Quickly, carefully, she removed the stick from the tablet and slipped it back into her bag.

Not a minute later Graves surfaced, followed by a waitress, who was blushing angrily and carrying two plates of gammon and chips.

"Let's get right to it then Miss Sekhmet. Cho. Do you mind if I call you Cho?" He said, sitting back down and checking his tablet to see if Kat had tried to open it up or move it with as much subtlety as he could manage. Seeing that there were no obvious fingerprints on it he assumed that Kat hadn't touched it and so set it up to record their conversation, leaving it on the table next to him.

"Sekhmet is fine."

"Sekhmet then- I get so many calls from girls like you every day saying they've got dirt on our glorious overlords. So, are you confident this is worth my time?"

"I'm fairly confident on what I've got, but it all depends."

"On?"

"If *you* think it's worth something." She smiled coyly at him, thanking the waitress by placing a tip of twenty pounds into her hand for her trouble and nodding for her to leave.

"Show him the envelope." Beth said in a low voice, "Don't show him what's inside though. Not yet."

He narrowed his eyes at her, saying nothing as he watched her swiftly lean down to the bag at her feet and produce a large and very thick brown envelope.

"Paper? That's pretty old fashioned."

"You can't hack paper."

"Fair point."

She set it on the table between them, beginning to tuck into the gammon. He tried to make a move to try to take the envelope to view its contents, but before he could even lay a finger on it, she pulled it away.

"I could quite easily take this elsewhere along with your chances at something bigger and better, so just remember that." She smirked coyly. The tease made him flush red. Holding onto the papers for a few quiet minutes as she licked the gammon grease from her lips, taking her time to savour the salty flavours. Clearly growing impatient, he began scoffing his own food as he waited for Kat to release the papers into his possession.

"How about you tell me something about it, or how such a lovely girl as yourself came to...*acquire it.*" He smiled at her, reaching over and brushing the back of her hand with his fingertips. "Unless you want to save the business talk until afterwards."

Disgust rose like bile in her throat. His behaviour was reminiscent of the actions and words she had heard men say when she had served her former owner. Lecherous and vile, trying to touch her when they shouldn't, thinking her as being gentle and naïve. Her hand tightened on the knife she held to cut the gammon, taking all her control not to put the blade through his hand instead of the meat.

"Keep it in your pants or loose 'em dickbag." Storm spat and snarled through the earpiece. "She's not your species."

It was hard to keep the smile from her face when she heard Storm speak, though she was grateful that it was enough to calm her. Kat put the knife down calmly, she began playing with her hair, keeping her hands occupied so that she wouldn't become to obviously threatening with the knife.

"I have my...sources." She hesitantly replied.

"So, you're just the messenger girl then." Graves snorted, cocking an eyebrow at her as he looked her up and down again. "You seemed a little too young and pretty to be a ...well, you know. To actually have gotten the information yourself."

"I can tell you that it involves three minor MP's." Purred Kat, being careful to wipe the grease from her mouth with the napkin rather than the back of her hand as she usually would.

He shrugged with disinterest. "If they're minor then it's not that important or worth my ti-"

"And five senior managers of a transnational company, who are all involved in human trafficking, organised kidnappings and assassinations, links to the Gibraltar incident, the truth behind the Portuguese virus, the Turkish mafia, paedophilia and some backhand investments which quite possibly led up to the massacre in Ukraine and Macedonia." She said rapidly, parroting the words Beth was speaking into her ear, making sure that he got a good dose of everything there was on offer.

His head snapped up to look at her, jaw askew and dribbling gravy down his chin. The ungracious look made Kat smile in amusement.

"He's gone quiet." Muttered Freeborn from the back. "Did she cut his throat? I hope so, he sounds like a douche-canoe."

"Not yet." Beth sniggered. "He's just trying to tell if she's bullshitting or not."

Graves took several deep breaths; she could smell the perspiration rising off him through the heavy deodorant.

"Well...I'd have to find out if any of this has...solid evidence."

"You're thinking about super-injunctions and compensations in case someone finds out you're going to publish, as well as the repercussions of exposing what in all fairness are *war crimes*?"

"Well we are near the Ministry of Justice. It's kind of hard not to think about how much it would cost and if it's even legal to publish or not." He laughed nervously, loosening his shirt as he started to think more about it.

His fidgeting behaviour and hesitance to take the bait made her uneasy. She flicked the microphone on the bracelet, hoping to prompt Beth into giving her some advice. The mic squealed and the sensitive eared recipients all shouted in pain at the screech they received through the speakers. Angrily Beth gave her a few suggestions as to what she could say to prompt him followed by several threats of what she would do to Kat if she damaged the microphone.

Kat sat up in her seat, sighing dramatically as she put her knife and fork together on her plate and rose to her feet.

"I'm sorry for wasting your time. I thought that I had something worthwhile for you to use, but it looks like I was wrong."

Graves lunged forward, eyes wide, arms flailing to try and stop her from leaving.

"Wait wait! I didn't say that I wasn't interested…"

"Well how much for it."

"Ah…money…" He hesitated again.

Unsure if he was intentionally hesitating or not, she sighed softly with exasperation and decided on a second prompt which Beth had suggested.

"Would reading the first page help?" She slid the first page from the envelope and passed it across to him, keeping the rest of its contents close to her chest. Eagerly he snatched it from her and begun reading down the page, his nose getting closer and closer to the sheet the further he read.

Kat had read it when Storm had shown her. In short it contained information and records of the people who were involved in the human trafficking, where it was coming in from and going too, and who was requesting it, although it as only one page of the story and it was one that he was clearly eager to learn more about.

"This is…deep." He swallowed and handed the page back to her, sweat glistening upon his brow. His eyes were wide in horror at the brief overview he had read and yet he was buzzing with excitement as he began to think about how much publicity something such as this would get, and how much of a pay rise he might gain from it, if not a promotion.

"Alright…how much do you want?"

"Fifty-thousand for each person involved in those stories, though there is about two hundred individuals involved."

"T-Ten million pounds? For the entire document?"

"Oh, you're good at maths." Kat grinned slyly, swiping up several chips with her fingers and eating them, forgetting her manners.

"Twenty-five thousand for each person published." He offered.

Beth laughed curtly. "Don't budge, Kat." She ordered. "If he tries to go any lower just seduce him. I'll fetch you some blackmail material to get you out of anything else he tries on after."

"A girl's gotta eat." Kat narrowed her eyes. Smiling shrewdly she leant forward and purred in a sultry tone, "*Fifty-thousand each.*"

He laughed awkwardly and tugged at his shirt collar again.

"You're not haggling with me here Miss Sekhmet."

"I'm pretty sure your competition will offer more." She pouted, fluttering her eyelashes at him and straightening up her shawl.

He opened his mouth to argue with her about the price. His eyes dropped down to her cleavage once more and he snapped his jaw shut as he considered the deal.

"Ten million it is then." He sighed in defeat, tapping the tablet. "Who do I make the check for?"

"Me. I'll get the money delivered back to my sources."

"Okay, give me a second to talk to my boss." He mumbled, typing away and falling silent. Kat leant back in the seat, shuffling slightly as her wings ached from being held close for so long. Through the earpiece she heard a sharp clap and laughter from Beth and Storm, who were spying upon the conversation between Graves and his boss upon her laptop.

"Bait taken, we've got confirmation from his boss. Now give it a few days and we'll have our distraction." Beth cackled. "Now all that's left is for the Daggers to gate-crash the Risio gala."

Kat grinned as she finished off the meal. She sincerely hoped that the Rogues would get to join in on that fun and not end up being ousted by the Rioteers wanting to do it for them.

Graves sighed and slid the tablet across to Kat to type in her details so he could transfer the money. Wiping her fingers clean on her skirt, she typed in the details Beth insisted that she should use for the transfer, sending the money to the Rogue's personal bank account.

"And there we go." She smiled, as the green processing bar ended with small sound and handing over the envelope of evidence. That was her job done and now she could leave. "Thank you for dinner." She said softly, slipping out from her corner, grabbing her bag and preparing to get to her feet.

"Wait!"

The girls groaned through the earpiece; they knew exactly what was coming.

"Would you mind if I…got your number? In case I need to get sources." He asked trying to sound as casual as possible. Kat grimaced, she had done her best to ignore his leching behaviour for the sake of the task, but now she had finished her job she could be as honest as she liked.

"All the sources you need are in there." She said coolly, letting the sweet innocent demeanour she had portrayed to him, drop for the Lioness beneath.

"My contact details are strictly confidential, available to my employer only."

"What about a drink sometime? I could even get you a job with us you know."

"*No.*"

He laughed and took her wrist. "Come on darling, you can't be all business."

Immediately Kat reversed his hold, twisting her arm grabbing his wrist in a vice like grip until he squeaked like a piglet.

"*Do. Not. Touch. Me.*" She snarled. Her blue wings strained, wishing to flare out to appear even more intimidating, but she forced them to remain shut.

"I'm sorry I-"

Kat smiled slyly as Beth begun to whisper things into her ear.

"I know for a fact that you have a wife, and two girlfriends on the side who you met from similar client interviews in the past, and who both think you're divorced." His face paled at her words. "Imagine what they all would say if I were to tell them that you were cheating on them all. Not to mention telling them about the drugs."

Graves swallowed and fell back into his seat, staring up at her in terror. "I wasn't intending to- All I asked for was your number! For journalism purposes only, I swear."

"And I said no. You really should have understood that." She sneered, flashing her long canines. His face paled and he retreated further into the seat. The switch from sweet girl to Lioness had petrified him.

"Do try and get those articles published soon. Your girlfriends might find out a little too much if you don't. Your wife, boss, and the police too. I'm sure they would love to know all about the *real* you." And with that she strode past him, blowing him a mocking kiss. "Thanks for dinner."

"I make that eight humans who have asked you for your number or other details." Asena chuckled through the earpiece as Kat strode across the pub, leaving a one-hundred-pound tip on the counter for the waitresses. They thanked her shyly, watching with caution as she stepped out into the sunshine.

Storm laughed. "Eleven actually, you weren't there for a few of them."

Out in the fresh air, Kat smiled and stretched her arms out behind her, aching to free her wings.

Having to put on an act of humanity was frustrating, and the tension made her wings ache. Looking around the road wasn't too busy and there was a shaded side street where she could cool herself off without too much worry of being seen.

"You're welcome to take a break Kat." Storm insisted. "That road down there is empty right now, so you can always shake off there."

Kat looked up to see the rounded street camera focused on her. Testing her theory, she twirled in the street, letting her flowing skirt fly up and her wings fan a little, but making Storm laugh and whistle through the earpiece and in so doing proving her right. Beth got into cameras far too easily.

Leaving the pub behind she snuck off into the side street, breathing deeply as she shrugged down the shawl and roused her feathers. Looking to the sky she stretched her hands above her to the blue above, extending the outmost primaries skyward. The breeze caressed the feathers with a gentle rustle, cooling them from the heat of anger and calming her.

Bright wings stretching out above her head, a voice interrupted through the earpiece, from what Kat guessed was, behind the girls.

"Asena, we just got a message. Some people in the Shard contacted the police about two giant birds and an unregistered military chinook, one took a picture and it looks like they're Avios."

"And they're bothering us with it because *why?*" Asena sighed loudly.

"Because they always do when they see Avios, and I don't recognise who they are in the pictures because of the quality."

"Well Kat is already out near there; she can always have a quick look to check. Beth do you mind having a look at the cameras."

"What should we do?"

"Tell the police to treat the chinook as standard. It shouldn't be flying in zone one anyway." And so, she shooed the interrupter away.

Sighing softly, Kat was a little disappointed that her break was short lived, but at least it meant an opportunity to be up high and closer to the sky. Without waiting for an order to search, Kat wrapped the shawl around her waist, held onto her hat then broke into a short run and leap, beating her wings down quickly to gain height. It wasn't the slow and elegant flapping with a graceful ascent that people assumed it to be, it never was.

Landing on the rooftop she kept low to the shadows and looked out across the city. Although it wasn't high, she could still see far with the wind turbines slowly turning in the park and on top of buildings, and flocks of pigeons flying low amongst the vertical forests of the skyscrapers.

Laying her hat and bag down on the eaves of the rooftop, she slowly made her way across the ridge of the tiles, wings half opened to help her balance and her dress and shawl swirling about beneath her as the strong summer breeze caught it. Her rounded ears twitched and turned, trying to distinguish the double-bladed thudding of the chinook over the sounds of the wind through leaves and the engines of cars.

"Is there anything on the cameras?" She asked, startling a lounging tabby from where it had been sunning itself as she walked on by, drawing closer to the city centre and its towering skyscrapers.

"Nothing much. No one seems to be staring and pointing at the sky."

"Maybe it was a false alarm?" Storm suggested. "Or maybe it was just Rai or someone forgetting not to fly by day again."

"You mean like *you* do?"

"I'm pretty sure my presence here rules me out as a suspect Beth."

"You're too fast for me *not* to suspect you."

Storm laughed aloud and from the yelling from Beth that followed, Kat assumed that Storm had taken her arm off again or at least interfered with the electronics that controlled it.

Leaping from building to building, she could begin to hear the chinook across the river next to the sounds of two more helicopters that were escorting it away from the city centre. Wary of how visible she was making herself to the towering skyscrapers before her, she made a quick assessment by ear, and still there was nothing. But there was no rhythmic flapping of giant wings of what she could hear, only the fluttering of pigeons, crows and gulls that scattered as she passed.

If there had been Avios, they might have been in an entirely different part of the city, and yet–

A shadow raced across the glass of the building to her left, far too large to have been a gull and too small and silent to have been a plane.

Kat froze, ears twisting and twitching. Another shadow crossed her path, too fast to catch immediately, but enough for her to have a direction. She strained her ears trying to close in on the sounds of air over feathers between the honks and rumble of traffic.

Slow and steady swooshing sounds were traveling away from her, she couldn't hear them for a moment, then the sound returned. They were gliding. Gliders were a nightmare to track by sound alone.

"I think I have them." She announced into the microphone on her wrist. "I'm going after them."

Throwing herself off the building and fluttering her wings hard to fly she struggled to keep the sounds in focus over the rush of wind.

Landing and running to the edge, she saw the tip of a black wing arc behind a cluster of buildings before their owner vanished again. They were keeping low enough to be out of view of cameras and out of sight from above.

Just as quickly as they had dipped out of sight, the sweeping arcs of black wings rose up above the buildings in an effortless swoop, rising high into the sky on a thermal.

"I see them!" She yelled into the microphone, trying to keep the other Rogues informed. "I'm flying after them."

"Do you recognise them?" Beth asked hopefully, voice being drown out by the rush of wind.

"No."

Chasing the Avio, she could barely keep pace. Kat cursed to herself, leaping and taking flight again after them. The repetitive take offs took up a lot of energy, and her muscles began to burn with strain and tiredness.

They didn't even seem to move their wings to flap, they only caught the air and surfed on the rising currents, spiking envy in Kat with her aching limbs rowing through the air as fast as she could manage. With an elegant twist they dove and then spiralled straight back up to the sky with an arc of black, sweeping their wings and tailfeathers out and giving them the look of a gigantic black swallow or kite against the bright sun.

Focused upon the gigantic kite, something huge streaked towards her in her peripheral. Before she could fully turn her head to face what it was, her wing had been grabbed and yanked hard through the air. The wind supporting her vanished and Kat fell spiralling towards the ground with a shriek. Twisting around, she righted herself, forcing her wings out to parachute and reduce speed, though still coming to a hard and heavy landing on her hands and knees as she hit the rooftop.

"Kat? Kat! What's going on?!" Beth bellowed into her ear, panic clear in her voice.

Shakily Kat raised the bead-microphone to her mouth, but before she could answer an impact caught her between her wings, slamming her face down to the ground with a crack and knocking the air from her lungs.

With black spots dancing before her eyes, Kat craned her neck to see who her attacker was.

Her strawberry blonde hair sliced short and yellow eyes glittering with glee, she crouched down on Kat's back, yanking her wrist up high to speak into the microphone.

"Hey Storm," Said the Vulture, Kathy, girlishly. "Let's play."

13

"Where are you Storm, come out and play," The Vulture repeated, singing into the microphone as Kat squirmed. "Come out or I'll tear your girlfriend's wings off."

Shaggy wings splayed either side of her; it was Kathy, though she now lacked her matted ginger hair and pregnancy bulge. The stolen dress now replaced by a military grade flight suit, made from the same SmartFabrics that Core used to protect their soldiers and designed to reduce drag in the air.

Wherever she had come from she'd come away equipped for a fight.

"She says go fuck yourself." Kat spat, repeating what Storm snarled within Kat's ear.

"Come out and say that to my face, bitch!" She snapped the clip from Kat's ear, placing it to her own only to hear the incoherent static of Beth cutting the feed.

Kat yanked her hand away, letting the beaded microphone slip from her wrist and rolling out from beneath the Vulture. She staggered with Kat moving, giving the Lioness time to get to her feet and move, bounding over the edge of building and onwards to the next platform. Kathy followed with a string of curses, throwing the microphone and clip to one side to chase her.

"Where is Storm?" Kathy snarled furiously, "Tell me!"

"Stick around and find out!"

Storm would have been on her way the moment she heard Kathy, she needed to bide time for her to get out the warren of tunnels in the headquarters and reach her by air.

She had six minutes at least.

Darting between the skylights and chimney stacks with her dress billowing out behind her, Kat led Kathy on, trying to draw her away from the city centre where they could be seen and to lessen any damage the crazed Vulture might cause.

As wildly confused as she was that Kathy was here, a snap judgement had to be made. Killing Kathy would mean they wouldn't know where she'd come from or where her baby had gone but keeping her alive might mean Storm would have a chance to redeem herself to Rex to bring her in captured. She needed to slow Kathy down and keep her out of the air.

Kathy drew in close, but Kat was ready. Drawing Kathy down close to a rooftop, she fanned her wings to slow herself, ears flicked back to follow the sound of Kathy's wings as the girl threw herself down upon Kat.

With a fast and flexible twist, Kat powered her wings down to throw herself round into a flip. Kathy gasped; arms outstretched as Kat brought her heels down onto Kathy's face. The kick sent Kathy crashing down upon the rooftop.

Kat smirked, though she regretted the choice of wearing the heeled sandals as she landed hard enough to sever the heel from the shoe. Tearing the strap off she kicked it at Kathy who was already staggering to her feet.

The heel caught Kathy in the side of the face hard enough to send her reeling and shielding herself with a wing as Kat kicked off the second shoe.

Barefoot, Kat charged forward, drawing her hand up her thigh to snatch a blade from a hidden garter sheath and slash it at her. The blade sliced through the SmartFabric, cutting into Kathy's chest, but as the fabric was designed to do, it sealed itself back together, protecting Kathy from bleeding out. Kathy retaliated with a hooked punch that struck Kat's face. The two scrappily struck and slashed at each other, driving themselves into a circling dance of fists and feathers. The Vulture was faster than Kat had anticipated, boosted by what Kat could see to be patches of EPI+ upon her neck. Kat snarled. She didn't have to kill the girl, only slow her down.

There was a sound like waves rushing over stones, and in swept the black-winged Avio, casting a shadow upon them both with his magnificent wingspan. The sun turned the silky ink black to a shimmering midnight blue, so sleek and neat next to Kathy's shaggy feathers.

Both girls faltered mid-battle to watch as the Avio they belonged to, land gently upon a thin stretch of railing that surrounded the building's roof. With a sybarite smile, Sabre winked a dark eye at Kat as he circled himself with his sleek wings.

Distracted by Sabre, Kathy punched Kat hard to the diaphragm, doubling her over before grabbing the pale blue feathers between her wings and pulling Kat forward to knee her in the gut again. Kat reacted in pain, throwing her wings forward as she had seen Storm do before and using them to punch the Vulture hard in the face and kicking them both apart.

"Cat fight!" Chimed Sabre excitedly, sitting to swing his legs and watch. "*Cat fight!*"

"Don't just sit there and watch!" Kathy yelled at him, wiping the blood from her nose. "Help me!"

"I don't see how I can assist."

"You're a muser! Read her mind! Find out where that bitch is!"

"I can't read what I can't see." He huffed, rustling his wings in annoyance. Ignoring her screeching, he took a picture of the two mid-fight with his phone. "Right now all she's thinking is about breaking your neck."

A smirk twinged at Kat's lips, and she inwardly applauded his chaotic neutrality and lack of involvement with the fight. Leaping off of Kathy, Kat forced herself into a vertical take-off before letting the wind catch and pull her away. Screaming in rage the Vulture followed, choosing to run and jump, sweeping the shaggy feathers out and gliding across the gaps between the rooftops.

The rushing of air over Kathy's wings was loud enough for the Lioness to tell how far behind she was. Drawing her knees up to her chest she waited until Kathy was right upon the hem of her dress to tuck and drop from her grasp into the gulley of a road that separated a block of buildings.

While her beautiful wings were not powerful or made to endure long, fast, or high flights, their short elliptical shape and her own flexibility meant she could out manoeuvre Kathy with ease.

Tightly twisting she looped before she hit the ground, spiralling skywards and dropping into a stoop that let her rip through the feathers of Kathy's wing, separating the interlocked fibres and forcing her to stall in the air as the aerofoil was broken. She fell forward, slamming hard against a glass skylight, shattering it and then rolling down into the gutter. Smirking at the dramatic flailing, Kat looked away for two seconds, trying to locate the black-winged Avio.

A beat like waves on rocks or a gust of wind through leaves caught her ear, and she turned to face him, knife out and ready to strike.

Blackness swirled before her eyes; all sound stopped and she was trapped in a solid muser induced silence. Gravity took hold of her as all feeling in her wings was numbed by a burst of pins and needles, and she fell from the sky. The suffocating helplessness of sensory deprivation didn't last long, as pain shot across her wing, drawing her back into consciousness. It was the black-winged Avio holding her by her wing and gliding with her as though she weighed nothing.

Dropping her on the edge of a sloping parapet that rimmed the buildings edge, Kat scrabbled furiously to keep from falling over the edge, claw-tips breaking as she dug them into the stone. Daring a peek below her, she hung over a narrow side road with the walls of the adjacent buildings lined with air conditioning units. Not enough room to twist and swoop away or to land without shocking her knees on impact.

Clawing at the stone to keep her grip, Kathy marched up to her, bloody faced and furious. Whipping a gun from a holster beneath a wing she hissed as she turned the safety off.

"Last chance." She threatened, gun pressed against Kat's head. "Where is she?"

Kat remained calm. She'd had a gun pressed to her head more times than she wished, it didn't scare her.

Dropping out of sight down the alley way might buy her time for Storm to arrive but landing in bare feet on whatever was down there sickened her more than the idea of being shot in the head.

Four minutes.

"You want to kill Storm? Why?" Kat asked, trying to stall for time. "You don't have to do this."

"She killed Teal! Of course, I'm going to fucking kill her."

"Kathy, hold on." Behind her, Sabre landed gracefully on the thin edge of the pyramid of skylights, watching unblinkingly and with an amused curiosity splashed across his face. He sat watching Kat as though he were a gargoyle, hands gripping the metal between his feet, tailfeathers twitching up and down to balance him. There was something in his posture that reminded her of Storm before she attacked.

Their eyes met. A prickle ran across her scalp as she remembered what had happened.

Storm grabbing Teal by his hair and snapping his back – Teal screaming – Malana slicing through his neck like paper.

"*Oooh.*" Sabre breathed, fanning his tailfeathers in intrigue. "You're wanting the wrong person Kathy."

The Vulture turned to sneer at him. "What?"

"The little girl. She killed your boyfriend." He blinked slowly; head cocked to one shoulder. His brow furrowed, concerned of something which showed more in the nervous shuffle of his wings.

'Who is that?' Kat heard him muse to himself, a soft whisper at the back of her mind.

"*Now* you read minds!" Kathy shrieked.

With her turned away, Kat risked snatching for the gun, trying to wrestle it from Kathy whilst clinging to the parapet. Face twisted in anger, Kathy beat her wings over Kat's head with the gun still pressed close against her skull, finger straining on the trigger.

The trigger clicked–

And nothing happened.

Wide eyed Kathy clicked the trigger several more times with a growing scream of anger.

It wasn't loaded. Sabre barked with laughter, jumping forward from his perch to take the gun from her hand in a swift movement before she could use it to bash Kat's skull in.

"Did you really think we'd give you a loaded gun?" Sabre purred mischievously, baring a set of curved lynx-teeth into a crafty grin.

"*YOU ASSHOLE!*"

Screaming and forgetting about Kat, she lashed out at him. With a simple and fluid motion, he had leaped over her head and gracefully landed back on his perch, pulling a round of ammunition from his pocket and loading the gun.

A rhythmic beating caught Kat's ear, growing louder with every beat. Storm she hoped, but the pattern was far too slow for the Rogue's sharp slicing beats. Sabre heard it too, ceasing in his tormenting of Kathy to snap his head to the sky as a shadow was cast on him.

Kat released her grip and dropped down the side of the building, wings straining hard as she beat them within the narrow alley space and forced herself to a slow. Her bones rattled, and agony shot through her legs as she landed hard in the dank darkness, the hem of her dress turning black with dirt.

"Oh shit!" Sabre yelped, darting from his perch with an effortless sweep of black as a thunderous roar of wings dove towards them.

Standing, Kathy turned, in time to have the wind struck from her lungs as from the sky bolted Amell, feet first and kicking her straight in the chest, driving her backwards across the skylight.

The sunlight glistening off his sweat soaked chest, he breathed heavily as he stood tall. Kathy glowered at him in pain as she dragged herself up. He shook his feathers down, a glossy purple sheen across his dark brown back, but with the whites of the undersides almost blinding in the sun.

"Amell." She snarled.

The Eagle didn't gratify her with a response of acknowledgement as he charged forward.

She leapt avoiding his attack, taking off into the sky with a fluttering struggle. Amell crashed against the glass, shattering it with his knee and sending the shards falling to the ground, leaving bloodied slices across his thigh. Hoisting himself out of the hole he had made, he ran and launched himself off the edge of the building after Kathy, focused so solely on her that he didn't even see Sabre looping back around in the sky and aiming his gun.

The pair of them slowly rising, fighting against the wind and straining to out manoeuvre the other with ungraceful twists of their bodies, Amell reached forward to snatch and grab at her ankles. Her lightness next to his bulky muscles made her the faster, but her panic slowed her down.

A bullet ripped through Amell's feathers with a resounding *crack*, narrowly avoiding the wrist of his wing, but puncturing through the muscle below it. He plummeted from the sky as he pulled the wing to his chest in pain. He crashed through the greenery and potted plants of a rooftop garden, sending its occupants screaming and running inside in terror.

"He's still after you?" Sabre scoffed as he arrowed up next to Kathy, turning the gun back onto safety mode to avoid shooting anyone by accident. "I thought he'd given up by now- also where's Regent's Park."

"What?" Kathy panted. The sun was burning hot on her dark feathers, and yet she wondered how Sabre wasn't even breaking a sweat.

"That's where the little girl is." He looked down at the squares of green between the unending greyness, "I hope you know where that is."

Fighting through the onset of sunstroke she righted them to face north and looking down at the familiar map of land below, led them both onwards.

Scrambling back onto the rooftops, Kat hopped to Amell's side, having found a route out that kept her from being seen by either the Vulture or Kite, but allowed her to see their direction.

"Are you alright?" She asked him hurriedly, ignoring all pleasantries and greetings. The humans in the apartment raised their phones from inside, recording and snapping pictures of them both.

"Sweet." He winced as he looked up at her, forcing himself into a sitting position before looking at his injured wing. The pain white hot and crippling for the few moments it lasted before he forced himself up and flexed it. Blood blossomed from the wound, staining the soft white ventral feathers crimson.

"It's just a bullet, I've taken plenty." He tried to laugh it off as Kat's eyes went wide in shock. "I think I can still fly with this."

"Good." She swallowed her shock. Grabbing his arm, she hauled him to the edge of the building. "Come on, we've got to go."

And without an argument they threw themselves out into the abyss, catching the wind and soaring across the rooftops after them.

-x-

Whilst the girls had been running their mission, Raoul, Wilny, Lana, and Comet were doing their best to find an unoccupied shaded area of the park to give them all some reprieve from the heat of the midday sun. The three Avios wings were sodden with sweat, and Raoul fared no better as they sauntered through the park. Wilny had to remove one tailfeather from beneath his shirt to fan himself with, wishing that he could mimic Raoul in going shirtless.

It had taken nearly two days to persuade Comet to come out. She had been wary of Raoul at first. Being around Canids made her anxious but she trusted Wilny, and as they traversed the zoo, she had relaxed more and more with him.

The zoo had been fun for all of them. Being able to see lions, tigers, and bears all in real life was an experience, and each and every animal was met with an awe filled "Wow!" of excitement from all of them.

The gentle breeze was refreshing, giving them a chance to cool down and relax before Malana spotted a playground by a flowered enclave garden and pleaded with Wilny to let her play while they sat down.

"I'll be right there!" She had assured him with deliberate words, looking to Raoul to make sure she had spoken correctly. "No panic. Please."

Seeing no reason to deny her a chance to play, he allowed her to jump over the fence – which she did so with a single bound – and climb up the rope tower that stood in the centre of the playpark, while he leant on the fence to watch.

One of the carers looked across at him warily, noting the wings on Malana. She had complained loudly that she was too hot to wear a jacket to cover her wings and had abandoned it the moment Wilny's back was turned, even after all his lecturing on how she had to keep it on.

"They're part of a costume," he assured them with a charming smile, "she begged me to get her them."

Smiling to himself he watched Malana play, lethargic beneath the hot sun and wondering to himself if he could simply say he was in costume too.

A hurried tap on his shoulder broke him out of the languid thoughts. He flinched but held back on swiping Raoul's hand away.

"Comet." Raoul said quietly, nodding to the other side of the playpark. With him distracted, Comet had begun to walk away towards the scarlet flowered bushes that formed a floral circle around a small hidden enclave, seemingly in a daze driven by heatstroke.

"Keep an eye on Malana for me." He asked Raoul before slipping away to follow Comet.

He was worried about her. She hadn't been alone outside of the headquarters before and he was worried that she might get lost or hurt either herself, or someone else, if she became spooked. It concerned him that the Rioteers and Synth groups had no safety or security in place for people like Comet who were highly traumatised and highly dangerous in their abilities. He had to be vigilant.

The enclave was peacefully quiet with several benches all facing inwards to a small fountain in the centre, and shaded by the tall rhododendron and magnolias, leaving the entire area with a warm and lightly fragrant air.

She paced peacefully around the circle, drawing a hand across the crimson, magenta, and white petals so that they danced behind her. She had let the light shawl she wore to cover her wings slip so that the sea-green feathers shimmered under the filtered sunlight.

Approaching her slowly, Wilny made sure to be within her line of sight so as not to startle her or infringe on her personal space.

"How are you doing Comet?" He asked gently. "Are you okay?"

"I'm fine I just needed space. It's quiet and there's flowers." She murmured, stroking the silky petals. "Do you know that humans can't see the markings on these? They just see them as being red."

"You see ultraviolet light?"

"Do you?"

"A little." Comet smiled, tilting her head to one shoulder to peek at the slip of tailfeather protruding from beneath his shirt. "They glow."

She turned back to the flowers to watch a bee land and shuffle down to the centre of a blossom. Several more buzzed around her, fumblingly bumbling along and bumping against her glossy black hair and shimmering feathers as they mistook them for flower petals. A few even buzzed around Wilny's own chocolate waves as they scented the honey on him, making him smile.

"You're really different to who you were."

Wilny blinked. As much as he was watching her, she was watching him with great suspicion and confusion.

"Sorry?"

"You're not a...Don't worry. It's not important."

"Don't remember? Huh?" Wilny watched her as she awkwardly pulled on her hair. Wings rolling, she shuffled from foot to foot.

"Lana wants ice cream." Comet said loudly, turning her head to face the playpark. "I can hear her from here. She's such a sweet girl."

Confused, Wilny strained his ears to hear for Lana's voice.

"I didn't say she was shouting. She's just thinking."

"You can hear her thoughts from over here?" He could barely hear the children shouting, let alone any thoughts. He couldn't even sense her musing.

"I've a radius range of thirty meters."

With a wide-eyed blink of surprise, he stared at his fellow Hummingbird, as she had said it as if it were nothing of note. It was a terrifying range. Most musers – himself included – could only reach out to five meters at most.

Suddenly her fearfulness in the headquarters and her response to dealing with Roux made sense if she was so sensitive that she could detect the thoughts of one little girl a hundred feet away, what must have she been dealing with when stood right before the Dragon.

"Do you listen to everyone's thoughts?" He asked gently, fearing what things she could have heard from everyone, himself included. Lashes falling, she closed her eyes to stop tears from welling in her eyes and drew her hands to her chest, clutching at her heart.

"Some people are too loud for me to shut out. They hurt too much and-" She swallowed down on her words, stopping them from wavering before she could sob.

"I used to be able to help people with their bad thoughts and pain. I even trained as a nurse while in ARCDA, because helping was all I wanted to do." The sorrow in her voice hurt him to hear, crushing his chest with sympathy. "But I can't even help myself now."

Through the weak and whimpering exterior, he could see the woman within the husk of sadness as her mind gently touched his.

Fleeting images of Synths crippled by PTSD and anxiety becoming calm, Transhumans laying half-formed in beds writhing in agony until she altered their mind to take away the pain better than any morphine. She could help people, she wanted to, but she was right. Without being first able to help herself how could anyone possibly rely on her.

Looking up to him she forced a smile upon her face before he could approach her with sympathy. "Go. You should get her ice cream, I'll be here."

"Are you sure?"

"I just want some time to myself."

It felt wrong to leave her alone, but he didn't feel as though he could argue with her without making her burst into tears, and so with a small nod he left her to the flowers and returned to Raoul and Lana, just in time to rescue Raoul from the scrutiny of the watching mothers. The relief in his eyes when he got back made Wilny smile.

Large groups of people still startled the Hound.

"Wilny! Malana would like-"

"Ice cream." He smiled, patting Raoul on the shoulder and digging into his pocket for some change. "I know. Would you like to try buying this time and I stay here?"

"I will try." Raoul laughed lightly before whispering a little breath of thanks as he escaped the women's frowning.

With a chuckle he watched Raoul before turning back to watch over Malana as she took a leap from the top of the wooden tower that made the mothers and carers gasp in a brief moment of terror before she landed gracefully. She was showing off, knowing that none of the other children could copy her without reprimand or injury.

To her credit, she was being very careful not to move her wings so much that they looked anything less than ornamental and her tail was safely hidden beneath her dress, but there was something else that drew his attention away.

A pair of shadows against the bright blue of the sky, too large to be seagulls. He squinted as one twisted away and dove towards the ground, streaking across the park towards them before performing an unexpected aerobatic twist and diving to the flowered enclave with a scream from Comet.

In the enclave, Comet had thrown her wings up over her head into a shield of metallic purple-green brushed with gold. Heart hammering in her chest she waited for the shadow to descend upon her.

'Comet?'

It wasn't said aloud.

'Comet is that really you?'

Cautiously, she drew her wings away from her face and squinted up at him, shielding her eyes from the sunlight.

Holding onto the pole, Sabre climbed headfirst down as deftly as a monkey, cocking his head to one side as he examined her.

A flicker of familiarity stirring from the depths of her memories. Long forgotten images of icy mountains and skimming the waters of a long silvery lake, blurred faces and muffled voices.

"You!" She responded in a small voice. "You shouldn't be here!"

He let go, dropping and landing before her. Tailfeathers fanning out behind him, he approached her on all fours with his wings arched behind him.

'Neither should you.'

Black wings between two different ermine-spotted white ones and silvery slate grey– nicknames of nicknames, different to the doctors– Arctic, Ghost, Shadow, and Silverbird, all getting shouted at again– 'don't fly over the mountain, what did I tell you all'– childish giggles following a defiant tongue stuck out at the doctors, the brothers pulling each other's tails again–

"Sabre…" She let her wings drop behind her, with a laugh of disbelief and feeling faint with shock. *'You were always the bad one, Shadow.'*

'I still am, Shiny.'

"Why are you here? *How* are you here? Where's Fell?"

No verbal answer only–

The image of a familiar dark eyed doctor staring her down, a fierce and determined pride– joy at getting to fly freely– 'Find me evidence that she's alive, I won't believe it until I have proof' – agnostic disbelief, sad memories of fire and screaming, so much screaming–

"Comet! Run!"

Sabre blinked, snapping back to formality and leaping up to his feet, powering his wings down to draw back away from Wilny to Comet's side. She ducked, avoiding brushing against the long black feathers, falling back into the rhododendrons with a second shriek.

Wings splayed into arches that took up the entire circle, he stared Wilny down, mouth agape in shock.

"B-Bluebird? *Wilny*? How the- They said you were dead!" He said aloud upon the sight of Wilny's iridescent peacock green and indigo wings. "They cremated you, we had DNA proof!"

"Well, they're wrong!" His wings swept out into a blur and Sabre backpedalled away as Wilny struck at him. He avoided and blocked the swinging punches before taking a bounding leap into the air. Taking out his phone, Sabre took both of their photographs and then catching the breeze he floated away without the slightest wingbeat.

"Comet!" Wilny scrambled to help pull the other Hummingbird out of the bushes.

"Sabre...Sabre's here..." Comet was paling from shock, drifting into a daze. Catching her before she collapsed entirely, Wilny did his best to rouse her as her eyes rolled in their sockets and she went limp in his arms. Pain seared across his frontal lobe as spikes of fear and drips of drifting consciousness projected from Comet started to hound him. Her range was thirty meters, a hundred feet. If she woke up in a panic–

"Comet, Comet stay calm." Wilny took her chin and lifted it for her to look at him. "Look at me. Focus on me."

He wasn't Crow. He couldn't project thoughts or emotions properly to trick her brain into staying calm. But he had to do something before she hurt herself.

Breathing slowly, he pulled the shawl she had dropped over her and gathered her up into his arms. Musing, he felt the growing inferno of white noise that was present on the edges of Comet's mind. Mental snapshots of blurry faces illuminated by an all-engulfing fire flashed across his mind.

'*Shhh.... shh...Stay calm. It's okay. It's okay.*' He mused loudly, hoping there was some semblance of consciousness in Comet still present and alert enough to respond. He tried to make himself calm so that he could make her feel calm.

'*I'm here, you're safe.*'

The inferno withdrew. She'd heard him. The light returned to her eyes, lashes fluttering and she gulped for breath, trembling at the sudden onslaught of terror. Looking up at him, she bit back tears of embarrassment and clung to Wilny's arms as though he would vanish at any second.

"I'm here, you're safe." He assured her aloud.

A collective scream rose from the playpark followed by the rending of metal and wood. Head snapping up, he gently let go of Comet and stood.

"Stay here." He ordered, ignoring the pleading pawing of his arm.

"Let me help…"

"Stay. *Here.*" He ordered her again with the softest of voices and before she could argue, forced himself into a vertical take-off, wings a blur and rose above the flowered enclave to see mothers and children scattering from Kathy.

Lana lay on the ground in pain, having been struck down, but using the invisible knife of her telkens to swipe and slash at Kathy, ripping through monkey bars and wooden steppingstones as she leaped and darted out of the way.

Without the ability to concentrate or being able to see what she was hitting; she risked the destruction of the entire playpark and surrounding trees.

Spiralling, Wilny snapped his wings to his sides and feet first he arrowed into Kathy's side, screaming with rage and knocking her straight from her perch on a slide.

The SmartFabric tore and restitched itself as she barrelled across the asphalt, feathers flying as they were ripped and torn from her wings during the tumble. But she wasn't of importance to him. Leaving her dazed, he rushed to Lana's side, helping her up and checking her over.

"Wilny." Malana murmured, reaching a small hand out towards his face before shutting her eyes and falling unconscious. Blood poured down the side of her face from a gash across her forehead.

Fury flared, along with the burning wish to rip out the Vulture's spine but needing to take care of the bleeding girl in his arms.

Raoul vaulted over the fence, launching himself upon Kathy. His claws shredded through her wings, ripping the feathers out. They scrapped in a quick and vicious tussle, stirring up dust, screeching and snarling at each other.

The wing smacked Raoul hard across the face, knocking him back. He drew back into a feral crouch upon all fours with a throaty snarl, the fur down his spine bristling and elongated teeth glinting sharp white in the sun. A metallic blur made him squint and pause for a moment, and Comet dropped in behind the Vulture.

"Don't hurt them!" Comet shrieked throwing herself forward and grabbing Kathy's wings by the arch that flowed from her shoulder. Pain seared across Kathy's back and her legs buckled from beneath her. With an ungracious fluttering and fanning of her tailfeathers, Comet collapsed on top of the vulture, still gripping her wings tightly.

Weakened by the sudden strike of pain, Raoul took a chance and snarling loudly, charged at the Vulture. Comet's eyes grew wide with terror, seeing the flashing teeth and clawed hands.

'No. PLEASE NO!' her voice sliced through their minds with a flashing pulse of twisted memories of terror swirling up into an inferno.

"Raoul, no!" Wilny yelled, but it was too late.

The inferno pulsed and exploded. Pure white blinding them into a black terror that flooded their minds, suffocating all rational thought in a heartbeat. Pure concentrated panic assaulting them.

"Traitor!" Voices screamed through Wilny's mind, "Traitor! Traitor! TRAITOR!"

"Kill them all."

"TRAITOR!"

Clamouring, suffering voices, all screaming in his head. All of them so real and so loud.

The terror ripped into his chest like a pickaxe, throwing his world into a swirling blackness. His chest wrenched in agony at the familiarity of the voices, the rage within them, the disgust. He couldn't breathe. Bloodstains blossomed upon his hands and flowing down his arms so hot and sticky that it felt like putrid crimson honey that seeped into every pore.

"Murderer." The voices, some whispering, some screaming, began to chant. *"Traitor! Murderer! Traitor!"*

"I'm sorry!" He choked, every strained breath burning his throat.

"Kill yourself! Kill yourself! You don't deserve to live!"

"No!"

"TRAITOR!"

The voices were right. He was a traitor. He'd done it before, what would stop him from repeating the mistake again– Suffocating– No air to breathe– Every toxic thought another stab into his heart.

'You deserve it Bluebird.' A singsong voice. He hated that voice. The Frigatebird.

"No. No, not you. You're not here. Please don't be here."

'Begging already? You won't make Diamond like that.'

"GET OUT OF MY HEAD!" He screamed at the Frigatebird's voice, "GET OUT! GET OUT! GET OUT!"

Clawing at himself, he felt for anything sharp, a knife, a key, something sharp to slice. Nothing. He begun to claw at his throat, driving his nails deep into his skin, trying to stop the Frigatebird from seizing control of him before he could hurt anyone else–

A blast of wind like the strike of a hurricane hit them all, felling those who stood with its wings. A bright slice of sunlit silver cut through the nightmare black and the intense screaming silenced for a brief moment. A winged beast with flashing fangs and crackling with static prowled before him.

"Wilny?"

Run.

Run!

Was it his own voice? He couldn't tell.

RUN!

IT'LL KILL YOU!

An uncontrollable scream left his throat and he fell onto his back, scrambling to get away from the silver beast. Every movement felt sluggish and numbed. The beast approached him, the striped feathers dazzling and tremoring before his eyes.

Thrashing about he tried to escape the beast, kicking wildly and scraping his wings so hard against the ground that he ripped several, making them bleed. It reached for him and he kicked hard against its arm with a crack. Its screeched with pain and reeled back only to pounce upon him and pin him to the ground before he could escape.

"I'm sorry." It said sorrowfully, grabbing his arm as he tried to shove it away. Electricity discharged through him and he dropped like a stone on the grass, staring at the sky which faded to black.

Ignoring her throbbing arm, Storm put Wilny into the recovery position, making sure to check his pulse and breathing before she did. He was safe, for now. Biting back the tears of pain she rose to her feet and surveyed the damage.

Many of the people had fled, but the few dumb idiots who had pulled out their phones to film had been caught in the radius and now lay quaking on the ground. Letting her wings hang limply Storm looked down upon the people she had taken down with a beat of her wings. She had come in so fast that she had broken several of Raoul and Comet's ribs upon impact, and left Kathy with a twisted wing. But she had no other way she could have stopped them from tearing themselves apart.

There was no less than fifty people lain on the floor in terror, some perfectly still, some still screaming and clawing to escape from invisible monsters.

"Storm!"

She looked to the sky, Kat sweeping in with a flagging Eagle beside her who skidded to his knees with a poorly executed landing.

"Oh god." Kat breathed, looking about the park. Swallowing down the initial shock and pain, Storm switched to business mode, forcing some order upon the situation. "What happened?"

"Owen's on his way, I need you to move Raoul and Malana into the recovery position and stem any bleeding." She ordered. "You, Amell right? I need you to hold Wilny down if he wakes up again, because he will try and hurt himself or anyone else who comes near."

Amell stood up straight, bewildered by the situation and Storm's sudden sharpness. He surveyed the devastation.

"Did Kathy do this or that other guy?"

"Neither." She looked to Comet laying limp and unconscious beside Kathy, so pale and still that she appeared nearly dead. Kathy who lay wide-eyed on the ground, staring, but unseeing in paralytic horror from being within the initial blast radius of Comet. Quickly, she rushed to their sides, checking their pulse and breathing and then carefully turned the girls onto their sides to put them into the recovery position, trying to make them more comfortable until the Rioteer medics arrived.

A shadow was cast across her as she moved Kathy and straightened out her wing. Storm knew who it was and before Amell could even make a move, Storm span on her heels and kicked his knee from under him, flattening him in an instant. She leapt between him and Kathy.

She flourished her wing out and pushed him back as hard as she could. He frowned at her in disgust as he tried to push past her to get to Kathy, only to have Kat leap behind her and help block him.

"Don't even try it." Storm warned, lip curling back into a snarl that revealed her sharp cat-like teeth.

"But-"

"We're going to need her alive."

"But she-"

"*I know!* I know what she did, and I know that you want revenge, but right now we need to get everyone to safety before this gets out of control!" She yelled, beating her wings and forcing him back.

"I need you to help me, help them. That is the most important thing right now and if you're not going to help then go sit down before I'll fucking *geld* you, got it?" Her voice so icily cold and severe that the Eagle dropped his eyes to his feet in submission. Their disparagement in size and strength meant nothing to her.

"Yes ma'am."

"Now tell me. Who was other guy that came with Kathy?"

Wiping away the shamefacedness he craned his neck to spot the Kite, before pointing to the swift-like shadow now sailing away back to the city centre high above them.

"Him. I don't know who he is but he came all the way from France with her."

Storm looked to where he was pointing.

The Kite was already a mile and a half away, but still clear within Storm's raptorial vision.

"Got it." She nodded. "Stay here. Take care of Wilny. Kat, you're in charge."

Without a moment of hesitation, she swept out her wings and launched herself into the sky with a single leap and downward stroke that kicked a cloud of dust into their eyes.

"Storm!" Kat screamed after her. "Where are you going!"

Ignoring Kat, she kept powering upwards through the blue until she was just a dot within their vision. She couldn't linger any longer on the ground, she needed to know what they were dealing with and fast.

Kathy here.

Stranger here.

How?

Her thoughts were sharp and fast, trying to connect the dots, but lacking in all the knowledge to piece together the reasons.

Why.

Something more-

Someone else-

Too many questions. What she needed was answers.

She homed in on the shadowy Avio, flying behind him and keeping her wings angled so that she was using the currents of air to make her approach fast and silent. He himself was sailing effortlessly through the sky upon the winds like a kite with barely a wing beat and making a beeline for a chinook that was slowly making its way out of the city.

Rising a little higher until she was flying directly above him, she prepared herself and examined the shape of his wings. It was always good to see who you would be against in a dogfight.

They were long and pointed, somewhere between designed for long distance soaring and quick agility, especially with elongated forked tail. He wouldn't be a fast flyer, but he would certainly be quick on the turn.

With a flick of her wings, she twisted and fell upon him with an avenging fury and a powerful kick that caught him between the wings.

Sabre howled in pain and surprise. The phone he had been messaging from fell from his hands, and slipping past him, Storm chased after it, but the Kite was quickly on her tail.

She caught the phone and in a quick flip, spiralled out of his way as he dove past her. Her lack of tailfeathers put her at a disadvantage, though she still tried to move as though she still had them, it wasn't enough and the Kite was steeply looping round after her.

The two scrapped and slashed at each other in the air, swirling and arcing with aerobatic speed as they fought for the phone, their fight and flight so fast that it put swifts to shame. Climbing, then diving into a steep rolling stoop, the Kite caught up with her, catching hold of her fluttering sash and pulling himself in. At arms-length with each other in a downward spiral, Sabre grabbed one hand for the phone, and the other to her throat, forcing Storm to release it so that she could pull him away from choking her. He almost laughed at her ballsiness as she kicked him in the gut, but then came the shock.

Electricity jolted through him, a biting pain that forced him to let her go.

Storm barked with laughter at him as he recoiled, and beating her wings, powered in for another kick just as Sabre pulled out his gun on her.

14

The resonating crack of the gun paralysed Storm in the air.

She reeled back into a hover, expecting pain and blood, but the bullet passed through her primaries and left a burn hole through them that coiled the fibres of the feathers up around the edges. He'd missed intentionally.

Her distraction was enough for him to snatch at her feathers, nearly ripping them from their follicles. Letting his huge wings billow and catch the wind, he dragged her along below him, pulling her up so that he was holding her more from the wrist of her wing than the feathers.

"Oh shit." He breathed, staring down at her in astonishment as she struggled to free herself. Like her, the thin third eyelid of the nictitating membrane was spread across his eyes, protecting them from the wind and dust in the sky.

"Silverbird! It really is you. Sweet fuck, the Professor is going to freak the fuck out about this! How the shit are you alive Storm? Where are your tailfeathers?"

Raising the camera, he snapped the picture of her being dragged beneath him by her wing, face darkened in anger.

"Who the fuck are you?" She yelled up at him. "Who sent you?"

He frowned, releasing her. Pulling back into a lazy glide with the long V of tailfeathers tilting and fanning to steady himself, wings wide and effortlessly floating on the breeze. She dropped then righted herself, rising to match his height and hover. She almost felt a little envious of his wingspan. Her entire length only just covered over one of his stark black and white wings, putting him at near-on thirty foot to her eighteen and a half.

Pocketing the phone, he made no indication that he was about to reach for the gun again and attack, his behaviour being one of confused curiosity rather than aggression.

"Silverbird, it's me. Sabre. *Shadow*. You should know me but why don't..."

He winced as he tried to focus on her. He was musing but it was like trying to hear a radio without signal; there was only angry static and a muffled echo of thoughts as she maintained her electrified field around her, blocking him out.

Baring her teeth into a snarl she, made a warning lunge at him.

"Trying to trigger memories isn't going to work with me."

"Yeah, it's you alright. You always were impossible when you were pissed off." He said to himself laughingly, cocking his head to the side in wild bewilderment. "You don't remember at all do you? What did they do to you to make you all forget?"

"Forget what?"

"*Loch Mullardoch!* I saw Rex shoot you! We all saw! Straight to the heart and then you fell from a hundred feet into the lake. How the fuck did you survive that?"

The mischievous slyness was gone from his tone, solemn shock replacing it, and it chilled her. He was so convinced of knowing her that it scared her.

Cold nauseating dread knotted her stomach at the name of the bunker she had come from, and she let go of her electrified charge. Flashes of fragments of memories flickered through her mind in a disarray of painful chaos.

"Oh. You remember...some." Wincing, he rubbed his chest. The same spot as where on Storm was a deeply pitted scar of a bullet wound.

"Why the fuck are you working for him, you know he's a monster right? He's why all of this is happening!" He was near on shouting, voice strained and wavering with frustration and grief. "Why does he have you? And Comet? And Wilny? You're all supposed to be dead!"

"I don't work for Rex." Storm hissed, knowing he was right. "I'm just trying to protect my family and keep everyone safe."

"From who?"

"Fr-from-"

"From us? From ARCDA?"

"From *everything!*"

"We're not the ones who hurt you!"

"If that's the truth then why is everyone so broken?" She bombarded him as he mused with rage, with flashes of memories of helping Wilny through his nightmares,

Crow angry at the very thought of Atlas, of the Old Rogues in pain and traumatised with haunted eyes whenever they came close to an ARCDA bunker.

Sabre reeled back, betrayed and distraught but quickly he gathered himself.

"Still vicious." He laughed softly. "Hate ARCDA all you want for what it has done, but please, *please*, keep Comet and yourself away from Rex. He's our real enemy here."

Without another word he fell from the sky in a graceful arc, sweeping his wings out at the lowest point and gliding out towards where the chinook slowly made its way out of the city.

She followed sharply after him, keeping pace and watching as he dipped below it, tucking his wings in tight and darting into the open door at its rear, avoiding the spinning blades. It powered on ahead, gaining speed. Storm caught its wake, angling her wings enough to ride it and keep speed.

The men in the back all saw and scrambled to get their weapons and aim, but much to her surprise, Sabre blocked them by extending his huge wings across the doorway, aiming his own weapon at her as she flew behind.

"I'm not here to fight you Storm, I really don't want you to think that's what I came to do." He shouted at her over the thunder of the blades. "Please don't make me shoot you."

"Then why did you come here?"

"Just to see if it really was you." He holstered the gun, holding on tight to the doorframe of the helicopter with a feral grin spreading across his face. "Now I just want to see how fast you can disappear again."

'*Retreat.*' His voice was surprisingly clear within her mind, that even the sound of the helicopter blades couldn't stop him from being heard. '*They'll shoot and then I'll have to eat them for being so rude.*'

There was no point in chasing them down or waiting to be shot. Folding her wings, she twisted and dropped back to earth, arcing up before she struck the ground and darting into the forest of skyscrapers and wind turbines, letting him escape.

There were too many questions now, some of which she began to dread getting an answer to with a fear that made her sick to her stomach. But what mattered above them all was her Rogues.

Owen's team had worked fast in getting enough ambulances to the human victims of Comet's attack, as well as getting the damaged Synths out of sight and into treatment before any news teams could arrive on the scene.

Wilny was unconscious still, barely breathing when they rushed him into the intensive care unit at the back of the headquarters medical ward. While Raoul and Malana were taken into the main area, both Kathy and Comet were sent directly into quarantine despite the injuries and the ongoing paralytic terror, as even when unconscious Comet could still be dangerous.

"What happened?" Asena asked Kat as the Lioness snapped and snarled at the Rioteers and residents to get out the way as they crowded the doors of the medical ward to watch what was happening.

"Comet projected her terror onto everyone and Storm took them out." She said quietly, showing her to the back room where Wilny lay unconscious. His hands had been forced into restraints and though he was heavily sedated, his wings would strain and force him to arch up off the bed to the point the restraints threatened to snap. Deep red scratches covered his throat and chin from where he had clawed at himself, and the nurses worriedly monitored the ECG which gave erratic readings for his heart rate.

They could give him medication, but the dosage for Avios and with him having heart problems would make it difficult to treat. For now, the most they could do was give him time.

"Let me see them."

"Beth, you need to stay back he could bite-"

"Richard, *I* will bite you and then rip out your spleen if you don't let me see my team." The Owl snarled at the headquarters head doctor. He tried to put his arms out to block her path, only to have Beth raise her metallic bird-shaped foot and threaten to kick him in the gut.

"Let her through." Asena ordered before Beth resorted to outright violence. Beth shoved past the doctor before he had a chance to respond and marched up to Raoul's bed where the Hound lay stirring from unconsciousness.

"Come on Puppy, wake up and bring yourself back to reality!" She snarled, taking him by the ear– "You're not letting bad dreams get the better of you."

"Beth!" Yelled the doctor, attempting to grab the Owl by the arm and pull her away from his patient.

"Richard, I will fucking end you! Back off and let me deal with my Rogues! I need to know what happened with all of them."

Eyes fluttering open, Raoul swayed and shakily forced himself into sitting up despite the sharp stabbing pain from his broken ribs. Bile kept rising in his throat, hot and acidic, threatening to come up.

"That's it, Puppy, wake up."

Disorientated, he had no idea where he was. His mind was a cacophony of images, sounds, smells and pain. There was no order and no one memory was worse than another. He could barely focus on the face in front of him.

Sharp clarity cut through as someone gently pushed upon his shoulder to lay him down, their voice angry and biting next to the deep sombre tone of the doctor. A blur of brown hair, rust eyes surrounded by red.

"Beth!" He yelped at her, bolting back upright to great agony and gripping her arms tightly. "Beth that's you, *oui*? Please say it is."

"Yes, it's me, now let go. You're cutting off the blood flow to the only arm I have left!"

"*Desolé.*" He swallowed again. "Where's Malana and Wilny? There was an Avio-"

A sharp stab pierced through his brain shocking his vision into blurred white, all sound drown out by a screaming tinnitus siren –

"Hound nummer P-zweiundzwanzig-vierundzwanzig, sie anzugreifen!" A commander barking at him, waving a cattle prod in the air as he stood on the platform over the arena. Afraid not angry; we can't all be dead.

'Can't breathe.'

White walls splashed with black– no, red, dried red.

'I can't breathe! Someone help me!'

"Hound V-twenty-two, twenty-four! Respond immediately–"

"Raoul?"

"Hey now son, stay with us–"

"Do you want to play? They said you're going to play with us."

A group of six small girls stood before him. Identical girls, the same yellow eyes and hungry smiles. They spoke as one, because they were one. "Do you want to play?" They repeated. He felt sick looking at them. Red uniforms— no, they were white once.

"I don't want to hurt you." He said aloud, both to the memory and to Beth.

He backed away and ran from the girls as they turned into fiery screaming banshees, slicing through his brothers.

"TUEZ-LES TOUS." A female doctor replaced the man with the cattle prod. She watches with her clipboard and doesn't interfere. Nose crinkled. "C'est un ordre."

Claws ripped into his shoulder, throwing him backwards to the ground. The big Wolf, circling and snapping at him. Teeth too large for his mouth.

"You are trackers now! Hunters!" He snarled, kicking him in the ribs as he passed. "Okay Runt? Desert or disobey me and I will skin you."

He turned, his face morphed into an abominable wolf creature that began to peel away the skin with fire, exposing raw muscle and fresh pink bone until it blackened and turned to ash. Around him the air was filled with the screaming and agonised howling of boys as they lay dying. The scent of burnt fur and flesh filled the air, the screaming grew into a solid noise-

"Raoul!"

The name more real than the memory, as was the shocking jolt across his leg. Eyes snapping open he found Storm gripping his leg with her talons hard enough to send blood running down his calf and staining the sheets he lay on whilst cradling her newly recast arm to her chest.

"Storm?" His throat burned to speak. She gave him a small smile which didn't reach her eyes.

He shuddered, picking up on the animosity in Storm as she turned to the doctor and demand that he bring Raoul some sedative patches to keep him calm and from being triggered off into another attack. Looking around, Beth was stood at the back beside the doors into the quarantine area in a deep and vicious argument with the Rioteers head of security.

A small tap on his shoulder made him flinch, and Malana stood and stared at him with tear filled eyes. The gash across her head had been given stitches and gauze, but the impact of hitting the ground still gave her a dark purple bruise across the side of her face. She sniffled bitterly, clearly holding her breath so that she wouldn't cry and reached her hands up to him.

Obligingly he lifted her up onto the bed beside him, giving no resistance when she flung her arms around his neck and quietly cried upon his shoulder.

"Hey hey hey, it's alright now." He murmured softly, trying to comfort the little girl. "I know…believe me I know."

"Aidez-moi, s'il vous plaît…"

"I'll help you, it'll be alright– *What was the nightmare?*" He slipped into quiet French for her so that she could speak easily.

"They kept cutting open my head to see how the knife works. Leilani too."

"Your telkens?"

"Yes. They kept cutting me and Leilani, so I cut them back. I didn't mean to, but they fell on the floor then I fell through the clouds and Rust didn't catch me. They didn't help me, and I couldn't help them and they were screaming and my knife couldn't reach-"

"Shh Shhh,"

"I don't want to fall any more, Raoul, I don't want to fall!"

He sat her up and gently brushed out one of her rusty orange wings so that the feathers splayed and cast shadows upon the floor. Rubbing her eyes, she followed his gaze to her wings as he drew a nail along the edge of a deep brown primary, bending it so that she could see the gold coming through on the edges.

"Look at your wings. They are so big now, as are you. You're not going to fall down anymore. Storm will teach you how to fly."

Storm forced a smile to her face and nodded, lifting Malana awkwardly onto her hip with one hand and nodded for Raoul to rise. Using a wing she curved it around each of them, helping to support the little girl as she walked with them to the back of the medical ward, as well as to comfort them with their warmth. She didn't seem to mind as he pulled on her wing to draw it closer to him.

Both were distressed to see Wilny restrained on the other side of the glass, but the sudden and violent thrashing made it clear why he needed them.

"What…what is wrong with him?" Malana asked hesitantly, frowning with pain through the bruise and stitches as she tried to recall English.

Storm sighed deeply. "He's having nightmares too, Sunshine."

"We help?"

"We're going to try."

-x-

"That was disappointing Bluebird." The doctor frowned at him, "Let's try that again."

The bulkhead doors parted, and Bluebird walked out into the darkened arena, back into the maze scenario for what felt like the hundredth time. The buzzer sounded, and the lights came on. It was a tall domed stadium, a ceiling that exposed the stars. His team scattered into the maze, following out their orders. Capture and neutralise the opposing team, using as few rounds of live ammunition as possible, and they would all begin their process of moving on up to become Diamond Elites.

They were matched up, Ruby-One versus the newly reassembled Sapphire-One.

Every run was the same and he remembered every entrance and shortcut in detail. He wouldn't fly up over the wall, all the combatants were armed with live rounds in their handguns. It may have been non-lethal practice, but he didn't want to be shot down, accidentally or otherwise.

Snapping and snarling resounded across the maze followed by a familiar howl.

'Feather's found their Canid.'

Leaping up onto the legs of the eastern watchtower he took a quick scan of the maze for any signs of movement. The longer he remained on the tower the more of a target he was. He tried to keep his long tailfeathers still, their large disks on the ends of them would catch in the light and draw attention.

A shadow on the wall, a slice of black streaking across the stadium. He looked up too late, the stars blotted out against huge wings and a pair of boots that struck him straight in the face. Blackness swallowed him for several seconds, reeling with pain as he tried to recover himself and push himself up off the ground.

"So, you're the one I've heard about. A hummingbird?" The Frigatebird-Avio laughed, face blurred by black smoke and voice echoed by a simple trick of perception distortion. A muser.

A cold prickle ran across Bluebird's scalp and his limbs jerked. In a disorientating clash of senses, he saw himself through the Frigatebird's eyes standing in a daze with his wings limply beside him. The Frigatebird laughed, itching at a patch of Nitro on his arm as Bluebird rose to his feet and unholstered his gun.

'Stop. STOP.' Bluebird screamed in horror, or at least he tried to scream. The words were strangled in his throat, his mouth wouldn't open. He could feel the Frigatebird's gleeful delight, a sour taste in his mouth caused by the Nitro and a poisonous aching pain in his bones.

"Be a good boy now and kill them all." The Frigatebird said.

The Frigatebird took off with a leap and Bluebird marched onwards through the maze, following the directions of the Frigatebird above. He tried to fight off the control, but the muser was boosted by Nitro and there was nothing he could do to fight back.

A flash of blonde hair and ghostly pale skin caught his attention. One of his teammates. Rainbow.

'No, please don't go after her!'

'Begging already? You won't make Diamond like that.'

Again, his body didn't respond to his wishes. He moved swiftly and silently to her, making his way through the maze, sticking to the shadows. Closing in on her, he got within two meters before she heard him. Her enhanced hearing as a Preternatural and the eerie silence of the arena made it hard for him to disguise his footsteps and the rustle of his feathers against his uniform.

Spinning on her heels, an invisible force struck Bluebird hard in the chest, knocking him to the floor. The telkens grabbed his arms and pulled them above his head so he was left dangling in mid-air, legs kicking wildly.

"Bluebird! What have I told you about sneaking up on me?" She breathed happily, recognising her teammate, dropping her guard and releasing him. One of many identical VE-RA Preternaturals with diamond skin and telkens, but she was unique in his eyes.

"I could have taken your head off."

Jogging the short distance to him she wrapped her arms around him and squeezed him tight in an affectionate hug, ignoring the arena protocol. She was so thin and delicate he always worried about breaking her bones whenever they touched.

'Don't hurt her! Please! She's not the enemy!'

'Aw you love her, don't you?'

'PLEASE!' He screamed. His body tensed and trembled as he tried to fight the muser's control.

He placed Bluebird's hands upon her shoulders. She frowned at him, sensing something wrong when he didn't speak.

A quick sweep of her legs and throwing his weight forward, she fell back with a shriek. He couldn't stop the Frigatebird using his hands to grab her neck.

Silver eyes wide with shock she kicked and squirmed beneath him, her own hands grabbing at his arms, nails cutting into his skin. Her telkens smacked him in the head and shoulders, trying to force him off, but the Frigatebird held tight.

'Stop it! STOP IT! I DON'T WANT TO DO THIS!'

'But I do.'

An invisible force clipped the side of his head, knocking him flying into the maze wall and dragging Rainbow with him.

"I'm sorry…" He choked, a tearful pained sob that slipped through.

Tears filled his eyes as he gripped her hair with one hand and with a sharp and sudden pull, snapped her head back. She fell limp in his arms, staring straight ahead. The Frigatebird released him for a few short moments, allowing him to sink to his knees and break into an anguished sob as he tried to shake Rainbow back into life.

"Don't do this! Don't be real!" He sobbed. "Don't be real! Please don't be dead, Rain-"

'She didn't even try to kill you, how romantic.'

"I'LL KILL YOU! I'LL FUCKING KILL YOU!" He screamed to the black sky above.

"Bluebird! What's wrong!"

He flinched at the voice, snapping his head round to see Eddie.

The other Avio watched him with dark green concerned eyes, dark grey Shrike wings marked by a single band of white across the primaries that were helping him to balance effortlessly on the wall. He stared down in horror at him holding Rainbow in his arms.

The Frigatebird's strings began to tighten again around Bluebird's mind.

Bluebird let Rainbow go, backing away from Eddie as fast as he could.

"Is she– Is Rainbow…" Eddie's voice wavered, "B-Bluebird? What-"

'Not Eddie!' Bluebird screamed to the Frigatebird, fighting against the control and writhing upon the ground in agony. The mental strings pulled tighter, crushing his chest to the point his heart felt as though it would burst from beating too fast. *'Please! Don't make me hurt him!'*

'Okay then. Then he can hurt you instead.'

The strings were loosened enough that Bluebird could yell.

"Eddie, move! Muser!"

The Frigatebird showed himself sweeping down upon the Shrike. Instantly, Eddie bolted out the way, the black wings swept over him. As always, Eddie had a knife with him, which he threw at the Frigatebird, slicing him across the wing and shearing off several black feathers.

The Frigatebird yelped with pain. He must have tried to use his muser abilities upon Eddie, Bluebird realised, only to find them useless against the bioelectric field that the Shrike emitted and swore in outrage.

"Ed-" Bluebird choked, his body jerked as he was forced to his feet. Eddie snapped his head round watching as Bluebird tried to resist pulling out the gun. Everything fell into slow motion as the Shrike, sprang into the air, driving his short wings down as fast as he could to get out of the line of fire, aware that he wasn't fast enough.

The boy snapped his eyes shut, and Bluebird pulled the trigger. The sound echoed for an eternity and Eddie dropped from the sky, the bullet shredding feathers that blustered and floated about long after his body fell from sight behind the wall.

The mental strings snapped, and Bluebird fell to the floor, gasping for air and catching at his chest. Tears blurred his vision.

'This can't be happening, this can't be happening,' he told himself.

Footsteps, sprinting towards him, but his vision too blurry to focus until they came closer. A Preternatural, dressed in the same red and black uniform as the one he wore. Fury.

"Blue-" Fury froze, catching the thought and immediately jumped backwards, hand reaching for the gun on his belt. "What-"

"I can't stop him! He's trying to kill us all!" Bluebird screamed from the floor. "I can't fight him! Help me please!"

"LEAVE HIM!" Fury roared, taking out his gun and turning the safety off, sighting the Frigatebird. Several rounds were fired, followed by a howl from the black-winged Avio and a crash as he hit the floor.

Bluebirds hand's jerked as the strings descended again, and Fury span and shouted something, but the world turned to a silent white.

White cleared, dazed and dizzy, the world was out of focus flashing amber to red to white, repeating over and over again. The siren was blaring with painful pulsing drones that flashed pain across his mind with every note. His right leg was broken, and hands felt heavy and sticky, and so raising them he squinted in pain trying to force his vision back into focus. Blood and black feathers covered over his hands.

'*What a fight,*' the Frigatebird laughed, leant against a wall for support, blood dripping onto the floor. '*What a fight.*'

Bluebird blearily looked around. Fury lay on the floor surrounded by black feathers at an awkward broken angle, his skull cracked against the concrete, blood splattering the floor and pooling around him. Bile rose in Bluebird's throat and he fell to his knees and retched.

"No…no this can't be-"

Bluebird snapped round at the voice and he raised the gun against his remaining teammate.

"Featherhead…" A sob caught in his throat as the Wolf stood before him, pale skin covered with scars and scarlet eyes narrowed in rage at the Frigatebird. Before he could move, Bluebird dragged himself to his feet, throwing his wings out either side of him. He couldn't let

Bluebird shook the gun before the Frigatebird in threat.

"Get back Feather! He'll make me kill you!"

'You love him too, how greedy. I should have made you choose between them. That would have been fun.' The Frigatebird trilled manically. He tasted the acrid spike of Nitro being used again by the other Avio. *'Maybe I should do this instead.'*

The weight of the Frigatebird lifted on him, but Featherhead suddenly doubled over with a howl of pain behind him, clawing at his head. He let rip a snarl from deep within his throat, vision twisted and distorted as he turned his sights onto Bluebird.

"He's stronger than you." Frigatebird laughed through both Featherhead's voice and his own behind him. "They love you so much, but it's not gonna stop me making him tear you apart."

Bluebird laughed hysterically, tears pouring down his cheeks. He fell to his knees, staring the Wolf down as he dug his claws into the floor, fighting the control.

"You don't need to make him kill me…" He said in a low and broken voice raising the gun to his head, "I'll do it myself."

Featherhead lunged at him with huge claws and sharp teeth. He swiped at Bluebird's arm, claws cutting through the SmartFabric suit and into his shoulder, then rammed him to the ground. Pain shot across his back as he landed upon his wings, but it was only the sharp claws slashing through the fragile propatagium and across his shoulder that made him scream.

The two wrestled for control of the gun, Featherhead's long teeth gnashing centimetres from his face. In the struggle the gun fired with a ringing crack that echoed across the stadium, and the big black Wolf slumped on top of him. Hot blood trickled down onto his face and neck.

"Feather?" Bluebird whispered hoarsely, shaking the body. There was no movement. Tears spilled down his face and his chest tightened. The Frigatebird hadn't controlled him that time, he'd killed him. He'd killed Featherhead.

He'd killed them all.

A thunder of footsteps and mechanical whir filled the air over the droning alarm, as the guards in their black mechanised ExoArmour dragged the Wolf's corpse off him. Gulping down air and trying not to sob, he forced himself to stand, biting back his tears of rage. The bodies of all four of his teammates lay before her and she paced before them, noting down the extent of their injuries into a tablet. She was speaking, but he heard nothing as he looked down at the blood and bodies, heartbeat ringing in his ears.

"Bluebird." The Doctor snapped, drawing his attention away from his team. She frowned at him, "Let's try that again."

And with her command he was turned around and forced back into the maze. Back into the darkness waiting for the bulkhead to open again with his team.

'Please...I want to stop,' Wilny begged himself, trying to stay still and not enter the stadium. *'I want to wake up, I don't want to remember.'*

But his legs wouldn't listen. They marched on through the maze, taking the exact same route as before. Back up the tower, struck down by the Frigatebird, unable to move on his own, spotting the flash of blonde again. Every detail was the same.

Rainbow turned to face him, lowering her fists and smiling like all the other times before.

"Bluebird! What have I told you about sneaking up on me?" She breathed happily.

'Stop. Please.'

His hands were trembling as she jogged up towards him–

-but then it changed.

The nightmare rippled around him, fading and distorting into hazy black and greys.

A deep and crackling *Caw-caw* shook the dream. The walls prickled and peeled inwards towards him, growing oily black plumes that moved, breathed, and shook, rattling like leaves against the wind as another *Caw* echoed through the transformed corridors. It swallowed him in blackness, but not darkness. Glittering black eyes, the size of tennis balls blinked at him between the feathers, huge black wings formed and melted into the walls as they beat. The temperature rose with a living heat.

He could barely breathe, barely move, an invisible weight sat upon his chest. Every attempt to twist and turn was like swimming in syrup and swinging his arm around as hard as he could he slowly and painfully twisted to face the wall. An eye blinked and burst before him, setting lose a flock of crows into his face that drove him to the soft ground.

"Wilny!" The crows cawed at him as one, clawing at his chest and scattering about him with noisy wingbeats. "Wake up! Wake up! *WAKE UP!*"

Wilny shrieked trying to push the crow off his chest.

"It's not real Wilny! Stop trying to hit me!"

A hint of familiarity about the voice, the rolling R and the warm Scottish twang within it that had grown to be comforting. The cloud of feathers scattered, and a soft peach light poured into his eyes.

"That's it, come on. Wake up."

"I am awake."

"You're *nearly* awake, just open your eyes."

Obeying the Crow's command, his eyelids fluttered open. Crow was leant over him, shielding Wilny's face from the glare of the medical ward's bright lamps. A wide smile spread across his face as Wilny blinked and reached up to feel the feathers on his face, trying to make sure it was real.

"Hey Willners." He laughed softly, placing a gentle hand on his shoulder, "Welcome back."

Wilny took a sharp breath as he realised, he was awake and in the present. Letting out a sob, he sat bolt upright and threw his arms around Crow, burying his face into his shoulder. Drawing his immense charcoal wings around them, Crow allowed him to be shielded from all onlookers to preserve what little pride he had left and let him cry.

"Thank you…" Wilny mumbled into Crow's shoulder, once he had calmed enough to speak, taking deep breaths and wiping his face upon Crow's shirt.

"Where's Malana and Raoul?" He managed to ask after swallowing down his terror.

With a soft smile, Crow withdrew his wings, revealing the Rogues stood behind him. Lana, Storm, Raoul, Beth and Kat. All of them were there.

Malana and Raoul ran to him the fastest as he reached out for them, nearly breaking his ribs as they ploughed into him to hug him, the pair of them sniffling, whilst the girls gathered at his feet. He breathed deeply, embracing the moment and letting their presence anchor him.

"Is he awake?" Asked the doctor, Richard, hiding behind Storm for defence, and taking a tentatively step towards him.

"Yes," she said curtly, "and Crow's got him, so you don't have to worry about being nearly killed, *again*."

Richard pulled a face as he approached Wilny's side, with a mumble of "Good."

Wilny flinched and glowered at the medic whilst he took his blood pressure and checked his eyes for any signs of malingering influence from Comet, until Wilny hissed at him and pulled Crow's wing across to shield him from the medic. Expecting to be hurt, Richard leapt back with a small bleat of panic, before running his fingers through his brown hair and recomposing himself.

"He's got his senses back. Can't say much about what happened mentally to him though…or how it'll affect him." He said in a low voice to Storm, "Nightmares and all that. Any issues he's got are just gonna be amplified, are you sure it's safe-"

"I know the risk. I can fix this." She assured him.

"I was getting better…" Wilny whispered, voice hoarse and quaking like a leaf. "I was doing fine and then— I saw them, I couldn't stop myself! It wouldn't stop— I can't breathe!"

Crow passed him an oxygen mask, allowing him to take in gulps of air.

"You can make me forget, right Crow?" He asked quietly once he could breathe again, looking to Crow with such bloodshot eyes that the little slice of red within his right eye was almost indistinguishable from what should have been his whites.

"They do that for Recovery. A hard reset."

"I can't do that." Crow sighed. "Mistakes and memories are what make you, I can't take it away from you."

"Then, please, please just kill me," He begged, grabbing Crow's arm tightly and pulling him in. "I don't want to remember, I don't want to remember."

"*No.*" Storm snarled, curling her lip back to bare her fangs, clearly disgusted that he even dare to consider it an option.

Wilny sobbed, curling up into a ball upon the bed.

"*I just want it to stop!*"

"There are things more important than memories right now Wilny." There was a growl within her voice that flowed beneath her words and made him cower beneath Crow's wings and pull Malana closer to him as if she were about to bite, "Raoul and Lana. They need you. You *promised* me that you'd take care of them."

She held his gaze unblinkingly until he looked away, ashamed of himself.

Run.

RUN.

Everyone could feel it. The electrified current in the air around them. There was a tension that filled the air around her as if she were charged and ready to unleash a wave of electricity upon someone at any given second. It wasn't the same smiling, laughing, calm Storm who told him he'd have to learn French and kept intentionally calling him by any name but his own. Storm was about to strike, and no one knew where she would hit.

"Wilny," Beth said softly to Wilny, shaking off a shudder from Storm's growing rage, "do you or Comet know who the man was?"

"Comet called him Sabre. He called me both Wilny and Bluebird, but..."

Crow's feathers gave a sudden twitch at the name, a subtle movement only caught by Storm's keen eyes.

"Did you know him?"

"Lots of people knew me as Bluebird, I…" He shook his head, not wanting to carry on speaking. He shuffled on the bed, letting Raoul sit beside him and hold his hand whilst Malana curled up against him on the other side.

The girls looked to one another with cold determination. They had work to do. Kat whispered something to Storm and Beth which he didn't catch, and they turned to leave.

"Please don't leave me." He gasped fearfully, reaching for them.

"We'll be right back. Crow is right here with you." Storm assured him, "I trust him to take care of you."

The girls left the room and made their way across the short distance to the hallway that went through to the quarantine rooms. Storm hung back a little, clutching her injured arm to her chest with a dark expression. She was angry, with her feathers bristling and falling with every fresh thought and theory. The behaviour caused Kat alarm. She was in no frame of mind to engage in argument, as she spotted one of the Rioteers ahead.

With a little nod from Kat, Beth sighed and marched on back to the buzzcut barbarian that was the Rioteers' head of security, Pete Joy. He stood statuesque before the cell that held Amell, staring the opposing giant down with an envious glower, despite Amell not being able to see him through the plated mirror.

"Feeling small there, Joy?" Beth joked snidely.

"How long are we quarantining him for?"

"I need to get his ID off of him, so he can be assessed, but first they want me to come up with a quick fix for what happened and why fifty people nearly died of panic induced heart attacks."

"Infrasound." Joy grunted, "Blame the panic on infrasound caused by augmented subwoofers the engineering college is working on."

"Will they believe that?"

"The moment they get a physicist or acoustics expert on the TV to explain it they'll believe it."

"How would that even work?" She took a small and subtle glance behind him to Kat as he quickly fell into an in-depth explanation of the mechanics behind it, declaring him distracted enough for her to talk to Storm without interruption.

Gently taking Storm's hand, Kat drew her to one side, raising her wings up to shield their conversation.

"Storm? Are you alright?"

She sighed heavily, voice wavering, she didn't meet Kat's eye.

"It's all going wrong. Horribly wrong."

"Hey now, you didn't know this would happen."

"No, but it is *my* fault."

"It's not."

"It is Kat. I should have gone after Kathy. It's my fault that-" Her wings brushed across the floor as they drooped. The electrified atmosphere that had been surrounding her had subsided. She swallowed, trying to keep her voice level.

"That other Avio knew me. He came to see if it was really me or not. He knew Wilny and Comet too."

"*What?* How?"

"I..." She trembled and drew her arms closer to her chest, letting her shoulders slump, shielding her face with her hair.

"I'm...I'm scared." Storm said in a quiet and trembling voice. "I'm scared I've just put everyone here in danger because of that one stupid thing I could have done better."

Kat's heart ached. It hurt to see Storm, fierce and cheerful Storm, plagued by such doubt and fear. She couldn't let her break, not here.

Gathering her into her arms, Kat hugged her tightly, curling a blue wing around her and resting her head atop of Storm's hair. Appreciating the comfort and safety of Kat, Storm reciprocated the hug and leant her head against the crook of Kat's shoulder, letting the Lioness brush her fingers through her grey hair.

"Shh, don't let anyone else hear that. You'll lose kudos as being the scary feral lightning goddess who can kick your ass into next Tuesday." She laughed gently, kissing Storm's forehead. "You must be pretty special if they send someone out just to see if you're real or not."

"I'm nothing special Kat, honestly. I don't want to be special."

"Well you are to me. You're an absolute force of nature."

A smile, warm and more like the Storm she was used to, but it faded quickly beneath the weight of worry on her shoulders.

"There's something about it that relates to where I came from. Sabre, he knew about…about Rex shooting me and got upset when I couldn't remember him."

"Do you remember what happened?"

"I know bits and pieces, not everything though, but I don't *want* to remember any of it." She shook her wings off in a small shudder.

"Whenever I even thought of learning what happened before I came here, my head just starts screaming and it makes me want to fly as far away as possible and never think about it again."

Kat watched her with concern. Storm never spoke about where she came from, not even in passing; she didn't think it was because Storm was scared of the memories or even the possibilities of what had happened.

"You know what you need to do. Even if it hurts." Breaking the hug and placing her hands upon Storms shoulders, Kat looked down upon her with glowing pride. "Find out who sent them. We have to keep people safe. Don't rely on Beth alone."

"But-"

"Storm. *Thunderbird.* You've got to do this, otherwise who knows how much Rex will fuck everything up."

The vote of confidence turned her cheeks red, but the comment on Rex made her chuckle and smile enough that she couldn't keep hold of the doubt.

"You're right, he'll blow the whole headquarters up by the end of the day if I don't sort this out."

Lifting her wings off the floor Storm shook them out and resettled the silver-edged feathers, standing straight again with her head held high. The little glittering *joie de vivre* returned to her pale green eyes, a sparkle of mischief and lightning.

That was the Storm that Kat knew.

"You've got this, and I've got your back. You helped me now let me help you." Said Kat warmly, gently tucking stray strands of grey behind the feathers that covered her ears, before leaning in and kissing her.

"You're not in this alone."

15

Rex marched down the corridor at a near sprinting pace, Asena hot on his heels ready to referee the argument before things got out of hand. The moment he caught sight of Storm his expression darkened. Quickly, Storm tidied herself up and recomposed herself, readying herself for another round against Rex.

"Not a fucking word Rex." Storm snapped fiercely. "I've got this."

"Oh, I can see that. So, you caught the runaway and let another go," Rex scoffed loudly as Storm passed him to go into the cell, beginning to clap sardonically. "Bravo, bravo. Now you can do what you were supposed to and *kill her*."

"I said I'm handling it."

"Handle it quicker! I can't believe you fucking brought her down here. Are you an amateur?"

Her rage flared, and she spun to face him with her fangs bared.

"Maybe if you pulled your dick out of your arse and stopped screaming at everyone for five minutes you might actually learn something, *sweetheart*." She said with such sweet charm that he was shocked beyond angry retaliation.

He took a moment to slowly try to process what she had said, whilst Joy and Beth raised their eyebrows and Kat beamed at her with relief, suppressing laughter behind her wing.

The fight was back in her again.

"Are you that ignorant? Are you an *amateur?*" She teased smarmily. "It's not like she just turned up on her own. She came in a chinook with another Avio all kitted out in the best gear that ARCDA has to offer. Are you not the least bit curious as to why and how that is? Now it'd be really, *really,* stupid to kill off a key source of information now, wouldn't it?"

There was a subtle change of Rex's expression, barely noticeable to the humans, but all of the Synths caught it. Curiosity, anger, concern, *fear*.

"Speak to me like that again and I'll-"

"Do what? Shoot me? You wanna try that again old man, since that worked out *so well* last time." She snarled coldly, stepping up to him. Rex was visibly shocked by her jab, drawing breath to shout at her.

"Stop it you two!" Asena interjected, stepping in before it escalated further, "Now is not the time to fight each other."

Following Asena's lead, Beth pulled Storm back by her wrist and Joy tapped Rex's shoulder and muttered something about having to delete over a hundred videos on the internet of the drama.

"Deal with it or else *I will*." He snarled before marching off, the Rioteers standing down and following him. "You've five minutes starting now."

Storm gave him an animalistic snarl as they left, arching her wings above her. Asena sighed, turning back to the glass to look in at the prisoner within, the other girls gathering behind her.

"Are you sure you want to deal with her?"

"I've got this." Storm nodded in assurance, quickly swallowing down on the rage and tucking her wings back once again. She felt Kat's wings brush against her arm as the Lioness stepped up to her side, the feathers soft and warm. Subtly reaching for the Lioness's hand, she gave it a little squeeze as well as casting her a small smile of thanks.

Kat frowned as she looked within the cell. Kathy lay curled up on her side with her wings limply sprawled across the floor behind her, still reeling from the aftermath of Comet's wave of terror.

"You two should get some rest for now." Storm insisted to the other two Rogues. "If things go sour, mum will give me a hand."

"We'll lend you Beth's if you need it." Kat laughed, earning herself a jab in the side from the Owl who held onto her bionic arm protectively.

With one final nod of reassurance, unlocking the door, Storm stepped inside the cell alone. There was barely enough room in the concrete grey cell for the both of them with their wings taking up the majority of the space.

"I wondered when you'd come and see me." Kathy said with a strained laugh, pushing herself up off the floor the moment she saw Storm.

Storm didn't answer. She remained by the door with her arms folded across her chest and an unforgiving glare as she examined the girl.

Kathy still trembled and twitched uncontrollably, Comet's effects still lingering on her, but also actively afraid of Storm.

"What...what do you want?" She asked tentatively, drawing away from Storm and pulling her wings up around her shoulders.

"Answers."

"You're interrogating me on your own? Don't I get a good cop or are they fine with me fighting you?"

"If you want to attack me then be my guest, it's your bones that'll get broken." She threatened calmly. "I don't have the time to deal with your shit. Now tell me, who sent you here, and where is your baby?"

"Like I'm gonna tell you anything."

"Okay then, I'll just call the Rioteers in here then. They're more than happy to interrogate you instead of me." With a shrug, she turned to leave.

"*Wait!* Don't bring them in here!"

"Do you want to answer?"

"They...they..." Kathy swallowed, trying to recompose herself. Storm flicked her wings out in a sharp and sudden movement.

"Start at the beginning. Why are you here? Who was that with you, and where is your baby?"

Kathy hesitated. Her eyes flicked from Storm to the one-way mirror that took up one wall of the cell. She knew she was being watched. Storm kept her raptorial stare upon her, letting her squirm uncomfortably until she spoke.

"I flew over to France and they– ARCDA- found me and took me in." She stated slowly.

"They helped me. Delivered my babies and kept them safe." She gave a little bleat of laughter. "This place was amazing. I've never been anywhere like it. It was an ARCDA nursery and the professor there, she was so kind. She said that I was amazing; they've never had second generation transhuman Avios before. She wanted me to stay until I said about *you*."

"Me?"

"She got really interested and scared when I told her about you and that you were feral."

Storm frowned; confused by what Kathy might have told the professor about her that would have gotten any interest. "Can you give me clear details Kathy? What was her name, what did she look like?"

"Eve Mira. Asian woman, dark eyes. She said that she was the boss of the bunker."

"What faction was it?"

"Aura."

"Aura?" Her stomach lurched. She had rarely encountered Aura bunkers before. They were rare to find, mythical almost, but something niggled at the back of Storm's mind as she processed the new information. The name sounded familiar. Where had she heard it before? A doctor?

"The guy you came with, who was he?"

"Sabre? He's an asshole. He kept taking pictures the entire time and didn't help at all."

"But do you know why they sent just him and not anyone else?"

"I dunnow." She shrugged. "To back me up, I guess. They said that you would have killed me if you had the chance."

There was a moment of silence between them both as Storm mulled over Kathy's story. Of course, there was more to what had happened than just that, she knew that the girl was being vague intentionally, but she had to piece together the facts and what it could mean.

A doctor in an Aura bunker who knew her, who sent a traumatised girl to go find her, who had someone inside – Sabre - who knew of her and had seen her get shot and fall from the skies a decade ago at the loch, who knew Comet. There was no way around it, the doctor had to have been in charge of her, and doctors could get extremely possessive about their project subjects, and it meant there was only one place that they could have all come from.

"*Loch Mullardoch.*" She breathed, letting her wings flex gently as she recalled what Sabre had said. Her stomach roiled and knotted in pain and anxiety, wings held so tight and tense that the muscles and tendons burned.

Letting out a low groan of exasperation Storm held her head in her hands, trying to keep herself calm as much as she possibly could, regretting Kat not being with her to help.

"Kathy, she sent you here to die. You're not valuable to them and the guy you came with only came with you for evidence."

"No! What! She hasn't! How do you know? How do you know that?"

"Because you're here and not being studied by her right now! If she thought you were *important* or *valuable*, like your babies are, she would have never let you go. Aura is like Atlas, and it's all about protecting important Synths to study."

Kathy looked horrified at the statement, then with a sceptical sneer she looked Storm up and down.

"You can't be that important. You're feral."

"*I really fucking hope I'm not important.* Either way, you weren't meant to go back."

"But she said I was important to her research! Why would she want me to die? Why would she want you to kill me?"

"Oh my god I'm talking to a child." Storm groaned loudly, beginning to pace. She needed to think of what to do next with Kathy. The Rioteers would want her dead. Amell would want her dead. Wilny and Malana too most likely.

Kathy staggering to her feet.

"I'm not a child, I'm sixteen!" She screamed.

"You're sixteen, and a tool."

With a shriek, she lunged towards Storm. Angry, Storm struck out with a sharp electrified palm-slap to Kathy's head, taking her down in a single strike. As she writhed upon the floor, Storm grabbed her by the feathers across her neck and dragged her back to the corner of the room.

"Ow! Stop it!" Kathy shrieked. Her limbs twitched uncontrollably as though her body were made of jelly as she tried to swipe at Storm and move.

"How are you doing that?"

Storm released the girl's head, holding her hand up for them both to see, her wings casting a shadow down across her.

"I'm bioelectric and your brain is controlled by electric impulses which I'm disrupting. I could put you into cardiac arrest or stop your heart if I really wanted."

Kathy backed up against the wall, drawing her shaggy wings around her and staring in terror at her. "You weren't even trying when you fought us."

"No. And I'm trying even less now." Storm tucked her wings back with a shrug.

Covering her reddened face, Kathy began to sob, humiliated and shaking in fear. Letting the girl cry, Storm crouched on all fours before Kathy, trying not to be as intimidating, but still in a position to knock the girl to the floor if she showed even the slightest hint of an attempt to lash out.

"I'm not getting them back, am I?" Kathy blubbered, scrubbing her face with her palms to try to wipe away the tears. "My babies?"

"No."

Her wailing intensified as she slumped back against the wall with her chest heaving as she took ragged breaths between her sobs. Storm stared down at the girl. For all her arrogant bluster, she really was still a child who thought she knew best and trusted kindness far too easily. The way that Teal had treated her, threatening to kill her then quickly turning it round to make it seem like he said it because he loved her. The professor she had met offering kindness too then throwing her out to be killed, she was little more than a victim of one person or another.

"I'm going to give you a second chance, even if you don't deserve one bit of it." Storm announced after a heavy sigh. "You are going to tell these people anything they need to know. The route you flew, what you remember of the layout of the Bunker you were in, what Synths were there. You do this, and I will get my people onto finding where your babies are and see if we can return them to you."

Kathy's head snapped up and she stared at her with shock. Snot and tears dribbling down her blotchy red face, she looked pitiful.

"But I swear–" Her voice turned so icily cold that Kathy shrunk down before her– "if you fuck up then that's it. You're on your own against whoever wants you dead first."

Nodding submissively, she scrubbed her face with her hands and tried to compose herself.

"You're really gonna try and get my babies back?"

"Trust me. I will." She gave Kathy a single affirmative nod and turned to head to the door. As she reached it and it slid open, from behind her she heard a small and teary "Thank you…" from Kathy.

Asena watched Storm's expression as the door shut behind her and she relaxed against it, staring up at the vaulted redbrick ceiling.

"Well?" She asked gently.

"She's an idiotic teenager, that's for sure. About as much sense as you can expect, but also a fuck ton of psychological damage going on in there too." Storm sighed, looking back through the glass at the girl who was now sobbing once again in the corner of her cell.

"I need to borrow one of the computers to look in the database for this Doctor Mira in charge of an Aura bunker. She's the one who found Kathy, and apparently knows me and Comet and is probably from Loch Mullardoch. I need to know just what she is and how much of a threat she is before telling Rex."

"Aura? *Wait.*" Asena's eyes widened as she recognised the name and her tone turned serious. "Did the girl say she was an Asian woman? Korean?"

"Yes."

"Not doctor, Storm. *Professor* Mira. And she is the director of Aura."

The name clicked.

Mira.

She knew a Mira. *Wilny Mira.*

Storm froze and took a slow breath, the gears turning and dots connecting in her head.

"As in Wilny Mira? My PTSD ridden Hummingbird." She said steadily, slowly folding her arms across her chest and scowling at the Empress. "You knew about that the entire time didn't you."

"Only after you arrived back with him," Asena's ears flattened against her head, "but I thought you were aware about it since he's on your team."

"Then how about you explain that to me, hm?" Storm dropped her shoulders forward, allowing her wings to arch behind her in aggression, filling the tunnel with them.

"Why I just so happened to get sent into a Core bunker at the very spot where he is, kick his ass and turn him Rogue, and then for his own mother – the boss of Aura – to show up?"

"Don't get sharp with me Storm, I am not Rex." Asena's sharp canines flashed under the fluorescent lights and the fur across her arms bristled. "This could just be coincidence, or maybe that girl in there let Aura know about Wilny."

Storm dropped her wings and lowered her glare to the floor away from the Empress, cradling her arm as she thought of how this could have happened. Kathy had never seen Wilny arrive, so she couldn't possibly have given the Professor information about him, it couldn't have had anything to do with Wilny, but it didn't feel like a coincidence that he was with them. It had been Beth's plan, coordinated with the Rioteers to attack the bunker that Wilny was in. Was it intentional? Was it an instruction from Rex?

The betrayal stung. She felt foolish for not knowing such seemingly basic information, but why would Beth keep such important information from her?

Composing herself, she took a breath to calm herself and held her head high.

"I need to know what Loch Mullardoch was and why I'm of interest to Miss Mira before Rex starts planning something stupid."

"You're going to- *Mullardoch*? Are you sure Storm?" Asena looked surprised, tail flicking in agitation.

"Are you saying that I *shouldn't* do it?"

"You've always been hostile to the idea of looking up Mullardoch. I'm just...worried that it'll hurt you, and maybe Beth feels the same way. You might not like anything you find."

"I won't let people be hurt because I didn't want to be hurt myself." She shook her head. Straightening herself up she cast Asena a wry grin, putting on a cocky confident air which Asena was more used to.

"*Know your enemy,* right?" She chirped and with a flick of her wings, quickly made her exit and sped off towards the Rioteers computer rooms. The march was short, but it gave her a chance to think about what she had to search for.

Eve Mira.

Mullardoch.

She'd heard it a few times in the past and every time had made her hate it and retreat from it. Ignorance is bliss, she had told herself, '*If I don't know what it is then it can't hurt me*', but it did.

The computer room was mercifully empty and silent, giving her the chance to breathe easy that she wasn't surrounded by watching eyes. Full of stolen Delta computers, it was often in use to gather intel, but with the disruption caused by Comet, everyone was busy. She left the lights off in the room and sat down with the chair turned around so that her wings wouldn't be trapped against the back of the seat. Then she logged in with Beth's account.

As private as Beth was, she often made the mistake of forgetting how powerful Storm's eyesight was and how quickly she processed visual information. Storm had often seen Beth type in her password, but she had never had reason to use Beth's administrators' account, until now.

"Let's see what we have on you Miss Mira." She said to herself, typing the name into the database as it loaded up onto the screen.

Shifting in her seat, she began to read the profile, hunting for information on what kind of person they were dealing with.

"Evelyn Mira, M.D. D.Sc. Professor of Genetics, Genomics and Anthrozoology, aged sixty-one, first began age twenty-four as part of the Synthetically Created Organism Research Team." She clicked her tongue as she scrolled down the page, skipping past the lists of achievements and titles.

Her heart nearly stopped as she scanned through it all. The Professor's profile showed a wide range of research. From new medicines, cures for various forms of cancer, cellular regeneration, the return of extinct organisms and their diversification, interstellar survival and more, but most importantly, the very existence of the Synthetic experiments was down to her work.

She had helped to build them Synths from the ground up, working with the likes of Atlas leader Amelia Samodiva to create template genomes for Synths that could be easily modified and adapted depending on what was required. It was very simple and very well organised, removing all of the flaws and correcting issues that organic life had through millennia of evolution.

Her specific area of expertise, however, was specialised in *Avios*.

Storm swallowed anxiously, reading through her list of projects. *Mistral, Sirocco, Gregale, Libeccio, Zephyrus, Inmyeonjo, Asteria.* Many were locked, with no way to access them whilst other smaller projects and accreditations appeared largely unimportant. The current research was the shortest section and was simply titled '*Second Generation Research'.* She didn't need much explaining as to what that meant.

Clicking onto it, the research was split into four categories, one each for *Mammals, Volants, Reptiles,* and *Preternaturals.*

Selecting the Volants category, the screen displayed an almost empty page with only six subjects posted onto it, split between the subheadings of Avios, Chiros, and Pteros. Storm frowned a little. She'd never heard of a Pteros before, but she skipped over it to keep on reading.

New studies, 2nd Gen Type 6 Avio (Transhuman) [Patented Study]

"Well, there are your babies Kathy." She muttered beneath her breath. She was glad that it was at least one thing solved. The Professor was a smart woman, secretive and shrewd, and the profile was so formal she could barely gleam a slice of what she was dealing with. There wasn't anything to suggest aggression, but it didn't seem like she would just sit by and let them go without some form of analysis.

Brain ticking over, she typed in Wilny's ID code into the search.

E.22.05:LoddiMirab-1-1

Up popped his profile, stating him as deceased in bright red letters across his photograph.

ID: *E.22.05:LoddiMirab-1-1* **Status**: *Deceased*

Callsign *[Current]: Bluebird* **AKA**: *Wilny Mira, Buzz.*

Creator: *AURA, Prof. Evelyn Mira* **Project**: *N/A*

Breed/Type: *Type-5 Avio* **Base**: *Marvellous Spatuletail Hummingbird (Loddigesia mirabilis) – Base adapted for additional features.*

Known Abilities: *UV Vision.* **Specialist Talent**: *Muser*

Training and Rank: *DIAMOND, RUBY-1 (AA-03), TOPAZ Training.*

Additional Notes:

-        *Creator/Mother: Professor Evelyn Mira.*
-        *Brother to Wilheim M. Mira, and Dr Willoughby P. Mira.*
-        *Muser Abilities added in additional edit.*
-        *No contact allowed from Prof. Eve Mira under instruction of G. Daniels.*
-        *Top horizonal speed 100mph. Base speed 60mph.*
-        *Digestion issues with meat. Vegetarian options only.*
-        *Short sightedness issue. Uncorrected.*

It made sense. The Professor was an Avio specialist, of course she'd make her sons as Avios and design them any way she wished. Pretty winged, handsome faced, intelligent – though Storm did question why on earth she'd give all her sons a name beginning with *Wil*.

Rage flared up within her. The children of doctors were better treated than most, but what had happened that she had just abandoned him in Core to become a broken soldier–

'*Stop this,*' she scolded herself, resettling her feathers. She had to focus. Insightful as it was, it was only partially relevant. The priority was knowing if this woman would find them and destroy them or not and what was so important that it was warranted sending someone to try and find her.

She typed again.

Loch Mullardoch.

An abandoned research facility popped up onto the screen, located in the highlands of Scotland, close to an old hydro-electric dam and reservoir. And as she read through the page, she discovered that whilst ARCDA had set up bunkers across the globe, this was its original heart for Synthetic created organisms but that had only been a tiny part of it.

At Mullardoch they had produced medicines, vaccines and cures, advanced Cyber bionics, discovered flawless transhumanism early on than what ARCDA had declared, perfect cloning, mutable ecology and biodiversity manipulation, and more. The summary spoke of technology and fields of research so advanced it would have put humanity in the stars already, building colonies upon several moons such as Europa, Calisto, Enceladus, and Titan, rather than them just starting to get the first Martian bases set up.

What had happened to all that technology? Had it all been destroyed in the fire? Why was ARCDA nowhere near as advanced as this summary suggested it should be?

As she continued on, Eve's name appeared once again along with, much to her gut-wrenching horror, the names of all the current and past leaders of the other factions of the Arcadia Corporation. Amelia Samodiva, Gaius "Guy" Daniels, Daniil Pavlov, as well as few other names she didn't expect to see there that included the doctor Richard, Jenna Hart, and Pete Joy.

She skipped through back to the relevant parts with the Synths and Eve Mira, though it took a long time to reach the right part. As part of her Synthetic Anthrozoology research, Eve along with several other lead doctors appeared to have conducted twin studies for identical and non-identical twins across all Synth species, based in Loch Mullardoch, Scotland.

A list of four hundred and ninety-eight children appeared on screen, sectioned in by species, all in pairs with their names written beneath each set of pictures alongside their species, each coordinated by a different team.

With so many children, Storm was surprised that Eve even knew who she was. Scrolling down, she reached a section labelled *Type-7 Avio Prototypes* which like all the others before it. From what she could tell there had been four initial prototypes made that had been deconstructed to improve the genome, and from that it had developed into two different studies: Variated, and Identical. Clicking onto the Identical section, she found there to be twelve rows of names to its list. The team however, was managed by none other than Eve Mira herself, and coordinated with one *Rex Brisbane*.

Her heart almost stopped upon reading his name, but she continued, hands and trembling with her blood pounding in her ears.

Avios; Type-7 Prototypes - "Aerials" [Identical]
Project Coordinators: *Eve Mira, Amelia Samodiva.*
Sub-Coordinators: *Rex Brisbane, Sang Min-Jin, Maille Lovat, Mikele Merlo.*

Location: *Loch Mullardoch, East Campus, Synth-AnthZoo Department.*

Project Brief: *Goal is to observe growth and adaptations between specialised bases, designed based upon highly distinct morphology bases to further adapt the genome for increased genetic diversity and future compatibility. All Prototypes are based on living species to ascertain viability of specific morphology and phenotypes and are not subject to accurate representation of designated base. Additional adjustments made to incorporate more diversity within the test group.*

Total Number of Prototypes: 24.   **Success Rate**: 100%

- ~~*Arsu & Azizos Kythera*~~ *– African Grey Parrot*
- ~~*Atlas & Helios Brabazon*~~ *– Wandering Albatross*
- ~~*Chase*~~ *& Swift Shun – Spine-tailed Swift - [Serenity F.F. – USA]*
- *Falchion & Sabre Merlo – Scissor-tailed Kite –[Unknown]*
- *Ghost &~~Spectre~~ Lihn – Snowy Owl –[Hoffell – ICE]*
- *Nil & Zero Nemo – Gyrfalcon –[Hrimfald, Svartisen – NOR]*

- ~~*Brook*~~ *& River Ilmatar – Northern Gannet – [Unknown]*
- ~~*Cadence &*~~ *Harmony Coe – Jackdaw – [Matala, Huila Prov. – ANGO]*
- ~~*Comet & Star Sang*~~ *– Anna's Hummingbird*
- *Frost &~~Storm~~ Fraser-Swann – Peregrine Falcon – [Unknown]*
- *Sketch &~~Trace~~ Ali - Rüppell's Vulture –[Mt. Shirakomori, Akita – JAP]*
- *Tawny & Umber Brown – Kori Bustard – F [Gibson Desert – AUS]*

"Comet?" She frowned, not sure if it were simply another Hummingbird called Comet, though she doubted the coincidence. She recognised the names of several others on the list too. Helios, Chase, Cadence, Brook, Trace, she knew them all as they had all been Rogues with her. From what she knew they were all still alive but it had been a few years since she had last seen them. Sabre's name automatically confirmed his connection. And then there was herself and her own sister. *Frost* and *Storm.*

Wrong.

Wrong name.

Cold.

She shut her eyes, the hairs and tiny feathers on the back of her arms stood on end, chest tight with panic and fear.

-Snowy mountains, smoke, waking up on the edge of a lake, her whole body so cold it burned, and a gaping bullet wound in her chest-

The cursor hovered over their names and the link at the bottom titled *Research Logs*. She tensed, clammy and cold and rebelling against her to click. She didn't want to know; she was too scared to know what reason Eve Mira would be interested in her but fighting against her own petrification Storm continued on.

The research log was filled with detailed notes and video logs, stretching back to nearly two and a half decades, archived from oldest to newest with approximately five-hundred and seventy video logs. In brief, it covered their activities, growth, behavioural and physical development, although much of it was censored and blocked from view.

She was almost thankful that there was so much as it meant that she wouldn't have to know too much. A little snapshot of a taste would be enough for her. Maybe it would give an indication of how this project was to the Professor. Stretching her wings out a little to relieve them of tension cramps, she picked a video with the most views upon it and clicked play.

Much to her surprise, the first person to appear on screen for the video was a much younger, much happier Rex.

Red hair spiked up with gel and without the creases of anger and worry marking his face, she nearly mistook him for a stranger. He was sat at a crowded research desk with what looked like a huge classroom that opened out onto a balcony behind him, the darkness of night obscuring the scenery in the far distance.

"You're really going with that name? Are you going to stick with it this time?" A woman's voice said from off screen, clear and exasperated. *"I'm not letting you change it again."*

"Just start the log already, Jin."

"It's already rolling. This is why we let Maille do these, you're so bad at them."

Spinning around dramatically in his chair, he grinned wildly and got comfortable. *"This is Doctor Rex Brisbane– Jin! Stop it!"* He snapped sharply, frowning to the woman off screen.

"It's a stupid name." She scoffed with a giggle. *"The King of Broken Bones."*

Snorting angrily, he lifted a heavily casted broken leg up onto the desk and gestured dramatically for her to look at it, to which her laughter intensified.

"Alright, alright. It suits you."

"This is Rex Brisbane with co-narration from Sang Min-Jin, and this is weekly log number three-hundred-and-forty-three, reporting on current findings and updates with the Avio twin study for the Type-Sevens…" he dropped off into a drawling sigh, languishing lazily in his chair and letting it spin, *"do I have to call them subjects still?"*

"Rex. Please. Don't drag this out, I want to go to bed."

"Fine. The subjects are now almost all four years old. They are still very slow growing, but are now capable of extended periods of flight of up to eight hours, are in full control of their talents, and scare me absolutely shitless." He said brightly with the largest smile he could muster and a clap of his hands, eyes glittering as he played to the camera and increased the drama. Swallowing he clicked quickly, his feed of the log shrinking to a corner whilst footage that had clearly been taken earlier that day.

The video was phone footage of two of the Avio children hovering and diving into the lake, white wings tipped with black folding back as they arrowed into the water and surfaced again. The doctors filming burst into peals of laughter as the Gannets landed back on the bank and presented their fish to the camera, before it switched at the sound of screaming to three older Hummingbird boys wearing a bumble bee coats, with one chasing the other two with a snail he had found.

"There's a distinct difference between the subjects, dependant on what their genetics are based on. The diversity has caused and specialisation is the likely cause of this. It's primarily stemming from the predatory bases versus non-predatory ones. We've seen it before in some of the mammalian-Synths. Although the predator bases are more inclined to behave like feral children or animals than the non-predatory ones, often exhibiting stalking-hunting behaviours, the predators are better strategists and are all round hardier."

A second clip played, five or six of the children, with black, grey, and spotted white wings, being filmed in the distance, all playfully herding a group of deer across the red-green heathland of a mountainous landscape, keeping them from darting into the dark green of the pine trees over the ridge of the hill.

"They're also better at teamwork even though its…well they're…" He dropped off as the video showed the group turn aggressive, as one of the stags caught an ermine spotted Avios

in its horns and tossed him to one side. The remaining Avios began to fly faster until they swarmed it as one and brought it down onto its side in a flurry of feathers. The footage cut sharply back to Rex's horrified face.

"Yeah," he said liltingly, *"they ate the deer. Raw. This stag weighed more than all of them combined and they still ripped it to shreds! Nil got gored in the side but was up and kicking immediately after. I'm glad they heal fast because if that happened to me, I'd be dead. Or have broken ribs."*

"What, so you think they could kill people if they wanted? They're only four."

"Oh, absolutely. They may be four now but think what they'll be like when they're ten or twelve. That's why I don't ever want to piss them off. Ever." He sighed and a glimmer of the serious bitter Rex, Storm was used to seeing, surfaced. *"But what worries me is if Gaius finds that out, he's just going to want to use the new batch tanks to mass produce them, ruin the genomes trying to make them grow fast and ship them out as super soldiers, or some shit like that. They're kids, not weapons. The whole point of making them was to find ways to diversify for the future, not to go all Il'ya Ivanov and make slaves of them."*

"Don't you dare say that name to me ever again or else I'll get Swann in here to break your arms." The doctor Storm assumed to have been Sang Min-Jin, snapped coldly, walking around into camera view for the first time that video to bat him across the head with a child's stuffed animal. She looked very much like Comet, albeit a much older version of her.

Storm's eyes flicked back to the list of names.

Comet and Star Sang, Sang Min-Jin. They were doctors' children? Looking again at the list, Sabre and Falchion's name matched another project sub-coordinator called Mikele Merlo. Swann, they had said. That was her name, but who was Swann? Did this mean that they were all doctors children? The thought made her angry.

"And don't you ever dare let him or Amy take the Sevens. Any one of them loose in their hands would be chaos. Even the Variated ones."

"Just you watch, he'll walk in here one day and confiscate them. I'm just hoping the kids will take him down like they did that deer." He laughed to himself and stretched out in the chair before adding nonchalantly. *"If not, I'll think of something or some way to stop him."*

It wasn't his indifference at what he had said that stabbed at Storm, but the fact of what *had* happened. He *did* do something. Something so catastrophic that it still had repercussions. What had turned him from a caring man to the paranoid maniac who would burn a building through of children to the ground.

Eve didn't feel to be much of a threat or danger, she was a scientist and she would watch and analyse. But Rex, now there was something chilling.

'Keep Comet and yourself away from Rex,' Sabre had said, and now she could see the danger of what he had meant. If Rex from a decade and a half ago was concerned about the use of the Type-Sevens, then he must have known what they were capable of to keep them – keep her – so close.

Her head was throbbing with trying to detangle the web.

There was something still missing. This couldn't have been all of it. There had to be more, more players in the game, more reason behind it. Something she'd overlooked.

Curiosity and terror combined, she took a breath and went back to the start.

-x-

"I told you to keep me updated on the situation!" Roared Eve at the returned Kite. *"Live tweeting the situation, isn't keeping me updated!"*

The photos he had taken were gathered across the three screens that surrounded her desk, displayed across overlapping windows so that every inch held some form of visual information. Sabre rolled his shoulders and let his feathers noisily rustle, not daring to look her in the eye and face her wrath or to even glance to his brother who was stood stoically beside him. She was so angry that he thought that she might stab him.

"Well Bluebird being alive was kind of a surprise I guess." He muttered.

"No Sabre! A surprise is the whole office getting you cake on your birthday, not finding out your son who was declared *dead*, to be *alive* and walking around London!"

"Mum, calm down." Heim said with a quiet voice. He was sat on the floor with his head in his hands from the initial shock, he had not moved or looked up to the screen once since his first glimpse of the photos.

The people who were once his friends. They were alive.

His brother too. *Alive.*

"Are you certain…it's him?" Eve asked slowly, steadying her breathing and looking sceptically to the polished jade urn that supposedly held her son's ashes.

"It was him alright. He has the same little mole as Heim and Bee." Sabre laughed lightly, tapping the right-hand corner of his mouth. "And that was definitely Comet, though she does look a little worse for wear. I don't know what the Rioteers have done to her."

"And this is definitely Storm? I don't see any tailfeathers…"

Eve played the footage back again, watching the movements of Storm's attack on them, taking them all down with a single wingbeat before landing immediately and pouncing upon Wilny. The lack of tailfeathers would have meant stopping without completely shattering her bones was difficult, but the Avio had pulled it off with flawless fluidity.

"Oh definitely!" Sabre laughed, rubbing his arms. "Electric shocks, silver feathers. She doesn't remember anything, and I couldn't trigger anything."

"Did she seem sane?"

"She was pissed off that's for sure."

"You could have brought her back here."

"Yeah, at the risk of losing my balls."

"*Sabre!*" She scowled at the Kite.

"Sorry Miss."

Taking a few breaths to calm herself, she stared up at the screen with sceptical disbelief. "How did she even survive? We all saw what happened…"

"The credit goes to you on how well you made us." Fell complimented softly, side-eyeing his brother for his informality. "You made us to survive, and she did."

The Professor tapped the glass with her pen. "I'm going to assume that if I found out every profile for every person in this footage, they'd all come back as dead under various circumstances."

Fell tilted his head to one side. "Then the Rioteers must have someone who knows the database and is at least an administrator on it." He suggested, seeing it as the only logical answer.

"Clever." Eve laughed at the screen. The twins looked between themselves with silent and confused glances.

"I'm not going to deny the cunning they've used." She smirked answering their silent questions. She flicked her fingers across the screen, searching for Comet's profile. Fell tensed and uttered a soft and pained gasp of horror as her image appeared on screen next to the most recent scar ridden images. He had only seen her a few months ago before she was sent off to work on a field expedition, and the difference was shocking.

"If most of these are from Core then they're not going to be looking for Synths which are dead." Eve continued, ignoring Fell's distress, tapping her foot quickly as she thought and questioned. "They're too stupid and too preoccupied to check. Atlas too."

How many more experiments were there in London hiding because of the system? Hiding may have been the wrong word for what they were doing, surviving would have been better. How many Synths had the Rioteers stolen? Declared dead? Was there more? How were they able to hide these unhuman creatures for so long? Were they brainwashed? She had so many questions. She was curious, but she knew it would be a big risk to investigate them right now.

"A good idea ma'am." Fell said softly, answering her idle self-musings. "We have to leave them be until they're calm, otherwise who knows what will happen."

"I can look into it if you want mum." Heim said softly, staggering to his feet and placing a comforting hand upon his mother's shoulder. "And tell Bee that Wilny's alright...if he hasn't lost his phone in a swamp again. Faraday too. He needs to know."

"Thank you." She drew him into a hug, taking a moment to let herself mother her son, brushing his long hair and sighing deeply. Releasing him, she composed herself and turned back to the screens. "Still…There's something wrong with all of this."

She had only wanted evidence. Something to prove a theory right and now she'd been given a situation with far more depth to it than she had realised. It was now more than just missing prototypes. Her son was involved. Rex was involved, and who knew what else there was beneath this first row of dominoes she had accidentally knocked into action.

"Leave." She ordered them. "I need to make a call."

With a polite dip of their heads, the twins strode out of the office with Wilheim in tow, whilst she snapped up her phone and brought up several profiles of different doctors and bunker contacts onto the surrounding screens. The door slid shut behind them with a hiss, the lights across its centre changing from green to red as it locked.

"God damnit!" Sabre snarled with a punch to the wall and an angry beating of his wings. Down the hall two doctors who were talking, snapped their heads round at the *thunk* he had made. "Fucking shit!"

His brother sighed and put a hand to his ruffled-up wings, stroking the feathers back down.

"Sabre, quiet."

"She's going to get them all killed if she goes after Bluebird."

"*Wilny.*" Heim corrected him sharply. "His name is Wilny."

"But she *will* get them all killed. Rex knows who he is, and there's no way that git will ever let him or Storm or Comet go to us without a fight."

"But we need to get them back!"

A sharp *fwip* of Fell's wings stopped them both before they could break into debate. He didn't need to make much noise to get their attention, but they knew well enough to listen. With a small gesture, he motioned for them to move on away from the doctors' stares and out of Eve's doorway.

'She isn't going to risk scattering them if it fails or having valuable experiments killed.' Fell explained quietly, trying to reason with them before musing to Sabre alone, *'I thought you were eager to kill the Rioteers.'*

'Tcht!' his brother rolled his shoulders in annoyance and persisted. *'The Rioteers yes, Rex yes, but not the girls.'*

'You miss those days.'

'Don't you? They were our friends; we were all family.'

'I know. But we have to stay calm. We cannot rush in and put them in danger.'

'You mean put Comet in danger.' Thought Sabre with a sour note of envy. Fell bristled, long tailfeathers flicking out sharply, sending a prickle of fear down Heim's spine.

'I mean all of them.' He mused coldly before extending the thoughts back out to include Heim once more. *'We can't risk going out of our way to see them again, we'll have to be patient.'*

Heim nodded. *'What do you want to do about it?'*

Fell sighed to himself.

'I'm not sure. But we'll think of something.'

16

Cherry Tree House, Battersea, London.

For days, the Rogues struggled to sleep, eat and think without having flashes of nightmares surfacing and crippling them all over again. Storm had spent most of her time down in the headquarters with them, refusing to sleep when they did so she could help as fast as she could if they needed her, whilst Kat and Beth had been trying to sort out the chaos Kathy had brought with her.

By the end of the week, they were begging Dr Richard to let Storm take them home. Being underground was driving them stir crazy, and after a very vocal threat made to Richard by Raoul, he allowed them to leave the headquarters.

The three traumatised Rogues instantly relaxed the moment they stepped outside the headquarters and into the sunlight. Foregoing public transport or a taxi, they instead walked the six miles home back to Battersea, their mood lightening every mile they drew closer. Malana with her little legs managed to walk a fair way, but eventually had to be carried by Wilny, and slept with her head on his shoulder for the rest of the journey.

"I'm going to have a long-ass bath and then I'm going to sleep for the next ten thousand years." Wilny sighed with relief, as they slowly stumbled through the gate and up the path to the door of the house. "I don't care if Kat is saving those bath bombs, they're mine."

Storm laughed lightly. "I'll make sure to bring some honey and sorbet up to you while you act like a diva."

"I desire as much mango as you can shove in the blender!"

"Of course, your majesty."

Beth opened the door for them before Storm even touched the handle, looking uncharacteristically flustered. Her usually pale complexion was a deep shade of abashed red, and rather than greeting them with a sardonic quip let out a small high squeak of, "Thank god," and let them inside.

Storm thanked her quickly and strode in to see what was wrong, and what had caused Beth to blush so hard. They had a guest.

"Whoa, whoa!" Amell shouted raising his hands, as Raoul recognised him and jumped forward with his teeth bared and snarling. Before he could do any harm, Storm darted towards him, grabbing him and holding him still with a warning growl. Disarmed he was by no means tempered by her intervention.

"What the fuck is he doing here?" Raoul snarled.

"Raoul stand down!" Beth barked, her soft wings ruffled too, though more from embarrassment than anger. "He's with us now."

Wilny scowled, holding Malana close with wary regard. He hadn't forgotten that Amell had hurt her family, even if it wasn't his fault.

"When did that happen? We never agreed to that."

"He attacked us! He tried to kill us!" Raoul added, baring his teeth in a snarl. Their shouting made Malana stir from her sleep and whine softly. His curled tail bristled and he gave the Eagle-Avio a flash of fang..

The Eagle frowned at them sadly, hurt by Raoul's reaction.

"I was being controlled. Whatever I did to you, 't wasn't *me* that really did it. I'm not the one to blame here, bro."

"I don't understand his accent, what is he saying?" Raoul muttered in an aside to Wilny, genuinely confused by Amell's Kiwi accent.

"*Stop.*" Storm snapped, brushing past them to shut the door which they had left wide open. The boys flinched at her slamming of the door and stood down, exchanging sceptical looks.

"Amell's with us because Rex has had one of his paranoia fuelled meltdowns about security and won't let him stay there." She explained in a hushed voice. "If you don't like mine and Beth's decision then you're free to contest it, but let me remind you that *both of you* have tried to attack me on first meeting so you are in no ways different to he is."

Raoul continuing to bristle angrily, looked away from her, mumbling a tiny apology.

"You two don't have to stay down here for his assessment" Said Beth. "you can go get showers and go to bed if you like."

The boys looked between each other, quietly discussing if they should stay or go, then with a small reluctant nod began to head upstairs, Wilny handing Malana over to Storm before he did so.

Kat passed them on the way down and on seeing their exhausted irritated faces, whispered to them both that she would bring food up to their rooms.

The boys thanked her then drifted off towards their rooms, grumbling to each other about how they didn't like the fact Amell had joined them without their input into the decision. The girls heard and rolled their eyes, choosing to ignore their whinging and carry on.

"Give them a week and they'll calm down." Storm sighed to Amell as way of an apology for their behaviour. "They've… just had a lot to deal with."

The Eagle shrugged and nodded in acceptance, running his fingers through his mane of hair and pushing it back out of his face.

"So, were we discussing anything important or were you just going over the assessment basics?" Storm asked, sitting down on the sofa beside Beth, Malana upon her lap. Malana scrunched her face up and squirmed, trying to find a more comfortable position to curl up and sleep in, settling to be cradled in Storm's arms forming a small cocoon of feathers around herself with her wings.

"Just the basics and explaining things to him. Seeing where he comes from, what he used to do in ARCDA, and all that jazz." Beth reopened her laptop, trying to compose herself enough so that her face wasn't scarlet.

"Original name: Amiri Ka'eo Rakena. ID code: *Muta-V:11:11:PithecJeffe-12-5*. He's been Transhuman for seven years, but is actually thirty-one years old from Tauranga, New Zealand, half-Hawaiian and part of the N… *Ngāti Ranginui iwi?*" Beth said hesitantly and gave Storm a small shrug of uncertainty on what that meant until a little glimmer in the crystal lens of her glasses gave her the quiet answer of '*Maori tribe*'.

"Maori, huh?" Storm looked intrigued. "What would you prefer to be called?"

"Amell is fine by me. I like that one the most."

Beth nodded and continued.

"He was a former medical student at the University of Auckland who was reported missing seven years ago after signing up to earn some money on a clinical trial. Surprise, surprise, who was running it but Atlas. Now, he's an Eagle based Transhuman Avio and beta tester for Atlas, given alterations to his MSTN genes and with boosted hyper healing to create all of that...*that*." She said gesturing to Amell's muscular physique. Amell puffed out his chest proudly and giving them all a flirtatious wink, to which Beth immediately tensed in aggression.

Storm snickered quietly at Beth's violent asexualism. The Owl did not like anyone flirting with her at all, much to other people's often painful discovery.

"So, there's quite the history to you. Is there anything else we should be aware of?"

"Other than my charm and good looks?" He chuckled, gently tracing the newly formed scar that ran across his face, so pale and light compared to his bronze complexion. "I'm not sure. I'll thank the little girl for this new scar she gave me though, makes me all the prettier and adds to my collection."

Storm couldn't help but laugh at his response to getting his face nearly cut in half by a child who didn't even come up to his waist. He was confident, she'd give him that, and now he wasn't anywhere near Kathy he was far more mellow than she'd expected. He had calmed to become himself once again.

"So other than the basics," Storm smirked, "how is it going? Any details you'd like to enlighten me on? Anything *salacious*?"

Beth's face reddened again to a deeply flustered shade of wine-red.

"Oh, it's that good?"

Beth shifted uncomfortably in her seat, looking between them. Amell hung his head in mischievous glee, trying not to laugh.

"He's been reprimanded seventeen times for sexual activities with other Synths *and* doctors." Beth stated in a low voice, aware that Malana was in the room with them.

Storm spluttered with laughter, trying with great difficulty to keep her voice down. Amell shrugged, his giant brown and white wings moving as well.

"Even though I'm sure it was more than that. More like thirty, maybe forty. The doctors used to call me Zeus."

"Ooh, so you're quite the man-slut aren't you, *Zeus*." Storm grinned. "How the hell did you manage that and not get sent to be recycled for all those reprimands?"

"I was a beta tester." He explained. "We'd test out new products and if we proved to be better than what we were pitted against and showed the docs what to improve on, we got rewarded with personal time to do what we liked. Testing was like once every two weeks or so."

"So that was how you spent your personal time? Those poor girls."

"They weren't *all* girls."

"*Oooh.* Nice!"

"Most the time I'd draw and paint unless other people asked me to entertain them. It was fun really." He shrugged again. "It was just the non-reward times that we got reprimanded on."

"Sounds like a pretty easy life."

"Hey now, it if it were easy, I'd look a hell of a lot different. I was the chubbiest bloke you ever saw when I first started and got my arse kicked nine times to a dozen. This is years of strength and endurance work!" He sat up and drummed his fists against his scar covered chest. The man had a body that could put gods to shame, they'd already seen him lift a car, but imagining him as a chubby medical student was near impossible.

"You don't get this from being a beach bum. So, if you ever need something big and heavy moved, I'm your man."

"I'm surprised you can even fit into anywhere without leaving a very Amell-shaped hole in the wall."

"That's uh, that's a point. I uh…had to come in through the kitchen." He laughed awkwardly, rubbing his shoulders. "I got stuck."

The house may have been redesigned to accommodate the wings of Avios and Chiros, however it had never been made to allow access to someone who was Amell's size.

"Well, I don't think it's safe for you to stay in Raoul and Wilny's room right now, and a single bed isn't really small enough for a guy as big as you are…" Storm pondered for a moment where else he could sleep in their house. He seemed far too tall and broad shouldered to fit comfortably into even a king size bed, and with the added extension of his expansive wingspan, the small bedrooms and doorframes would pose a bit of trouble for him fitting through easily without possibly knocking down walls. She didn't want to force anyone to change rooms or give up her master bedroom at the top of the house, and which she had coveted for years prior.

"There are two spare rooms, so I guess you can go pick whichever one you can fit into comfortably. If not there's always the basement. We can clear it out and bring two mattresses down for you."

"Wherever you think's best."

"I'll show him to the spare rooms then." Kat offered, listening in from the kitchen where she had been preparing food. With a nod of permission from Storm, he rose to his feet and followed Kat as she led him up, doing his best to manage his huge wings and squeeze his shoulders through the doorways.

For a short while Storm and Beth sat in silence, Beth typing away on her laptop whilst Storm braided Lana's hair and preened her wings. The tiny hairs across Beth's arm prickled as a tension began to grow between them, raising the alarm bells in Beth's mind as she felt the electrical field rise around Storm.

"So, there's this one crackpot on the vox pop section of the news who thought we were mutants after some of the videos slipped through the net." Beth laughed awkwardly to herself trying to break the silence. "*Mutants*! I mean, fucking really? They seriously don't know the meaning of that word, do they?"

"Most of them don't *actually* know what we are Beth." Said Storm coolly, running her talons through Lana's feathers.

"Mutant would imply we're natural. We're Synthetic."

"Well I'm sure if they *knew*…about *things,* then they could get it right.*"*

It wasn't until Beth looked out the corner of her eye did, she notice Storm watching her with a cold and unreadable expression.

"What." She asked nervously, not sure what had caused the sudden change in her mood. "Why are you giving me that look?"

"Whose side are you on Beth?"

Beth's wings tensed at the sharpness in her words. Her breath had caught in her throat. The two hadn't spoken in the few days Storm had been busy with the boys and Lana, and she hadn't informed Beth of what she'd learnt.

"I mean, I let you take charge of the plans and you somehow seem to keep directing us to things related to Mullardoch." Storm didn't move, she only stared straight at her

Stormbite

without so much as an alien blink. "Explain it to me. Why? Why Wilny and Comet? Or all the others we've just so happened across."

Forcing down the sudden terror, Beth swallowed and shut her laptop slowly, placing it on the glass coffee table in front of her.

"You told me you never wanted to look into it. You've always been *blasé* about ARCDA's clockwork."

"Needs must. I've already marathoned a fifth of the videos in the archives on the Type-Sevens to see why it was so important to Eve Mira that she would send someone out to confirm my existence, and the only thing that doesn't make sense is why would *you* direct *me* to these Synths specifically. Did Rex tell you to get them for him?"

"Why-"

"Don't lie to me Beth. I know Rex worked on the project I was on."

"I was…curious." Beth said slowly and deliberately, inching away to the corner of the sofa so that there would be some space between them both. "I grew up hearing about what happened. The Rioteers attacking and the fire wiping out the entire campus and facility. They used to call Mullardoch the Monster Factory where I was, since all of the survivors were basically insane or horribly disfigured by burns, and we had to make sure that there were tabs kept on all former inmate– *experiments*– to a point where it is still ingrained in me, which is why I still search for them even now. Honestly, I'm very good at finding people. But most of them are beyond help, locked in Hrimfald, or in private projects where they can't be used for anything new and are strictly monitored."

She rolled her shoulders from the strain of suddenly being under Storm's scrutiny and let her bionic hand flex involuntarily. She did well to keep eye contact with Storm so that the Rogue knew that she was telling the truth. With such acute eyesight she made it easy to detect a lie from the twitches of a person's face.

"And then I find you five years ago or so." Beth continued, swallowing again. "Presumed dead after being shot out of the sky, but flying around in plain sight, in a fist fight with another Avio that ended in a city-wide blackout. I wanted to know how this monster had survived, how they'd gotten past me and everyone else."

"So, me being off radar hurt your ego?"

"No, it piqued my curiosity to the point I risked my life to walk out of Delta to know more. Knowledge, Storm, I love it like nothing else and I'm always hungry for it. You hunt from the skies, I hunt from right here-" She stopped herself before she let her passion take her out of control into a lecture, holding her hands close to her chest to stop herself from making exaggerated gestures.

"I'm a bitch, I know, but I'm on your side Storm. I swear it. You are the first person I'd have called my friend and family. I don't trust anyone else, but you."

"But clearly not enough to tell me what's going on."

"I never knew this would happen, and I've done my best to stop the likes of this from occurring. I know it upsets you when I bring up the past. All I wanted to do was save and free people because I know that's what you wanted to do. I wanted to find the so-called-monsters. I wanted to help."

"And now the monsters you sought to free are being hunted, so thanks for that."

"That's how the world turns Storm." Beth assured her. "Professor Mira won't hunt us if we don't give her reason to. You think she would dare risk trying to attack us knowing that Rex is here?"

"And you're sure about that? We have a reason, *many* reasons in fact."

"As sure as eggs is eggs."

With a sigh and a well overdue blink, she stated how stupid the phrase was and let Beth relax. The tension dropped, but Storm was still huffing and frowning.

"So why are you being angry exactly?" Beth asked cautiously, wiping the tiny display crystal of the glasses clean. "It's not just because of me is it?"

Brushing her grey-blue hair back in aggravation, Storm groaned loudly.

"It's lots of things. I'm pissed off with Kathy. Contemplating Rex's murder. I wanting to help everyone get better from all the shit that's happened to them but feeling like I'll never be able to. And I just…really, *really*, want to get the hell out of the city before someone does *something*. What do I focus on Beth?"

"Break it down. Prioritise what the problems are."

Storm leant her head back and stared at the ceiling, deconstructing what there was and taking deep breaths before she spoke.

"Comet and I are part of an old prototype study, owned by Eve Mira – Wilny's mother– which Rex was part of and subsequently ruined by being his cordial self. We're not killing Kathy, because fuck Rex. Not only that, but I'm also far more scared of Rex doing something dangerous than I am of some Aura boss popping up to pick up her son now she likely knows that he's alive– who I now don't know how to handle, since Comet royally fucked up his mind with her own brand of trauma."

"Okay, now what are the things that you can influence and solve?"

She shut her eyes, trying to focus.

"The priorities are the others. I need them better before we make any kind of plan to run or fight. They were doing so well…"

They had all been doing well, Raoul the best of them all and adapting fastest to his new situation, but as far as Malana and Wilny were concerned, they seemed to be feigning a lot of the time. Occasionally there would be smirking and cheery sarcastic quips from Wilny as he grew more comfortable with the Rogues, but with Malana it was far harder to tell. Storm wasn't sure if she was too young to process all that had happened or if she was cleverly bottling it up. Either way she wanted to make sure Malana felt safe enough with them that she could tell them her feelings.

"You can try and talk them down, do your thing, but you can't force them to change and get better." Beth sighed regretfully. "This is something they have to work through in their own time."

"I don't think I *can* talk them down. I can barely manage myself."

Cocking her head to one side, Beth contemplated what she could do or say to Storm that might help her or at least make her feel more certain.

"Professor Mira will probably hold back and watch or send another man in to investigate further before doing anything – that's what I'd do anyway. And if I were her and I had a son in the clutches of a known terrorist, I'd share none of this knowledge with any of the other factions because sure as shit, they'd fuck it up."

It wasn't much of an answer, but it seemed to reassure Storm enough to make a smile break across her face.

"Should we go on the defensive and prepare for the worst?" Storm asked, rolling her head to the side to face Beth. "Rex is just upping his paranoia levels to *'let's put military grade C-4 on every door to barricade ourselves in if someone comes knocking'*. Meanwhile, Joy is just going with it rather than talking sense into him."

"We stay defensive, maybe not to Rex's extreme, but at least we know who the enemy is now."

Storm nodded, looking to the staircase as Kat padded down the stairs. Her ears were flicked back, having heard everything. Amell, they could assume was exploring the house alone or was in the bathroom since he wasn't with her.

"Don't worry Storm." Reassured Kat. She leant over the sofa and wrapped her arms around Storm to hug her. "You can handle it."

Storm smiled softly and pawed at her arm, gesturing for her to sit down beside her. Kat obliged, squeezing onto the sofa next to her, wrapping an arm around her shoulder and letting Storm curl up against her.

"I hope so." Storm sighed, leaning her head against Kat's and allowing her to play with her hair whilst she preened out the loose baby feathers from Malana's wings. "All I want for the next few days is some peace and quiet."

-x-

Dark and taunting memories looped in endless circles as Wilny slept. The faces slicing into sharp focus against mismatched hallways, a huge black shadow running its talons down the back of his neck. Spinning around he tried to catch sight of the face of the Frigatebird only to fall backwards through the darkness.

A jarring pain shot across his back as he hit the floor, trapping a wing beneath him sparking bright flashes of white before his eyes. Gulping for air, Wilny slammed his fists down against the carpet, digging his nails into the fibres and letting the rough feeling anchor him back in reality.

The deep blue shadows of his and Raoul's room grew slowly into focus, lightly illuminated from the white streetlamps outside. His eyes adjusted to the low light as he counted beneath his breath in order to calm himself down. He was so hot he felt sick and had been sweating so much that his feathers were soaking wet. The bed sheets were in a tangled knot around his feet and the pillows were cast across the floor.

"Just a dream." He assured himself, untangling his legs from the sheets and tossing them into the laundry basket. "Just a dream."

He looked round to Raoul who lay face down in his bed. The streak of fur down his spine was bristled in his sleep, one leg hanging off the bed while he hugged a pillow so tightly it looked like it would burst. It seemed Wilny wasn't the only one having bad dreams.

Not wanting to go back to sleep, he picked up his reading glasses and wandered to the bathroom to wash his face. Then went down to the kitchen in search of some honey and to find a book to read to distract himself.

Surprisingly, the living room was dark and absent of Beth who was usually awake all night, though he put it down to being a rare occasion her actually having gone to sleep. He picked a book out in the low light, scoffing at the title as he found it to be one of the trashy-romance novels that Kat loved to read, and taking it with him to the kitchen.

The kitchen light was on, but the room was empty and the sliding doors to the decking outside open wide, letting a cold refreshing summer breeze in.

A prickle of suspicion ran down his spine and quietly he removed a knife from the rack and padded softly to the doors. A hulking dark shadow sat on the stairs, huge dark wings draped back across the decking and staring up to the sky with a shaggy mane of hair.

'*Frigatebird!*' his still nightmare startled brain screamed, but on approach the feathers were dark brown with an edge of creamy white to every single one and a glossy plum sheen to the feathers between his shoulders. He didn't recognise the colours.

The figure turned, hearing the sharp rustling scrape of Wilny's tailfeathers as they brushed against the wood, sweeping a wing across the decking.

"Fuck me!" Amell yelped, shattering the silence. He lept to his feet, back peddling away from him with several flurrying beats of his huge wings. "You scared the crap out of me there bro!"

Wilny approached him cautiously, letting his knife hand drop slightly.

"What are you doing out here?" He asked.

"I wanted to see the stars." Amell smiled, craning his neck to look to the sky. "They're not very clear in the city. Too much light pollution."

The sceptical disbelief across Wilny's face was still visible even in the low light. Amell rolled his shoulders, lifting the tips of his wings off the ground and refolding them again.

"Look, I know you don't trust me, bro," He said softly, "but Storm thinks that it'd be good for us both for me to be here."

"Why the hell would she think that?"

"Because then you have someone who knows what you went through and can relate."

Wilny's lip curled up into a snarl and the glossy feathers along his shoulders rose in anger.

"You killed Lana's family." He spat, letting his tailfeathers rattle noisily, "You tried to kill me. We have nothing in common at all! Why would she even think-"

"Because I had no control in it either."

"Oh, so you all know about it now. Fantastic. Fan-*fucking*-tastic."

Brandishing the knife, he advanced slowly on Amell, quietly sizing him up. Even a foot up on the decking, Amell still seemed taller than him.

"You have no idea what I went through!" He snapped, "And she has no right to interfere, this has nothing to do with her."

The Eagle stepped up to the angry Hummingbird. The huge wings gave a warning flare, with a flex that spread across his chest and shoulders showing the near spider web of scars and wounds that gouged out ridges across his bronze skin. He was no stranger to a fight.

"Oh yes. Of course-" He kept his voice softly level and held Wilny's eye without a blink- "how could I possibly know what it's like to be forced to kill your own family. To have no control over your own body. To be screaming at yourself to stop while the people you love are dying right in front of you. And I'm sure as hell not going to be able to understand what it's like to wake up remembering every damn detail about it as if it just happened. *How could I possibly understand any of that at all?*"

It was a low blow, and immediately Wilny's gut hollowed in shame. The Frigatebird only had control of him for a few short minutes, but Amell had been under for months. It hadn't even occurred to him what he must have gone through, or who he might have lost, and all of his own morose misery suddenly seemed insignificant.

He dropped the knife with a clatter.

"I'm...I'm sorry..." He said weakly, trying to stop his voice from wavering.

"I'm sorry too. I didn't bring it up to make you feel bad, I didn't even want to talk about it at all, but I just want you to know bro, that you're not alone." Amell softly assured him.

"Look. I know this is probably not what you want, me being here, and I'm sorry that our first interaction was me nearly crushing your skull, but I had no choice in that, but right now we have a choice and opportunity." He held out his hand for the Hummingbird with a reassuring smile.

"Can we start again from the top?"

There was such warmth in his mellow voice that Wilny was in disbelief that anything terrible could have happened to this man.

He dropped his gaze, tears pricking at his eyes. Looking down at his open hands, Wilny stared at them and then slowly he reached out and shook Amell's hand. The two exchanged a small moment between one another, before Amell gave him a firm and comforting pat on the shoulder, picked up the dropped knife and headed inside with a smile.

A small weight lifted from Wilny's shoulders and breathing became easier. Taking a slow and steady breath he let the cool breeze tussle at his waves of hair and disturb his feathers, taking off his glasses and looking out to the few stars that could be seen.

"I'm proud of you, giving him another chance." A quiet voice said from above. Turning around he squinted up to the top of the terrace house to see a pair of scaled legs swinging through the bars of the upper floor's balcony and a pale face illuminated blue by the glow of a laptop screen.

"What are you doing awake?" He asked Storm in a hushed whisper. Hard to see her in the low light, the gentle rustle of feathers gave him the indication of a shrug.

"Come on up." She said. "I've something to ask you."

Taking a few steps back, he put his glasses back on and gave himself a short run up before powering up the short way to the second floor and grabbing hold of the balcony where Storm reached out her hand and pulled him up and over.

He peeked into Storm's room. Aside from the basement it was one of the few places where he had only been in once, out of respect for Storm's privacy.

Painted blue and white, it had a messy charm to it with clothes and feathers everywhere, photographs pinned to the walls between several ornaments gathered from years of traveling with the Rioteers, and with the ceiling painted in such a way that it looked like the sky. In the huge bed that sat beneath a veil of netting he could see the faint outline of a small body sleeping soundly in the nest of pillows.

"Malana?"

"Shh, let her sleep." She hushed him, patting the balcony floor beside her for him to sit. "She had a nightmare."

Brushing his tailfeathers back, he knelt next to her on the little space that the balcony provided, adjusting himself so that he was able to see the screen.

"What are you watching?"

"Something important."

There was something '*off*' with her demeanour which unnerved him, especially how she didn't meet his eye. Headphones around her neck with purple shadows forming beneath her eyes, she didn't look as though she had slept in several days and was close to ripping out somebody's jugular with her teeth.

It had to be serious.

"Wilny." She asked. "What's your earliest memory?"

"I…I…" He hesitated with a frown. "I don't know."

"Do you remember how you ended up in Core? Or if there was anything before that?"

"Storm? Are you okay?"

"This whole situation led to me re-learning a lot about myself and what I am, and along with it I learnt a lot about other people too. Like Comet and yourself. Do you know anything about Mullardoch?"

"*What?*"

"Here."

She brought up a video, clearly filmed by drone, which flew over a large grey lake penned in by mountains either side. The footage tried to focus on figures racing about the sky, until one with black wings snatched the drone from the air and dragged it with him on a chase against the other children. A man could be heard screaming in the footage from below and the boy laughed as he dove towards the man, letting the drone clatter to the floor before shooting off again to play. She sped up the footage up to a point where all the children had landed and were gathered in frame for a very wing filled class photograph, which was where she paused the video.

"That there is me and my sister." She said flatly, pointing to the pair of green-eyed, grey-winged girls who were engaged in pulling the hair of a pair of black-winged girls.

"Comet and I were prototype Avios, designed very differently from how you are and even from how Crow is."

Wilny stared at the faces of the kids with a wide-eyed look of disbelief, then looked back at Storm for comparison.

"How…different?" There were so many questions he wanted to ask, but that was the only one which came out.

"So many things… They specially engineered the muscle fibres to be fatigue resistant. Increased healing processes. Smaller but more powerful and efficient organs; they completely redesigned the circulatory and respiratory systems from all other Avio types, and completely altered the structure of my brain and nervous system. And that's not even half of it."

"That doesn't sound too different."

"It's like the difference between a hyena and a wolf. Both look like dogs but are part of very different families." She explained, eyes never leaving the screen. A shudder ran across the length of his arms, the tiny hairs rising as they felt the electricity radiating off Storm. Ignoring the risk of an electric shock he gently pawed her shoulder.

"Are you alright?"

"Not really. No. I started watching hoping to understand what might happen and what did happen and now…now I'm just so tired." Letting her shoulders droop, she rubbed her face to the point that the tiny little feathers across her cheeks were in disarray.

"I…" She gave a heaving sigh. Her wings drew up tight to her shoulders semi-shielding her against the world.

"I can't remember any of it, and I see myself there with my sister and friends, all just so happy and I can't remember any of it." Her voice wavered. "I hate knowing that it was all Rex's fault. Helios, Chase, Cadence, Brook and Trace were all rescued during the fire by the Rioteers– sorry, it wasn't a rescue… it was a kidnapping. They sometimes talked but I didn't want to look and learn because I didn't want to be afraid. I wanted to be ignorant, so I could be happy."

"I'm honestly shocked that you're still working with the Rioteers after everything that happened."

She gnawed on her lip, refusing to look at him. "It's not like I have any choice in staying. It's my responsibility to look after you all or else Rex might..."

Comforting Malana was different to comforting Storm. He wasn't sure if he could or should put an arm around her or give her some reassuring words, not that he knew of any that could help.

Giving her a gentle nudge and a small silent tilt of his head in question of if she needed anything, she shook her head and leant forward to change the video, bringing up footage of a different log where a Korean woman sat with her three hummingbird-winged sons, showing them how to write their names in the Korean Hangul alphabet.

"This here is you." Said Storm, pointing to a boy with teary blue eyes and a mole on the right side of his chin, trying his best to hide his face beneath a woollen hat meant to resemble goat ears and horns, while his two brothers, dark eyed and wide smiled, ran up to the camera and attempted to steal it from the cameraman. Both had short tailfeathers that ended in small glossy disks, and narrow shimmering wings of golden-green to blue tipped with icy white.

Wilny's skin drained of colour, leaving him ashen and faint.

"No...no that can't be right."

"Your brothers, Wilheim and Willoughby. Your mother, Professor Eve Mira, head of Aura, and her assistant researcher Rex Brisbane."

His stomach hollowed again, and the world felt as though it were falling into a spin around him. Lightheaded he leant back on his hands, wings slumping.

"Eve...Mira?"

"Yes."

"But that's...how? I thought that Beth said that my last name was just part of my ID. And that Wilny was just another callsign I used in the past."

"That's what I thought too."

"H-how did- how long have you known about this?" He asked hoarsely.

"Honestly, just three days. Beth's known all along, and I just– I want to make sure that everyone is aware of what's happening. I don't want there to be any secrets or miscommunication on it."

He drew the video back and watched it again, listening to the soft gentle cooing and staring as Eve fussed over him, drawing him up into her arms the moment he got scared. There was no shouting or ordering as the man had done with the class full of Avio children, only sweet mothering affection.

"She loved me." He said softly, not even realising that the tears were spilling down his cheeks. The little weight that had been lifted after his talk with Amell was thrown back on with crushing force.

"Then…how did I end up in Core? Did…" Voice breaking he stared at Storm, blue eyes glistening with tears, "Did she abandon me? Did she leave me there to make me tougher? Were my brothers there too?"

"I don't have the answer to that I'm afraid. It might have been because of the fire at Mullardoch too. That's my theory at least."

"Why would she abandon me if she loved me, I was her son!" Pain seared across his chest, forcing him to curl up into a ball, hearing nothing, but his thundering heartbeat in his ears. One of Storm's heavy wings fell across him, startling him out of his agony with the softness and blistering warmth.

"Beth's been lying to us." He croaked, rubbing his face furiously to wipe the tears from his eyes. "She's the one who plans, she knew this all along!"

"She's not been giving us all the facts." Storm sighed, "She didn't tell me that you were the son of a doctor when she sent me to get you. She didn't tell me Comet was on the same study as me when she said we should help her."

"You didn't look into it?"

"I trusted her judgement and was respectful of everyone's privacy. I didn't want to dig into everyone's graves."

"What if she sells us out."

"She won't."

"You trust her?" He scrambled to his feet, unable to keep the disgust from his voice. Storm didn't so much as bat an eyelash and stared him down as he stood with his wings semi-flared.

"I trust you, don't I? I trust you not to hurt Raoul or Malana, or anyone else in my family even though you're tearing yourself up trying not to think about what happened."

"You trust me?" His wings dropped with a rustling *fwump* of feathers, all the anger in his voice extinguished immediately. "I don't trust myself. You...you shouldn't have given me this responsibility. I'll kill them."

"*Wilny.*"

"I was abandoned by one family. I killed my second one. What am I going to do to this one?" His hands felt clammy and sticky, though he feared looking down at them just in case a nightmare surfaced to show them covered in blood.

Shutting the laptop, Storm rose to her feet and took hold of his hand, giving it a gentle and reassuring squeeze.

"First off, you're going to get some sleep. Then we'll figure out what we're going to do with you in the morning." She assured him, drawing him in to a gentle hug. The warmth of her wings radiated through into his bones with an anchoring realness to their heat and weight; nothing would get a chance to harm her family, she wouldn't let it happen. He almost didn't want her to let go and leave him on his own, but she did. Releasing him she mumbled about heading to bed herself, allowing him to leave.

Staggering down the stairs to his room, the house felt a lot colder than it had done outside in the breeze, the shadows darker. The whole world felt out of place, as if his balance was shifted and he was in danger of slipping into the abyss.

Raoul still slept, curled up tight into a shivering ball with all the covers kicked onto the floor in a bundle. Sighing, he rescued the sheets and covered the Hound over before heading to his bed where he sat deep in thought.

Icy cold panic sparked along his spine at thoughts of the dangers at could happen if he stayed, what he could potentially do.

He didn't want to hurt them. Any of them.

"I'm sorry." He whispered into the darkness, "I'm so sorry."

-x-

The call tone on her phone rang barely the moment she had begun to drift off to sleep. Glowering angrily at it for several moments, Storm squinted at the caller ID before she placed it against her ear, rolling over to check that the sound hadn't startled Malana awake beside her.

"Bit late in the night for a booty call Roux. Can it wait?" She slurred with exhaustion.

There was the sound of a drums and cheering crowd in the background of the call, the Dragon was at her usual haunt of London's late-night bars, working her way around the city until she got cut off.

"Storm. Are you having a night flight with your group?"

The heavy suspicion and sobriety in Roux's voice made her swing her legs out of bed and sit up immediately. Alert and awake.

"No. Why?"

"Then why have I just seen Wilny?"

17

As much as Storm loved to fly at night, this was one time she wished she didn't have to. Not wanting to wake any of the others, she dragged Amell out with her to where Roux had seen Wilny flying overhead.

Even at night the city was still as bright as day; soaked in golden light that filled the network of capillary-like roads. Storm kept an eye on the rooftops and high peaks of buildings where he would possibly perch. There was no sign of Wilny yet.

Following Roux's directions, she quickly reached the neon lit nightclub which resided beneath a railway arch. Although very late at night it was still alive with pulsating bass from the speakers within, people pouring out onto the roads as they began to leave and move on to continue the party elsewhere or hunt down a kebab shop that would still be open.

Here everyone was drunk to a point where the few people that noticed them cheered the arrival of a pair of winged people landing on the wall above. Ignoring them, Storm homed in on Roux lurking across the road next to a building held the sign *British Interplanetary Society*, dressed in little more than a bikini top, hot pants and painted with fluorescent orange body paint. Jumping down Storm greeted her with a hug, with Amell following shortly behind.

"What happened? Did you guys fight?" The Dragon asked, with more worry than she'd let anyone in the headquarters hear her speak.

"Not exactly. Which way did he go?"

"Northeast-ish. I sent Free after him, but who know where that idiot Chiro went. *Pinche culero.*"

"Free? As in Freeborn?" Amell gave her a frown, tearing his eyes away from the band of drunks staggering across the road. "That Aussie bastard is still alive?"

"You know him?"

"Unfortunately." His face scrunched in disgust and he shook his wings out with an agitated beat as a few of the partygoers began staring at him.

"Well, he's probably drunk in a tree somewhere now. He got pretty hammered." Roux sighed, stepping back away from the vomit and pulling out her phone with a small and angry curse. "If I hear anything, I'll text you."

Thanking the Dragon, Storm leaped into the air with a flick of silver feathers. Not having expected such a swift and sudden exit, Amell was left gawking up as she disappeared into the dark sky. Breaking into a run and beating his wings down, he slowly sailed up after her though he struggled to match her pace.

Up in the sky, a deep rumble rolled across the city as the dark and heavy clouds drew in, threatening to strike them with a lightning storm and a torrential downpour. Storm shuddered. She could feel it growing, the electricity in the atmosphere and the metallic taste upon the back of her tongue. The summer lightning was always impressive, and always arrived after an extended heatwave, however if it started raining then they wouldn't be able to fly far or for long without their wings becoming sodden.

Soaring past the tower of a church, the buildings parted around a large park-like area in which stood the Imperial War Museum, maned out front by its turquoise blue dreadnought naval guns.

Lightning crackled to the east, its light half blinding her with the sudden flash and leaving an after image upon her retina.

Iridescent blue caught her eye.

She banked sharply, circling the museum and examining the rooftop and all its eves and crevices. A fluttering blue disk hung over the edge of a small shadowy ledge, and the hunched feathery forms of wings gave themselves away with the faintest metallic shimmer of feathers even in the low light.

It was definitely Wilny. He hadn't spotted her and so she dove at him, Amell awkwardly following behind.

"The fuck do you think you're doing?" She snapped loudly, landing on the ledge beside him, barely buffeting her wings to brake. Wilny flinched at her arrival, raising his fists and leaping up into a crouch.

Lightning crackled again, followed seconds later by the sound of rolling thunder. In the brief moment of lilac-white light, she could his bloodshot eyes, his tear-streaked face and a small rucksack sat beside him, round and nearly bursting with clothes and food crammed into it.

"Leave." He ordered them, his voice harsh and cracked.

"Hey now Wilny, it's alright." Amell tried to assure him as he stumbled across the ledge. "We're here to help."

Wilny looked between Amell and Storm hesitantly, before taking a deep breath and slowly standing up straight.

"I've decided I'm going back to Core." He said calmly, directing the statement more towards Amell than to Storm, cradling his arms to his chest.

"You *what?*"

"It's safer for everyone if I go back to Core. I was sent there and so I should go back. I can go to Recovery and they can give me a hard reset so I don't remember anything. And maybe if I'm there, then Professor Mira won't come here and hurt any of you."

Storm's jaw dropped in disbelief, astonished by his logic and decision.

"Wilny." Said Amell, cautiously stepping forward. "You don't have to do this.

"I do. What if I kill somebody? What if I hurt Malana or Raoul?"

"But you wouldn't."

"What if– I don't- I don't want to risk it. I'm sorry." He hung his head and reached for his bag, only to be stopped by sudden and animalistic snarl from Storm. Even Amell flinched, nervously backing away from her and edging closer to Wilny.

"So, you're going to run away?" She growled. Her wings arched out above her, the city-light catching on the scales of her legs and the silvered edges of her feathers and turning them to steel and leaving her pale green eyes almost fluorescent.

"You're going to run and hide because you're afraid of what *could* happen rather than let us help?"

"You can't help me. None of you can. Crow won't take away the memories, what else can I do?" Wilny swallowed, backing away from the bag and Storm as he caught sight of her cat-like teeth and flexing talons. "I don't want to remember it."

Wilny's heart began to beat wildly, its rhythm erratic and painful in sudden fear. An electrical tingle ran across his skin as even from where he stood, he could feel her electrical charge, and for a brief moment, he was sure that she was musing as he felt her anger, her exhaustion and frustration, and a savage ache in his chest and teeth. The terrified voice in the back of his head screamed for him to run with sudden hyperawareness and terror that he was staring down an apex predator who *could* and *would* kill him.

He didn't even get a chance to blink as she pounced at him, slamming him down onto the edge of the ledge with a powerful kick.

"Do you think you're the only one who's suffering and dangerous?" She barked down at him, one foot on his chest and letting the talons at the end of her four long toes, dig into his skin.

"You think it's less painful to be Lana, or Raoul, or Amell, or fuck- even *me*? You'd rather take a shitty, easy way out than come to terms with what happened? What about us? Do you think we don't want an easier option to help us with what we've been through? Your team would be ashamed of you– no, *disgusted* with you."

"You know nothing of how they would think!"

"You're right. But *I* expected better from *you*." She blazed with anger. He felt it. Her anger was violent and deadly, and infectious, turning his vision red with undiluted fury.

"How dare you talk to me like that! You know nothing about me or what happened!"

"Because you won't talk to me! I want to help you, but I can't if you won't fucking talk about it!"

"I don't want your help! You're nothing but a *Feral*."

He rolled out from beneath her, twisting to use his legs to capture hers and bring her down. She fell with a flurry of wingbeats, whilst he bounced onto his feet. The impact rattled her, giving Wilny time to grab her by her shirt and arm, he lifted her up, span her round and threw her from the ledge.

Quickly before she hit the ground, she twisted and righted herself in time to glide across the grass and rise again, flipping round to face Wilny who was now stood on the ledge. His eyes were icy, the pupils little more than beads of black against opalescent blue.

"Wilny! Let me help! I am not your enemy!" She shouted down at him as she pulled into a hover. "But if you go back to Core then I will be, and I will fight you."

He didn't respond.

Wings flaring out, he crouched and pounced from the ledge. His wings blurred and thrummed loudly as he flew at Storm. Snapping her wings in quickly and letting herself drop, Wilny streak past her in an uncontrolled charge. Twisting deftly beneath the gigantic naval guns, she took off over the treetops of the museum park, leaving Amell still standing on the roof in a state of shock at how fast they had moved.

Wings flashing out, she twisted and surfed across the rooftops of cars in the street below, luring him across the city as the wind picked up and thunder began to shake the air as it drew overhead. Enthralled in anger, he gave chase.

Up, round, over, down, through, and between, she led him on a chase, the world flashing black and gold to white and lilac as the lightning began to strike the skyscrapers and casting light across the entire city. Banking back towards the river, Wilny barely realised where he was going, his sights were locked on Storm.

The focus he had was so strong he nearly crashed into the spokes of the London Eye, not nearly as agile as Storm who deftly avoided the moving metal and sprinted up towards the clock tower on the other side of the river as a bolt struck the lightning rod of the building behind with a deafening crack.

She perched and watched Wilny stumble onto the ledge below, gripping onto the façade for dear life with ragged breaths.

Even in such low light, with her sensitive vision she could see the veins in his neck pulsing an uneven tempo and trembling in his hands. She didn't know if he could put his heart through the strain.

"You need to stop. You're gonna damage yourself like." Storm snarled down at him, crawling down the near-vertical roof towards him with the deftness of a snow leopard on a mountainside. "Stop acting like an arse and I can help."

Breathing ragged, he clung to the gold and black gothic decors for dear life, feathers catching on the tiny ornate fencing on the edge of the roof.

"I don't need your help."

"Then I guess we'll just have to carry on until you realise you have to stop." Then she pounced. Wilny ducked, thinking she would tackle him from his precarious position, but instead she dove over him and lazily glided away. With a flurry of enraged flaps, Wilny followed her, practically falling off the clocktower though managing to awkwardly level out his flight and chase her down across a park.

Skirting the treetops, Wilny caught up with her. His hand extended before him to grab at her ankle, just as they reached the edge of the park, but only caught air as she spun out of his way, circling the grand golden statue that stood before the palace. Storm looped around the statue several times as Wilny tried to predict her movement and swiped at her, before she took off down the road to the right of the palace that was protected by towering maple trees. Flying in a straight line, Wilny picked up speed and pushed himself to sprint through the air after her.

Whilst she could have flown like this for hours, Wilny was quickly tiring. His fast-beating wings were beginning to slow and become irregular in their fluttering. She'd need to make him land soon or risk him dropping from the sky. She kept low, hoping that if Wilny did need to stop the fall wouldn't be as rough as falling from a great height and at speed.

Between the thunder she heard the blades of a helicopter drawing close to them. Storm cursed under her breath. Another problem to deal with. She didn't need more attention drawn to them or to give Rex another reason to be furious at them. Without a clear view of where it was, she had no clue as to what direction she'd need to take Wilny in to get him away from it. Flying so fast and so low through the trees made it hard to fix on sounds, especially against the backdrop of a thunderstorm.

Taking a risk, she darted up through a gap in the trees in order to find where it was coming from and almost immediately collided with it.

The helicopter veered sharply as its pilots spotted her, Storm backpedalling in the air yelping a streak of curses as its tail swung about to stabilise it. Focused on not having her head cut off by the helicopter blades, her hesitation gave Wilny the chance to tackle her in the air, hitting her in the back and throwing his arms around her neck and waist to hold her.

The two struggled briefly, falling through the air back towards the ground, but Storm wasn't about to let them both crash-land. With a sharp and sudden shock of electricity she forced him to let go then twisting round painfully she grabbed Wilny by a wing and flapping as hard as she could, dragging him through the air and out of the park towards several grand old buildings. She hid them in the eaves of the Natural History Museum, crouching between the gargoyles as the helicopter flew over them in its search before turning back to escape the oncoming weather.

Tucking her wings back, Storm released her grip on Wilny and took several deep breaths to try and calm herself after the panic of nearly being decapitated. Wilny slid limply to his side upon release. Concerned by his lack of movement she shook him a little but had no response. Fingers to his neck she checked his pulse and held her ear to his mouth, looking down his chest to check for breath.

Nothing.

She reeled back as she realised that all of the strain and her sudden shock had stopped his heart. Heavy drops of rain began to splash across her wings and hair, slowly building into a torrent.

"Shit…What the fuck did I tell you, you fucking idiot!" She bellowed at him, shaking his shoulders to try to get a response. Wilny remained limp.

Taking a deep breath, she moved his body so that he was laying comfortably on the ground, tilting his head back to open his airway, and opening out her wings to keep the rain off him, trying to be as swift as possible in performing CPR.

CPR on Avios was difficult with their large sternal keel, but she knew what she was doing and how important it was to get his heart beating again. The longer he remained without a heartbeat or air, the less oxygen there would be for his brain, and the more likely he would be to suffer permanent brain damage.

It was arduous work keeping the rhythm going, but after several sets and breaths she heard a little cough from him and could feel a weak heartbeat. His chest rose and fell as he began to breathe again and when she placed her fingers over the arteries in his neck, she could feel his pulse beginning to strengthen.

His back arched as he took a dry rasping breath, eyelids fluttering open to stare up at the orange tinted clouds.

"Wh-where am I?" He asked her feebly, trying to sit up with an aching groan. Storm pushed his arms down with a wing, so she could keep her hands on his heart and neck to check his pulse.

"Don't."

"Storm I-I'm sor-sorry."

"Quiet. Don't get worked up, I've still not got your heart settled."

Wincing in pain, he remained still as Storm checked him over, taking his pulse and rolling him onto his side to check his wings, flexing them out and brushing the barbs of the feathers back into alignment after dragging him.

"You brought me back…again…" He stated softly, watching her out the corner of his eye, rainwater beginning to drip down his face. She shrugged and mumbled to herself something about being clinically dead versus being actually dead, continuing to check his vitals.

"You should have just let me die."

Her head snapped up and she locked eyes with him in a statuesque stare, then without the slightest indicating twitch punched him square in the face, snapping his head back against the stone. Black spots danced before his eyes and he curled up clutching at his head.

"S-Storm!"

"*Shut the fuck up.*" Her hand gripped his jaw, forcing him to look her in the eye. The tiny feathers across her cheekbones and ears had raised themselves in fury as had the ones on her wings. Steam rose from her skin in a fine swirling mist.

"Please just-"

"*You should have just let me die.* Really?" She snarled, letting the talons pierce his skin, every R a rumbling rolling growl.

"Don't be such a selfish fuck. Do you really think dying will solve anything? Do you think it'd be easier than going back to Core? Do you *seriously* believe any of that? Are you incapable of thinking about the consequences of your actions? How would Malana feel? Raoul too."

"I- I just-"

She released him, leaping to her feet and shaking the rain from her wings in a beat. She wanted to help him, she truly did, but in that moment, rage took over.

"DOES ALL OF THIS MEAN SO LITTLE TO YOU THAT YOU'D RATHER BE DEAD?"

The thunder echoed her roar, yet all he could hear was the sound of his own heartbeat in his ears. She towered over him with a backdrop of a lightning-struck city behind her. Frightened, Wilny backed up against the battlement and hugged himself, looking like a pitiful child covered in scrapes and bruises.

"I've killed people Storm. They were my friends, my family, I loved them, and I killed them. I shouldn't be allowed to live." His voice wavered. Tears were welling up in his eyes in disgust and pity at himself, but his wallowing was met with fury from Storm.

"You think you're the only one who's killed someone they love? Who's lost people?" She let out a curt and humourless laugh. "Raoul. Kat. Amell. Malana. Me. We've all killed and lost people, do you think we don't understand? We know how you feel! We want to help!"

"You don't know anything! I'm dangerous. I've trained to kill people."

"Fuck off. I'm way more dangerous than you *and you know it.*" She spat, letting her wings flare to their fullest extent so that they caught the light and the feathers rustled against the wind. "You're just a scared little boy who's been taught to fight, but I'm a force of nature."

He cowered beneath her. She was right, of course she was. For all his training and tactical knowledge, he couldn't compete with her in terms of raw power, they were made completely differently. If she wanted to, she could have killed him at any point, ripped his throat out with her teeth, stopped his heart and fried his brain with a burst of electricity, broken his bones and let him drop from the sky.

The anger in her eyes died down, replaced with cold contempt. Letting her wings softly droop and sweep back in against her back, the rain running off the sleek feathers she turned to face the city. The cold began to seep into his bones even beneath the radiating heat of his wings that were slowly becoming sodden with water.

"I want to help you get better, I really do," she sighed, hugging her arms tight to her chest, "but I can't help you if I don't know what you want. So, tell me. Do you really want to feel this way forever?"

"No. I-"

"Do you really *want* to go back to Core?"

"No."

"Do you really want to die?"

"I...I don't know..."

She stared down at him, exhaustion leaving her gaunt and pale with bruised purple rings around her eyes. It was hard to tell what she was feeling; her face was a stoic mask disguising something he'd not seen in her before.

Resignation.

"I think you need to go away for a while and think about what it is you want."

The suddenness of her words shook the ennui from him with a sudden gut wrench.

"A-away?" He swallowed. "Wha-what do you mean *away*?"

"Out of the country. Somewhere that you can go clear your head."

Silence fell on the world around him as the words sunk in.

"Storm please. Please." He begged her, hoarse voice wavering as a fresh rain of tears fell from his eyes, "You can't just send me away! I need help! Wh-wh-what if I kill people! What if I try and kill myse-"

"*Don't.* Don't you dare even say it, I have too much respect for you to even hear those words from you."

"Then please! You have to help me!" He clawed at her wingtips, scrambling after her on his knees as she began to walk away from him in search of a good place to fly from. "I can't do this on my own!"

"I can't help you!" She snarled down at him, snatching her wings away from him, "I've been trying for months to help you. Getting you therapy, antidepressants, several forms of sleep medication and helping you calm down when you wake up screaming with nightmares, trying to get you to talk and come to terms with what happened, all of it but you won't let me help. I can't do it anymore. I want to believe I can help you, but I...can't." Her voice broke. "I need to take care of my family. And you need to take care of yourself. I'm sorry."

"Please don't leave me here! Don't send me away! Please Storm! *Please!*" He begged. "How will I get back home? M-my heart hurts...I don't think I can..." He clutched at his chest, breathing raggedly.

"Walk. Fly. I don't care. If you fall out the sky call someone to drag your arse off the pavement."

"Storm-"

But he never got to finish his pleading as in a flurry of wingbeats that sprayed the rainwater off in an arc of droplets, she had taken off into the sky.

"Storm!" He screamed at the sky, "STORM! PLEASE! COME BACK!"

But she was high above him, beyond his reach. Up, up, up, she went, higher and higher, her muscles aching and chest heaving. High, she needed to be up high and away from him lest she allow his begging to soften her, but she refused to allow herself to be gentle.

Distraught, Wilny screeched at the sky, begging her to come back until he began to choke on his sobs, and fell onto his side in exhaustion. His earlier flight had left him weary and sore and the things that Storm had said, the words that she had used, ran around his head, winding him up into a ball of despair.

She'd given up on him.

He lay shivering on the rooftop for many long minutes, clutching at his chest until Amell finally arrived.

When he asked where Storm was, Wilny could barely speak, let alone move. Staying still for too long in the meant that his core body temperature had dropped and where his feathers would usually have kept him warm, they now felt as each was edged in frost despite it being summer.

"She wants me gone." He whispered hoarsely, barely even looking up at Amell when he crouched beside him. "She wants me gone."

Unable to get him to stand, Amell was left with no choice, but to lift the limp and shattered Wilny off the ground into his arms and leaped from the roof with him, gliding out across the city back to Cherry Tree. The Hummingbird was absolutely silent as the despair had overwhelmed him.

A journey that would have taken little under two minutes took an extra five with the rain and extra weight and drag caused by sodden Wilny being in his arms. Reaching the river, he put as much of his remaining strength into flying across and aiming to try and glide over the few dozen terrace gardens and into Cherry Tree, landing with a stumble.

"Are you alright to walk bro?" He asked the Hummingbird, helping him to stand steady. With a hiccup and a nod, he patted Amell's arm, ushering him to leave him be and stumbling up the slippery decking to the kitchen.

Sat at the table were Kat and Beth, both dressed in their pyjamas and who seemed to have been in the middle of a conversation, interrupted by Wilny awkwardly tripping through the sliding doors face first onto the floor. The pair quickly rose from their seats and went to his side.

"B-Beth." He snivelled pitifully, trying to stand.

"What's wrong with your face? What happened?"

"S-Storm told m-me that I…I…" His voice broke and he fell against the wall in floods of tears, unable to move once again. Amell went to his side and helped him up once again, bringing him to sit at the table. A small silent exchange between the girls and Kat disappeared to fetch towels and a hairdryer to warm the boys up while Beth flicked on the switch for the kettle and made him some sweet coffee.

Giving him some time to calm down and helping to dry his soaked feathers and hair, they waited until his breathing was level enough that they could talk to him without too much broken sobbing.

"What did Storm say?" Beth asked tentatively, drying his hair with a towel so that the soft waves of brown were messed up into a damp tangle of curls.

"She thinks I sh-should go away for a while."

"*Away?*"

He nodded, wishing that he could just project his thoughts to them rather than tell them everything aloud. Talking about it hurt too much.

"Of course," Beth sighed. She made a small gesture for Amell and Kat to move back from him as she helped him to his feet and wrapped a towel around his shoulders. "I'll make the arrangements now."

"I'm gonna pack…" He mumbled bitterly, staggering off through into the living room and up the flight of stairs to his room at a trudging slow pace, leaning against the walls and banisters for support.

On the second floor he passed Kat's room where he could hear Raoul laughing with Malana.

The laughter made him pause and he peeked in through the ajar door. Both were sat on the bright blue beanbags Kat owned and in a circle around Malana were several open books with sticky notes indicating lines for her to read. It was one of Raoul's ideas to help Malana learn English as well as improve his own vocabulary. Though it was barely light outside, he was sure that it was Beth's suggestion to distract them both from the girls fretting until they found out what was going on with Storm and Wilny.

"*Arrête de me faire rire*, Lana! I'm trying to teach you." Raoul chucked, tapping the page to get Malana to read. Malana whined, fluffing up he downy feathers and cocooning herself in her wings.

"*Désolé! J'ai mal à la tête!*" She cooed, unable to contain her giggles.

"You can't use that excuse every time."

"I have tel-kens y'know, ma head coo-ed explode!" Malana chirped, mimicking Storm's accent and making Raoul laugh again.

As wonderful as it was to see them getting along, he couldn't shake the feeling of disgust and despair as he knew how damaging he could be to them. They were safer with him gone.

Sighing, Wilny shuffled past, hoping that they didn't see him. There was a pause in their conversation as he reached the stairs, but then Raoul continued with his lesson.

Upon reaching his room, he shut the door behind him and rummaged through his drawers finding a rucksack and tossing in all the clothes he could carry. Shirts, shorts, a flying jacket, he didn't know if he would be dropped off in Spain and left to fend for himself or not, if he would be gone forever or if it was just a short-term thing.

The hinges of the door creaked behind him as he stuffed into his bag two bottles of honey he had been keeping in the back of a draw of socks.

"Hey…are you alright? I heard you go past." Raoul asked tentatively, padding softly up behind Wilny.

"Go away…"

"Are you crying? Why do you smell like-"

"*Don't talk to me. Leave me alone!*" He snapped at the Hound. Raoul recoiled slightly, confused by Wilny's behaviour. Reaching out, Raoul tried to put his hand on Wilny's shoulder in an attempt to comfort him, but Wilny threw his wings out and beat them rapidly to keep Raoul back.

"Don't touch me!" He yelled, "Don't come near me and don't talk to me!"

"Raoul." Storm's sharp voice made them both flinch. "*Here.*"

Raoul turned to face Storm, fur bristling with nervousness at her voice.

Her usually grey-blue hair was black and tangled from flying in the rain, and face burning red from the cold.

Out of fear and uncertainty as to what was happening, Raoul obeyed, darting behind Storm's wing as she stood at the door to his room. Kat, Amell and Malana had all rushed upstairs the instant Wilny started shouting.

Wilny's shoulders drooped. "Stor-"

"Don't forget to say goodbye to everyone before you go." Cold sharp words that made him cower.

She blustered past the rest of the Rogues gathered at the door to scoop Malana up into her arms and carry her away before she could see. Quickly following her lead the other Rogues followed after Storm, hoping for answers.

-x-

Several minutes later, Wilny emerged from the house to find a minivan taxi hailed by Beth waiting for them. Amell was already in and waiting, having insisted on going with Wilny just to make sure he got there safely. After carrying him through the sky in the rain, he felt duty bound to keep an eye on him. Beth bundled Wilny and his bag into the back then ordered the driver to take them to Gatwick.

The journey was tense and quiet, only interrupted by the occasional snot-ridden sniff from Wilny. As mellow and chatty as he had been earlier in the evening, Amell was somewhat subdued and silent as well, not knowing what to say to Wilny and not wanting to pry into what had happened. Beth, sitting in the seats in front of him, glanced back at him from her phone where she had been asking Storm for details on what she had said to him to reduce him to tears.

"You've been crying for the entire journey." She noted aloud. Wilny sniffled and wiped his nose on the sleeve of his jacket much to Beth's disgust.

"Sorry."

"I've made some arrangements with Crow and he's contacted Xana."

"Xana?" It took a while for the name to have any form of meaning to him, such was his state. "Oh, the Spanish group."

"You're to meet Adonis at the airport when you arrive. He'll look after you until he thinks you're ready to return to us."

"Adonis?" Having never met any of the group members, in his despair-clouded mind he tried to subdue his sadness and focus on trying to know what the group leader might be like from his name alone.

"Adonis as in the god of beauty?" Amell laughed softly with a smirk, "Did he name himself that?"

"Actually, Crow named him that. Do you know a lot about gods Amell?"

"Well, I am one, so of course." Amell purred, winking at Beth and blowing her a kiss. Beth glared at him so ferociously that the Eagle gave a startled honk of fright and leant back as far as he could so that he was out of punching range of Beth. Satisfied with his fear, she looked back to her phone.

"What does he look like?" Wilny asked gently. "I've never met him or seen a picture; how will I know who I'm looking for."

Beth laughed loudly, as they hit the motorway, not taking her eyes off her phone and pulling on a pair of headphones.

"Oh, you'll know."

Seeing as though the usually talkative Beth had now gone onto shut down mode and plugged into listen to music, Wilny turned to Amell. The taxi driver was squinting at Amell's huge wings splayed out across the back of the taxi and quietly questioning if they were real or just very well constructed cosplay features, leaning towards the latter. It almost made him laugh at how confused he was getting by them, to the point he was barely paying attention to the road and Amell was getting visibly worried that they might crash.

"They're controlled by remote micro-hydraulics." Wilny said loudly to the driver. "We're going to a convention."

The driver's eyebrows raised, and he relaxed with a soft chuckle to himself, quietly assuring himself that '*of course they aren't real*'.

"You doing alright bro?" Amell asked gently, relaxing once again.

"How do you stand it? Stand yourself, knowing what you did."

The words fell out of his mouth before he even realised what he'd said. Amell however, didn't seem to be too taken aback by them and shrugged calmly, returning to mellowness.

"I take the time to remember them happily." He said with a calm certainty. "We didn't have much, most of my family had spent their entire lives in Atlas as testers, but we did plan to travel if we ever got the chance. I promised my friend, Spice, that I'd learn to cook and paint, so while I'm here, I plan to learn that and live up to my promise."

"But they're gone…"

"Yes, but what matters is that I did something for them, and I can remember them by it, even if it makes me sad."

Wilny looked down to his hands, thinking over what Amell had said for several long silent minutes. The pale teal-green tinge of dawn was spreading across the horizon as they slowed on arrival to the airport. Sliding the door open he stopped before he got out and turned to the Eagle.

"Fury liked to fish. He'd tell us about going out to the rivers and lakes with his father and spending the entire day fishing." He said slowly, expecting the words to hurt as he thought about his friend, but there was no stabbing pain. Allowing himself a small smile, he looked to the Eagle. "Thank you Amell."

"I'm here to help, any way you need." Amell purred with playful slap to Wilny's ass as he got out of the car, a sybarite wink as the Hummingbird turned around with a gawking frown. Amell laughed, ushering for him to head on out.

Throwing a well-meaning pair of middle fingers to Amell, Wilny thanked Beth for taking him to the airport, picked up his bag and headed inside to catch his flight.

18

Ruidera, Ciudad Real, Castile-La Mancha, Spain

Being on an aeroplane was a strange experience for Wilny, gazing out a window and watching clouds roll by. Patchwork lands of city and green farmland rolled away beneath him, giving way to snow-streaked mountains and solar panel covered deserts. It seemed so barren and dry compared to England.

It was an experience, and it took his mind off the pain. Beth had booked him a flight upon a private charter jet for him and having never been on a plane before he had idea what to expect. Still being teary eyed and bruised, the lone stewardess paid him great attention, offering him first aid and free food. He politely declined all their offer of help and tried to focus on keeping his wings hidden and not breaking his flight feathers from sitting on them.

After arriving in *Ciudad Real* airport, departing the plane and negotiating the security, he followed Beth's instructions, making his way to arrivals to find Xana group's leader, Adonis Oola.

He scanned the small crowd of people waiting at the end of the gate, families mostly, some holding up tablets with names written on the screens, so their loved ones could find them. He almost felt envious of them, especially when he saw a young man run to the barrier and throw his arms around what Wilny assumed was his parents.

However, stood in the arrivals was the least surreptitious looking man he had ever seen, dressed in a trench coat with its collar turned up to hide his face and hat pulled so far down over his eyes that he could barely see. He towered over most of the people waiting in arrivals and held a cardboard sign with a hummingbird drawn on it. Dull yellow reptilian eyes blinked slowly at him from beneath the hat.

This had to be the right man.

"Adonis?" Wilny asked him cautiously. The man nodded and beckoned him to follow, his hands oddly textured, yellow with banded black, and ending in long black talons. Wilny quickly followed after him, noticing that the airport security was watching them closely and dressed as they were it was hard for them to be anything but suspicious.

Making it out of the airport and into the bright hot sun, Adonis led him across the mile-long carpark to a large four-by-four with tinted windows which he opened and beckoned Wilny into before sitting in the driver's seat beside him.

"Finally. Now I can take this damn thing off." Adonis breathed, in a gravelly voice, taking off the hat and coat and throwing them into the back of the car.

"Whoa…" Wilny stopped to stare at him as he scrubbed his short ecru-grey hair and stretched. The man was as tall as Wilny, incredibly lithe with a long whip of a tail that uncurled from around his narrow waist, but what drew his attention was Adonis's skin. Textured with fine grey reptilian scales that darkened along the backs of his arms and neck into black, but was broken by organised spots of pale yellow, ringing his arms and fingers in contrasting bands. Even his long heavy tail that was now sprawled across the floor had these spotted markings.

A Reptile synth.

Adonis smiled, showing off a set of thin backwards curving teeth.

"Surprised?" He asked softly. "Never seen a Tlaloc Reptile before?"

He flicked out his long-forked tongue and held his hand out to shake. "Adonis Oola. Xana leader."

Slowly taking his hand, Wilny shook it and continued to stare at the man, enthralled by his alien appearance. He could see why he was called Adonis; the man was captivating. Having barely looked away from the man, Wilny didn't realise that they had already begun to drive.

"Beth tells me that you are to stay with us for a week or two. You don't seem like a bad kid, so we should get along amiably." He said softly after a few minutes, aware Wilny was still gawping at him out the corner of his eye.

"Yeah…"

"Do you know how to fish?"

"Vaguely…"

"Can you speak any Spanish?"

"Some…"

"Some? Well, I'll teach you a few phrases. The girls don't speak any English, so I'll probably have to translate to start with."

"Yeah…"

"Do you know how to talk in extended sentences?"

Beginning to realise how stupid he sounded, Wilny tore his eyes away, muttering an apology. Adonis chuckled softly and held an arm out to Wilny.

"Go on then. I know you want to."

His cheeks flushed in embarrassment. "S-sorry?"

"You're curious about the scales, it's alright you can touch."

"A-are you a muser?"

He laughed. "No. I'm just used to people staring and asking me where my ears are."

Graciously, he took Adonis's arm and gently ran his fingers across the scales. He expected them to be rough and hard, but they were entirely the opposite, smooth and supple.

"Happy?"

"Y-yes."

"At least you're not as bad as Crow was when I first met him. The idiot tried to rip my tail off." He shot a fanged smile across to the still awestruck Hummingbird. There was no malice in the smile, despite the teeth, and the warm and gentle tones made Wilny feel at ease.

"You know Crow?"

"Yes, he was the one who got me into the Rogues back when it first began. He was the one who named me actually."

His ears pricked, and he sat a little straighter in intrigue.

"You were a Rogue?" Storm had never mentioned this. Adonis nodded, pulling the car off at a junction and swearing loudly at a speeding sports car which had dashed out in front of them, with the same level of angry enthusiasm that Roux showed when she swore.

"I'll tell you more about it later if you like, but firstly, you should know, two of us are Marines – the Risio made ones, not the armed forces sort, so we spend a lot of time in the lakes."

Looking out at the desert scrubland that stretched for miles in all directions, Wilny found it hard to imagine any water at all being present in such an arid place.

"There's five of us at the moment. Me and the four girls. You'll be the only Avio. A word of warning; don't be surprised if Asia and Ceto pull your feathers, they've never seen an Avio before. Diana and Inanna might be a little wary, but they should be fine after a while."

Wilny nodded sagely, trying to remember the names and imagine what the home might be like if there were Marines living with them. He had never even seen a Marine before in real life and all that he could think was that they looked like mermaids, though he was sure that he was wrong.

"Another thing you should know about us Xanas, our house rule is that you have to be perfectly honest about everything. Even if it offends or insults a person, you have to be honest."

"Why? Doesn't that just cause arguments?"

"Communication is key to having a functioning family. I'm not sure how Storm runs the Rogues, but the way its run for us is more about talking honestly and finding ways to fix thinking."

His face scrunched up as he considered how little Beth would tell them of what she knew, how often Storm would lie about where she was when she went out or how much Kat had spent when shopping. They were spontaneous at the best of times, chaotic at the worst, and any trouble they had would be dealt with quietly and out of everyone else's knowledge, although Storm now seemed to want to try to change that.

"It's...different." He sighed. Catching the tone of his voice, Adonis' smile stopped, and he glanced at Wilny with concern and sympathy.

"If there's anything you want, you need only ask."

Staring ahead at the road he thought about what Amell had said to him in silence for several minutes.

"In the Elites," he said in a small voice, trying not to waver or choke up, "we used to get letters from people outside. I'd get letters from a friend who travels the world. He'd send me little pressed flowers, drawings, honey, and little books on bees and Fury would get photos of his family fishing and he'd cry and talk for hours about the different fishing trips he went on with his dad."

He trailed off feeling his chest tighten but swallowing down the pain he turned to Adonis. "I want to go fishing."

Adonis smiled and nodded affirmatively, continuing the journey on in a comfortable and peaceful silence.

Upon arriving at the villa of the Xana group he was greeted by four very curious girls who thronged around him the moment he stepped out the car and refused to back away until each were each introduced to Wilny in turn, their greetings being translated by Adonis.

Ceto and Asia were twin Marines, who launched themselves at him first to shake his hand and welcome him. The mental image of long-haired mermaids with beautiful, scaled tails was a far cry from what they actually looked like. Their hair was little more than short velvety brown fur, with faces that looked more similar to the Anubis-headed Canids, long whiskers surrounding their upper lips and a mouth full of surprisingly sharp teeth. Although they didn't have the fluking tail, he had imagined their webbed feet easily made up for it the moment he saw them in the water. It hadn't occurred to him that there would have been mammalian-based Marines, but the more he thought of it, the more rational it seemed, although Adonis assured him that Risio had truly fish-tailed Marines somewhere in the Risio farms.

After he had finished gawping at the Marines, he was introduced to Inanna the Lioness, far different to Kat with her beautiful black skin, long flare tipped tail and large yellow eyes. She greeted him with less suspicion than what Kat had given him, even leaning in to kiss his cheek as a greeting, before being pushed to one side by Diana, a fair and newly designed CY-NX Preternatural who was the youngest and smallest, but was the second in command, as she declared very loudly much to Inanna's chagrin.

When the introductions had finished, he was shown the villa, welcoming and protected by a large wall overgrown with grape and wisteria. It built over the edge of one of the many chains of lakes surrounded by rolling red hills, with its own short pier which stretched out from a decking and over the lake. With two Marines he could see the reasoning behind them being so close to the water, there was even a small pool inside the house where the girls spent most of their time.

-x-

"Storm!" Kathy sat bolt upright in her bunk; eyes bright with delight the moment the Rogue entered the cell. Grinning at the change of reception from their initial greeting, Storm gave the girl a wave.

"Aww, look at you all starry eyed at seeing me." Storm teased. "You're not getting a crush on me, are you?"

"*Maybe?*"

With Wilny gone and Rex on a rampage, Storm had been determined to do some good. She had visited Kathy every day to talk with her and even been able to get Jenna in to give her an evaluation and some counselling in order to help her. It was small steps, but it had made a difference.

With a little laugh, she stepped to one side, allowing Kathy to see behind her.

"I've brought a friend."

Comet clutched at Storm's feathers in wide-eyed fear as Kathy slowly began to recognise who she was. Kathy cringed a little, looking Comet up and down and rolling her shoulders awkwardly.

"Oh uh…weren't you the girl who was there when…"

"Storm why'd you bring me in here?" Comet hissed, drawing her metallic wings around her. "What if she tries to kill me."

"I've told her to behave." Storm assured Comet sitting on the floor with her wings splayed out behind her.

"I just wanted you two to meet and apologise to each other, then just talk."

"What about?" Kathy tried to play down her suspicion.

"Anything, that's up to you two. I did bring food."

Instantly dropping her suspicion, Kathy gave a delighted squeal and slid off her bunk and sat on the floor beside Storm, laying her wings out behind her as Storm did. Comet refused to move from the door, watching Kathy carefully as she tore into the meats with ravenous hunger.

"What's your name again?" Kathy eventually asked, once she had swallowed down the food.

"Comet."

"Kathy Grey." She smiled and offered a hand up to shake. "I'm sorry about what happened. I was not in a great place."

The Hummingbird refused to shake and instead stood glowering down at her with her wings quivering behind her. There was an awkward yet tense silence as the two girls warily watched each other, only broken by Storm who tutted and rummaged through the bag.

"Comet are you going to say sorry too?"

"Why should I apologise? She attacked me."

"You were the one who ran into that fight of your own accord." Storm sniped sharply and held out the bottle of honey to the nervous Hummingbird.

"Do I have to be here?" She asked sharply, her short fan of tailfeathers flicking open and shut. Rolling her eyes at Comet's cold sourness towards the Vulture she sighed and pulled on one of the pearlescent white feathers along the upper arch of Comet's wings.

"Yes, because I want to piss Rex off as much as possible." Said Storm dryly, "And it's good to socialise, but also because I want you two to keep an eye out on each other."

"Why?"

"Because you both need purpose in your life. Milling about with nothing to do is terrible for the mind. And when you improve then you might be able to get out of here and have a house of your own," She reached over and patted Kathy's shoulder reassuringly, smiling warmly as the girl almost teared up at the idea. With a sly grin, Storm threw the bottle of honey gently at the Hummingbird.

"Now, buck up before I tell Roux you're whining again."

Cautiously, Comet took the honey, inspecting it before sipping it. The thick syrupiness made her choke a little at first before she drank the rest of it without stopping for breath when she found the taste pleasant. The other two girls chuckled, waiting for her to finish.

"Sorry if I gave you nightmares." Comet eventually grumbled.

"I would say no problem, but what you did was terrifying. Are you a muser?"

"Yes."

"Huh. You're pretty badass for somebody who looks like they cry all the time." The Vulture snarked, tearing into more of the food, speaking as she chewed. She looked Comet up and down, staring at her bare feet with curiosity.

"Are you the same as Storm?" She asked, nodding to the four toes covered with tiny grey scales. Storm gave a firm nod.

"Yes, Comet was from the same project as me."

"Oh, so she is a Type-Seven like you? Is that why she's weirdly strong?"

"Yep, that's right."

Comet's head whipped round to stare at Storm. The more she stared the more dawning realisation spread across her face. It was the same shocked expression as what Sabre had.

'Not now. I'll talk about it later.' She heard Storm muse, clear as a bell. It came as a shock to hear her so clearly when usually she was rebuffed by her bioelectricity.

"Yes. And I don't cry all the time." She frowned at Kathy.

"There's no need to glare. I'm on my best behaviour here, aint I. If it gets me my babies back, then I'll do whatever– except talk to that nob in charge."

Comet nodded in understanding, having heard for herself the various arguments between Rex and Storm, but then began to frown as she noted something that Kathy had mentioned.

"I'm sorry, but did you say *babies*?" She asked, looking the girl up and down with a critical eye.

"Two of 'em." Kathy smiled sadly down at her lap, voice softening. "Boy and girl, but I don't have names for them yet. I was going to call my little boy Teal after his daddy, but Teal was a manipulative bastard now that I think about it."

"How?" Her face scrunched in disbelief. "You're transhuman. That should have meant you'd be sterile."

"I'll never not be amazed how you people know that right off the bat." Kathy sighed loudly and pulled her shaggy wings closer to her back. Though she now took their observation with less offence, it was still mildly aggravating that they had to point it out.

"It's incredibly obvious. Transhumans all lack tail-feathers, meaning you're worse at flying." Said Comet. "No offence."

"Storm doesn't have any though."

Storm winced. "I do but they haven't…grown back." She said cautiously as Comet squinted at her back with the same curiosity as Sabre.

"Where are they now?" Asked Comet with a frown, looking away from the Rogue when she saw her grey feathers bristle at the scrutiny.

"With Professor Mira in France."

Comet blinked, purple eyes wide at the mention of the name and her tense wings dropped for a moment, the gold tips bending against the floor.

"Eve Mira?"

"You know her?"

Comet's jaw clenched and she stared hard at Storm.

"Professor Mira ran our project." Storm shrugged. "That's why she was so interested when you told her about me."

Comet's eyes widened as she began to scream internally at Storm but was met with the static buzz of Storm's electrical field blocking her concerns out.

"But enough about that, I've an idea. How about we go outside." The Rogue said with a coy smile.

19

With the majority of the Rioteer headquarters asleep, it wasn't too difficult to get Kathy and Comet outside and take off with them into the night sky.

Kathy's large heavy wings and Comet's lack of practice made their take-off's somewhat awkward and ungainly, but they managed to remain airborne.

"Just glide. Hold your wings steady and find the warm air." Storm taught them, flying between them both. Their technique was so poor that she was constantly checking and adjusting the angle of their wings with gentle hands so they were flying correctly.

"How do we find warm air?" Comet asked hesitantly, struggling to keep aloft. Her long narrow wings were designed for high energy flight, not for soaring like Kathy could do.

"You'll know when you hit it. It'll be like walking into the sun."

After half an hour of airtime, the two girls had somewhat grasped the main elements of flight though they were still very wobbly. A hundred-thousand lights glittered beneath them as they flew, illuminating the estuary beneath them, mapping out the land in glittering gold rivers. The warm air carried them far down the river, over bridges and past the skyscrapers and wind turbines.

Even as the city gave way to the countryside, there were still rivers of light traveling in every direction, mapping out the landscape and illuminating various landmarks. It was so bright in places that Kathy recognised where she was, though her own recollections began to trouble her.

"Kathy?" Storm noted the growing frown on the girl's face as they drifted over the towering pillars of a suspension bridge.

"I know that place." She pointed downwards to a dark area, only vaguely illuminated by the crescent moon and soft glow of lights from across the river. Not stopping to explain, she fell towards it. Reactively, Storm chased after her, and with a panicked shriek Comet followed out of fear at being left behind in the sky.

Landing with stumbling steps, Kathy disappeared into the darkness as Storm landed behind her. She squinted into the darkness, trying to follow Kathy's movement, muttering a small curse under her breath.

"S-Storm help!" Comet yelped, hesitantly and badly hovering in the air several meters above the ground. "I don't know how to land like this!"

"Get closer and I'll catch you."

"I can't see you!"

"I'm right below you, I can hear you. Just stop fluttering and I'll catch you."

Stopping her wings, Comet dropped like a stone into Storm's arms. Storm caught her round her waist and staggered backwards before setting her on her feet. Even in the low light, Comet's embarrassment was plain to see.

"T-thank you." She breathed.

"Back pedal faster next time. Use your tailfeathers and bend your knees so if you do drop you won't hurt your legs as much."

She nodded and squinted into the darkness to try to pick out Kathy's shape. Though their sight may have been better than a humans, neither could see in the absolute darkness, reliant on the glow from the lights on the other side of the river to give them a silhouette to focus on.

"Where are we?" Comet asked as Storm cautiously, holding tightly onto her arm. She squinted into the darkness, trying to figure out where they were.

"Not sure. A park maybe?"

The two walked tentatively through the dark, stones crunching underfoot until they came upon a slope. At the top a figure moved between barely illuminated strange metal structures. They advanced up the steep slope, and upon cresting it found themselves looking out across the river and stood beside ancient anti-aircraft guns.

Walking between them they found Kathy perched on a one, staring wistfully out across the water.

"Kathy?" Comet asked gently. "Are you alright?"

There was a small pregnant silence between them all with nothing, but the sound of the water lapping against the sea wall and the distant sound of cars to fill the silence.

"I used to come here with my dad and brothers about twice a year. We used to play that we were spitfires and run around with our arms out pretending that we were flying." Kathy answered sadly, letting out a small bittersweet laugh and patting the old artillery. "Y'know, I used to enjoy history and visiting places like this. I think I wanted to be a historian…or something like that."

She jumped down and calmly walked along the bank to the next gun, crouching beside a crank and turning it so that the gun swivelled slowly in its base. Storm cocked her head to one side, watching Kathy's behaviour warily.

"Few Transhumans remember their lives before. Sometimes they remember languages they used to know and obscure facts, but it's rare to remember everything. I'm not sure if you're lucky or unlucky with that."

"Unlucky is the answer. It's like–" She shook her head and scoffed, frowning at Storm. "You've not been human; you wouldn't understand what it's like to know…you weren't…you just…"

"You're right, I wouldn't understand. And I won't pretend to try."

Her acceptance of her statement took Kathy by surprise; she had half expected Storm to try and be sympathetic and make it seem like they had some level of equality. She felt relieved that she didn't understand.

"I had a fight with my dad. It was over something stupid like leaving the door unlocked or something. He told me to leave and I did. There was a youth hostel near where we lived so I stayed there for the night and woke up with some other guys from there, in a white room. We were all in the same cell and being sick," Kathy murmured, "like being so sick that everything in your body burns and aches to the point you want to die."

"Transgenic virus. Made to destroy your human cells and forcibly mutate them." Explained Comet, her soft timid voice filled with sympathy.

"Chiro and Avio transgenics are the worst ones to watch and take care of. They have to break your shoulder blades in half to get the sockets and bones to form. The same with your sternum. The screaming was the worst bit when the anaesthetic wore off."

"You've seen people like me…grow?"

"I trained as a nurse. For a long time, it was my job to help keep people going through transgenesis calm. I hated watching it, but I wanted to help them. I still do."

Kathy looked across at her. Tears welling up in her eyes she gave a little pained laugh. "It's weird that I'm the mutant here and yet you're both freakier than me." Kathy joked, making the girls smile.

Comet climbed onto the artillery, fluttering her wings a little to keep her balance as she looked out across the river then behind them at the rest of the star fort.

"You visited place's like this?" She asked Kathy with genuine curiosity.

"This and a few other forts and castles. This is tilbury fort. It's one of the few star-forts left. I remember getting on trains and visiting big houses with giant gardens and old ruins with trees growing through walls…can't remember all of the names, but I enjoyed it. Bayham Abbey was my favourite."

"Lucky. I've never been to a castle before."

"I suppose I was…I just didn't realise what I had." Her voice wavered. Swallowing down her breath she tried to stop a sob from escaping her but failed. Bursting into tears, she fell to her knees, startling Comet and Storm who dropped down beside her and placed their hands on her shoulders in reassurance.

"I just…I'm so fucking stupid and I fucked everything up!" She wailed, shielding her face with her arm. "Everything I get I ruin! I want to go home! I want to be me again, but I can't! I don't know what I'm supposed to do! I even messed your lives up! I keep making mistakes and I don't know what to do! What do I do?!"

"Kathy, we're all fuck ups in one way or another. You can't change what happened, but you shouldn't blame yourself for it." Storm said with assurance, Comet nodding. She gently soothingly stroked Kathy's shaggy wings.

"We'll get your babies back and get you a home. We've just got to fix it all one step at a time."

"But I led Aura to you and the Rioteers! How can you just say that you'll fix that? I've ruined all their lives if they-"

Storm hugged her tightly, cutting her off. The girl gasped and began to sniffle, burying her head against Storm's feathers as she drew her wings around them.

"I'll fix it somehow. Trust me."

The comment took Kathy by surprise.

"You still want to help me?" She had to ask, looking up at her with a snotty face and bleary eyes.

"Hell yeah."

Shaking her head, the Vulture gave a curt and humourless laugh. "I don't understand you Storm."

"What?"

"Why do you care so much?"

"Is there a reason why I shouldn't care about helping others?"

"Is that your purpose out here? To help others. Why help?"

Storm grimaced a little as she tried to explain herself. Even Comet was looking at her questioningly.

"The Rioteers they have good intentions; it doesn't mean I trust them to do the right thing. Half the time they focus more on the saving part than the caring for you guys after and expect everyone to be alright and fall into line without trouble. Someone has to give a shit and do something; it might as well be me."

"So, none of your groups follow the Rioteers?"

"Only when it suits us." She laughed. "It doesn't matter why. What matters is that I can do something."

Kathy stared at her silently for a little while, then gave a little chuckle.

"So, what can I do to help?"

-x-

The Xanas' villa was far larger than Cherry Tree, but much quieter and far more secluded. The nearest town was two miles away and leaving them surrounded by low hills forested hills and interconnecting lakes that were the home to a myriad of water birds and fish. It was refreshing and peaceful compared to the business of London, and Wilny enjoyed the tranquillity.

The Xana girls passed their days laying in the sun in their walled garden or playing in the crystalline lakes, between lessons taught by Adonis. He was their teacher as much as he was their leader. Even though they had a lot of freedom, Adonis made sure they all kept the villa in order, gardening, washing up and cooking, much as Storm had done for the Rogues or as he imagined it would be like if his team, had been given the opportunity to be free.

Over the three weeks that Wilny stayed with them, he had somewhat overcome his awestricken starry-eyed fascination with Adonis's appearance, enough that he could hold a conversation without being distracted. Sticking by the rules, he spoke to Adonis honestly about many things, exchanging anecdotes with him on how they grew up. He slowly began to talk about his old team. Of Eddie, Fury, Rainbow, and Featherhead. It was hard to talk about them at first without feeling sad, but following what Amell had told him, he did it for them to remember them.

Sitting by the lake as the sun began to set on Wilny's last day, the radio played softly through Adonis's phone as the two talked, occasionally tugging at their fishing lines to see if they had a catch and sipping from their bottles of beer.

"...and then there's just a dead silence as Asena just walks into the room and sees Marlowe, Helios, and Crow, flat on their faces and groaning pain, Anthony balls-out naked and flexing on the table. The girls just all point at him and start blaming him for all of the broken chairs and dishes, trying to hide all of the bottles they were throwing, but Asena says nothing. Instead she just walks over to Anthony, takes a bottle and downs what's left, then sits down puts her arm on the table and challenges Anthony to wrestle her."

Wilny snorted with laughter. "You're shitting me."

"I shit you not sir!"

"Did she win?"

"It's Asena. Of course, she won."

His laughter intensified to the point where he fell onto his side in stitches at the very thought of the scene.

Adonis had been telling him stories of his days in the Rogues. Wilny had assumed that before he had joined, the Rogues consisted of only Kat, Beth and Storm, but the way Adonis told it there had been at least twenty-five Rogues before him and much to Wilny's surprise, Adonis had only left and diverged into his own group several weeks before Kat had arrived.

"W-was it always like that?" Wilny asked between giggles. "Always chaos and crime?"

"Always." Adonis laughed, but the good humour faded from his voice as he nodded solemnly. "But eventually things changed as we got older and we went our separate ways for one reason or another. Storm was the most troublesome though. Stealing, fighting, streaking through the city, occasionally vandalism. It got to the point where if anything went wrong, Rex would just instantly blame her."

"He still does."

Adonis chuckled. "Does she still fly off whenever he drops by to lecture?"

"Occasionally. She never says where she goes though."

"To see Nike and Victoria most likely. She goes and talks to the various uh...Winged Victory statues, or if things are really bad, she goes to Cornwall."

Wilny cocked a scar-spilt eyebrow at him, unsure if Adonis was joking or not.

"She goes and talks to statues?"

"I'm not sure if she still does, but she used to when she was about fourteen, I only found out through Mesi." He tugged a little on his line, reeling it in several notches. The name sounded familiar, another old Rogue Wilny presumed, but from listening to the stories Adonis told he couldn't quite remember if he had mentioned Mesi before. Curious, he gave Adonis a nudge with his elbow in order to get him to continue.

"Mesi was an Avio and her girlfriend for a long time." Adonis explained with a sigh, rolling his eyes and taking a huge swig of beer. "Very gorgeous, but very vain. She always liked to act like her talents were rare and special."

"And were they?"

"No. She was just a basic muser. You can probably do more than her, but she thought she was something divine. But *fuck*, they were a nightmare together."

"I've never heard Storm mention her." Wilny shrugged, sipping at his beer.

Adonis sighed deeply again, running his clawed fingers through his grey hair.

"It was a very bad breakup. It was partly because Rex wanted an operative out in North Africa and Mesi offered to take the role as far as I know and because she was also cheating on her with Rai. It ended in a blackout across London, one broken wind turbine and at least three hundred smashed windows."

He gave Wilny a moment to think about the image, watching him frown as he tried to recall if Storm had ever told him the story or even mentioned her before.

"I'm not surprised that she hasn't told you about it." Adonis cut through his thoughts, reeling in a small fish on his line. "She either purposefully forgets what happened, or she does the '*So I fucked up, I'll deal with it*' and carries on."

"There you go mind reading again." He chuckled brushing his own hair to one side and feeling about for the small pinfeathers growing back from where he had plucked them in stress.

Adonis shrugged. "It's probably you, you know."

"Me?"

"You're a muser. You're probably projecting thoughts towards me."

"Yes, but I never learnt how to do the telepathy stuff. I don't think I could really do that, and the idea of getting into someone's head is just…urgh, I don't like it." He shuddered so hard that his tailfeathers rattled.

"Well, the telepathy stuff is pretty basic, and it's not like you'd be seeing every detail of their thoughts, just loud conscious ones."

"Fury used to say that to me, but I could never do it."

Adonis shot him a cautious look at Wilny with the mention of Fury.

"There's nothing to stop you learning. You'd have to talk to Crow about it though, I've got no idea how it works."

The radio crackled with static, the soft music being interrupted by a newscaster's voice speaking far too fast for Wilny to pick out the words. Adonis, however, understood perfectly and gave a small cheer and raised his beer bottle to the sky.

"*Buena suerte y cuidae!*" He shouted to the stars, swigging the beer and laying back with a laugh. Staring in confusion between him and the stars, Wilny prodded Adonis in the side for an answer.

"What are they saying?"

"The seventh colony fleet to Mars has just had lift-off from Toledo and the sixth has landed without trouble."

"There are people on Mars?" He stared up at the sky, hoping to catch a glimpse of the rocket leaving the atmosphere.

"The first crew have been there for about eight years now." Adonis nodded. "A lot of them are actually Preternaturals. Core and Delta had almost all the shares in the project and thought that it'd be good to send them out there."

"Wait...you mean Project Astra?"

"Oh, you've heard of it?"

Wilny's wings gave a little flutter as Adonis gave him an impressed smile. He still wasn't used to such sincerity or kindness from such an attractive individual and found himself repeatedly having to stop himself from staring at him.

"Rainbow talked about it; she loved the stars." He started to smile too, breaking into a small laugh. "But she always made it sound like they were going to the Andromeda galaxy. That and that Preters and other Synths would take care of the humans during the journey so that there'd be whole generations of humans used to them. Man, she used to get Eddie so worked up about it, he wouldn't sleep for days because he'd be training so hard to get on that project."

He looked from the stars back to the Hummingbird. "How are you holding up?"

"Hm?"

"You're talking easier about them now."

"I...I am aren't I." He paused and contemplated himself. "I never wanted to talk to Storm about them...I think because it felt like she wanted me to forget them —or at least that's what I thought."

"But you're assuming that's what she wants from you. Has she ever told you to forget about them?"

Tears began to roll down his cheeks before he even realised. Embarrassed at the sudden tears, he scrubbed his face hard, hoping that they would go unnoticed. Adonis sat up quickly, reaching out a hand to comfort him with, but was blocked by Wilny's wing being drawn up to shield himself.

"I've got it now." He hung his head, laughing at himself. "I don't want people to feel sorry for me. I don't want to feel cold and dark all the time, it hurts to feel like this every day." He choked, doing his best to stop his voice from wavering.

"I don't want to forget them or pretend I'm not sad they're not here even if sometimes that's what I want to do."

"It's alright to feel that way. It hurts, but you shouldn't pretend that it's nothing. Doing that..." Adonis trailed off, giving a little twitch of his long tail.

Wilny looked up at him, drying his eyes as best he could, realisation dawning upon him as he watched the Reptile tense in frustration.

"She's lost people. Hasn't she. That's why she wants to help."

"That's Storm's pain. Not yours." He said firmly. He looked at him, flat yellow eyes hard with soft anger.

"She deals with it in her own way and tries her best to help others with their own problems -sometimes to her own destruction in my opinion, but for you, it's down to what you think and feel is going to be the most valuable way for you to help yourself. You are not Storm. You shouldn't think you have to dedicate yourself to something such as huge as revenge or healing others to get better or distract yourself from the pain. You shouldn't destroy yourself to fix something beyond your control. Helping others does not always help you heal yourself; it only radicalises you into thinking that you are the only one who can solve others pain because you won't let your own pain heal."

Wilny nodded slowly, startled. Adonis had managed his anger well, but he didn't know if he was talking about Storm or Rex, or both.

The Reptile relaxed, breathing slowly and sipping his beer.

"But enough of how I feel. What do you feel you need?"

"I…I know I need to carry on and do something to make my team -my family-proud or do something they never got a chance to do. I know I need to change, not just for myself, but for my family."

"And how do you feel you will be able to do that?"

"I…"

The tears stopped flowing and a weight lifted from is shoulders. A spark ignited in him, the same he had felt when Storm had ordered him to protect Malana. The same that had driven him to defend Raoul and help him fit in with the Rogues. They were his family now and they needed him, and he needed them.

He took a deep breath and looked to the stars starting to come into view, then slowly exhaled.

"You can do it. It won't be as easy, but you'll get there." Adonis smiled softly at the young man, bumping his shoulder with a gentle fist. "I know you can. Just remember to take it one day at a time. It's a marathon not a sprint."

"Thank you." Said Wilny quietly, swallowing down the lump in his throat as the milky way began to glitter into view. "I appreciate everything you've done for me, but I should really get back."

"Back?"

Smiling softly, Wilny rose to his feet, brushing the dust from his wings and looking towards the rainbow hued sky of the setting sun.

"Home."

20

Montpellier, France.

Adonis had agreed to take Wilny to the French border on the mountains, but after there and as per what Wilny requested, he was on his own. He had insisted on making his own way back to England, wanting to see the landscape first-hand as well as have some time to himself to think and remember.

Given a spare phone with a GPS set to take him back to Cherry Tree along with a light rucksack with some money for food and shelter, he had all he needed to travel.

The GPS had instructed him to fly north east towards a city called Montpellier, Adonis had insisted that finding main towns would make it easier to navigate his way back and use the thermals from the roadways to head north or provide him with the alternative of the aeroplanes or trains if he got tired.

Not built to be a distance flyer with his narrow and high-energy wings, he kept at a steady cruising speed that utilised the air-currents and thermals to save energy and timed himself to fly for only two hours at a time with half an hour rests in between. He questioned how tiny birds managed such long-haul migrations without stopping for food. There was no rush to the flight, but he knew that Adonis had told Storm to be expecting him and he didn't want to disappoint her by not returning home at all.

The thermals carried him much further than he thought they would, although his wings began to ache to the point of collapse by the time he reached the outskirts of the city. With a clumsy landing on top of the roof of an ancient church that sat isolated on a spit between a small lagoon by the city and the rest of the sea.

Breathing heavily from his flight, he laid down in the midday sun with a smile, wings fanned out behind him and admired the glittering turquoise sea, taking his third rest of the day. In a moment of restful peace, he surveyed his surroundings lazily. The warm sea-salt air, the soft breaking of waves on a white sandy shoreline, and distant hum of the city provided a calming atmosphere. An array of wind turbines spiralled lazily out at sea as ships of all shapes and sizes travelled about the Mediterranean, their images rippling under the heat of the early-July sun. Whilst the gulls soared high above him, a crow flew up onto the cross beside him with a flutter, and with beady black eyes, watched him intently. He noticed it out the corner of his eye but kept watching the sea. After a while with the crow not moving, he rolled his head to look at it.

"Bonjour?" He said with a smirk to it, letting his wings flutter and expecting it to be startled and fly off.

It hopped forward, cocking its head from side to side before opening its beak.

"*Hello hot lips.*" It said with a croaking voice.

"*Holy shit.*" Wilny leapt to his feet pointing at the crow, "*You.* I know you."

The bird cawed in such a way that it sounded as though it were laughing.

He knew it was one of Crow's crows, one of the ones that ARCDA had altered many generations ago, and which had been hand raised by Crow himself. Blackheath however, named after the area it was meant to live in, was one of the most intelligent of his birds, enough so that he could mimic a human voice and of course Crow had taught it to recognise and name people. And the name that he had given in association to Wilny was Hot lips.

He "Go away! Go away Blackheath!" He ordered it, flourishing his hands at the bird. "You're not supposed to be here!"

The crow cawed at him, hopping down and following him across the tiles as he backed away with watchful intelligence.

He turned away for several seconds, then turned back to shout at it when he heard the fluttering getting closer. Several more crows had arrived. Frowning he backed further away along the rooftop before he stopped before he realised how silly he was to be afraid of a bird. Shaking his head, he began to laugh at himself and sat back down, pulling his long feathers onto his lap to brush of the dirt that would have gathered on them from flying.

Ignoring the crows, he preened his feathers, running his nail across the barbs and scratching off a surface of grime with a disgusted look. Brushing the dirt off his fingers he snuck a look back at the crows.

"What the fuck?" He gaped in fright at how many more crows had gathered. Near enough the entire rooftop end had been covered with crows, all watching him silently.

He scrambled to his feet again and the crows flurried towards him. Their rush startled him, driving Wilny to charge off the rooftop and with the birds giving chase.

Beating his tired wings hard as he could manage, he took off towards the mainland, hoping that he could run beneath the cover of trees or throw them off with the buildings. His muscles screamed as he twisted and drew himself into a downward spiral, a semi-practical manoeuvre he had seen Storm perform, but proved to be far more difficult and spraining in practice. Dizzy, he twisted out the way of an oncoming block of flats and arcing sharply back around it. The muscles in his back strained in pain, unaccustomed to such acrobatics.

However, he had no chance of out flying the crows.

They darted at him, mobbing him and diving through his feathers to break their barbs apart, forcing him to land with an ungainly stumble into an overshadowed side street.

Wilny sprinted through the streets, he ignored the fact that his wings were still out in the open, more preoccupied with the birds, rushing across roads and only narrowly avoiding cars.

Disorientated, he couldn't tell which way he was going, but they drove him towards derelict grass covered lot, where an old warehouse stood stoic in the centre. Wilny sprinted towards it, hoping that there might be some cover he could take within only to find the building a gutted wreck. The crows only rushed in after him and began to spiral into a black whirlwind around him, cawing incessantly.

Panicked and unable to see a way through, he dropped to his knees and drew his wings over his head, cursing himself for running from some birds. Then with a beat of panic to their cawing, the crows scattered in a flurry of black, filtering out through the skeletal roof and leaving a dusting of feathers on the ground around him.

Pulling his wings away from his face, he peeked out at to see a young woman, dark skinned with pointed blacked furred ears aside her head, and a twitching black tail behind her, a Pard striding purposefully towards him.

"Please don't hurt me! You're with the Rioteers right? Right?" He tested, rising off the ground with his hands up. "You know Storm, right? I'm part of her group."

The woman cocked her head at him saying something in French too fast for him to catch, black ears flicking back as a van drove through one of the open walls towards them. Two Preternaturals swung out the back of the van alongside an Anubis-headed Canid with his claws and fangs bared.

Panic hit Wilny quick, and with a mental pulse he attempted to temporarily blind the four as he made a dash to escape. In his haste to dive through the wall, he forgot that on the ground both Pards and Canids were far faster than he was, even with a delay driven by blindness, and he was roughly tackled to the ground by the Canid.

He elbowed the Canid in the muzzle causing him to yelp, before twisting and pulling his knees up to his chest and kicking him off. Wilny rolled to the side, trying to scramble to his feet, but wasn't fast enough to react as the two Preters grabbed him, grappling with him on the ground and trying to force his arms behind his back.

Forcing himself to focus he tried to bring his minds-eye up, attempting to use his talents against them, wanting to stun them for a second and give himself time to get away. A blinding pain shot through his skull as his musing was rebuffed. One of the Preters was also a muser and they were blocking him.

Blinded by the pain, he swore between rasping breaths. Beating his wings as hard as he could he knocked the two Preters backwards, pushing himself up off the ground to sprint away.

The Pard was faster.

She leapt back onto her haunches to avoid his beating wings, then sprung at him before he could get away, grabbing him by the waist and tackling him back to the ground. Head slamming face first against broken concrete and winded by the girl, he lay stunned. All his panic faded, leaving him somewhat serene and dazed on the floor. Quickly his vision became tunnelled and he felt the muser smother his consciousness. There was no way to fight against it. The two Preters spoke to each other, though their voices felt distant, muffled and interrupted by the sound of his own slowing heartbeat in his ears.

They lifted him off the ground and carried him towards the van. A slow thought crossed Wilny's mind about not wanting to go but it faded quickly. Blurry shapes and colours blended together into one mass of shifting beiges and greys and, all sounds were nothing more than tonal drones that swallowed him in darkness.

-x-

Laying blearily on his side, his head hit the floor of the van every time they drove over a bump in the road. The hits brought him back to consciousness quickly, though it did nothing for his pounding headache.

He was glad to be alive and aware, even if he was in the process of being kidnapped. Frowning to himself he quietly thought about what had happened with, one of Crow's own birds being there, then the sudden kidnapping from a Pard. Whilst he wasn't sure they were on the same side, he strongly suspected that Adonis had something to do with it. Or Crow. Or both. They were both former Rogues and if Beth's criminal behaviour was anything to go by, kidnapping wasn't a far cry from something she would plan.

They had blindfolded him, and when he gently tested his ankles and wrist found them to be cuffed twice, hand to ankle. His wings ached, bound with elasticated chords so that whenever he tried to stretch one out, they would snap painfully back against his back again.

Aware that one of the Preternaturals was also a muser he tentatively pushed his mental field out around him to detect if he was alone in the back of the van or not. The gentle buzz of a mind at rest told him he wasn't alone though the person was sleeping.

The other three must have been in the front, though he could hear no music or muffled talking coming from them, though if one of them was the muser then they wouldn't need to. It also meant that there'd be little to keep him entertained during his kidnapping which greatly annoyed him.

After several hours of tediously long and uneventful driving, Wilny drifting in and out of sleep when the road was kind, he felt the van rumble to a stop and the engine cut out. He listened carefully to hear the crunch of feet on gravel approaching, then the van door opening and the exchange of greetings before they moved towards the back of the van.

The Preter in the back with him sighed with relief and opened the doors to them, speaking in French though slow enough that Wilny could pick out the words *'badass'* and *'piss'.* He was grateful that Raoul had eventually gotten to give him some translations for vulgarities even if the boy did squirm in embarrassment and disgust at speaking them.

"You have him then? Was he much trouble?" The voice of a young man, Australian? He didn't sound familiar.

"No trouble. But I was disappointed. I thought he'd be tougher." A girl speaking in a very heavy French accent, he assumed it was the Pard.

"He's had a few weeks leave, give him a break." A second man laughed with a deep and grating cackle.

Wilny knew that laugh.

"Well, here's the two-grand we owe ya."

"Keep half, he's only worth one."

"Inks, *please.* You'll hurt his feelings."

"Crow?" Wilny said cautiously, shifting about on the floor of the van, trying to face the voices. "Crow is that you, you fucking asshole?"

There was a pause between them, followed by the sound of rustling feathers. He was sat up, with the cuffs from his ankles and the blindfold removed. Barely half an inch away from his nose, Crow was leant before him with a cocky smile across his feathered face.

"Hey there Willners." Crow laughed, petting Wilny's head and ruffling his hair up.

"You. Mother. Fucker!" Wilny lunged forward head-butting him hard in the nose, nearly tumbling headfirst out of the van. *"You could have killed me!"*

Crow reeled back holding his nose and cackling in pain as the rest looked on in shock. "Calm ya' tits, we know what we're doing, we're professionals."

Angrily, Wilny swung his legs out from under him, snap-kicking Crow in the gut and tumbling out into the daylight with a squawk of rage.

The sun burnt his eyes, low in the sky, but bright and hot already, he had no clue as to where he was, though he was sure he certainly wasn't back in England. A figure stepped into the sunlight, shading him, although the sun still shone through the pale membrane of his wings showing off all the veins in dark red. The Chiro broke into a smile and his huge rabbit-like ears twitched back and forth.

"You'll want to uncuff him now." He said smoothly looking down at Wilny with solid black eyes, spinning a set of keys round on his finger, "He's going to ruin his pretty face at this rate."

"And we don't want that do we." Crow gave Free a smirk and snatched the keys from him. He knelt beside Wilny with a rustle of feathers.

Wilny glanced around. To one side stood the three who had kidnapped him, smirking and laughing to each other at him. On the other side stood two motorhomes with their canopies out and figures moving about inside, presumable Bubbles and Jett. They looked to be camping in a scrubby woodland off the edge of a small country road caught between dusty rolling hills of vineyards and olive groves. The Monkey, Saffron and the Dagger's own Canid, Prince, lounged in hammocks strung up beneath the trees, seeming uninterested in Wilny's arrival.

"Where am I?" He asked aloud, rubbing his wrists the moment they were loose, flexing his wings too when the straps were removed and thrown into the back of the van. He stretched, furious at the irritating itching of his feathers that they had caused.

"Lombardy, Italy. Not too far from Milan actually," Free answered him with a chirp, tossing him a bottle of water which he drank thirstily. "Though I think we just missed the fashion week. Shame."

Wilny didn't realise how dry his throat was until the water hit, cool and refreshing.

"So, is there a reason I was bagged, gagged and thrown into a van? And chased by your birds?" He asked Crow angrily after taking a gulp of air. In the tree above, the crows cackled in an oddly sentient way at him, flapping down to land upon a stump beside Crow beginning to make begging noises for food.

"Well, we didn't know your exact mental state. As much as I trust Ada, he's not always good at reading people." Crow shrugged, crouching to feed the birds dried fruit and nuts that he kept on his persons for them. "And Inks wanted to see what you were made of."

Wilny scowled. The Old Rogues were all in cahoots with each other, just as he had suspected.

"Don't worry, I'm better now. Not cured, but better." He assured Crow, rising to his feet and dusting himself down.

"Good."

Crow gave his shoulder a playful slap, then dropped his shoulder and rammed him. Knocked back and winded, Crow grabbed him by his throat and lifted him clean off his feet, pinning him against the door of the van and fanning his wings out into a shield around them both. The little finger-like digits on the wing wrists flexed, gripping the roof of the van, the claws scraping noisily against the metal. Neither the Pard, Preters, or Free made a move to help him and instead stood back to watch.

"If ya' ever hurt my sister again then I'll be killing you before she does. The same goes for if ya' hurt anyone else, Rogue, Dagger or Rioteer. *I will rip your head off.*" Crow snarled, his voice low and menacing. His already dark eyes were black and every feather across his scalp and shoulders was raised in fury. He'd never seen Crow so angry.

Wilny choked, unable to speak or breathe from the grip Crow had on his throat.

'I didn't hurt her!' He thought as loud as he could, feeling a crushing pain strike his mind. *'I'm not going to hurt anyone!'*

"No, but you made her give up and I've never known her to give up or refuse to help anyone, not even Rex."

'I'm sorry. I'm going to try to do better I swear, I don't want to lose anyone else.'

"I don't want you to try, I want you to *do*."

"Crow, let him down." A voice chimed and immediately he was dropped. Bubbles strode across to them, her usually flowing pink mane, braided back. Reaching them, she yanked hard on Crow's tailfeathers, scolding him telepathically. The anger that was in Crow's eyes vanished and he crouched a little, shrinking down before the tiny Gecko.

"I wasn't gonna kill him. I was only reminding him not to be a dick." He muttered in a low voice, pawing at her arm. She continued to scowl at him, watching silently as his hair-feathers fluffed up.

Thinking himself safe with Bubbles now present, he turned to his kidnappers only to be immediately slapped across the face by the Pard. He reeled back in shock, rubbing his face and staring wide eyed at her.

"Nara Inxter. Matagot." She said coldly, introducing herself.

"Ex-Rogue?" He asked, though he knew he didn't need to.

"Of course."

"Njce swing you've got there."

He was beginning to see a pattern with the Rogues and understand that no matter how far apart and how far across the world they were, they were a family, and no one fucked with their family. He just hoped that he was still one of them.

"We can take him from here Nara." Bubbles assured the black cat. The lack of emotion in Bubbles veined blue eyes and the mouthful of needle teeth seemed to unnerve her and force her to step back. Pointed ears flicking back she swiped again across Wilny's other cheek, allowing her claws to graze the skin.

"Pass that on to Rex when you see him." She spat, spinning on her heels and signalling for the two Preternaturals to get into the van. Giving Wilny one last critiquing look, she huffed an arrogant, "*Au revoir,*" before getting into the van herself.

"Ah, Inks, you are one of the nicest ladies I know." Crow sighed as the Matagot group drove away.

Wilny shot him an incredulous look, still not quite able to grasp what had just occurred. Shaking his head so that the feathers settled, Crow pulled Wilny over to the second motorhome by his shoulder and rapped his knuckles hard on the door.

"Once a Rogue, always a Rogue. We're the best at what we do." He chuckled. "Which is why we brought you one to work with."

There were some low irritable mumblings before the door swung open and out stumbled Raoul.

His cream-grey hair and fur was sun-streaked tousled mess and his freckles starkly dark against sun bronzed skin, he'd clearly been out with the Daggers for several days. His green eyes lit up and a smile spread across his face the moment he saw Wilny and overjoyed to see a friendly face, Wilny threw his arms and wings around Raoul, laughing and lifting the smaller Hound off his feet and spinning him around.

Reluctantly, as Raoul started to cough and choke mid-laughter, Wilny let him go, though he couldn't stop himself from ruffling Raoul's. Laughing lightly at the two, Crow swept past them, ducking into the motorhome with Bubbles, leaving them to talk.

"I go away for three weeks and you've already grown an inch." He laughed, patting his shoulders and measuring the shortening height difference.

"I got forced into '*working out*' with Amell." The Hound laughed, rolling his eyes. "He made me run with Kat and him. They tricked me into running in a marathon."

Wilny's joyful smile quickly faded and he slumped as he remembered how he had behaved before they had parted.

"I'm so sorry for what happened, I didn't mean to–"

Raoul caught his hand and squeezed gently in reassurance.

"You were having problems, I understand. You don't have to tell me about it if you don't want to."

A light wave of relief washed across Wilny's chest, making it easier to breathe. He was grateful for Raoul's gentle empathy and respect for his privacy.

"How is everyone? Did I miss anything fun?" He asked, resettling his wings as they sat down on the two stumps that were being used as stools and taking another swig of water again.

"Well, other than me accidentally running a marathon," Raoul clicked his tongue. "We got a motorbike which I'm still learning to ride, though Beth is the one who owns it. Kat wanted to try dying her hair and it went bright blue. I puppy-sat Asena's son Caesar for an evening which was fun, he chewed through the sofa. Beth is still the same though now she just screams and throws stuff at Amell because he doesn't wear – or can't wear– shirts."

Wilny smiled with pride at the Canid at how much his vocabulary had grown. His French accent was still strong, but there was a noticeable difference on his pronunciation and speech with it, now being faster and more fluid.

"They could never get Zeus to wear a shirt, I doubt that little Bionic bird is gonna do it." Free chirped, ducking beneath the canopy with them and lathering his pale skin with sun cream, as well as applying some to the pale membrane of his wings.

"I forgot you two know each other." Noted Raoul.

The Chiro chuckled, sweeping back his dark auburn hair back.

"I'd say we know each other *intimately*, but alas I am one jockey that stallion would never let ride him. Such a shame since it would have been so much fun to use a whip on him."

Raoul stared blankly at him.

"I am so grateful that I know what you were implying."

"Well, I could show you-" Free purred, only to be quickly cut off by a sharp wingbeat to his gut from Wilny.

"You touch my son and I will end you." He snarled to the Chiro.

Laughing, Free threw his hands up and backed away, strolling back out into the sun and leaving the two Rogues to themselves.

"Malana misses you a lot, she asked me to give you this." Raoul said softly, pulling a folded piece of paper from his pocket and passing it to Wilny. On it was a stick figure drawing of them both drawn in colourful marker pens and a '*GET BETTER SOON*' scrawled in black along the top of the page. Tears sprung to his eyes and he held the page close to his chest.

"Does she…" He could barely speak, throat choked with emotion.

"Storm told us all about it."

Casting his eyes down to the ground he felt a knot of trepidation in his gut; what had Storm told them, he wanted to ask. The truth? Had she told them he was a dangerous psychopath? He wanted to know what they now thought of him and if they still trusted him, but more importantly, did Storm trust him at all. He felt sick and dizzy. The world suddenly shifted beneath him and he fell forward, almost hitting the ground nose first though fortunately caught by Raoul.

"Get him some more water Crow, he's dehydrated." Bubbles ordered sharply, racing out of the motorhome to Wilny's side and helping to prop him up. "And starving."

Crow didn't waste time, shouting for Prince and Jett to find some honey or fruit, whilst he brought a bottle of water for Wilny. They crowded him as he ate, watching in anticipation as he ate and drank until he gave them a thumbs up of being alright again.

Then with a twitching of their ears, Prince and Jett darted out of sight with frantic hushed whispers, whilst Free's head snapped round to face the road.

"She's here." He muttered, clapping his hands and fluttering up onto the roof of the motorhome. A deep rumble of an engine drew near, rounding the corner with a plume of dust a lone rider on a flame-streaked motorbike pulled into their little motorhome park.

"You're late!" Free shouted at the rider. "What took so long, I've been out here for a day already."

The rider flicked up their middle finger to Free and removed their helmet, shaking out her mess of black hair. Wilny gawped in shock as Roux strode across the gravel to them.

"What is she doing here?"

"Roux is going to be our cover." Bubbles said calmly, squeezing his shoulder before he tried to make a run for it, away from Roux.

Giving his shoulder a little tug, she guided Wilny into the closest motorhome. Sitting him down on one of the chairs at the narrow table, she handed him a damp flannel to clean the dust and sweat from his face. Raoul joined him at his side giving a little nod to Jett who was aggressively trying to button a white dress shirt, cursing every time he realised, he had buttoned the wrong hole.

"Okay so why are they with us?" Wilny questioned, cautiously pressing up against Raoul's shoulder in an attempt to get further away from Roux as he could manage in such a small space, his wings awkwardly angled from the lack of room. She glowered at him and feeling slightly intimidated he grabbed a pillow from behind him and clutched it to his chest.

"We can't go into the bunker like this."

"What? We're doing a mission?"

Bubbles nodded, pulling out of a suitcase that was jammed under a table a gold dress wrapped in a plastic cover and handed it to Roux.

"We're going into a Risio Gala." Roux said calmly, one eye on Wilny as she removed her motorbike leathers and boots, she was wearing before sitting down before Bubbles for her hair and makeup to be done.

"We're going to see what they're up to right now and get as many leads and blackmails out of everyone attending as possible."

"It's bullshit we have to dress up though." Jett complained, worrying the fur around the opening to his trousers where his tail was. "The pants are riding up something fierce."

"If we're trying to fit in what's with…"

"Free? He's originally from Risio so he'll be able to tell us who to look out for and which to bug. And Roux is human looking enough that she can get us in, and we can be passed off as her, err…*pets*."

Jett laughed aloud, flumping down into the chair opposite Raoul and drumming his fingers on the tabletop.

"Ah yes, glittering diamond skin and smelling like a bonfire. Very human."

"That won't matter much, it's more about being an almost identical clone of a doctor so we get free passes." Bubbles rolled her eyes at him, pulling out a set of hairbrushes and curlers to attack Roux's tangled hair with. All of the boys looked in surprise at Roux.

Jett cleared his throat awkwardly. "You're really a doctor's clone?" He asked her nervously.

"Yes. More or less."

"Then how come you're all magical and shit if you're a human clone?"

"There's no such thing as a pure-human clone, *tu pinche cabrón*." Roux sneered at Jett's use of the word *magical*, rolling her eyes at her reflection in the mirror whilst Bubbles sighed behind her. "They're Preternaturals that have been based upon an individual's genetics. It's the closest that Atlas can get to human clones without all the issues of aging and death."

"What? Really?"

"They've always had problems making proper clones, they have done for nearly a century. The telomeres shortening through aging, the general human genome being too small and full of too many epigenetic changes and mutations which causes so many issues when an attempting to copy and replicate it. And then you have the ethical issues of 'is it right to clone a human' come up-"

She huffed and shook her head.

"Just stupid."

"You could have spoken Spanish, and it would have made as much sense as you just did to me right then."

"It's very simple you-"

"No no! Please, I'm not going to get it so stop right there!" Jett held his hands to his large ears, shaking his head and refusing to listen to the explanation. He knew he wasn't going to understand, and he didn't want to have to be humiliated by her explaining it to him like a child.

Glancing at Raoul, Wilny was prepared to whisper an explanation if the Hound didn't understand, but Raoul just smiled and gave a gentle hand signal to Wilny that he understood. Wilny was surprised, Raoul certainly seemed to have a different aura to him. Calmer, more confident though there was a slight gleam of cockiness to it. A little like Beth. It worried him a little that his adoptive son might have spent a little too much time around the Owl if he was beginning to pick up her mannerisms.

"And why would they pay attention to you?" Raoul asked gently, head tilted to one side as he watched the makeup blossom across her eyelids with dark bronze shadows.

"Who even is your mother?"

"Amelia Samodiva."

"*Merde.*" Raoul swore, wide eyed and the colour draining from his skin. Wilny drew breath, as the name sunk in and he fell back against the narrow chair as Raoul continued to swear.

"*Putain de merde!* Your mother is head of Atlas?"

Roux nodded firmly, only increasing the terror on the boy's faces.

They had heard all kinds of horror stories and fairy tales about the head of Atlas throughout their lives. Some said that she self-experimented so much she'd become an abomination who only had to know your name to kill you whenever she chose, and would start a war on a whim. Others said that she was a self-made goddess who had saved hundreds of thousands of people from both epidemic and pandemics with her medical research and funded the education of college students who had gone on to help the world with their inventions and creations.

The truth was often overwhelmed by fiction, and they were more inclined to believe the stories of Samodiva eating the still beating hearts of men than the ones of her hand in helping to eradicate the spread of disease driven by El Niño cycles and other natural disasters.

The door to the motorhome swung open and Free pulled himself through the frame awkwardly. Even with his pale wings folded as tightly against his back as he could manage, he struggled to stop himself from bumping against the walls and cupboards.

"Are you playing nicely Roux?" He said with a sharp grin, giving a wink towards the boys still staring in fear at Roux. She smirked across at Free, mockingly kissing the back of her hand to remove the excess lipstick, before wiping it away on her shirt.

"Always."

"Is the dress the right style for her?" Bubbles asked as Free inspected the clothing.

"Yes, most of the people working in Risio don't know Samodiva personally so some might notice a few missing details like claw-rings, gold tattoos and hair style."

"Aw crap. I knew we forgot something. Are you sure people won't notice her missing rings?"

"If they comment I'll think of something for you to tell them."

"How did you even end up with the Rioteers?" Wilny blathered, cutting through the conversation. "You should be living like a princess on a private island with a full Ruby team as your body guards."

Roux shrugged, not wanting to explain herself to him. But Crow wasn't as private. While Wilny absorbed his shared information with little more than a shocked blink, a rush of images, smells and emotions washed over Raoul, doubling him over in pain as the shock crushed his chest.

Men in black masks at the window. Breaking glass. Tear gas filling the bedroom. The terror and pain as it burned at his eyes, screaming for help until his throat was raw as the men dragged him from his home. They shouted in English at each other, words he didn't understand. Then pure burning hatred, so hot that his hands set aflame and seared his captor before a sharp pain at the back of his head sent black across his vision.

Pain throbbed behind Raoul's eyes, blinding him and he clutched his chest where his heart felt as though it were about to burst it was throbbing so fiercely. He fell against Wilny's shoulder dizzy and wheezing at the intensity of the rage; He had never felt this angry before. He couldn't breathe. He knew that they couldn't be his memories, but it just felt like they were, like he was there.

"Raoul!" Wilny yelped, supporting the boy as he struggled for breath. "Crow stop!"

"Oops. Sorry kid," Crow shrugged, and the crushing pain stopped. "I forgot you're very emotionally sensitive."

Wilny gathered Raoul up into his arms and fussed over his head, worrying in muttering words about Crow messing with his mind and hoping that he hadn't done any damage to him.

"What happened?" Voice slurred and vision blurry, Raoul's head lolled from side to side, feeling too heavy to lift, "I was burning…"

"He fucked up is what. Crow, get your musing in line and stop being rude." Roux's voice from across the room; She hadn't risen to help him.

A confused thought of broken Spanish tumbled through his mind as Raoul tried to process the memories and assure himself that they didn't belong to him. He hated the sensation so much.

"Oh…oh they –Rex, kidnapped you?" Raoul softly questioned, hand still clutching his chest. The throbbing subsided slowly, but the overwhelming hatred and disgust lingered. "I'm…I'm sorry."

Roux rolled her shoulders, her hair tamed into long silky black waves by Bubbles. "I don't need your pity," Roux sneered in disgust, her voice venomous with rage, but he didn't flinch. Her fury was understandable to him now.

He leant limply against Wilny's shoulder, questioning to himself if all the older Synths and Old Rogues felt such intense loathing for Rex. From the way they all acted around him, there was more to their hate than just being angered by his behaviour. The memories from Roux only proved it right.

'*We play a slow game against Rex.*' Raoul heard Crow muse, the sentiment of apology colouring his thoughts. '*We know what he is, what he does, but we know the risk of being direct with him.*'

'*Then why do you stay?*'

'*To do better than him. To help those that fall by the wayside because of him.*'

They were quickly shooed out of the motorhome by Bubbles to give Roux the privacy to change.

Head still reeling Raoul laid down on the ground under the shade of the canopy with Wilny while Bubbles openly scolded Crow for invading Roux's privacy and inflicting her memories upon Raoul. Crow's feathers flattened back, and he turned to Bubbles with the look of a sad puppy, pouting and trying to gain sympathy from her. With a scoff, she put her hands to her hips.

"Don't give me that," she tutted, "now get your act together, we have to be ready soon. Wilny and Raoul have to get dressed into their suits then I have to do their make up too."

Wilny's laugh cut off as he stared up at Bubbles, suddenly feeling nervous again as he noticed the glint of mischief in her eyes.

"Suit?"

21

Lake Iseo, Lombardy, Northern Italy

"I don't like the suit."

"Quiet."

"And this eyeliner is too thick, it's sticking my eyelids together."

"Blame Bubbles, she put it on ya'."

Seven of them were piled into the back of a hired limousine, slowly making its way round the winding bends of the Italian roads, weaving its way through the mountains. The journey seemed to take an eternity for Crow as everyone had a complaint and as the boss, he was the one who had to take them with the growing aggravation of a father on a long road trip.

The boys were complaining about their earpieces being squeaky and popping. The girls were complaining about their clothes, and back at the motorhome monitoring the situation were Free and Bubbles, who were also in on the complaining about the expenses and how much time they had before they would be caught.

"Roux stop fidgeting." Crow sighed wearily.

"Ugh! *Cojeme*; This dress is making me feel like I've got someone's hands on my tits." She snapped, tugging at the bodice of the dress. "Who in their right mind even wears this shit, I can't breathe."

"Your mother apparently. It's part of her fall collection for parties involving the ritual sacrifice of virgins."

"I said in their right mind, Prince, not in their semi-megalomaniacal mind."

"You need to wear the dress Roux, punk isn't in fashion right now." Crow sighed in exasperation, his glossy black feathers quivering from where he was straining himself trying not to fidget and lay on the floor with the pain shooting up his lower back.

Living with tailfeathers had its benefits when flying, but at all other times were an irritating inconvenience when it came to clothing and chairs, and even sitting on the edge of the seat meant that he would have to bend the feathers to one side and in doing so pulling at the little nerve-ends of them. Wilny however, didn't have this trouble since he had the benefit of having only four feathers, two which were too small to be a bother, and two which were flexible enough to adjust as he wished.

"She's got a body like a battle-axe, Crow." Saffron cut in, idly twiddling at the hem of her dress and pulling at the gloves she had to wear to hide her gnarled monkey hands, irritated by her palms sweating in the heat, "Battle-axes don't need dresses."

"Saffron!"

"That's Bubble's words not mine!"

"*Bubbles!*"

There was a peal of laughter through the headsets from Bubbles and Free, echoed by Prince and Jett who had both obviously thought too loud about something which earnt them both a clip round the back of the head from Crow.

The tunnel ended with an abrupt burst of sunlight and all turned to gaze out of the windows at their approaching destination, winding down an avenue lined with towering Cyprus trees and silver leafed eucalyptus. There was a break in the trees allowing them to see the villa for the first time.

"Wow…" Wilny breathed. "Just…*wow*…"

The villa was perched right on the edge of Lake Iseo, whitewashed walls with archways to support extended balconies and verandas, and terracotta orange roof to match the region's aesthetic.

It was no vast sprawling castle, but still exuded wealth and beauty, and with the tall green mountains surrounding it, the warm fragrant air and little white sailboats bobbing about the blue of the lake.

Why couldn't the Rogues live somewhere like this, both Wilny and Raoul wondered together. London was noisy, cramped, and smelt of iron; there was no room to breathe, but here was somewhere where they could have the freedom to act and do as they wished.

"*Merde alors.* Is this…*normal* for Risio?" Raoul asked tentatively, breaking through Wilny's awe.

"This is just a ballroom with displays and nurseries. It's not an actual working farm, but it will hold some more things underneath. It has got blueprints for surgeries and spa rooms, so it doubles as a beauty clinic." Free crackled over the earpieces, still tuning the frequency. "I'm sure you could use a bit of a face lift couldn't you, eh Crow?"

"Rex needs it more than me, Free." Crow snorted. "But I think all the surgery in the world wouldn't be able to remove that stick from his arse."

The limo pulled up, waiting for the ones ahead of it to move and leave before the crew slid out. Brushing down their suits, they stood to attention, knowing their parts to play. Almost immediately, the eyes of the crowd were on them, watching with minimal subtlety as Crow stood before the door of the limo whilst Jett held a hand out to aid Roux in getting out of the car.

The boys in their black and gold tuxedos with several buttons loosened for show, all with their feathers and fur groomed into a shine. Saffron with her golden hair and furred tail brushed into to a sheen and wearing innocent smile and a crown of red and gold flowers in a golden-yellow dress to match Roux's.

As she was leading the procession, Roux was dressed in an overly extravagant gold to red mullet-cocktail dress, with the motifs of glittering phoenixes, fire and suns in red printed into it. It flared out behind her as she walked, a light sheer train floating gently in her wake shimmering red and gold in the sun giving the illusion of fire, as did her accompanying mask and fan, patterned with the same phoenix motif. Her black hair had been tamed into a sleek trailing coif that Bubbles had artfully streaked with strands of gold to match the shimmer of her skin. It was flashy and drew attention, but the more attention paid to her meant the less that was paid to the boys and Saffron.

They followed Roux as she sashayed up the red carpeted stairs, straight past the other guests waiting in line who hissed and tutted at the rudeness. A white suited waiter assisting the doorman descended to try and halt them. Roux flicked her fan in the waiter's direction and he buckled, dropping to his knees. The guests gasped, thinking that she had done this and begun whispering amongst themselves in hushed unnerved tones.

Crow grinned to himself as the waiter crawled off the floor shaking his head from the sudden mental attack, swaggering to the forefront of the entourage and smirking at the guests.

"Invitation." The doorman stated barely looking up at the parade, as the couple before them wearing their Venetian masks were ushered into the villa. The doorman was an unusual looking Tribrid, with gaudy patterned green, orange and red parrot wings and a very long black prehensile primate's tail covered with black and white stripped fur that opened and shut the door. A Risio commissioned product.

'How much you want to bet he performs as one of the monkeys whenever the Wizard of Oz rolls into town?' Roux shot to Crow with a smirk from behind her fan. With a cocky smile, Crow stepped up with the invite, pulling it swiftly from his tuxedo and flashing it before the doorman's eyes.

'Do I want to know how you got that invitation?' Wilny thought loudly so that Crow could hear.

'No. It's not even the real thing.'

"Scan please." The doorman said monotonously, giving Crow an uninterested look over. Crow frowned as he took the small black swipe machine and pretended to scan the invite. A cold yet melodically laugh erupted from Roux and she stepped forth, drawing the attention of the doorman away from Crow who inserted a tiny device in to the charging jack of the scanner before handing it back, musing to make everyone think they heard the noise of an affirmative from the machine.

"Is that necessary, *mi querido?*" Roux's voice raised several octaves and sweetened in tone, to the point of which all Wilny wanted to do was shout for everyone to start running and screaming in terror. "Do you know who I am, *mi muerto pequeño mariposo?*"

"Um...It's compulsory-"

She gave the doorman a condescending laugh, cutting him off mid-sentence, "I'll make this easier for you." Handing her mask to Jett, she gracefully removed a glove and with a flourish of her wrist and click of her fingers, she let a small flame dance across her skin with a sultry smirk. The doorman's eyes widened at the flames and he dropped into a bow so deep his nose touched his knees.

"Señora Samodiva! Oh my- please accept my deepest apologies for not recognising you sooner."

"You were just doing your job. Commendable. Now am I and my entourage allowed to pass? I am ever so eager to meet Señora Langley, it's been too long."

"Do go in!" the doorman leapt to the side opening the door with his tail and bowing once again so low he nearly rolled headfirst down the stairs.

"Thank you." Waving her hand, she sauntered through, the rest of the crew in toe. Crow, smiling, handed the scanner back to the doorman, and gave his shoulder a friendly slap. The doorman looked confused for a second then smiled, allowing Crow in.

"We're in." Prince whispered into the mic hidden on the inside of his collar, confirming their status to Bubbles. "Scanner information is done."

"Keep it safe." Bubbles chimed. "Next is the database for clientele and security control. Saffron, if you would please."

"I'm going to play." Saffron declared loudly with a smile, tugging on the sleeve of Crow's tuxedo. Crow smiled down at her, gently brushing a hand across her hair.

"Make sure you make some friends, and don't scare the other children so much."

"*Yes dad.*" And with a wink, she skipped between the guests without attracting a single glance of suspicion and disappeared into the crowd.

Roux's entrance caught everyone's attention, drawing stares of awe and fear from those who recognised Samodiva, parting before her. Wilny was impressed, he had only ever seen this level of immediate respect from the survivors in the Rioteer headquarters whenever Asena strode by.

No one questioned if she was really Samodiva or not, they believed what they saw and had heard.

The main hall gave way to a large marble room, elegantly furnished with gold leaf flourishes. They were overwhelmed by the scent of jasmine and vanilla; Raoul felt as though he were going to suffocate in its sweetness.

A black and white chequered floor took up the centre of the ballroom where several guests danced, or chattered in groups, whilst above them reams of white and gold cloth hung, connecting from the corners of the ceiling to the glittering chandeliers. There were other rooms leading off from the main hallway under archways lit with different colours depending on the climates inside, orange for a hot room, green for a tropical jungle, blue for a room filled with ice sculptures.

The guests milled enthusiastically between vivariums and aquariums that stood floor-to-ceiling either side of the connecting hallways which were filled with rare plants and fish, giving the black and white rooms colour, but there was something else amongst them.

Flashes of colour darted and fluttered amongst the emerald jungle foliage of the vivariums, keeping still for only the briefest of moments for Raoul to realise that they were raptors; one of ARCDA's critter Synths. Raoul had seen the larger ones known as Drake Raptors which were used by Core to chase down deserters and patrol compounds. Huge black and red beasts with yellow eyes that could bite through bone, but Risio had made these ones into chicken-sized pets. They were a rainbow of colours, from azure blue to sunflower yellow, to shiny crow black and delicate pearl with a feathered tails like a bird of paradise. They were certainly beautiful.

In the aquarium however, there was a Synth large as a seal yet with limbs too elongated and spindly to be flippers, swam swiftly, gracefully through the towers of bright green kelp, making Raoul look twice at what he had seen. It passed again, and his jaw dropped at the sight of a girl, skin and hair the colour of mother of pearl, swam up to the glass. Gills with red lamellae frills pulsated along her neck and naked body covered with scalloped pale scales and long frilled fins that turned to the red striped pattern of a lionfish.

Seeing his shocked face, she mockingly kissed the glass then flipped round, shooting off to the other side of the tank with a few quick kicks of her elongated webbed toes.

"Are those…" Raoul started, trailing off as he stared into the water.

Crow chuckled, gently pushing the stunned boy along. "Marines? Yes. Risio likes to have their living decor."

"Now that's a mermaid." Wilny muttered to himself, remembering the two Marines in the Xanas. Raoul looked at him in confusion.

"There's different kinds of Marines like there's different kinds of Avios."

Raoul nodded slowly, eyes wide as he looked around the room in a bewildered daze, gently ushered along by Wilny.

It was a cacophony of colour.

All around them there were the most exotic Synths and Preternaturals he had ever seen, bright flashing colours in their hair and skin marked by colourful patterns of stripes and spots, hypnotically beautiful eyes, some sat upon pedestals playing instruments or posing, others on the floor mingling with the guests.

The fashion that some of the guests were equally as exotic the Synths on display, and equally as brightly coloured as the raptors that hopped from branch to branch in the vivariums with clothes that had glowing threads or shifted colours with the temperature changes between the various rooms.

The security guards were easy to spot amongst all the excessiveness, wearing simple black SmartFabrics. They stood against the wall and in pairs at every archway, all of them either humans or Preternaturals and each wearing golden plague doctor masks and with their hands behind their backs. They weren't heavily armed and they didn't seem at all suspicious of the Daggers.

The atmosphere was brightly jovial, everyone involved was either dancing or laughing to one another. It was an oddly infectious mood on Raoul, suffocating his initial worry and discomfort in a multi-coloured wave of enjoyment radiating from almost every attendee.

Prince nudged Raoul in the ribs, to get his attention before directing him to look at what he was seeing with a small nod of his head towards a room that looked to be like a crèche area, filled with children who appeared no older than six or seven. They got a little closer to the crèche so that he could see, Prince keeping one eye on the rest of the group so that they did not get separated within the crowd.

Each child had almost shimmering skin, their shades ranging from ivory white to deepest ebony black, with a rainbow of eye colours mirrored by tiny wings of similar shades and a myriad of patterns, fully feathered and yet none that looked big enough to fly with.

"They call those ones cherubs." Prince muttered in a low voice, unable to keep his large ears from twitching wildly.

"Avio children?"

"Not quite. They're a really stunted, creepy kind that only Risio makes."

Prince shuddered as one of the cherubs joyfully sang on the command of guest. They looked too perfect, calling out and politely greeting the gala attendees in a range of languages. There were no freckles, no feathers sprouting from their cheeks or shoulders, no scales upon their legs, no frowns or fighting between any of them; Malana was nothing like these Synths.

"Half of them are as old as you are, they stunted their growth, so they'll remain childlike for longer. Your girl Malana is probably healthier and better made than any of these ones."

Raoul turned to the Dhole with a frown at the statement.

"Why would they want to keep them as children for longer?" He asked, confused as in his own experience with Core, those who grew into adulthood fastest were the ones in highest demand.

"What are they made for?"

"Anything their owners want of them. Some just want them as decorations, others use them as target practice or *worse*." Prince winced, ears flattening back against his head. The strained look on his face told more than Raoul wanted to know of their purpose and his gut hollowed in horror.

Their charm had been ripped away from them and now even just the sight of them gave Raoul nausea at the thought of what would happen with them, and at the people in the room who propagated this trade.

"Stop worrying and enjoy yourself, we're here to party after all," He tried to reassure Raoul taking a gold edged wineglass and handing it to Raoul. Already feeling nauseous eyed it suspiciously, as it was a luminous blue and glowing, and hardly looked consumable. Rolling his eyes at Raoul's suspicion, Prince sipped at it and wandered off back into the crowd.

"*Hai sete, signore?*" The waitress asked, offering the tray out to Raoul. Not wanting to be rude, he turned to the waitress and took a drink for himself out of politeness more than thirst.

"*Merci.*"

"Oh, *Francais.*" The waitress blinked at Raoul, then cleared her throat and smiled widely, visibly thinking hard about what she was about to say, "*I'm...always happy to help. Is there anything else you need? There's nothing I can't do.*"

There was no attempt to hide his cringing at the overly peppy tone of the girl. With a quick glance around to make sure that none of the guests were within earshot, he ushered the girl to lean in so he could whisper to her.

"*You are happy like this?*" He questioned, continuing in French, the fur beginning to prickle through his skin the more repelled he grew. "*Honestly?*"

"*Yes. This makes me happy.*"

"*You don't ever wish for anything else?*"

"*I only wish that I make Madame Pavo happy and the guests give me high recommendations.*" The girl beamed happily. "*I could get my price raised and serve abroad! Oh, I would love to go to America one day.*"

"*You don't want to live freely? Out in the real world where you're not someone's property?*"

She gasped. "*I would rather be dead.*"

Raoul's mouth dropped open and he gawped at her in disbelief. He could not even think of a response to her he was so appalled by her reply that he had to retreat to the others, shaking his head in disgust.

Being with the Rogues had made him see the world differently, and now he couldn't even remember what he was like when he was in Core. Had he been so blissfully happy like that? Living and only wishing to serve?

Walking back to Jett and Wilny's side, he flinched as a passing guest reached out and gently brushed his curled tail. His hackles rose, and he gritted his teeth, wanting to break the hand of the person who had done it, even if it would have been damaging to the mission.

He nudged the Avio's shoulder to draw his attention away from a strange looking Synth parading around the main ballroom to the violins playing a warm melody, her body covered in black scalloped feathers with orange avant-garde hair like a fan of fire. Two pairs of short glossy black-green wings flexed as she moved, giving her the look of a feathered dragonfly, but Raoul was too disturbed to be as awestruck.

"She's so beautiful. Not like Kat is, but still..." Wilny muttered, nodding back at the Synth who was now performing a one-woman ballet, twirling and revealing an array of softly plumed tailfeathers in the same orange as her hair.

"I wonder if I can go talk to her. Do you think I can?"

Raoul couldn't help but sneer.

"She'll probably want you to order her to speak first."

"What?"

"They only seem to think they're worth as much as they cost." Raoul hissed venomously. "Everyone here is *just*…was…was I ever that…brainwashed?"

He nodded back to the waitress. Wilny looked at the distress on Raoul's face, then back at the beaming smile of the girl and shrugged subtly.

"I don't know about you Raoul, but I was at one point. I carried out orders without a thought and I guess they're the same." He admitted, gently pulling Raoul out the path of two women waltzing around the ballroom to the music.

"But it's wrong."

"I know, I know but- *wait*, where's Saffron?" Wilny asked quietly, finally noting the disappearance of the Dagger's youngest. Free's voice cut in over his earpiece, nearly scaring Wilny out of his skin he had been so quiet for so long.

"She's off to do her thing. Bubbles is directing her."

"Isn't she a child? Is that safe for her to be on her own?"

Jett scoffed, overhearing Wilny's question and nodding to the crowds around them. The guests took very little notice of them, speaking more to Roux than anyone else. With her there, the rest were ignored as much as the waitress was.

"She's fine; she can handle this with no problem." He assured Raoul with a smirk. "I've seen her shank people in the gut at these things before without being caught. No one is going to notice one more little girl here."

Wilny did not doubt Saffron's capabilities, but he could not help but feel worried for her, as he would for Malana if she were ever to be on a mission like this. He wasn't going to question the plan, but he did feel uneasy with the Daggers allowing a little kid off on her own to steal and sabotage without support.

"Boys. Heads up." Roux murmured behind her fan, giving a small nudge to Crow. From the top of the arcing stairs, their hostess surveyed her guests. Dressed in beautiful mermaid dress, bejewelled with tiny crystals with its skirt made of two-tone glimmering organza and peacock feathers that shimmered from bronze and green to orange and blue with every movement.

From head to toe, the Synths could see her for what she was as the rest of the guests swooned at her beauty. A fake. Her agelessly perfect alabaster skin, her coif of black hair braided into a crown knotted with glowing flowers, even the sweet jasmine scent that clouded her constantly, it was all down to the various Risio based products and treatments sold to those who could afford them. Even her eyes were fake, with their aquamarine-blue sharpness.

"We found Langley." Jett whispered into his collar, trying not to stare as the hostess began to survey them all with a critical eye.

"Good, now the main thing to remember is to not drool," Free chuckled through the headset, "Nerissa Langley loves to flirt, but she loves making men beg even more."

"Noted."

Then the hostess turned. The Synths gasped quietly as there on her back, looking quite out of place, was a pair of deep glossy vivianite-green and flame orange feathers shimmering beneath the warm light of the chandeliers.

"She's an Avio?" Prince hissed to Crow, nudging him sharply in the ribs. "What the shit?"

Crow glanced up and frowned at the woman, giving a small shake of his head, cautiously watching the way that some of the other partygoers were admiring his feathered-hair and reaching out to stroke his wings.

"No…" He trailed off, but the sound of his voice echoed across their minds, dark and full of fury. *'She's still human, not even transhuman. Those are grafts and she's treating them like hair extensions. What the hell is she thinking?'*

They stared in horror at Crow.

"Grafts?" Wilny whispered. "Like…just sewn on?"

'From an Avio.'

Wilny felt his gut hollow, and his wings pull a little tighter against his back. Beside him he could feel the ever-growing burning loathing from Raoul.

'It all starts with looking beautiful, and then they want to look ethereal. Heavenly.' Raoul and Wilny heard Crow think loudly. *'Just you wait, in five years' time all of these people here will be wearing wings like it's high fashion and everyone who can't afford it will be clawing each-others' throats out to get a pair.'*

'And what will that make us?'

'Servants? Spouse Stock? Donors? Who knows?'

Horror gutted him. All his awe at the four-winged Synth dissipated as he imagined how the surgery for both parties would have gone. He could see a dozen things going wrong with the grafting; the incompatibility was a main point. Was the *donor* dead, did they allow it or were they just taken into surgery before the gala and had their wings removed?

"Well at least now none of you are going to drool." Free laughed over their ear pieces.

Removing her phoenix mask, Roux looked up to the balcony, giving a little wave to their hostess. The hostess's unnatural blue eyes met Roux's and with a smile, she gracefully descended the spiralling staircase.

"Amelia Samodiva, I didn't expect to see you here." She chimed with a gentle Irish brogue, gracing the floor and exchanging a small kiss on the cheek in greeting.

"But you should have expected me immediately Langley, *mi querida*, I enjoy these little galas Risio throws even if you are so spontaneous with their seasons." Roux smiled coyly, tucking a loose coil of hair back behind her ear. "They give me time to look at the market and take my mind off my work for a while."

"Who can deny a girl some fun." Looking over Roux with a warm and welcoming smile, examining her attire, her gaze lingering on Roux's bare hands. There was a slight narrowing of her altered-blue eyes and she snapped her head up, with a smile. "And please, it's Pavo now, not Langley."

'She's seen there's no rings,' Crow warned Roux, *'but she's taking it as a peaceful sign and wants to try and rope Samodiva into selling her some Atlas tech for chameleon and diamond skin. Be prepared to politely resist, only use threats only when necessary.'*

Roux, flicked her fan out and fluttered it flirtatiously.

"Pavo? For peacock? Those *are* peacock if I'm not mistaken."

The hostess gave a small melodic laugh, turning a little and showing off her grafted pair of peacock wings. A few small red marks along her back where the feathers met the skin showed that they were recent additions. There was no muscle mass to them, it seemed as though to Wilny that she had simply had them sewn on, on a whim, and sincerely doubted that she could even control them or open them, even if she wanted to.

"These? Based upon a Javan peafowl with a little Risio twist, I didn't want to go through with the whole transition yet. I'm still waiting for the details of the *Mistral* project is released before that happens and I can get a reliable design for something unique for myself – so I took a pair from a willing donor." She smiled as she spoke. "The sweet thing was more than happy for it, such as we make them."

A flame of rage arced through Raoul. It took all of his willpower not to lunge for the woman's throat. As much as he wanted to grab her and throttle her till she screamed, he knew how badly it would go if he did, so instead he snatched a honey glazed chicken leg from a passing waitress and bit through the bone with a crunch.

'I'm surprise she hasn't lit the place on fire already.' Wilny thought loudly to Crow, noting Roux's tenseness. She was the centre of attention and could not take her anger out as Raoul could.

'She's planning to. Seeing this place on fire would make me a lot happier about being here. Your boy is in the same mood, but I'm not sure if it's just him emphasising with Roux.'

'If we have time could you please teach me some basic telepathy, I really want to know what's going on in these freaks heads.'

'I'll teach you, but it won't make it any clearer I'm afraid."

"These are your men? They're very pretty, although I thought you only liked pretty women." Pavo asked, reaching out and brushing her fingers across the feathers in Wilny's waved hair, then took him gently by his chin to turn his head and examine him. "You must give me the genome details to this type, he's very handsome."

"Limited edition, I'm afraid." Said Wilny smoothly. "One of only three made in the world."

"Oh, these are just my boy scouts." Roux interrupted as Pavo began to pout bitterly. "Boys, this is Nerissa Pavo, be polite and no showing off. We don't want to upstage her party now do we?" They nodded politely, keeping their smiles as best they could and not allowing them to turn into snarls.

"They're helping me scout for potential clients as well as keeping an eye on the conversations. They are my best eyes and ears."

"Stalking out fresh meat?"

"Potential is everything."

"I'm surprised with all your self-improvement you haven't gotten yourself a pair of golden wings or changed your skin colour. Something whiter perhaps?" She leant in coyly, dropping her voice down to a deep sultry tone.

"Or how about your eyes? Brown is so dull, why not make them a better shade? Lilac perhaps? We could make a goddess out of you."

Roux snapped her fan out with a startling crack, making several of the nearby guests flinch and look round.

"Too much hassle, and besides, *I like my skin and eyes the shade they are.*" Pavo seemed oblivious to the deadly edge to Roux's tone at the suggestion of bleaching her skin, laughing her response off as a well-humoured quip. "But I'm not here to talk about me, I'm here to spy on you and Risio with my boys."

"Well, you don't have to rely on just them." She chimed, hooking her arm through Roux's. "Let me introduce you to some people."

"Boys, you're free to mingle."

And without a second look at the boys, Pavo led Roux off into the crowd alone. As soon as she left Raoul let out a snarl in Pavo's direction, snapping his teeth together and cursing under his breath.

"Bubbles, we're lose," Crow muttered into the mic on his lapel as they casually wandered towards through the halls trying to find the one with the service doors that led to the rest of the base. "How's our situation?"

"Better since Roux started mingling with Pavo, break up and get your jobs done. Saffron is almost finished with her job."

A waitress strode past them holding the hand of a very excited looking cherub and with a subtle nod from Crow, Prince and Jett casually strode after her, watching where she went.

"Raoul, tail Jett and Prince and keep an eye out for anyone looking too closely." Crow ordered Raoul quietly.

"What will you two do?" Raoul asked, looking between him and Wilny.

"*Dance.* Now off you go." He shooed the Canid away with his wing and a smirk, rousing and settling his feathers with a subtle shake.

With a sceptical frown, Raoul nodded and with his jaw clenched in fury and frustration, he followed after the two Daggers, trying to catch up with them before they got out of sight.

Crow cleared his throat and held out his arm for Wilny to take, then with a growing smirk led the Hummingbird back to the ballroom. Roux spotted them from across the hall and gave a small glance to the crowd that Pavo had trapped her in, with two absurdly dressed men who were wearing what looked like wolf skull hats.

Making their way through the waltzing dancers on the floor, he brought Wilny to the centre of the ballroom. He took his hand and placed his hand on Wilny's hip, with a small gesture for Wilny to copy.

'Follow my instructions and you'll not trip over and cause a scene.'

'Why are we dancing? Don't we have work to do?' Wilny asked glancing down at his feet as Crow waltzed with him to the music.

'We are but you're going to learn some telepathy and the best place to learn and work is here on the dancefloor.'

-x-

Whilst the others had been mingling, little Saffron had been busy at work.

Skipping down the hallways, she was young enough and small enough that the waiters ignored her and security guards with their golden masks, politely asked her where she was going and if she needed to pass on a message or required any assistance.

"I've been sent to exchange something for Miss Pavo," She kept on telling them with a smile, "which way is the technology suite?"

And each time they'd give her the answer, albeit with some suspicion the further from the gala floor she got. Away from the main villa, the rest of the place looked like a spa resort. Clean white walls, glass doors that led to different departments and pots of bamboo growing amongst the occasional water feature that dwelt in the crossroads of corridors, it was a pristine and calming place.

Through one hallway she had seen porters wheeling clients out of surgery rooms, no doubt in there for the beauty treatments and gene therapies, whilst in another corridor there were white suited paediatricians leading a classful of children in and out of vaccination areas.

Risio, the home of beauty and perfection in all areas. Saffron scrunched her face at the children, disgusted by their bright-eyed joy of the way they lived.

Bubbles kept track of her through the digital blueprints and linking to the cameras one at a time to watch where she was heading. As the Dagger's equivalent to Beth, she was a skilled technician and saboteur. As soon as Saffron hit the restricted area corridor, the security guards lost their charm and masks.

"Bambina—" A tall bitter looking guard snapped at Saffron as she flounced past him with her head held high.

"Child." Bubbles in her ear clip translated, helping Saffron to understand and speak Italian to get her through the villa's backstage.

"Where did you come from? You're not supposed to be back here."

"I was sent to exchange this." Saffron said slowly, listening carefully to Bubble's pronunciation and parroting what she said. She held up the mnemonic, a small flexible data-strip, meant for quickly placing orders and recording numbers and addresses for quick acquisition of clients.

"Miss Pavo is adamant it did not work."

"Give it here."

The guard snatched it from her hand, pressing the narrow button on the side to try and activate it, not that he could as Free had broken it before they arrived by pouring saltwater into its charging jack. The guard frowned and shook his head.

"May I come with you to replace it?" Saffron chirped, keeping calm and trying not to fidget with her tail. *"I need to get it back as soon as possible. She is very busy. She has the gold-lady with her."*

"Gold lady?"

"Miss Samodiva."

The guard's eyes widened, and he stood a little straighter, understanding the urgency of a request from their boss.

"Ah! Right this way."

Smiling as he led her through the hallways, she paid close attention to the path she was taken along, keeping an eye on the floor names and numbers until they arrived. Barging into the office without knocking the guard said something loudly to the technician making the tech throw the sandwich he was eating at him. One huge screen filled the back wall he was facing, split into smaller screens each of which displayed footage from a different camera in the building and at the gala. Every now and then green boxes would frame the faces of the guests, bringing up a small brief client description with a star rating, before moving onto the next guest.

Saffron kept watching and waiting as the technician and guard talked over the mnemonic, pressing buttons and plugging into one of the wall of jacks to try to charge it up again. Eyes on the screen Saffron spotted Pavo leading Roux off to a crowd, the camera fixing on her face and bringing up the real Samodiva's client profile with a five-star rating.

She smirked to herself, nimble tail reaching under the hem of her dress as she slowly walked towards the technician and guard as they bickered at each other, pulling out two small tubes filled with a clear liquid.

They flinched at the sharp sting in their legs, both rubbing at what felt like a mosquito bite, then several seconds later the guard staggered, falling to his knees and whacking his head upon the technicians' desk, whilst the technician slumped in his chair and let the faux-mnemonic fall to the ground with a clatter.

Saffron wiped the small needleless injectors clean, before hooking them back onto the thigh belt she had been keeping them on beneath her dress. Pushing the technician from his chair, she sat down at the set up and began the data exchange with Bubbles.

"And Jett thinks this is hard." Saffron giggled in excitement. Bubbles laughed over the mic.

"Very good my little chickadee, know you know how to bring up the access files for the server right?"

"Easy." She typed away until she had exactly what she wanted onscreen, locating the external source, which was Free and Bubbles lurking on the other side of the lake and extending the access to them. "Rerouting the cameras and stuff to you, Bubs."

The camera recordings on the screen, flashed as they re-set and began re-photographing every attendee to put the names of the guest list to faces and share their details with the Daggers. Over a hundred-and-fifty guests all accounted for as well as two hundred products on display. Bubbles started cackling to herself on the other end of the mic, clapping her hands.

"This is a gold mine, we're good to go! Get back to Crow now Saffy."

"And the boys?" She looked up at the cameras. Prince, Jett and Raoul were walking down the hallway, Free directing them towards Pavo's office.

"They're on their way."

22

Lake Iseo, Lombardy, Northern Italy

"Down the next set of stairs, second door on the left. That should be the way down to the resources."

"Thank you Free." Prince muttered into the microphone on his lapel. Raoul felt uneasy with their task. There were far too many things that could go wrong with just three of them.

Plague masked guards chatted idly to each other, ignoring the three well-dressed Synths for the most part, occasionally giving them suspicious glances, but never saying anything to them.

"Remember, we're looking for Pavo's tablet, laptop, and data core, anything that will give us details on the rest of Risio."

"We know, we know."

Already on edge, every little sound or scent grated on Raoul's senses. Perfume filled the hallways from the gala's ballroom with sickly sweetness battling against the antiseptic cleanness of the surgeries. Surgeons who talked in low murmurs through doors and across hallways seemed as clear as if they were standing right beside him talking normally, or children giggling or arguing in their nurseries, or crying in pain.

Raoul's fur stood on end at the sound of the crying. It grew louder, as they went past a hallway before going down the stairs towards Pavo's office.

"Free, there are kids down here." He hissed into his own mic, hesitating at the top of the stairs.

"Leave them."

"But Free!"

"We're not here to rescue."

"But–"

"No." His earpiece let out a piercing screech as Free blew into his microphone. Flinching Raoul ripped the earpiece off, shaking his head at the ringing in his ears. Prince and Jett also flinched, the sound from Raoul's earpiece carrying. They stared up the stairs at him, angrily ushering him down to join them.

"You think we're cruel, Raoul?" Jett asked coolly, taking Raoul by the collar and dragging him down the hall to the second door.

"Yes. Why don't–"

"–We help them? We don't have the time or resources to pull out seventy kids and deal with them. They're not worth the risk." His tone shifted from calm to snide at the latter end of his response, sending a fierce burst of fury through Raoul. Never had Raoul felt the urge to head-butt a person more.

"I'm sure Storm could do it." He snarled, slapping Jett's hand off. "She'd get them out and even get the guards to help her."

"I'm sure she could." Jett laughed down at him.

Fist clenched, Raoul visualised himself swiping a clawed hand across Jett's smug face for bad talking the Rogues, they were his family and he had gained far too much self-respect to be spoken down to.

"Shut up Jett." Prince scolded, yanking hard on the Pard's tail. "Stop riling him up, this isn't the place for it."

"I'm only teasing him."

"Boys! The stuff!" Free barked through the earpieces. "Second office, the access key is five-nine-four…"

Raoul sneered as the two boys toyed with the door, turning away from them and turning down the volume on his earpiece so Free was barely a whisper. Glancing off towards the stairs, he considered to himself what would Storm have done. He imagined her head high, wings outstretched, ignoring all orders and striding off to help any way she could.

The ideal he had of the Rogue may have been more fanciful and wishful thinking than what Storm might have actually done, but he wanted to help. And so, with his head held high, he marched off down the hallway and back up the stairs, following the sound of whimpering, Prince and Jett barely registering his disappearance.

Breezing through the doors, he felt nervous about being alone, questioning his decision as two guards passed him. They didn't look twice at him, but it didn't make him feel any more confident.

In the rooms around him he could hear the low discussions of doctors talking with patients in for treatment or giving directions to porters on the care of the clients, it was a very different atmosphere to the ballroom. Even the smell was different; antiseptic and faintly smelling of magnolia. It was nothing like Core and its permanent stench of metal and oil, he almost missed it.

A sharp yelp of pain came from a room to his left. He flinched at the sound, teeth on edge and hackles raised. He lunged to the door, watching warily from the corner of the round window into the white room at what they were doing.

A plague-masked guard and a nurse crowded a low table, both pinning down a squirming shrieking Canid-cub dressed in simple white clothes as a tattooist tried to ink a code on the back of the boy's neck. Raoul was familiar with this sight, it was common practice in ARCDA to mark products with their identification code and a microchip once they had been sold or moved, but never had he seen it being done to someone this young.

"Stop wriggling!" The tattooist scolded the boy in English.

"I don't want it! It hurts!" The boy shrieked, face red and scrunched from crying.

"It'll hurt even more if you keep moving!"

His arms flailed out and he screamed the moment the needle drew close to his neck, the nurse and guard struggling to wrestle him still, earning herself a sharp puppy nip through the gloves to the back of her hand. The tattooist yelled, reeling back as a drop of blood began to well up on the injury, the nurse and guard seizing him tighter as he twisted and struggled.

"Sol-fifteen, stop, or we'll get the alphas to punish you." The nurse snapped, calling the boy by what Raoul assumed to be his batch name and number.

"Do you want us to tell Mr Yzaaks that you're broken, and he has to pay less?"

"No! No, I'm not broken!" The boy wailed, taking deep blubbering sobs between breaths. "I'll be good, but I don't want you to hurt me!"

The Canid-cub let out a distressed whine and claws digging into the door, it took all of Raoul's willpower to not slam the door open, lunge in and rip their throats out. The sudden fury caught a more civil part of him, grounding him with a sudden pinch of reflection.

'*Think Raoul.*' He told himself, taking deep breaths to calm his anger and control himself. '*What would the girls do? How would they handle this?*'

Storm would be smiling, charming, and calm before she snapped her teeth and attacked; Beth would be remote and logical, talking rationally so she would be believed whilst never revealing too much; and Kat would be sneaky and subtle, walk in and lie with a smile letting her appearance distract them from her intentions.

Whilst he was none of the girls, he could at least pretend to be them.

'*Think like the girls*' he told himself, smoothing his hair back he steadied his breathing, mimicking the calm and crafty poise that the girls held themselves with, before pushing the door open and sliding into the room. The guard's masked face snapped up at his entrance, and for a brief moment he thought that he would be caught out as he saw a twinge of suspicion in his eyes behind the mask.

"Ah good, the cavalry has arrived." The tattooist laughed with relief, seeing the curled tail and furred ears that made him easily distinguishable as a Canid. "I didn't think they'd send a Dog so soon."

He may not have been a beautiful Risio blond, but he was going to give being sultry his best shot.

"Do you require assistance, *Signore?*" Raoul asked in a low smooth voice, swallowing down his fear and pretending to be Kat. "I was sent by Signora Pavo, she was getting concerned by how long you were taking."

The Italian accent wasn't too difficult to mimic and calling people by signore and signora was simple enough. The tattooist seemed to buy his act, though she was busier with disinfecting the injury she had sustained.

"We're having a hiccup. Can you get this child under control? He's wriggling like crazy."

Raoul looked down at the boy with a warm smile, putting his finger to his lips and gently hushing him. Sol-fifteen stopped crying and stared at Raoul with odd eyes. The left eye was a bright yellow, the right a dark brown. He was incredibly cute with his blonde curls and round face. Raoul couldn't believe that Risio could make Canids look so adorable, and he was likely a dog-based Canid. But the little cub was also very wary. He knew that this wasn't his usual Alpha.

Rubbing his face Sol-fifteen mumbled. "Sorry, Alpa," sniffling and trying to regain his composure, whilst all the while watching Raoul with subtle curiosity.

Head held high Raoul took two steps further into the room, arms behind his back and remaining as still and calm as he had seen the waitresses, trying to not let his smile get too smug. "Signora Pavo said that you were taking too long with the coding and that we need to pass Sol-fifteen over soon before his buyer leaves."

"I'm not surprised. But we need to get this done." The guard said, voice muffled by his mask though his Italian accent still audible.

"Who is he going to?" Raoul asked calmly, brushing off a few stray hairs from his shirt idly, switching from Kat to Beth, becoming sharp and curt.

"You don't know?"

"I was ordered to pass on the message and collect the product as soon as possible, I wasn't told who the buyer was."

"Mr Martien Yzaaks, he was wearing a panda-skin jacket and had quetzal feathers in his hat."

"I'm sure Mr Yzaaks wouldn't want Sol-fifteen to be crying when he's handed over. That would be bad for our image." It felt a little odd channelling Beth's personality, but he was sure he'd done her justice. "He's already misbehaved once, and if he goes out in a bad mood then it will only increase the chances are that he might be brought back. We're already on the edge with the Rioteers and Core watching us for signs of weakness, we don't want to make a loss, nor do we want to give Core an excuse to take the products as faulty stock."

"You're being very forward there, Dog." The guard warned. With a disinterested snort, Raoul folded his arms and stared the guard down.

"I'm just doing my job as an Alpha." He stated coldly, keeping with Beth's sharp tone. "Unlike you *signore*, I have a far better understanding of how products react if they're mishandled initially and having seen so many well-made products end up at Core and Atlas for petty and idiotic reasons such as *crying too much*, I feel as though you need to understand my concerns for my subordinates."

The guard squirmed. It took all he could muster not to laugh at the sight of it, a Dog like him pulling rank over a human.

"He's only got half an ID done, and I haven't chipped him yet." The nurse protested, but Raoul kept on smiling, looking across to Sol-fifteen with a subtle wink.

"There's no harm in cutting a few corners with procedure. I'm sure he'll behave himself and not run away." Raoul assured the nurse. He tilted his head to one shoulder with a smile, charming like Storm. "We do have the reputation for having the best standards of behaviour. We need to maintain that as best we can."

He had no idea if it were true or not, but it felt like it'd be the sort of thing that Risio bosses would say to stroke the egos of their employees.

The Canid pup looked up at the nurse and gave a little whine.

"I promise I'll be good." He insisted.

"Fine. Take him up." The tattooist gave a sigh of resignation. "But if he gets broken or runs away, I'll pass on that you're to blame."

"As you should." Raoul shrugged, lifting the boy up into his arms, letting him wrap his arms around his neck and burry his face into his shoulder. "*Alpha Cerisier Vingt-quatre*, if you need my code." He smiled, thinking of the first words that came to mind that sounded like they'd be part of Risio's naming system based on Sol-fifteen's name.

The nurse and guard seemed to accept it, and without any further protest he turned on his heels and strode out of the room and back towards where the two Daggers would still be sabotaging Pavo's office. Proud and riding on a wave of adrenalin from his first real crime, Raoul let out a small laugh, realising what he had done.

"Who are you?" The boy whispered into Raoul's ear, short tail gently wagging, "You're not my Alpa."

"Raoul Hunter. I'm a secret agent, *shh*." He murmured with a grin, padding down the stairs with him. The boy's odd eyes grew wide with wonder, and a smile spread across his face.

"How old are you?"

"Two months!"

"*Merde*." Raoul shuddered. His teeth ached in anger. What person would by a two-month-old Canid-cub?

"Do you want to go with that man?" He asked cautiously.

The Canid-cub shook his head. "No."

"Would you like to come with me instead?"

"Yes."

He didn't seem to have been conditioned to the same extent as the waitress, though being quite young, Raoul wasn't sure if the boy fully knew what he was agreeing to. However, he didn't feel as though he could just leave him here, especially with what he had learnt. Hoisting the cub up onto his hip a little further, he hurried on back to the Daggers.

Rounding the corner, he found Jett and Prince both carrying laptop cases with– what Raoul assumed to be containing– Pavo's personal laptop. With their backs to him, they were busy bickering between themselves as they locked the door. Raoul tried not to roll his eyes as he snuck up upon them. They were only transhuman, their senses not as developed or as heightened as his.

"Have we got what we came for?" Raoul asked.

"Raoul!" Prince span round, clutching his chest in fear as Raoul took him by surprise. "You were told to keep-" He stopped mid-sentence as he saw Sol-fifteen in his arms, jaw snapping shut and gripping Jett's shoulder, so he would look.

"Raoul…please." Jett stared at the boy, speaking slowly and quietly as he realised what Raoul had done. "Don't do this. Put it back where you found it."

Sol-fifteen hugged Raoul tightly, as Raoul curled his lip back and snarled.

"He is not it! Now we have what we came for, we should leave."

Free's voice crackled quietly over the headset, as the two quickly tailed Raoul, as he strode off towards the stairs they had arrived down.

"What has he done? Prince? What has the Dog done?"

"He's got a kid."

A crackling series of curses were hurled at Raoul before he turned the volume back on, on his earpiece.

"Raoul put him down! You're going to blow the entire mission."

"Storm is my boss." Raoul declared forcefully. "You can take this up with her."

"Prince, stop him."

Prince lunged forward, attempting to swipe at Raoul who lightly stepped out the way with a calm smile as he heard the approach of footsteps. He remained calm and composed as the two Daggers froze. Down the hall were four of the masked guards, walking towards them.

"Try to touch me or him again, then I will make sure neither of you leave here alive." He snarled softly, holding the puppy close, teeth flashing threateningly in the light. The masked guards walked by Raoul giving them a reassuring gesture that they accepted and continued on their way.

"You- you can't-" The Daggers began, but Raoul cleared his throat, a cunning smile playing at the corners of his lips as he raised his voice.

"Excuse me." He stated loudly in Italian to get the guards attention. They turned to face them. Both Daggers held their breath as Raoul spoke, paling at the threat.

"Has Mr Martien Yzaaks left yet, I believe he was the man in the panda skin suit? Is he still here?" Raoul spoke quickly, certain that neither of the transhuman synths spoke any Italian to understand.

"Yes, he should still be here."

"Thank you. Which way is the fastest to reach him do you know? I last saw him by the front door."

"Ah yes. Head up that corridor on the left."

"Thank you."

"What did you say?" Hissed Prince.

"I only asked which way the exit was." Raoul snorted with laughter. He shook his head at the pair and continued onwards, the two Daggers fearfully rushing after him, grinning from ear to ear with glee.

-x-

"Okay, I admit it; you're worth more than just a grand." Crow sighed, swiping a drink from a waitress's tray and sipping it bitterly as Wilny beamed gleefully at him.

"A million!"

"It was just that man's opinion."

"One. *Million.*"

"Don't get excited, it's not that much."

Having grown tired of dancing, Wilny had decided upon a game where they each would make a guess of how much people would buy them for, the loser having to drink the glowing blue cocktails if they weren't close enough.

It had been easier to learn how to muse upon people's thoughts than Wilny had first expected. It was different to what he was used to with altering their perceptions, and he wasn't too comfortable yet with pushing his own thoughts out to others but *hearing* them however was something else.

Words were distant whispers, abstract and incoherent, but the emotions were clear as crystal and infectious.

'Feelings are stronger than thoughts. Better. You can adapt to how someone feels and change how you act.' Crow had told him. *'Start with a feeling, and then thoughts and reasoning become clear. And the more you know a person, the more like their voice their thoughts will sound, you might even feel the colours of their minds.'*

The band played a lively tune, a rhythm that drew many guests to the floor to dance with the Risio products, creating a changing sea of colour from gowns and hair, scales and feathers, as the dancers span and waltzed with one another. They even had glimpsed Roux in the crowd, clearly having been drawn in against her will to dance with the hostess, briefly before escaping back to the edge for drinks.

Crow rolled his eyes.

"Are ya' done gloating?"

"Hold, on I want to talk to that girl over there."

Crow followed Wilny's gaze back to the four-winged Synth he had been so awe-struck by earlier. She was dancing on the edge of the crowd, laughing with an albino Pard with hair so long it brushed the floor.

His eyes nearly rolled back into his skull he was so exhausted.

"*Willners–*"

"If you won't let me talk to her can you at least let me try and make out what she's thinking?"

He lunged for Wilny, dragging him back by his wing as he made a move to speak to the girl who was surrounded by men all leching over her.

"You better reign your dick in there kiddo." He hissed, tailfeathers fanning quickly and sharply in irritation. He regretted letting Wilny drink some of the blue cocktails and was certain that he was getting a little tipsy.

"I just want to talk to her!"

"*No.*"

"She's out of your league anyway." Saffron scoffed, sidling over to them with a plate of only semi-identifiable *hors d'oeuvres*. Wilny stared down at her aghast, before swiping a small leaf roll filled with rice from her plate. Gently pulling her to his side, Crow glared at a passing guest who was watching the girl with a saytric smirk.

There was a slight prickle across Wilny's head as he felt Crow and Saffron talking mentally to each other, only able to roughly distinguish a few words from their exchange. Crow was pleased. Saffron was tired, and hungry, and wanting to trip up the next person who touched her without her permission. He itched at the base of his tail feathers, feeling the ghost of a prehensile monkey tail that didn't belong to him and shuddered. Mental tracing was weird, but eye opening in how others perceived the world through their senses.

"Time to leave boys." Bubbles chimed over the earpieces. "We have what we need and then some."

"That bloody kid-" Free's voice snapped in the background. "This is all because I said no isn't it?"

With a shared frown between the boys, Crow discreetly muttered into the microphone on his lapel, "What's Batman squeaking about?" paying heed to the crowd and scanning it for the return of the others.

"Raoul."

"*Raoul?*"

"They're heading out to you now."

Scanning the crowd, they looked for the boys, curious as to what Raoul had done. Pushing past an overly drunk parade of dancing guests, Prince made a beeline towards them, an exasperated Jett in tow whilst bringing up the rear strode Raoul carrying a small puppy.

With his eyes almost rolling back into his skull once again, Crow took a deep breath trying to calm his ruffled feathers.

"Raoul, why do you have a toddler?" He asked calmly, noting the continued swearing from Free on the earpiece and the other boys' minds. "You do know that we're here to gather information, not to kidnap children."

"I know." Jaw clenched Raoul stared Crow dead in the eye, a look Wilny had seen Storm give Rex whenever she intended on pissing him off and refusing orders.

"Raoul's part of my team, I'll deal with it." Wilny hushed Crow before he could lecture him. Sol-fifteen just observed wide eyed, smiling obliviously to the situation, tiny tail wagging back and forth. Holding the cub a little closer Raoul warily watched Wilny as he stepped up to him and put a hand on his shoulder, unsure of what to expect. Turning with a wild grin to the Daggers, Wilny pulled Raoul to his side with his wing and ruffled the boy's hair.

"I'd like all of you to meet my new grandson." Wilny declared proudly, casting a smile across the Hound's face.

The expressions from the Daggers was unanimous in anger. The black feathers on Crow's head rose in anger, shouting '*Bloody Rogues*' in his head loud enough that Wilny heard it as if Crow had screamed it aloud into the room.

"Let's go...before you start a revolt," Crow sighed, shaking his head, "You lot head to the door, I'll get Roux and meet you out the front."

The group shuffled off through the crowd, slowly making their way through the black and white halls to the main doors.

Smoothing his feathers down, Crow set off on the hunt for Roux. Pushing through the guests, most of whom were bordering on drunk, it took a bit of searching to find Roux, but when he did he found her standing before a group of men and making them all cower before her.

"Yes, have them shipped to my villa." Roux declared loudly, waving her hand towards four young men, each with a mane of golden-brown hair and swishing brush ended tails. They looked at one another in relief, whilst two human men looked defeated at each other and shuffled off towards a vivarium full of raptors to brood.

'*Did you really just buy four Lions, Roux?*' Crow asked her. She tensed at the sudden invasion of thoughts from Crow, quickly giving him a side glance as Pavo fussed over the Pards, relaying them their orders.

'There's a guy here who's "broken" several young men from Risio and was aiming to buy these. My mother won't mind a bit. She loves a repair job.'

'At least you aren't bringing them home with us.' Out the corner of his eye he noticed a plague masked guard approaching, a gleam of worry and fear on his mind as he approached. 'It's time to go. Now.'

With a frown she turned to Pavo, patting her hand gently.

"If you'll excuse me a moment, *quierda*, my pets are misbehaving." She said with honeysweet charm, then proudly glided off down the hall to Crow before Pavo could get a word of protest in, dress flowing out behind her like fire.

"We good to go?" Roux whispered, voice dropping back down several octaves to her regular snarling tone.

"We're good. Just move faster."

"You move faster! You're not the one wearing stilettos."

"Signora Samodiva!" A guard called to them, as they picked up their pace towards the exit. Head high, Roux blanked him. Behind them she could hear Pavo starting to shout and order guards to her. With so many guests it was difficult for them to keep up, but they were closing in.

Gracefully plucking a glass of blue cocktail from a passing tray, Roux filled her mouth with as much as she could, then drawing her hand to her mouth, she span round, clicked her fingers and blew the guards a fiery kiss. A ball of fire plumed from the spray of the alcohol as it crossed her aflame palm. Guests shrieked and reeled back, blocking the guards from getting any closer as they retreated from the fire.

Grinning wildly as they reached the door, she blew another fireball kiss that startled the door attendant, kicking her heels off and sprinting down the stairs with Crow. The limo had already pulled up, the others all crowded inside with the door open and prepared for Crow and Roux to bail in and drive away.

They leapt inside just as the guards burst through the door, trying to chase after them and tripping over the heels Roux had left behind, sending the first few stumbling and tumbling down the stairs. Panicked the driver hit the accelerator, engine revving, dust and stones kicking up as the wheels span and the limo launched away, door still open.

"Are they going to chase us?" Raoul asked, staring out the back window as they raced along the driveway, holding the Canid-cub close.

Free crackled over the earpiece with a laugh. "They're trying. It's a bit hard since I've still got a grip on their security. If anything, they'll harass the real Samodiva about it?"

"Any ideas how she'll respond to that?" They looked to Roux, now sitting smugly in her chair and pulling her hair down.

"She's not an idiot. She'll know it was me, but what she'll do about it I've got no idea." She shrugged. "But for now, let's go home."

23

Cherry Tree House, Battersea, London

The Dagger's motorhome pulled slowly into the parking bay before Cherry Tree, the doors opening and allowing the boys to tumble out into the fine drizzling mist of rain. They stretched from the long journey, having had a three-day drive back to England from Italy, with little chance to get out and walk. Roux had long since raced off ahead of them on her motorbike with Free the moment they reached France.

"Well, I hope you kids had fun." Crow smirked at the boys, tossing their bags out of the motorhome to them. "We'll have to do a holiday like this again sometime. Just maybe a little less kidnapping next time, okay?"

Raoul laughed, ruffling the hair of his new protégé, renaming him from Sol-fifteen to Palmer after an extended debate during the journey home.

"Are we home now?" Palmer asked curiously, looking up at the terrace.

"Yes. This is your new home."

"It's small."

Raoul laughed again, looking up at the tall terrace house with a smile, "No its not. It's perfect. And it's home."

The sight of Cherry Tree House gave Wilny an overwhelming sense of bittersweet belonging. He stood staring up at the climbing vine that crawled up the redbrick and through the wrought iron balcony across the first floor as the door swung open and Kat greeting them all with a wide grin across her face, pleased to see them return. She leapt down the stairs in a single bound, pouncing upon Raoul and gathering him up into her arms, fussing over him and brushing his hair back.

"We're back!" Raoul laughed. "With a few extra people."

Kat stared down at the toddler hiding behind Raoul nervously, and grinned.

"New puppy?" She asked, a rounded ear flicking back in caution.

"His name's Palmer." Said Raoul firmly.

Kat crouched holding her hand out tentatively for the Canid-cub to take.

"Hello there." She said softly, letting him see her twitching round ears and blue feathers along her tail. "I'm Kat."

Palmer stared in awe at her, Raoul smirking to himself as he as he realised that he had worn the exact same expression when he had first been introduced properly to Kat.

"You have bright hair!" He barked, pointing to the still pastel blue shade that stained the lighter streaks of her failed hair-dye attempt. "Could I have that hair?"

"If you're a good boy and if Raoul says you can, then maybe you can pick which colour you want." Kat laughed, brushing her fingers through her blue-streaked hair with a little flourish. Palmer's tail wagged excitedly as he nodded his head, looking to Raoul with bright eyes of promise.

"He must be hungry after coming all that way." Wilny flinched at the sound of Storm's voice, casting his eyes to the damp ground and not daring to look up at her. "Bring them inside Kat. Wilny and I have to talk."

Wordlessly Kat ducked inside the house with Raoul and Palmer, leaving Wilny on the path with Storm.

There was an all-consuming silence between them for several long seconds until tentatively, he glanced up at her, holding his breath and preparing for her snarling rage, ordering him to leave. She stared down at him from the top of the stairs, arms folded across her chest, tartan blanket draped over her wings and shoulders like a cape.

"Hello." She said. A simple greeting, but it was ice cold.

He'd much rather have had her fury bearing down on him than her calm ire. He felt the anxiety build in his chest, struggling to take a deep breath and calm himself before speaking as Storm took a slow step down towards him.

"Storm...I..." His voice cracked, and he flinched at his own hesitation.

"Is there something you wish to say?"

"I'm- What I want to say is- I...I let you down." His shoulders dropped, wings releasing and sweeping the weed strewn pathway. "I let the Rogues down, you just wanted to help me, and I was an ass. I'm sorry. I was angry and depressed, and everything just made me think of them, and how they died. It just hurt too much for me to think about moving on from what happened, and I thought you were trying to make me forget them. They were my family and I loved them, and I killed them and there is nothing that can change that or how I feel."

Tears stung at his eyes with the mist of rain, blurring his vision as he tried to blink them away, chest burning in pain at the sudden stress. He remained still, clutching his hand to his heart.

"I still blame myself for killing them, and I understand if you don't trust me. So, if you think I'm still a risk to everyone's safety then please, *please*, just tell me to leave now because I don't want to do anything to hurt you or Lana. Especially Lana. Please…I don't want to hurt any of you."

She remained on the second step, high enough to make direct eye contact and be level with him, but he still felt small and beneath her. Her pupils dilated and contracted rapidly as she analysed the minute changes in his expressions, nictitating membrane flicking across her eyes. The scrutiny was intense.

"Lana cried for the first few days you were gone and was angsty for days after." Calm, soft, but still threatening. "One of the little kids in the headquarters nursery said I'd killed you. She head-butted them and broke their nose."

"Did she…"

"Believe it? No. I told her what happened. Raoul too. I told them that I sent you away because you weren't feeling world and needed to think."

He looked lowered his gaze to the floor, letting the droplets of water roll off of his nose.

"I'm sorry."

"I'm sorry too." Storm sighed, tilting his chin up to look at her. She looked exhausted and careworn. "I was selfish and childish about it all; I wanted you to get better quickly so that I could have that victory of having helped. I went about this all the wrong way thinking that it was going to be easy, and all you needed to do was to just talk to someone about what happened, and you'd start to recover within days. I tried everything I thought you needed to get better and change, when all you needed was time."

"You did what you thought was right by me, that's more than I could have done."

"But I disregarded your wellbeing and how much you needed to grieve. I should have done better, and I want you to know that I don't expect you to be instantly magically cured of the grief and pain you've been going through, Will. I'm sorry for trying to make you move on when you're not ready to do so." She said, drawing her wings up and almost cocooning herself in shame and trying to keep the tears from her eyes. "I'm sorry I rushed you to get better. I can't force you to talk to people about what happened, I can't force you to take medication, I can give you all the advice I think you need, but I can't make you change and get better. Only you can do that."

"But I'm…" He hesitated, unnerved by seeing Storm looking so vulnerable. It wasn't the Storm he was used to. Clearing his throat, he held his head high. "What do you expect me to do?" He asked politely.

She looked a little surprised but lowered her wings.

"What I expect you to do is for you to make a conscious effort to talk and ask for help." She said. "No more trying to shrug it off or keep people away, you are not alone in this. Come talk to me or someone you trust and feel safe with, immediately. And if you start to feel stressed or like an attack is about to begin, just say and we'll try and get you into a safer environment."

"I'll try. I can't promise-"

"I don't need a promise. I need your confidence and trust, because this is my home, my family, and I will not allow it to be broken by anyone. I can't help you if you don't trust me to help you." She let her hands drop so that they were outstretched towards him. "Now…do you trust me?"

The Rogues both old and new were dangerous, reckless scoundrels, but one thing he had learnt from them all was that they had an astounding amount of dedication and loyalty to one another no matter how far away they went. The Rogues needed him, and he needed them.

With a slow and steady breath, he placed his hands in hers, letting them curl and close.

"I trust you, Boss." He nodded, a weak smile forming, "More than I trust myself."

"Boss? Is that who I am now?" A smile slowly spread across her face at his new name for her. Warmth blossomed across his chest at the sight of her smiling, glad and comforted to see the Storm he knew again.

"My teammate, Eddie, he used to call me Boss, and since you're my boss…I thought I might…I'm sorry, I'll-"

"It's fine, call me what you like."

A sigh of relief escaped him. "Thanks Boss."

"Come on home." She smiled, tugging him by the hand to lead him through the door. "We've missed you."

He resisted a little, uncertain and then let go to wrap his arms around her. Storm paused as he gave a deep sigh of relief, letting her wings unfurl from beneath her blanket and surround him with warmth.

"Thank you." He murmured softly. "Thank you."

"Are you crying on me?"

"No." He sniffled, releasing her and trying to scrub his tear-reddened face dry on his arms. Taking his hands gently she put his arms down. His wings trembled he was holding them so tense.

"It's alright." Said Storm. "You can cry if that's what you want to do."

"Bu-but I don- don't w-ant to cry."

"Deep breaths then." She brushed his hair from his face and dried his tears with the cuff of her shirt, giving him several moments to get his breathing under control and stop crying. Gently taking his hand when he had calmed, she led him up the stairs and into the light and warmth of the house.

The house was quiet as he entered, the rest of the Rogues gathered in the living room and watching him warily as he entered, waiting for Storm to officially give her sentence on his situation, even though from the smug grin on Beth's face they already knew. He could smell bacon grilling from the kitchen and saw honey on the coffee table waiting for him.

"Welcome back." Beth said with a nod, her usual position on the sofa exchanged for a new armchair that allowed her to drape her wings over the sides and put her feet up.

Looking about nervously, he noticed that one person was missing.

"Where…where's Lana?" He asked in a quiet voice.

"Lana! *Ah enfin rentré!*" Raoul shouted up the stairs.

There was a thundering of feet, and with a single leap down the staircase came Malana. She skidded to a halt beside Storm, looking up at Wilny anxiously. In the near three weeks he had been away she seemed to have grown an inch and her grey baby down had all but fallen out, replaced by clean tiger-orange feathers, some edged with iridescent-bronze. Even what was once a short tail that usually remained beneath her skirts were beginning to show as the tailfeathers grew longer. The growth and change of the little girl hurt his heart at how much he had missed whilst he was gone.

Kneeling before her, he tentatively held his hand out.

"I'm sorry for not being there for you, Sunbeam." He apologised, "I wasn't well. But I'm home now."

Malana stared at him critically for several moments, analysing his face and tone of voice. Watching her pupils rapidly dilate and constrict against the bright amber iris in the same raptorial way in which Storm's eyes did, it was hard to tell what she was thinking, though he didn't want to intrude on her thoughts.

And then filling with tears she let out a sudden burst of bawling, then flung her arms around Wilny, burying her face into his shirt. Arms around, he hugged her gently, her wings shuddered as she cried on him, incoherently whimpering between sobs.

"What did she say Raoul?" Wilny asked quietly, hoping that Raoul could distinguish what the girl had said.

"Not sure, there was too much crying."

"Why is she sad?" Palmer asked loudly, letting go of Raoul to go to Lana's side and paw her arm, "Don't be sad!"

Lana looked down at him in teary confusion as Palmer pulled her back and hugged her tightly, repeatedly cooing to her to stop being sad, making the others laugh a little and even drawing a smile from Malana.

"Lana, why don't you show Wilny and Palmer your drawings. I'm sure they'll want to see what you've been up to while he's been away." Storm suggested gently, running a hand down her rust and gold wings. Wiping her eyes on the back of her arm, Malana nodded, taking Palmer by the hand and leading him across to the toy box that sat next to the television.

"Amell's been teaching her how to draw. Lana's still a little uh…sharp with him, but she's slowly understanding what happened wasn't his fault."

"Amell?"

At the mention of his name, Amell's head popped out from the kitchen.

"*Kia ora*, how ya' doing bro?" He asked with a wide grin.

Throwing a thumbs up to the Eagle, Wilny laughed a little, seeing his hair tied back into a knot and wearing a novelty apron which read *Check Out These Buns* across it. He'd been learning to cook as he said he was going to do. Seeing Amell following through on his promise was extremely admirable to him, and he only wished he could do likewise.

"Better now I'm home."

"Well, I'm glad you're back, these girls haven't shut up about you." He laughed, rolling his eyes. "You must have been quite the ladies-man."

"Yeah right." Kat laughed, dragging Wilny down onto the sofa beside her and fussing over his hair and wings. "I'm glad you're back K-Pop. With you gone I had no one to torment or fight about guns with; Raoul is far too nice to argue with me." She mocked, brushing through the tiny little feathers. Relaxing, Wilny leant his head so that Kat could groom the feathers along his neck and shoulders with a comb and letting his long tailfeathers sprawl across the floor.

"More like you start speaking Japanese so I have no idea what you're talking about and surrender." The Hound sighed with a shake of his head.

"I guess you'll have to learn Japanese then."

"Kat. I speak seven languages already. One more won't bother me."

"It's not a challenge Raoul."

"*Yes, it is.*"

"Alright, if you learn Japanese by the end of August, you'll get one big favour from me. Now, come on and tell us all about the holiday."

"The Daggers were fun and noisy, but they're not you guys." Raoul laughed softly, sitting on the other side of Kat who was seemingly comfortable enough with him to allow him to lean against the red feathers of her under-wing.

Raoul shuffled up enough that Storm could squash in beside him on the very end of the sofa, allowing her to stretch her legs across Raoul and Kat's laps so that she could allow her own wings to drape over the arm of the sofa.

"Was there a lot of dancing? Oh, and the clothes! Tell me about the clothes!" Kat said in delight, hazel eyes glittering with excitement as her imagination began to run wild.

"The Gala was…*something*…lots of people, lots of alcohol, very, *very,* strange clothing, you would have loved it Kat." He said, and gave a look to Wilny to see if the Hummingbird wanted to explain anything about their adventure. Wilny started to speak when Malana rushed forward to him.

"Look!" Malana said, thrusting a densely filled sketchbook of drawings into Wilny's lap. "Look what I made for you!"

"That is very good English Lana, well done." Praised Raoul, seeing the surprise on Wilny's face before adding in an aside to him. "She's been practicing."

Diligently, Wilny flicked through, musing at the pictures as Malana did her best to explain the stories behind the bright colours and figures within, flicking between French and English the more excited and happier she became.

Some were very clearly animals and critters, others were people.

"What's that?" Palmer asked, pointing to a striped four-legged animal that Malana had drawn.

"A Zebra!"

Palmer didn't seem to fully understand but nodded away happily regardless.

"Who's that?" Wilny asked pointing to a round figure with a tiny head getting kicked – or at least he assumed it was getting kicked- by what appeared to be a frowning face with two strange antennae sticking out of its back.

"That you kick- uh, *kicking,* him." Malana explained pointing at Amell.

"That's her favourite thing to draw." Amell sighed heavily.

Between complimenting Malana's drawing skills and warning Palmer not to detach Beth's legs, Raoul and Wilny told them all about the Gala, the cherubs and the ballroom, trying to remember the outfits for Kat's benefit and then the technology for Beth's before Raoul went into his adventure on saving Palmer. The girls laughed and hugged him as he told them about how he put himself in their shoes to pull it off, to which they stood him up and had him doing impressions of them all.

"The Daggers told me to leave Palmer." He lost all joviality in his explanation, "But I couldn't just…put him back after I told him I would help."

Storm gave his shoulder a light punch, beaming at him. "I heard from Free that you threatened Jett and Prince with sinking the mission and allowing them to be caught. You didn't really do that did you?"

"I did. I was still in a what-would-the-girls-do mind set."

"Well, I know *someone* who's already done that once in the past." Storm chuckled, looking at Beth who winked mischievously.

"Let's not go into that story just yet."

Raoul smiled, looking down at Palmer and Malana on the floor as Malana showed him how to colour inside of the lines, wings splayed out behind her.

"I couldn't just leave him."

"And you didn't." The pride glittered in her pale-green eyes and she drew him into a swift tight hug, cocooning her wings around him. Raoul initially tensed in surprise, but he liked that it made him feel warm and safe, even when she let him go and ruffled his hair up. "I am so very proud of you. I'm sure we'll really make an alpha out of you yet Raoul."

In a childish fit of jealousy, Palmer leapt up from the floor, yapping at Storm to keep off of his '*alpa*'.

"You're gonna go far kid." Said Wilny.

"He's not going to go far unless he eats properly." Amell laughed, striding into the living room with a tray full of freshly made bacon and egg sandwiches for the girls and Raoul, and peach sorbet for Wilny and Malana.

"They told me you were a vegetarian and I had no idea what that was." He said with an embarrassed smile and catching a sly look from Kat. "You are able to eat fruit, right? Not just vegetables?"

"I am. Thank you."

"Yeah, if he eats meat or dairy, he throws up everywhere and acts super dramatic about it."

"*Kat!*"

"It's true." Kat said with a shrug, squirming a little as Wilny elbowed her in the side, to which she retaliated by pulling out an iridescent feather and the two called it even. The tormenting brought a flutter of relief across him, glad that despite the changes and things he had missed from his weeks away, not everything was different. However, he was still uneasy as the Rogues tucked into their lunch and chatted about the various things that had gone on, Amell sitting and joining them on the remaining armchair, doing his best not to knock anything over with his huge wings.

"How's Ada?" Storm asked, switching from her squashed perch on the sofa to sit on the floor and preen Lana's wings. "Did he finally finish up his fishpond?"

Wilny nodded nervously, pinching the bridge of his nose as the brain-freeze set in from the sorbet. "Y-yeah it's all finished. Though he kept on going on about how hard it was to find authentic statuary and mosaic tiles for the inside ponds."

"He is such a history geek."

"He offered for us to go visit him at some point in November."

"Nice. And since both you and Raoul speak Spanish it shouldn't be too hard to get around."

"Spain in winter is cold though." Complained Beth, lightly slapping Palmer's hand as he reached up to try and play with her bionics again. "Puppy, no." She scolded, "I need these legs unchewed."

"But you aren't using them." He protested with a squeak. Shooting the Canid-cub a sharp glare and a vicious hiss, she sent him leaping into Raoul and Kat's laps for safety from the Owl.

"Beth don't be so mean." Kat laughed, comforting the toddler with Raoul.

"I don't like small people."

Lana looked up at Beth and lightly hit her leg with a wing.

"Oi." She said, pouting angrily. "I am small."

"You're stellar Lana, so long as you stay in my good books."

"Beth. *Idioms.*" Raoul sighed. "We've talked about this."

Lana continued to pout until she noticed Wilny on the end of the sofa, looking very sombre and contemplative. Shuffling across the carpet to him she tugged on his shining feathers until he looked up at her.

"*Ça va?*" She asked, tilting her head to one side in curiosity. He grimaced to himself and cleared his throat, speaking in a soft voice.

"I know this is going to be a little off topic – sort of –, but I kind of feel that it's time for all of you to know about my team."

The adults in the room all fidgeted awkwardly, knowing how much of a sensitive topic it was for him.

"You want to talk about it?" Beth asked tentatively, keenly aware of the sharp warning look in Storm's eye.

"Will," Storm cautioned him, "you don't have to right now if you're uncomfortable."

"I probably never will be comfortable with it Storm. But it's about time I did." He took a moment to breathe as the Rogues grew quiet, giving him their full attention and support before he began to speak. Palmer wriggled a little in Kat's arms, wondering why the atmosphere had changed so quickly, and Malana patiently sat on the floor at his feet, staring up at him with curious golden eyes.

He was hesitant, doing his best to stop his wings from trembling in anxiety and fixing his gaze on the corner of a painting on the wall in front of him, afraid to meet anyone's eye.

"Their…their names were Fury, Eddie, Rainbow, and Featherhead. And they were my family. Together we made up the last Ruby-One team. AA03." He began. "We…we were a bit eclectic and worked well together in our own way. Featherhead was a Canid, Rainbow a VE-RA Preternatural, Fury a transhuman DRACO Preternatural, and Eddie an Avio."

"Why did you call your canid Featherhead?" Asked Kat gently, passing Palmer to Raoul so that he would sit still. "Wouldn't that have suited an Avio more?"

Wilny gave her a little nervous laugh and knotting his fingers together around his knee to stop his leg from bouncing.

"We all named each other for kinda silly reasons because we didn't really have much of a gage of what names were meant to be, so we had some really odd ones like Shoe, Arris, Hamburger, and Zyzzyva. On the first night I knew him, he ripped open a pillow in his sleep and woke up covered in feathers, so we called him Featherhead from there onwards."

"And Eddie? That's quite a human name compared to those ones."

"It was short for Thomas Edison."

"What?"

"Well, we called him Shrike to start with, but then when we had a science class we learnt about electricity, and because he could shock people like Storm could, we called him that instead because it was funny at the time." He began to laugh a little more, running his fingers through his hair and scrubbing it up into a mess of brown and iridescent blue waves. "Though his full name was actually Thomas Tesla Kelvin Einstein Westinghouse Hertz Volta Bell Faraday Ohm…Edison. Or Eddie for short."

"You're joking."

"It was a joke." Wilny shrugged. "Every time he messed around or do something stupid, we'd add another name to the list- well it was actually Fury who was our proto-dad and the oldest, was the one who kept adding names."

Raoul gave him a gentle little nudge, clearing his throat to speak though there was a slightly constricted tone to it.

"Fury was the oldest, but you were leader? That seems strange to me."

"That's not that much different than what we have here Raoul." Storm shrugged, shifting sitting positions on the floor so that she could tie Lana's hair up into thick bunches.

He looked surprised. "Really?"

"Yeah, I'm twenty-two and technically in-charge, while Beth is twenty-four and Wilny is twenty-six."

"You're twenty-six?" Raoul asked in shock, staring agog between Storm and Wilny. "I thought that you were the same age as Kat!"

"It's his pretty face. It's a trick." Kat mused, reaching across and pinching Wilny's cheeks. "Though I'm kinda surprised it hasn't been mashed up some more after being through Core."

"Excuse you J-Pop! I took great care to make sure I kept these good looks." He said dramatically, breaking his focus on the wall to cast Kat a playfully disapproving face. A spark of his usual self, returning.

"You don't get to be top of the Ruby ranks without some resilience and good self-preservation techniques."

"Or maybe people thought you were too much of a delicate little hummingbird to harm."

"I'll have you know, the Aztecs believed their warriors would be reincarnated as hummingbirds, so ha! That makes me the best kind of *warbird* they could have ever had!"

"So, what was it like to be a Ruby?" Amell chuckled. "Was it really as raunchy and chaotic as everyone makes it out to be?"

Wilny threw his head back and laughed.

"Oh, let me tell you…" He said with a nostalgic smile. The Rogues relaxed, listening to several of his stories from Core, allowing him to go on into ramblings about his first memories of being a new recruit with the rank of Quartz as well as going off onto a tangent into smaller missions they were sent on, being careful not to be too graphic in front of the two children.

"We…we had never actually been against Sapphire-One before but we had met and argued in the past. Their team leader, god I hated him so much. Friend he was called, but if ever I had a nemesis it was him. If I ever come across like I hate lions, Kat, I'm sorry, but it's entirely his fault." He was still chuckling, but it had turned to a nervous edge. "Sapphire teams are trained for stealth and support and thought they were so much superior to us Rubies who are trained as shock troops and built to go in hard and fast. Joke's on them because we beat their asses at almost everything."

He stopped chuckling and swallowed, gaze becoming fixed upon the painting corner again and leg tremoring. Heart drumming, his chest tightened in pain, vision becoming blurry as tears bubbled up again.

"This…this event though…we had rumours that it was going to be part of the Diamond selection and they would be watching how well we performed. We were meant to be evenly matched. Fury was our primary muser, and I was the second."

"You don't have to overwhelm yourself bro." Said Amell, giving Wilny's shoulder a warm reassuring shake, "You can stop for now if it's getting too much."

"You don't understand! I loved them all– Feather and Rainbow especially– and whenever they got hurt, I'd attack those that hurt them, and he made me- I never wanted to- it was that fucking Frigatebird!" He choked, head pounding from the stress. "They must have cheated, given him Nitro or something. I couldn't even move! I couldn't-"

Lana climbed up onto his lap, hugging him tight.

"S'allright to cry." She cooed in a soft voice, gently stroking his hair. "You can cry."

Sobbing, he held Malana tight as she did her best to calm him down. Without even realising it, he found himself surrounded on all sides by the Rogues in support and comfort, all there for him.

Kat leant against his left shoulder, with Raoul reaching across her lap to take his arm, while Amell took the right and covered his shoulder with a huge warm wing. Beth couldn't reach and wasn't prepared to throw herself into the group hug, but she still extended one robotic bird leg out and patted his knee carefully to show her support. Storm knelt before him with her hand upon his knee also, sweeping out her own wings over them all in a blanket of feathers.

They remained with him until is sobs had quietened, offering tissues, water, and honey. None of them pushed him to calm down, he needed to cry to take away some of the pressure that had built up. After a few minutes he stopped, snotty nosed and sniffling.

"When my brothers were...were murdered," Raoul started quietly, breaking the quiet, "I thought; *This is it. There is nothing else for me in life.*"

Wilny's breath caught in his throat. He snapped his head up with the other Rogues to look at Raoul, finding the Canid with a thousand-yard stare and tears pouring down his face.

"I could have fought back against those CY-NX clones. I could have helped turn the tide...or died with them, but instead I froze up and watched, then said I didn't attack on principle when really, I was just scared. I should have just done as I was ordered to do." He said with a breaking voice.

"Raoul..."

"Alpa?" Palmer said in panic, unsure of what to do. Alphas never cried as far as he knew.

"*Desolé.*" He choked, shaking his head and recoiling away from the Hummingbird. "I didn't mean to take anything away from you Wilny. It just...made me think of my brothers."

"It could have been different if I stayed with my family too." Kat sighed, rubbing Raoul's furred ear and shoulder and showing Palmer how to calm his Alpha down. "Maybe I'd have been killed, or caught, or held them off long enough for Storm to arrive."

"At least you tried to do something." Grumbled Raoul, scrubbing at his eyes.

Lana looked down at her hands.

"I could have helped…" She whispered.

They had all lost family, Wilny realised with a sudden shock of cold horror. Kat had spoken about it in passing and was more open about her regrets, but he had not thought much of how much it hurt her to talk about it. Raoul had never spoken about his brothers beyond Beth's initial needling, and Wilny all, but forgotten what was said, and Lana; She had said nothing at all. He'd been far too caught up in his own loss to realise they were all in the same boat.

Even Storm, though she didn't include her own regrets into the discussion and remained quiet throughout it all. Wilny could see from the white knuckles, the hard-set jaw, and her cold calmness, that she was thinking about every decision that she had ever made, though he knew little of what they could have been.

"We all could have done things differently and it's easy to work yourselves up with saying '*What if, what if*.'" Amell said in his calm mellow tone, soothing them taking hold of Wilny's hand with a reaffirming smile. He was clearly pained in thinking about his own losses, but he kept control over his voice. "I could have tried harder with all of it. But I'm here now and I can always make the future better rather than letting regret chain me down."

Raoul laughed bitterly. "I wish I had your optimism and *c'est la vie* attitude, Amell."

"I wouldn't call it optimism, but it's the only practical thing left that I can do." Amell said with a self-conscious shrug. "I've already told Wilny here about the promises I've made and intend to keep. I've no lofty goals of world peace, just small things that I hope can give me peace and closure."

The Rogues nodded, looking to one another with quiet glances of reassurance.

"Do you regret anything Beth?" Kat asked across to Beth who, like Storm, had remained uncharacteristically quiet throughout the conversation, even leaving her phone and laptop to one side so that she was entirely focused on the Rogues.

"No."

"Wow. You've the body, heart, *and* mind of a machine, Beth."

"Because I've made it my purpose to keep you lot safe and I don't have time to regret every bad choice I've made when I could be preventing future ones from happening." She responded sharply.

It was an unintended jab, which Storm scolded her for silently with a sharp tilt of her head. There was a mute exchange between the Rogue and her technician that the others didn't fully understand, but it caused Beth to wither beneath Storm's cold ire. Composing herself, Beth sat up in her armchair, adjusting her uneven wings and avoiding Storm's gaze.

"You all need closure in your own ways. If that's finding where you came from, helping your friends, whatever it may be, I can do my best to help, but I can't promise I can solve it for you or that it will make anything better." Beth said calmly, folding her hands across her lap. They looked between each other, slightly bewildered at her offer.

"I'd like to find my family." Said Amell eventually, rolling his shoulders and rousing the feathers across his shoulders. "My human one. Before the wings. They may be a world away, but I want to see where I came from and if all's well."

"I can do that." Beth nodded. "Kat? Do you want me to keep on trying to find Tanto and Tachi?"

Kat shook her head after a small moment of contemplation.

"No." She said, wiping her eyes of the tears threatening to boil over. "You've done your best."

"I can still have the Japanese groups search for them regardless. Raoul? Is there anything to help you."

"I want to help the Rogues. In any way possible."

"Well, you can start by house training your new puppy not to steal my bionics."

Palmer stuck his tongue out at her, earning him a hiss in reprisal from Beth. There was a small laugh from the Rogues, the mood lightening as the burdens were shared among them all. He looked to Amell with a smile and small thanking nod, realising that he was still holding his hand tightly. Bashfully, Wilny let go and cleared his throat.

"I want to try and talk about my team a little more in future, some of the good and funny stuff at least." He said gently, avoiding Amell's eye. Sitting up a little he brushed a loose feather back down into line on Lana's wing.

"Do you want to talk about anything Lana?" He asked her gently.

Lana shook her head. "I want to help."

"That's sweet of you, but are you alright?"

"I am. I have you." She said softly, hugging Wilny tight. Tears immediately poured down Wilny's cheeks and the ex-soldier choked up in emotion all over again.

Storm smiled at her family of teary-eyed rogues, all comforting one another with reassurances and offers of help.

"I'll get some tea and honey." She said with a grin, getting to her feet and shaking her wings out. Leaving them together she picked up the left-over plates and headed to the kitchen. Half listening to the ongoing conversation, she put the kettle on and began to wash up.

'Thank you for helping' She texted Beth from the kitchen.

Beth responded quickly and subtly.

'Only doing what you would have done. You didn't need to put me on the spot like that.'

'Help them with what they need.'

'You're angry. Do you need to talk?'

Storm regarded the text with a clenched jaw, using the boiling kettle and rummaging around the kitchen for mugs to disguise her hesitation at responding.

'No. I'll be fine.' She sent.

24

A glimmer of normality had returned to the Rogue's lives since Raoul and Wilny's return. A steady routine of learning, helping to keep the house in order, exercising and engaging in hobbies. It took them both a while to help Palmer adjust to the less than extravagant lifestyle, he had been living in Risio. However, he did enjoy amount of freedom he was allowed, driving him and Malana to spend almost every day outside in the parks running around and adventuring. When they couldn't stay outside, they would head to the headquarters and use the gym and crèche, though Raoul grew increasingly hostile and agitated when faced with the Rioteers. Knowing what Rex had done had enraged and concerned him.

"What if he does something to hurt the Rogues?" He had said Wilny in a hushed whisper. "I need to be strong enough to help. Train me to fight like you."

Reluctant at first but seeing an ever-growing necessity for Raoul to be able to defend himself, Wilny accepted with the help of Kat and Amell. The headquarters did have a gym and its sparring rings available for them to use, but at Storm's suggestion they would use the city as an open arena for more in-the-field training. Within a fortnight of intensive training there was a marked difference from the combat skills he had received from Core. Leaning on the edge of the ring, Wilny watched Raoul's footwork carefully as he spared with Amell, whilst the kids stood with Kat and Anthony also watching the sparring and cheering Raoul on.

"Go Alpa! Go!" The Canid-cub yipped, wiggling his hands and feet manically from Kat's shoulders whilst Caesar watched in confusion at him.

"Alpa? Wassat?" The other cub asked, bushy tail thumping hard against Anthony's back.

With the widest grin as Raoul swept his leg low beneath Amell, sending him crashing to the floor, Palmer cheered. "He's my Alpa!"

With a small '*ah*' of understanding, Caesar reached down and patted Anthony's cheek with pride.

"He's *my* Alpa."

Leaping back onto his feet, Amell swore loudly as Raoul landed a solid punch to his floating ribs, earning him a cheer from Wilny. Ducking and rolling, he was doing well to avoid Amell's heavy blows, keeping light on his feet and now allowing himself to resort to Canid-like attacks of swiping and biting as he was trained to do.

"He needs to straighten his wrist out and bend his knees more." A familiar voice commented from behind Wilny. "At least that's what Roux would say."

With a smile, he turned to face Comet and did a double take at her new appearance.

"Comet! How are you?" He asked, looking her up and down with pleasant surprise. Dressed in what looked like clothes borrowed from Roux, with their dark punk style covered with spikes, and her once waist length black hair had been cut into a short pixie-cut to complete the sharp look.

"Better. Not cured, but better." She smiled, embracing him warmly. Surprised by the softness and warmth, Wilny gently reciprocated the hug until she let him go and brushed his hair from his face, checking him over. "But how about you? You travelled to Spain, right?"

"Yes, it was relaxing. And I'm about the same. Better, but not cured."

Comet gave him a sympathetic nod, brushing her fringe from her plum-coloured eyes and joining Wilny in watching Raoul, although he struggled to look away. She seemed different from when they had walked in the park. Head held a little higher, eyes a little brighter, wings no longer trailing along the ground. The scars that were once raw and pink were little more than shiny strikes across her skin, healed and fading.

"You look...different." He noted with a nod to her attire.

"It was Roux's idea. It actually makes me feel a lot better. Safer"

The leather jacket with the silver spikes did seem to help with her, '*Don't touch me*' aura, as no doubt her new teammate did.

"So, I hear you've teamed with Kathy." He stated, eyeing the Vulture in the background, lingering beside Storm who appeared to be in the middle of a discussion with Free and Roux.

"That's right."

"You're okay with being with her?"

"Of course. She's just a scared teenager and wants to have her babies back and feel safe. She needs help and helping her gives me purpose."

"And if she tries-"

Comet shook her head. Certainty in her eyes as she gazed up at him. "Kathy's got too much love for Storm to do anything bad."

"Love?" He let loose a bark of uncontrolled laughter that drew Raoul's attention away for two seconds and earning him a clip round the head from Amell to concentrate. "Kathy's in love with Storm?"

"What's the word...admiration. She feels believed in by her and wants to be better to make her proud. She likes having this as her purpose in life."

Now distracted from the fight, he turned away and began to walk with Comet around the ring towards the doors. Upon seeing Wilny abandon his job, Kat swore under her breath at him then began to cheer louder for the Hound as he was once again thrown down by Amell.

"Come on Raoul! Up off your arse! You don't want to be shown up in front of Palmer now do you?" She shouted, bouncing Palmer up and down on her shoulders so he waved.

Wilny snorted in bewilderment. "Sure. As if she's being honest about that."

"Watch her face." Comet sternly directed him. Humouring the other Hummingbird with a reluctant sigh, he did as she bid. Analysing Kathy's behaviour. Dancing a little as she spoke to Storm, smiling coyly, with hopeful eyes fixed solely upon the Rogue.

"Hmm..." Contemplative, he bit his lip. The display seemed genuine, but he wasn't convinced that she was completely trustworthy and didn't feel comfortable with Comet being with her. "I'm sure we all look at someone like that."

"She may not seem like it, but she's very loyal."

"Even to her psychopathic boyfriend?"

"Hey now. It took a lot of talking with Jenna to help her realise that Teal was abusive and manipulative to her, she's understanding that now and regrets following him. She doesn't regret the babies though."

With a suspicious glance at Kathy, he double checked her behaviour. She still had a puppy eyed look about her and seemed eager to talk to Storm. It was hard for Wilny to imagine Kathy as being a good mother, but he had no way to judge it.

Comet scrunched her face up as she tried to alliterate a thought, "It's like…Storm's a werewolf."

It came so left out of field that Wilny burst into laughter at her comment.

"I-I mean like- *Don't laugh!* I'm being metaphorical!" She shoved him hard enough in the chest to make him wobble a little.

"Okay, Comet, explain what you mean please."

"What I mean is, werewolves supposedly bite, or scratch people and they turn into werewolves too, yes?"

"According to movies they do." It took a lot of effort to bite back his amused smirk.

"Well, that's what she does, except they don't turn into werewolves o-or Avios…I uh…it…sounded better in my head." Embarrassed she tugged at her hair. Narrowing his eyes and mulling the concept over in his head, he tried to gleam what she meant from the analogy.

"So, you're saying Storm *metaphorically* bites people and turns them into Rogues?"

"She uses words and charm rather than fangs and claws, infecting people with thoughts and feelings so that they change. Influences them somehow."

"I…guess?"

"You're laughing at me. I shouldn't have said anything."

"I'm not laughing, I swear." He tried to assure her before bursting into another fit of giggles again. Provoked by his laughter at her, she beat her narrow wings on him, making him shield his head with his arm and forcing him still laughing to the ground.

"Comet! I got your honey!" Kathy shouted, running over to the two Hummingbirds. Desisting in her assault on Wilny, Comet turned to the girl and smiled warmly, accepting the gift from her. Being so close to Kathy made Wilny tense.

"Thank you! Also! I thought of some more boy names!" Said Comet, placing herself between the two and pushing Wilny back with the slow extension of her wings. Kathy's eyes widened expectantly, beaming at Comet.

"Mika, Ryker, or Theka."

"Theka?"

"Because it's an anagram of Kathy."

"I spell my name with a Y not an E, but I like it." The girls smiled amicably between each other, before Kathy glanced past Comet, seemingly just noticing Wilny and handing out a bottle of honey towards him.

"Here. You like honey too, since you're a…y'know…hummingbird." She said with thinly veiled nonchalance that attempted to disguise either wariness. It was an attempt at civility at least.

"Thanks." He reciprocated the cool indifference, pocketing the honey for later. "Did you apologise to Amell."

"I tried. He didn't accept it."

"You killed his family, I'm sure he won't."

"I didn't kill them personally." She shrugged.

"But you helped." He seethed, the feathers across his neck and shoulders rose in anger at her disregard of her actions. "Are you completely oblivious to the consequences of your actions?"

"I did what I had to do to survive at the time, but I've learnt from my mistakes."

"I'm sure you have. What a wonderful example you'll set for your kids."

Baited by his goading, Kathy's shaggy wings half-flared of their own accord and she drew her fist up as though to strike him.

'Stop. Please. Don't fight here.'

It was a clear and forceful thought, ringing in his ears with Comet's stern voice and temporarily dazing him. Realising what it was, he pushed back against the thoughts cast by Comet.

"Both of you, stop." Comet chided aloud, pushing Kathy gently back by her shoulder. "Now we really should go, we're meant to be keeping an eye on the crèche today."

The sudden burst of imposed thoughts seemed to daze the Vulture, leaving her with a doe eyed gaze. The expression gave Wilny the faintest theory, from having seen it earlier, that there was a reason Storm had prompted Comet and Kathy to form a group. A loud pained yelp from the rings drew Wilny's thoughts back to what he was meant to be doing and he stepped back from the girls.

"I'll talk to you later Comet." He said with a smile to the girl.

"Will you tell me about Spain later?"

"Of course." And as he spun on his heels, he was just in time to see Raoul be thrown across the length of the ring like a ragdoll much to his horror. The boy slammed down hard, bouncing across the rest of the ring.

"Be gentle Amell!" Wilny shouted, charging back to his spot by the ringside to help, "He's just a kid!"

"He was running away!" Amell called back, flourishing his arms and wings wide. "Throw him back at me, he's still conscious!"

"Raoul, *as-tu besoin d'aide?*" Malana asked, leaning over the boundary ropes and looking down at the dazed Hound. Raoul shook his head, clutching at his bruised ribs and trembling with exhaustion.

"*Anglais*, Malana, *Anglais.*"

"Help?" She repeated, giggling as Raoul rolled slowly onto his hands and knees. Wilny lifted the ropes up, reaching out a hand to help Raoul as Amell heckled the Hound whilst he rolled out of the ring and onto the floor with a thud.

With a loud and aching groan, Raoul stuck his hand up into the air with a lone middle finger raised high for Amell to see, before letting it collapse down onto his chest.

"Kick his arse." He commanded the girl in a hushed whisper, tentatively touching his arms, hissing in pain at each new-found bruise. Lana's smile grew, and she flexed her wings and fingers in excitement.

"Whoa there Lana, you're not going to fight Amell are you?" He caught the girl by her feathers, pulling her back before she slipped all the way under the ropes.

"*S'il te plait laisse-moi jouer avec Amell.*" She smiled coyly, amber eyes bright and glittering with mischief. Storm's influence had rubbed off on her too much.

"I will do, but let me warm him up for you first, Sunbeam." He brushed her hair back, swinging his leg over into the ring.

With an energized clap of his hands and a bounce in his step Amell danced about the ring.

"Finally!" Amell laughed, rolling his shoulders and bouncing on the balls of his feet enthusiastically with little punches being thrown at the air. "I get to make you sweat."

A grin growing across Wilny's face he flexed his fingers, curling them into a fist as he strode towards Amell.

"You won't get a chance 'cause you'll be on your back the whole time."

"One of my favourite positions. Give me your best shot pretty boy." He smirked, stretching his arms and wings wide, exposing his scar covered chest to Wilny for him to strike. Obligingly Wilny lunged at the man, fist striking at his lower ribs with a forceful thwack that rippled down the length of Wilny's arm.

Amell barely blinked at the hit. With a disappointed sigh, Amell caught his arm, sweeping his legs out from beneath him and tossing him across the ring. Rolling onto his feet, Wilny gathered himself up and rushed Amell again, darting under his swinging arms to throw some hits to Amell's side. He barely even tried to block the kicks and punches that Wilny was landing with growing fury, his pectoral muscles were so dense that it acted like armour.

Enraged, he kicked Amell's inner knee, knocking his leg out from under him, aiming to elbow him in the throat as he toppled, but Amell lashed his arm out. Fist connecting with the side of his head, Wilny reeled back clutching his face, barely having the chance to block the second incoming punch from Amell. For such a large man, he didn't expect that Amell could move with such speed.

Amell grabbed at his ankle as he stumbled backward, gripping tightly and with little effort put into it, flung Wilny across the room.

"Will! Wings out!"

On command, his wings fwooshed out and thrumming, Wilny caught himself before he flew into the brick wall, hovering several feet above the ring with a blur of green and indigo. The boys looked round to see Storm perched on the edge of the ring, grinning at them both.

"They're limbs! Not accessories!" She barked. "Use them!"

Wisps of training echoed back on him as Wilny scrutinized what weaknesses and advantages there were to flying.

There was no room in the vaulted chamber for Amell to fly and catch him in the air, but there was also no height for Wilny to mimic Storm's aerial attacks, though he had a nimbleness that Amell lacked.

Speedily lapping the chamber several times from above, he looped over Amell's head and with a hard kick, took the Eagle' legs out from under him and gave him a wink of triumph as he scored a solid punch upon Amell's face before he hit the floor. The small audience within the gym cheered as Wilny took off again. As he grandstanded proudly, the Eagle had gotten back up onto his feet, jumped up and plucked him from the air and with a flourishing spin, flung Wilny back out of the ring.

Frustrated and heart beginning to reach a painfully fast rhythm, Wilny landed on his feet, he came in to attack again, darting under and behind Amell's huge wing into what he believed to be a blind spot on the giant Eagle. Amell swung a left hook down across at where Wilny should have been standing, his momentum on his swing spinning him round, brown and white wing sweeping out and slamming Wilny across the back.

Tumbling forward with the force, Wilny fell to his hands and knees. A laugh and a sharp slap across his arse shocked him into standing and grabbing where Amell had hit. Throwing his head back Amell laughed heartily as the tips of Wilny's ears turned red and flustered he struggled to regain his stance.

"You're a fun fight bro," Amell grinned, sweeping his dark hair back from his face, "but you can at least try a *little* harder, you'll enjoy it more."

A prickle ran across Amell's scalp followed by a sudden dizziness as everything in his vision suddenly became incomprehensible for several seconds. As soon as he felt the pain of being both uppercutted in the jaw and simultaneously kneed in the crotch, the dizziness abated.

Out of surprise at the sudden mental and physical attack, Amell threw his left wing out before him, clipping Wilny's head hard as Wilny tried to get in closer. Black spots across leaped before Wilny's vision and he hit the decking nose first, trapping a wing beneath him.

Amell's head throbbed, and the world seemed to spin still. Then the ground withdrew from beneath his feet and Amell was wrenched into the air by his ankle with a shriek, face slamming against the ring floor on the way up.

"Time out! Time out!" He slurred cradling his head and flailing his wings as he hung upside down, suspended in mid-air whilst the watchers cheered. Rolling over to free his wing, Wilny frowned at the ceiling until Malana's face appeared above him and she began pulling at his arm to help him sit up. It wasn't a mystery at what had happened then.

Patting the little girl's shoulder, he gave her a bleary smile. "Lana, you didn't have to." He said to her, to which she just shrugged and scurried behind him to check on his feathers that had become tussled in the fight.

"You know Amell...I prefer you this way." Wilny chuckled, looking up at the upside down Amell and wiping the blood from his lip and nose.

"Well hung you mean?" Amell winked playfully. Wilny spluttered, face flushing red.

"Wha- No! I mean- fuck you Amell."

"Please Wilny, there are children here, maybe later."

"THAT'S NOT WHAT I-"

"Alright, I think Lana's proved she's the strongest." Storm clapped, leaping over the ring ropes in a single bound. "Time to clear out. Lana. Put Amell down."

Reluctantly, Malana dropped Amell as she helped Wilny to leave the ring and tagging Kat in to fight with Storm.

Whilst the boys cleaned up after their fight, the others watched transfixed by Kat and Storm's sparring. Quick, fluid movements, sweeping legs and powerful kicks, blocking punches and wing flourishes that aimed to sweep the other's feet out from under them or knock each other back.

Palmer quickly lost interest in the girls' capoeira and began tugging on Raoul's shirt.

"I'm go play with Cease." He stated, pointing to Caesar who began to squirm impatiently on Anthony's shoulders.

"With the other children in the crèche?"

"Sí!"

"Do you want me to walk you over there?"

"No. Cease knows the way." His tail wagged excitedly behind him as Anthony set his son down onto his feet. Both Cubs bounced energetically, waiting for an answer from both of the older Canids. With a glance to Anthony, they shared a smirk.

"Alright, be good both of you."

Both Cubs yipped with glee and Raoul watched as Palmer trundled off down the hall behind them that led to the crèche after the slightly older Caesar, making sure that the toddler didn't trip and fall as he regularly did whenever he walked too fast.

Seeing the flag of caramel that was Palmer's tail, disappear through the doors, Raoul turned his attention back to the fight. Or at least he would have done.

A strange scent caught his attention.

To the left-hand hall that joined into the gym and rings, he noticed what he thought was a Coyote-Canid walking towards them, at a slow yet purposeful pace. It stared blankly ahead with glazed orange eyes; head cocked awkwardly with maw agape. The hair on the nape of his neck stood up as it drew closer. He recognised the Coyote.

The Rogues had killed it.

Snarling, Raoul rushed the Coyote and tackled it to the ground. He tried to seize the Canid's jaws and force it to the floor, but for a dead Canid it was surprisingly strong, able to throw him back. It squirmed on the floor, unable to stand as Raoul relaunched himself at it with swiping claws and tearing into its chest like it was paper. His claws hit plastic and metal within the chest and a sickly lavender stench gushed from the wound followed by putrefied flesh.

If he hadn't of been grabbed about his waist by Amell he would have stumbled back from the overpowering smell. He knew what the smell was now, and it horrified him.

"Raoul! What are you-"

"Cybers!" Raoul gagged, wiping his hand on Amell's bicep in disgust. "Delta's infiltrated the headquarters!"

Amell dropped the boy and stared down at the corpse.

"*Oh shit.*" He said softly, crouching and peeling back the skin that Raoul had sliced open with his claws. The Coyote lunged up, jaws snapping and arms flailing with the rigidity of an animatronic. As it snapped at Amell's face, his response was a single swiping punch to its head and crushing it against the floor like a grape.

No blood was spilt from either its crushed head or its chest as steel alloy replaced the ribs and sternum. The only organic thing about it was the head, a death mask of flesh taxidermied to a robotic skeleton to give the appearance of life.

Bounding over Storm examined the Coyote quickly with a taloned foot, with Kat, Wilny and Malana cautiously following close behind with a few of the more curious Synths in the room. Wilny's eyes widened at the sight of the exposed metal ribcage and he held Malana close to him, although she herself didn't bat an eyelid. Other Synths were just as horrified by the sight as Wilny was.

Many had only heard of Cybers through rumours, that this was the fate of any Synth who didn't behave or who ARCDA had no need of any more. Seeing it for themselves, seeing the skin of a Canid wrapped around a metal skull, its body powered by mixed hydraulics and electronics was horrifying to see.

"I recognised him. We- Storm fought these dogs before." Said Raoul, trying to justify his reasons for attacking.

Kat looked down, both horrified and enraged by the Cyber, taking a knife and gently slicing open the skin along its cheek to reveal foam padding over a mechanical jaw directly beneath.

"But…Owen said he cleaned the bodies up after we killed them." She said looking to Storm with dawning realisation. "If they used these bodies, which means the other three might be-"

Storm straightened up, her feathers bristling in fury.

"Do you remember what their scents were?" She said quickly to Raoul.

"I remember the Wolf, but there was another Coyote and a Fox."

"Kat, Amell, hunt the Fox!" Ordered Storm quickly. "Wilny, you and Malana on other Coyote! Raoul, Wolf with me!"

"Take Lana?" Wilny looked incredulous. "But she-"

"If she can fuck up a car then she can fuck up a Cyber, now go!"

"What should we do?" Asked a Preter who had been standing close by. Other onlookers, other Canids, Preters and Pards nodded, wanting to help the Rogues to defend the headquarters.

"If they sent one then there's going to be a whole bunch more." Storm said firmly to the attentive Synths, looking to Anthony for reassurance. "Be sure when you think someone is a Cyber before you do anything."

Anthony gave a low growl of approval, beginning to assist in directing people to help, instructing several people to go guard the creche and the most vulnerable of the headquarters' members first and as their priority, sending them scattering throughout the warren of tunnels. Storm grabbed Raoul by the shoulder and proceeding to drag him forward to find the Wolf as the knowledge of the Cyber intrusion spread.

Kat swiftly found the Fox-Canid, lurking quietly in a group of other Canids. The scent of lavender amongst the dogs was easy to detect now she knew what she was looking for, but with so many Canids and people, individual scents became masked and blended together. It was only the strange twitch of its eyes and tail that gave it's cyber-nature away, and she quietly disabled it with a jab to the base of its neck, which she then snapped as it fell to its knees.

Wilny and Malana however, were not so discreet as upon finding the second Coyote lurking in the main hall, Wilny body slammed it to the floor in an attempt to restrain it.

It gave a distorted screech, head turning around unnaturally to snap its jaws on Wilny's face, only to be saved by Malana who decapitated it. Its head rolled across the floor slightly and the limbs continued to twitch for several seconds whilst all around respondent screeches echoed across the headquarters followed by screaming, howling, snarling, and clatter of gunfire.

"There's more than four!" Shouted a Preter to Wilny as she tackled a Cyber wearing Rioteer clothing and masks, after he had turned and shot his comrades in the head.

With the chaos ensuing around them, it was now impossible to tell who was an infiltrator and who was just a panicked bystander as automatic weapons were fired, spraying everywhere upon the Synths and Rioteers alike.

Leaping to his feet, Wilny span to grab Malana to drag her to safety, but found her running headlong at a Reptile, wrestling a gun away from a Rioteer.

"Lana stop!"

Ignoring him she tore the two away from each other, and flung them to opposite ends of the room, and slicing up the gun.

"No blood, no person." She nodded, to the two both of whom were beginning to bleed. "They bleed."

Her calm resolve was terrifying, but he felt proud that she was so quick to understand and make a judgement, far better than most of the adults in the room.

Elsewhere, Raoul and Storm had tracked the Wolf down, chasing it from the armoury which had been ransacked by the infiltrators and residents alike, and between scattering startled people towards the crèche. The crèche monitors had been quick enough to close the bulkhead doors, but not quick enough to stop a Cyber from being caught between them and keeping it open with its steel bones. The children inside were all screaming in terror, trying to hurry out of the warren boltholes, which were only small enough for one person to run through at a time, making the evacuation of the frightened children far too slow.

The Wolf wrenched the doors apart with a semi-mechanical roar, forcing itself into the room as Raoul leapt on the Cyber trying to tear through the thick ballistic weave that surrounded its body to get to the wiring.

Comet was frozen to the spot on the sight of the Wolf. Pale faced with horror and trauma, she didn't even hear as the remaining kids began to scream and cling to her and Kathy at the sight of its mechanical snapping jaws.

"Comet! Get the kids out of here!" Storm shouted down the as the Wolf threw off Raoul and began to try charge towards them, only for Storm to assist by pouncing upon it. "They can get out through the medical ward!"

She ducked under its arm, shocking it with a punch to the chest and disabling it for several seconds, giving her enough time to kick it onto its back and for Raoul to lunge forward and tear off its lower jaw.

Slapping Comet on the back, Kathy urged the kids forward to the door, able to get the remainder of the children out and around the Wolf Cyber, save for Palmer who kicked the Cyber in the shin until Raoul snatched both him and Caesar up and ran with him after the crowd of children, leaving Storm to deactivate it with a powerful electric shock.

They scrambled along the corridor trying to avoid the still scattering panicked people and the injured lying on the floor. Two children holding hands slipped in a splash of blood across the floor and fell, falling at the feet of an armed Cyber, disguised as a

Rioteer in full uniform who had been prowling an adjoining hallway. The kids struggled to their feet to race after the group, only to fall again as the Cyber robotically turned to assess what had collided with it and aimed at them.

Kathy spun on her heels, driving her broad shaggy wings down to cover the distance in a single bound. She pounced over the two fallen children to kick the infiltrator onto its back, before scooping them up into her arms and running after the rest.

The Cyber sat up and fired at them, and Kathy was brought to the floor.

"No! No, no, no!" Comet braked hard with her wings and skidded to a halt. It fired three more times in short bursts, struggling to

"Raoul get the kids to safety!" She ordered as the children and Raoul passed her. Fist clenched Comet ran at the Cyber and struck it square in the face with a harsh metallic thunk. The Cyber's head snapped back as Comet wrenched the gun away. Turning it upon the Cyber she shot the Cyber several times in the head until there was nothing, but the empty click of the trigger and an unidentifiably mutilated corpse that reeked of lavender and sandalwood.

"Kathy?" Comet threw the gun down and raced back to her friend. "Kathy are you hurt!"

"I'll be fine, make sure the kids are okay." The Vulture wheezed, trying to push herself up off the floor as blood pooled, and passing the kids to Comet. "Just make sure the kids are alright."

"Storm!" Shrieked Comet, carefully gathering the bleeding, choking boy up into her arms whilst the little girl clung to her leg with pained sobs. The bullets had ripped through Kathy's body and hit both of the children. "Storm help me!"

Sprinting around the corner, covered in blood and scratches, Storm slid to her knees beside Kathy, wrapping her arms around her to pull her up.

"Medical ward. Now!"

25

The medical ward was overflowing with the injured. The few doctors and nurses that the headquarters had on staff were overwhelmed, leaving many with no choice but to lay the wounded down in the hallways and try and treat them their selves however they could. Raoul offered his assistance in his skills as a Crisis Aid Responder, showing others how to help bandage limbs properly and create tourniquets with whatever they had available, and snarling at them angrily whenever they tried to remove the bullets.

Storm and Comet propped Kathy against a wall, blood still pouring from her wounds. Storm had tied her sash around Kathy's back and stomach from where the bullets had punctured through, doing her best to make sure that the bleeding stopped.

"No." Kathy gasped at Storm as she tried to put pressure onto the wound, already pale and shivering from blood loss. "Take care of the kids first. I'll be fine."

"Keep pressure on it." Storm ordered, voice wavering as the shock began to set in. She took Kathy's hands and placed them hard over the wound. "Can you do that for me Kathy? I'll make sure you get help as soon as possible, but you need to keep pressure on it."

Kathy nodded slowly, eyes beginning to roll backwards.

"Hey now!" Storm warned, shaking her shoulders. "Stay awake. Just stay awake for me okay?"

"Worry about them... not me."

Storm nodded, stepping away from Kathy to help with the children.

Comet held their hands, soothing them as best she could with her muser abilities to stop them from perceiving the pain, whilst Storm tried her best to tightly bandage the wounds to stop the bleeding, hands shaking as she did.

Their hearts were beating far too fast, their skin growing cold as they continued to use blood which they were struggling to stem. They didn't have the skills or equipment to deal with such trauma, and despite their best efforts when the children shut their eyes and their breathing slowed, Storm and Comet realised that they stood no chance against the effect that shock and blood loss had upon their tiny bodies.

Comet kept on trying her best to resuscitate them until Storm had to pull Comet away. Comet fought her with vicious screams that she was wrong, believing that there was still a chance at saving them until she pressed her ear to their chest and found no heartbeat and she had to give up.

By the time they turned their attention back to Kathy, she too had already shut her eyes and stopped breathing. In denial, Comet tried to shake her back into consciousness and beginning to scream hoarsely at her to wake up, forcing Storm to have to drag her away and restrain her on the floor. She thrashed and shrieked, clawing at Storms arms and wings until they bled.

"She tried! She tried so hard to make it right!" Comet sobbed into Storm's feathers as she tried to calm her.

"I know..."

"It's not fair! Why did this happen? Why! She was sixteen! She was a kid!"

"I don't know..." Storm muttered numbly, staring ahead unseeingly as she held Comet close to comfort her.

It wasn't fair. It was never fair.

The initial panic subsided and the headquarters began to clean up the carnage as quickly as they could. They couldn't be certain at how long it would take before ARCDA came at them again for a second attack, and they needed to make sure everyone who could be helped was helped and they needed to be ready to move and escape.

The injured soon overflowed into the sparring rings and canteen, whilst the dead were laid in the main hall. The Cybers were separated from the rest of the bodies, most of which had been mangled by those that had attacked them.

"Thirteen Cybers. Thirteen." Asena spat, pacing the length of the row of stinking taxidermied corpses. "They all should have been checked!"

The Rioteers who had been on duty to maintain security had been brought before her, their weapons taken from them by the members of Asena's pack.

The Rogues stood to one side, Palmer with his face buried into Raoul's chest to hide from the sight of it all, Wilny and Malana comforting Comet as she crouched next to Kathy's body. Both children that she had tried to save were laid out next to her, both having died from shock and blood loss even after all of their efforts.

"They were checked ma'am." Joy assured her, trembling in his boots.

Snarling, Asena grabbed the skull of the Coyote and ripped the skin from it to show the Rioteer.

"You call this *checking*? It has a camera in its eye. How did your men miss this?"

"The control team did check them."

"Then your control team is fucking useless." She slammed the skull into the floor, where it shattered on impact, leaving a jelly stain of grey matter and electrodes everywhere. "Seven of these things were your men! And now we've less than half an hour to get everyone out of here and away safely!"

"We can-"

"You're not doing anything until I say so. Understood? I need to know the damage before anything else happens."

"Toll is at thirty-four dead so far. Fifty-three injured. Nine are in critical." Storm told Asena bitterly, staring distantly at nothing and scratching at her hands as the blood from trying to save other people began to dry upon them.

"Doctor Richard doesn't think he can handle any more patients and wants to send the Preters and Rioteers to a human hospital."

"And if the Preters need blood transfusions? They're not human."

"I know. These are his thoughts, not mine Wolfie."

"What about you? Your team? Are they injured as well?"

"No, my team are fine. We've had worse."

"I know, I know, Rogues are always tough as Diamond Elites…just…*shit*. How could this have happened? We've been so careful with everything." Asena sighed sadly, sweeping her blonde hair back as she paced between the Cybers and the Rogues. She turned to Raoul and put her hand on his shoulder.

"Thank you, Raoul. You were the quickest to spot them and react and have been invaluable as a medic. I'm proud of you and your team."

Palmer peeked at her from behind Kat's vivid wings where she had shielded him and Lana, and sniffled.

"Alpa did good?"

"He did indeed."

The Hound smiled weakly, in shock and nauseous from the sight of all the blood but gave a modest nod. "I was just doing my job. Although the only reason I knew something was wrong was because I recognised them and knew they were dead."

"Owen said he cleaned the bodies up." Kat pointed out. "At least that's what he told Beth."

Asena's face darkened, lip curling into a fang-bearing sneer and fur bristling across her body. The Rioteers had not been doing their jobs right and now people had died from it.

She turned to her second in command, keeping her tone steady and controlled.

"Anthony, which of the external locations is easiest to relocate to for the time being."

Anthony thought quickly, holding his son close to his chest and keeping his eyes averted from as much of the blood as he could.

"Chancery, Parliament Hill, and Goodge."

"Chancery is too far and too crowded." Contested Storm. "The injured need to go to Parliament Hill."

"But we don't have the equipment to transport the critical ones."

"Then we'll just have to make do." Asena nodded, taking it into consideration before issuing her orders to her awaiting pack, pacing again with furious snarls beneath her breath.

"Anthony, alert the East Europe side, specifically Silver Vesik with code STENDEC. Ask her to relay with the others." Asena ordered, before turning to the rest of her pack. "Timber, Akela, McKenzie, assist in having all of those who are not on medical duty up and ready to change locations as fast as they can to either Parliament Hill or Goodge. Monty, Marius, Blake, Byron. I want you to get all the computers offline and packed up as fast as you can, use only Synths that have been checked for being Cybers first. I will meet you at Goodge."

Anthony nodded and then whistled for the named canids of Asena's pack to get moving as fast as they could, keeping Caesar close to him and continuing to shield him from the devastation.

Asena frowned as she counted off her pack. "Jack, where are the others?"

"Tiber and Sly are injured." A scrawny Jackal Synth said. "The others are doing final rounds to make sure there are no more infiltrators left."

"Find me Ranger, Riggs, and Kazan, they're to scout the other entrances and to keep alert and in contact with you at all time. Rogues, you should all head home and make ready to clear out to your secondary home."

Roux stepped forward, unscathed with the help of her diamond skin. Several Rioteers backed away as she shot them furious glowers for their slow pace at following the instructions, they clearly heard from Asena.

"Do you need me to do anything?" She asked.

"Roux, if this is a scouting mission there's likely to be a control point nearby. They can't run Cybers underground without being close by." Said Asena, "I want you to find them and eliminate them."

"But if they've already got a message back to their base-"

"They likely already have, but their roaming upload data is always limited at long range, so they wouldn't be able send all information in one go."

"I should do it." Storm offered. "I should go find their hub."

"Storm no."

"They already know that an Avio is about the city from Professor Mira, and if someone who looks like Samodiva appears and they call that in it'll draw too much focus. I can do it."

"You're in no state to-"

"Asena!" At the sound of Rex's voice, Storm's eyes rolled back, and her feathers roused up in anger.

"Here comes the King." She snarled beneath her breath to Roux.

Rex strode out from the elevator with Owen, and his entourage of armed guards and daughter.

"What happened?" He paled in horror at the scene, trying to hide his daughter behind him. Bodies everywhere, smashed glass, the injured staring blankly ahead in shock and Asena standing over the decapitated and mauled bodies of the Cybers.

Asena bared her fangs, striding up to the Rioteer leader and hoisting him off his feet by his throat.

"Oh, I don't know Rex, how about- *YOUR MEN ARE NOT DOING THEIR FUCKING JOB RIGHT!*" She roared, slamming him into the closest column of the main hall. His guards flinched, and half raised their weapons, uncertain if they should try to threaten the Empress or not.

"Russel! Russ! Triss!" His daughter, Imogen, shouted, shoving past the Rex and ran to the bodies of the two children that Comet and Storm had failed to save before Rex could stop her, throwing herself down next to them and trying to shake them awake. Her hands came away bloody and she screamed and stumbled backwards, tripping over Kathy's wing. Angrily with tears in her eyes, she rose to her feet and kicked Kathy's body as hard as she could.

"How dare you!" Comet snapped furiously. "She tried to help save them!"

"She hurt them! Daddy said she was evil!"

"You don't know anything! You weren't even here."

Imogen began to wail loudly and tried to hit back at Comet.

"You shouldn't have let her out! She got my friends dead!"

"Stop!" Snapped Lana, shoving Imogen away hard enough to throw her onto her back and flaring her wings out. Wilny pulled Lana away before she started a fight with the other girl. "Stop hurting Com! You don't know nothing!"

"You should have killed her in the first place! Look at what you've done!" Rex snapped at Storm, staggering to his feet and drawing his daughter back away from the dead. "This is all your fault!"

Storm gawped, stunned by the accusation, and then slowly she began to laugh.

"My fault? *My fault?*" She cocked her head sharply from side to side, quick bird-like movements that forewarned an attack. Her bloody hands flexed and closed into fists.

"Our position has been compromised because you're too fucking lazy and immature to get a job done properly." He jabbed a finger at her. "You let that girl go back to

ARCDA. You didn't take out those others when they came back here with her. They know where we are because of you! All these people are going to die because of *you!*"

"How? I can't control what other people do."

"You're in charge of the Rogues. You should be using your team to do your job properly and efficiently."

"The way you run your missions has always been careless." Joy added, stepping a little closer to Rex and Owen, puffing his chest out. "This is all because of your carelessness."

"*How fucking dare you.*" Storm snarled dangerously, advancing with Roux.

"Back off Joy." Roux warned, bristling and ready to take a swing at the men. "Lose your attitude or loose the balls you've suddenly grown now Rex is here."

Asena took both the Rogue and Dragon by their wrists and pulled them behind her.

"Girls stop." She scolded calmly, knowing that they were more than ready to brawl with the men. "We don't have time for you all to be casting blame, we need to move everyone to a new location as soon as possible."

"Agreed." Rex nodded, gently rubbing his daughter's back as she continued to sob and cling to him.

"I've already ordered them to their stations. Rex, you and your men are going to King William Street. Separate from the Synths."

"These are my men Asena-"

"Seven of *your men* were part of this attack," Storm snapped, unable to keep quiet. "Four were Canids that Owen said he had cleaned up!"

Owen blinked out of his silent petrification. He was used to cleaning up bodies, but there was a difference between them being strangers and them being people that he knew.

"From when you ran that unauthorised mission against those Canids?"

"Who cares if it was authorised or not, you said you cleaned it up!"

"My team did yes, not me personally, girly." He murmured, casting his eyes down away from the bodies.

"If my men are responsible for this then I'll make sure they're dealt with."

Rex scoffed and shook his head.

"Your team are not the problem Owen." He said in Owen's defence, giving the man a reassuring pat upon the shoulder.

"It was his cleaners that gave those corpses back to ARCDA!" Storm snarled, the animalistic undertone coming through with a fierce and feral viciousness.

"Storm, you need to-" Asena began, knowing that she wouldn't be able to call Storm off if Rex provoked her any further.

"You are the biggest compromise to security for us all."

"How is this her fault?" Roux spat, stepping forward and shoving Rex in the chest, leaving burning scorch marks upon his jacket. "You are the one in charge here and the fucker who's fucked off Arcadia the most! You're the biggest danger to us all."

Rex stood his ground.

"This is none of your business, bitch! I have done all I can to protect and help you Synths and all you lot seem to do is to undo it all!"

"I didn't see your ass down here helping us, *cabrón*."

"My men were down here to protect you all."

"Your men panicked and started shooting people who weren't even Cybers!" She shoved him again, harder this time and knocking him back against Joy. "You don't want to protect people you want to kill. Well congratulations, you've killed people!"

Asena grabbed Roux by her arms and dragged her back from the men before she set them all on fire. It hadn't gone unnoticed to her that Rex's hand twitched towards his belt, tempted to go for his gun.

"My men did what they thought was right in the situation." He yelled back at her as Asena quietly ordered Roux to go outside and leave it to her. "It was *her* who drew them here in the first place!"

"People have died because of Storm." Joy added with a nod. "Not us."

Asena didn't have time to react.

"You fucking cowardly shitbag-" Storm launched herself at Rex and Joy with a powerful down stroke of her wings, accidentally knocking Imogen to the side in the process. She struck Joy first kicking him as hard as she could in the chest, before vaulting off him to strike her heel into Rex's jaw, felling him before he could even bark out an order.

"Don't you fucking blame me you piece of shit!" Storm snarled down at Joy as she sliced him across the face with her talons while he shrieked in terror, "You're meant to oversee security here! You let thirteen unscreened Cybers walk in and murder people and you're screaming at me for it being my fault? People have died because of you! Not me! YOU!"

Rex scrambled to stand, but she jumped forward again, a powerful kick taking him off his feet.

He flew backwards onto shattered glass with a crunch, Storm leaping after him and pinning him down to the floor with a foot to his throat. Malana broke out of Wilny's arms and jumped on Imogen to stop her from trying to intervene, holding her down on the floor as she squirmed and yelled.

Rex choked and grasped at her clawed foot.

"Asena! S-stop her!" He coughed, but Asena walked silently past him to join the Rogues in their ranks as did all the surviving Synths in the hall.

A few of the Rioteers made lunges forward to try to pull her away, only to be stopped by Kat, Wilny, and Roux on Asena's order.

"I run the Rogues! Not the Rioteers!"

"Fucking Synths, it's always been your fault! After everything I've tried to do to protect you all from them."

"It was you who bailed on ARCDA, stole their work and started this entire war. There wouldn't be this problem if you didn't start it!" She dug her claws into his collarbone, threatening to snap it with the slightest kick downwards onto it, "You only care about us when it helps you feel like a fucking hero."

He struggled to loosen her fingers from his neck, unable to move her. His grey eyes were sharp with hatred, pure loathing, and voice barely above a hoarse whisper.

"Maybe I should sell you to Core so they can see what you're made of and tear you apart."

"Then why don't you? Wouldn't that solve your problem with me?"

There was a split second where his expression changed subtly, far too quick for anyone else to see it. '*You don't understand*', his eyes said, '*I can't.*'

But it wasn't because of his beliefs and morals, she realised, he wanted to sell her to Core, he wanted to get rid of her, but there was some other reason that he wouldn't, or couldn't, do that and she was sure it wasn't because he was afraid of Asena or the Synths turning against him.

As quickly as the expression changed, it vanished again replaced by hatred once more as he dragged her foot out from under her, forcing her off and attempting to grab at her feathers to rip them out. Furious, she slashed Rex as hard as she could in the face with her talons, feeling the rip of skin, and then with a hard kick, leapt backwards, landing on all fours.

"I should have killed you." Rex spat at her. "You've always been more trouble than you're worth."

"Oh, you did try to. But I guess I'm made of the right stuff aren't I doc."

Rex snorted and muttered something under his breath that only Storm could hear. With a snarl, she arched her wings above her head.

Kat knew the poise.

"Storm stop!" Kat shouted. "Amell, grab her!"

Amell moved fast with Kat. Rushing forward, he wrapped his arms around Storm's waist, wrestling her away as best he could with her frenzied flapping wings hitting him hard in the face, her nails digging into his arm and her shrieking insults reaching ear piecing levels that became outraged raptorial screeching. Rex's own men and daughter rushed to his side, having been too frightened of Storm to intervene beforehand.

Brushing them off him, Rex wiped his bloodied face on his arm, the cuts so deep they would leave scars. He spat out a mouthful of blood, cursing her under his breath with vitriol. Pushing Imogen out of the way as she tried to hug his waist, he reached for his belt–

And then Rex's body went rigid, arm frozen in place at his hip in the middle of drawing his gun. In a sudden and fluid movement, he was flung backward across the chamber.

Malana shot to Storm's side, throwing her arms around her and snarling at Rex as he lay stunned against the wall from where he had been slammed by her telkens, with Katana, Roux, and Comet charging up and placing themselves before Storm, and Wilny and Raoul flanking her.

There was a ripple of murmurs amongst the Synths who had been watching as they realised how close Rex had come to shooting one of their own people, terrifying some and enraging others. Jaws snapped, and wings beat as they drew rank, the human Rioteers doing same and causing a deep division through the entire headquarters.

"Stop this!" Asena roared at them all, finally deciding to be democratic before it descended into a brawl. "We've lost enough people today without everyone turning on each other. You have your orders and we have no time so *move or else!*"

Reluctantly, they all backed down, returning to taking care of the injured if not for their shorter tempers and occasional snapping at each there.

"You. Amell is it?" Asena pointed to the Eagle, still holding onto the squirming and spitting Storm to stop her assaulting Rex any further. "Bring her with me."

-x-

"I'm going to tear his throat out one day, I fucking swear it."

"Storm. Stop." Asena scolded as they climbed up the stairwell to street level, pushing ancient trollies and empty cans of beer out of the way.

"Did Rex really try and kill you once before?" Amell asked softly, still carrying the Rogue. Storm laughed sharply.

"Yeah, one of the first memories I have is of biting the fucker's finger off and then getting shot in the heart."

"How the crap have you put up with him?"

"I've no idea, especially since I've always been his scapegoat." She snarled as Asena flung open the hatch door and pulled them up, speaking in a mock-Irish accent to mimic Rex. "*But of course, I blame you for everything, because I never make mistakes! Oh no, not me because I'm a human and you're a Synth-o, I made you and I can do whatever I want with you!*"

"Okay, you need to get skyborne." Asena snapped, pushing Storm forward out into the alleyway.

"But Wolfie-"

"I know you're upset. But you need to get some air. *Please.*"

She opened her mouth to argue with Asena, but she couldn't bring herself to speak; she had far too much respect for her, and the people needed her to take charge and find out what had gone wrong.

"I'll go." Storm sighed. "Amell, can you give me a boost please?"

Cupping his hands, Amell knelt to one knee.

"Oh, and if you should so happen across say, a control point with some ARCDA assholes inside." Asena said with a vengeful growl. "Do with them as you see fit."

Storm nodded, then putting her foot into Amell's cupped hands she let him toss her up into the sky.

The second she rose above the buildings, she thrust her wings down and rocketed skywards. Her anger powered her ascent, heart pounding in time with her wingbeats until she burst out through the top of the clouds and screamed at the top of her lungs.

If she couldn't tear out Rex's throat, she could at least do the next best thing.

She circled, half a mile up above Camden, aware of what she was searching for, being as fast as she could manage. The sun was setting, the twilight drawing in. It was the worst time to hunt for anything with indigo shadows everywhere and the traffic picking up as people began to make their way out of the city.

She knew the types of vehicles they used and how they used them. Simple white vans for camouflage, with a small solar powered satellite dish on top when they were using Cybers. Main roads with a place to park were essential for getting away, as well as so that the drivers didn't get lost. And of course, somewhere to get food relatively close by.

With such complex machinery and finesse, and since they were used as spies similar to drones, Cybers needed a control hub to relay information to, and if they were sending these Cybers underground they only had a short range in which they could operate in, of less than one thousand meters.

There were too many white vans, and so she had to think with more specifics. To get in to the headquarters, they would have needed an entrance. Mornington crescent was close by and had a service line that ran to one entrance of the catacombs that the Rioteers occasionally used as she recalled; it must have been how they had accessed the headquarters.

She did a second sweep by as she spotted a white van parked in the side street close to three identical black motorbikes, before perching upon a rooftop. Two men strode quickly across the park towards the van, both wearing black shirts with the little red accents of Core on them. The back of the van opened and inside she could see the lights of a control panel.

Bingo.

They argued for a short few seconds between themselves before another man scrambled to the back to scold them all. With them distracted by one another, Storm quietly swooped into the huge trees above them, gripping the smooth bark.

"-about food orders when we have actual orders to continue with." The chastising sergeant snapped at the two delayed men. The two men who had been out getting food for them all both looked at each other and shrugged, passing out the orders to everyone.

"Have you sent whatever was gathered yet?"

"We've only managed two files out of thirteen in the last ten minutes."

A spark of hope ignited in Storm. Two videos may have already been too much information leaked and she had no way of knowing what they might have already seen, but she could stop more from being sent back to ARCDA. She did her best to creep closer to them, bloodied hands struggling to maintain a grip on the tree branches and using her wings to help support herself as she moved in closer. Her wing snagged on a branch, dislodging an already loose feather and dropping it to the pavement below before she could stop it.

The men froze mid-argument as the silvered feather spiralled down between them. Freezing in recognition of it being an Avio feather, they looked up at Storm who was poised like a lynx above them. There was a beat of silence between them, and then there was panic.

"Shit-!"

"It's *that* one-!" Their sergeant shrieked, shoving the others into the van and reeling back as she dove at them.

Wings beating down she flattened all five of them, slashing with talons and shocks of electricity.

A smoke grenade was thrown at her, striking her in the head much to her shock, allowing them time to scramble into the van and onto their bikes as she coughed and spluttered. With a squeal of tires, they took off. Charging forward, she broke clear of the smoke grenade and shot upwards above the trees and buildings, nictitating membrane flicking across her eyes to protect them.

The van and its flanking motorbikes were already heading south towards the main road. She tracked the small fleet at a steady pace, knowing they couldn't go too far too fast in the city. There was chaos within the van, all injured and panicked by the sudden appearance of a blood soaked Avio.

"We have sight of an Avio. I repeat; we have sight of an Avio." The sergeant yelled breathlessly into his phone, blood dripping down his face from where Storm had sliced him with her talons. "They are chasing us right now!"

"Sergeant-" the dispatcher on the other end began, only to be cut off immediately by the rest of the team.

"Hard left! You two, keep an eye on the sky!"

"Where is she? Where did she go?"

"We don't know how many there might be with her."

"We need more details sergeant," the dispatcher pressed, "what does it look like?"

The sergeant stole a glance out of the window as Storm shot past them, kicking out the glass of the drivers' side window and sending shards all over the passengers.

"Very angry sir!" The sergeant yelled into the phone.

Distracted by the traffic, Storm searched for a weapon to use against them. Sweeping by a construction site, she doubled back quickly, seeing exactly what she needed before resuming her tailing of the van.

"Keep her in your sights!" He roared. "Don't let her surprise us!"

"Can you contain her?"

"Negative sir! We're prioritising sending the information gathered back to the command post!"

There was a metallic thunk from above them with a distant crashing behind.

"She's taken out the aerial sir."

A rod of black metal pierced through the roof of the van, missing the sergeant by inches, but plunging straight into the Cyber handling station. Sparks erupted from the station, the screens cracking and glitching wildly before fizzling into blackness, followed by smoke beginning to flood the back of the van. They all screamed as a second black rod pierced through the bonnet of the van like a spear, striking the engine. A huge ball of fire erupted from the bonnet, shooting up into the inside of the cab through the radiator vents.

"Where is she! Where did she go?" The sergeant howled blindly, the smoke from the ruined station beginning to sting at his eyes.

A blur of silver-grey swept past them, kicking the rear end of the lead motorbike, throwing the biker from his seat and sending it on a collision course with the van as it turned sharply. The bike was crushed beneath the wheels, jolting the van and sending it careening uncontrollably down the road, hitting other cars as it skidded. The van rocked as it veered right, colliding with an oncoming car, spinning and rolling onto its side with a shattering of glass and rending of metal.

The two in the back leapt from the van screaming, shielding their faces from the burst of fire, they were blinded and burnt by the sudden shock of flames. The two in the front seats however had no such luck with escaping, abandoned in the smoke-filled van, coughing and howling for help.

The second motorcyclist screeched to a stop and looked back in time to see Storm swoop in and strike the third biker with such force, that he heard his ribs and skull shattering on impact. His bike toppled onto its side as he himself was thrown across the road where he rolled limply to a stop, unmoving and unresponsive.

Storm dropped down to the road, wings buffeting the flames and ignoring the onlookers who were already calling the emergency services.

Pulling the long piece of rebar that had been impaled into the roof of the van, Storm struck with it at one of the men who had escaped out the back, rendering him unconscious and broken before throwing it like a javelin down the road at the sergeant, who had broken into a terrified sprint to escape.

The last biker snapped his head away from the sight of the sergeant being impaled through the back, revving his bike and taking off along the pavement in a blind panic.

He glanced her reflections in windows, saw her shadow sweep across his path, terrified at the realisation that he was being hunted, with no way to escape.

A flash of silver feathers caught his attention out the corner of his eye and he looked back for only a moment but by then it was too late to react. The oncoming lorries at the crossroad struck him before he even realised, he had run the red light.

Circling up above, Storm watched quietly as the bike shattered and the traffic came to a halt around it with people rushing forward to help. It was a mess, but not one she was going to clean up. Rex would find out about it of course, and would be furious over how she handled it, but it was done.

Her phone vibrated in her pocket. Beth undoubtedly, but she didn't feel like answering. Her anger had burnt its self out and now everything felt cold and distant, unreal.

Out.

Out.

Need to get out.

Switching her phone off, she banked in a full circle again, setting her sights on the western horizon towards the sunset and flew as fast as she could.

26

Heels sharply clicking on the tiled floor, Eve Mira marched furiously down the hallway with her son and two of her security consultants in her wake, sending the consulting doctors and nurses scattering. Even the critters in the terrariums scurried away from the glass as she strode past.

"Zevallos, double regulation on the station to Milan, get Mercer to stop playing with his toys and to check on the import lines. Give all your men stun guns only, I do not want one of them gunning down any innocents."

"Sì signora, but what about *my* gun?" The taller of the two men, a dark-haired Italian with deep brown eyes and an even deeper set of scars, asked, holding on tight to the strap of his rifle. Eve rolled her eyes. Parting boys from their toys was always troublesome.

"You can keep it, just don't use it on anyone. Aden is your team doing background checks on all of the nurses again?"

"Yes Miss M."

"Keep it up. Be as thorough as you can, I want to know any motivation for any of them to talk, and please keep an eye on Deltas shipping movements. No doubt they will be mobilising with Core as we speak."

Aden nodded, peeling away from the group to do his research.

"You really think that it was more than one person?" Wilheim asked, twitching the long disks of his tailfeathers about as he strode along behind her, approaching the doors to the holding cells.

"I'm not sure. One person is all it takes to screw everything up, but you can never be too careful- Did you find her?" Eve curtly asked Sabre and Fell who had been standing guard at the door. Her security consultants were good, but there was no pair she trusted more than her Merlo twins. Sabre smiled. Zevallos shift uncomfortably as the Avio flashed his fangs, very familiar with how sharp they could be.

"Oh yes." With a low sweeping bow he opened the door for her with a gentle hiss. "Right this way Prof."

Head held high the Professor stepped into the dark room, lit by the dim orange emergency lights.

"You've disappointed me Patrice." Eve snarled down at the captive nurse who had been strapped to the surgery table, circling her. The Avios and Italian however, remained by the door, arms folded and waiting for instructions to be given.

Her leopard print heels had been removed, the heel of one sheared off from her attempted escape of the twins. She whimpered a little as Eve switched on the powerful overhead light, then off again, dazzling the woman and leaving her temporarily blinded.

"I don't know anything, I swear! I swear!" Doctor Kelly snivelled, her red lipstick black under the orange lights. "I didn't send those Cybers to attack them!"

"No, *you* didn't, but you told someone about them and they responded by attacking."

"But I-"

The Professor swooped down upon the pinned woman, pinching her jaw and holding her head still so that Patrice could look her in the eye.

"Do you realise what you've done? Do you not realise how valuable those Synths are? *I had a plan!* We could have saved them, cooperated with them, but no. Do you realise how difficult it will be now for them to trust us?"

"I...It wasn't- I don't-"

'She's lying.' Fell mused to them all. There was a sharp feeling of fear from the woman on the table, that they all felt.

The trepidation of what she was doing, sneaking into the office to find what Sabre had seen, recording overheard conversations with her phone, nervousness, hunger, 'They should know about this,' pacing back and forth trying to remain calm.

The fear gave way to defeat and she shut her tearful eyes, knowing that there was no way out of it now. No lie could escape Fell's muser abilities.

"How much were you paid?" Eve asked curtly.

"I-I-"

Zevallos stepped forward with his rifle, swinging it round and holding the barrel against her knee.

"Answer the professor or-"

"Zevallos, please. I can handle this myself." Eve snapped viciously.

The Italian stepped back with some reluctance and lowered his weapon. Behind him Sabre gave him a smug grin which earnt the Avio an angry middle finger. Eve ignored the boys, removing an ornate scalpel from the breast pocket of her lab coat and twirled it, letting the orange lights shine of it into Patrice's eyes. She pulled against the restraints holding her down, trying to twist her head away from the blade.

"Answer. *Truthfully.*"

"I have family!" She pleaded, hoping to appeal to Eve's maternal side, but Eve only shrugged and grazed the scalpel along the side of Patrice's temple.

"We all have a family somewhere. Is that why you sold information?"

"T-they offered to pay for my niece's tuition fees and synthetic gene therapy and for my brother!"

"They?" Eve patted the blade on Patrice's cheek, the edge facing down and leaving delicate little slices.

"Every second you fail to answer me properly, I cut a little deeper."

"*Core!* I sold it to a someone who works in Core."

"Just Core?" She paused for a moment as the twins mused to her, and then she seized the woman's ear and cut into the soft skin behind it. "Are you listening to me Patrice? Did you sell them to *just* Core?"

Patrice bit her lip, nodding furiously, then screamed as Eve sliced the ear off with a single swift movement. Blood dribbled from the wound splattering the white of Eve's coat, black as her lipstick under the orange light. Patrice screamed and thrashed against the restraints, begging the professor to let her go. Wilheim recoiled, looking away sharply at the sight of the blood, tapping his finger to his ear to silence his hidden hearing aids so that he wouldn't have to hear the screaming.

"I told you to answer me honestly and you did not." Eve snarled, tossing the ear to the floor. "Was it so bad here that you had to sell out valuable information to both Core *and* Delta?"

"I didn't know- I- I'm sorry! I'm so sorry!" The woman sobbed. "Please! Please don't kill me!"

"I'm bored of her now." Eve huffed in disgust, spinning on her heels and making her way out. She ushered for everyone else to leave.

"Sabre, deal with her and make sure you clean up any mess you make; I would like the room back in order when you're done."

The Avio flashed his fangs and let his long sleek wings rustle in excited anticipation as he took Eve's blade in hand. As soon as the door hissed to a close, they could just about hear the muffled screams of Patrice as she was abandoned in the vindictive talons of Sabre.

Without so much as a hesitant look back, Eve ordered the remaining men to follow her as she strode back to her office, encountering Aden who sprinted to catch up to them as she reached the door. He handed her a tablet of intel on the attack at the Rioteer headquarters.

"The handiwork was Core, but the insurgents were Delta." He confirmed for her, "Old model Cybers which were meant to go to Hasekura as sleeper agents but were somehow redirected to the Rioteers."

"They're working together then?"

"Quite possibly. They did make a new alliance for a trade off, and they're going to make a second deal later today."

"Aden, find out what bunkers were key in this attack, pull strings and sweet talk your way through them, buy them dinner and a happy ending if you have to. Work your magic. Zevallos, tell Malva to report in as soon as she can. I need her."

Both men bowed curtly with a *"Yes Miss M,"* and a *"Sì signora,"* between them before they parted ways. Eve scanned through the report again, waiting until both men were out of earshot before turning to the remaining twin.

"Fell, please make sure our other bunkers are safe." She asked him softly. "I doubt she gave away our location, but please make sure. I don't want the babies to be hurt, any research stolen, and I *do not* want another Loch Mullardoch happening again."

"I fully understand. I'll be discreet." He assured her gently with a flare of his forked tailfeathers, before he too left.

Heim watched after him as he departed, admiring the beautiful long feathers he was struggling to keep of the ground.

Enviously, he flashed out his own iridescent purple wings, fluttering them loudly in a sharp and erratic movement. Usually, the loud fluttering would have got his mother's attention, but she was far too concerned with the report to the point she kept her hand on the lock pad of the door, failing to notice that the door was open.

"Mum?" He prodded, as her brow continued to furrow in anger. "Did you really have to cut her ear off? Don't you think that was a bit dramatic."

She looked up at him, blank faced for a moment before she realised that he had spoken.

"I have some things to take care of sweetie." She smiled softly. Sidestepping the question, she lovingly tucked her son's long hair back behind his ears and kissed his cheek.

"Please make sure that none of your own projects have been hacked into."

"I'm sure they're fine. I would have already heard about Griffin rioting already if anything had happened." He rolled his eyes and sighed at the thought of his Gregale project. "I'll double check anyway. I love you."

"I love you too sweetie, remember to get to dinner on time okay." Then with a small wave she stepped into her office, the door swishing shut behind her.

Much like the décor throughout the facility, her office was white with blue accents, less of an office and more of a humid botanical greenhouse. Islands of tall Jurassic ferns, moss, ginger, bamboo, and jacaranda trees entwined with vanilla and vines, reached the high towards the ceiling and glass dome that let in the sunlight. One wall was full of unusual Synthetic rainforest flowers that she had made herself continually being water by a mist, whilst another corner held an aviary full of equally colourful songbird-sized raptors and other bird-based critters that trilled and whistled noisily.

Making her way through the tropical office she sat herself at her desk made from the sawn-off cross section of a once giant tree, logged in to her computer and sent out a message to order a meeting.

Now it was time to round the culprits up.

They eventually assembled before her upon her screens, the leaders of the factions of the Arcadia Corporation, each with their colour accent and faction symbol at the bottom of their camera frame.

"This better not take long, I've a schedule to keep to." Grumbled one of the two men present. Grey streaked hair and the deeply furrowed face of a man who was in a perpetual state of anger, he was Gaius Daniels, the eldest of them all and the director of Core.

"I'm sorry Gaius, this shouldn't take too long, it's just a quick meeting."

"Not proposing silly requests again are we, *Evelyn*? What was the last one on? You demanding that we not sterilise all the Elites in case you wish to use them? Yes, I think it was. I don't have time for your silly whims for your *so-called-research*."

His plummy Eton English made the hair on Eve's neck stand on end. As if she didn't dislike the man already, his condescending voice just made her hate him even more, not that she liked or respected any of the other leaders, particularly not the newest leader of Delta.

"Why isn't Pavlov here?" The second man asked, sweeping his white-blond hair back, eyes darting about as he observed his own multiple screens for the Risio leader's face.

"Because, *Cedric*, this isn't his area and only you two are stupid enough to pull shit like this." She snapped, ignoring the need to be civil.

"I have no idea what you're talking about."

"Don't play dumb with me. Patrice Kelly sold you information about the Rioteers."

"Oh that!" He feigned a gasp.

Eve bristled at his arrogance. All the past leaders of Delta had always been arrogant pricks, but out of all that had come and been killed, Cedric Wardens was the one she wished to pull the trigger on all by herself. Even Gaius couldn't stop his eyes from rolling at the tone of his voice.

"We did haggle with her for what kind of reward she wanted from each of us. I'm sure her niece will flourish and get a nice job offer in the near future. We're in great demand of promising young engineers." Cedric span in his chair, beckoning a Synth with a bruised face to him, drinking the wine he was served.

The sight made Eve's skin crawl, but she could only deal with one tragedy and crime at a time.

"You *both* set the Cybers on the Rioteers, together. Delt and Core."

"Actually, they were meant to target Hasekura shipments initially before they were… *intercepted*." Cedric laughed, toasting her mockingly as he drank. "It's funny how that goes, right?"

"I'm surprised you didn't deal with those vermin right away Evelyn." Gaius' voice cut through her disgust, anger colouring his tone. "You had a pin on them for several weeks! You could have done something!"

"I am a *researcher*, not a militant."

"You'd allow them to carry on existing when you *know* what they do to the organisation?"

A musical laugh cut through the speakers as the Atlas leader joined in the conversation.

"*Dejar de ser una puta,* Guy." Amelia Samodiva sighed, spinning around in her office chair. "The Rioteers- they're flies to us. Wasps even. Their existence has little impact, but annoyance. Don't waste your time with them, *mi querido.*"

Her brown eyes glittered mischievously. For a woman who was in her mid-sixties, the same as the other leaders, she didn't look a day over twenty-five nor did she act like it.

"They destroyed five of my key bunkers this year." Gaius snarled, leaning in close to the camera on his screens.

"I've lost the lives of four hundred men and women. Do you know how much that costs me in compensation funds for those worker's families? The trust that gets broken when my employees are put at risk? Not only that, but there's also been at least three hundred Synths be released into the wild, half of whom come back nearly dead and broken when they're recaptured. Thirty of those three hundred were Elites! All the wasted money and time on raising those products, to have them lost and destroyed, and don't even get me started on the corrupted genome sequences."

"I've told you this already." Eve snapped again, slapping the desk in fury. "The sequence files you have are *not* corrupted! It's your machines not reading the sequences properly and not building the genomes correctly; that's a technological issue, not a creation issue."

She gave a pointed stare at Cedric.

"Or you've just not preserved the data correctly." Samodiva pointed out in her defence. Both men were technologically minded, and it didn't surprise either woman that subjects of biology were troubling them. They had had this argument many times before.

"They keep dying!" Gaius's voice rose to a crescendo, slamming his desk hard enough to shake the camera. "How am I meant to produce Elites who cannot live for any longer than two years! Or go insane! Or who are better off as scrap! I haven't had a decent Preternatural origin since the LYNX origin was produced. We're back to square one on almost all Synth productions!"

"You have Canids and Pards, they work fine."

"I want *Preternaturals!* I need to sell something that looks human! I need Transhumans that don't lose their minds!"

"Then why are you shrieking at Eve? Preternaturals are my department and Eve has had nothing to do with your products for nearly a decade, it's not her fault your technicians aren't doing their job correctly." She rolled her eyes childishly.

"Risio produces them just fine. *You* produce them just fine."

"Risio is full of paedophiles who dedicate a *considerable* amount of time to their production. She sneered at him through the screen, kicking her legs up onto her desk and braiding her waves of brown hair nonchalantly.

"I want your research, Amelia."

"Hah! You're not having anything of mine until you can learn to behave, *tú pequeño putos idiota.*"

"Well, if we didn't keep every file we had in a single server room, or store the backups in chromostorage, then let the only person who could decrypt them mutiny then maybe we wouldn't have this problem. We could all have the toys and tools we need." Cedric prodded maliciously and teasingly, raising Gaius's ire. A vein pulsed across his temple, face nearly purple in fury.

"Ruadri is a paranoid little fuck!" The Core leader snapped, slamming his desk so hard the camera shook. "It's not my fault that he-"

"He was always *a paranoid little fuck*, that's why we let him encrypt the back-up codes into a DNA format!" Snarled Eve. "That's why *you* agreed to it!"

"And now none of us can read them! It took nearly three months to translate the binary on the Brown twins and another three to sift through the nonsense and find the information, and then it wasn't even there! We couldn't even clone them to get the data."

"You still believe that theory? That he coded the backup data directly into them?"

"Every investigation we've had points to yes, that Ruadri hid that data in the Type-Sevens? Yes! We need that data back Evelyn!"

"Well, I'm sorry to tell you this that you can't! You know why? Because the technology for the Type-Seven Avios was lost from the Mullardoch servers, with all the sequences for how they were made and coded, and for the machines to produce it and read it, which was on the blueprints, which you agreed to be-"

"Do you need to remind me-"

"*Yes! I do!* I'm sorry you can't play toy soldiers as well as you hoped you could, Guy. But this is ultimately your fault for being an aggressive asshole who wants to fight everything, and Cedric's fault for not keeping all of our technology up to standard so we can recover what we lost."

All four leaders were now lent in close to their cameras, ready to snap and fight each other. Their civility had waned over the past few years with each other, but now it was non-existent. With Hasekura growing as a competitor and the Rioteers sabotaging them, there was very little that stopped them from attacking and stealing from each other.

"Do not think to attack the Rioteers again, Boys." Said Eve coolly. "Your factions are already in danger because you're careless with your work."

"We know where they are Eve, you think you're going to stop us from wiping them out?"

"Wiping them out? Ah yes, you've been saying this for years, how well has that gone so far?" Amelia purred, drumming her golden claw-like rings on the desk.

"Do you really believe that they'll not vanish after this? I thought you two were strategists."

"I'll not tolerate their existence or your criticisms, *Evelyn*. I funded your faction and I can destroy it. The same goes for you Amelia."

"This isn't Mullardoch or even Broken Arrow, Gaius." Eve leant into the camera with a coy smile. "You've no power over Aura and you wouldn't dare risk losing all the research I've provided you. You do want to have functioning Preternaturals and transgenics, yes? Or do you want me to release a literal plague upon your people and everyone associated to them. Because I can, you know. One little virus and there goes your empire."

Gaius flinched at the threat.

"You wouldn't dare resort to pathogenic warfare, you'd lose everything too. All the data for the cures and vaccines on those viruses was lost at Mullardoch."

"Push me and see. How fast would your shares drop; how fast would Astra and Hecate fail if there were to be a sudden pandemic sweeping across your new colony on Mars or Europa? Oh my, all those recruits would abandon ship. Profits and progress would drop, and then we'd see you both crash and burn." Her dark eyes sparkled at his discomfort and horror at the thought of losing money.

"You've been so busy in your little game of toy soldiers and reaching for the stars, you have no idea what we have been achieving down here on earth."

"My darling Eve is quite right, *querido*." Samodiva smiled, goading him, drawing a golden claw across her lip. "You really ought to start using some aether, your memory and logic seem to be failing you."

"You've lost as much as I have! You should be wanting to destroy them!"

"Where's the fun in that?"

"This isn't meant to be *fun*! This is a battle and I will take both of you girls down too if you just do nothing!" He slammed the desk again, making Samodiva chuckle.

"Girls he says. He really should know; *La hembra de la especie es más mortal que el varón.*"

"Don't you dare quote-"

"Ladies, please," Cedric cut through with a drawl, sipping on his wine, "bickering is so very unbecoming of you girls."

"Ladies? There are no ladies here," Said Samodiva coyly and snapped her fingers, causing a flame that raced across her brown skin and flashing yellow eyeshine across her eyes in an unnatural glint. "Only goddesses."

Both the men paused, Cedric mid sip and wide-eyed at her, having both forgotten to what extent she self-experimented. She was the original *Preternatural*, her favourite word. Not above natural, but *beyond*.

Gaius writhed in his chair, letting the leather creak noisily until Samodiva blinked and behaved humanly once again.

"I'll not tolerate the Rioteers, Eve."

"Then don't tolerate them or me at all, all I'm telling you is that these Rioteers, like Amy said, are wasps. You've stirred them up with your stupid attack, and now they're going to be alert and ready to destroy anything you throw at them and scatter if you get too close."

"So, what then? Should we wear bee keeper clothes and use smoke to calm them?" Sneered Cedric, rolling his eyes.

"Yes. Stay on guard and keep far away from them." Eve straightened up in her seat, glad that they were back on topic, "I know Ruadri is dangerous, but the value of what he has is greater than revenge, for now."

Gaius stopped and frowned.

"Value? What could possibly be of value amongst his scraps of broken products and mongrel Hasekura-Ferals."

"Like you said. Ruadri is a paranoid little fuck, and he always has a plan. And as a researcher, I would like to discover that agenda because– if my theory is correct– then all the problems you've been having can be rectified."

"And what is your theory?"

"That among the collection of prototypes and rare Synths he has, that he still has the back-up data from Mullardoch. Either in a hard copy or in chromostorage as transcribable DNA." She didn't want to give the information away, but she revelled in the fact that Gaius went wide-eyed and pale at the theory. She could see the spark of greed in his eyes; all his problems would be solved, but she could also see him thinking it through very carefully.

"If you move too fast, he could destroy it, and Ruadri, *Rex*, whatever he wants to call himself, he will destroy it. You know he will the moment he even suspects we might be on to him." She warned, watching Gaius nod slowly and Samodiva raise her eyebrows in intrigue. "If I find out what his game is then I promise I'll make sure you're informed along with specific details of numbers of products in his command."

"In exchange for what."

"For you to keep your hands to yourself."

It wasn't a deal he wanted, but he seemed to accept it. Of them all, and though he would be reluctant to admit it, Gaius trusted Eve to keep to her word the most.

"Oh and, don't openly ship anything about Europe for a few weeks." Eve smiled, "They have people working on our outer systems and will pick up any activity. You don't want to lose a whole ship full of Exo-Armour or Hercules to the Rioteers. They'd put it to use right away."

With a final shared sneer, the men left the screen, leaving only Samodiva and Eve.

"They're not going to listen to you, *Cariña*." The Spaniard purred affectionately.

"Of course not, they're men. It's all about dominance and territory with them, even these many centuries down the evolutionary chain. I'll have one of my boys keep an eye on Core shipments."

"Strange to see humans acting in similar ways to some of our research subjects isn't it?"

"The sooner he gets off this planet the happier I'll be." Eve sighed, leaning back in her chair, pulling her tight bun loose and shaking out her hair.

"You should keep an eye on activity too Amy, you were deliberately provoking him."

"My ladies know what to look for, and I'm *always* aware of what's going on."

There was a coy smile there that worried her. The men's intentions were simply profit based, but past experience had taught her that Samodiva only cared for entertainment, which could take any form at all; including baiting people against each other.

"I understand that you don't want to attack the Rioteers for reasons of a research-based nature," she needled with a sultry grin, "if it were anything less than that, you'd have vivisected them all by now. Or is there something *special* there perhaps that has your interest and is holding you back?"

"I thought you were aware of what's going on."

"Yes, but I want to know your reasoning." She tilted her head from side to side cattishly, and stared dead down the camera. The deep brown of her eyes flashing gold like tigers-eye with eyeshine. Eve half expected to see a membrane flick across her eye rather than for her to blink she was so inhuman.

She was certain that Samodiva knew that her son was there. The woman was too cunning, too sly, that Eve didn't believe that she didn't know a thing.

"I want to see how they've adapted and survived. How they've changed." She answered in a half lie.

"Oooh. Please study them *mi amiga*, I want to compare them to El Dorado and see what the differences are between human and natural environments."

"Project El Dorado is still running?"

"We had a few... *hiccups* in the last two years, some of the subjects got out during the expansion, and we had a problem with careless students not wearing the correct clothing and infecting the subjects, so we had to vaccinate the population on the second ecosystem."

El Dorado was one of Samodiva's personal projects that she had started back when they first began making Synthetic organisms. The aim was to build entirely synthetic ecosystems, filled with plants, critters, and even more sapiential synths like Canids and Pards; a step towards terraforming that had been succumbed to a number of setbacks in later years.

"So why haven't you attacked them if you know what's going on." Eve asked, trying not to sound overly suspicious.

"Where's the fun in it?"

"That can't be your whole reasoning."

"No, I really am that shallow." She clapped her hands together. "But enough about work, let's talk about dinner."

"Dinner?"

"You and me, let's go have dinner together soon. In person. You can come up to my villa!"

"Amy, I've told you I'm busy."

"You're always *busy*," She winked playfully. "Come on, I'll get you that red wine you like. Your son can come and play with my computers, and we can bitch about how much of a whore Guy is until we're too drunk to be coherent, what do you say?"

It had been too long since she had seen Samodiva in person, in which the last time resulted in her poisoning the third delta leader at a dinner conference. The dessert was lovely but had ultimately been ruined after he had keeled over into the meringue.

"I'll think about it."

Samodiva grinned and blew her a kiss before signing out and leaving Eve all alone with her greenhouse office, with nothing but the sounds of the raptors in the aviary to fill the silence. Slouching back in her chair she slowly counted to ten, trying to be calm after the frustration of dealing with the other leaders. All of them were trouble and although Samodiva was willing to help and defend her, she mistrusted her.

Dealing with a fickle Preternatural in person was a risk, but if she knew anything, if she was planning or plotting anything against herself or anyone else, Eve wanted to know. Especially if it concerned her son.

"For his own safety," she told the trilling songbird-raptors, "I will bring him home."

-x-

"Stupid, jumped up, little leach!" Beth snarled, punching hard into Amell's palm. "Mother-fucking piss bucket, he can eat a maggoty phallus and choke on it!"

"You're telling me." Kat sighed, scrolling through her tablet whilst lounging in the sun. The hot summer days had forced the house out into the garden, the children playing with water balloons and the garden sprinkler, whilst the older Rogues lounged in the sun, wings half spread to soak up the sunshine.

All were out, save for Storm who still had not returned.

Kat looked up from the screen and frowned at the Owl as she burnt her rage out on Amell.

"Beth, straighten your arm out when you punch, you can hit harder and it'll hurt less."

"Bionic arm remember!" *–thwack-* "I can't feel a thing," *–thwack –* "just like lord ass-butt Brisbane."

"Yes, but you still have one fleshy arm which can feel. I just don't want you breaking your fingers, we might need them for some side jobs."

"Ow...okay that's enough hitting for now." Amell winced, rubbing his palms together. "I didn't think that you were one for violence Beth."

With a final *thwack* she finished her pummelling and rolled her shoulders in relief.

"That man drives me to it." Beth growled, stepping into the kitchen to grab an iced smoothie that Amell had been preparing for them all before slumping down in a sun lounger. "Fourteen and half a million that we've built up over the last few years, and he just turns around and says, '*Cough up!*' and takes ten million like the tight-assed little parasite he is."

Wilny's head snapped up from the book he'd been reading as he sunbathed.

"Wait. He took our money?" His reading glasses slid down his nose in shock.

"As a '*community donation*' towards paying for building contractors to clear out one of the old tube stations for a new headquarters and equipment in the remnants of the British Museum Station." She sneered, draining her glass until there was only ice left in the bottom. Holding it up to the sun, she clinked the cubes about until Amell took it from her to refill it. "I've half a mind to sell him out on his next trip and be rid of him."

"Well, we don't really need him now do we." Kat winked, waving her tablet. "I've recovered some of the funds we lost at the price of a few photos of my feet and a little light extortion and racketeering. There's a few other jobs going."

"Sure," Beth shrugged, "so long as they don't involve children or animals."

"Well, there's three who want some blackmail material, two who want information regarding both a double homicide and a kidnapping, seven who are asking for some extortions to be carried out, and one asking for some smuggled goods to be brought across the continent for him."

"I'll take the blackmail and kidnapping info. You can deal with the extortion cases, right? The banket ban on smuggling still stands."

"Good. They were wanting to traffic rare reptiles taken from the wild."

"Fuck no. Sell that person out for me, will you?"

"On it."

"How...how do you girls even find these things?" Amell asked, handing out glasses full of ice-cold blueberry smoothies, but the girls only laughed it away, assuring him that he didn't need to know how.

Both Palmer and Malana slurped quickly on their drinks, giggling to each other as they both held their heads in pain from the brain freeze it brought with it. Raoul passed them both a new box full of freshly prepared water balloons that he had been filling for them and smiled as they grabbed the ammunition with excited thanks.

Despite the horrors of what had happened, the children didn't seem to have dwelt on it. Many of the survivors who had escaped through the warren of bolt holes had still not surfaced and were likely to remain hidden for another week until things had calmed down.

"Storm's still not back..." Raoul sighed, looking away from the children chasing each other around the tiny garden with water balloons. He sat down on the steps, tossing balloons into the air for Palmer to catch and throw.

"She'll come back." Beth assured him nonchalantly. The calm indifference that both Kat and Beth had shown at Storm's disappearance had made him uneasy as much as their absolute lack of knowledge of her whereabouts or willingness to search for her.

"It's been three days. What if she's hurt?"

"She probably is, but she'll be back soon. She doesn't stay away for more than three days."

"She does this often?"

"Not really. The first time I saw her do this was when I first arrived here. She went out and just went feral in the New Forest for several days, and apparently ate a horse or deer. Her friend Rai brought her back though..." Beth grimaced, giving Raoul a moment to imagine the sight of it, which wasn't difficult in the slightest. "The times after that were either when Rex aggravated her or when she lost... a friend."

After the display he had seen between Storm and Rex – who Raoul was surprised that he had escaped with not even a single broken rib– he felt that Storm running off was a more common occurrence than what Beth let on.

In all truth as he and Wilny had come to realise, Storm rarely talked about herself or what she was feeling, and everything they knew about her were from others telling them stories. For such an outgoing person, she was highly private.

"She's probably talking to a statue. Nothing dangerous." Wilny tried to assure Raoul.

"A...statue?"

"Adonis told me she used to go talk to some of the statues to vent off whenever Rex lectured her."

"*Vent off?* Ah. Shout."

There was shriek followed by a sobbing wail as Palmer ran into his arms, dramatically pointing at his scuffed knee. After gently chiding him for running too fast and tripping over his own feet, Raoul gave the little pup a comforting hug, ignoring how damp he was. With Palmer too busy being cuddled, Malana was left without anyone to play with, and so sat down in the sun to try and dry her wings off with little luck, resorting to patting Wilny on the thigh to get his attention.

"What is it Lana?"

"Wing scratchy. Stormy gets rid of scratch, but she's gone. Can you?" Her English had improved greatly, however the eclectic mix of accents among them had an influence on her. She extended a wing out, the feathers damp and gathered from the water fight, and pouted up at him.

"Let me help."

He creased the corner of the page and set it to one side. Happily, Malana let her wing drape on the ground as Wilny tried his best to pat the feathers dry and make them fall back into line. Storm usually dealt with all of their wings, preening them and making sure to pluck out loose feathers, making it look very simple and easy to do, when the reality was that keeping them maintained took up a lot of time. Wilny's grimaced at how cleaning feathers made his hands feel greasy.

"You're doing it wrong." A voice scolded from above them. Amell shrieked and fell backwards into the kitchen at the surprise, earning him a peal of relieved laughter from Beth and Kat.

"Storm!"

Storm jumped from her perch on the roof and circled gracefully round the garden before alighting gracefully upon the patio. Her wings were trembling with exhaustion and she looked horrendously fatigued from what they assumed to have been a long and fast flight back home.

"You've got to dry them all first." She instructed in a hoarse voice, tossing a towel over to Wilny with a small smile as Malana rushed up to her to hug her.

"Hang on Sunshine, I need to clean up first."

"But you're back."

"And I'm all messy and need a drink first, give me a moment please sweetie."

Kat rose to her feet and quickly got Storm a smoothie from the kitchen to soothe her throat, pushing her down onto the lounger to rest. She downed the drink thirstily, ignoring the silent stares of the others until she finished the second drink.

The three days away and she was bloodier and even more injured than when she had left, though most of it had dried a dark and rusty brown on her skin and ripped clothes, her hair was a tangled mess, and yet her feathers were immaculately clean.

"Better?" Amell asked warily, handing her the garden hose to wash herself down with.

She shrugged, shaking her wings off as she took a cooling birdbath and scrubbing at her skin until it was clean.

"Calmer...not happier, not better." She smiled hollowly, trying to act as though nothing was wrong. Lana pouted as she watched.

"Stormy? Are you okay?"

"I'm fine Sunshine, nothing to worry about." She put on her best smile for Lana. "Is your wings scratchy?"

"Yes."

"Come on then, lets show Wilny what to do."

Wilny slid over, allowing Storm to take his place, shrugging her own wings out, letting them fan across the deck. The others started to relax once again, except for Raoul who watched her carefully whilst Palmer wiggled in his arms.

He wanted to ask her if she was alright, what happened, but it felt inappropriate. If she didn't want to tell them, then she wouldn't tell them.

"Raoul can you do Wilny's wings." Storm instructed to Raoul, ignoring his twitching whiskers and ears.

"Are you sure?"

Wilny slapped his shoulder, scooting down onto the steps beside Malana and flourishing his wings out. "Come on, I trust you."

"Palmer, do you want to learn?" Storm asked the cub.

"Yes!"

She laughed, as he shoved his way out of Raoul's arms to take on Wilny's other wing, patting the iridescent feathers gently. Both Canids watched in earnest as Storm scrubbed Lana's rusty wings down with her fingers, rousing the feathers. She then ran a finger beneath a row, gently lifting them up and blowing on the revealed skin beneath to dislodge any dust or grit from the bases of the quills. The grey down of her baby feathers gently came away in her fingers, revealing little feather buds and pin feathers just showing the tips of newer plumage. Some of the feathers had already grown in, a warm orange slightly edged with an iridescent bronze that looked golden when it caught the glint of the sun. Even her long dark brown flight feathers had this gold along their leading edges.

They did their best to mimic what Storm did, though Wilny ended up wincing as Palmer tried to pull feathers out that he thought were loose.

"You guys are next." Storm chimed, sticking her tongue out at Beth.

"Do we have to?"

"Maintenance is important Beth. You wouldn't neglect to clean your hard drive regularly, would you?"

"Fair, but why?"

"Two words Beth. Bird mites."

"Ew." She cringed and curled up into a ball on her lounger in disgust. "God, some days I wish they'd made me a Preter, rather than an Avio. Flying isn't for me, neither is bird mites or any other bugs."

Quietly, they attended to the feathers, Amell sitting on the grass so that Wilny and Malana could preen his own huge wings, taking instruction from Storm as to what to do. After a while, Storm spoke up again.

"You know, we should hold a birthday party for Malana soon." She said.

Kat and Wilny gasped in delight. "Yes! That's a brilliant idea!"

Both Raoul and Malana looked to each other in confusion.

"A what?"

"Well, her ID says she was born on the second of August. *X.02.08.* Which means she's going to be five, so we should do something for her like we did for you, Wilny."

"Please yes! Can we do it? She deserves it!" Wilny beamed eagerly. "You take her to the top of the towers and show her to fly, while you do that, we'll make a cake like you did for me, have lots of food, lots of honey, invite some of the kids from the headquarters. It'll be fun!"

"I'm sure we could."

His tailfeathers thrashed about excitedly, hitting Raoul and Palmer repeatedly as he began explaining to them what was involved in hosting a birthday party. Both Canids looked confused but nodded along politely as Wilny enthusiastically began planning the day.

"Storm, do you mind if I practiced cleaning your feathers?" Kat asked sweetly, crouching beside Storm and brushing a lock of honey-brown hair from her eyes. Giving extended a wing for Kat to treat, she let the Lioness sit close behind her, leaning back against her.

"Are you alright?" Kat whispered as she stroked and preened the feathers of her mantle. Storm shook her head.

"Not really. I don't know what to do…"

"It'll be fine," she whispered to her, affectionately kissing her shoulder. "You'll think of something."

27

Cherry Tree House, Battersea, London.

Just as Kat had said, it didn't take long until Storm had come up with a fully-fledged plan. When she shared it with the Rogues there was a sudden and united rebellion that ignited in them all. They were going to stop the Rioteers and take all the Synths they had in their command away from them. It was a risky plan, as not all of the Synth groups were as hostile with the Rioteers as they were but with recent events, they felt that others would take their side and join them.

However, Storm's fierce rebelliousness was infectious. Even Malana and Palmer were feeling defiant, playing in the park and gathering an audience of children and dogs and showing off their talents before them. Before the end of the week, they had invited several children into the house, letting them in on the Rogues secret existence. The children knowing their secret had worried Beth, but the moment she mentioned to Storm '*how pissed Rex would be if he found out*', Storm had invited the neighbours to dinner.

Much to Beth's surprise the dinner went smoothly after their initial shock of explaining the existence of Synthetic non-human people to them. Their neighbours handled it very well, however they were careful to make sure that no knowledge of their dinner party got back to the Rioteers.

Whilst the girls worked away in their clandestine criminal ways, drawing allies together across the world and forewarning other groups, the boys had taken to exercising outside whilst the summer was still bright and hot. They made use of the city and the prospect of Rex's eyes watching them to use it as an opportunity to practice their athletics, stealth attacks, and parkour skills.

Returning home from a late afternoon's session of training with a ten-mile parkour run in the scorching summer heat, all whilst Raoul carried Palmer on his back, the four boys were stopped at the gate by Malana who vehemently hushed them all, before whispering "Mission!" and allowing them inside.

What they found was nothing short of a military operation being run.

The girls were crowded before the TV, all with their phones, tablets, and laptops out as they cross-referenced times and dates, scribbling down notes onto paper or bookmarked into various coloured notebooks that were strewn about the coffee table.

All were intent in their work, cooperating quickly and efficiently together as they passed notes and relayed messages between devices. Even Malana appeared to be helping as she scurried back to her place beside Storm and began passing notepads between them when they asked. When she wasn't helping, she was sat drawing enthusiastically drawing stick figures with big fluffy wings.

"So that's five pre-planned attacks by the Rioters and a shipment of Hercules armaments being dispatched from New Jersey docks. It's all Delta and Core based equipment on board. That's what Hábrók found for us at least. Y'd all best be careful if they float your way because security is going to be tight." The disembodied voice of an American echoed through the room.

Creeping a little further in, cocking their heads as they looked at the television, they found the speaker to be a blonde Avio with dove-grey wings. Her two assistants were a muscular bull-horned Synth – a Tauro - who was manning two laptops himself, and a dark-haired woman who they assumed must have been a Preternatural.

"Five attacks? *Shit.*" Swore Storm, hastily grabbing at a list from the table and passing it to Beth.

"That's the second worst thing he could do, after trying to make a pact with Hasekura. Are you sure that there's no more shipments going out across the Atlantic?"

"Hábrók's been good with his info so far. Better than Sun." The blonde Avio stated as she pinched the bridge of her nose in aggravation, reading through a new notification on her phone. "Also, Rex sent an order for us to destroy a Core weapons store about four days ago. Hábrók checked it out for us and found it was just an Atlas Geo-modding centre, not a store at all."

"Quill, please tell me that you refused to take it out. Those are some of the few good things that ARCDA has produced."

"We did, Butcher and Barron refused too. But then Rex brought the hammer down and put the rules on them, and now they've got a guard watching them and have a hack monitoring their systems."

With equal frowns of confusion and suspicion, the boys slowly crept into the room.

"Wow…These girls are so…*Mafiosa.*" Amell breathed quietly to Wilny, awestruck by the girls and their efficiency. The Hummingbird stared at him in confusion.

"How do you know the word *Mafiosa,* but not *orange*?"

"Firstly, it's *karaka,* not orange." He shrugged, then with a grin and a wink he leant against Wilny's shoulder. "And secondly, I may not know many things, but I do know is that we are damn handsome together."

With a grunt of exasperation at his flirting, Wilny brushed Amell away with a wing and began to take his sweat drenched shirt off to throw into the laundry. Arms aching from their workout as he unclasped the hooks that held it together beneath his wings.

"Hey. Hey Wilny?" Amell grinned, flexing his muscle-bound arms and rousing his feathers up to make himself appear even larger. "Am I handsome?"

"*Amell.*"

"Answer the question Mira!"

"You're more like a horse on steroids dressed in a feather boa."

"Well….it wasn't a no." He said, then ducked as Malana threw a cushion at him. She loudly shushed him, pointing to the TV to show that they were busy working. After an apologetic smile from Amell, Malana sat back down to carry on colouring between passing notes, letting Kat give the boys a small nod to allow them to join in on their operation.

"Kat, what's going on?" Raoul whispered as Beth and Storm continued to focus on the video call and various maps and lists. Her hazel eyes glittered in glee.

"Beth and Storm are on a warpath, even more so now since Rex just gave a long list of rules to the groups in America."

"More rules?"

"Pretty much a big, long list of '*Do nothing unless I say so,*' which Rex has gone and slapped everyone with like a helicoptering phallus."

Palmer looked up with tired confused eyes and asked loudly with a yawn. "What's a phallus?"

The girls on the other end of the stream burst into laughter, as did Wilny who slow clapped at the new addition to the toddler's vocabulary.

"It's what Rex is, Puppy." Raoul said, catching a slight smile out the corner of his eye from Storm. Ever since she had returned, she hadn't smiled properly, nor had she really been as cheerful as she usually was. The stress of it all was beginning to gnaw at her. The cuts and grazes from her time away hadn't healed as fast as they should have done, and her pale face gaunt with purple bruises forming beneath her eyes.

"Do you girls need help with anything?" Asked Raoul gently, hoping to help take some of the pressure off them all.

"No, we've got it. You lot though…" Kat grimaced as she sniffed the air and gave Raoul a shove, "You need a shower. You smell like sweaty dog."

"I *am* a sweaty dog." He said chuckling softly, then teasingly, raised his arm so that Kat could smell his armpits. She grimaced and gagged, shoving him away, demanding that he go wash. Laughing, Raoul he backed away before Kat could think to use her claws, hoisting Palmer up and leaving the girls to their work to shower. Amell and Wilny however were far too intrigued by the girls at work, and instead remained to watch them run their operation.

"*Ko wai rāua?* Who's the horny guy and the blondie?" Amell frowned, leaning in to frame to stare into the camera. Beth rolled her eyes as Amell took up the entire view of the camera with his broad shoulders and huge brown and white wings.

"Kia ora koutou, weirdos."

"*Blondie's* name is Silver-Quill." Beth stated, trying to kick Amell out of the way, "She's a US Sapphire Elite and leads the Varren group, our north-American equivalent. Maira Foley, second in command and medic. And the *horny guy* is Fatal Killington, is a more muscular Artadactylian version of me, now please get your nipples away from my camera."

"Did… did they name themselves?" Amell couldn't hold in a snort of laughter at the image of a buff and tall version of Beth.

"Yes, we did, and we can hear all've ya'll in there." Fatal snapped getting up and taking up the entire camera frame, earning him exasperated groans from both girls on his end. "What's your name even meant to be birdbrain?"

Amell cocked his head, noting the tone of aggression in the male's voice but kept smiling. However, from behind him, Wilny could see the dark brown feathers down Amell's spine bristle.

"Amell Rakena, also known by the callsign: Zeus. Pleasure."

"Zoos?"

"Zeus! As in the god, you philistine."

"How pretentious, naming y'self after a god."

"Well why wouldn't I? I mean look at me, look at this body, you don't get that from sitting on your ass all day at a computer." Amell snarked, flexing dramatically for the benefit of Fatal who only sneered condescendingly at him, long bovine ears flicked angrily either side his head and he lowered his horns with a snort.

"Oh impressive, for a *five-year-old*."

Amell leapt back and flourished his arms towards Malana. "Hey! I've a five-year-old right here who could drop kick you to Tasmania."

"Aw, why? Because you couldn't do that yourself buddy?"

"You know, it's a good job you're a bull-Synth because you're just full of-"

Storm whistled shrilly, snapping the boys to attention before pulling Amell back by his wings and kicking him out of the view of the camera. "Not right now boys. Reign your dicks in or I'll cut them off."

"Focus Fatal. We don't need a transatlantic testosterone match right now." His own leader snapped.

"He started it." Fatal grumbled, retreating back to his spot on the sofa and flinching as the dark-haired woman, Maira, pulled on his short, tufted tail with a disapproving glare at his behaviour. Once he had his laptops back at hand, he shook off the bitterness.

"The Vipers are with us on this." Fatal announced. "Just confirmed. If you can get them to move south out of Illinois, then that puts them in the same area as a cache and safe house. Relay the dates and locations again for me Beth."

"There's no solid date yet," Beth scanned her information with a frown, using the tiny optical crystal to help locate the key details, "but the locations for upcoming ARCDA recruitment and supply runs are, Cisco, Manti-la Sal, and Salt Lake."

"That's all in Utah. It's not our turf Beth. We're in Washington."

"I can't remember who takes care of Utah anymore since Nailer abandoned their house, and you guys have more contact with the US groups, or at least you're *supposed* to." Said Beth. Silver-Quill pursed her lips, detecting a subtle jab at their management style. "There's a convoy going through Olympia if you're that particular about only taking care of shit in Washington."

"We're not stealing from convoys on supply runs."

"Why not? Use your backgrounds. Isn't this what you trained to do?"

"Varren is not a unit meant for subterfuge, not theft." She flicked her blonde hair over her shoulder proudly. "We're specialists."

"And we're not?"

"No."

Wilny frowned at the former Sapphire Elite, fully aware that she was insulting them. His expression noted by Storm who gave a curt laugh.

"Half of you *are* criminals, come on. You can do it." She gave a pointed nod towards the dark-haired Preternatural who blushed shyly, tucking a curl of black hair behind her ear. The bull-horned Synth beside her bristled at Storm's charming and snorted loudly.

"*Ex-criminals*, we're trying to have a good streak here."

"Then steal from the Rioteers to protect your smaller groups out there, if you're going to be so squeamish about taking from ARCDA." Storm announced loudly. Only Amell and Wilny seemed shocked at the statement.

"Isn't this quite…I don't know…backwards?" Amell nudged cautiously. Wilny frowned and nodded, his long tailfeathers swaying slightly behind him.

"Amell is right. I know Storm wants to rip Rex's dick off, but how will this help? Aren't we meant to be against ARCDA as well? We spend most of our time messing their stuff up. It seems a bit redundant to protect them."

"ARCDA isn't pure evil and the Rioteers are *not* good guys." The dark-haired woman, Maira, finally spoke, her accent a sharp Irish one which contrasted the Americans.

"Despite what my uncle makes them out to be, they are in fact terrorists. The Rioteers have killed more innocent people and Synths with car bombs, assassinations, kidnappings, and trigger happily tearing through bunkers than they have saved people, whilst ARCDA has helped to save so many people and even the world on multiple occasions through their exploits. If it weren't for ARCDA we would have been wiped out years ago by natural disasters, famines, energy and water wars, even pandemics. You should *not* feel guilty or traitorous for stealing from or lying to the Rioteers in order to protect the parts of ARCDA that are helping the world, or to protect other Synths who the Rioteers forget about as soon as they rescue them."

Wilny blinked slowly, allowing Maira's alternative view point to settle upon him until he noted something she had said.

"Wait. Your uncle?"

"Yes, Rex is my uncle."

"*Condolences.*"

"Maira's mum is a doctor in Atlas." Storm explained swiftly. "Sometimes Mai goes in and pretends to be her. She's like Roux."

"*Oooh.* Got it." Wilny stared hard at the Preternatural until she noticed and began to laugh bashfully and her skin lightly flushed with iridescent green to violet stripes, the change made Amell, Lana, and Wilny all gasp. Camouflage skin. She didn't match the appearance of any Preternatural origin bases that he knew of, at closest she may have been a GEMINI, but then if she was a prototype like Roux, then it was likely the origin base had come from her.

"I don't *always* pretend to be her." Insisted Maira, settling her skin back to a neutral and fair complexion. "Sometimes I go in as *me*. ARCDA has a revolving door for me for the amount of times I've been kidnapped by the Rioteers and returned to ARCDA."

Her two teammates rolled their eyes and gave sighs of forlorn exasperation. Maira nodded, and pointed her pen at the camera, gesturing towards Wilny with an inquiring look.

"I know you from somewhere, don't I? Have we ever met?"

"No, sorry."

"Wait. I got it. Your mum is Professor Mira, right?" She said with a victorious smile.

There was a pause between them all, and Wilny became suddenly acutely aware that Storm was analysing his expression in a very raptorial way. Keeping perfectly still and calm, she was watching him for any twitch or hint to indicate emotions he might be hiding, eyes sharp and unblinking.

"Yes, yes she is. You might have met one of my brothers, not me. Uh…have you ever met Professor Mira?"

"I've met her a few times actually." Maira declared, smiling brightly, "She's very nice and very determined. I'd have loved to have worked in Aura with her."

A bizarre and awkward feeling came across him, which he had no other way of describing other than '*odd*'. Odd at that he didn't know how to feel and was conflicted. He'd not forgotten what he'd learnt.

"Well…" He said slowly, trying not to betray the conflicted feelings to any of them. "If you see her again, tell her I said…hi."

Maira nodded, not seeming to have noticed the awkwardness and passed over a note to Quill, moving on. Fatal drummed his stomach loudly, slouching back in the sofa and looking between them all.

"So, what is your plan then ladies?"

"You guys need to get your things prepared." Storm sat up, taking command of the operation. "Take the supplies and make a cache. Box it and store it so you can make a dash when the Rioteers try and strike that Core bunker. The evacuation code is still STENDEC."

"You think they're gonna get caught?"

"Of course, they are. The attack made them angry and now they're gonna fight hard, not smart." Beth pointed out. "Remember that whole troupe who went out of their way to get revenge on that one doctor and all ended up being caged and tortured because they didn't think it through."

Quill frowned. "The Melbourne crew? Yeah, I remember."

"It'd be that, but on a larger scale."

"Got it. Think, don't feel; sights on the horizon and don't stop until you get there."

"And the ships. Do you know which port they're heading for?"

"All I've got is *checkpoint is in England, move on to Denmark*. With a two-week window in which they'll be there for one night only."

A glance at Kat's screen showed the boys that she'd already brought up a list of ports that handled transatlantic cargo ships and sent it to Storm. They hadn't noticed how fast the girls were handling the information as they'd been so busy watching the TV.

"We'll try and take it, but we'd need a clearer time frame." Said Storm, looking at all the ports with a frown. "If we're out of the city for more than two days then Rex will take a shotgun to my head."

"I'll see what I can do and if I can get Hábrók to contact you directly."

Storm yawned loudly, extending her wings out above her head. "Right, I'm gonna take a break now, I'm getting a headache."

"I'll take charge." Beth announced, shooting her hand up to tag Storm out with a high five.

"The Oceania and Pacific groups are next right? Tag Amell in to help with the accents and slang then send the notes to me later."

"Thanks for your help, *Wing Commander.*" Quill smirked, allowing their screen to close as Beth called up the lead Oceania group. Uncoiling her legs and arching her back, Storm left Kat and Beth to handle the next round. She stumbled towards the kitchen behind them, letting Amell jump over the sofa to take her spot, eager to see who was part of the New Zealand group.

Wilny however, quietly followed Storm to the kitchen out of concern.

He watched quietly as she leant against the counter with a deep and exhausted sigh. Her slate grey wings drooped across the floor. The feathers were misaligned and tattered in places, as though she had been in a fight not long before. She was always meticulous with her wings, never allowing them to become damaged or dirtied.

"Boss?" He said gently, running the back of his hand down a wing to straighten the feathers.

Glancing at him over her shoulder, he noticed how bloodshot her eyes were. Raoul had noticed her haggard look before and commented to him about it during their run, which he'd passed off as Raoul being overly concerned, but now he knew that the Hound was right.

"What's wrong? You look like shit."

Sighing heavily, she ran her fingers through her hair and shook her head.

"Just...come with me." She said softly, taking him by his wrist and tugging him towards the door. "I need you to come with me."

Her voice was so quiet he was almost certain that he had heard her thoughts rather than her voice.

"I'm not really dressed for flying." He pointed out gesturing to his lack of shirt, but she didn't seem to care.

Leading him out onto the decking, in two strides and a leap, she shot upwards with a flurry of wingbeats to clear the ancient old cherry and willow trees that lined the back of the garden. He followed, running and leaping onto the trampoline they'd bought Malana to bounce himself up into the air to catch up with her. Storm circled slowly, waiting for him and when he managed to slow his frantic wingbeats down to a steady glide, she led him onwards.

They arced over the river and the old power station cruising out towards Brixton, where she began to cruise on a thermal until she found what she was looking for.

Without any indication, she spiralled down towards a monolithic bronze statue that stood atop the building, adorned with what Wilny first thought to be a bird. He landed before its wings that arched forward like a hawk shielding its prey and scattering the roosting crows. The stern face of a woman stared down at him from beneath her plumed helmet, crouched with a spear in her eagle talons pointed out over the edge of the building.

"I don't think I've seen this statue before." He noted between gasping breaths and sitting on the façade to let his heartrate return to a regular beat.

"Bellona. Roman goddess of war. Though this statue is just so people know where Club Bellona is."

"She has bird arms."

"Yeah, it's part of the landmarking pattern that Crow, and I cooked up. Whenever you see a statue with wings, there's a chance of a secret cache there."

He watched her awkwardly crawl beneath the statue, pulling out a tightly sealed metal case only slightly larger than a shoebox. The crows that had scattered began to return to their roosts on the back and arches of the statue's wings, calm and indifferent to the presence of the two Avios.

"Your cache?"

"Crow's actually." She nodded to a large crow that dropped in beside Wilny and began pulling at his tailfeathers. "Evening Brixton."

The crow cackled as Wilny tried to shoo it away and instead landed on his head to pull at his hair and feathers and didn't leave until Wilny noisily beat his wings.

Normally it would have made Storm laugh to see him being accosted by a bird, but she didn't even crack a smile as she released the clips on the box to unlock it.

"Are you alright? Why are we out here?"

"Beth knows our cache-and-dash protocol, but you need to learn it too."

"Me?"

"You're protecting Malana, Raoul, and Palmer, you'll need to be on the ground with them if anything happens." She was deadly serious in tone. "Beth will be too busy wiping files and quick-routing our trail to stop others following. Kat and Amell will probably follow me, but the means it will cause us all to separate. In case of emergency, you need to know where these boxes are, what's in each of them and how to use them."

"In case of emergency? Wow, you really do think that the Rioteers are going to turn on us."

"I don't doubt it." She popped the box open and brought it to the level top of the façade for Wilny to examine.

"Here. These maps are cache locations with directions to different safe havens. Some are occupied, some aren't, the books will tell you what to do."

Alongside the traditional paper maps there were notebooks of names and numbers, wads of money in what looked to be five different currencies, painkillers, a small bottle of disinfectant, bandages, a Swiss army knife, and a small black case with a golden bird on it. All neatly organised and ready to use, she'd clearly thought ahead and had safe guards in place.

"You're impressive."

"Is that a compliment?"

"I'm being serious."

"I can trust ARCDA to attack us. But I can't trust the Rioteers not to fall, switch sides and sell us out."

"Betrayal never comes from your enemies."

"Exactly." She gave him the first clear smile he'd seen in a fortnight and passed him the notebook and maps of Europe. "Whenever you get the message STENDEC come through on your phone, you just dash to the nearest cache and pick a location written in the book. There's directions and money. Here are our main safe houses; one in Cornwall where I've just been to, three in France and one in Luxembourg."

"Which one will we know to use."

"The trick is you don't. Spontaneity helps." She then removed the black case from the box and swapped it for the maps he held.

"Storm? What is this?" Wilny frowned, trying to remember where he had seen the little golden bird symbol before. He flipped it open and gasped as inside lay a sleek black and red handgun along with several cartridges of ammunition.

"You know I said a while ago that I don't think we need or should have guns. I've changed my mind, you need one."

Starry eyed, he gently lifted the gun from its place and examined it in the dying amber light of the sun. Sliding the tiny safety lock off, the red on the gun glowed softly and a small LED sights flicked up. She rolled her wings and sat herself on the façade next to him, watching as he tentatively turned the gun around.

"Is this a-"

"A *Fénix X4-2*. Yeah."

"Ooooh maaaan…oh this is beautiful. Look at this! EMI guns are so beautiful!"

He aimed up at a plane flying overhead in the pink sky, watching it through its sights, drumming his feet excitedly on the club roof. Even his long tailfeathers were dancing about in excitement. Although Core trained all of their Elites to use standard firearms, they had a preference towards EMI -Electromagnetic Incapacitators– based weapons now that Hasekura was using them. It had all the effect of a bullet, with the stunning capabilities of a tazer.

"I didn't know they were out of the prototype stage! Saw them at a tactical village display, such a beautiful gun. *Look at it!*"

His excited sentiments were lost on Storm.

"Honestly, it's just a gun to me. I've no idea what the butt from the barrel is, but Roux is the one who got me it to give to you. Though, *got* is the wrong word. What's it called when you kill someone and take their stuff?"

"Tuesday, but Storm…why?" He asked, neatly putting the gun back in its case and returning it to the cache box. "Why are you giving me this?"

"You're the only one qualified to handle it."

"That's not what I meant."

'It's because I trust you to keep them safe.'

Wilny blinked slowly.

He'd heard what she said, but she hadn't moved her lips to say it. Several stunned seconds went by as he took a moment to realise what she had done.

'Can you hear me?' she said silently again, a smirk spreading across her face as Wilny's eyes widened. *'Is this thing on?'*

"How did- I heard you!" He shrieked, nearly falling backwards off the façade. "I heard you!"

'That's because we're far out of other people's way so you can focus more easily.' She smirked, tilting her head to one side. *'And I've lived with a lot of musers, enough that I can make myself heard to them when I want to. It helps a lot with persuading.'*

"You did it again." He stared in awe at her. It was so odd to hear her.

"Wait. If you can make musers hear you –also *how can you do that* –then why didn't you do this with me earlier."

"Because I didn't want you to feel like I was intruding on your privacy, and I didn't want to do your brain any damage. All musery stuff is, is just electricity and detecting the frequency of brain activity and translating it to words. Crow could explain it better, but back to this–"

"What colour am I thinking of?"

"It doesn't work like that. I can't see what's in *your* head, I can only broadcast to musers."

"Damn…Think of a colour!"

"Wilny."

"Please. *Pleeeeeeeease.*"

Laughing she shut her eyes and scrunched her face up, trying to picture a colour for him. Focusing all his attention on her, he tried to see what she was visualising. He tried to remember that Crow had told him about trying to detect emotions, but it felt different trying to see a colour someone else was thinking of. Wisps of thoughts played on the edge of his mental field, but he could see no clear colours, instead there was sounds more akin to an old radio being tuned with a static and high-pitched tinnitus as well as the feeling of exhaustion.

The frequency became clearer the longer he tuned into it and soon he was able to hear the word she was thinking of.

"Ver...vermillion?" He said slowly, catching the little twitch of a grin and beginning to dance where he sat. "I'm right, aren't I?"

"You're lucky you're adorable or I'd have pushed you off this roof right now."

"So, I was right!"

She shoved him gently and the two laughed. The red of the sunset bathed the city in a contrast of red on blue, turning the clouds to a glowing orange against the aqua sky. With their backs facing the sun, the warmth soaked into their feathers.

It had been a trying time between them with one thing happening after the other, neither had really had the chance to talk.

"Storm..." Wilny began slowly, trailing off as he thought carefully about what he was going to say to her. Now she trusted him a little more, he could finally ask her what he had been meaning to for the last several weeks without a total shut down or sarcastic comment.

"I uh...asked Beth if I could see my profile so I could see why I was left in Core." He warily watched her expression, "And some of the files from the twin studies. I only watched one or two of the vlogs and I kind of understood what it was about."

"Did you learn anything?" She was being calm and unreactive, though he knew that acute watchful look. Hiding her worry by being perfectly still and expressionless.

"Not really. All I learnt was that I loved bees even as a kid and that I was a real cry baby."

"Well, that hasn't changed."

"How dare you. Bees are some of the most important creatures ever to evolve!"

She laughed a little, recalling his occasional outburst of knowledge on bees or aggressively defending them from Beth whenever one lost its way into the house.

"You did have a lot of bee outfits" She said with a smirk, "I liked the one of you in a little black and yellow raincoat best."

"Did you watch all of them?"

"I marathoned just about every video of the Identical Avio studies and some of the Variance studies, from the very beginning to the very end with the fire." Every feather on her wing bristled, and a sudden and familiar rageful feeling crept into Wilny's mental field, the almost exact same level of rage that Roux had held. He withdrew from trying to see what she had seen.

"I can't make sense of the fire or what happened. I can't even remember much of it." She sighed, gripping her hair in frustration. "It was a critical point to where we are now, but I can't- it's just- what the hell happened for it all to go the way it did. I know Rex caused it, but I don't know what was going on with him to begin with."

"What can you remember?" Wilny asked gently.

There was a pregnant pause between them, Storm taking her time to calm herself and let her feathers settle before she spoke. She shifted slightly in agitation, scrunching her face up as she forced herself to recall what she could of the fire before slowly she started to tell him of what she remembered. The broken fragmented glimpses between waking and black unconsciousness, blood in her mouth and needing to get out.

"I'm sorry I can't remember anything about what happened to you during it."

"It's alright, I didn't expect you to know." Wilny assured her. "From the sounds of it, it was chaos."

"But what I can't see why your mother put you in Core after all of that." She contemplated with a frown. "From the videos she made, she just seemed to adore you."

"I saw. I...don't know how to feel about it."

"You must have been put into Recovery or something. I think that's more likely than you willingly signing on at fifteen to be a soldier; no offence, but you were a real cry baby."

"That's true. They do Hard Resets, which means they essentially destroy all your memories so nothing that hurt you continues to hurt you." He shifted uncomfortably at the thought. "Maybe...it's just a theory but it does make more sense than for her to have just abandoned me there but keep my brothers."

Storm shrugged and slouched forward, allowing the silence to grow with nothing but the constant low rumble of engines and distant music to fill it. It wasn't awkward, more rather that it was difficult to talk on the matter without knowing if they were going to upset the other.

"So...you have a twin somewhere? Is that right?"

"Yes and…I'm not sure how to feel about it. Should I be sad? Hopeful? I've no idea." Letting her shoulders drop, she looked away from him, sadly staring out across the city. "It scares me that one day Rex or Beth might find her and I have to find out how she feels about me. She must hate me."

"I'm sorry, I'm sorry, just…are you alright?" He asked tentatively, restraining himself from reaching out and taking her hand.

She didn't answer, neither did she seem to *want* to answer, and her expression betrayed very little as to what she was feeling but she was clearly thinking about what had happened. Curious, he mused upon her, trying to catch a glimpse of what she was feeling and thinking.

The high-pitched tinnitus whined piercingly through his head for several seconds with the wisps of thoughts, followed by a cacophony of colours and emotions all flooding his head in a single screeching torrent. It was all sharp, fast and painful, alien in that it was not his thoughts, and intense.

With a shriek of pain, he gripped his head and bolted away from her side and hid round the back of the statue's wing, hoping that the distance would lessen the intensity.

"Holy shit. Storm!" He gasped as his head cleared. "Is that what you meant about giving me brain damage because I totally believe it now."

She didn't even seem to acknowledge him speaking and instead just stared ahead at the sky. Shaking his head, he padded back cautiously and sat back down beside her.

"I know you're fast and flighty, but you can slow down Storm."

"I can't do that."

"Why not?"

"Because there's a million things I need to keep track on. I don't have time to worry about me. I'm not important, everyone else is."

"Then can you at least let us worry about you?" He took her hand and gripped it tightly. "I know you want to help and keep everyone safe, but you're exhausted and need to stop thinking about all the shit going on with Rex, it's going to destroy you."

"You sound like Ada."

"And Crow."

There was no attempt made to snatch her hand away or take off into the sky, instead just the drooping of her wings, letting them hang down the side of the building.

"Look at us." Said Storm hoarsely. "Monsters missing memories and made to murder."

"At least there's a bright side."

"And that is?"

"We may be monsters," Wilny grinned widely, "but we're also hot as hell."

Then he raised his arms and flexed for her. The spluttering laugh that followed from Storm echoed between the statue's metallic wings, and she shoved him playfully. Bouncing to his feet, Wilny peacocked around, flashing his tail disks in the sunset and mimicking everyone in the Rogues until there were tears in her eyes from laughing so much.

"Are we good Boss?" He asked when he was finally done showing off, holding his hand out to her. Wiping the tears away she took it with both hands and smiled warmly up at him.

"We're good, but we do have to make a plan for a certain special someone."

"Who? Oh! Yes. So, I have an idea."

28

The Obelisk, Southwark, Central London.

The heat of the day had left behind a swelteringly hot August night. From their high perch on the Obelisk, the newly crowned tallest skyscraper in London, they looked out across the city that glittered and shone far into hazy purpling horizon of the sunset, sound tracked by a low thunderous rumble of engines. The Obelisk was an impressively tall spire, decadent in design and completely outfitted in solar glass that generated electricity to power the building with, and with wide balconies that allowed plant life to cascade down the sides of the building. It represented new growth and change within the city and at night, like many of the newly planted trees in the city, the leaves and flowers of the plants glowed with blue and green bioluminescence as well as releasing a refreshingly scent across London.

The Rogues had given Malana a birthday to remember. Half of her gifts had been opened or experienced already, and now it was time for the main event before her party. With Storm, Crow, Amell, and Kat all having helped fly her up to the very peak of the tower, they were readying Malana for her first free flight. It was the perfect place to let her practice freely, as it was a high enough point that she would have enough altitude for the older Avios to help if anything did go wrong.

Storm had been training Malana everyday by exercising her wings and muscles in preparation. The little girl had taken the training very seriously, and even as she waited at the top of the spire for everything to be readied, Malana had already had a warm up, practicing running and jumping to flap and gain lift. Now however, it was time for the real thing.

"High." Malana gulped. She held onto the railing tightly, whilst Storm wrapped around her waist a beautifully patterned length of gold sari material that trailed across the floor, glittering with rhinestones.

"Well high places are the best places to learn to fly from." Storm assured her, observing her as her gold eyes flashed in the light. She had talked Wilny down from getting Malana large flight goggles to wear as she had pointed out to him that like herself, Malana had a nictitating membrane which would protect her eyes and would– hopefully– work on instinct.

"I really hope we don't ruin these." Katana mumbled, draping her own beautiful blue length of cloth about her arm and tail, twirling gracefully around with it. Each of them – apart from Crow- wore one, each a different colour. "They're expensive. And beautiful."

"So why are we wearing these?" Asked Amell. He had been eager to go with them but was confused by the fact that he had to stretch and warm up with Malana, practice breathing exercises and wing extensions and movement, and now wear a sash.

"Do you know how kites work Amell?" Crow asked him shrewdly and fanning out his own long tailfeathers rapidly.

"Sort of."

"Well, these sashes act like the tails of kites, they'll balance you out and keep you aloft and in your case with your big-arse wings, will help ya' turn since you lack tailfeathers like me. Storm found that sari cloth is actually the best to use when training people to fly. Long, nicely made, accessible and durable." He shot a grin towards Storm. "Even though Miss Nagarkar nearly killed her for it. Ruining all her silks."

Storm pulled a face and straightened up her own purple sash, mumbling to herself, "I can still hear her screaming *chutiya* at me."

"Fucking loved that woman."

"I didn't."

"Yes, but you were a brat."

Amell looked to Kat for an explanation on who they were talking about, though all he got was a confused shrug in response.

"Who's Miss Nagarkar?"

"She was a transhuman who helped to fix our clothes up so that we weren't constantly flying shirtless." Storm said, preening Lana's wings for what must have been the fiftieth time that day.

"What happened to her? She didn't die, did she?" Questioned Kat nervously.

Crow laughed, nearly tipping over the railings he was perched upon.

"No, she's now running a Rioteer headquarters in Mumbai. She's like the West Asian equivalent to Rex, but with minus Rex's bullshit attitude."

"Oh, so Asena then."

Amell still looked a little confused. He gave Storm a little nudge with his wing.

"So why don't you have a full set of tailfeathers like Crow? I thought all Avios that weren't Transhumans had tailfeathers."

"I *used* to have them."

"Really? Then why don't you anymore?"

"Because-" She stopped and scrunched her face up into a distressed grimace as she tried to answer, before giving up and turning to face her back to him and Lana, who was also watching and waiting for an answer. Raising one wing up she twisted around and moved her shirt and the layers of sari out of the way so that they could see her short feather covered tail.

"Well, *this* is why." She said, ignoring the slight twinges in her back and wings as she twisted. "They've just not grown back yet."

Amell, Kat, and Malana gathered closer to inspect the short tail. Deep claw marks sliced through the grey feathers, across both the tail as well as her hip and the small of her back. It looked painful, bald in places from where it looked as though she had plucked out some of the feathers. A shudder ran down Kat's spine at the very sight of them; they were the lacerations of either an Avio's talons, or a Pard's claws, either one made her feel sick to her stomach to see and upset that Storm had kept them hidden from her.

"*Ouch!* Those are some deep scars." Amell winced, stepping back and rubbing his tailbone sympathetically. Both Malana and Kat looked horrified at the mutilation.

"You...you didn't do this, did you?" Kat whispered, bristling all over.

"Of course not." She covered her tail again quickly, uncomfortable with them staring at her.

"What happened?"

"I'll tell you another time." She said, shaking her wings off roughly. "But don't worry. They'll grow back."

Amell shrugged and went back to looking out at the city, however Kat noticed Storm shooting Crow a dangerous glare, a warning to him to not tell them. Noting the seriousness of Storm's look, Kat made a quiet note to herself to ask Storm again later, when the Rogue was feeling more comfortable to talk about herself.

Prepared and ready to go, Storm gave the others a wave of her hand, drawing Malana across to one corner of the platform so that she could watch and take instruction.

"Keep your eyes on Kat and Crow." She said, nodding to the Lioness to go first. Taking a deep breath, Malana fixed her gaze and watched them intently, trembling slightly with the anxiety of knowing she would be jumping off the building too.

Smiling brightly and giving the little girl a reassuring wink, Kat rolled her shoulders to loosen her wings and jumped up onto the bar of the railings, brushing out the long blue sari out behind her. Even though she didn't need to wear it, it was for Lana's support.

Extending her wings out behind her, Kat drew her breath and kicked off the railings into a swan dive. Malana watched as she fell away, down along the glass side of the building before extending out her wings, swooping out and arcing up, the blue kite-tail flaring out behind her. Crow followed swiftly after, launching himself out into the abyss sweeping his wings out. Broad wings catching the hot rising air, he spiralled effortlessly up. There was no need to flap when the wind was carrying him.

Malana's eyes grew wide and her jaw dropped behind the bandana, as Crow twisted and tightly corkscrewed downwards into a tight spiral, one hand reaching out and brushing across Kat's blue wings as they passed each other. The two soared in circles around the tower and through the adornments that topped it, Crow tilting his tailfeathers and changing his direction with minimal effort, Kat flitting about like a butterfly with her brilliant wings.

Shaking his head and laughing, Amell drew himself up onto the railing and leapt out over Kat as she passed, throwing all twenty plus feet of wings out with a loud crack against the wind. The rising heat caught him too and following Crow, he spiralled upwards around the tower without so much as a wing beat, laughing to himself as he soared.

Malana's fears dissipated in a flash as she watched in wide eyed awe of the three wheeling through the sky. Giddy with excitement to feel the wind on her feathers and experience the same joy they were feeling she flexed her wings, quickly running her hands down the primaries to align them properly as Storm had just done.

All but a few of the baby grey feathers had fallen out. The dark brown primaries were no longer sheathed in their grey casings, faintly marked by lighter coloured bars. Gold edged each warm copper-orange feather in an iridescent gloss whilst the feathers between her shoulders shifted between pink and bronze lustres.

She could already feel the turbulence buffeting the soft undersides, trembling each feather gently. Looking down at the light streams below, her scalp prickled with anticipation. Amell rushed past, his tail-cloth cracking like a bullwhip in the wind as it trailed behind him. Soaring up on the banks of rising heat, it was as though he weighed nothing. Awe inspired as she was, Malana held onto the railing tightly.

Storm crouched to her level, noting her apprehension. "What's wrong Sweetie?" She asked tentatively.

"My wings are too small…" Malana responded in a timid whisper, golden eyes filled with worry. "I'll fall."

"No, you won't."

"I will!"

"Only if you allow yourself to. And even if you do, we'll catch you." She promised, gently tucking a curled lock of hair behind her feathered ear tufts. "You trust us, right?"

With a hesitant nod, Malana loosened her grip on the railing. Giving the little girl a boost up, Storm held her hand as she balanced upon the bar.

"Remember to breathe in when you lift them up, and out when you bring them down. In and out. Just like we practiced." Storm reminded her, slowly letting go of her hand.

"Ready?"

"Ready."

The world seemed to slow down around her; every detail of the city below began to come into hyper focus. The bar of the railing felt icy cold beneath her bare feet compared to the hot rising air. Heartbeat drumming faster and faster in her ears, Malana crouched, drawing her wings back behind her. Arms out either side, she shut her eyes and drew breath.

In a heartbeat, Malana sprung out leaping forward into the sky, throwing her wings down to her sides with a crack of feathers against the wind. The wind hit her like a sucker punch, forcing her to open her eyes, which were immediately protected by the translucent membrane flicking across her eye. The air caught her wings almost immediately, keeping her aloft in the sky.

Daring to look down, building rolled beneath her. Her toes curled at not being able to feel anything solid beneath them, but the feeling of the air across her feathers and chest told her that she wasn't falling. She was flying! She was actually flying!

Holding her wings firm, she glided across the river towards where Crow was hovering, her golden kite-tail fluttering out behind her while her true tailfeathers awkwardly and jerkily twitched to tilt and alter her course. The muscles across her chest and back ached with the effort and her heartbeat was so loud in her ears she could no longer hear the wind. Twisting her body, she banked in long sweeping arcs from side to side, just as Storm had practiced with her, wings wavering slightly as she strained to keep them out. The older Avios drew in, surrounding her in an arrowhead shape, keeping her within the middle so that they could see her.

There was a sharp whistle to her right-hand side, where Kat was steadily beating her wings. The Lioness made a gesture for Malana to copy the rowing motion, moving them a little slower so that she could see the technique. Mimicking the movements steadily, she found herself moving forward and the air resistance lessening.

Crow laughed loudly and fell back, allowing Amell to take the lead of the arrowhead. Smiling she beat her wings a little harder and faster, following in the wake of Amell's path. She could feel the difference in the airflow as he made vortices with wingtips through his slow and steady flaps, with each beat helping her to maintain her altitude. Even when they changed direction in a smooth arc, she kept up with the others.

Bright ecstatic delight overwhelmed her. She only wished that Wilny had come out with them, so he could see her fly.

Caught up in her joy, she gave a short scream as Storm arrowed past her with a whistle of feathers, almost too fast for Malana to focus on against the lights of the city. Darting at speed in circles around them, Storm drew her wings in to gain speed and then snapped them back out just as quickly to loop-de-loop and corkscrew through the air, using the velocity to go from barely scraping the rooftops to sling-shotting herself far above them without a single beat.

She was showing off.

Having only seen Storm fly from the ground, Malana never realised how dynamic her flying was, using every twist and change in the air to manoeuvre. Effortless, in her element and in full control without fear of falling.

So distracted by Storm, Malana lost her rhythm and stalling in the air. She began to drop, slowly at first, but then she noticed the loss of altitude as the others began to get further and further away from her. Beating as hard as she could she felt the turbulent wind catch the feathers, the muscles in her lower back twinging sharply with the strain, but she couldn't get the air to flow over them.

As she began to panic, a rough hand pushed down on her legs and wings, levelling her body out so her wings could catch the air once again. Craning her neck round, she glimpsed the black feathers of her rescuer. Crow.

He gave her a wink and then tucking his wings back, he dropped like a stone, diving towards a band of trees before sweeping his dark wings out, a shadow in the twilight.

Crow let out a loud piercing whistle as he darted low across the tree tops circling round as he caught another vent. A black cloud erupted from the trees chasing up after him with a sound like the wind rushing through the leaves of a forest. A thousand crows took to the sky as one long black river, joining the flock of giants.

Lana's breath hitched as a large raven flew across her wing, cocking its head briefly to watch her with a dark eye, and then matched her speed before her. Its wingspan was barely the length of one of her own wings. Watching its black feathers beating slowly and rhythmically, she copied it, trying to match its strokes to keep moving forward.

"Her name's Temese."

She flinched as Crow sailed alongside her, tilting his long arc of tailfeathers so that he drifted in a full circle around her to meet the raven's side. Flying at a lower level meant the wind was less deafening and she could now hear her own wingbeats and panting breaths. In on the upstroke, out on the down.

"She's the only raven here, the rest are in the tower."

"They all have names?" She asked as an ungainly young bird landed on Crow's shoulder, holding its wings out in an attempt to surf upon him. Crow nodded, rolling onto his back in the air, surfing with ease as he pointed out a small flock of seven birds flying in a uniform V just slightly behind him.

"These are my main buddies though. We've got Marylebone who's the boss, Mayfair, Kensington, Belgravia, Brixton, Poplar, and this little bast- um...*idiot*, this one's Blackheath." At the sound of its name, the bird swooped past and pecked at Crow's head.

"Did they teach you to fly?"

"I learnt from different crows, but we teach each other. I learn from them and they learn from me. There's no better teacher than a bird."

Kat swooped beneath Malana in a flash of blue, spiralling round with her long tail, some of the crows veering off to join her in the diving, clearly playing as they tried to dart beneath her wings on her down strokes. They didn't mind the fact that they were flying with creatures three hundred times their size and who could take them out with a single wingbeat.

"Watch a bird, then copy them." Crow instructed, leading Malana into a thermal to soar. She nodded and began watching intently at how the birds would swoop and spiral.

Seeing that Malana was safely surrounded on all sides again by advanced fliers, Storm swooped down to land upon the top of the BT tower to call the boys at home who had been busy finishing off preparations for Lana's party.

"How's it going." She chirped into the phone, watching as Kat and Crow showed Malana and Amell how to use dynamic soaring to climb into the air, with aided demonstration provided by the crows.

"WHERE'S THE FIRE EXTINGUISHER?"

Storm jerked the phone away from her ear at Wilny's screeching.

"Wha-"

"EVERYTHING'S GONE WRONG! HELP!"

"Whoa whoa! What's happened?"

"OH GOD! RAOUL'S BURNT HIS HAND!"

"What are you two-"

"*Palmer!* PALMER PUT THAT DOWN RIGHT NO- AH! Oh god. OH GOD! BETH HELP US!"

With a groan she hung up and jumped from the tower to catch up with the others. Wilny had assured her that everything would have been fine, but she had underestimated just how bad their baking skills were and just how unhelpful Beth could be.

"Amell, Crow, I'm gonna need you two to go back to the house and rescue Wilny and Raoul." She directed, swooping round between them and drawing herself into a hover, letting the others circle.

"What's the damage?"

"House on fire, Beth being Beth, Raoul's got burns and I think Palmer might have had too much sugar already."

Crow winced.

"I'll get my crew in to help." He assured her, whistling to the crows and veering off southwards to Battersea.

"I'll help." Kat trilled, pulling back into hover before Storm.

"Are you sure Kat?"

"He needs someone who has good taste as well as someone who knows how to cook."

"That's true. Alright then I'll meet you all back at home." She laughed, giving the three a wave to send them on their way.

As Crow left, the flock of corvids slowly dispersed, returning their roosts in the trees below, leaving Storm and Malana to glide over a glittering sea of lights together.

The temperature dropped the higher they flew, and the colder it grew, the emptier and more silent the sky became. Malana also began to realise how tired her chest and wings were becoming as her rhythm started to falter and become more erratic. She almost wanted to let them stop and just glide softly after the crows and fall asleep in the trees. Flying was more exhausting than it looked.

Distracted by her exhaustion and watching the crows, a sudden gust struck Malana hard. It snapped her right wing back, wrenching her backwards and ripping all support away from her. She fell, tumbling through the sky just as she had done before. She saw it all over again, her previous family struggling in the sky above as Miel struggled to catch up to her.

"Storm!" She shrieked, reaching up towards the Rogue as she plummeted. "Help me!"

Storm dove, easily keeping pace.

"Malana. Malana listen to me." She said curtly, half shouting over the rush of wind. "Malana you have to twist round onto your front."

"Help me! *Please!*"

"You have to help yourself. You have to learn to fly."

"Storm!"

"Copy what I do." She ordered quickly. Tucking her sleek wings in close to her body she reduced air resistance and twisted so that she was angled correctly, and then when she was ready, she flung her wings out and swept upwards in a controlled arc.

Quickly taking her lesson in, Malana mimicked Storm, forcing her wings close to her body. She twisted, aiming her head towards the ground and using her short tailfeathers to adjust her position. With a gulp, she swept her wings out and sharply she was pulled into a steep arc as she was catapulted back towards the sky by her own velocity, giving her a chance to beat her wings and fly level once more.

Shaking the dizziness of panic off and breathing deeply Malana looked below at how close the ground was with a sudden realisation at how close to crashing she had come.

"See? That wasn't so hard." Storm chirped, soaring along beside her, brushing her fingers across the top of the grass and rising with her, guiding her back up to the sky.

Malana glowered at Storm, her wings and hands trembling.

"Why did you not *help*?"

"Because you could save yourself." Storm said with a gentle shrug, leading her back up above the buildings on a thermal. Malana watched her carefully, doing her best to mimic Storm's movements.

"Did…did you learn this way?" Malana tentatively asked after a short silence. "Falling out of the…*la ciel?*"

"Yes. I had to learn how to do this all by myself and broke almost all of my bones doing so." Storm shrugged and then dipped beneath her with a gentle tilt of her primaries. "Hold onto my shoulders and flap with me, we're going up."

Doing as instructed, Malana held onto Storm and lay on her back, letting Storm do all the work. Catching the wind, Storm surged upwards. From where she lay, Malana could feel the tough powerful muscles of her back and shoulders beneath her as they powered on upwards through the damp layer of clouds that covered the city.

Emerging on the other side, Storm surfed across the top of the cloud base stirring up little vortices of disturbance in her wake, gliding steadily through the unending sky whilst Malana looked up at the full moon above them.

Malana gasped.

Just as when she leapt from the Obelisk and the world below came into hyper focus. Staring up in awe at the sky, the details of the moon and the more distant stars began to reveal themselves to her, a billion pinpricks of light against the velvet blackness of space. "Pretty." Malana breathed, suddenly overcome with dizziness at how big the sky was and how far she was from the ground.

With the world above and below, a spine-tingling awareness dawned upon her as she realised how much there was to see and how there were so very few people in the world who had such freedom as to explore all of it.

"You should see what it's like to fly under the northern lights." Chuckled Storm, hoisting Malana back up on her back before she slipped off. "Now that's really pretty."

"Storm."

"Hm?"

"Teach me to fly."

"Fly like a bird?" Storm smirked, fanning her primaries out and realigning them. "That's not too hard."

"No. Fly like a Storm."

She looked over her shoulder at the little girl, heart aching with pride.

"Well, to fly like a *Storm*," she said slowly, breaking out of surfing and beating her wings again, "you first need to know how to fall without fear."

Lana looked frightened.

"Fall?"

"Well. *Stoop.*" She grinned as they rose up and looped, the stars beneath them and the clouds above. "Hold on tight."

Wide eyed, Malana clung to Storm's shoulders, pulling her wings in tight as she could. With a whistling crack of feathers, Storm powered through the clouds, picking up speed as they went into the dive.

Bursting through the other side of the cloud cover the ground rushed towards them. Malana held her breath in terror as they became level with the top of the Obelisk, prepared to scream until Storm pulled up at the very last second above the river, diving beneath London Bridge and speeding across the top of the water. She arced up following the curve of the river as she took Malana past the riverside landmarks, letting her enjoy the sights.

In steady flight, Malana could breathe again and did so followed by a fit of giggles at how silly she felt in herself for thinking that Storm would let them crash.

"Fast!" She laughed, hugging Storm tightly. "So fast!"

"That wasn't *that* fast. We were only going one-hundred miles an hour."

"Quoi!"

"When you get a little braver, then we'll go higher then and then we'll go faster." Storm assured her with a wink. "But for now, we've a party to go to."

29

Cherry Tree House, Battersea, London.

They circled above Cherry Tree House, the garden illuminated by lights strung about the trees and busy with people setting up the table full of food upon the decking. Crow had done as he had promised, bringing his entire team as well as, Comet, Asena, Anthony and Caesar along with some of the members of the pack and kids from the headquarters. Between the Daggers and Asena's pack, they had managed to rescue the house and garden, transforming it into a warm golden themed party area with toys and music. Storm was certain that she had Asena's organisational skills to thank for it all.

Storm let out a high-pitched whistle to alert them to their arrival, hearing the faint voices of "Here she comes!" from below and watching them clear an area for her to land. She let Malana go and left her to flutter by herself for a moment before showing her how to land in such a small area. Malana did her best to copy Storm as she beat her wings back and splayed her primaries to break and land softly. Afraid that she might hit the trees she stayed wavering in the air several meters above the garden, then dropped like a stone with a yelp. Fortunately, Wilny had been waiting below and caught her, spinning her round into a hug as the guests clapped at her arrival.

"Sunshine! You did so well!" He praised, brushing her hair gently. She kicked her legs and squealed in joy.

"I flew! I flew!" She declared, tiredly flapping her wings.

"I saw! I'm so proud of you Sunshine!"

"Next time, you come with me, okay?"

"Of course! There'll be plenty of time to go out and fly together."

"Promise?"

"I promise." He chuckled., "Now go say hello to everyone, they've all been waiting here for you."

He set her down so that she could run and receive presents and share her adventure with the gathering of children that had arrived for the party. The tears of pride in Wilny's eyes made Storm chuckle as she stepped over to his side, with a bottle of honey for him from the table.

"Look at you, getting all emotional over Lana's first flight." She said with a grin, placing the honey bottle into his hand. "I think you've now ascended to '*Dad*' status."

"H-how did she do?" Wilny asked, clearing his throat and watching Amell as he brought the cake out to the table on the decking. The man was a culinary artist and with help from Kat, they had successfully rescued Wilny from catastrophe with the cake, turning their mess into a work of art with rock candy and marbled gold and white royal icing.

"She was fantastic." Said Storm. "She only had two minor falls, but she sorted herself out and caught herself in time on the second one. Now she wants to fly like me."

"You're going to teach her, right?"

"Of course I am." Storm laughed, bumping him with a wing as he took a sip of honey. "Do you really think I'm going to let her be as terrible at flying as you are?"

"Hey, I'm not *that* terrible."

"Well, you can get off the ground, so I guess that is something."

Wilny returned the wing bump playfully and the two burst into laughter, though Wilny quickly grew solemn again, casting a glance around him before leaning in to speak more softly.

"Thank you for this. All of it. I mean it."

"You don't need to thank me, we're family. Keeping everyone safe and happy is just what we do for each other."

"Urgh," Wilny groaned loudly, blue eyes glittering gleefully. "Your bleeding-heart sweetness is killing me."

Unable to think of a quick retort, Storm stuck her tongue out at him and messed up his hair, to which he retaliated by pulling on the feathers of her cheekbones and tweaking her nose. Calling a truce after one final playful whack with one of Storm's wings, the two shared a short and thankful hug.

"Go on," Storm said giggling and giving him a small shove, "go and try Amell's dipstick."

"*Dirty.*"

"I meant the sweets!"

"Sure you did Boss."

Snickering, she watched Wilny saunter off to thank Amell for his help.

The atmosphere was refreshingly jovial and so Storm took a moment to admire the scene of all of her Rogues, happy and at ease. Kat was showing off the butterfly patterning of her wings to a shy Canid who was in awe of her beauty. Palmer was on very good behaviour, playing with the other kids by getting them to throw sweets to him which he caught in his mouth. However, she was very impressed that Amell had managed to find a shirt that covered his chest, and that Beth had managed to tear herself away from her computer for more than ten minutes to socialise. There were no arguments between the kids, and all of Asena's Pack and the Daggers were behaving themselves.

Despite the recent events, almost all were seemingly calm and recovered.

Almost.

Weaving in and out of the guests with short greetings to each person, Storm padded over to the metallic-winged Hummingbird as she finished a flower crown for a child and sent them on their way to join the party. Comet's feathers rose in agitation and she tensed in Storm's presence, casting her gaze to the flower beds beside her rather than look at Storm.

"How are you holding up Comet?" She asked softly as the child ran off. She knew that after what had happened with the attack upon the Rioteer headquarters, Comet had taken it all badly. She felt so sorry for her, knowing that she had already lived through the Mullardoch attack as well as a number of other tragedies and traumas.

"I'm...I don't know to be honest..." Comet murmured, cradling her arms to her chest and her wings quivering.

"If it helps, you can always stay here with us for a few weeks."

"I don't want to be a burden to anyone here."

"It's no trouble to me." Storm assured her with a friendly smile, trying to get Comet to look up at her. "There used to be twelve people living here at one point, so what's one more? We'd be more than happy for you to join us."

"I don't want to."

"You don't need to snap at me, I'm just trying to help."

'You don't have to help everyone Storm.' Comet mused to her loudly, rising to her feet and shaking her head. The clarity of the thought surprised Storm, as did the sharp bitterness behind it. It was a sting and it set Storm on edge, feathers bristling and talons curling up against her palms.

'Well, like Kathy said; Helping people is my purpose out here. It gives me something to do.'

'And what help have you actually done? How has anything you've done ever helped? You can't fix things by faking a smile or by fighting them. You have no idea what you're doing.' Comet responded coldly, suddenly looking sharply at her with a fierce and feral glower, the likes she had never seen before from Comet. An echo of her own behaviour. There was no attempt to hide the sentiments of her thoughts and all at once, Storm realised how Comet felt about her.

Angry. Envious. Suspicious. Bitter. Afraid.

It was understandable. Comet had lost people, but then so had Storm.

'It's a bit hard to try and take the high ground when you're squatting in a sewer, sweetheart.' Storm's feathers bristled angrily, and she pushed back at Comet's feelings with her own fierce wrath. She had dealt with enough musers to know when to turn their own feelings back upon themselves.

'You're right, of course I don't know what I'm doing, but at least I'm trying to make an effort. You've done nothing, but hide away and complain, and whine, and isolate yourself on every occasion. Stop trying to blame people for trying to do something when you are doing nothing.'

Comet squirmed under Storm's intensity, drawing her wings in so tight to her body that they hurt.

'If you want to blame me, be angry at me, sure go ahead, it doesn't mean shit to me. You could be anywhere else, doing something that you want to do, but instead you're here sulking.'

'I never wanted to be here in the first place! I never wanted the Rioteers or you to help me.'

'Alright then. Go.' She snorted aloud. *'If you don't want to be here then go ahead and leave, but don't you dare ruin my Lana's day with your own selfish misery.'*

She was aware that they were both glaring at each other silently with their hackles raised like a pair of alley cats about to fight. Those who were closest to them were beginning to look uncomfortable and afraid, caught in the radius of Comet's muser abilities.

"You need to find something to do with yourself." Storm said aloud, her irritation towards Comet increasing the electrical field around herself, blocking out Comet's thoughts and feelings. Comet scowled, attempting to send a message to her silently, but only being met with interference.

"Go abroad, get a group, learn something new, just do *something.*"

"Like you?"

"No. Absolutely not." She snapped her wings in and out sharply. "We may be the same type and from the same project, but you're not built like me and you shouldn't try to be me. You're not made for it."

Comet's scowl flickered into shock.

Giving up trying to muse, she shook down her tense wings. She muttered despondently, folding her arms across her chest and looking away from Storm.

Out the corner of her eye, Storm was aware that Asena was watching them with wary suspicion coupled with a motherly frown. She had seen this look multiple times when she had been under Asena's warnings to not antagonise Rex and to just back down from another fight. If Comet hadn't been so close by and with her electrical field bristled up to full, she would have sent an inward groan towards Asena for that look.

"Just find something that makes you smile." Storm patted her shoulder firmly, smiling warmly at her. "You're far to pretty to be scowling all the time."

Comet blushed furiously under the compliment, feathers rising and her short fan of tailfeathers twitching in confusion. Before she could respond, Caesar sprinted up to them. Tackling Comet's wings, he began dragging her towards the trampoline whilst chanting *"play, play, play,"* along with several of the other children accosting her. Laughing, Storm gave a small sweep of her wing to sign for Comet to do as they asked.

Shaking her head as the troubled Hummingbird left, she headed on inside to get herself a drink. Although the kids had juice on the table outside, they were being sure to keep the alcoholic drinks far out of their reach and sight. As she browsed the selection of beers, wines, and spirits in the mini fridge, out the corner of the eye she caught sight of Crow with a glass of wine in hand. He was taking a rest with a post-flight drink, musing to keep himself invisible to everyone as he lounged in the living room.

Crow smirked at her; his crest of black feathers raised as he watched her. His coy expression didn't go unnoticed.

"Whatever you're doing with your face right now, you can stop it." Storm snarled in a low voice, rustling her feathers. Chuckling, he rose to his feet and sidled over to her, drink in hand.

"Do you think she's pretty?"

"Who?"

He pointedly looked out through the doors and across the garden to where Comet now amazed the children by blowing bubbles for them, something that few of them had ever seen before.

"Comet. Do you think she's pretty?"

"Yes. What are you getting at?"

"I'm just saying that you better not be considering her as a future girlfriend, considering how your last few relationships went. Maybe it'll only end in a coma this time." He was always a torment after a drink. He began to laugh to himself, then nearly choked on his drink as Storm thwacked him hard with her wing.

"Shut up. I've grown out of freaking out over every pretty girl or guy I meet."

"Oh, have you now? I can see, you'd be all over Kat if you still were. And Wilny. He counts as a pretty girl to me."

She rolled her eyes and found herself a bottle of IPA to drink, slamming the mini fridge shut.

"They are pretty, but after Mesi, Rai, and V... *Vesper*, I've decided not to date another team member again. The breakups get too messy." She tried to pass it off as a half-hearted joke, but her tone had a sharp edge to it.

Crow winced at the mention of the No-Go topic between them all with an uncomfortable shuffle. It was serious enough to sober him and he flattened his feathers down apologetically as she avoided looking at him and drank. What happened with Mesi was on public record, what happened with Vesper however, was not.

"Pretty or not," Storm continued as soon as her bottle was finished, ignoring the look he gave her at the mention of Vesper's name, "it's much better for everyone if we all just stick to being a team regardless of who we all fancy."

"True, though I can't say the same for my team."

"Bubbles owns you."

"That she does. What a woman." He sighed dramatically, blowing a kiss out to the garden where she was. "My team is great but you've done better than I expected with running the Rogues on your own. Congratulations."

"Better than you expected?" She took his glass from him and drained it, grimacing at the taste of wine before passing the glass back. Rolling his eyes, he poured the remainder of the bottle he had brought with him into his glass.

"Only that I thought that after all the shit you've pulled in the last two years that Rex would have tried to shoot you...*again.*"

The doorbell sounded, and Beth barrelled on through to answer, then immediately rushed upstairs to her room in a flustered hurry. As the late arriving guests entered, a cunning grin spread across Storm's face and she slapped her brother so hard on the shoulder that he spilt his remaining wine all over his feathers.

"Well, he might do if he hears about this."

A young human woman entered the house, thanking Beth before she disappeared, and letting her two children run past out into the garden with their gifts for Lana. Crow laughed softly, waving to the woman then hid his mouth with a of his wine so he could hiss at Storm.

"Oh my god. You invited the neighbours!"

"Be nice, Ms. Barret makes the best brownies and is also a primary school teacher. Wilny and I talked to her about getting Palmer and Malana tutored, or at least for her to give us a starting mark as to where to go with educating them."

"Storm you absolute sh-*sweetheart.*" His tone went from anger to cheery and sweet within a second, as the woman trotted over to them, wide eyed in awe.

"Hello there! Storm! Lovely to see you, I was worried I might have arrived too late and that Camille and Preston would have been too tired to come." She was trying so hard to look at Storm's face and had her arms folded tightly across her chest to keep her hands from reaching out and touching the feathers. Crow silently commended her for her restraint.

Storm chuckled cheerily, "I was worried too, Preston adores Lana."

"He really does!" She leant in to whisper, "he asked me if he could have wings himself, so I bought him a pair of costume ones online."

"So adorable, although, I think he might have a new-found adoration for Comet."

She gestured with her wing out to the garden where Ms. Barret's son was pawing at Comet's wings and bouncing excitedly as she spread them out to show off their metallic gloss.

"Ah, kids." Crow said with pensive sarcasm. "I remember when Saffron was that age, the little monkey."

Ms. Barret jumped and covered her mouth to stop herself screaming, having been fooled by Crow's muser tricks of making himself invisible within her perception. She stared fixedly at his face and hair, mouth agape in a mixture of shock, awe, and alarm at seeing Crow for the first time. Storm often forgot that Crow's appearance was so impactful upon humans who had never encountered Synths before; his face wasn't particularly human looking, and the solid black eyes and face full of feathers could even be considered disturbing to some.

Crow smiled.

"Yep, they actually do move." He said, wiggling the crest of feathers.

"D-did I say that out loud?" She covered her mouth and backed away, looking down at his bare arms and the tiny black pinfeathers and scales along the backs of his hands. He revelled in the shock on people's faces whenever they saw him, even if it was more terror than shock at times.

"Oh, this is Crow." Storm announced, loudly mentally scolding him to behave. "My brother."

"Adoptive brother." He winked with the nictitating membrane followed by a slow blink, just to emphasise the inhumanness. Ms. Barret nodded slowly.

"It moves…"

"Just like a cockatoo." Noted Bubbles, entering with a glass of wine for the woman. Mid-thanks Ms. Barret's shock-struck gawping returned as she came face to face with the slitted eyes and scaled skin of Bubbles, almost dropping the glass in the process.

Storm could have beat them both with her wings for startling her guest with their introductions. Breaking humans into understanding the concept of Synthetic people was very different to letting them see and come to grasps with them in person. Instead, she went for a sweet voiced, "Don't be weird guys," rather than a full-on threat towards the two Daggers.

"Bubblegum Pink, and yes, these are scales." Bubbles chimed taking Ms. Barret's hand and placing it on her arm to feel them.

"Oh my." She breathed, stroking Bubble's hands gently, turning them over and tracing the red and black rosette patterning's. "How…tropical? I'm sorry! I hope I wasn't being offensive! I-I just- I'm not sure what to say."

"Don't worry. I've had worse said to me."

"Did you get called cold-blooded again babe?" Crow asked quietly.

"Several times actually." She said sweetly, brushing her pink hair back over her shoulders and linking her arm with Ms Barret's to lead her into the garden for the party with Crow.

"I'm sure you're dying to ask questions Ms. Barret. Ask away. I am all ears. Well, if I had any ears." She laughed, showing her the tiny holes in the side of her head.

Excitedly, the human began babbling pointing to their scales and feathers, wings, and tails, asking a barrage of questions.

"You Daggers." Storm sighed to her brother. "Always a pain in the arse."

"Yes, but ya' love us really."

Allowing Crow to drag her outside, they joined the rest of the party where Kat was busy gathering everyone together around the garden table for them to sing happy birthday to Malana and cut the cake. The little girl was dazed by how many people there were, the cake and all the gifts, resorting to pulling her wings over her head to hide her blushing until the singing had ended and she had received a plate full of cake after blowing out the five candles.

Every present was received with excited and grateful thanks. Whilst her glowing smile never left her face, the adults talked softly to each other on why they chose certain gifts.

"Kat. You got her a *knife?*" Wilny chided the Lioness, watching as Malana held the amber stone in the hilt up to the light to smile at the little flecks of black inside.

"Pretty, isn't it? Though actually it's more of a hair-pin that can double as a dagger."

"She's five."

"And? I got a knife when I was five, what's the problem?"

"*I got her a knife too!*" He whispered bitterly. "That's so embarrassing! I wanted my present to be special."

"They're different, and since yours is from *you*, of course its special." She purred giving him a reassuring hug, then leant in close to whisper. "Although, for the record, mine is prettier though since I'm the only one between us with a sense of fashion and taste."

"Wanna bet?"

Lana didn't care though that she had received another knife as when she opened Wilny's box, she admired the beautiful needle-point dagger with bouncing joy at the whorls of gold in the black steel, and the small, engraved sun on the blade. She thanked him graciously with a tight hug and in near tears with happiness, being careful not to stab him in the process.

By the end Malana had amassed a collection of four knives, many small rings, chains, pendants and other sparkling trinkets found by the children, new clothes, adjustable aviator goggles, a variety of toys, books, and an expensive set of pens and pencils to draw with. Palmer and Caesar admired the haul with childish greed, loudly yowling to their parents that they too wanted a birthday party, and with Caesar on the brink of bursting into howls of complaint, Anthony took them both into the open space of the garden and coaxed them into dancing with him.

His distraction worked and soon the other children and several of the adults joined in with them, including Storm and Wilny who danced as a trio with Malana. To the side, Kat took photographs, showing and sharing them with whoever wanted them.

"Mind if I join in?" Amell asked as the three Rogues spun by to the lively music. Storm looked to Wilny with a smirk, watching him as his cheeks turned a delicate shade of pink.

"He's all yours." She laughed, pushing Wilny forward into Amell's arms before he could answer, only for Malana to immediately squeeze between them both and hug Wilny, giving Amell a jealous glare. Amell held his hands up retreating immediately from the little girl with a smile.

"You can't have me all to yourself, Sunshine." Wilny said softly, brushing her hair. She looked up at him with big golden eyes and a determined smirk.

"But it's my birthday." She said coyly. Pausing thoughtfully, Wilny gave her a small smile.

"I have an idea." He said and lifted her up onto his shoulders where she squealed in delight at being so tall, fluttering her tired golden wings for balance, whilst Wilny obliged Amell with a dance.

Storm stepped back to one side, out the way of those who were dancing, and joined Kat who had been taking pictures of them all throughout the party.

"This is great!" She giggled to Storm, skipping through the photos her brush ended tail twitching gleefully and setting the new pictures to her contacts with them. "I hope you do something like this for my birthday, *Thunderbird*."

"Well, I'll do my best." Storm promised her with a smile, "I'm sorry I didn't do anything for you last year. We didn't know each other to well and you were a *little* stressed."

"You know me better now."

"Is there anything you really, really, want, *Sekhmet*?" She asked playfully.

Kat's eyes glittered but before she could say anything, she was interrupted by Beth who came charging through into the garden where she leapt off the decking, very nearly tackling Storm and Kat to the ground.

"Storm! Storm! Good, you're here!"

"It's a party Beth, why wouldn't I be here?"

"I've gotta tell you something." The bright eyes and wide grin were a rare sight on Beth, she was very rarely so visibly excited. It was almost disturbing.

"Wait. Beth, are you drunk?" Kat asked, ears flicking back in disbelief as she smelt a whiff of caramel whiskey on Beth's mottled feathers.

"Hábrók got into contact with me!"

"Oh. And?"

Beth clutched at Storm's shoulders, looking over her thick glasses into Storm's aquamarine-green eyes.

"*A whole container ship*. We've got a whole container ship coming our way." She said slowly, as she shook Storm's shoulders. "With about nine-thousand containers on-board full of Hercules, bioprinters, bioClensers and Alter-Organics, purifiers, solar glass, SmartFabric, boosters, meds, transgenic serums, and a whole shit tonne of the latest Delta-ware."

Both Storm and Kat made a shared slow gasp at the summarised list, calculating a rough estimate as to how much of the cargo was useful to them. Any one item from the list could have vastly improved their lives, but coming across an entire cargo ship could potentially make them as self-sufficient as any of the colonies on mars, if they didn't sell any of it to start with. Beth drummed her feet and squealed in happiness seeing Storm's own realisation, then led Storm into a giddy spin around the decking to the music.

"You're such a happy little criminal." Storm laughingly sang, forcing Beth to stop spinning before she tripped them both over.

"You're damn right I am! When should we-"

"*Girls.*" The Empress barked from behind them, catching them all off guard. The Rogue flinched at her sudden appearance, Beth clutching Storm's arm so tightly she thought that Beth would break her arm all over again.

"Make your plans later." Asena said softly, smiling as she gestured out to the garden, "For now, enjoy the party."

-x-

The night wore on with great joviality, passing into the dark early hours of the morning. Anthony and the Daggers took the exhausted and sleepy Synth children back to their temporary bolt hole, whilst Ms. Barret took her own children and their collection of feathers, back home. Only Asena, Comet and Crow remained to help clean up after the party with the Rogues, which by the end of left only Storm, Beth and Raoul awake.

With the others in bed, and Amell deciding that he was going to sleep outside on the decking behind them as they sat and talked, as he was too exhausted and inebriated to go down into the basement which had become his room, the remaining Rogues sat outside as dawn broke, to discuss Beth's new intel, sharing the last dregs of alcohol and food between them.

"And it's all medicine and technology?" Asena asked, gently rocking her sleeping son in her arms.

Beth nodded, still buzzing with glee and caramel whiskey.

"And possibly a few things transferred from Delta. There could be weapons and a team of Elites to protect it, but I'll get the details down and verified as soon as I can. It'll be passing through the channel in six days."

"It'd be a great haul for us. After what happened at the HQ, we're all out of medicine and I'm sure our equipment is at least five years out of date." Crow added in, feathers rising and falling as he contemplated the notes that Beth had made.

"I wonder if I can get Jett to replace the motorhome's windows with some of the solar glass. Hm. I'd love to do a heist but a big ship is hard to target for my crew."

"My team can handle it." Said Storm proudly. "Most of us can fly, and we have Beth, and now Raoul too. Although I think we might need a few boats to load off into, there's no way I'm able to carry anything as heavy as what they're packing."

Asena nodded.

"I agree. If it's out in the channel, then your team would be able to access it and secure it the fastest and with the most stealth."

"Team Sienna has access to boats and almost all of their team can pilot them, so between that should be a small fleet of about six to nine ships if they had one each or teamed up." Raoul pointed out, getting them back on subject as he remembered his notes on the different groups.

"They'd need a few extra hands to help load, and we'd need control of the cranes on the ship, if it even has cranes."

"It does, Hábrók checked."

Crow was grinning gleefully, tailfeathers flicking up and down as he paced with his wine. "What if we get Fen and Matagot in on this too. I know Inks will want to do this, and she owes me one last favour as it is."

"If you can keep them from fighting, yes."

"I know how to handle them mum, don't worry. All we need to do is tell Marlowe and Inks that they can get new toys each and they'll play nice enough together."

"And if we get more than we bargained for we can spread it out to all the groups, cache the left overs and then we can break the fuck away from Rex whenever shit goes down again!" Said Beth. She was wiggling her bionic feet in glee so fast that the claws scraped up the dry grass into small dusty clouds.

Comet looked shocked when the rest began to laugh and nod in agreement. She'd never been a part of any meeting before and the way they spoke, so quickly and forthright, left her lost and feeling out of place amongst them as she struggled to follow their line of thinking, even with her muser abilities.

"You mean you aren't going to get help from Rex?" She asked, turning to Crow and watching as his head feathers flattened back across his scalp. "Wouldn't something this big mean you'd need the Rioteers to assist?"

There was a collective noise of indignation between them all at her comment.

"Fuck no!" Beth nearly yelled, swigging the last of the wine to limit her volume, whilst Raoul shook his head and snarled. "*Jamais de la vie.*"

"If he knew we were doing this, he would just take everything for the Rioteers only, not for any of us." Crow spat venomously. "Like fuck he'd give us assistance anyway, even if we asked."

"And he did help he'd probably sink the ship." Storm added in snidely, clinking bottle against Crow's in agreement.

"That guy's such a tight-arse, if you shoved a lump of coal up his gooch, two weeks later you'll get a diamond."

"Charming Crow." Asena said with a roll of her golden eyes. Comet pulled a face at the image, beginning to laugh with the others until they were hushed to stop Caesar from waking at the noise.

"What do you think mum?" Storm questioned, glancing at all of the excited and mischievous expressions of all who were present. "Do you think we can manage this? We won't be able to access everything, but maybe it will be enough."

Asena looked down thoughtfully at her son in her arms, stroking his red hair gently, weighing up the risks and rewards.

"Let's do it." She said with a determined smirk to her two feathered children. Beth cheered silently with righteous vindication, her hands raised to the sky and soft wings flaring wide, whilst Storm and Crow exchanged high fives with such vigour that it left them both clutching their palms in pain.

"Beth, get back into contact with Hábrók and see how narrow this timeframe is for its arrival. Daggers, you can help by getting Sienna to get some boats ready manning the harbours for receiving it. See if you can all drag Avarken up to play too, there should be time for them to get their asses here." Asena smiled coyly, watching Beth leap and run for her notebook and tablet with enthusiasm. "Whilst you lot coordinate, I'll find something to keep *the King* busy with."

"*Pas question*, we're actually going to capture a ship?" Raoul laughed, curled tail wagging excitedly. "As pirates?"

Storm looked at him in surprise, delighted by the idea.

"Well, when you put it that way…yeah, we're going to be pirates. *Dashing Rogues*."

"The *dashingest* of Rogues with our c-captain!" Amell hiccupped, stirring from where he was sprawled across the decking and raising a sleepy salute to Storm.

"Captain Lady Thor Thunderstormington!" Then he let his arm flop to the ground again before breaking into a loud snore.

"How much has he drunk?" Crow had to ask, looking down at the bottle he had in his hands. Beth shook her head slowly, forgetting how many bottles she had collected.

"Let him sleep. It'll metabolise."

"So, it's agreed then." Storm grinned, bringing them back to the conversation. "It's a heist?"

Asena nodded. "It's a heist."

30

A waning gibbous moon glowed brightly through the mackerel clouded sky, creating spots of light across the calm sea. In the distance, summertime thunder rumbled across the open water, disrupting the rhythmic gentle crash of waves against the base of the cliff.

The caravan they had rented on the edge of the cliff had quickly been converted into a communication hub by Beth with multiple computers set up, some holding blueprints to the ship and an updating list of its inventory, some holding contact information and various livestreams from the other groups who they were working with. Everything had come together quickly with the combined efforts of the European Synth groups, and soon they were all battle ready and waiting for their target.

Since they had arrived that morning, Storm had been brimming with a zealous excitement that overflowed into every movement she made. It was infectious.

A considerable amount of her energy had gone into grooming her feathers, running her fingers deliberately and methodically down every single vane, aligning the barbs and testing the flex of the quills for any slight fracture or bend. Every now and then as she preened, her head would snap up, pupils dilating and contracting rapidly as she watched birds in the distance and focused on the slightest movements of the grass in the fields around, a wry smile cast across her face.

It was nothing like how Raoul had ever seen her behave, it was perfectly Feral, but he could understand it. This was the prelude to a hunt, and she was designed to be a thoroughbred aerial predator.

Amell may have been an Eagle, but he was Transhuman. Kat may have been an agile Lioness, but she wasn't a skyborne hunter. And Wilny for all his training as a soldier, was still a pretty hummingbird and not cut out for air-based combat, particularly when he had a troublesome arrhythmic heart.

Whilst Kat, Amell, and Wilny had been practicing their sparring and targets with the handguns, Storm had raced up and down the entire length of the coast, surfing low across the waves and circling above any shipwreck she came across, practicing her dives and pivots until she could turn on a dime, with Malana attempting to copy her.

Ridge lift, advection, anabatic and *katabatic winds, crosswind, wind shear, drag,* there were so many new words that Malana had learnt that in the end Raoul had to write them down for her.

Even though the Avios were raring to go, Raoul couldn't help but feel as though he was being left behind because he wasn't one of them.

He enviously watched them getting prepared, dressing in their stolen and very old SmartFabrics, trying to activate them so that they could help protect their bodies in case of emergencies.

Wilny argued loudly that they should wear helmets with the armour to better protect themselves, and that if there was any Avio fitted armour on board that they should take it, so they could upgrade to something that would cover and protect their wings. Whilst Beth agreed with the idea, she then got annoyed as he began to lecture them all on how badly maintained their equipment was compared to Core's standards, to which Kat jokingly called him an Elite-Elitist, and so the two engaged in a small, but quick practice fight with their respective weapons.

When Raoul saw that Storm had a moment to spare from her grooming and changing into her '*battle gear*'— as she called the ragged black flight suit that already had a number of tears and bullet holes in it – he took her to one side away from the others.

"Storm," he said, puffing out his chest and trying to look tough, "I want to help! I'm part of this team and I want to go with you."

"You are helping Raoul." She assured him as she tightened the straps of her armguards for the fifth time that hour. "In fact, you've probably got one of the most important jobs."

"But I'm not coming with you." Raoul complained. "What if one of you needs medical support? How can I help if I can't even go with you all?"

"As useful as you would be as a medic for when we got injured, it's your communication skills we need more. We need you to keep in contact with all of these technicians to deal with for us Puppy because Beth sure as hell can't. So, don't think for a second that you're not doing something worthwhile."

He gave her a doubtful look. Gently draping a wing around his shoulders with a sigh, Storm guided him to the cliff edge. A cold updraft rose from the sea, gently lapping at the white chalk of the cliff base only fifty meters below. On the horizon was the lights of cargo ships, and in the further distance towards the east, a faint glitter of the French coast.

"That's where they're coming from Raoul." She pointed out across the dark water, trying to reassure him of his usefulness.

"They've got eleven small boats and three big ones, and even though Grace can speak English, you'll be dealing with Velvet, Kirsche, Gabbiano, Looper, and Bordeaux, who are all the technicians from Sienna, Fen, Matagot, and two or three smaller groups I can't remember the names of. There's something like sixty or seventy of us all in on this, and all relying on you to help communicate between us all."

Raoul hung his head reluctantly. "They speak only French then?"

"French, German, Italian, and I think Kirsche is the one who likes to slip into Russian when he gets upset. None of us can speak that many languages apart from you. So, don't think that you're useless to us here. You don't have to fight or fly or have special talents to be useful, we just need you to be *you*."

"Actually, I need you to be me as well." Beth's voice made him jump.

For a woman with two bionic legs, she had crept up behind them so stealthily. He glanced round to see Beth standing behind them, her soft mottled wings almost cream coloured in the blue light of the moon, with Palmer and Lana looking poutily up at him. She pushed the kids forward and they ran towards him and hugged his legs to try to comfort him.

"You're also helping because I need to keep a monitor on the ship, the security, the coast guard, Core and Delta communications on-board. I can't do all that at once by myself. I've tried it and it's only through *sheer dumb luck* that we've pulled some of these stunts off." She said, giving Storm a pointed look, before continuing. "That and I can't take care of the kids. But you can."

Raoul knelt beside the two children, hugging them as they cooed and brushed his hair, trying to make him feel loved. Palmer threw his arms around his neck and hugged him tight, leaning up to his ear to whisper to him not to look sad.

"I wanna help too!" Malana announced, flaring out her wings to show off her shiny new feathers. She jumped a little, fluttering her wings and managing a short hover, trying to prove she was capable of flight now and making Storm smirk.

"Lana, I know you do-"

"Me too! Me too!" Palmer barked, trying to jump up and down in Raoul's arms, wriggling excitedly.

"You can't come with us this time. This is a job for adults only."

The children glowered at her. It was enough to make Raoul break out of his despondent scowl into a little laugh and smile.

"However! You can help make sure that no stragglers come and hunt us down though, protect the base." Laughed Storm, shooting the Owl and Hound a wry grin. "And if you ask Beth nicely, she might even let you two play with the headsets and use them like we're doing."

This seemed to appease the kids and they ran up to Beth, bouncing about before her both squeaking *'please,'* at her until the Owl surrendered and led them inside the caravan to keep them busy.

"We're changed!" Kat announced, exiting the caravan with Wilny and Amell. They beamed at her each with an excited smiles.

Whilst Wilny and Kat wore combat armour over their SmartFabrics that fitted snugly against their bodies, giving them suitable protection whilst freeing up their wings. Amell however had to wear a makeshift patched together armour from various SmartFabrics and spare Kevlar which barely covered his vital organs, since there wasn't an armour big enough to fit his shoulder and chest breadth. Storm had to laugh at them however, noting them all wearing a purple sash at their waists like the one she wore.

"We're almost set up and ready to go." Kat declared, brushing down her skirt and twirling for Storm, her collection of knives sheathed at her hips and the vivid blue in her feathers gleaming beneath the patchy moonlight.

As much as Storm wanted to question her logic behind the choice of skirt, if Kat felt comfortable fighting in a skirt and carrying the weight of so many knives, she wasn't going to stop her, though she was glad that Kat had the sense to *not* fight in heels, and to tie her hair back so that it wouldn't be caught or grabbed.

"How long do we have until either Core or Rex catches on to us?" Amell asked looking out across the sea, kneeling on the grass so that Kat could preen his huge wings, his own weapons being his fists which were wrapped tightly up to his elbows with the remaining strips of SmartFabric to protect the wrists.

"At least until seven in the morning," Beth confirmed watching the kids try to put on the headsets and microphones. "Roux and Free will be keeping the Rioteers and Rex busy in a cross-country chase in about an hour."

"What?"

"You'll see the videos and news tomorrow." She grinned wildly at him.

A gentle sound caught Beth's attention, and her smile disappeared, head snapping up and watching the sky. Craning his neck, Amell squinted into the sky to try and follow what Beth was looking at, though he could see nothing as the black shadow arced in across the clifftops, dropping into land with pitch-black wings. Even with the moonlight, he was so dark he was almost invisible.

The Rogues tensed, Wilny drawing his gun and Palmer barking at the intruder as he caught the sounds of feathers against the wind.

"It's alright," Storm assured them. "He's with us."

Amell looked across at Storm warily. "Who is *he*, exactly? And why didn't you warn us? Wilny could have shot him."

"Ex-Rogue?" Wilny glanced to Kat, hoping that she might have an inkling towards who it might be. She shook her head, squinting into the darkness at the man.

Ignoring the question, Storm ran at the unfamiliar Avio, throwing her arms around him and laughing heartily with him as he picked her up and span her around.

"Sorry for the delay," The stranger apologised, "the wind's picking up and I overshot this place."

"Oh, you sensitive jenny wren."

"Hey. I'm not a haggard hawk like you who can fly through all weathers, Stormy."

"What's the assessment?"

She led the Avio into the light and Amell's jaw dropped open. Eyes still fixed on the man, he grabbed both Kat and Wilny by their shoulders. He turned them sharply, pointing at the young man. With the light now on his face, they could admire him.

"Holy shit." Kat breathed, tucking the stray hairs back from her face and gawping at the Avio man approaching them. Wilny was no better, staring slack jawed with Amell, and hurriedly smoothing out his roused feathers.

"He's hot."

"Too right. Look at them cheekbones."

"Look at those shoulders."

"What type of bird is he based on? A hawk?"

"He's just my type that's for sure."

Storm made a shushing gesture as the man winced under their scrutiny. "Guys! Behave!" She barked at them, hugging the man tight and patting his head. "He's delicate!"

"Introduce us first! You can't keep him all to yourself!"

"Yeah! Sharing is caring boss!"

Rolling her eyes, she quickly whispered an apology to the man before she ushered them over, showing off the newcomer to them.

"This is Raiquen. We're loaning him for the moment since he's the only Avio I know of close to us with some level of night-vision."

"*Loaning*, since I'm in between groups right now." He smiled, shaking their hands as Storm darted off to the caravan to get him his body armour. "Please. Call me Rai."

Tiny black feathers spread across his sharp cheekbones to his ear tufts and running down his shoulders into void-black wings. The most striking thing about him however, had to be his solid yellow eyes, stark against his earthy complexion, even in the low light. The dark pupil constricted and dilated in rapid succession as he analysed the Rogues, and a pale membrane flicked across his eye.

"So," Wilny asked with as smooth of a tone as he could muster, slicking his hair back, trying to appear cool, "how do you know Storm?"

Rai gave a curt, but awkward laugh, brushing his dark hair from his face, some of the feathers within it twitching slightly with the change of expression.

"It's messy, but we know each other because of our mutual ex-girlfriend. Mesi."

"Eh? Messy?"

"No, *Mesi*." He shrugged, his feathers rustling.

"Oh, her ex-girlfriend." The name clicked. "Adonis mentioned her."

"Ooh, so you've met Ada. Did he tell you that they broke up because she wanted to move groups?"

"Yeah, he said it was something like that."

"Huh, well then he left out the other half of that reason is because Mesi was cheating on her, with me, and on me, with her. Storm was a tiny bit offended with that."

"At least we dealt with it." Storm shouted from the caravan as she rummaged through their bags. Shooting a quizzical frown over at her through the open window, Rai scoffed loudly, folding his arms across his chest.

"You threw her through a window after she punched you in the nose for calling her a bitch. How is that *dealing with it*?"

"I was sixteen and she started it!"

"Most sixteen-year-olds deal with breakups by crying, not destroying a wind turbine and causing a blackout across London by throwing a motorbike into a transformer."

"I was aiming for her! The transformer got in the way!"

"I'm still curious as to how Rex's bike managed to end up there for you to even throw it in the first place."

Swinging out of the caravan, she threw the remaining Kevlar at him and aggressively stuck her middle fingers up, as she sauntered past to sit on the ground beside a small camping lantern, ushering Kat to join her.

The boys watched in confusion as after carefully braiding Storm's hair back– tying into it one of her own red and velvet blue feathers– Kat lined Storm's eyes with eyeliner from her makeup compact, before smudging a dark purple dust across her forehead and eyelids, then down her nose to create a sharp, dark mask. The smoky makeup only made her pale eyes seem brighter and her already sharp face look more angular.

"You're wearing make up? At night? *For a fight?*" Asked Wilny, helping Rai with the belts and arranging them to lie beneath the lower feathers of his broad back.

"War paint." Kat chirped, applying some to her own face with artful finesse. "Gotta look hot for a heist."

"It also throws off facial recognition from cameras." Storm added in, rolling her eyes. "You can add some to your wings and make them less...shiny."

"No, I think I'm good.

"Well, you probably should have some on your face, regardless." Said Kat, shooting him a mischievous smirk. "Someone as *pretty* as you is bound to be recognised by any higherups."

Wilny grimaced, understanding immediately what she was insinuating, but he along with Amell and Rai agreed to the war paint, all be it with the greatest reluctance. Like with Storm, she masked their eyes and used the shadows to contour and change the shape of their faces slightly before applying some to her vibrant wings and the stray feathers along her tail to dull the brightness of the blue.

"The ship's coming by in about twenty-five minutes Storm. Seven miles out, that makes it about a steady twelve-minute flight to reach it for everyone who isn't you."

"Thank you, Beth. Time to warm up everyone!"

The group stretched their wings out, flexing and extending them, warming the muscles like athletes before a race. Amell hopped near to the edge of the cliff, following Rai's lead in what he did, buffeting his wings against the turbulent ridge lift to gage how fast he would have to run to gain lift off. With very little light to illuminate him, the Hawk was near invisible, leading Amell to accidentally thwack him several times as they practiced, not that Rai seemed to mind.

A few metres away from them, Storm stood with her long toes gripping the edge of the cliff, extending her wings out and letting the sea breeze and updraft rustle the feathers. Sidling over to her, Wilny watched as she adjusted each long flight feather, changing the shape and angle of her wings.

"You've got your gun on you." She noted out the corner of her eye with a slow and gentle wingbeat. The paler feathers were softly glowing a pale moon-blue with the patches of light shining through the gaps in the clouds, whilst the slate-grey dorsal feathers were so dark they were matched to the colour of the sky.

"Yeah, the Fénix you gave me."

"Make sure you conserve the ammo. EMI cartridges are hard to get. Also remember that when you fly out, glide so you save energy and keep your heartrate low. I don't want you busting an aorta out there."

The wind whistled over the leading edge as she drew the feathers close together, then silenced as she splayed them; he couldn't tell how she had such control over every individual quill enough to know how to change them without looking.

"It's not going to rain on us is it?" He asked, trying to seem nonchalant as he watched. She smiled; her eyes were fixed on the sky.

"No, but you can smell the charge in the air. There might be a little lightning. The wind should be with us, we've got a nice cloud road to get us out there then it's just a float along the gulf stream. Colder than London, but you'll fly faster." She chattered, more to herself than to Wilny, lightly stepping into the updraft and floating before dropping back onto the cliff. "What a great night to fly."

Wilny marvelled at her, envious of her physical power, her instinct and control over her wings. Musing gently, he reached out to see how she felt and dealt with it all, and immediately he staggered backwards, overwhelmed by the sensory overload.

The awareness of herself and everything around her, burning with excitable wrath and euphoria, it was so different to when he tried to hear her on the top of club Bellona. He could feel every subtle breeze buffet her feathers. Even her concealed tail was reactive to every slight movement of fabric upon it, so much so that the base of his own tail tickled and stung as he felt the breeze jostle the huge iridescent disks at the end.

It made him dizzy to feel what it was like to be her.

"So, what's the angle of attack, Boss?" He asked, with a smile though his head still reeled, and tailfeathers still itched with every slight movement they made.

"Well let's find out, shall we?" Rolling her shoulders, she made her way back to the group, summoning them all to the camp light to discuss their plan.

"There's three Avios out on the cranes right now, two in the air." Said Rai rubbing his hands together as he explained the observations. "There's also several humans and Preters walking around the deck and a dozen or so more below, plus three in the bridge. These ships only need five people, but since this is an important cargo, overall, I'd say there's about twenty to thirty individuals in total from my initial scout out."

"That's about five a piece then? Perfect." Smirked Storm. "I'll take down the Avios if someone wants to detain them."

"They also have some powered down Hercules AutoMech, a Poacher on the prow, and new suits I don't recognise out on deck, but I'm not sure if anyone was in them or if they were drones. I didn't know if they had any heat sensors or anything, but I didn't want to get too close to set them off."

Storm looked to Wilny, a slight tilt of her head and a little push at his mental field prompting him to talk.

'You're the one who knows this stuff,' he caught her muse to him, *'What's your advice for dealing with AutoMechs and any potential Elites?'*

Without trying to look too surprised, Wilny cleared his throat.

"If they're new then the chances are, they're recharging since they're out at sea. Some might be useable right now, but that means they'll have to get their asses into the things first. Other than that, for the Hercules AutoMechs their weakest points are on the joints of the arms and the turret can only do three full turns before it jams and has to rotate back. Spin it around fast and it'll shear off."

He clicked his tongue as he thought back over the lists of Armour plans, he once had to commit to memory to pass his exams.

"If you somehow get an automatic weapon, don't bother hitting the main body, its titanium alloy with ballistic fibre coating. You can't pierce it, you can't electrocute it, but if you can trap it in between a stack of containers then the restricted movement should give you a chance to disable the arms. They do have a recharge rate of five seconds though, keep that in mind if they do fire. As for the Poacher, it's a drone. It's not dangerous to people since it's meant for hunting other drones and foreign electrical signatures."

"I can trick the Poacher and security systems into thinking that the earpieces are related to the ship's system." Beth noted from the side where she sat, all ready and calculating timings.

"As for the Elites…" Wilny glanced across to Storm quickly, giving her a small gesture that he was alright before she could worry about how he felt with them taking them on. Her toes dug into the ground, but her face remained impassive.

"What colours did you see Rai. Were they in black or grey suits?"

"Grey."

"Then they're not Rubies or Sapphires. It sounds like they're going to be lower ranked Elites, however if you find the handlers first and they should yield quickly."

The others nodded sagely. He hadn't expected such easy cooperation from what were usually a highly opinionated and argumentative group of Synths.

"I'm glad you know how to handle all of this." Chuckled Amell, putting a hand on Wilny's shoulder and giving him a small and friendly shake. "I don't think I've fought anything other than prototypes and beta-testers before. It's nice to know things."

"T-thank you." His cheeks flushed, but he was thankful that it was too dark for them to notice. "We should probably stick to callsigns too, rather than use our names."

"That's a good idea." Said Beth, looking impressed with Wilny. "So long as you remember to use them."

Storm nodded in agreement, looking over to their technician with a smirk. "Are you keeping yours as *Strix*, Beth?"

"Yes."

"Okay then so we've got, *Thunderbird* - me, *Sekhmet* - Kat, *Zeus* - Amell, *Mach* - Rai, and...." She paused and gave a little click of her tongue as she tried to remember which callsign Wilny wanted to use.

His eyes glittered; bright blue intensified by the dark shadows of the war paint.

"*Huitzilopochtli*." He said smugly.

"I...cannot say that."

"Well, that's the callsign I want."

"*Hweetszeropochley-? Hertz*...Nope. Can't say it." She shook her head, "If I yell Mirabel then assume I'm yelling at you."

They laughed a little as Wilny stuck his tongue out at her.

"Fine, I'll go with Horus then."

"Getting back to what we were doing," She said, shaking her wings down in anticipation. "All of you fly out whilst I'm heading up and wait just behind the ship. I'll dive down, Rai it's your job to see my signal and that'll be your queue to go."

"I don't see why you can't take the whole ship alone." Amell laughed heartily, slapping her lightly on the shoulder. "You're living lightning! Super-fast and able to command electricity! The Thor of the team. Can that be your callsign instead?"

"Flattering as it is to be called Thor, *Zeus*," Storm chuckled, "I'm only fastest in a high-altitude dive, I'm diurnal so I've no night vision like Rai here, I can't control electricity I can just create it, but glad you think so highly of me."

"Don't be modest! You could still take it alone."

"I still need you all, since all three of you are professionally trained fighters." She gestured to her boys and Kat. "Raiquen, go with Amell since you can't fight for shit and need a big strong man to protect you."

Rai shrugged, nodding and accepting her statement.

"Kat and Will, you'll be fine together. Just subdue everyone in the hold and take out the dangerous ones."

There was a small tug on Wilny's feathers. Turning around he was met with Malana smiling up at him brightly.

He knelt before her, "Yes Lana?"

"I drew a picture for you." She declared and thrust a paper out at him, watching his face carefully as he examined it. It was of the Rogues all flying with Palmer and Raoul included and all easily identifiable as who was who. Beth with her glasses and frowning eyebrows, Wilny with long tailfeathers coming off his body, and Amell taking up a quarter of the page she had drawn him so large.

"It's beautiful."

"Don't hurt it!"

"I'll try not to." Wilny smiled, delicately folding the picture up and tucking it beneath his Kevlar against his heart. Satisfied by the gesture, Malana gave him one last tight hug before running back to Raoul waiting by the caravan with Palmer and showing him how to set up a headset.

"Ready?" Storm asked her group. Beth gave her a thumbs-up from the caravan window, Raoul too as he gathered Malana and Palmer into the caravan to keep an eye on them. Raoul was still looking despondent but was already busy translating and relaying what was being said across to the other teams on the continent with fierce determination.

Looking to Kat, Rai, Wilny, and Amell, each dressed in black SmartFabrics, each with a floor length purple sash wrapped about their waists to balance them whilst they flew. Wilny slotted the gun that Storm had given to him onto a thigh holster, Kat adjusting the belts across her waist, whilst Amell stretched out his arms and flexed his muscles, making the feathers closest to the limbs rustle. Armed and ready to go.

"Any final questions?"

"I suppose you want us to show mercy?" said Kat, flicking her long braid of hair over her shoulder. "No killing unless necessary or unless by accident?"

"Correct." Storm's smile dropped for a second. "We'll give them a chance to surrender and live, but we can't have a repeat of what happened with Kathy. This time we detain them all."

There was a shared nod of agreement between them all as Beth called out that it was time for them all to get ready for take-off.

She gave them all a thumbs-up, priming her wings.

"See you all soon." Storm promised. "And if you don't know what to do, just wing it."

Taking a deep breath, she charged off the cliff, beating her wings hard and throwing herself out into the dark abyss. The cold salty updraft caught her wings and she accelerated effortlessly upwards.

She glanced down to watch the rest of them take off after her, before the darkness swallowed them as they flew out across the sea.

Powering on upwards she rowed her wings steadily, using the strong westerly wind blowing across the sea to take her higher. She searched for stars through a break in the clouds above, not wanting to fly through and dampen her wings. Thirty-thousand feet was her target. It would be horridly cold, and the air would be thin at that altitude, but she needed it. She needed time to gain speed and to select a target path to take the Core Avios out as fast as possible and coincide her arrival with the others.

'If geese and vultures can get that high, so can I,' she told herself as she shot through the low-level clouds into a sea of broken moon-bathed white rolling waves. Above her now was nothing, but thin streaks of cirrus clouds illuminated by the moonlight and a billion scintillescent stars above.

Up, up, up she flew. The pressure gradually changed the higher she flew, the air becoming less dense and making it harder to flap her wings. The colour gradient of the sky changed, the horizon beginning to show a visible curve.

A sharp drop in the temperature signalled the border of a sky stream. Tilting her wings slightly she let it catch her, snatching her across the sky carrying her eastwards. Levelling out she used the stream to her advantage, taking several deep breaths whilst she still could, then catapulted herself higher out of the top of the sky stream to the top of the world.

At thirty-thousand feet she was higher than Everest. The night sky spread before her, an archway of stars which cut through the sky. It had been a long time since she had seen the Milky Way so clearly.

Gently floating on the wind, she gazed down at the world below. The wind was gentle against her feathers, enough to keep her buoyant whilst she let her muscles recover. The land was a glitter of gold veins and spidery threads of light, broken by moonlit clouds rolling on below, bright against the midnight blue of the sea, even the coast of France behind her was illuminated in gold. A billion little stars, above and below.

She was alone in the sky with nothing but the sound of her own heartbeat in her ears. She drank it all in. The colours, the peace, the freedom.

Her chest burned with the lack of air to breathe and she became dizzy as she began to reach her limit. She hadn't flown at altitude in a long time, she was out of practice.

The faint white wakes of ships, lit by their own lights and the moon, marked their locations, but pointing out the correct target was aided by the golden map of light. Lightning flashed across some of the clouds below, illuminating them in electric purple, followed by muffled thunder.

'My kind of weather.'

Another flash below made her awe-struck smile broaden into an excited grin as she thought to herself on what Amell had said. *Living lightning.*

Another muffled rumble of thunder against the silence.

It was time.

With one final deep breath she twisted round, pulling her arms in tight against her chest and angling herself towards the ship below. She beat her wings hard, gaining momentum before tucking them close to her body, bolting from the sky.

Every feather pulled in tight to reduce the drag, the nictitating membrane across her eyes protecting her sight.

'One…two…three…four…' she counted the seconds in her head, timing her descent. The rush of air whistled past her ears, the force of the pressure changes almost crushing her lungs. She breathed quickly, forcing herself to regulate the pressure as she burst through the thunderclouds.

'Forty-six… forty-seven…'

The ship was half a mile to the east of where she was diving.

Perfect.

Even at speed, she could see the tiny gliding figures of the Core Avios, stark under the moonlight. She calculated her distance and her path. There was no need to kill them, hitting them would be an instant death at this velocity, but flying past them would cause a wake strong enough to throw them and bring them down.

'Seventy-seven…seventy-eight…seventy-nine'

A flash of lightning to her left illuminated the world perfectly for the briefest of seconds.

"There!" Rai shouted to the others over the thunder as they soared over the waves, spotting the silver flash of moonlight and lightning on her steely feathers, "There she goes!"

The group grinned, powering forward as the silver arrow curved through the sky.

'Eighty-nine…Ninety!' Storm rushed in low across the stern of the ship, powering over an unsuspecting Gull-Avio gliding calmly on the wind. The wake vortex hit the Avio before he had even registered Storm flying past, knocking him out of the sky and sending him tumbling into the sea.

In less than two seconds she had shot across the entire length of the ship, ripping all five Avios from the sky and their perches on the cranes. Two of the five were in the sea, the rest fell stunned to the deck of the ship. Bolting upwards, Strom let her primaries flare and slowed herself down from over two hundred miles per hour to just eighty, breathing deeply to reoxygenate her body, loop-de-looping and assessing the deck for herself.

She saw the Poacher on the bow of the ship, a spider like drone the size of a large dog, spin its camera and launchers round, following her as she moved.

Kat and Wilny darted forward, watching where the three Avios fell and pouncing on one apiece. Wilny zip-tying the arms and legs of a lanky long-winged Avio behind his back, whilst Kat did the same to a second Gull Avio, both knocking them unconscious.

Looping round Storm pounced upon the remaining Avio, a struggling Osprey-Avio rolling about on the top of a container stack, trying to shake the shock of the impact from her head. Grabbing the girl by her wing, she kicked sharply down upon her shoulder to dislocate the wing, stunning her before restraining her arms and legs.

Crawling on her hands and feet to the edge of the container, she caught a glimpse of iridescent blue as Kat and Wilny snuck down into the hold below, unseen by the patrolling guards. Looking back across towards the bridge of the ship, a flash of white and brown indicated where Amell was, with Rai no doubt right with him and heading to their targets.

Everyone was on-board. The clock had started.

The heist had begun.

31

With his ink-black wings, keeping track of Rai was difficult. For the entire flight, he had been gliding with quiet effortlessness, but the moment Rai saw Storm stoop through the sky, he had broken into a sprint. Next to him the rest of them were somewhat clumsy and unsteady, but even Rai couldn't hold a candle to Storm's flying prowess.

Gracelessly landing on the roof of the bridge with a thunk, Amell ducked low to avoid the spinning radar and clumsily closed his wings. Catching his breath, he leant back against the barrel of the fog horn.

"Careful!" Rai hissed at him from the shadows. "Try not to make too much noise."

Amell frowned back at the dark Avio.

"I can't help it. There's a lot of me to control." And to which to prove his point he gently flexed a single gigantic wing. The sea breeze caught it and like the sail of a ship, it tugged him across the deck until he closed it.

"Your headset is connected to the ship now, *Zeus.*" Beth muttered into Amell's ear. "Remember, we're going to do this calmly. No rushing in."

Giving each other a signalling nod, Amell followed Rai's directions as he jumped down to the landing outside of the bridge door, perching above it on the railings. Composing himself and holding his wings tight against his back, Rai stepped forward and tapped on the door several times. There was a short grumbling between the ship's pilots from within, followed by a short pause as one left their seat to answer the door.

Rai leapt back and saluted. The pilot looked him up and down and sighed deeply.

"What is it?" The pilot asked, clearly exhausted.

Rai smiled, throwing on his best American accent.

"My captain asks if you could take us further out to sea. He don't like the fact that we're so close to the shore. 'S getting worried that we'll run aground."

"And he didn't think to radio up?"

"He said you'd blocked him."

The pilot called back into the cabin to see if it was true. The other crewmember tested it to find that there was no response, thanks to Beth's input.

"If your boss wants to be angry about how I do my job he better come up and tell me himself next time. I'll take us further out into the water if he gets your birds to stop messing around out there."

"Alright, but one more thing." Rai bobbed his head and stepped back. The pilot looked up as Amell dropped down on him, knocking him unconscious and throwing him back into the bridge. The co-pilot scrambled from his seat, unable to move fast enough to slam down on the alarm or shriek as Rai rushed him and tackled him to the floor.

Rai chuckled and tipped an imaginary cowboy hat to the unconscious men. "I don't best appreciate being called a *Bird*." He said. Amell gave him a bemused look.

"What the hell was that accent?"

"I like spaghetti westerns." Rai shrugged.

"You'd think they could have done better than this though. Their security is as bad as your accent, bro." Amell laughed as he glanced round and bounded to the other door to make sure no one was on the other side. "Only two people in here?"

"It's a cargo ship which no one would have known about, and there's always a minimum of two people on the bridge." Beth sighed over his earpiece, "plug the jack in *Mach*, I need to deal with turning off the GPS, unless you want to do it."

"I'll do it."

Amell gave a sweeping gesture for Rai to get to work whilst he dragged the unconscious pilots to the back, and zip tied their hands together. He watched Rai out of the corner of his eye as he set to work on the large flat-screens, deft hands dancing across its surfaces as soon as he plugged in the jack.

"All done, Strix." Rai confirmed aloud, giving Amell a thumbs-up and continuing to calibrate the coordinates to help Beth override the steering and turn the ship into one oversized drone that was at her command.

Delta had done an excellent job of equipping the ship's bridge with technology to keep the ship on course, keeping the designs sleek and simple. A light overlay spanned the entire window, recording the speed and heading of the ship as well as laying out a path before them and outlining the coast and other passing ships in white against the darkness. On one of the smaller piloting screens that stood at the deck chairs, they could see the security cameras recording in thermal imaging across the decks. He could tell where the others were, as Avios radiated so much heat that they were beacons of white next to the dull oranges of Preternaturals and humans. Storm was the easiest to spot and a quick comparison from the screen looking up to the cranes he could pick her out even in the darkness, whilst the white dots that were descending the stairs he could tell to be Kat and Wilny. Some of the containers held spots of light; there was living cargo on-board too.

A loud piercing screech echoed across the ship and from Amell's ear piece. Amell yelped at the suddenness of the noise and clawed at his head, trying to pull the headset off to avoid the sound as it rang through again.

"What the hell was that?" He snarled as Rai looked up from his calibrating.

"That was on Horus's speaker." Beth said sharply, meaning Wilny. There was a slight buffing noise as she moved her mic down to talk to Raoul, leaving Amell to go to the window. More piercing screeches followed, louder this time and echoing through the hold of the ship. On the thermal screen, the clustered spots of light were moving fast, following the other bright moving spots.

"What has that prick done now?" Beth snapped loudly.

"He's not answering me."

Amell looked up from the screen to across the deck as the white dot signals left the hold. Across the deck upon the top of a stack of containers he could almost make out the figures of Kat and Wilny, only semi visible without the floodlights of the ship directly on them.

He could still hear the muffled sound of Kat screaming at Wilny from Raoul's receiver, followed by Beth and Raoul snapping at each other. The edge they'd had was gone, they had been compromised.

"He's startled the guard dogs." Beth, growled. He could almost hear her holding her head in her hands. "Not even three fucking minutes."

"Those don't sound like guard dogs Beth."

"They're not. They're *worse*."

A flash of silver flew across the window, as Storm flew in to help. A there was more screeching and clamouring of metal, followed by a clattering hail of bullets which thundered and echoed about the containers.

"Amell, go help them!" Ordered Beth, a sudden streak of panic in her otherwise angry tone. "They need some brute force."

Amell leapt back from the screen, stumbling over his own wings to try to run to the door, which he slammed into when he came to an abrupt stop to try and explain to Rai how the plan had disintegrated.

"Strix said-"

"I heard her." Rai smirked, continuing to work on the technology. "Go. Help your family."

Amell nodded, spinning on his heels and breaking into a sprint out the door, skidding and slamming against the railings before hurling himself and his gigantic wingspan out and clumsily gliding across the containers. Rai tapped in the final commands on the screens, glancing up to see Amell banking across the wide window, picking out a place to land without trouble.

A shot rang out from behind him, and Rai fell heavily to the floor.

-x-

The cargo hold of the ship was as equally filled with containers as the upper decks. Dark, confined, and smelling of sea salt, Wilny felt uneasy especially with the ship moving beneath him. Rows upon rows of stacked containers in boxes of brown, green, and white ran almost endlessly from prow to stern of the ship, only divided by the bulkheads. It was so packed and crowded yet was practically silent aside from the rumble of the ships engines and rotating fans.

"*Mach* and *Zeus* have the jack in. You should be safe now." Raoul assured him quietly through his ear piece.

"Good. How long until Sienna get here?"

"Approximately one hour."

"I guess we can take it slowly then." Wilny smiled.

"Not too slowly or they'll figure out something is wrong."

Carefully making his way down the stairs to the lower level, he patted his chest where he still had hold of Lana's drawing beneath his breastplate, feeling a little glow of comfort at having it by him.

In the crew areas between the containers, he could hear the low talking of people and the chink of chains scraping against the floor. With the acoustics of the hold, it was hard to tell how many people there were and where they were exactly. Kat would have been able to discern it more easily, but he made an estimate of about five to eight individuals. Creeping slowly closer, he padded softly as he could manage down the corridor, keeping his wings tight against his body and his tailfeathers high off the floor to keep them from rustling. There was little he could do to keep out of the spotlights that made his peacock-blue feathers glow.

There was a slight gap in the arrangement of the containers, an indent where it appeared some were missing. He slowly peeked around the corner. Several of the containers were open and through the narrow gap between them he could see a light. Most of the shadows were of figures laying down to sleep with only a few sat up talking, but he could count at least seven by the shadows.

Wilny cursed internally, wishing that he had been better equipped to deal with them all. A grenade would have taken them all out, but all he had was zip ties and a gun. As he recalculated his plan of attack, he listened in to the conversation the few that were awake were having.

"I'm telling you, it's not real." He heard one laugh teasingly. "The people are actors. If it were real, then they would know how to drive a car without blowing it up."

"But everything's always exploding!"

"Its special effects." A third joined in, struggling to stifle laughter. "Just like all those people using *magic*. It's not real."

"You're a liar, it is real! It's all real! Magic is real!" The second protested in a high childish voice. "Just like telkens! They're magic 'cause you're lifting things without touching them!"

"Telkens aren't magic, they're-"

"LA LA! Not listening! I'm *not* listening!"

The first person chuckled and from what Wilny could hear, shoved the second off the box they were sat on. The interactions reminded him of his old team and how they would talk exactly like this with each other. Fury laughing at Eddie for saying he wanted to be a racing driver or a cowboy, and Rainbow teasing Featherhead whenever he asked about flowers in gardens.

Pain racked his chest. All the questions and wishes they had; he missed them.

Wilny forgot his plans of grenades or resorting to killing them and angrily scolded himself. These were people, and all had lives and had their family as much as he had his. He was better than that to destroy what little they had.

He backtracked, eyes darting around the area for a point of inspiration. If he could get closer or climb onto the containers and be above them, he could drop down between them all and stun them with his talents and tied them all up safely. No one would be hurt.

But as he made a quiet step forward, in the darkness of the closest open container, a pair of yellow eyes snapped open, bright and reflective in the gloom. Panic froze Wilny in place upon the low and angry hiss, and out the corner of his eye saw the quills of maroon feathers rising. He knew that sound very well. Wilny held his breath as it scraped its scaled legs against the floor, the hissing turning into a throaty growl.

Wilny mused to try and make himself invisible to its perception. Its thoughts were sharply alien, with no spoken language, but instead thinking in image in which he found himself looking through the creatures' eyes at himself.

The creature lunged at him with a piercing screech that cut through the silence, panicked by the prickle of disturbance across its skull. Sharp needle like teeth snapped inches from his face as Wilny reeled back. Bringing its self into the spotlight of the corridor, the colour drained from Wilny's face as he came nose to nose with one of ARCDA's favourite synthetic critters.

A Drake Raptor.

It strained at the harness and chain it was hooked up to, striking its long neck out at him to bite, scraping the paint from the deck with its powerful talons and beating its short broad wings.

"Woah! Woah!" Their handler yelled, as the several other Raptors in the dark began to stir. The Elites stirred too, shoving each other out of bed and scrambling to snatch up their weapons.

The Raptor he woke snapped at him again, followed by another screeching alarm call that hurt his ears. Abandoning all plans, Wilny bolted just as their handler shouted something. A series of clicks were then followed a thundering of talons against metal and skittering crashing sounds as they took the corners round the containers too fast.

"Wilny, what's going on?" Raoul asked through his earpiece, though Wilny barely heard him through the sound of thundering feet on metal. The bulkhead doors were open and leaping through he swung himself on a railing and tumbled up the set of stairs beside it.

"Wilny!" Raoul shouted as the Raptors skidded to a stop then began leaping up the stairs in quick scurrying bounds after Wilny. "What the *fuck* is going on?"

"Guard dogs! They've got guard dogs onboard!" He shrieked back as a set of teeth gnashed upon the ends of his tailfeathers. "Raptors! Harrier types!"

"Oh shit."

Drawn by the commotion, up ahead of him he saw Kat pop her head out from a diverging path that led across the hold.

"Go! Go! Go!" Wilny yelled wildly gesturing for her to run as he raced towards the open door. She didn't need telling twice upon seeing the Raptors behind him. Both threw themselves through the door, flaring out their wings with the speed as soon as they hit the sea air, but the Raptors kept chasing.

Their excited shrieks and whistles echoed across the entire ship and across the open sea. It Storm's attention and she abandoned the Osprey Avio she had captured to leap up onto the cranes to pinpoint from above where the sounds had come from. No sooner had she landed when she saw Kat and Wilny escape from the hold, sprinting and darting up and between the containers, when the Raptors emerged after them.

Storm's eyes widened in awe at the Raptors as they stalked out onto the deck, shaking their feathered crowns and flexing their clawed wings out, their majesty highlighted by the floodlights of the ship as they scented the air and circled the containers, calling to one another with throaty barks.

"Oh, you beauties!" Storm gasped, slowly creeping around the edge of the crane to follow them as they moved.

Each of the six Raptors stood taller than Amell on long scaled legs, nearly four meters long from tip to tail. They were based upon prehistoric raptors, but with ARCDA's own flair added to them. Feathers covered their bodies all over, maroon-reds and blacks, from their toothed dinosaur-like heads all the way down their long stiff tails and their taloned arms and wings; they were six limbed like an Avio.

"What the fuck did you do?!" Kat shrieked at Wilny, leaping up to join him on the top of a container, the Raptors leaping and clawing at the bars of the stacked containers, circling them as a flock. They tried to jump across the gap to get to the next stack and barely missed having their tails snapped off by a leaping Raptor.

"Nothing!" He shrieked back, grabbing and holding his torn tailfeathers close to keep them out of reach of the snapping jaws. "They just woke up!"

"HORUS YOU MOTHERFUCKER!" Beth roared into his ear, as he scrambled to draw his gun. "WHAT THE SHIT DID YOU DO?"

"I didn't do anything! ARCDA brought Raptors with them!"

"Oh you...Good job, Horus! Great! *Great work!* NOW YOU HAVE TO HANDLE NOT BEING *EATEN* AS WELL AS NOT BEING *SHOT!*"

"I KNOW!"

With a beating of its wings, one of the Raptors managed to climb its way up to reach the top container adjacent to them, with another quickly following after. With a throaty hiss, the Raptor flared its wings out and leapt across the gap at them. Wilny fired once to its head, rolling out the way as it skidded past, electrocuted by the EMI bullets and rolling unconscious onto the deck below. The second Raptor however leapt across, and as Kat swung her foot at it to kick it from the top of the container, it grabbed hold of the tips of her right wing in its teeth as it slipped on the metal. Pain shot up her wing and Kat screamed at the top of her lungs.

"STORM!"

Snapping herself back into the moment at the sound of her name, Storm launched herself off the crane and slammed feet first into the side of the Raptor, sending it crashing onto the deck where it lay stunned.

The rest of the Raptor flock recoiled as Storm span round, throwing her wings high above her and hissed at them. They hissed back, bowing low with their short wings fanned in aggression, keeping their distance as she threatened them with powerful beats of her wings.

Their handler came charging out of the shadows with heavy thudding *clanks*, carrying in a long crackling cattle prod and whistle. The ExoArmour he was wearing made him a walking fortress that towered above the Raptors on mechanical legs. Tilting his head at Storm he frowned beneath his gold visor and sneered, then blew on his whistle with a single extended note, commanding his Raptors to run forward and attack. When they made a move, Storm leapt forward at them with a series of quick swipes across the closest Raptor's snout and beating it across the head with her wings, driving the pack back to their master.

Mechanical whirring and a heavy metal thunk, sent a cold streak down Wilny's spine and flaring up every feather on his body. They'd been alerted and powered up the Hercules, which was now angling its arms between the containers on their other side. The AutoMech was built like a small tank, raised up on two broad legs with a large, armoured body and four arms, two of which were armed with gatling guns with the barrels already beginning to spin and warm up. There was no way she could take on Raptors and a Hercules.

As it began to move forward towards the feral commotion, Wilny fired at the cockpit several times to get the attention of the pilot inside. The gunshots silenced the Raptors for a moment, and he saw Storm look up to where he was.

"THUNDERBIRD! FLY!" Wilny screamed at her, drumming the top of the container loudly. She didn't argue, in a flurry of wingbeats, she bolted over the head of the Raptor-handler, kicking him hard in the face. With a muffled yowl, the Raptor-handler blew his whistle several times, sending the pack after Storm.

The cockpit of the AutoMech tilted as the pilot within looked up to the top of the container where Kat and Wilny were lurking, the thermal sensors picking them up in the darkness. Wilny cursed himself for not remembering to tell them about the sensors.

"Don't waste your ammunition." Kat snarled as she pushed him to change position and pick a new spot from the top of the containers to aim. "I thought you said you've dealt with this stuff before?"

"I panicked."

"Oh, you *panicked?* Weren't you an Elite?"

"Yes, but that was in a clinical environment!"

"What's happening! Byrnes! What's going on?" Shouted a man from below. "Why aren't you receiving on the radio!"

Both Kat and Wilny flattened themselves against the top of the container. Kat's round ears flicked back and forth as she counted the number of footsteps she was hearing, the click of guns and the hushed confused whispering of people as they gathered. The Elites were out and armed.

"There's fifteen Elites down there right now." Kat whispered. "Plus big-boy in the Exo and the Hercules."

The pilot in the Hercules, whirred his machine round, keeping the guns trained on where Kat and Wilny were lurking.

"Walker's pets were chasing something, I think it was an Avio, but not one of our ones sir." His voice crackled through a speaker.

"What have we got?" Raoul asked on behalf of Beth. "The cameras are on night mode, I can't see colours. Do we have any Ruby or Sapphires here?"

Wilny risked a glance as the handler began to instruct them to move. Three teams each with a different colour accent to their grey SmartFabrics. Green, pale orange, and pale yellow. Four per team plus a fifth as their handlers. Unlike the yellow and orange team in their body-hugging SmartFabrics, the members of the green team wore heavy duty armoured suits with helmets.

"Two sub teams. Quartz level, fifth year oranges, sixth year yellows. One team of Emeralds. Handlers have Ruby badges on them." Wilny pointed out to Kat and alliterating to Raoul as he sized them up. He was a little relieved that they weren't dealing with higher level Elites such as the Rubies and Sapphires, however, he was a little shocked that what were essentially school aged Synths were being put to work. Quartzes weren't even Elites yet.

"They're letting baby *Quartzes* out now?" Raoul tutted, equally as shocked. "Wow, things have really gone downhill."

"This is probably a work experience crew. They do these things for aptitude tests."

"Hm. True. Make sure they don't get killed, they're just kids. What about the AutoMechs?"

"The ExoArmors, those are Beowulf models. SmartFabric lining under a plated shell, so even if a bullet does go through it'll stop them from bleeding out."

"What about your gun?" Kat asked with a small nod.

"If we're going to stop them we need a high velocity rifle, this is a handgun with EMI bullets. If I were closer, then maybe I could get a clean shot at their necks, or even hit their visors I could."

"What about a knife?"

"Sure. If you can get at their armpits, necks, or crotch then you can hit soft tissues." He sighed heavily, watching as they spread out into their groups. "No offence Kat, but I don't think you're fast enough to get close and-"

Kat's claws dug into his leg sharply to get his attention so that he would look her in the eye.

"It's *Sekhmet*. And I bet you three month's supply of honey that I can take more down than you." She said with a smirk. "But if you lose, I get to dress you like a Ken-doll and you can't complain."

"Done." The two shook hands in agreement on the bet.

"Mach is down!" Raoul barked over the ear piece, snapping the pair back to attention. "We need to get back in control of the bridge."

"Crap." Wilny spat. "*Sekhmet*, you've gotta get to the bridge. I'll cover you."

Kat nodded, taking out her knives and calculating a path to get to the other end of the ship.

"The bet is still on K-Pop."

"You're damn right it is J-Pop."

And with a shared fist-bump between them, Kat was off. The containers were level enough to run across, high enough that the Elites couldn't climb them easily, but it wouldn't be quiet. However, she was sure that Storm was making enough noise with the Raptors and Hercules to keep her covered. She could hear the Elites shouting to each other and skidding as they tried to sharply turn corners and communicate with each other, that was now more difficult since Beth still had control over their radios.

The Hercules had her heat signature locked and began following her and none of the shots Wilny fired drew its attention away.

"There!" A Quartz in orange shouted as Storm flashed past him, skidding to a halt at the crossroads of a long open pathway. The group aimed and made a short run to follow when the Raptors bolted past them, body slamming them and tearing them down like skittles before scampering off after Storm once more. After quickly picking themselves up, the orange team cautiously followed the Raptors at a steady jog, nervous and struggling to plan without the aid of their handler's orders coming through to them.

Storm whipped by the AutoMech, giving a rough kick to one of its arms as she did so, drawing the pilot's attention away from Kat and making it spin round to face her. The Raptors bounded past it, leaping on its arms and propelling themselves off with flurrying wingbeats, leaving it wobbling behind them with loud curses crackling through its speaker.

The Hercules fired a round of bullets, panicking the Raptors chasing Storm and sending them into a blind sprint. A bullet ricochet and caught Storm in the leg just as she leaped over the railings of the ship, flaring out her wings and swooping in an arc, the Raptors following her. They were far heavier than Storm, unable to take a vertical leap into the air for flight, but with their broad wings they could glide and use their fan-feathered tails to help them.

More bullets whizzed past her, the orange Quartz team this time, now able to take aim without the containers being in their way. Dropping low to avoid another volley, Storm clipped the side of a container with her foot, swearing and tumbling forward across the deck into an open and exposed area. The remaining Raptors pounced at her back, slashing through her feathers with their sharp talons, her SmartFabric doing little to protect her.

Storm rolled onto her back and kicked up hard against its muscular chest and forcing it back for a moment before it struck at her again as she raised her hands to defend herself. Sharp needle-like teeth snapped shut upon her left hand, piercing through the skin and bone, whilst it clawed at her and trying to beat her with its wings. Storm screeched in pain, shocking the Raptor in retaliation. The creature reeled back with a screech, crashing into a container as it shook its head, its two remaining flock members hesitant to rush forward again.

Her hand bled profusely from where the Raptor had bitten through the SmartFabric gloves, to the skin and broken the fingers, her arm and face sliced multiple times by the sharp talons. It was white hot in agony and throbbing with every heartbeat, but feral vengeful rage quickly drowned out the pain. Forcing herself onto her hands and feet, she lunged at the Raptor that had attacked her, snarling and snapping her teeth, kicking out hard at it in fury, slamming it against the container. In the shadows behind the Raptors, the orange Quartz team were watching her in wide eyed terror as in a feral rage she dragged the Raptor by its nostrils down to the ground and bit it hard upon its neck.

Three loud gunshots echoed through the containers, the EMI bullets striking three of the orange team, leaving the remaining one to bolt in panic at the sound. The screams and shouts of the orange team rolling about on the deck, drew the remaining Raptors attention away from Storm and they began to stalk forward towards the Quartzes.

Wilny reloaded, firing again and scratching past the face of the remaining member of the orange team just as they spun to face him. The Elite shrieked and let loose a clip of bullets that skittered and scattered off the containers, panicked by the sudden attack.

"Shooter on the roof- uh! Top! There's someone shooting from above!" One screeched into a radio microphone upon their collar as the two Raptors stalked closer, seeing them as easier targets than the enraged Avio.

The heavy clumping footsteps vibrated through the metal as the AutoMech moved, getting Storm back into its line of sight over the orange team as they squirmed and kicked at the Raptors they were inadvertently goading. Too busy in her fight with the Raptor, she didn't even acknowledge the Hercules approaching.

"Thunderbird, get out of there!" Wilny shouted, risking himself by crawling to the edge and shooting again at the machine.

The Hercules, turned its barrels up to where Wilny was hidden, using its thermal sensors to pin his location down. The sound of the guns whirring alerted Wilny immediately and he rolled away from the edge of the container, moving quickly to get to a new and safer location. The pilot was reluctant to directly hit the containers as the bullets would have torn straight through the metal and destroyed whatever cargo was inside.

Guns raised, the barrels began to spin again, ignoring Wilny's and focusing on Storm. A huge speeding object struck the AutoMech hard in the back, knocking it forward onto its barrels, before jumping from it and skidding to a halt. The Raptors shrieked and trilled in fear as the Hercules crashed to the deck and scattered into the maze of containers. Even the one Storm had been fighting panicked. Storm gripped it tightly by its crest of feathers, ignoring its hisses and screes as it scrambled up to its feet. Jumping and swinging her leg over the arch of its neck she kicked it hard, sending it into a sprint as it chased after the rest of its remaining flock, carrying her off.

"Am- Zeus!" Wilny cheered almost forgetting to use his callsign. He had never been happier to see the Eagle. Looking up to him Amell saluted with a wide smile and a wink.

He watched in glee as the Hercules picked itself up, only to have Amell charge it. Amell grabbed it by a barrel and swung himself at its joint, severing it from its body before slamming it against a leg, denting and staggering it. The pilot made a grab for him with one of the grasping arms, but the Eagle caught it with a laugh and pulled. Wilny was in awe. He knew Amell was a strong man, but he'd never seen him tear a half-tonne arm from an AutoMech before, not that there'd been much opportunity to witness that.

A bullet whizzed past his head, as a better trained Emerald Elite fired at him. Immediately he rolled off and swung himself down to the side of the container, holding onto the bars and keeping out of the shooters line of sight as another bullet hit the container behind him. Pulling himself up to peek quickly he located the origin point of the shooter. The Emeralds who were climbing up into the cranes.

"You got this?" Wilny shouted down to Amell.

"I've got this!" Amell roared with laughter, dropping and pulling the arm he'd caught down and throwing off the balance of the Hercules and making it spin on its undented leg. "You deal with the Elites."

The Hercules pivoted, in time for the pilot to see Amell swing the broken arm forward at the cockpit and slam the machine down onto its back where it turtled.

Wilny nodded, relaying what was happening to Beth as he disappeared between the containers in a flurry of wingbeats, to take the Emerald Elites out.

Amell turned to the orange Quartzes as the remaining unhurt member tried to help drag his teammates away, watching him with wide eyed fear. They weren't worth chasing or hurting any further and so turned his attention back to the Hercules. The pilot had regained its footing and the Hercules grabbed Amell by the head with one of its grasping arms, lifting him off the ground and squeezing his head. Gold flashed across the Herculeses' line of sight and the arm holding Amell was sheared off at with a flawlessly clean cut. Amell fell to the floor, the arm on top of his chest and found himself staring up at his saviour with her copper orange and gold wings.

Malana had entered the fray.

32

"Lana!"

The little girl bounced off the broken arm, pirouetting on the balls of her feet and turning to face Amell and the Hercules. The AutoMech's severed arm rose into the air off his chest, levitated by the invisible force of her telkens. The AutoMech pilot didn't know how to react, and in his confusion was knocked onto its back by the force of Malana hurling the floating arm at him. Amell, getting to his feet and rubbing his aching head, stared down at the little girl in relieved bewilderment.

"Lana…how the hell did you get out here? Why are you here, you're just a—"

Malana ignored him and leapt to perch on top of the upturned Hercules. The pilot inside staring up through his plated windscreen at her in shock. Without so much as a blink, she sliced off its remaining two arms, leaving the pilot wildly trying to wriggle the machine out of the gap and back into standing position.

Malana smiled down at Amell from her perch and giggled.

"Oh yeah, forgot about *that*." Amell swallowed, trying not to picture what she could have done to him with her telkens when he was being manipulated by Teal. A scar across the face was nothing if she could cut through titanium alloy like paper.

"Lana, why are you here?"

"Beth sent me." She turned her head to tap her ear tufts. Like him, she was wearing a headset and SmartFabrics that had been rolled up to fit her like the rest of the Rogues, though she wore her golden sash over her still short tailfeathers.

Amell smiled, hiding his shock as best as he could.

"She what?"

"Beth thought it might be fun for her and Palmer to play." Raoul sighed over the headset. In the background he could hear Palmer yell "I'm helping!" followed by laughter from both children. The microphone buffered and hissed slightly as Beth lent in to talk through both his and Wilny's ears.

Wilny was furious.

"YOU LET LANA FLY OUT ACROSS THE SEA ON HER OWN?"

"She's fine. I also thought you might need back up, or at least some sort of secret weapon."

"*SECRET WEAPON?*" Screeched Wilny through Beth's headphones. "SHE'S MY DAUGHTER! NOT A WEAPON!"

"She's also four times deadlier than all of you, excluding Storm."

"She's five, Beth! *FIVE!*"

"Then if you do your job quickly, you can make sure she stays safe. She's with Amell right now, she'll be fine." Beth said dismissively. Malana bounced off the Hercules and immediately began preening her wings and adjusting her sash, looking alert and eager to help.

Even after Beth pulled away from Raoul's mic, Amell could still hear Wilny's irate screaming although he was certain that it was because Wilny was literally shouting from the crane ladder, loud enough for the entire ship to hear him.

Amell sighed, putting his hands to his hips and looking to the stranded Hercules then back down at the tiny child. He was fully aware that if anything happened to her on his watch, that Wilny would never forgive him, not that he would ever forgive himself either.

"Well, Malana. Are you ready to have some fun?"

Her golden eyes lit up in glee. "Yes!"

"Then let's go."

With a roll of his shoulders, he strode off through the containers at a steady pace, Malana skipping along behind him to keep up. Keeping to the shadows they carefully crept around the ship, Amell took care to keep Malana within arm's reach so that he could grab her and pull her back if needed. With the Raptors busy with Storm, they were safe from sudden attack, but with the sound of their scratching and hissing so far away, the deck was oddly quiet, even with the constant tonal drone of the engines.

Amell's ears pricked at the sound of people talking and a steady and fading clank-clank of the AutoMech. Stealthily, Amell and Malana peeked cautiously out from behind a stack of containers.

The yellow team of Quartzes– a Canid, a Pard and two Preters– were keeping formation at the base of the crane as their handler climbed it. The Green team, the higher ranked Emerald Elites, were already up high along the crane arms and searching, but as their subordinate team the yellows had to follow their orders to remain where they were. They were positioned so that they could see up and down the deck and with the main corridor between the containers covered, although weren't doing a particularly good job, having not noticed that Malana and Amell were watching them.

Amell smirked and tapped Lana's shoulder, pointing out to the black sea. With a grin and a nod, she knew exactly what to do, and disappeared into the darkness. While she flew, Amell climbed the containers as quietly as he could manage, keeping his huge wings close to his back.

Reaching the top of the stack, he didn't wait for the Elites on the crane to give away his position. He leaped down upon the yellow team, driving his wings down and flattening them all with one huge sweep of his twenty-foot wingspan.

With dazed shouts and fumbling, the yellow team struggled to stand and fight back, not that Amell gave them the chance as he grabbed two of the team of four, one in each hand and knocked their heads against each other, as the remaining two scrambled to their feet. They had no time to aim or balance themselves, as out of the shadows Malana raced across the length of the railings on the wing, and struck the third down, clipping the fourth across the back of his head with her wings.

Their handler yelped in shock as he watched his team be flattened and leapt down from the crane and drew his gun on the two Avios, fearfully pacing backwards as Amell held the pair of his dazed teammates off the ground as though they weighed nothing whilst Malana threw their guns into the sea.

"Drop them! Drop them or I'll shoot!" The panicked Preter warned, shakily pointing his weapon at Amell's wings.

A set of eyes flashed in the darkness behind the Handler and the sound of claw on metal grew closer. Immediately, Amell dropped the two captives to the ground, leaping back to grab Malana and keep her protected within his huge wings.

"Get down!" One of the Yellows screamed from the floor to the handler before he could say another word.

The handler shrieked and threw himself and his gun to the floor, covering his head with his hands as the Raptor leaped over him. Its high-pitched *scree* sent an electric jolt of fear down their spines and the Quartzes curled up into balls and threw their arms over their heads as they had been taught to do, protecting their necks from being bitten.

The three Raptors' russet wings splayed and their bodies slinking low, they hissed to each other, ignoring Amell and Malana and keeping their yellow eyes fixed on the team.

"We surrender! We surrender okay!" One of the team yelled, a Canid with a torn ear. He pulled his hands away for the fraction of a second and a Raptor snapped its wide jaws around his neck. Two piercing short whistles stopped the Raptor from sinking its teeth into the Canid's flesh, and the other two Raptors looked up and backed away as Storm came gliding in between them all. Fanning her wings, the creamy white and charcoal barring now reddened with a smear of blood, she mimicked the Raptors body language, walking on her toes with purposeful steps and intermittent bounding leaps, sharply turning her head, and hissing at them in their same low echoing manner. They stepped away, allowing her to walk between them.

"Storm, how did you..." Amell marvelled, watching Storm step up and tug sharply on the Raptor's crown of feathers, making it pull away from the Canid. It released his head from its jaws with only pin pricks of blood from where the teeth had pierced the skin, letting him scramble to his teammates. The yellows all huddled together, back-to-back as the Raptors circled and watched them, nudging their snouts at Storm's arms and wings for attention.

"Don't touch them." She warned, gently running a finger down the neck of the Raptor closest to her and preening some of the loose feathers. "They might bite your fingers of."

"But how are you controlling them?"

She smirked. "Their handler just trained them with simple signal commands and whistles like you do with falconry birds, it's not that hard to figure out. And if they don't listen then they get an electric shock."

Amell nodded sagely and took a step back with Malana as he caught the yellow eye of a Raptor.

"If you don't want to be eaten, stay *exactly* where you are." Storm snarled to the yellow team, rubbing the neck of the Raptors and calming them. The Quartzes didn't so much as nod as Storm stepped away with three short sharp whistles, leaving them to be contained by the Raptors.

"Lana." Storm said sternly, looking down at the little girl with a serious frown and folding her arms across her chest. Malana bowed her head slightly, shuffling out of the protection of Amell's wings. If Wilny was mad with her for flying out across the sea on her own, then she was sure that Storm would lecture her as well.

"Your flying skills are better than I expected."

Lana looked up in surprise to find Storm grinning with pride. Storm gathered her up into her arms and hugged her tight, ignoring the blood smears she was getting all over her golden wings. Malana blushed and pulled her wings to her face, hiding her cheeks in embarrassment at the praise.

"Orange team is down. Hercules is down. Wilny's taken out most of the Emeralds with only their handler left, and Kat's got back control on the bridge." Beth confirmed to Amell. "One of the crew shot Rai."

"*What?*" Storm looked horrified at the news, as Amell relayed what was said to him.

"Kat's dealt with it; she's now just going to get the left over Avios."

"But is Rai okay?"

"Beth says he's alive, but what do we do now boss?" Amell asked. He kept his distance from the Raptors, as much as he trusted Storm to be able to control them, they were still savage hungry beasts. One seemed particularly aware of his caution and hissed at him, bearing a sharp backwards curving teeth and letting its crown of feathers flare up.

"Round up whoever surrenders and stick them in this container." She signalled for the surrendered Quartz to enter the open container. "We'll treat Rai and anyone else of them who've hurt after we've got them all contained."

"Got it."

With four short whistles from Storm, the Raptors withdrew to her side allowing the Quartzes up. Under threat of the Raptors, they quickly stumbled into the container, which was full of boxes of SmartFabrics, pushing themselves to the back. Between the thought of staying out in the open with the Raptors and Rogues, the container seemed much safer. Before they could all enter Storm grabbed a Preternatural by the collar of their suit and held them back.

"Where is your boss?" She asked, letting a Raptor hiss into the Preternatural's ear.

The terrified Preter was trembling so much his teeth were rattling.

"They all went up there." He gulped, pointing towards the crane and pulling away as far as he could from the Raptor as it began to sniff at him. Releasing him, the Preter shot into the container to hide from the Raptors. Tilting her head to the side, she looked up towards the cranes, searching for the last one.

-x-

Wilny had been busy.

Angered by Lana's arrival and fearful for what could happen to her if she got hurt, he had picked off the Emeralds on the cranes, one by one, mimicking Storm's stealth attacks by flying high and swooping in sharply out of the dark to knock them out before they could hear him coming. The strategy worked surprisingly well, and he cursed himself for not having thought of the method himself during his time at Core.

Gliding on the wind, keeping above the floodlights so that his glossy feathers didn't draw any attention, he allowed himself a moment of reprieve, making sure that he didn't over exert his heart. As he soared, he watched for signs of movement below, witnessing Amell and Lana's joint attack and Storm running with the Raptors.

The Emerald's handler, a Preternatural, was setting up a position high above the deck on the upper tower of the frontmost crane with a rifle. He was being quick, but Wilny was already onto him, falling into a rapid dive.

He struck at the Elite, his foot connecting with the barrel of the riffle and the force pulled the Elite forward. Arms wind milling, the handler managed to grab the edge of the crane and hold on, swinging his legs as he tried to pull himself back up. Wilny landed across from him on the crane. The Elite drew a handgun but wasn't fast enough to fire it as Wilny kicked it hard out of his hand before moving forward to knock the helmet from his head, staggering him once again. The Preternatural swore, clutching at his face as Wilny gave an uppercut to his nose, blood splurging everywhere.

With a light-footed bounce Wilny whipped up into the air, noisy wings a flashing blur of golden-green and indigo, landing behind him.

Lunging forward he struck at the Elite's neck before he had a chance to turn, aiming to snap it before remembering that he was not meant to kill any of the crew if it couldn't be helped. Curling his fingers up mid strike he punched the Elite across the face. He swore loudly and uppercutted Wilny in retaliation. Wilny's footing on the bars slipped and he fell hard to a knee, just as the Elite brought his foot up to kick. Snatching his hand forward, he dragged the Elite forward, turning him up onto his back against the bars.

'Use your wings,' he could hear Storm muse to him. 'You have them so use them.'

Shrugging the pain in his shin off, Wilny's wings blurred and helped him to stand as the Elite came at him again. Using his wings to balance himself and keep him slightly off the bars, reducing his risk of slipping and falling as the two wrestled. The wind whipped around them as the storm clouds rolled over, a deep echoing thunder reverberating through the metal, followed by a creaking groan from below. A blur of metallic grey flew towards them from the deck. Wilny only had a split second to shove the Elite back before one of the Hercules broken arms arced between them, only to crash into the sea.

"What is that?" The Elite yelped, staggering to his feet again, looking down at where it might have come from. Wilny clawed at the bars, locking his fingers tight as he held on and looked below.

"Sunbeam!"

Malana sailed over the containers, the sash a tail of gold flaring out behind her as she chased down an Emerald Elite on the run.

Wilny snarled at the Elite before him as he began to spit and swear at Malana. In a sharp strike, Wilny swept his wing forward, catching the handler in the knee. The handler slipped on the poles, foot taken out from under him and dragging Wilny down with him by the collar of his SmartFabrics. He dropped a wing down to the bars, trying to keep himself up as the Elite started to slip through.

Taking out a tazer from his thigh holster, the Elite jabbed Wilny in the chest with it hard. Electricity shocked him and Wilny gasped in painfully for breath. The Elite prodded again, several times in quick succession. Wilny stumbled back, trying not to let his footing slip, and looked down for the briefest of seconds only to be met with a punch across the face when he looked back up again.

His chest throbbed, lightheaded from the shocks and unable to focus upon the Elite, he clung to the metal, dizzy and disorientated. Fury lined the Elite's face, and he could see the Elite's vision tunnelling as he focused solely upon him.

Ignoring his injuries, he lunged forward, attempting a final assault. Wilny beat his wings hard and took off, forcing himself to muse as he did so.

The world became slow and acutely detailed as Wilny mused, everything feeling as though it took minutes to happen despite it only being several seconds, giving Wilny time to think and calculate before the handler could kill him. Every shining filament of every feather and hair was in perfect detail, the what-should-have-been, blur of feathers slowed to a gentle sweep. Even the sound seemed slowed, which only drew attention and focus to the looming *vwom-vwom* sound, growing closer and closer to them, almost keeping pace to the fluttering and uneven beating of his heart. Out the corner of his eye, ignoring the Handler swinging a wild flailing arm to grab at his feathers, he saw a thin wire silver in the light and held taut between two half-spheres whirling towards them.

The Poacher drone's bolo.

It had detected the taser as a foreign electrical field.

The Elite could see it too, the panic in his eyes immediate and slowly his muscles beginning to tense as he too tried to pull away. Wilny beat his wings hard, arching back to escape the whirling weapon drawing closer to them, though his muscles didn't feel as if they were responding to him at all as he moved so slowly.

Wilny couldn't keep the perception change going much longer, but he knew now what he could do to escape. He waited until gravity had pulled them just out of the line of fire when he broke his focus. The world blurred into normal speed again for them both as they fell backwards out of the arc of the bolo and dropped from the crane like stones.

The Elite hit the deck hard and fast, whilst Wilny struggled to beat his wings and gain lift spiralling in a flat spin downwards. He landed knees first onto the deck with a bone rattling thunk that threw him face first down to the ground. Black spots danced before his eyes, body throbbing with pain. He stumbled forward onto something soft and sticky; the crumpled heap of the Elite looked less like a person and more of a crushed rag doll, skull and spine fractured by the impact.

Nausea swept over him as he backpedalled as fast as he could away from the corpse, and disorientated he collapsed onto the deck, heart beating erratically and struggling for breath as he stared up at the floodlights.

A huge set of wings shielded him from the light. He couldn't tell who it was until he felt himself being lifted from the deck and saw a familiar glint of gold close by.

"Wilny!"

"Dad!"

"Help…Me." Wilny rasped, weakly reaching up to hold onto Amell. Vision tunnelled and the voices distant, panic and shock set in. His eyes rolled in his head.

Amell and Malana began to panic, looking down at the pale and clammy Wilny, trying to put him into the recovery position as best they could whilst explaining to Raoul what was happening.

"He's not breathing Raoul!"

"Is he conscious?"

"Yes- no, sort of."

"I knew I should have gone with you!" Raoul growled over both headsets. "You need to keep him breathing, make sure that he's on his back when you give him recovery breaths. Wilny, I'm going to need you to try to relax your muscles as much as you can so you can breathe easier."

"Do I need to do CPR?"

"Has he got a pulse?"

"Yes, but it's all over the place."

"Then not yet, just keep him breathing."

Amell swore, rolling Wilny onto his back. He looked round trying to find something to trigger his memory of what to do. He spotted the dead Elite and his small pockets and saddlebag.

"Lana." Amell said, leaning down to check Wilny's chest for breathing. "Get that guy's bag."

Leaving the little girl to do as he asked whilst he gave the Hummingbird recovery breaths. Malana ignored the bloody mess and tore open the saddlebag of the Elite that Wilny had taken down with him and brought it over to Amell. They riffled through the contents.

"Nitro, aspirin, painkillers, boosters." He mumbled to himself, flicking through the tiny square patches. "Raoul! Elites have epinephrine. EPI+. I can stop the attack with it right?"

"What? You're going to flood him with adrenaline?" Raoul barked. "Amell, don't! It could stop his heart completely. Focus on keeping him breathing and relaxing his chest! Beth get Kat or Storm to find a defibrillator! There should be one at the front of the ship, we can check his heart rate with that."

Shots were fired, cutting Raoul off. Amell howled in pain and shock as he was hit in the shoulder.

The Raptor's handler was still walking about. He stomped towards them, snarling under his breath as he reloaded his gun with fumbling fingers.

Lana leapt to her feet and flared her wings out, letting the quills rattle as she hissed at the armoured Preter. He stopped to laugh, but his amusement was short lived as the gun was ripped from his hands by an invisible force and the red tipped cartridges rolled and scattered about the deck. Stunned, the Raptor-handler backed away with his hands up in self-defence, and with a triumphant grin, Malana ran at him.

"L-Lana…Lana no-" Wilny gasped weakly, reaching out after her, but she wasn't listening.

Malana charged the Preternatural, aiming to slice through his chest, but was tackled one of the gull-Avios that Storm had taken down and ditched into the sea.

Malana skidded across the floor, the impact sending black spots darting about her vision. The Gull-Avio held her still, gripping her tightly by her wing. Before she could even think to use her telkens upon the Gull, he swept her up into the sky and over the containers. Amell charged after him, trying to beat his huge wings in the narrow gap. The Preter swung his arm around, clipping Amell across the face with his elbow before shooting him in the shoulder with a handgun and letting him drop to the deck.

Snarling, Amell ignored the pain and lunged forward and grabbed the Preter by his saddlebag, only to have the bag rip away from the belt as the Preter kicked him back down once more. With a vindictive laugh, he retreated with the Gull, leaving both boys behind writhing in pain.

Amell hissed and put his hand to where the first bullet had struck him, only to find a red tipped syringe of a tranquiliser, intended for use on the Raptors. He would have less than a minute before he was unable to move.

He plucked it out and brushed away the dribble of blood now flowing down his shoulder, tearing open the saddle bag to find it packed with little packets of Nitro, booster patches, morphine and adrenalin.

"Raoul, what do I need to do! We don't have time for a defibrillator, but Wilny is breathing and I'm on a timer here before I'm paralysed. I have two field med kits with me now."

"Okay! In this order." Raoul spoke quickly. "Booster packs to the jugular, one above the heart and below, morphine and aspirin to the right arm, wait ten seconds then put the Nitro on his jugular also but only for *twenty seconds,* then half an EPI+ followed by another two boosters to his left arm. It will only be a quick fix and Wilny you're going to hate me tomorrow for it."

"Stop, get…Lana." Wilny slurred as Amell ripped open Wilny's SmartFabric to do as Raoul instructed, holding the squares between his teeth. "Save her."

"You first." Said Amell, doing as instructed with the medical patches, letting the chemicals flow into his bloodstream. The pain across Wilny's chest subsided rapidly with sweet relief and his breathing slowed. He could feel the boosters beginning work, a strange tingling sensation as it mended the bruises across his face and cooled his aching muscles.

"This won't last long." Said Raoul. "He'll have five minutes before it'll wear off."

"It should be enough."

Feeling the tranquilisers begin to set in, his wings and legs beginning to go numb, Amell worked as fast he could to get the order and timings right, as he ripped the back off the final patch and slapped the square down onto Wilny's arm.

A golden warmth spread throughout Wilny's veins and all the exhaustion from the fight and flight were washed away.

"Fuck me!" Wilny coughed. He flexed his toes and wings, the pain now distant and faded. Energy from the Nitro buzzed him into life as he stood up and stretched. He knew that for the next week he'd be bed ridden from the aftershock of injuries, but for now he was on a fresh high.

"Heh, later if you're still up for it." Amell joked, slipping down against the wall of the container he was leant against. Wilny's cheeks flushed and he laughed a little.

"Thank you Amell. Do you need me-" Wilny slurred as he extended his wings out. His pupils were dilated to the point where his pale baby blue eyes were now almost completely black.

"No. You go on ahead bro…" Amell breathed heavily, fumbling through the saddlebag for a spare adrenalin patch, "I've gotta…shake this off."

"I'll come back and get you once I've dealt with this." And with a snarl Wilny too off, feeling the warm energy flood his wings.

"Beth. Where's Kat and Storm? I need them to cover me, they've got-"

"Lana, yes, Palmer told me. I've got the security monitors." Beth snarled, "Storm and Kat are driving him up to the top. Get up there and flank them."

High on adrenaline, Wilny's wings blurred into action in a burst of energy. He shot up over the containers without a second thought or question of Beth's orders. The floodlights lit everything up, but the drugs made everything sharper, more contrasting. The Gull-Avio had landed on top of the bridge, lurking behind the radar with Malana snapping and squirming in his arms. He heard the Raptor-handler blowing on his whistle trying to command his beasts again, and from the echoing snarling and screes that followed he wasn't sure if it was the sound of the Raptors attacking him or Storm.

Wilny's muscles shuddered and his wings twitched, wanting to beat and fly again. Barely thinking about it, he was almost immediately up in the air, racing up towards the crane and looping over, focused and reactive. He dive bombed the Gull, the wind whistling through his primaries and his tailfeathers flaring out behind him.

The Gull ducked and launched himself off the bridge, arcing sharply with minimal effort with his long wings before catching the wind and shooting upwards. Wilny followed, wings thrumming, chasing after him as the Gull carried Lana, her own golden wings hanging limply below them, across the ship, goading Wilny to shoot at them.

Flying at speed whilst shooting at a soaring Avio with a hostage in his arms was something he hadn't done in a *very* long time. The adrenaline had narrowed his focus and vision down, but now his hands were shaking and his breathing ragged, trying to be steady whilst fluttering erratically was impossible. He could feel the strain he was putting on his heart again.

He crashed upon the containers, skidding and pulling himself into a controlled roll that could allow him to leap to his feet immediately after. Wobbly and light headed, he fired at the Gull, aiming for the long wings. All his shots missed, but it drew the Gull to turn back to face him. Slowly drawing his breath, he focused through the light-headedness and aimed slowly. He had to focus.

'Breathe in. Breathe out.' He could hear Fury's voice.

The target was within the glowing red crosshairs of the sights. He pushed himself to muse and slow the world around him once more.

'Breathe in. And shoot.'

The bullet ripped through the wrist of the Gulls left wing, forcing him to stumble and drop in altitude, landing heavily onto the containers below. Blood blossomed across the feathers, brightly crimson under the floodlights and exposing pink bone. The gull twisted and squirmed with Malana in his arms. She was still fighting and was nearly free.

The Preter hauled himself up onto the container beside the Gull, holding a bloody hunting knife, which Wilny could only hope was covered with Raptor blood and not Storm's. Wilny fired again, catching the Preter's shoulder, but the bullets ricocheted off the armour.

"Stop!" The Raptor-handler barked at him, voice echoing throughout the containers, snatching up Malana before she could escape. He held the little girl in front of him as a shield from Wilny's bullets. The Gull staggered to his feet, also drawing his gun and aiming at Wilny.

"Stand down or I gut her!" He snarled, grabbing a fist full of Lana's hair and pressing his bloody hunting knife to her chest. Feeling the sharp point to her chest, she became paralysed in wide eyed terror.

Wilny froze to the spot, finger on the trigger.

"Don't hurt her, don't you dare hurt her!"

"Gun down! And don't even think about using any talents or wings."

Wilny bared his teeth at the Preter. His wings trembled behind him., his chest was already straining again for his last use of his muser talents. The drugs were metabolising fast and letting the pain seep back in.

He couldn't risk it.

"Wilny, on your knees." Beth said softly. "We've got you covered."

In the background he could hear Raoul talking in a low voice to Amell, too quiet for him to hear. Across the deck he heard the sharp scrabbling of talons against metal and the fading whistling whoosh of wings that were lifting their owners up to the sky.

Though he wasn't sure what they were planning, he had backup.

Gently, he placed the gun down after turning the safety on and kicked it off the top of the container. Slowly he sunk to his knees, holding his hands in the air and keeping his wings flat out either side of him to show that he wasn't going to take off without warning.

He trusted them to do the right thing.

"I surrender. Just let her go."

"Not until all your friends come out of the shadows. I've seen all you Avios lurking, I know how many there are of you. Now where are the other three." Although he couldn't see the Preter's eyes beneath the gold visor, he could tell that he was scanning the area around him for any signs of movement. "Come out!"

Behind him and the Gull, two pairs of eyes caught the light with an eerie green shine, prowling closer to them within the semi-darkness of where the floodlights failed to shine. A small wry smile twinged at the corners of Wilny's lips.

"I'll call them out." He said, "I'll get them to come here for you."

The Preter sneered, threateningly lowering the knife from Lana's chest to her gut and the Gull tensed, focusing his aim.

"*Sekhmet. Zeus. Thunderbird.*"

The Gull gagged quietly and fell to his knees, blood dripping from his throat. The sound of his body hitting the floor made the Preter jump and he spun to face Kat with a holler of shock. She blocked the Preter's arm as he lashed at her with his knife and drove her own blade hard into the soft exposed area of his raised arm, releasing Malana in pain. The Preter shrieked, trying to grab the knife, but found the heavy armour restricted his reach, sending him spinning round like a dog chasing its tail.

Kat immediately scooped Malana up off the floor and sprinted to Wilny's side, placing the little girl into his arms.

"Go!" She ordered, drawing a knife for each hand and turning to defend them whilst they escaped.

She gave a sharp whistle and Amell dropped in upon him from the crane above, slamming him into the ground with all his weight and a loud echoing thunk. With the Preter down, Kat ran back at him and helped Amell to pry the clips free with her knives. The Preter shouted and squirmed, lashing out to try and throw the pair off only to be punched hard in the face by Amell.

The Preter lay stunned on the container, the golden visor cracked. With a few slices from Kat's knives along the seams and belts, Amell ripped his armour in half, the Fibres separating too far for them to reconnect and repair themselves, releasing the Preter from his shell.

Kicking frantically at them, the Preter scrambled to his feet, slashing wildly with the bloody hunting knife, the other arm limp beside him. A slice caught Amell's arm and Kat lunged forward to engage in a knife fight with him. Both were equally as quick and skilled as the other, but with Amell behind her, Kat drove the Raptor-handler back and forced him to jump across the gap between the containers. He chanced a look back to see where they were, right as Kat ducked and allowed Amell to leap over her, slamming his fist hard into the Preters face with a crunch as teeth were broken and his nose splurged blood everywhere.

Then, with a high-pitched whistle that echoed across the ship, Amell dove out the way, exposing the Raptor-handler to Storm's stooping attack. She kicked him hard in the chest at high speed, his ribs cracked with a meaty crunch, and he flew backwards several meters across the containers, rolling heels over head as he clipped the edge and fell to the deck. With no ExoArmour to protect him, his spine shattered, and he was left staring up at the sky, the pain of the fall throbbing through his body.

Storm leapt down upon him, landing hard on his chest. Wings spread before him, she snarled viciously, baring her mouth full of fangs. The yellow eyes of the Raptors gleamed in the dark as they stalked closer. Hungry, angry, low hisses between the three.

Their wounds still bled from where their former master had slashed and stabbed at them and their crests of feathers trembled.

"No! No, please!" The Preter begged, wheezing between breaths of his crushed chest. Storm blinked slowly, taking his whistle from his neck and tossing it into the sea.

"I won't kill you." She said calmly, and slowly she rose to her feet and leapt off him. Looking down at him with her wings splayed either side of her with the Raptors stalked around to stand by her side, cocking their heads, watching them both with interest.

"But they will." And she whistled a single extended note that was drowned out by the shrieks of the Raptors as they charged forward to attack.

33

The Hercules skittered and span across the deck as Amell tried to bash open the cockpit with one of its broken arms, so that they could round up one of the last few soldiers that remained. Those who had witnessed what had happened to the Raptor-handler had quickly surrendered and entered the container, leaving only a few of the crew and the still trapped AutoMech pilot on deck.

"Need a hand, Zeus?" Storm asked, staggering into a landing beside him. Her hand and leg throbbed with pain, but she was glad that the SmartFabrics had stopped her from bleeding out as they formed a tight sticky gauze when the fibres knitted themselves back together.

Amell laughed and examined the door of the Hercules, watching as the pilot inside continued to yell and throw multiple rude gestures at him between instructions on how to open the damaged door.

"You're still doing the callsigns?"

"We're still working."

"If you can unlock the door then that will help, but are you going to be okay, *Thunderbird?*" He asked, looking at the injury, broken AutoMech arm still in hand.

"Well, it's not killed me yet, so I guess I'm good." Storm laughed, clutching at her thigh as she limped towards the mangled mess of the Hercules hanging precariously off the edge of the ship. "Let's get this sardine out of his can."

The pilot kicked hard against the door, trying to open it frantically before the AutoMech plummeted into the sea, despite shaking it each time he did so. With a small jump onto the machine, Storm put her hand over the lock and gave it a small electrical burst to release it and help Amell yank open the jammed door.

"D-don't kill me! I surrender!" The pilot shrieked, throwing his hands up.

The machine groaned as it tipped slowly towards the black water. Grabbing the pilot by his arms, Storm powered backwards with a wingbeat dragging the man back onto the ship as the Hercules tumbled into the sea below with a gigantic splash.

Throwing him down, she let Amell restrain him and taking him to the container. Weary, Storm sat down upon the ledge with her wings draped over the railings and attempted to pull the bullet from her thigh.

"Well, that could have gone- *ow*- worse." She mumbled to herself, clawing at the SmartFabrics to loosen the fibres that kept on reknitting themselves together.

"We're alive, aren't we?" Kat laughed, strutting across the rails towards her, greeting Storm with a smile. Half of her knives were missing from her belts, either buried into the fallen Raptors and its handler to confirm their deaths.

A pang of regret struck Storm. She really admired the Raptors and wished she didn't have to attack them. The remaining Raptors they had locked up once again into their container and reattached their harnesses so they wouldn't escape. She half-wished that she didn't have to send them back to Core, but then there wasn't anywhere that they could keep them.

"You know you shouldn't remove bullets by yourself." Kat said pointedly, folding her arms across her chest. "Raoul will get mad."

"I know, but if I go back to the headquarters with it still in my leg Rex will add another five to it."

"How are you still smiling?"

"Still running on adrenaline. Give it five minutes and I'll be out cold on the ground just you wait." She laughed, wincing as she started to feel the bruises from her fight with the Raptors. Abandoning her attempts at self-surgery, she allowed the fibres to pull together again and removed the SmartFabric gloves to inspect the damage to her hand. "Where's Rai? Is he going to be okay?"

"He's fine. He's had a few boosters and some morphine."

"And what about Horus?" Storm squinted at her, taking Kat's arm and allowing her to help her up onto her feet.

Kat gave a little nod and led Storm around to the container where they had detained the Elites. On the floor beside it lay Wilny with Malana at his side. As Storm drew closer, she could see that Kat had fetched a defibrillator and stuck the pads to his chest, following the instructions the machine provided to check his heart.

Upon hearing their footsteps, Malana looked up and gave Wilny a little shake so that he opened his eyes.

"Did we get them all?" Wilny wheezed, looking up at them blearily. After all that had happened to him, he was very pale and weak, shivering as though he were cold, so Malana had covered his shoulders with her wings. Several more booster patches had been applied to his arms and chest by Malana in an attempt to heal him faster, though she didn't realise that it was exhausting for him to be using so many at once.

"Almost." Storm smiled down at him as the defibrillator gave him the all clear and shut down without shocking him. "Zeus is looking for whoever is left."

Groaning, Wilny tried to sit up, pulling off the sticky pads.

"I should probably go and help him."

"You've done enough for today."

"But I want to help."

"You keep your arse on the floor. That's an order."

He gave a scoff, but did as she asked, laying back on the floor.

"Looks like someone is going to be my dress up doll for the next month." Kat purred, crouching beside him and poking his cheek.

"I had a heart attack, *Sekhmet*." He said sternly, narrowing his eyes at her though unable to keep himself from smirking at the playful jab.

"The excuses of a looser."

"Hey Storm, there's still AutoMechs on the ship, right? I think Kat should have a solo round against me in one."

"Sunshine, sit on him and make sure he doesn't get up." Kat ordered the little girl, leaping to her feet as Storm laughed. Malana smiled and threw her arms around Wilny, holding him down in a hug and covering his face with her wings.

"I am very, *very*, angry with you, Sunbeam." He growled softly, stroking her wings. Malana tensed and hid her face against his chest. "You could have been killed rushing in like that, what on earth were you thinking?"

"I wanted to help too."

"And you did, but next time, please don't run in without back up. I don't want to see you get hurt."

She looked up at him apologetically, golden eyes wide and threatening to burst with tears. "Were you scared?"

"Very. I was so scared that he might…" He stifled a sob and hugged her tight, curling his wings up and around her in an iridescent shield of peacock blue. "Promise me that you won't ever do that again."

"I promise."

He smiled and let her go, pulling away so that he could reveal to her the drawing she had given to him, still tucked under the Kevlar. Despite being a little moist from his sweating, it was untorn and undamaged. She gave a little gasp of happiness and took it from him.

"You have it!"

"I promised you that I wouldn't get it hurt." He reminded her, taking the picture and tucking it safely away again. "Next time, you stay back and keep yourself safe, okay?"

With an affirmative nod, Malana scrubbed her face hard, trying to keep the tears from bubbling over, but resigning to crying on Wilny with quiet heaving sobs. Looking up at Storm, Wilny gave her a silent smile, and a quiet whisper within the back of her mind of *'thank you'* as he comforted the little girl.

There was a heavy beating of wings and in dropped Amell, carrying a man ungraciously beneath each arm.

"Woo! I think we got everybody now." Amell grinned as he hauled the two once again unconscious ship pilots into the open container to join the rest of the soldiers. The various battles had shredded Kat's attempted SmartFabric armour for him and left thin slices across his chest and arms, but he ignored them as much as the other Rogues ignored their wounds. The tranquiliser had been metabolised quickly, but Amell was still very languid and leaning against the container for support despite the several patches of EPI+ that were still attached to his arms.

"Nice work." Storm congratulated them all, ruffling Lana's hair as she helped Wilny to his feet. "We didn't do too badly for a bunch of Ferals."

"Sienna should be there on us in thirty minutes. B-uh *Strix* is getting the inventory up for the containers. And *Hunter* says to do your thing on our captives. See how many abandon ship to us." Amell assured them all, holding his hand to his ear to receive the instructions, mouthing to her that Hunter meant Raoul. She nodded.

"Well then. Let's give these kids their warning."

Tightening the sash around her waist, Storm dusted herself down and realigned her feathers before opening up the container and advancing on the group of soldiers, Kat and Amell at her back for support.

Bruised and battered, the Rogues had been brutal with them, leaving none without injury and with only four of them dead, although two of the deaths were caused by the Raptors rather than the Rogues. Both teams of Quartzes trembled as the Rogues entered the enclosure. The majority of them were Preternaturals with only seven of them being Canids or Pards. The four remaining Avios were all Transhumans as far as Storm could see from their lack of tailfeathers. a little jab of sadness struck at her as she remembered when they first met Kathy and how she had refused to go to the Rioteers. She knew she had to be careful in how she would persuade them.

A yellow-eyed Preter in grey and green Emerald Elite uniform nudged the others around him as Storm drew closer, whilst the Osprey-based Avio girl tensed and drew her bound wings in tighter around her, watching her with unblinking terror.

"They're Rioteers! Say nothing to them." The Preternatural hissed. "They can offer you nothing remember."

With a cheery honeyed laugh, Storm knelt before the captives.

"Oh, you don't need to say anything, *sweetheart*, only to listen. It'll be better for you if you just cooperate with us." She said softly, sweetly to them though the menace in it remained. Raoul remembered the tone well and smiled to himself as he heard Storm throw on her Mullardoch tone. The Quartzes and Emeralds all quivered as she flashed her fangs at them.

"You." She nudged another Emerald elite with her wing, making him flinch as she turned her gaze upon him. "Your ID code please. Or your name. I like hearing people's names."

The yellow-eyed Preter tried to twist and hiss at his comrade to be silent, attempting to muse but being blocked by Storm. She dug her talons sharply into his cheeks, musing to him in warning and watching as his skin pulsed into a terrified wave of grey and blue from his camouflage skin ability.

"T:ORION-ACE-302." The other Preternatural said hesitantly. "They- m-my team, Emerald-Twelve, calls me Valiant."

Storm nodded slowly. A T generation ORION Preternatural with the ACE suffix meant that he was a transhuman. ORION Preternaturals themselves had been discontinued in production for quite a number of years. It didn't sit comfortably however how young this transhuman looked, approximately eighteen to her. So young. It made her think of Kathy.

How young were they taking these kids when ARCDA made them transhuman?

"Well Valiant, we are not Rioteers, so you're safe. However, if you have any sense then you'd listen carefully to what I'm going to say and try to understand that the moment we leave this ship, the Arcadia Corporation, Core, will kill you."

"Bullshit!" The yellow-eyed Preter snapped, twisting his head out of Storm's grip. "Don't listen to her, she's lying to you."

Storm rose to her feet and let her wings flick out, catching several of the Synths across the top of their heads with her feathers.

"Quite the cynic aren't you." She said sharply. "What's your ID code and callsign?"

"He's Diogenes." Valiant said quickly. "U:SIRIUS-676."

"I have *literally* been out of ARCDA longer than you've been alive, Diogenes. Eleven years in fact, and in that time I've seen exactly what they do to you people." She stated looking back over her shoulder and nodding for Wilny to join her. "I've played this game for far too long. I don't expect you to want to leave, but I am giving you the *choice* to make your own decision on if you think you should or not."

Wilny dropped his gaze a little with a reminiscing frown before stepping forward, gesturing for Malana to remain outside. As he joined Storm, his posture changed. Ignoring his fatigue and still aching chest, he drew his shoulders back and saluted with sharp professionalism.

"None of you will know me, but you will know of me." He said curtly. "I am Hummingbird-E-One-One, also known as *Bluebird*, commander of the previous Ruby-One team, AA03. And as far as ARCDA is aware, I'm dead. Killed by a *rogue* Avio." He gave a little nod to Storm who smirked.

All eyes widened and there were several gasps at the realisation of who he was, along with the immediate understanding of the lowliness of their rank. The shocked gasps gave way to a ripple of murmurs between them, which Storm could only assume was a discussion of what had happened to the Ruby-One team. It was more common knowledge than she had first thought. Even the cynical Diogenes straightened up in front of Wilny.

"Emerald-Twelve. This is not a practice test; this is a real-life field mission that has been failed by all of you." He continued addressing the Elites, beginning to pace slowly before them. All eyes were fixed upon him in fear and respect.

"She's not lying. We're giving you a choice that Core wont since Core doesn't allow failures to live. Emerald-Thirteen will move up to your place as Emerald-Twelve and no one will ask where you've gone. If you're lucky you'll end up dead...if not..." He shook his head, and his voice became choked. "They'll make you fight your own team to the death to take out the weak ones and the lone survivor will go to whoever wants you. If they want you, that is. They did this to Sapphire-Four and Ruby-Nine, and they will do the same to you."

There was a pregnant silence amongst them as the teams looked between one another, some reaching with their bound hands to hold each other. The teams were more of a family than they would have admitted to their superiors, to the point that even the Diogenes looked to his teammate Valliant, distressed at the idea of killing him or letting him suffer because they were out matched by these Feral strangers.

"I'm not ordering you to join us. I wouldn't want to make you do anything you didn't want to, however," Wilny's voice was soft and wavering, "what comes next well- the nightmares don't stop as fast as they make you believe. Trust me, if you love and respect your team then there is no going back to Core after this."

"And if we joined you? What then?" A Tiger-Pard in a yellow-accented Quartz uniform, asked tentatively, the only one to speak up. The rest of her team looked to her and nodded.

"We'd make sure you had a chance to get away." Storm answered, patting Wilny on the shoulder and allowing him to stand down and return into the fresh air with Malana.

"We'd get you a lifeboat, some rations and supplies so that you can fix yourselves up and vanish...If you wanted to that is. We wouldn't chase you down, wouldn't tell the Rioteers where you went. Yes, ARCDA might chase you but we'd help you if you let us. But ultimately, it's your decisions."

They looked shocked. The younger, more inexperienced Quartzes all muttered to themselves but the Emerald Elites however, were more sceptical, all who could muse trying their best to see if Storm was lying or not. With a soft smile, she lowered her bioelectric guard to let them in on the honesty of her sentiments, then with a delicate flourish of her wings, she turned to leave them.

"I'll let you discuss it amongst yourselves." And with a smile she left them to be guarded for the moment by Kat.

His speech to the Elites had left Wilny in tears. He sat on the floor in the shadows with Amell and Malana, letting her preen and pat his wing in comfort as Amell put a wing around his shoulders and held his hands, speaking gently to him. It would be a wound that would never heal, but it could at least be tamed by their joint efforts and affections.

"He'll be fine in a few minutes." Storm assured Rai, feeling his presence at her side despite his silent arrival. When she turned to look at him she sighed deeply, looking him up and down with his fresh bandages.

"Really Rai?"

The Hawk-Avio laughed, still nursing the bullet wound.

"I'm a lover not a fighter. You should know that Stormy. They took me by surprise." He joked, trying to laugh before he sat down heavily on the floor with a pained groan. "I think the bullet is still in here somewhere."

"Keep sat down Rai. My guys have got this."

"*Me* sit down? You're the one limping here. Did you get shot again?"

"Ricochet." Storm shrugged, giving her thigh a slap. "Not so dramatic as last time, but hey, on the bright side I didn't break my arm again."

"You're still pretty injured."

"Injured, but still pretty." Storm joked with a wink at Kat. Kat burst into laughter and reached over to playfully pull on the tiny cheek feathers across Storm's face until she swatted her hands away.

"So, do you have the inventory?" Asked Storm, flattening down her cheek feathers and running her fingers through her feathered ear tufts. "I may need something to sort my hand out with."

"Yeah." Nodded Rai. "Beth sent it on through. I took the liberty of getting a sample for us while we wait. Lucky for you, there's a whole section of containers that are just full of medical supplies."

He showed her the list of medicinal supplies, pain killers, anti-inflammatories, vaccines, boosters, bandages, disinfectant, gloves, and dormant synthetic stem cells all kept within cooled crates. One of which he found had dragged out for them to use.

Letting Rai and Beth discuss the logistics of moving it all through the headset, Kat and Storm rummaged through it to find something to bandage Storm's hand with. Instead, they found something less expected.

"There's...folded up bags of skin here." Kat declared holding it up for Rai to see.

"Nice." He said nonchalantly, beginning to mark the containers around them with various letters so that the others would know what they were taking. "Put some on your cuts. Just clean up and disinfect your skin first."

"I don't much fancy having a skin suit Rai."

"It's like gauze made of epidermal mimic cells. Synthetic of course." He explained, taking a bottle of disinfectant to clean his hands before taking a bag and opening it to show them. It was thinner than paper, with an odd translucent quality to it.

"It creates an unbroken layer to protect your skin and it'll stop scarification and blood loss, when your skin is fully repaired beneath it just flakes away like natural. Try it on your hand there Storm. It won't fix the bones, but at least you can stop bleeding and reduce any scars."

"What if I like the scars?" Said Storm sweetly.

"You're already a bloody mess as it is Storm." Kat sighed, taking hold of the Rogue's hand, pulling back the damaged SmartFabric uniform and gloves, and disinfecting it. "Okay, okay, Kat. I'll remain pretty for you."

Storm winced at the stinging sensation, tears prickling her eyes, but allowed Kat to carry on. She draped the strips of dermal skins across Storm's arm, wrapping it up carefully pressing it upon the cuts and bites she had received from the Raptors. A tingling sensation raced the length of Storm's arm as the cells activated, reacting to the heat of her arm, bonding together and smoothing out the skin.

"Don't do too many layers," warned Rai, "you don't want to end up with air bubbles being trapped in there or having too thick of a skin layer, it'll turn into a callous."

Impressed by its works Storm wrapped the skins around her finger tips, after spraying them down with tears stinging her eyes in pain, leaving her left hand smooth, even though the fingers were still broken. Kats ears flicked back as she inspected Storm's hand and arms with suspicion.

"Okay, I'm sold on this." Storm chuckled, painfully trying to wiggle her fingers. She stopped as an idea came to her. "Hey Rai. Does it work on old scars too? And feathers?"

Rai's jaw clenched.

"You can...try." He said carefully, the black feathers prickling, eyes flicking to Storm's back and tail.

"You should test it on Amell and Wilny." Suggested Kat, sensing Rai's uncomfortableness and doing her best to quickly draw them away from it before it became awkward. "They've more scars than you."

Storm nodded, giving Kat's hand a little squeeze of thanks before taking what was left of her bag of dermal skins, as well as a couple of spares and returning back to the other Rogues.

Wilny had calmed down and was now sat beside the open container of Elites with Amell, talking with them and trying to explain to them of the gloriousness of a hot bath and unrestricted access on the internet, whilst Malana span in circles trying to reach over her shoulder to preen her feathers.

"How's the talks going? Have they decided what they want to do?" She asked Wilny, showing off the medical packs and handing them out to the Elites in the container. A few of the more relaxed Synths thanked her although the Emerald Elites were still highly cautious of her intentions.

"They're still discussing it." He smiled looking in as Amell flexed and began telling the Elites the story of how Malana split a car in two and how he chased Kathy across France and back again. Malana demonstrated, lifting up Amell and then slicing off one of the doors to the container, showing off.

'You know. Sometimes I worry about Malana.' Storm mused loudly to Wilny, letting a subtle sentiment of nervousness and suspicion colour her thoughts. *'Do you think they knew what they were doing when they made her?'*

'Did you ever look into her project?'

'Not yet.'

'I can't imagine why-' Wilny jumped suddenly, cutting her off and nearly hitting her in the face with his wing, hand to his ear as he received an alert from Beth.

"*Thunderbird,*" He yelled at her, eyes wide in panic, "one of them has just contacted Core!"

"So, we didn't get everybody?" She looked back to the Elites and did a headcount. It was none of the ones within the container. It must have been another handler. "Who's he talking to? A Commander?"

"Yes- wait no, the call's transferred."

"Tell Strix to patch me in through the ship's radio."

Leaping up to her feet she beat her wings and leapt into the air in a single bound, charging towards the bridge. "Sekhmet! Sunshine!" She shouted back to her Rogue girls, "Find him!"

Kat shot out of the stack of containers with a blur of blue, with Malana scrambling to take off after her to help search.

Skidding into the bridge she quickly searched the place for any hiding person. Empty. Ignoring the flashing white lights on the security display and bloodstain from where Rai had been shot and fallen, Storm grabbed hold of the headset, slipped it on over her feathered ears and held down the call button on its side.

"*Strix*, I'm here. Patch me in. I want to know who they've contacted."

"On it." The Owl's voice hissed through, "He won't hear me, but he'll hear you if you speak."

There were several short clicks as she changed the channels before she heard the voice of the captain.

"- swear it on my life!" He whimpered in a hushed whisper. "The others- they just turned like that when the girl spoke to them! They have their own ex-Elite with them too, a Ruby-One member. He told them that you'll make them kill each other for failing. They're organised and-"

"I don't care about your life. I care about my cargo!" A cold voice filled with venom in its rich Eton English spat at the Synth. The feathers down her spine and mantle rose at his tone. Intelligent and cruel. It sounded familiar, or at least reminded her of Rex.

"Sir please!"

"Finest captain in the north-east my eye; you beg like a child. If these terrorists don't feed you to the Raptors, then *I will do so myself!*"

"But sir! I'm out numbered here! I need back up!"

"I do not care about your reservations! You are meant to be an Onyx! We hired you for this very reason! You *will* regain control of the ship or else-"

"Well, I'm glad to hear you won't have a problem with us killing your man here." Storm cut through with a purr, rolling her R's into a growl. There was sudden silence from both ends, followed by a shriek and a shout as the Synth was pounced upon by Kat and Malana before the sound cut out.

Storm smirked. She could hear a creak of what she presumed to be the man on the other end, sinking back into a chair along with a soft sigh of humiliation, as well as the sound of Beth letting her head drop heavily onto her desk in aggravation.

"Well...this is rather embarrassing."

"Just a tad." She teased, shaking her feathers off. "Who only sends one team of Emerald Elites and two Quartzes to protect a cargo ship? I am so disappointed. I expected far better from Core in all honesty. Now, which higher up am I speaking with? Are you high-up important at all?"

There was a pause before the man sighed bitterly, clearly humiliated by the scenario.

"I am of the *highest* importance, young lady."

"The highest?" It was cryptic, but then it clicked as she paired the familiar cruel voice to its owner. "Wait. *Gaius Daniels?* Seriously? The head of Core, *wow*, I expected someone lower than you if I'm honest."

"Instead, you got me."

She couldn't believe it. An uncontrolled laugh escaped her whilst Beth and Raoul swore a panicked blue streak between them both that echoed through to the rest of the Rogues.

"This must have been some important cargo for you to chew that guy out."

"Indeed, it was. I'll have you know that my shipment is satellite tracked, I know exactly where you are, girl. I will have you *exterminated.*"

"Check again and you'll find it isn't where you think it is."

"I-"

"See. This is the problem with relying too much on technology. It can get hacked."

"You repugnant-"

"Save your breath. You can make all the threats you want about killing us, *boy*, but I can match them and raise them with actions. You don't scare me." She warned cheerfully, leaning against the control panels and looking out across the water. The sky was beginning to be tinged with teal green as the sun began to rise and set fire to the horizon, whilst to their left flashing red and green lights of several boats were drawing closer. Sienna and the others would be by them soon and they could unload what they needed from the containers.

"You Rioteer bastard terrorists-"

"We're not with the Rioteers, Daniels, so don't you dare lump me in with those idiots. They would have sunk the entire damn ship." She snapped. "Now if I remember rightly, it'd take you five hours to get here from your closest major control point, two and a half if you pushed it. We'd be long gone by then with what we need."

"And what *do* you need?"

"Stuff which I'm sure you won't miss. Don't worry you can have most of it. We're only after the bare necessities. Medical supplies, new equipment."

"He's trying to plug into the security cameras." Beth whispered through the left ear of the headset. With a curt laugh Storm swung her arms out and looked up to face the camera poised above the console.

"Let him see me." She snapped, sweeping out her wings. "Get a good look arsehole, because you won't know me from basic scientific ethics."

"Storm hang up and stop pissing him off!"

"No don't." Raoul cut through. "We can trace Daniels down to a general area and forward it to Varren and Hábrók through the line he's trying to get to the ship with."

"Wait. Shit. You're right Raoul. Storm keep talking to him for another minute."

"Is that fearlessness or is it arrogance?" It was a subtle switch from humiliation to analytical in Daniel's tone, trying to find something to keep her talking.

A red light flashed on the camera, and the image of a bloody war paint covered Storm came into view upon his screen. Standing tall she flared her wings out either side of her and deliberately rose her middle finger into the air.

"Take a gander old man."

"Look at you. Oh, *look at you*." He marvelled, ignoring her rude gesture. "What a beast you are. *Though she be, but little, she is fierce.* I'm guessing you were Mullardoch made from the look of you, and from the voice, though I can't see any tailfeathers."

"Damn right I am, and that alone should tell you as much as you need to know about what manner of monster I am."

"Monster? You're a masterwork and incredibly…valuable."

"Compliment me all you like Daniels, I much prefer girls."

Daniels laughed in disbelief. The camera zoomed and moved slowly, and she could hear the Core leader mumbling to himself.

"What is your name?"

"*Thunderbird.*" Storm smirked, tucking her wings back in. Daniels scoffed.

"And who are you working for, *Thunderbird*?" She could almost hear him pressing his nose against the screen as he tried to analyse her, he was curious. "Samodiva? Hasekura? That wretched piece of shit, Ruaidrí Foley?"

"Who?"

"I believe he still calls himself Rex Brisbane. Ridiculous name."

"Oh, *that fucker.*" She spat reactively, letting her feathers flare up and arch in anger. The Core leader burst into a fit of laughter at her words, having not expected such an outburst. "You've got a cargo of ExoArmours and Elites, plus a load of meds and you really think I'm going to let the Rioteers at this shit? *Fuck no.*"

"You sound so much like Swann." Daniels chuckled to himself.

Storm's gut hollowed with a sickening feeling of panic as for a moment she thought that he had figured out who she was, before realising that he wasn't referring to her.

Who was Swann?

"I doubt you're working alone, even if you're not with the Rioteers." He said, carrying on, not having noticed the sudden tension in her pose.

"You think I couldn't take an entire ship on my own? I am offended! And if we're being honest I'd sell Rex to you for a nice slab of Kobe beef and a holiday in Hawaii."

"That can be arranged."

"Well then, if I meet Rex again then you, good sir, will be the first to know. The world will be better off without him." She smirked. "If you want your ship back then come collect it at Goodwin Sands."

"And what is to stop me from hunting you down afterwards?"

"My sparkling personality of course."

Beth and Raoul held their breath as silence flooded the line between them.

"You have a five-hour head start, *Thunderbird.*" Then with a small chuckle, Daniels hung up. She didn't know what the man was like beyond his reputation, but she was sure that he was somewhat impressed by the trouble they had caused him.

"The ship is ours." Raoul declared, sighing with relief.

The little red light on the camera blinked off and Beth growled, laying her head down upon the desk in exhaustion, Raoul almost crying beside her.

"Storm. Just so you know. I hate you so very, *very,* much."

Storm laughed. "You love me, and you know it." And with a mock kiss she set down the headset and stretched her limbs out.

A rush of wings startled her as she left the Bridge, nearly slamming her fist into Rai's face in surprise.

"Sienna and the others are here!" Rai declared, balancing with his wings on the edge of the railing, pointing down to the boats pulling up alongside the ship. Eleven small fishing boats and three larger tug boats just as planned, all temporarily acquired for the night.

Storm smiled, shooing Rai off to glide down and help, whilst she took a moment to herself to admire them all working together. The other groups greeting everyone with enthusiasm. Amell let down a ladder to the boats, although several of their Avios and Chiros had already flown up onto deck to help take instructions and orders from Rai as to where everything was.

Leaping out over the railing, she lapped the boat in a steady soar upon the sea breeze, watching for a moment as the groups emptied the containers and passed the crates in an efficient quick moving swarm across the deck and down into the boats, loading them up one at a time. Some of the Elites had been allowed out of the container watching with astonishment at the scene before them of sixty or so Synths all working together. Some even began to help move and lift the cargo with the new arrivals.

At the prow of the ship, she found her Rogues taking their well-earned break together, with Amell just sprawled across the deck with his wingspan draped across the entire beam of the ship as he lay flat on his face to sleep. Kat was preening her wings and cleaning up her warpaint. Wilny and Lana were laughing together.

Her family.

She was so proud of them all.

"Hey Lana! Look at me!" She heard Wilny hoot, picking up a leg of the broken Poacher drone and wielding it round like a sword. "I'm a pirate captain! *Avast!* Hand over ye treasure!"

The little girl snatched up a leg of her own.

"Arrr! Never!"

Laughing, Storm descended upon them both as they began to hit each other's *swords*.

"You're not planning on mutinying against me, are you?" She asked playfully, taking a bottle of water from Kat to drink and wash the warpaint from her face with.

"Nah boss, we'd never turn against you." He smiled, then gave a playful scream of pain as Malana poked him in the chest and dramatically collapsed to the floor.

"Betrayal! Treachery!" He cried with his fist raised to the sky, then with a heavy thunk he lay motionless on the deck as Malana poked at him and laughed victoriously.

'Thank you Storm.' Wilny mused to the Rogue as he lay still on the ground, trying to limply resist Malana pulling on his arms to remain *'dead'* until she got closer where he captured her and tickled her until she screamed laughing.

'For?'

'For keeping me alive and letting me stay.'

'I wouldn't thank me yet. I've already killed you twice and kicked you out once.'

'And yet I'm still here.'

She buffed him with a wing and smiled.

The sound of seagulls screaming from the cliffs drifted across the water over the sound of Malana and Wilny's laughter. Storm dried her face and tilted her head towards the sky to see their white forms drifting along the coast. Her wings tensed in anticipation.

"Go on." Wilny sighed, rolling his eyes. "Go fly."

"Are you gonna be fine captaining the ship for a while?"

"I can manage boss." He saluted and stuck his tongue out at her.

Grinning she strode past, giving him a gentle and loving punch to the shoulder and gently brushing her fingertips across Kat's blue wings as she sat cleaning her knives.

Standing proud on the prow of the ship, Storm looked up to the purple tinged clouds as the last of the night was being drawn away by the pale turquoise light of dawn.

"Lana, do you want to come with me?" She asked the little girl. Malana didn't need asking twice as she scrambled to the railings in excitement, priming her golden-edged wings and drumming her feet upon the deck in glee.

With a thumbs up to the rest of her Rogues, Storm threw herself out across the sea with a rush of wings, Malana following after her.

Surfing across the teal-green crests of waves in the light of the dawning sun with no sound other than the steady beating of their wings and the smell of sea salt, a wave of calm washed over her. Malana beat her wings harder to power ahead of Storm, drawing them in and snapping them open again to arc sharply up when she was just inches above the waves. Heart in her throat, Storm watched proudly. Malana was going to be a fantastic flyer; she could already tell.

Giggling with glee Malana levelled out from her diving and arcing and followed Storm up on a sharp wind shear that propelled them up high into the sky.

"Higher?" Storm asked her, making sure that Malana could keep pace.

"Higher!"

A golden glow of growing euphoria spread throughout her veins, and they powered on higher, wings straining, hearts pounding as they burst up over the clouds, flying towards the sun together, its light edging their feathers in silver and in gold.

"Where are we going?" Malana asked with a smile, dipping her hand into the clouds beneath her. Storm grinned wildly.

"Wherever the wind takes us, Sunshine. Are you ready?"

"Yes!"

"Then let's go!"

34

Villa del Guayota, Mount Teide, Tenerife, Canary Islands.

Out of the bunker and out of the country, Eve Mira had taken Samodiva up on the offer of dinner. She was incredibly pleased by the outcome of the Rogues attack on the ship that left her dying to call Gaius up and say, "I told you so".

Usually, she would have considered herself above such pettiness, but she would always make an exception for him.

As their car wound its way up to the villa perched on the sunniest side of the volcano, Sabre and Fell were gliding leisurely on a thermal overhead, admiring the glittering blue ocean around them and challenging each other to spot lizards from their aerial view whilst they monitored the progress of Eve's car. They were the only guards that Eve would allow to travel with her and her son, and the only pair she knew that Samodiva wouldn't have shot on sight.

The bright hot sun scorched their black feathers and hair, but it was ignored by the experience of flying over a volcano. Old black and grey pyroclastic remains stained the red sandstone in trails down the mountain, the rocky terrain broken by dark green pine trees and scrubland bushes. Soaring up on the ridge lift, they spiralled around the ashy crater, watching the fumaroles rising like steam from within.

With excited glances shared between each other, they grabbed each other's hands as they knew the game they were about to play. Tucking their long sweeping wings back, they spiralled down towards the crater, playing *Chicken* with each other. Fell released first, letting his long wings catch the wind like a parachute. Sabre, on the other hand, kept diving and with a flare of his long swallowtail, pulled up at the last second, lightly grazing the rocky surface with his foot and rising back into the blue skies above.

"Well…She lives on the side of an *active* volcano." Sabre coughed hard at the sulphur he had inhaled. "As if I wasn't scared shitless of her enough already."

Fell, rolling his eyes and lunged at him with a playful kick. He was always much more relaxed when flying.

"You should have held your breath."

"And miss out on the opportunity to tell Heim that volcanoes smell like farts?"

"You're such a child." Fell banked sharply, the long swallow-tailed feathers fanning out either side and letting him twist into a descent as Eve's car drew up to the front of the villa.

They landed before Eve and Heim exited. Both Kites shook their aching wings and clumsily folded their thirty feet of length back. With wings so long it allowed them to soar endlessly and tirelessly for hours as they had done to get to Tenerife, their only flaw being that when they weren't in the air they had to carry them carefully around and keep the tips off the floor to prevent them from being damaged.

"Thirty-six hours to get here, Prof." Sabre announced, helping Heim balance as he stretched out after the long journey. "With two four hour breaks in between."

Eve appeared genuinely impressed and handed each twin a bag of chorizos and churros for them to eat as treats as well as to state their calorie loss after their long-haul flight. Wind tunnel tests and speed-distance-time theories were very different to when they were using their skills out in the real world, and over three-thousand kilometres on paper was far different to flying it.

"Make sure you downplay it to Amy," She insisted, tucking back her black curls of hair. "Otherwise she'll try and steal you again."

"Of course. Being kidnapped by Samodiva is the last thing I want." Fell smiled, sweeping a wing out to gesture for them to move forward up to meet Samodiva, all of them sharing a level of reluctance to do so.

'And I thought you liked Amy.' Sabre prodded to his twin, trying to keep the tips of his long wings off the floor as they walked close behind Eve and Heim, and keep from being dragged across the rocks when the wind caught them.

'I'm polite. It doesn't mean I'm friendly or that I like people.' Fell shrugged his wings, face impassive once more.

'Much to everyone's sadness. Do you know how many people cry over you being 'mean' to them?'

'Well, they and Samodiva, can all continue to cry.'

'Cruel bastard.'

The villa exterior was a stark and shining white against the volcanic grey-red backdrop, in-keeping with the traditional island aesthetics, with a tall stone wall that surrounded it. The tops of yellow and purple flowering trees peeked out from above it and against the quiet they could hear birdsong from within.

"Why a volcano?" Heim asked sourly, dragging his feet like a child. The claustrophobia of a car had done nothing for his mood, as had having to leave all of his robotics behind at Beaufort. He didn't like joining his mother on trips, especially when he had his own projects to work on.

"She chose to live here because it's four of five things she likes." Eve remarked, checking her phone for the time as they strode up the gleaming white steps. "Gold, islands, myths and or legends, fire, and living dangerously."

"Myths and legends?"

"Or other stories and poetry. She chose this as her home because of a legend that a monster or devil locked away the sun here."

"And she believes that?"

"She doesn't need to believe it to enjoy the references. Check anything she's worked on or with and there's a link to at least one myth or legend or story. She even changed her last name to some sort of fire fairy." She rolled her eyes. "She and Gaius would always compete with testing each other on their literary references."

The boys snickered amongst each other as Samodiva's doorman bounced down the stairs to greet them with a broad smile. A golden-haired Ram Synth – A Capra, a subtype of other Artadactylian Synths - with a curling set of horns that had a beautifully intricate set of carvings inlaid with gold.

'Golden Fleece?' Heim wondered, trying to spot Samodiva's references as well as force himself to remember what little mythology he could. He set himself the challenge that he would at least try to get all the references there were by the end of the trip.

Fell and Sabre stepped forward, bobbing their heads in greeting. They spoke quickly in Spanish to the Ram, too fast for Heim and Eve who were unfamiliar with the language to pick out anything more than basic words such as dinner and swimming pool. With a gracious nod and a *"Sí,"* of agreement they followed the doorman in through the villa.

Inside it was minimalistic in furniture, but grandiose in décor, in keeping with Samodiva's love of grandeur and flair. White, gold, and black were the key colours, with living plants and flowing water traveling throughout the ground floor. Day lilies and unusual black and white blossoming flowers with golden leaves grew on cultivated islands amongst the water features in every room, flowing down the hallways with golden koi swimming beneath them under the transparent walkways. Gold mosaic murals depicting phoenixes flying through flames decorated the walls, as well as the work of Gustav Klimt hung in elegant dark frames. Glass balconies passed above the larger living areas with more abstract-contemporary art on podiums throughout the hallways, the scent of ambergris and mandarin everywhere. It was more of an art gallery than a home, but the boys were sure that in the rooms below was her personal laboratory with an unknown amount of horrors or treasures within them.

'What are you willing to bet that she has several rows of clones of herself in tanks down there' Sabre mused to his brother, smirking as they passed an imposing oil painting of Samodiva that was hung above a wide stone fireplace.

'My right wing and three years of my life. That's what I'm willing to bet.'

The lilt of a guitar strummed from somewhere up the stairs, and as much as Heim craned his neck to see if it were from another being in the villa, he could see nothing.

The doorman hurried them along outside into the garden. The villa's swimming pool sat overlooking the rest of the island within a private and lush garden that looked as though Samodiva had stolen a little piece of rainforest for herself, with many tiny sparkling jewel-coloured raptors hopping through the branches like birds, whilst leopards no bigger than cats prowled through the undergrowth.

And there amongst it all was Samodiva.

The twin's hackles rose out of compulsion rather than fear. They held their wings as tightly as they could manage to stop the black quills from rattling or from launching themselves high into the sky to escape. They stepped to the side, allowing, or more rather pushing, Eve to the front to greet the mistress of the villa.

Acknowledging their presence, she abandoned her grove to greet them with a wide smile. A mane of dark brown hair flowed untamed behind her as she strode over, and her airy white camisole barely fulfilled its role of keeping her from being nude. It was odd to see her so underdressed, though she did retain her claw-like rings.

"*Cariña*. You finally came to dinner then? And here I was thinking that I'd have to kidnap you to get you here." She joked, taking Eve's hand and kissing it.

"I said I'd think about it. I didn't realise I would have to go through a public airport to get here."

"Oh no! How dare you walk amongst common people, though I am glad you've come to see my Eden, *Eve*."

"*Hilarious*. Truly."

Dropping Eve's hand, she stepped past Eve and embraced Heim before he even had the chance to speak, brushing his long hair back and squishing his cheeks as though he were a child again. The clipped purple feathers fluttered out in surprise at the sudden groping and his tailfeathers thrashed about, glinting violet on black in the sun.

"Heimy! Look how much you've grown." Samodiva cooed, spinning him around and playfully tugging at his feathers until one came away in her hands. "You've gotten taller again."

"Thanks, that's partly because of the new legs, but you already know that." He gave his legs a pat. Eve pursed her lips as Samodiva smugly grinned. Her son's Axolomeh therapy for replacing his bionic legs had been almost wholly due to her work. She was as grateful for it as she was resentful for how much it now meant that she owed Samodiva.

"No Willoughby again?"

"Bee's in the Philippines right now. Busy with his bugs."

"As always. Now where are my boys? Sabre and Falchion Merlo." Samodiva smiled at them, ushering them to come closer.

She gently brushed her hand across the soft black feathers along the tops of their wings. Eyes wide with wonder she examined their wingspans, gesturing for Fell to open them out to their fullest. The breeze tugged at the feathers, tempting Fell with the urge to sweep them down and power off into the sky away. He resisted the urge to escape, though he did give a small wing beat that sent a gust through the jungle-garden.

Samodiva clapped happily.

"What a beautiful pair you are," She laughed, tucking the black curls of hair back behind their feathered ears. "Do you still have your talents? I'd love to know if you've managed to develop them any further."

Sabre glanced to Eve, seeking her approval to discuss themselves with her.

'Only the stuff she'll want to fix, nothing else. Don't tell her anything that will make her curious.' Eve sent to him silently with a nod. If anything made Samodiva curious then it would be a battle to get her to back off.

"My talents are fine, but Fell's noticed behaviour changes in me. He said I get irrationally angry and almost feral at times, and since there's been teratomas in other Avios he thinks it might be that."

"Have you not had an MRI?"

"Acute claustrophobia and having such large wings make it hard to get scanned."

"Ah yes, that is an issue. Although correlation is not causation, and you were made differently to the standard Avios that Core uses." Samodiva pondered. "No matter. I'll get that seen to right now if you'd like, it'd be best to find out if you have one or not, before it develops into something more serious. DeLucas!"

With a clap of her hands, four identical Lion-Pards emerged from the jungle garden. Both Fell and Heim cocked an eyebrow at the sight of the quintuplet Risio lions, Sabre breaking into a wolf whistle of approval, whilst Fell wondered how to tell the four apart.

"Hot damn! Look at them-"

"Sabre!" Snapped Eve before he had a chance to finish what she predicted to be a very crude innuendo. "I don't care how pretty they are, don't catcall the Pards, it's rude."

The quintuplets didn't seem to mind.

"Yvain, Arlsan, *puede por favor llevarse a Sabre a la cirugía?* You can go with them too Falchion, take care of your brother. Feel free to go and explore, Heim." She instructed the boys. Two of the four bowed and gestured for the Kites to follow them back into the villa, which they did so with some reluctance. Heim however, shot off into the jungle garden with the remaining two lions beaming at the opportunity to explore, leaving Eve to hold her head and sigh deeply.

"New men?" She asked, trying not to look sceptical.

"A gift from my daughter." Samodiva smiled, striding out along the pathway towards a rocky natural pool with neon green moss and yellow flag irises, where there were more chicken-sized raptors trying to fish for koi from it. A small jasmine covered patio overlooked it with a pair of loungers and table overflowing with open books, feathers, a box of pinned insects, and glittering amber fossils, from where it appeared she had been working before being distracted by her garden. With her own botanical garden-office back in France, she could understand the appeal of working in a natural living environment as opposed to a clinically clean corporate room.

Shooing a little cherry-red raptor from her lounger, Samodiva sat down only to have it leap back onto the arm and demand attention from Samodiva with trilling squawks. Running her golden claws through the feathers of its neck, she gestured for Eve to join her.

Not wanting to be rude, Eve sat awkwardly on the edge of the lounger, peeking into the books to see what Samodiva was studying this time, until Samodiva closed them and allowed the raptor to walk across the table.

"She went onto a little excursion to a Risio Gala a month or so back and bought them while she was there." She noted loudly to Eve. "Nerissa Pavo couldn't tell the difference. Do you remember Nerissa? Very loud, always wanting to be the world's muse for fashion."

"I remember her." Eve grimaced, recalling several tiring encounters with the woman. Samodiva rang a small glass bell, summoning one of the servants to her, before continuing nonchalantly with her gossip.

"She got a pair of peacock wings grafted onto her back. Such a waste to go to such lengths to create an Avio only to take its wings for yourself."

"*Grafted?* Why not become transhuman if she wanted wings that much."

"Because she's a silly human elitist, who thinks you can just stitch a pair on and not change anything about yourself for them. That and she'd have to wait an entire year for them to grow, then spend another year and a half learning how to move them." She smirked at the shallowness and vanity of the woman. "There's nothing special to being human, I don't know why she insists on remaining as such."

A young woman carrying a golden platter with two crystal glasses and a decanter of wine arrived, quickly and neatly tidying the table to make room for the wine without so much as a chink of glass. Like the ram and lions, she seemed happy and eager to please Samodiva, but the thought of owning servants was not one that pleased Eve, though she was glad that they were treated with far more kindness and care than what Cedric would have shown them.

"I'd have thought that you would view her as a Preter, she's had so many gene therapies."

"No, she's *nothing* like me." Gold flashed across Samodiva's eyes, and she sneered at the concept of calling her a Preternatural. It was far too easy to forget that Samodiva was no longer human and hadn't been for years, and now calling her human was a point of insult to her. "Really she is nothing more than a little girl playing with her mother's make up box to make herself prettier."

"So, your daughter-" Stated Eve, taking her wine and trying to drive the conversation back to the fact. As always with Samodiva she loved to dance and flirt around a topic before getting to the real reason for it.

"*Roux.* Please use her name, *Hye-Jin.*" She smiled sharply, a cold and quickly threatening twitch to warn Eve to be careful of what she said.

Eve bristled at the use of her old name, biting her tongue before she snapped and caused an argument between them both.

"Roux...broke into a gala and used your name and you didn't do anything about it?"

"She's a big girl, she can do what she likes. Nerissa did kick up such a fuss about the people who went with her infiltrating her security, but I told her she only had herself to blame and that she really ought to be more careful in future." Her eyes glittered mischievously. "She went with your son actually."

Eve's head snapped up from her wine mid-sip. Of course Samodiva had a reason to inviting her to dinner, she always had a motive. Smirking slyly, Samodiva produced the photo evidence on her phone, holding it out for Eve to see. The picture was from a security camera of Crow, Wilny, Roux and several others talking to Nerissa Pavo.

"He does wear a tuxedo well, doesn't he? Even Crow, you remember him, don't you? Although I really do wish I had been there myself now, I'd love to see them all up close."

None of Samodiva's words sank in as she stared at the photo, mind racing at what she could possibly be planning. Was it blackmail? Ransom? What else did she have and what was her endgames if she even had any.

"You've known about them for a while, haven't you?" Eve swallowed, "You knew about my son being-"

"I found out about them a week after you did, so who really is the one who's known for a while here?"

"Then you know-"

"About the boat? Yes! Now that was hilarious!" She pressed her hand to her chest as she laughed. "Don't look so shocked. I know which pockets to fill to find things out, but come now *Cariña*, you're here for dinner, not work. You still like barbeque, yes?"

She withdrew her phone from Eve, beginning to text the chef for their dinner plans, ignoring Eve's rigidity and wary stare from over the tops of her glasses.

"Why are you always so nervous around me Evie?" Samodiva finally said with a sigh, "Why don't you trust me?"

"Because I can never tell what you're going to do next, or who's side you're on."

"*Amiga*, I'm on *my* side in this octagon of sides which we have going on here."

"Octagon?"

"You're right, it's a dodecahedron really." She shrugged, sipping her wine and pointing for Eve to keep drinking.

"The ship. Did you help them? What would you gain from this?"

"Humiliating Gaius is gain enough for me, *Cariña*, but I didn't give any information out about it to the Rioteers or these little groups."

The nonchalant lack of interest, but awareness of what had happened worried Eve. She *always* had something going on in the background, there was nothing Samodiva could resist more than adding players and pieces to her games.

"Amy," She said slowly, trying to keep from raising her voice. "If you're planning anything, please leave Wilny out of it, I-"

"Oh, you care about the safety of your son *now*? After you left him in Core and made no attempt to collect him within the last ten years, I thought you didn't care about him at all."

"I DIDN'T LEAVE HIM! *I DIDN'T HAVE A CHOICE!*" She had leapt from her chair, her crystal glass falling from the table and smashing upon the floor.

The noise sent the raptors scattering with panicked trills, back into the foliage of the garden, and stopped Eve from any further shouting. She stood looking down at the broken shards and red splash. Samodiva frowned at the outburst, though seemed more annoyed that the glass had shattered than being screamed at.

"You don't understand. You really don't." Eve sighed deeply, slowly sinking back down onto the lounger and regretting her display.

"Don't ruin your pretty face glaring at me. Have some wine and relax. *Cágate*, you're always so emotional when you're sober." She held her own glass forth in offering, smiling snidely. "We both want what's best for our children, even if it means staying out of their lives completely. Besides I'm sure he's doing fine with Storm, maybe he'll even make it back to you in one piece. Or at least…a piece."

Eve slapped the glass from her hand, sending it spinning and shattering across the stone patio, then snatching up a shard of broken crystal from her own glass, she struck at her Samodiva in anger. She didn't even realise she had done it until Samodiva caught her wrist, yanking her forwards so they were nose to nose. The shard didn't even so much as graze her skin.

"Really Evie? *Really?*" Samodiva purred, drawing a golden claw down Eve's cheek and leaving a white trace of a scratch along it. "Stabbing me in my own home? Is that what you've reduced yourself to?"

She took the shard from Eve's hand and crushed it into dust, letting the fragments fall onto the table in a little pile. Eve held her breath waiting for Samodiva to threaten or twist and break her arm, and yet all Samodiva did was gently release her and summon a servant with a chime of her bell to clean away the shards before any of her pets were harmed by the fragments, leaving Eve to awkwardly sit in silence under her unblinking gaze until the girl had left.

"You would do well to get yourself some anger management classes there Evie, or at least take a holiday every now and then." She said coolly. "All of this stress is doing you no good."

The noise had drawn Wilheim out of the jungle garden, frowning and cautiously making his way round to the patio.

"Did you break something?" He asked, letting Eve take his hand and mother him by tucking loose hairs back behind his ears and wiping mossy green dirt from his cheek.

"Just the raptors," She lied, as Samodiva smirked, "the little devils ran over the table and knocked the wine everywhere."

Wilheim looked sceptical, seeing how pale faced his mother looked. With a swish of his tailfeathers, he went to her side to make sure that she was okay whilst Samodiva gave a little chuckle.

"I'd hate for our friendship to be ruined Evie." Samodiva chirped, stretching out her legs, she rang the tiny bell beside her again to a different pattern of three slow chimes.

"A gift then, to show that I do mean no harm."

Eve tensed and pulled her son close to her side, sensing a malicious undertone to Samodiva's sultry voice.

"If you don't like it then I'm happy to keep hold of it for a while longer."

The sound of huge beating wings cut through the air, growing louder over the sounds of the waterfall, drawing Eve and Heim to look up. A dark shadow flashed in front of the sun, then looping round the tops of the jungle trees with a gentle bank, the Avio dropped down onto the top most rocks of the pond, sending the colourful little raptors scattering in panic, fanning out her arc of long tailfeathers as she did.

She moved on all fours with the grace of a jungle cat, four long toes gripped the rocks, each ending in a hooked talon. Slate-grey feathers glinting under the sun with an edge of steel to them, peering out at them from beneath her hair of the same shade, with cold aquamarine-green eyes.

"No...no that can't be-" Heim shook his head in shock, eyes widening and retreating behind his mother, from the young woman as she flexed and flared her wings, hissing raptorially at him with a mouthful of fangs. "What is she doing here?"

Horrified, Eve turned to Samodiva, her face equally as pale as Wilheim, but Samodiva only smiled and gestured out to the Avio.

"Frost, don't be rude, say hello."

Made in the USA
Coppell, TX
09 October 2022

84301088R00329